DON QUIXOTE

DE LA MANCHA

" *O happy era, happy age!* " *he continued,* " *when my glorious deeds shall be revealed to the world! deeds worthy of being engraven on brass and sculptured in marble!* "

DON QUIXOTE
DE LA MANCHA

TRANSLATED FROM THE SPANISH OF

MIGUEL DE CERVANTES SAAVEDRA,

By CHARLES JARVIS.

WITH ONE HUNDRED ILLUSTRATIONS.

BARNES
&NOBLE
BOOKS
NEW YORK

This edition published by Barnes & Noble, Inc.

1995 Barnes & Noble Books

ISBN 1-56619-731-7

Printed and bound in the United States of America

M 9 8 7 6 5 4 3 2 1

INTRODUCTION

In 1607, at the Globe Theater in London, a character in a comedy by George Wilkins spoke the following words: "Boy, hold this torch for me, for I am armed and ready to fight a windmill." Did the audience catch this allusion to a foreign book published only two years before and not yet available in English translation? Whether they did or were only expected to, obviously the fame of Part One of *Don Quixote* was already spreading in England—a fact remarkable but not astonishing: All Europe at this time read Spanish books, not only because of their quality but because of Spain's prestige as the premier power of Europe.

This prestige had, however, already climaxed before Cervantes wrote a single word of his masterpiece. Spanish culture, enjoying its Golden Age, peaked twice in the publication of the two parts of *Don Quixote* in 1605 and 1615, and continued to dazzle the world almost until the end of the century; but all the while Spanish power was sinking further into a decline the next century failed to reverse. By the 1800s the former political titan, shrunk almost to invisibility, had been relegated to the periphery of the European mind, and most foreign readers had simply ceased to take an interest in Spanish books, even those that had once enjoyed a wide currency outside Spain.

Don Quixote proved the sole exception to this rule. As if to make up for their indifference to the whole remainder of Spanish culture, foreigners not only still read this strange mock epic in prose, they idolized it, paying it every sort of compliment from scholarly annotations and splendid illustrations for new editions to searching, often passionate essays on its meaning.

The most striking proof of the book's enduring success abroad is its influence on novelists of many countries in every period since its publication. Except that they did not take it literally, these novelists seem to have been almost as enraptured by *Don Quixote* as the knight himself was by his books of chivalry. Let us look at a few examples. In *Joseph Andrews* and *Tom Jones*, Henry Fielding guided his heroes on their own adventurous roads in a spirit of tolerant satire caught from *Don Quixote*; he also borrowed—directly or indirectly—many of its burlesque devices. For Gustave Flaubert, Cervantes was a novelist without peer and his masterpiece the touchstone of novelistic art; Flaubert's own Madame Bovary is an updated female Quixote, her head turned by steamy romantic novels rather than dreamy chivalric romances. In Prince Myshkin, the hero of *The Idiot*, Fyodor Dostoevsky offered a Don Quixote shorn of his lance: The feistiness is gone; the otherworldly virtue remains. A more recent novelist, John Kennedy Toole, exhibited true Cervantean gusto in Ignatius J. Reilly, the hero of *A Confederacy of Dunces*. With his blustery grandiloquence, hankerings for the Middle Ages, and surrealistic schemes to rescue the oppressed and save the world, Ignatius is an unmistakable offspring of The Knight of the Sorrowful Figure. (His misogyny is merely an inversion of Quixote's reverence for Dulcinea and all other damsels of forty-carat virtue, just as his gluttony is an inversion of the knight's abstemiousness.)

But Cervantes is not only a novelist conversing across the centuries and the continents with other novelists and literati. He has always reached the international popular audience as well, whose response to *Don Quixote* has been just as ardent, if not as inspired, as that of Flaubert or Dostoevsky.

W hy has *Don Quixote* triumphed so spectacularly over the prejudice that has kept Spanish literature under virtual boycott outside Spain and Latin America for the last two centuries? (The works of a few "moderns" have been the only other exemptions.) The paramount reason is, of course, Don Quixote himself—a fictional archetype with the power to instantly grip the imagination regardless of particular cultural conditioning. (How much do the social contexts of Dostoevsky and John Kennedy Toole have in common?) What exactly this archetype represents is, however, a much-debated question.

Those who know the book only by reputation usually have an answer ready at hand: Don Quixote stands for the eternal romantic in all of us, emerging ever hopeful from all of life's sordid misadventures and heartwrenching disappointments. Besides its human warmth, this view has another attraction: It can trace its ancestry to the judgments of some great critics of the nineteenth century.

But does the book itself support such a reading? Having gleaned their Don Quixote from the general culture, many people experience a shock—

like a blow in the head from a windmill—when they actually confront Cervantes's hero. How could the subject of so many endearing knick-knacks and sentimental poems, not to mention one Broadway musical, behave so often like a belligerent egomaniac? His comic grandiosity drives him to hair-raising violence on at least two occasions: when he attacks and pounds the Biscayan until "the blood began to gush out of his nostrils, his mouth and his ears," and when he wreaks havoc among a funeral procession, severely wounding one mourner, breaking the leg of another, and thrashing the remainder. Egomania also drives those long speeches (the narrator calls one a "harangue") in which this most talkative of warriors holds forth on the code of chivalry and other lofty subjects in exhaustive and exhausting detail.

Are we then dealing with an antihero? The flip side of his belligerence is the altruism he also exercises as part of the chivalric code; the flip side of his pedantry is his occasional hardheaded eloquence. His hallucinations spring from a fertile though diseased mind, and his fanaticism gives him an enviable resilience. When he challenges the king's lion and tries to make peace between the warring villages, he is foolhardy but also courageous. Is it possible to form a coherent attitude toward this baffling mixture of faults and virtues?

The crazed knight's knack for keeping the reader off balance is one of the sources of his fascination. A good example is the scene in which he liberates the convicts in the name of a higher justice, commands them to bring his respects to the nonexistent Dulcinea, and as a reward for this blend of chivalry and Spanish anarchism is attacked by the same needy and oppressed to whom he has just given succor. True, he has saved the convicts from the inhumane punishment of the galleys, but he has also left this dubious bunch free to recirculate in society. (One convict he knows to be a career criminal, another a pimp; half of the group he knows nothing about.) Moreover, we cannot tell whether he was motivated only by a desire to carry out his ridiculous chivalric program, or if he also felt genuine sympathy for the convicts' lot. He ends up where we have already found him more than once at the end of an adventure: stretched out helpless on the ground, with that peerless nag Rozinante stretched out beside him. Is the reader supposed to laugh at Don Quixote in this episode, weep for him, admire him, or condemn him? (There is no harm in doing all four.) The same question occurs to us in another case—when our world-reformer-on-the-spot rescues the servant boy from the whipping being dealt him by his master, yet only succeeds in doubling the victim's suffering in the long run.

The wide range of possible reactions to the hero's antics is the key to another reason for the book's lasting universal appeal: an ambiguity that has allowed readers and critics of every period, background, and temperament to find in it what they wish to find. *Don Quixote* may have inspired more widely divergent interpretations than any other classic novel. (One possible competitor is another novel it influenced: *Moby Dick*.) The most divergent opinions contradict each other flat out, and some make the fantasies conceived in the sizzling brain under the barber's-basin helmet seem sane by comparison.

Yet we have Cervantes's own guarantee that his book is not ambiguous at all. In his Prologue to Part One, he casts himself as a mere entertainer, whose only serious purpose, if one can call it serious, is to puncture the pretensions of books of antique chivalry. However, we must be careful: The prologue to a book served in Cervantes's time the role that a talk-show appearance serves in ours; it was self-promotion, not self-elucidation, and seldom an artistic manifesto. Nor should we be overly concerned that Cervantes reiterates his prologue's statement of purpose in his farewell to the reader, since by then his ironic habits have been firmly established. And even if Cervantes was both candid and accurate about his conscious purpose, postmodern criticism has taught us that the meanings of a text can be multiple and even indeterminate in spite of an author's intentions.

The Spain of Cervantes's time seems to have taken his modest claims at face value. There is no record that any of the readers who sent *Don Quixote* through sixteen Spanish editions before Cervantes's death groped about in its entrails—as would many future critics—for the key to human destiny or the Problem of Spain, or saw it as anything but a knee-slappingly funny puppet show spoofing an escapist genre. The litterateurs who dictated taste (if not buying habits) did not encourage rumination over mere novels—especially those that struck out, as did *Don Quixote*, in realistic new directions instead of clinging to the ancient Greek models then held in reverence—and now almost wholly forgotten. Put in today's terms, the judgment of these highbrows on Cervantes's comic spree probably was: Dazzling pop fiction, yes—Art, no.

The book's popularity abroad dates from the first translations, and remained strong even in countries hostile to Spain, where readers came to take the hero's slapstick tumbles and bizarre projects as metaphors for Spanish incompetence. Don Quixote sold off "many acres of arable land" in order to buy fatuous books of chivalry; Spain let its fields lie fallow in order to chase pipe dreams of universal dominion. Don Quixote tried to violently impose the code of chivalry on an unbelieving world; Spain tried—with much more violence but as little success—to impose its rigid Catholicism on its subjects in Holland. And could the rough-handled hero have looked any more crestfallen when he returned vanquished to his village than the admiral of the battered Armada must have looked when he returned in defeat to Spain?

By the mid-eighteenth century, Rationalism and Empiricism dominated the culture of Europe; they did not, however, monopolize it. A countertradition of Sentiment and Enthusiasm also flourished, exemplified in such works as Samuel Richardson's five-handkerchief novel *Clarissa*. The intellectuals who scorned this trend took *Don Quixote* as a prophetic satire on its excesses—and read it avidly. They especially appreciated what Tobias Smollett, in a note to his 1755 translation, called the "ludicrous solemnity" in the portrayal of the knight. Moreover, these enemies of Absolute Monarchy saw an ally in a satirist they took as the great derider of feudal chivalry. (Actually, Cervantes had satirized only *books* of chivalry, not chivalry itself—erasing the line between them was an oddly quixotic error for these dispassionate reasoners.)

With the nineteenth century—the Age of Romanticism—*Quixote* criticism outside Spain switches into reverse. The vast, instructive joke of the eighteenth century becomes something approaching a straight epic romance. The sallow, gangly, grandstanding, pompous actuality of the pseudo-knight—the foil during the Age of Satire to his gorgeous self-image—is now picturesque; it also points paradoxically to the splendor within—somewhat as Quasimodo's repulsiveness in Victor Hugo's *Hunchback of Notre Dame* is an inverse sign of his loving heart. The Knight of the Lions' zeal for the restoration of chivalry is not food for mirth to the Romantics, who view it as the mirror image of their own yearning for the Age of Unity, Faith, and Little Science to Speak Of. Foreseeably, the ever-out-of-reach Dulcinea is now the equivalent of Petrarch's Laura, with the result that her champion's love penance changes from an exercise in futility to a kind of weird mystical masochism. The Rationalists accepted Don Quixote's many beatings as proper spankings for a grown-up boy who insisted on defying the rules of reason. Now the same beatings represent the lashings-out of philistinism against Poetry. The hero's abandonment of chivalry on his deathbed—which the seventeenth century must have seen as a return to the Christian virtue of humility, and the eighteenth saw as a return to common sense—is bewailed by the Romantics as the consummation of a tragedy. In their minds *Don Quixote* is only secondarily a comedy, and the joke ultimately cuts against such prosaic persecutors of the visionary hero as the tight-fisted innkeeper in Part One.

It was the Argentine writer Jorge Luis Borges who pointed out that the distancing effect of time had played the trick of turning *Don Quixote*'s gritty, sharply etched Spain—the ironic backdrop to the knight's fantasies—into a place as romantic as any of the magic kingdoms the book derides. But the aloof shepherdess Marcela and the other beleaguered beauties who cross Don Quixote's path; the charming, memoir-writing rogue Gines de Pasamonte; the swashbuckling "Captive's History" interpolated into Part One; Don Quixote's moving tributes to Dulcinea before the mocking Duke and the Duchess; and the truly chivalrous outlaw Roque de Ginart all show that Cervantes had already mixed a great deal of romance with his realism. Inspired by these elements of the book, as well as by a soft-focus nostalgia for a bygone Spain, the Romantics painted a portrait of a Cervantes who revered the whole world of dreams and who gave his readers Don Quixote to revere as the noblest dreamer of them all.

Yet we have only to think of this exalted personage dangling by the wrist from the hayloft door after his courtly rejection of Maritornes, or in the cage complaining about the uncontrollable event about to sully his knightly dignity, in order to dismiss him as a living hymn to the Ideal. As for the tributes to Dulcinea mentioned above, what seems heartfelt in them may arise merely from his demented role-playing. Moreover, typical examples of the knight's pedantry and staggering gullibility surround these passages, undercutting a straight reading of their intent. However assessed, a few hundred words cannot make us forget the void we feel behind his usual rhetoric about Dulcinea, which many readers have been anxious to fill with their own imaginings. For these gentle spirits, what seems obvious about Dulcinea—that she is an elaborate bookish sublimation of the yen Alonso Quixano felt for a farm girl—is too disillusioning to be accepted. Just as hard to live with is the thought that all the slapstick and parody that seem to disparage the knight's egocentric fantasyland are intended by Cervantes to do just that, faulting the dreamer no matter what the real world may be.

As the pleasant, instructive satire it had turned into during the eighteenth century, *Don Quixote* might have lost its international audience as soon as that century passed. The Romantics' belief that the book was a grave parable and hardly a burlesque at all insured its fame in their own time, and also—by allowing us to see it as a burlesque that transcends the genre—made possible its fame in ours. Today, readers continue to turn to this dauntingly huge novel because they know it offers serious themes to grapple with, not just hilarities to revel in.

To try to describe these themes is, first of all, to try to crystallize the meaning of Cervantes's delicious and exasperating protagonist. At the same time, we might keep in mind those twentieth-century critics for whom *Don Quixote* is an example of an open text, inviting an infinite number of equally valid interpretations and excluding only a definitive one. According to this approach, a nihilistic view of the book that construes it as satirizing the human imposition of value on a meaningless universe would be as respectable as a Romantic view.

As an archetype, this monkishly wasted, overtopping figure with a lance and helmet can be said to stand for virtue rendered useless or destructive by deluded egotism. To give Don Quixote this significance makes him sound like the hero of a tragedy, or of a comedy of a disturbing kind— which is exactly what Cervantes's masterpiece is. And doubly disturbing since it insists that the virtue in human beings cannot survive without the distortions of self-exaltation.

In Part Two, the puckish university wit Sampson Carrasco sets out to check the knight's reckless career. Sampson has many affinities with Don Quixote—learning, experience of the world outside the village, restless energy, stubborn determination—while his wit turns on the combination of Quixote-related fantasies with the reality principle. Sampson is Quixote without the fatal literal-mindedness.

Perhaps understanding that too rapid a cure may kill the patient, Sampson has no intention of giving the rambunctious cavalier the equivalent of a strong dose of hellebore or primal therapy. His plan is to bring Quixote back to safe anchorage in the village, where he can recover slowly; to execute it, he needs only to bend Quixote's will to his own, thereby hurting nothing but his ego.

So far gone is the hero at this point that Sampson must proceed by accommodating himself to Don Quixote's magic kingdom. He manages to do this with great finesse and accomplishes his mission, but by quelling the rampaging ego of his friend he has done more than he foresaw. The old man ("bordering upon fifty" was old in the Renaissance) who left the time-bound world of his village for the timeless world of fiction succumbs to despair soon after he loses his fictional supremacy. In this state, he no longer has the strength to support the system of delightful unrealities he constructed, and it quickly collapses. Now his mind is clear and his virtue shines undistorted through his every word—but not for long. In the last pages of the novel, the pathos of old age that lay between the lines of all those chapters of adventure becomes the explicit pathos of a disillusioned death.

From treating the delusions of the ego, the book naturally expanded its scope to take in general questions of appearance versus reality, and of the slippery nature of truth. With remarkable deftness, *Don Quixote* even exposes its own artistic "fakery"; Cervantes seems to leap from his time to our own, where self-referential novels and stories abound, reflecting an uneasiness about fictional "lying" that in turn reflects anxiety in the midst of a welter of conflicting reality readings and value systems. That Cervantes also felt such insecurities should not surprise us if we consider the age of intellectual tumult in which he lived.

When Don Quixote, Sancho Panza, and Sampson Carrasco discuss, in Part Two, the chart-topping popularity of Part One (published ten years before), they are breaking a cardinal rule of fictional illusion: Characters cannot refer to the work they are themselves a part of. Yet perhaps they are not breaking any rule, since the work they appear in is not to their minds a novel but a history. The self-infatuated knight even protests the use of "novels and irrelevant stories" (*i.e.*, the interpolated tales) in this veracious history of himself: If the author, he believes, had included only "my thoughts, my sighs, my groans, my laudable intentions, or my actual achievements," he would have produced a far better book. Later, master and man join in attacking an apochryphal Part Two (a travesty by a writer with a grudge against Cervantes) for its gross inaccuracies—the author is a disgrace to the historian's profession! The true Part Two must be the one we are reading, squarely based like Part One on the original work of the Arab historian Cide Hamete Benengeli, whose rocklike authority (neither he nor his book ever existed) is appealed to again and again throughout *Don Quixote.* ·

All these devices absurdly underlining the book's truth as history have the calculated effect of shattering the fictional illusion. Cervantes seems confident that each time he shatters it we will quickly put it together again with his help—that our appetite for illusion is as insatiable as his hero's. "Truth," psychologically considered, is what any individual mind happens to believe is true, whether temporarily as in the case of the credence a reader lends to a novel, or very temporarily as in the case of Don Quixote's belief that the three peasant girls on their mules are—three peasant girls on their mules. When Sancho gives him the lowdown—that the boorish trio are actually Dulcinea and her ladies-in-waiting, whose splendors her champion cannot see because his vision has been tampered with by evil magicians—Don Quixote soon goes down on his knees (literally) before the new "truth." For the priest, the barber, and other fellow villagers of the chivalry-mad Alonso Quixano, "Don Quixote" is an invented personage who behaves preposterously; for people outside the village, Don Quixote is an actual person who behaves preposterously and sometimes alarmingly; for Alonso Quixano, Don Quixote is an actual person (himself) who behaves magnificently—unless, as some critics have argued, Quixano is merely pretending to be mad. The Duke and the Duchess are smart and witty aristocrats in their own minds, and spoiled idle mockers in the mind of the reader—unless a particular reader happens, unlikely as it seems, to find them charming. Meanwhile, throughout the book we have the inimitable Sancho busily sorting wild improbabilities into two piles labeled "True" and "False."

Cervantes was not a radical skeptic, but an ironist who relished showing the mercurial and often falsifying perspectives of the passional creatures of his imagination. His great satire shows truth as apprehensible, but does not flatter the human ability or willingness to perceive it.

The comedy of *Don Quixote* has widened the audience that its seriousness has maintained. Unlike the Romantics, we laugh out loud at the book without feeling we are betraying its gist. In this we resemble the first international audience, which we only fault for missing the darker implications of the unpredictable and irresistible humor. Exactly when the comedy is at its unsurpassable best, the meanings become most grave. The Cave of Montesinos chapters can stand for the many sections illustrating this correlation—all of them disturbing in their complex disillusion yet full of pathos, with a timing any nightclub comic might envy, and a sublimity whose tragic equivalent can be found in the climaxes of *King Lear*.

—Paul Montazzoli
1995

AUTHOR'S PREFACE

—◇—

Loving reader, thou wilt believe me, I trust, without an oath, when I tell thee it was my earnest desire that this offspring of my brain should be as beautiful, ingenious, and sprightly as it is possible to imagine; but, alas! I have not been able to control that order in nature's works whereby all things produce their like; and therefore, what could be expected from a mind sterile and uncultivated like mine, but a dry, meagre, fantastical thing, full of strange conceits, and that might well be engendered in a prison—the dreadful abode of care, where nothing is heard but sounds of wretchedness? Leisure, an agreeable residence, pleasant fields, serene skies, murmuring streams, and tranquillity of mind—by these the most barren muse may become fruitful, and produce that which will delight and astonish the world.

Some parents are so hoodwinked by their excessive fondness, that they see not the imperfections of their children, and mistake their folly and impertinence for sprightliness and wit; but I, who, though seemingly the parent, am in truth only the step-father of Don Quixote, will not yield to this prevailing infirmity; nor will I, as others would do, beseech thee, kind reader, almost with tears in my eyes, to pardon or conceal the faults thou mayest discover in this brat of mine. Besides, thou art neither its kinsman nor friend; thou art in possession of thine own soul, and of a will as free and absolute as the best; and art, moreover, in thine own house, being as much the lord and master of it as is the monarch of his revenue; knowing also the common saying—"Under my cloak, a fig for a king." Wherefore, I say, thou art absolved and liberated from every restraint or obligation, and mayest freely avow thy opinion on my performance, without fear of reproach for the evil, or hope of reward for the good thou shalt say of it. Fain, indeed, would I have given it to thee naked as it was born, without the decoration of a preface, or that numerous train of sonnets, epigrams, and other eulogies, now commonly placed at the beginning of every book; for I confess that, although mine cost me some labour in composing, I found no part of it so difficult as this same Preface which thou art now reading : yes, many a time have I taken up my pen, and as often laid it down again— not knowing what to write.

Happening one day, when in this perplexity, to be sitting with the paper before me, pen behind my ear, my elbow on the table, and my cheek resting on my hand, deeply pondering on what I should say, a lively and intelligent friend unexpectedly entered ; and seeing me in that posture, he inquired what made me so thoughtful. I told him I was musing on a preface for Don Quixote, and frankly confessed I had been so teased and harassed by it that I felt disposed to give up the attempt, and trouble myself no further, either with the preface or the book, but rather leave the achievements of that noble knight unpublished. " For shall I not be confounded," said I, "with the taunts of that old law-maker, the Vulgar, when, after so long a silence, I now, forsooth, come out at this time of day, with a legend as dry as a rush, destitute of invention, in a wretched style, poor in conception, void of learning, and without either quotations in the margin or annotations at the end : while all other books, whether fabulous or profane, are so stuffed with sentences from Aristotle, Plato, and the whole tribe of philosophers, that the world is amazed at the extensive reading, deep learning, and extraordinary eloquence of their authors ? Truly, when these wiseacres quote the Holy Scriptures, you would take them for so many St. Thomases, or doctors of the Church ! And so observant are they of the rules of decorum, that in one line they will cite you the ravings of a lover, and in the next some pious homily—to the delight of every reader. In all these matters, my book will be wholly deficient ; for Heaven knows I have nothing either to quote or make notes upon ; nor do I know what authors I have followed, and therefore cannot display their names, as usual, in alphabetical succession, beginning with Aristotle, and ending with Xenophon, or Zoilus or Zeuxis—the one a painter, the other a slanderous critic. It will also be ungraced by commendatory sonnets from the pens of dukes, marquises, earls, bishops, ladies of quality, or other illustrious poets, though, were I to request them of two or three humbler friends, I know they would supply me with such as many of higher name amongst us could not equal. In short, my dear friend," continued I, "it is plain that Signor Don Quixote must lie buried amongst the musty records of La Mancha, till Heaven shall send some abler hand to fit him out in a manner suitable to his high deserts ; since I find it impossible to perform that duty myself, not only from a want of competent talents, but because I am naturally too lazy in hunting after authors to enable me to say what I can say as well without them. These are the considerations that made me so thoughtful when you entered, and you must allow that it was not without sufficient cause."

On hearing this tale of distress, my friend struck his forehead with the palm of his hand, and, bursting into a loud laugh, said, " I now see I have been in error ever since I have known you : I always took you for a discreet and sensible man, but now, it appears, you are as far from being so as heaven is from earth. What ! is it possible that a thing of such little moment should have power to embarrass and confound a genius like yours, formed to overcome and trample under foot the greatest obstacles ?—By my faith, this is not incapacity, but sheer idleness; and if you would be convinced that what I say is true, attend to me, and in the twinkling of an eye you shall see me put those difficulties to the rout which you say prevent your introducing to the world the history of the renowned Don Quixote, the light and mirror of all knight-errantry."

" Say on," replied I, " and tell me how you propose to fill up the vacuum which my fear has created, or how brighten up the gloom that surrounds me." " Nothing so easy," said he : " your first difficulty, respecting the want of sonnets, epigrams, or panegyrics by high and titled authors, may at once be removed simply by taking the trouble to compose them yourself, and then baptizing them by whatever name you please : fathering them upon Prester John of the Indies, or the Emperor Trapisonda, who, to my certain knowledge, were famous poets. But suppose they were not so, and that sundry pedants and praters, doubting that fact, should slander you—heed them not ; for should they even convict you of falsehood, they cannot deprive you of the hand that wrote it.

" Now, as to your marginal citations of those authors and books whence you collected the various sentences and sayings interspersed through your history, it is but scattering here and there over your pages some scraps of Latin which you know by heart, or that will cost you but little trouble to find :—for example, when treating of liberty or slavery,

' Non bene pro toto libertas venditur auro ;'

and then on the margin you clap me down the name of Horace, or who-ever said it. If your subject be the power of death, then opportunely comes

' Pallida mors, æquo pulsat pede pauperum tabernas
Regumque turres.'

If friendship, or loving our enemies, as God enjoins, forthwith you look into the Holy Scriptures, and without any very curious search you will be able to take the identical words of the sacred text .

'Ego autem dico vobis, diligite inimicos vestros.'

If you should be speaking of evil thoughts, recollect the Evangelist :

'De corde exeunt cogitationes malæ.'

On the inconstancy of friends, Cato will give you this distich :

'Donec eris felix, multos numerabis amicos,
Tempora si fuerint nubila, solus eris.'

By the assistance of these, or such-like driblets of learning, you will at least gain the credit of being a scholar—a character which in these times leads both to honour and profit.

" As for annotations at the end of your book, you may safely manage it in this manner : if you should have occasion to speak of a giant, let it be Goliath, for there you will have, at a small expense, a noble annotation, which will run thus :—' The giant Golias, or Goliath, was a Philistine whom the shepherd David slew in the valley of Terebinthus, by means of a great stone which he cast from a sling '—as recorded in the Book of Kings, where you will find both chapter and verse. And, in order to prove yourself skilled in literature and cosmography, take an opportunity to mention the river Tagus, on which an admirable note will present itself, to this effect :—' The river Tagus was so named by a king of Spain : its source is in such a place : after kissing the walls of the celebrated city of Lisbon, it is swallowed up in the ocean. Its sands are reported to be of gold '—and so on. If you would treat of robbers, I will furnish you with the history of Cacus, for I have it at my fingers' ends ; and if of courtezans, there is the Bishop of Mondonedo, who will accommodate you with a Lamia, a Laïs, and a Flora, which annotation cannot fail to do you infinite credit. If you have to speak of cruel females, Ovid will supply you with Medea ; if enchanters and witches be your theme, Homer has a Calypso and Virgil a Circe ; if valiant commanders, Julius Cæsar and his ' Commentaries ' are at your service, and Plutarch will give you a thousand Alexanders. If love should chance to engage your pen, with the two ounces which you possess of the Tuscan tongue, you may apply to Leon Hebreo, who will provide you abundantly ; or in case you dislike to visit foreign parts, you have here, at home, Fonseca on ' The Love of God,' which contains all that you, or the most inquisitive, can possibly desire on that subject. In short, do you only contrive to introduce these names or allusions, and leave both quotations and annotations to me; for I will engage to fill up your margins, and add four whole sheets to the end of your book.

" We now come to the list of quoted authors—another of your grievances, which also admits of an easy remedy ; for you have only to look out for some book containing such an alphabetical list, from A down to Z, and transfer it bodily to your own ; and should the artifice be apparent from the little need you had of their help, it matters not: some, perhaps, may be silly enough to believe that in your plain and simple tale you really have made use of every one of them ;—at all events, such a display of learned names will give your book an air of importance at the first sight, and nobody will take the trouble to examine whether you have followed them or not, since nothing would be gained by the labour.

" Yet, after all, sir," continued my friend, " if I am not greatly mistaken, none of these things are necessary to your book, which is a satire on the extravagant tales of chivalry ; a subject never considered by Aristotle, overlooked by St. Basil, and utterly unknown to Cicero. The minute accuracies of true history, the calculations of astrology, the measurements of geometry, and subtleties of logic have nothing to do with it ; neither does it interfere with ecclesiastical concerns, mingling divine and human things—from which every good Christian should abstain :— to Nature only do you refer: she is your sole guide and example, and the more closely you attend to her suggestions, the more perfect must be your book. Books of chivalry are your game, and your chief purpose is to destroy their credit with the world; you therefore need not go begging for sentences from philosophers, precepts from Holy Writ, fables from poets, harangues from orators, nor miracles from saints, but simply endeavour to express your meaning in a clear and intelligible manner ; and in well-chosen, significant, and decorous terms, give a harmonious and pleasing turn to your periods ; so that the perusal of your history may dispel the gloom of the melancholy, add to the cheerfulness of the gay, and, while it affords amusement even to the simple, it shall be approved by the grave, the judicious, and the wise. In fine, the downfall and demolition of that mischievous pile of absurdity which, though despised by some, is admired by the many ; and, if successful, believe me, you will have performed a service of no mean importance."

I listened to my friend's discourse in profound silence, and so strongly was I impressed by his observations, that I acknowledged their truth, and immediately converted them to my use in composing this Preface ;

wherein, gentle reader, thou wilt perceive the judgment of my friend, my own good fortune in meeting with so able a counsellor in the crisis of my distress, and at the same time thou wilt confess thy own satisfaction in thus receiving, in so simple and artless a manner, the History of the famous Don Quixote de la Mancha, who in the opinion of all the inhabitants of the Campo de Montiel, was the chastest lover and most valiant knight that had appeared in those parts for many years. I will not enlarge on the benefit I confer in presenting to thee so distinguished and honourable a personage; but I do expect some acknowledgment for having introduced to thy acquaintance his faithful attendant, the famous Sancho Panza, in whom are combined all the squirely endowments that are to be found scattered over the pages of knight-errantry. And now, may God give thee health!—not forgetting me. Farewell.

CONTENTS

BOOK I.

BOOK II.

BOOK III.

Contents

BOOK IV.

Contents

SECOND PART

BOOK I.

Contents

BOOK II.

BOOK III.

Contents

BOOK IV.

Contents

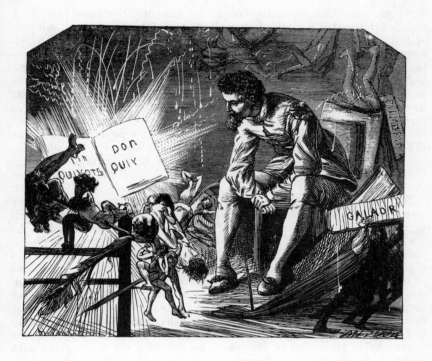

ADVENTURES OF DON QUIXOTE

BOOK I.

CHAPTER I.

Which treats of the quality and manner of life of our renowned hero

Down in a village of La Mancha,* the name of which I have no desire to recollect, there lived, not long ago, one of those gentlemen who usually keep a lance upon a rack, an old buckler, a lean horse, and a coursing greyhound. Soup, composed of somewhat more mutton than beef, the fragments served up cold on most nights, lentils on Fridays, collops and eggs on Saturdays, and a pigeon by way of addition on

---

* Partly in the kingdom of Arragon, and partly in Castile.

Sundays, consumed three-fourths of his income; the remainder of it supplied him with a cloak of fine cloth, velvet breeches, with slippers of the same for holidays, and a suit of the best homespun, in which he adorned himself on week-days. His family consisted of a house-keeper above forty, a niece not quite twenty, and a lad who served him both in the field and at home, who could saddle the horse or handle the pruning-hook. The age of our gentleman bordered upon fifty years: he was of a strong constitution, spare-bodied, of a meagre visage, a very early riser, and a lover of the chase. Some pretend to say that his surname was Quixada,* or Quesada, for on this point his historians differ; though, from very probable conjectures, we may conclude that his name was Quixana. This is, however, of little importance to our history; let it suffice that, in relating it, we do not swerve a jot from the truth.

Be it known, then, that the afore-mentioned gentleman, in his leisure moments, which composed the greater part of the year, gave himself up with so much ardour to the perusal of books of chivalry, that he almost wholly neglected the exercise of the chase, and even the regu-lation of his domestic affairs; indeed, so extravagant was his zeal in this pursuit, that he sold many acres of arable land to purchase books of knight-errantry, collecting as many as he could possibly obtain. Among them all, none pleased him so much as those written by the famous Feliciano de Silva, whose brilliant prose and intricate style were, in his opinion, infinitely precious; especially those amorous speeches and challenges in which they so abound; such as: "The reason of the unreasonable treatment of my reason so enfeebles my reason, that with reason I complain of your beauty." And again: "The high heavens that, with your divinity, divinely fortify you with the stars, rendering you meritorious of the merit merited by your greatness." These and similar rhapsodies distracted the poor gentleman, for he laboured to comprehend and unravel their meaning, which was more than Aristotle himself could do, were he to rise from the dead expressly for that purpose. He was not quite satisfied as to the wounds which Don Belianis gave and received; for he could not help thinking that, how-ever skilful the surgeons were who healed them, his face and whole body must have been covered with seams and scars. Nevertheless, he commended his author for concluding his book with the promise of that interminable adventure; and he often felt an inclination to seize the pen himself and conclude it, literally as it is there promised: this he would doubtless have done, and not without success, had he not been diverted from it by meditations of greater moment, on which his mind was incessantly employed.

He often debated with the curate of the village, a man of learning and a graduate of Siguenza, which of the two was the best knight, Palmerin of England, or Amadis de Gaul; but Master Nicholas, barber of the same place, declared that none ever came up to the Knight of

---

* *Quixadas* signifies "jaws."

the Sun: if, indeed, any one could be compared to him, it was Don Galaor, brother of Amadis de Gaul, for he had a genius suited to everything: he was no effeminate knight, no whimperer, like his brother; and in point of courage he was by no means his inferior. In short, he became so infatuated with this kind of study, that he passed whole days and nights over these books; and thus, with little sleeping and much reading, his brains were dried up and his intellects deranged. His imagination was full of all that he had read—of enchantments, contests, battles, challenges, wounds, courtships, amours, tortures, and impossible absurdities; and so firmly was he persuaded of the truth of the whole tissue of visionary fiction, that, in his mind, no history in the world was more authentic. The Cid Ruy Diaz, he asserted, was a very good knight, but not to be compared with the Knight of the Flaming Sword, who, with a single back-stroke, cleft asunder two fierce and monstrous giants. He was better pleased with Bernardo del Carpio, because, at Roncesvalles, he slew Roland the Enchanted, by availing himself of the stratagem employed by Hercules upon Antæus, whom he squeezed to death within his arms. He spoke very favourably of the giant Morganti, for, although of that monstrous brood who are always proud and insolent, he alone was courteous and well-bred. Above all he admired Rinaldo de Montalvan, particularly when he saw him sallying forth from his castle to plunder all he encountered, and when, moreover, he seized upon that image of Mahomet which, according to history, was of massive gold. But he would have given his housekeeper, and even his niece into the bargain, for a fair opportunity of kicking the traitor Galalon.

In fine, his judgment being completely obscured, he was seized with one of the strangest fancies that ever entered the head of any madman: this was, a belief that it behoved him, as well for the advancement of his glory as the service of his country, to become a knight-errant, and traverse the world, armed and mounted, in quest of adventures, and to practise all that had been performed by knights-errant of whom he had read; redressing every species of grievance, and exposing himself to dangers which, being surmounted, might secure to him eternal glory and renown. The poor gentleman imagined himself at least crowned Emperor of Trebisond, by the valour of his arm; and thus wrapped in these agreeable delusions, and borne away by the extraordinary pleasure he found in them, he hastened to put his designs into execution.

The first thing he did was to scour up some rusty armour, which had been his great-grandfather's, and had lain many years neglected in a corner. This he cleaned and adjusted as well as he could; but he found one grand defect: the helmet was incomplete, having only the morion; this deficiency, however, he ingeniously supplied, by making a kind of vizor of pasteboard, which, being fixed to the morion, gave the appearance of an entire helmet. It is true indeed that, in order to prove its strength, he drew his sword, and gave it two strokes, the first of which instantly demolished the labour of a week; but not altogether approving of the facility with which it was destroyed, and in order to secure himself against a similar misfortune, he made another vizor, which, having fenced in the inside with small bars of iron, he felt assured of its strength, and, without making any more experiments, held it to be a most excellent helmet.

In the next place he visited his steed ; and although this animal had more blemishes than the horse of Gonela, which "*tantum pellis et ossa fuit,*" yet, in his eyes, neither the Bucephalus of Alexander, nor the Cid's Babieca, could be compared with him.   Four days was he delibe-rating upon what name he should give him ; for, as he said to himself, it would be very improper that a horse so excellent, appertaining to a knight so famous, should be without an appropriate name ; he therefore endeavoured to find one that should express what he had been before he belonged to a knight-errant, and also what he now was : nothing could, indeed, be more reasonable than that, when the master changed his state, the horse should likewise change his name, and assume one pompous and high-sounding, as became the new order he now professed. So after having devised, altered, lengthened, curtailed, rejected, and again framed in his imagination a variety of names, he finally deter-mined upon Rozinante,* a name, in his opinion, lofty, sonorous, and full of meaning ; importing that he had been only a *rozin*, a drudge-horse, *before* his present condition, and that now he was *before* all the *rozins* in the world.

Having given his horse a name so much to his satisfaction, he resolved to fix upon one for himself.   This consideration employed him eight more days, when at length he determined to call himself Don Quixote ; whence some of the historians of this most true history have concluded that his name was certainly Quixada, and not Quesada, as others would have it.   Then recollecting that the valorous Amadis, not content with the simple appellation of Amadis, added thereto the name of his kingdom and native country, in order to render it famous, styling himself Amadis de Gaul ; so he, like a good knight, also added the name of his province, and called himself Don Quixote de la Mancha ; whereby, in his opinion, he fully proclaimed his lineage and country, which, at the same time, he honoured by taking its name.

His armour being now furbished, his helmet made perfect, his horse and himself provided with names, he found nothing wanting but a lady to be in love with ; for a knight-errant without the tender passion was a tree without leaves and fruit—a body without a soul.   " If," said he, " for my sins, or rather, through my good fortune, I encounter some giant—an ordinary occurrence to knights-errant—and overthrow him at the first onset, or cleave him in twain, or, in short, vanquish him and force him to surrender, must I not have some lady to whom I may send him as a present ? that when he enters into the presence of my charming mistress, he may throw himself upon his knees before her, and

---

* From *rozin*, a common drudge-horse, and *ante*, before ; as Alexander's horse was called Bucephalus, from his bull-head, and the Knight of the Sun's, Cornerio, from a horn in the forehead.—JARVIS.

in a submissive, humble voice, say, 'Madam, in me you behold the giant Caraculiambro, lord of the island Malendrania, who, being vanquished in single combat by the never-enough-to-be-praised Don Quixote de la Mancha, am by him commanded to present myself before you, to be disposed of according to the will and pleasure of your highness.' " How happy was our good knight after this harangue! How much more so when he found a mistress! It is said that, in a neighbouring

A horse so excellent should not be without an appropriate name.

village, a good-looking peasant girl resided, of whom he had formerly been enamoured, although it does not appear that she ever knew or cared about it; and this was the lady whom he chose to nominate mistress of his heart. He then sought a name for her, which, without entirely departing from her own, should incline and approach towards that of a princess or great lady, and determined upon Dulcinea del Toboso (for she was a native of that village), a name, he thought, harmonious, uncommon, and expressive—like all the others which he had adopted.

CHAPTER II.

Which treats of the first sally that Don Quixote made from his native village.

As soon as these arrangements were made, he no longer deferred the execution of his project, which he hastened from a consideration of what the world suffered by his delay : so many were the grievances he intended to redress, the wrongs to rectify, errors to amend, abuses to reform, and debts to discharge ! Therefore, without communicating his intentions to anybody, and wholly unobserved, one morning before day, being one of the most sultry in the month of July, he armed himself cap-a-pie, mounted Rozinante, placed the helmet on his head, braced on his target, took his lance, and, through the private gate of his back yard, issued forth into the open plain, in a transport of joy to think he had met with no obstacles to the commencement of his honourable enterprise. But scarce had he found himself on the plain, when he was assailed by a recollection so terrible as almost to make him abandon the undertaking : for it just then occurred to him that he was not yet dubbed a knight; therefore, in conformity to the laws of chivalry, he neither could nor ought to enter the lists against any of that order ; and, if he had been actually dubbed, he should, as a new knight, have worn white armour, without any device on his shield, until he had gained one by force of arms. These considerations made him irresolute whether to proceed; but frenzy prevailing over reason, he determined to get himself made a knight by the first one he should meet, like many others of whom he had read. As to white armour, he resolved, when he had an opportunity, to scour his own, so that it should be whiter than ermine. Having now composed his mind, he proceeded, taking whatever road his horse pleased ; for therein, he believed, consisted the true spirit of adventure.

Our new adventurer, thus pursuing his way, conversed within himself, saying, " Who doubts but that in future times, when the true history of my famous achievements is brought to light, the sage who records them will in this manner describe my first sally : ' Scarcely had ruddy Phœbus extended over the face of this wide and spacious earth the golden filaments of his beautiful hair, and scarcely had the little painted birds, with their forked tongues, hailed, in soft and mellifluous harmony, the approach of the rosy harbinger of morn, who, leaving the soft couch of her jealous consort, had just disclosed herself to mortals through the gates and balconies of the Manchegan horizon, when the renowned knight, Don Quixote de la Mancha, quitting the slothful down, mounted Rozinante, his famous steed, proceeded over the ancient memorable plain of Montiel ' (which was indeed the truth). O happy era, happy age ! " he continued, " when my glorious deeds shall be revealed to the world ! deeds worthy of being engraven on brass, sculptured in marble, and recorded by the pencil ! And thou, O sage enchanter, whosoever thou mayest be, destined to chronicle this extra-ordinary history ! forget not, I beseech thee, my good Rozinante, the inseparable companion of all my toils ! " Then again, as if really enamoured, he exclaimed, " O Dulcinea, my princess ! sovereign of this captive heart ! greatly do you wrong me by a cruel adherence to your decree, forbidding me to appear in the presence of your beauty ! Deign, O lady, to think on this enslaved heart, which for love of you endures so many pangs ! "

In this wild strain he continued, imitating the style of his books as nearly as he could, and proceeding slowly on, while the sun arose with such intense heat that it was enough to dissolve his brains, if any had been left. He travelled almost the whole of that day with-out encountering anything worthy of recital, which caused him much vexation, for he was impatient for an opportunity to prove the valour of his powerful arm.

Some authors say his first adventure was that of the Pass of Lapice; others affirm it to have been that of the windmills; but, from what I have been able to ascertain of this matter, and have found written in the annals of La Mancha, the fact is that he travelled all that day, and as night approached, both he and his horse were wearied and dying with hunger; and in this state, as he looked around him, in hopes of discovering some castle, or shepherd's cot, where he might repose and find refreshment, he descried, not far from the road, an inn, which to him was a star conducting him to the portals, if not the palace of his redemption. He made all the haste he could, and reached it at night-all. There chanced to stand at the door two young women on their journey to Seville, in the company of some carriers who rested there that night. Now, as everything that our adventurer saw and conceived was, by his imagination, moulded to what he had read, so in his eyes the inn appeared to be a castle, with its four turrets, and pinnacles of shining silver, together with its drawbridge, deep moat, and all the appurtenances with which such castles are usually described. When he had advanced within a short distance of it, he checked Rozinante, expecting some dwarf would mount the battlements, to announce by sound of trumpet the arrival of a knight-errant at the castle; but finding them tardy, and Rozinante impatient for the stable, he approached the inn-door, and there saw the two girls, who to him appeared to be beautiful damsels or lovely dames enjoying themselves before the gate of their castle.

It happened that, just at this time, a swineherd collecting his hogs (I make no apology, for so they are called) from an adjoining stubble-field, blew the horn which assembles them together, and instantly Don Quixote was satisfied, for he imagined it was a dwarf who had given the signal of his arrival. With extraordinary satisfaction, therefore, he went up to the inn; upon which the ladies, being startled at the sight of a man armed in that manner, with lance and buckler, were retreating into the house; but Don Quixote, perceiving their alarm, raised his pasteboard vizor, thereby partly discovering his meagre, dusty visage, and, with gentle demeanour and placid voice, thus addressed them:

" Fly not, ladies, nor fear any discourtesy, for it would be wholly inconsistent with the order of knighthood, which I profess, to offer insult to
any person, much less to virgins of that exalted rank which your appearance indicates." The girls stared at him, and were endeavouring to find
out his face, which was almost concealed by the sorry vizor ; but hearing
themselves called virgins, they could not forbear laughing, and to such a
degree, that Don Quixote was displeased, and said to them : " Modesty
well becomes beauty, but excessive laughter, proceeding from a slight
cause, is folly : but I say not this to humble or distress you, for my part
is no other than to do you service." This language, so unintelligible to
the ladies, added to the uncouth figure of our knight, increased their
laughter ; consequently he grew more indignant, and would have proceeded further, but for the timely appearance of the innkeeper, a very
corpulent, and therefore a very pacific man, who, upon seeing so ludicrous
an object, armed, and with accoutrements so ill-sorted as were the bridle,
lance, buckler, and corslet, felt disposed to join the damsels in demonstrations of mirth ; but, in truth, apprehending some danger from a
form thus strongly fortified, he resolved to behave with civility, and
therefore said, " If, Sir Knight, you are seeking for a lodging, you will
here find, excepting a bed (for there are none in this inn), everything in
abundance." Don Quixote, perceiving the humility of the governor of
the fortress, for such to him appeared the innkeeper, answered, " For
me, Signor Castellano, anything will suffice, since arms are my ornaments, warfare my repose." The host thought he called him Castellano
because he took him for a sound Castilian, whereas he was an Andalusian,
of the coast of St. Lucar, as great a thief as Cacus, and not less mischievous than a collegian or a page ; and he replied, " If so, your
worship's beds must be hard rocks, and your sleep continual watching ;
and that being the case, you may dismount with a certainty of finding
here sufficient cause for keeping awake the whole year, much more a
single night." So saying, he laid hold of Don Quixote's stirrup, who
alighted with much difficulty and pain, for he had fasted the whole of
the day. He then desired the host to take especial care of his steed,
for it was the finest creature that ever fed : the innkeeper examined
him, but thought him not so good by half as his master had represented
him. Having led the horse to the stable, he returned to receive the
orders of his guest, whom the damsels, being now reconciled to him,
were disarming : they had taken off the back and breast plates, but
endeavoured in vain to disengage the gorget, or take off the counterfeit
beaver, which he had fastened with green ribbons in such a manner that
they could not be untied, and he would upon no account allow them to
be cut ; therefore he remained all that night with his helmet on, the
strangest and most ridiculous figure imaginable.

While these frivolous girls, whom he still conceived to be persons of
quality and ladies of the castle, were disarming him, he said to them,
with infinite grace, " Never before was knight so honoured by ladies
as Don Quixote, after his departure from his native village ! Damsels
attended upon him ; princesses took charge of his steed ! O Rozinante

Therefore one of the ladies performed that office for him.

—for that, ladies, is the name of my horse, and Don Quixote de la Mancha my own; although it was not my intention to have discovered myself, until deeds, performed in your service, should have proclaimed me; but impelled to make so just an application of that ancient romance of Lanzarote to my present situation, I have thus prematurely disclosed my name: yet the time shall come when your ladyships may command, and I obey; when the valour of my arm shall make manifest the desire I have to serve you." The girls, unaccustomed to such rhetorical flourishes, made no reply, but asked whether he would please to eat anything. "I shall willingly take some food," answered Don Quixote, "for I apprehend it would be of much service to me." That day happened to be Friday, and there was nothing in the house but some fish, of that kind which in Castile is called abadexo; in Andalusia, bacallao; in some parts, curadillo; and in others, truchuela.* They asked if his worship would like some truchuela, for they had no other fish to offer him. "If there be many troutlings," replied Don Quixote, "they will supply the place of one trout; for it is the same to me whether I receive eight single reals or one piece-of-eight. Moreover, these troutlings may be preferable, as veal is better than beef, and kid superior to goat. Be

---

* The fish called *poor John*, or little trouts.

that as it may, let it come immediately, for the toil and weight of arms cannot be sustained by the body unless the interior be supplied with aliments." For the benefit of the cool air, they placed the table at the door of the inn, and the landlord produced some of his ill-soaked and worse-cooked bacallao, with bread as foul and black as the knight's armour : but it was a spectacle highly risible to see him eat ; for his hands being engaged in holding his helmet on and raising the beaver, he could not feed himself, therefore one of the ladies performed that office for him ; but to drink would have been utterly impossible, had not the innkeeper bored a reed, and, placing one end into his mouth, at the other poured in the wine ; and all this he patiently endured rather than cut the lacings of his helmet.

In the meantime there came to the inn a sow-doctor, who, as soon as he arrived, blew his pipe of reeds four or five times, which finally convinced Don Quixote that he was now in some famous castle, where he was regaled with music ; that the *poor John* was trout, the bread of the purest white, the strolling wenches ladies of distinction, and the innkeeper governor of the castle ; consequently he remained satisfied with his enterprise and first sally, though it troubled him to reflect that he was not yet a knight, feeling persuaded that he could not lawfully engage in any adventure until he had been invested with the order of knighthood.

CHAPTER III.

In which is related the pleasant method Don Quixote took to be dubbed a knight.

AGITATED by this idea, he abruptly finished his scanty supper, called the innkeeper, and, shutting himself up with him in the stable, he fell on his knees before him, and said, "Never will I arise from this place, valorous knight, until your courtesy shall vouchsafe to grant a boon which it is my intention to request : a boon that will redound to your glory, and to the benefit of all mankind." The innkeeper, seeing his guest at his feet, and hearing such language, stood confounded, and stared at him, without knowing what to do or say : he entreated him to rise, but in vain, until he had promised to grant the boon he requested. "I expected no less, signor, from your great magnificence," replied Don Quixote; "know, therefore, that the boon I have demanded, and which your liberality has conceded, is that, on the morrow, you will confer upon me the honour of knighthood. This night I will watch my arms in the chapel of your castle, in order that, in the morning, my earnest desire may be fulfilled, and I may with propriety traverse the four quarters of the world, in quest of adventures for the relief of the distressed ; conformable to the duties of chivalry and of knights-errant, who, like myself, are devoted to such pursuits."

The host, who, as we have said, was a shrewd fellow, and had already entertained some doubts respecting the wits of his guest, was now confirmed in his suspicions; and, to make sport for the night, determined to follow his humour. He told him, therefore, that his desire was very reasonable, and that such pursuits were natural and suitable to knights so illustrious as he appeared to be, and as his gallant demeanour fully testified; that he had himself in the days of his youth followed that honourable profession, and travelled over various parts of the world in search of adventures; failing not to visit the suburbs of Malaga, the isles of Riaran, the compass of Seville, the market-place of Segovia, the olive-field of Valencia, the rondilla of Grenada, the coast of St. Lucar, the fountain of Cordova, the taverns of Toledo, and divers other parts, where he had exercised the agility of his heels and the dexterity of his hands : committing sundry wrongs, soliciting widows, courting damsels, cheating youths; in short, making himself known to most of the tribunals in Spain; and that finally he had retired to this castle, where he lived upon his revenue and that of others; entertaining therein all knights-errant of every quality and degree, solely for the great affection he bore them, and that they might share their fortune with him, in return for his good-will. He further told him that in his castle there was no chapel wherein he could watch his armour, for it had been pulled down, in order to be rebuilt; but that, in cases of necessity, he knew it might be done wherever he pleased; therefore he might watch it that night in a court of the castle, and the following morning, if it pleased God, the requisite ceremonies should be performed, and he should be dubbed so effectually, that the world would not be able to produce a more perfect knight. He then inquired if he had any money about him. Don Quixote told him he had none, having never read in their histories that knights-errant provided themselves with money. The innkeeper assured him he was mistaken; for, admitting that it was not mentioned in their history, the authors deeming it unnecessary to specify things so obviously requisite as money and clean shirts, yet was it not therefore to be inferred that they had none; but, on the contrary, he might consider it as an established fact that all knights-errant, of whose histories so many volumes are filled, carried their purses well provided against accidents; that they were also supplied with shirts, and a small casket of ointments, to heal the wounds they might receive; for in plains and deserts, where they fought and were wounded, no aid was near, unless they had some sage enchanter for their friend, who could give them immediate assistance, by conveying in a cloud through the air some damsel or dwarf, with a phial of water, possessed of such virtue that, upon tasting a single drop of it, they should instantly become as sound as if they had received no injury. But when the knights of former times were without such a friend, they always took care that their esquires should be provided with money, and such necessary articles as lint and salves; and when they had no esquires, which very rarely happened, they carried these things themselves upon the crupper of their horse, in wallets so small as to be scarcely visible, that they might seem to be something of more importance; for, except in such cases, the custom of carrying wallets was not tolerated among knights-errant. He therefore advised, though, as his godson (which he was soon to be), he might command him, never henceforth to travel without money and the aforesaid provisions, and he would find them serviceable when he least expected it. Don Quixote promised to follow his advice with punctuality; and an order was now given for performing the watch of the armour in a large yard adjoining the inn. Don Quixote, having collected it together, placed it on a cistern which was close to a well; then, bracing on his target and grasping his lance, with graceful demeanour he paced to and fro before the pile, beginning his parade as soon as it was dark.

The innkeeper informed all who were in the inn of the frenzy of his guest, the watching of his armour, and of the intended knighting. They were surprised at so singular a kind of madness, and went out to observe him at a distance. They perceived him sometimes quietly pacing along, and sometimes leaning upon his lance with his eyes fixed upon his armour for a considerable time. It was now night, but the moon shone with a splendour which might vie even with that whence it was borrowed; so that every motion of our new knight might be distinctly seen.

At this time, it happened that one of the carriers wanted to give his mules some water, for which purpose it was necessary to remove Don Quixote's armour from the cistern; who, seeing him advance, exclaimed with a loud voice, " O thou, whomsoever thou art, rash knight ! who approachest the armour of the most valiant adventurer that ever girded sword, beware of what thou dost, and touch it not, unless thou wouldst yield thy life as the forfeit of thy temerity." The carrier heeded not this admonition (though better would it have been for him if he had), but, seizing hold of the straps, he threw the armour some distance from him; which Don Quixote perceiving, he raised his eyes to heaven, and addressing his thoughts, apparently, to his lady Dulcinea, said, " Assist me, O lady, to avenge this first insult offered to your vassal's breast, nor let your favour and protection fail me in this first perilous encounter." Having uttered these and similar ejaculations, he let slip his target, and, raising his lance with both hands, he gave the carrier such a stroke upon the head that he fell to the ground in so grievous a plight that, had the stroke been repeated, there would have been no need of a surgeon. This done, he replaced his armour, and continued his parade with the same tranquillity as before.

Soon after, another carrier, not knowing what had passed, for the first yet lay stunned, came out with the same intention of watering his mules; and, as he approached to take away the armour from the cistern, Don Quixote, without saying a word or imploring any protection, again let slip his target, raised his lance, and, with no less effect than before, smote the head of the second carrier. The noise brought out all the people in the inn, and the landlord among the rest; upon which Don Quixote braced on his target, and laying his hand upon his sword, said, " O lady of beauty! strength and vigour of my enfeebled heart! Now is the time for thee to turn thy illustrious eyes upon this thy captive knight, whom so mighty an encounter awaits!" This address had, he conceived, animated him with so much courage, that, were all the carriers in the world to have assailed him, he would not have retreated one step.

The comrades of the wounded, upon discovering the situation of their friends, began at a distance to discharge a shower of stones upon Don Quixote, who sheltered himself as well as he could with his target, without daring to quit the cistern, because he would not abandon his armour. The innkeeper called aloud to them, begging they would desist, for he had already told them he was insane, and that, as a madman, he would be acquitted, though he were to kill them all. Don Quixote, in a voice still louder, called them infamous traitors, and the lord of the castle a cowardly, base-born knight, for allowing knights-errant to be treated in that manner; declaring that, had he received the order of knighthood, he would have made him sensible of his perfidy. " But as for you, ye vile and worthless rabble, I utterly despise ye! Advance! Come on; molest me as far as ye are able, for quickly shall ye receive the reward of your folly and insolence!" This he uttered with so much spirit and intrepidity that the assailants were struck with terror; which, in addition to the landlord's persuasions, made them cease their attack. He then permitted the wounded to be carried off, and, with the same gravity and composure, resumed the watch of his armour.

The host, not relishing these pranks of his guest, determined to put an end to them, before any further mischief ensued, by immediately investing him with the luckless order of chivalry: approaching him, therefore, he disclaimed any concurrence on his part in the insolent conduct of those low people, who were, he observed, well chastised for their presumption. He repeated to him that there was no chapel in the castle, nor was it by any means necessary for what remained to be done; that the stroke of knighting consisted in blows on the neck and shoulders, according to the ceremonial of the order, which might be effectually performed in the middle of a field; that the duty of watching his armour he had now completely fulfilled, for he had watched more than four hours, though only two were required. All this Don Quixote believed, and said that he was there ready to obey him, requesting him, at the same time, to perform the deed as soon as possible; because, should he be assaulted again when he found himself knighted, he was resolved not to leave one person alive in the castle, excepting those whom, out of respect to him, and at his particular request, he might be induced to spare. The constable, thus warned and alarmed, immediately brought forth a book in which he kept his account of the straw and oats he furnished to the carriers, and, attended by a boy, who carried an end of candle, and the two damsels before mentioned, went towards Don Quixote, whom he commanded to kneel down : he then began reading in his manual, as if it were some devout prayer, in the course of which he raised his hand and gave him a good blow on the neck, and, after that, a handsome stroke over the shoulders, with his own sword, still muttering between his teeth, as if in prayer. This being done, he commanded one of the ladies to gird on his sword, an office she performed with much alacrity, as well as discretion, no small portion of which was necessary to avoid bursting with laughter at every part of the ceremony; but indeed the prowess they had seen displayed by the new knight kept their mirth within bounds. At girding on the sword, the good lady said, "God grant you may be a fortunate knight, and successful in battle." Don Quixote inquired her name, that he might thenceforward know to whom he was indebted for the favour received, as it was his

The other girl now buckled on his spurs.

intention to bestow upon her some share of the honour he should acquire by the valour of his arm. She replied, with much humility, that her name was Tolosa, and that she was the daughter of a cobbler at Toledo, who lived at the stalls of Sanchobienaya; and that, wherever she was, she would serve and honour him as her lord. Don Quixote, in reply, requested her, for his sake, to do him the favour henceforth to add to her name the title of don, and call herself Donna Tolosa, which she promised to do. The other girl now buckled on his spurs, and with her he held nearly the same conference as with the lady of the sword. Having inquired her name, she told him it was Molinera, and that she was daughter to an honest miller of Antiquera: he then requested her likewise to assume the don, and style herself Donna Molinera, renewing his proffers of service and thanks.

These never-till-then-seen ceremonies being thus speedily performed, Don Quixote was impatient to find himself on horseback, in quest of adventures. He therefore instantly saddled Rozinante, mounted him, and, embracing his host, made his acknowledgments for the favour he had conferred by knighting him, in terms so extraordinary, that it would be in vain to attempt to repeat them. The host, in order to get rid of him the sooner, replied with no less flourish, but more brevity; and, without making any demand for his lodging, wished him a good journey.

CHAPTER IV.

Of what befell our knight after he had sallied from the inn.

LIGHT of heart, Don Quixote issued forth from the inn about break of day, so satisfied and so pleased to see himself knighted, that the joy thereof almost burst his horse's girths. But recollecting the advice of his host concerning the necessary provisions for his undertaking, especially the articles of money and clean shirts, he resolved to return home and furnish himself accordingly, and also provide himself with a squire, purposing to take into his service a certain country fellow of the neighbourhood, who was poor and had children, yet was very fit for the squirely office of chivalry. With this determination he turned Rozinante towards his village; and the steed, as if aware of his master's intention, began to put on with so much alacrity that he hardly seemed to set his feet to the ground. He had not, however, gone far, when, on his right hand, from a thicket hard by, he fancied he heard feeble cries, as from some person complaining. And scarcely had he heard it when he said, "I thank Heaven for the favour it does me, by offering me so early an opportunity of complying with the duty of my profession, and of reaping the fruit of my honourable desires. These are, doubtless, the cries of some distressed person who stands in need of my protection and assistance." Then turning the reins, he guided Rozinante towards the place whence he thought the cries proceeded, and he had entered but a few paces into the wood, when he saw a mare tied to an oak, and a lad to another, naked from the waist upwards, about fifteen years of age, who was the person that cried out; and not without cause, for a lusty country fellow was laying on him very severely with a belt, and accompanied every lash with a reprimand and a word of advice: " For," said he, " the tongue slow and the eyes quick." The boy answered, " I will do so no more, dear sir; by the passion of God, I will never do so again; and I promise for the future to take more care of the flock."

Don Quixote, observing what passed, now called out in an angry tone, " Discourteous knight, it ill becomes thee to deal thus with one who is not able to defend himself. Get upon thy horse, and take thy lance" (for he had also a lance leaning against the oak to which the mare was fastened), " and I will make thee sensible of thy dastardly conduct." The countryman, seeing such a figure coming towards him, armed from head to foot, and brandishing his lance at his face, gave himself up for a dead man, and therefore humbly answered, " Signor cavalier, this lad I am chastising is a servant of mine, whom I employ to tend a flock of sheep which I have hereabouts ; but he is so careless that I lose one every day ; and because I correct him for his negligence, or roguery, he says I do it out of covetousness, and for an excuse not to pay him his wages ; but before God, and on my conscience, he lies." " Darest thou say so in my presence, vile rustic ? " said Don Quixote. " By the sun that shines upon us, I have a good mind to run thee through with this lance ! Pay him immediately, without further reply ; if not, by the God that rules us, I will dispatch and annihilate thee in a moment ! Unbind him instantly ! " The countryman hung down his head, and, without reply, untied his boy. Don Quixote then asked the lad how much his master owed him ; and he answered, nine months' wages, at seven reals a month. Don Quixote, on calculation, found that it amounted to sixty-three reals, and desired the countryman instantly to disburse them, unless he meant to pay it with his life. The fellow, in a fright, answered that, on the word of a dying man, and upon the oath he had taken (though by the way he had taken no oath), it was not so much ; for he must deduct the price of three pair of shoes he had given him on account, and a real for two blood-lettings when he was sick. " All this is very right," said Don Quixote ; " but set the shoes and the blood-lettings against the stripes thou hast given him unjustly ; for if he tore the leather of thy shoes, thou hast torn his skin ; and if the barber-surgeon drew blood from him when he was sick, thou hast drawn blood from him when he is well ; so that upon these accounts he owes thee nothing." " The mischief is, signor cavalier," quoth the countryman, " that I have no money about me ; but let Andres go home with me, and I will pay him all, real by real." " I go home with him ! " said the lad ; " the devil a bit ! No, sir, I will do no such thing ; for when he has me alone he will flay me like any Saint Bartholomew." " He will not do so," replied Don Quixote ; " to keep him in awe, it is sufficient that I lay my commands upon him ; and, on condition he swears to me by the order of knighthood which he has received, I shall let him go free, and will be bound for the payment." " Good sir, think of what you say," quoth the boy ; " for my master is no knight, nor ever received any order of knighthood : he is John Aldudo, the rich, of the neighbourhood of Quintanar." " That is little to the purpose," answered Don Quixote ; "there may be knights of the family of the Aldudos, more especially as every man is the son of his own works." "That's true," quoth Andres ; " but what works is my master the son of, who refuses me the wages of my sweat and labour ? " " I do not refuse thee, friend Andres," replied the countryman : " have the kindness to go with me ; and I swear, by all the orders of knighthood that are in the world, I will pay thee every real down, and perfumed* into the bargain." " For the perfuming, I thank thee," said Don Quixote : " give him the reals, and I shall be

---

* A Spanish phrase for paying or returning anything with advantage.

satisfied: and see that thou failest not; or else, by the same oath, I swear to return and chastise thee; nor shalt thou escape me, though thou wert to conceal thyself closer than a lizard. And if thou wouldst be informed who it is thus commands, that thou mayest feel the more strictly bound to perform thy promise, know that I am the valorous Don Quixote de la Mancha, the redresser of wrongs and abuses. So farewell, and do not forget what thou hast promised and sworn, on pain of the penalty I have denounced." So saying, he clapped spurs to Rozinante, and was soon far off.

The countryman eagerly followed him with his eyes; and, when he saw him quite out of the wood, he turned to his lad Andres, and said, "Come hither, child; I wish now to pay what I owe thee, as that redresser of wrongs commanded." "So you shall, I swear," quoth Andres; "and you will do well to obey the orders of that honest gentleman (whom God grant to live a thousand years!), who is so brave a man, and so just a judge, that, egad! if you do not pay me, he will come back and do what he has threatened." "And I swear so too," quoth the countryman: "and to show how much I love thee, I am resolved to augment the debt, that I may add to the payment." Then, taking him by the arm, he again tied him to the tree, where he gave him so many stripes that he left him for dead. "Now," said he, "Master Andres, call upon that redresser of wrongs; thou wilt find he will not easily redress this, though I believe I have not quite done with thee yet, for I have a good mind to flay thee alive, as thou saidst just now." At length, however, he untied him, and gave him leave to go in quest of his judge, to execute the threatened sentence. Andres went away in dudgeon, swearing he would find out the valorous Don Quixote de la Mancha, and tell him all that had passed, and that he should pay for it sevenfold. Nevertheless, he departed in tears, leaving his master laughing at him.

Thus did the valorous Don Quixote redress this wrong; and, elated at so fortunate and glorious a beginning to his knight-errantry, he went on toward his village, entirely satisfied with himself, and saying with a low voice, "Well mayest thou deem thyself happy above all women living on the earth, O Dulcinea del Toboso, beauteous above the most beautiful! since it has been thy lot to have subject and obedient to thy whole will and pleasure so valiant and renowned a knight as is and ever shall be Don Quixote de la Mancha! who, as all the world knows, received but yesterday the order of knighthood, and to-day has redressed the greatest injury and grievance that injustice could invent and cruelty commit! to-day hath he wrested the scourge out of the hand of that pitiless enemy, by whom a tender stripling was so undeservedly lashed!"

He now came to the road, which branched out in four different directions; when immediately those cross-ways presented themselves to his imagination where knights-errant usually stop to consider which of the roads they shall take. Here, then, following their example, he paused awhile, and, after mature consideration, let go the reins, submitting his own will to that of his horse, who, following his first motion, took the direct road towards his stable. Having proceeded about two miles, Don Quixote discovered a company of people, who, as it afterwards appeared, were merchants of Toledo, going to buy silks in Murcia. There were six of them in number; they carried umbrellas, and were attended by four servants on horseback and three muleteers on foot. Scarcely had Don Quixote espied them, when he imagined it must be some new adventure; and, to imitate as nearly as possible what he had read in his books, as he fancied this to be cut out on purpose for him to achieve, with a graceful deportment and intrepid air he settled himself firmly in his stirrups, grasped his lance, covered his breast with his target, and, posting himself in the midst of the highway, awaited the approach of those whom he already judged to be knights-errant; and when they were come so near as to be seen and heard, he raised his voice, and, with an arrogant tone, cried out, "Let the whole world stand, if the whole world does not confess that there is not in the whole world a damsel more beautiful than the Empress of La Mancha, the peerless Dulcinea del Toboso!"

The merchants stopped at the sound of these words, and also to behold the strange figure of him who pronounced them; and both by the one and the other they perceived the madness of the speaker; but they were disposed to stay and see what this confession meant which he required; and therefore one of them, who was somewhat of a wag, but withal very discreet, said to him,

"Signor cavalier, we do not know who this good lady you mention may be: let us but see her, and if she be really so beautiful as you intimate, we will, with all our hearts, and without any constraint, make the confession you demand of us." "Should I show her to you," replied Don Quixote, "where would be the merit of confessing a truth so manifest? It is essential that, without seeing her, you believe, confess, affirm, swear, and maintain it; and if not, I challenge you all to battle, proud and monstrous as you are: and, whether you come on one by one (as the laws of chivalry require), or all together, as is the custom and wicked practice of those of your stamp, here I wait for you, confiding in the justice of my cause." "Signor cavalier," replied the merchant, "I beseech your worship, in the name of all the princes here present, that we may not lay a burden upon our consciences by confessing a thing we never saw or heard, and especially being so much to the prejudice of the empresses and queens of Alcarria and Estremadura, that your worship would be pleased to show us some picture of this lady, though no bigger than a barleycorn, for we shall guess at the clue by the thread; and therewith we shall rest satisfied and safe, and your worship contented and pleased. Nay, I verily believe we are so far inclined to your side, that, although her picture should represent her squinting with one eye, and distilling vermilion and brimstone from the other, notwithstanding all this, to oblige you, we will say whatever you please in her favour." "There distils not, base scoundrels!" answered Don Quixote, burning with rage, "there distils not from her what you say, but rather ambergris and civet among cotton; neither doth she squint, nor is she hunchbacked,

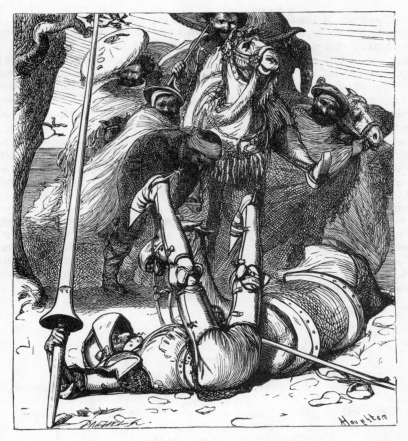

Rozinante fell and his master lay rolling about the field.

but as straight as a spindle of Guadarrama :* but you shall pay for the horrid blasphemy you have uttered against so transcendent a beauty !" So saying, with his lance couched he ran at him who had spoken, with so much fury and rage that, if good fortune had not so ordered that Rozinante stumbled and fell in the midst of his career, it had gone hard with the rash merchant. Rozinante fell, and his master lay rolling about the field for some time, endeavouring to rise, but in vain, so encumbered was he with his lance, target, spurs, and helmet, added to the weight of his antiquated armour. And while he was thus struggling to get up he continued calling out, " Fly not, ye dastardly rabble !

---

* A small town nine leagues from Madrid, situated at the foot of a mountain, the rocks of which are so perpendicular that they are called "the Spindles." Near it stands the Escurial.—Jarvis.

stay, ye race of slaves! for it is through my horse's fault, and not my own, that I lie here extended." A muleteer of the company, not over good-natured, hearing the arrogant language of the poor fallen gentleman, could not bear it without returning him an answer on his ribs; and coming to him, he took the lance, which having broken to pieces, he applied one of the splinters with so much agility upon Don Quixote, that, in spite of his armour, he was threshed like wheat. His masters called out, desiring him to forbear; but the lad was provoked, and would not quit the game until he had quite spent the remainder of his choler; and, seizing the other pieces of the lance, he completely demolished them upon the unfortunate knight; who, notwithstanding the tempest of blows that rained upon him, never shut his mouth, incessantly threatening heaven and earth, and those who to him appeared to be assassins. At length the fellow was tired, and the merchants departed, sufficiently furnished with matter of discourse concerning the poor belaboured knight, who, when he found himself alone, again endeavoured to rise; but, if he could not do it when sound and well, how should he in so bruised and battered a condition? Yet he was consoled in looking upon this as a misfortune peculiar to knights-errant, and imputing the blame to his horse; although to raise himself up was impossible, his whole body was so horribly bruised.

CHAPTER V.

Wherein is continued the narration of our knight's misfortune.

VERY full of pain, yet, soon as he was able to stir, Don Quixote had recourse to his usual remedy, which was, to recollect some incident in his books, and his frenzy instantly suggested to him that of Valdovinos and the Marquis of Mantua, when Carloto left him wounded on the mountain: a story familiar to children, not unknown to youth, commended and even credited by old men; yet no more true than the miracles of Mahomet. Now, this seemed to him exactly suited to his case; therefore he began to roll himself on the ground, and to repeat, in a faint voice, what they affirm was said by the wounded Knight of the Wood:

> "Where art thou, mistress of my heart,
> Unconscious of thy lover's smart?
> Ah me! thou know'st not my distress,
> Or thou art false and pitiless."

In this manner he went on with the romance, until he came to those verses where it is said—"O noble Marquis of Mantua, my uncle and lord by blood!" Just at that instant it so happened that a peasant of his own village, a near neighbour, who had been carrying a load of wheat to the mill, passed by; and, seeing a man lying stretched on the earth, he came up, and asked him who he was, and what was the cause of his doleful lamentation? Don Quixote, firmly believing him to be the Marquis of Mantua his uncle, returned him no answer, but proceeded with the romance, giving an account of his misfortune, and of the amours of the emperor's son, just as it is there recounted. The peasant was astonished at his extravagant discourse; and taking off his vizor, now battered all to pieces, he wiped the dust from his face; upon which he recognised him, and exclaimed, "Ah, Signor Quixana" (for so he was called before he had lost his senses, and was transformed from a sober gentleman to a knight-errant), "how came your worship in this condition?" But still he answered out of his romance to whatever question he was asked.

The good man seeing this, contrived to take off the back and breastpiece of his armour, to examine if he had any wound; but he saw no blood nor sign of any hurt. He then endeavoured to raise him from the ground, and with no little trouble placed him upon his ass, as being the beast of easier carriage. He gathered together all the arms, not excepting the broken pieces of lance, and tied them upon Rozinante; then taking him by the bridle, and his ass by the halter, he went on towards his village, full of concern at the wild language of Don Quixote. No less thoughtful was the knight, who was so cruelly beaten and bruised that he could scarcely keep himself upon the ass, and ever and anon he sent forth groans that seemed to pierce the skies, insomuch that the peasant was again forced to inquire what ailed him. And surely the devil alone could have furnished his memory with stories so applicable to what had befallen him; for at that instant, forgetting Valdovinos, he recollected the Moor Abindarraez, at the time when the Governor of Antequera, Roderigo of Narvaez, had taken him prisoner and conveyed him to his castle; so that when the peasant asked him again how he was and what he felt, he answered him in the very same terms that were used by the prisoner Abindarraez to Roderigo of Narvaez, as he had read in the "Diana" of George of Montemayor, applying it so aptly to his own case, that the peasant went on cursing himself to the devil, to hear such a monstrous heap of nonsense, which convinced him that his neighbour had run mad, and he therefore made what haste he could to reach the village, and thereby escape the plague of Don Quixote's long speeches; who, still continuing, said, "Be it known to your worship, Signor Don Roderigo de Narvaez, that this beauteous Xarifa, whom I mentioned, is now the fair Dulcinea del Toboso, for whom I have done, do, and will do, the most famous exploits of chivalry that have been, are, or shall be seen in the world." To this the peasant answered, "Look you, sir, as I am a sinner, I am not Don Roderigo de Narvaez, nor the Marquis of Mantua, but Pedro Alonzo your neighbour; neither is your worship Valdovinos, nor Abindarraez, but the worthy gentleman Signor Quixana." "I know who I am," answered Don Quixote; "and I know, too, that I am not only capable of being those I have mentioned, but all the twelve peers of

France, yea, and the nine worthies, since my exploits will far exceed all that they have jointly or separately achieved."

With this and similar conversation, they reached the village about sunset; but the peasant waited until the night was a little advanced, that the poor battered gentleman might not be seen so scurvily mounted. When he thought it the proper time, he entered the village, and arrived at Don Quixote's house, which he found all in confusion. The priest and the barber of the place, who were Don Quixote's particular friends, happened to be there; and the housekeeper was saying to them aloud, " What do you think, Signor Licentiate Pero Perez " (for that was the priest's name), " of my master's misfortune? For neither he, nor his horse, nor the target, nor the lance, nor the armour have been seen these six days past. Woe is me! I am verily persuaded, and it is certainly true as I was born to die, that these cursed books of knight-errantry, which he is often reading, have turned his brain; and, now I think of it, I have often heard him say, talking to himself, that he would turn knight-errant, and go about the world in quest of adventures. The devil and Barabbas take all such books, that have spoiled the finest understanding in all La Mancha!" The niece joined with her, adding, " And you must know, Master Nicholas " (for that was the barber's name), " that it has often happened that my honoured uncle has continued poring on these wicked books of misadventures two whole days and nights; then, throwing the book out of his hand, he would draw his sword and strike against the walls; and when he was heartily tired, would say he had killed four giants as tall as so many steeples, and that the sweat, which his labour occasioned, was the blood of the wounds he had received in the fight; then, after drinking off a large pitcher of cold water, he would be as quiet as ever, telling us that the water was a most precious liquor, brought him by the sage Esquife, a great enchanter, and his friend. But I take the blame of all this to myself, for not informing you, gentlemen, of my dear uncle's extravagances, that they might have been cured before they had gone so far, by burning all those cursed books, which as justly deserve to be committed to the flames as if they were heretical." " I say the same," quoth the priest; " and, in faith, to-morrow shall not pass without holding a public inquisition upon them, and condemning them to the fire, that they may not occasion others to act as I fear my good friend has done."

All this was overheard by Don Quixote and the peasant; and, as it confirmed the latter in the belief of his neighbour's infirmity, he began to cry aloud, " Open the doors, gentlemen, to Signor Valdovinos and the Marquis of Mantua, who comes dangerously wounded, and to Signor Abindarraez the Moor, whom the valorous Roderigo de Narvaez, Governor of Antequera, brings as his prisoner." Hearing this, they all came out; and, immediately recognising their friend, they ran to embrace him, although he had not yet alighted from the ass; for, indeed, it was not in his power. " Forbear, all of you! " he cried, " for I am sorely wounded, through my horse's fault: carry me to my bed;

"Carry me to my bed; and, if it be possible, send for the sage Urganda, to heal my wounds."

and, if it be possible, send for the sage Urganda, to search and heal my wounds." "Look ye!" said the housekeeper immediately, "if my heart did not tell me truly on which leg my master halted. Get upstairs in God's name; for without the help of that same Urganda we shall find a way to cure you ourselves. Cursed, say I again, and a hundred times cursed, be those books of knight-errantry, that have brought your worship to this pass!" They carried him directly to his chamber, where, on searching for his wounds, they could discover none. He then told them, "he was only bruised by a great fall he got with his horse Rozinante, as he was fighting with ten of the most prodigious and audacious giants on the face of the earth." "Ho, ho!" says the priest, "what! there are giants too in the dance? By my faith, I shall set fire to them all before to-morrow night." They asked Don Quixote a thousand questions, to which he would return no answer. He only desired that they would give him some food, and allow him to sleep, that being what he most required. Having done this, the priest inquired particularly of the countryman in what condition Don Quixote had been found. The countryman gave him an account of the whole, with the extravagances he had uttered, both at the time of finding him and during their journey home; which made the licentiate impatient to carry into execution what he had determined to do the following day; when, for that purpose, calling upon his friend Master Nicholas the barber, they proceeded together to Don Quixote's house.

CHAPTER VI.

Of the grand and diverting scrutiny made by the priest and the barber in the library of our ingenious gentleman.

LONG and heavy was the sleep of Don Quixote; meanwhile the priest having asked the niece for the key of the chamber containing the books, those authors of the mischief, which she delivered with a very good will, they entered, attended by the housekeeper, and found above a hundred large volumes well bound, besides a great number of smaller size. No sooner did the housekeeper see them than she ran out of the room in great haste, and immediately returned with a pot of holy water and a bunch of hyssop, saying, " Signor Licentiate, take this and sprinkle the room, lest some enchanter of the many that these books abound with should enchant us, as a punishment for our intention to banish them out of the world." The priest smiled at the housekeeper's simplicity, and ordered the barber to reach him the books one by one, that they might see what they treated of, as they might perhaps find some that deserved not to be chastised by fire. " No," said the niece, " there is no reason why any of them should be spared, for they have all been mischief-makers : so let them all be thrown out of the window into the courtyard, and having made a pile of them, set fire to it ; or else make a bonfire of them in the back yard, where the smoke will offend nobody." The housekeeper said the same, so eagerly did they both thirst for the death of those innocents. But the priest would not consent to it without first reading the titles at least.

The first that Master Nicholas put into his hands was " Amadis de Gaul," in four parts ; and the priest said, " There seems to be some mystery in this, for I have heard say that this was the first book of chivalry printed in Spain, and that all the rest had their foundation and rise from it ; I think, therefore, as head of so pernicious a sect, we ought to condemn him to the fire without mercy." " Not so," said the barber ; " for I have heard also that it is the best of all the books of this kind ; therefore, as being unequalled in its way, it ought to be spared." " You are right," said the priest, " and for that reason its life is granted for the present. Let us see that other next to him." " It is," said the barber, " the ' Adventures of Esplandian,' the legitimate son of ' Amadis de Gaul.' " " Verily," said the priest, " the goodness of the father shall avail the son nothing : take him, Mistress Housekeeper ; open that case-ment, and throw him into the yard, and let him make a beginning to the pile for the intended bonfire." The housekeeper did so with much satisfaction, and good Esplandian was sent flying into the yard, there to wait with patience for the fire with which he was threatened. " Proceed," said the priest. " The next," said the barber, " is ' Amadis of Greece ;' yea, and all these on this side, I believe, are of the lineage of Amadis." " Then into the yard with them all ! " quoth the priest ; " for rather than not burn Queen Pintiquiniestra, and the shepherd Darinal with his eclogues, and the devilish perplexities of the author, I would burn the father who begot me, were I to meet him in the shape of a knight-errant." " Of the same opinion am I," said the barber. " And I too," added the niece. " Well, then," said the housekeeper, " away with them all into the yard." They handed them to her ; and, as they were numerous, to save herself the trouble of the stairs, she threw them all out of the window.

" What tun of an author is that ? " said the priest. " This," answered the barber, " is ' Don Olivante de Laura.' " " The author of that book," said the priest, " was the same who composed the ' Garden of Flowers ;' and in good truth I know not which of the two books is the truest, or rather, the least lying : I can only say that this goes to the yard for its arrogance and absurdity." " This that follows is ' Florismarte of Hyr-cania,'" said the barber. " What ! is Signor Florismarte there ?" replied the priest ; " now, by my faith, he shall soon make his appearance in the yard, notwithstanding his strange birth and chimerical adventures ; for the harshness and dryness of his style will admit of no excuse. To the yard with him, and this other, Mistress Housekeeper." " With all my heart, dear sir," answered she, and with much joy executed what she was commanded. " Here is the ' Knight Platir,'" said the barber. "That," said the priest, " is an ancient book, and I find nothing in him deserving pardon : without more words, let him be sent after the rest ; " which was accordingly done. They opened another book, and found it entitled the " Knight of the Cross." " So religious a title," quoth the priest, " might, one would think, atone for the ignorance of the author ; but it is a common saying, ' the devil lurks behind the cross :' so to the fire with him." The barber, taking down another book, said, " This is the ' Mirror of Chivalry.'" " Oh, I know his worship very well," quoth the priest. " Here comes ' Signor Reynaldos de Montalvan,' with his friends and companions, greater thieves than Cacus ; and the ' Twelve Peers,' with the faithful historiographer Turpin. However, I am only for con-demning them to perpetual banishment, because they contain some things of the famous Mateo Boyardo, from whom the Christian poet Ludovico Ariosto spun his web ; and, even to him, if I find him here uttering any other language than his own, I will show no respect ; but if he speaks in his own tongue, I will put him upon my head." " I have him in Italian," said the barber, " but I do not understand him." " Neither is it any great matter whether you understand him or not," answered the priest ; " and we would willingly have excused the good captain from bringing him into Spain and making him a Castilian; for he has deprived him of a great deal of his native value, which, indeed, is the misfortune of all those who undertake the translation of poetry into other languages; for, with all their care and skill, they can never bring them on a level with the original production. In short, I sentence this, and all other books that shall be found treating of French matters, to be thrown aside and deposited in some dry vault, until we can deliberate more maturely what is to be done with them; excepting, however, 'Bernardo del Carpio,' and another called 'Roncesvalles,' which, if they fall into my hands, shall pass into those of the housekeeper, and thence into the fire without any remission." The barber confirmed the sentence, and accounted it well and rightly determined, knowing that the priest was so good a Christian, and so much a friend to truth, that he would not utter a falsehood for all the world.

Then, opening another book, he saw it was " Palmerin de Oliva," and next to that another, called " Palmerin of England;" on espying which, the licentiate said, " Let this 'Oliva' be torn to pieces, and so effectually burnt that not so much as the ashes may remain; but let 'Palmerin of England' be preserved and kept, as an unique production; and let such another case be made for it as that which Alexander found among the spoils of Darius, and appropriated to preserve the works of the poet Homer. This book, neighbour, is estimable on two accounts: the one, that it is very good of itself; and the other, because there is a tradition that it was written by an ingenious king of Portugal. All the adventures of the Castle of Miraguarda are excellent, and contrived with much art; the dialogue courtly and clear; and all the characters preserved with great judgment and propriety. Therefore, Master Nicholas, saving your better judgment, let this and 'Amadis de Gaul' be exempted from the fire, and let all the rest perish without any further inquiry." " Not so, friend," replied the barber; " for this which I have here is the renowned 'Don Belianis.'" The priest replied, " This, and the second, third, and fourth parts, want a little rhubarb to purge away their excess of bile; besides, we must remove all that relates to the Castle of Fame and other absurdities of greater consequence; for which let sentence of transportation be passed upon them, and, according as they show signs of amendment, they shall be treated with mercy or justice. In the meantime, neighbour, give them room in your house, but let them not be read." " With all my heart," quoth the barber; and without tiring himself any further in turning over books of chivalry, bade the housekeeper take all the great ones and throw them into the yard. This was not spoken to the stupid or deaf, but to one who had a greater mind to be burning them than weaving the finest and largest web; and therefore, laying hold of seven or eight at once, she tossed them out at the window.

But, in taking so many together, one fell at the barber's feet, who had a mind to see what it was, and found it to be the " History of the renowned knight Tiraute the White." " Heaven save me!" quoth the priest, with a loud voice, " is 'Tirante the White' there? Give him to me, neighbour; for in him I shall have a treasure of delight and a mine of entertainment. Here we have Don Kyrie-Eleison of Montalvan, a valorous knight, and his brother Thomas of Montalvan, with the knight Fonseca, and the combat which the valiant Tirante fought with the bull-dog, and the witticisms of the damsel Plazerdemivida, also the amours and artifices of the widow Reposada, and madame the empress in love with her squire Hypolito. Verily, neighbour, in its way it is the best book in the world: here the knights eat, and sleep, and die in their beds, and make their wills before their deaths; with several things which are not to be found in any other books of this kind. Notwithstanding this, I tell you, the author deserved, for writing so many foolish things seriously, to be sent to the galleys for the whole of his life : carry it home and read it, and you will find all I say of him to be true." " I will do so," answered the barber; " but what shall we do with these small volumes that remain?" " Those," said the priest, " are, probably, not books of chivalry, but of poetry." Then opening one, he found it was the " Diana " of George de Montemayor, and, concluding that all the others were of the same kind, he said, " These do not deserve to be burnt like the rest, for they cannot do the mischief that those of chivalry have done: they are works of genius and fancy, and do injury to none." " Oh, sir!" said the niece, " pray order them to be burnt with the rest; for should my uncle be cured of this distemper of chivalry, he may possibly, by reading such books, take it into his head to turn shepherd, and wander through the woods and fields, singing and playing on a pipe ; and, what would be still worse, turn poet, which they say is an incurable and contagious disease." " The damsel says true," quoth the priest, " and it will not be amiss to remove this stumbling-block out of our friend's way. And, since we begin with the ' Diana ' of Monte-mayor, my opinion is that it should not be burnt, but that all that part should be expunged which treats of the sage Felicia and of the enchanted fountain, and also most of the longer poems; leaving him, in God's name, the prose, and also the honour of being the first in that kind of writing." " The next that appears," said the barber, " is the ' Diana,' called the Second, by Salmantino; and another of the same name, whose author is Gil Polo." " The Salmantinian," answered the priest, " may accompany and increase the number of the condemned—to the yard with him! but let that of Gil Polo be preserved as if it were written by Apollo himself. Proceed, friend, and let us dispatch, for it grows late."

" This," said the barber, opening another, " is the ' Ten Books of the Fortune of Love,' composed by Antonio de la Frasso, a Sardinian poet." " By the holy orders I have received !" said the priest, " since Apollo was Apollo, the Muses muses, and the poets poets, so humorous and so whimsical a book as this was never written: it is the best and most extraordinary of the kind that ever appeared in the world; and he who has not read it may be assured that he has never read anything of taste. Give it me here, neighbour; for I am better pleased at finding it than if I had been presented with a cassock of Florence satin." He laid it aside with great satisfaction, and the barber proceeded, saying, "These which follow are the ' Shepherd of Iberia,' the ' Nymphs of Enares,' and the ' Cure of Jealousy.' " " Then you have only to deliver them up to the secular arm of the housekeeper," said the priest; " and ask me not why, for in that case we should never have done." " The next is the ' Shepherd of Filida.'" " He is no shepherd," said the priest, " but an ingenious courtier: let him be preserved, and laid up as a precious jewel." " This bulky volume here," said the barber, " is entitled the ' Treasure of Divers Poems.' " " Had they been fewer," replied the priest, " they would have been more esteemed. It is necessary that this book should be weeded and cleared of some low things interspersed among its sublimities : let it be preserved, both because the author is my friend, and out of respect to other more heroic and exalted productions of his pen." " This," pursued the barber, " is ' El Cancionero' of Lopez Maldonado." " The author of that book," replied the priest, " is also a great friend of mine: his verses, when sung by himself, excite much admiration; indeed, such is the sweetness of his voice in singing them, that they are perfectly enchanting. He is a little too prolix in his eclogues; but there can never be too much of what is really good : let it be preserved with the select. But what book is that next to it?" " The ' Galatea' of Miguel de Cervantes," said the barber. " That Cervantes has been an intimate friend of mine these many years, and I know that he is more versed in misfortunes than in poetry. There is a good vein of invention in his book, which proposes something, though nothing is concluded. We must wait for the second part, which he has promised : perhaps, on his amendment, he may obtain that entire pardon which is now denied him; in the meantime, neighbour, keep him a recluse in your chamber." " With all my heart," answered the barber. " Now, here come three together : the ' Araucana' of Don Alonso de Ercilla, the ' Austriada' of Juan Rufo, a magistrate of Cordova, and the ' Monserrato' of Christoval de Virves, a poet of Valencia." " These three books," said the priest, " are the best that are written in heroic verse in the Castilian tongue, and may stand in competition with the most renowned works of Italy. Let them be peserved as the best productions of the Spanish Muse." The priest grew tired of looking over so many books, and therefore, without examination, proposed that all the rest should be burnt; but the barber, having already opened one called the " Tears of Angelica," " I should have shed tears myself," said the priest, on hearing the name, " had I ordered that book to be burnt; for its author was one of the most celebrated poets, not only of Spain, but of the whole world: his translations from Ovid are admirable."

They closed in with him, and by main force conveyed him again to his bed.

CHAPTER VII.

Of the second sally of our good knight Don Quixote de la Mancha.

ON a sudden, while they were thus employed, Don Quixote began to call aloud, saying, "Here, here, valorous knights! Here you must exert the force of your powerful arms, for the courtiers begin to get the advantage in the tournament." All rushing out at once to the place whence this noisy exclamation proceeded, the scrutiny was suddenly interrupted; and therefore it is believed that to the fire, unseen and un-heard, went the "Carolea," and "Leon of Spain," with the "Acts of the Emperor," composed by Don Louis de Avila,* which, without doubt, must have been amongst those that were left: and, perhaps, had the priest seen them, they might not have undergone so rigorous a sentence. On entering Don Quixote's chamber, they found him already out of bed, and continuing his outcries and ravings, with his drawn sword laying furiously about him, back-stroke and fore-stroke, and as broad awake as if he had

* Generally supposed that this is intended for Don Louis Zapata.

never been asleep. They closed in with him, and by main force conveyed him again to his bed, where, after he was a little composed, he said, turning himself to the priest, "Certainly, my lord Archbishop Turpin, it is a great disgrace to us, who call ourselves the Twelve Peers, to let the knights-courtiers carry off the palm without more opposition, after we the adventurers have gained the prize on the three preceding days." "Say no more, good sir," said the priest; "it may be Heaven's will to change our fortune, and what is lost to-day may be won to-morrow. Mind your health for the present; for I think you must needs be extremely fatigued, if not sorely wounded." "Wounded I am not," said Don Quixote; "but bruised and battered, most certainly; for that bastard, Don Roldan, has pounded me with the trunk of an oak; and all out of mere envy, because he sees I am the sole rival of his prowess. But let me never more be called Rinaldo of Montauban, if, as soon as I can rise from this bed, he pay not dearly for it, in spite of all his enchantments. In the meantime, give me some food, for that is what I am now most in need of, and leave to me the care of avenging myself." They complied with his request, and gave him something to eat; and he then fell fast asleep again, leaving them in astonishment at his madness.

The same night the housekeeper set fire to and burnt all the books that were in the yard and in the house. Some must have perished that deserved to be treasured up in perpetual archives; but their destiny, or the indolence of the scrutineer, forbade it; and in them was fulfilled the saying that "the just sometimes suffer for the unjust." One of the remedies which the priest and the barber prescribed at that time for their friend's malady, was to wall up the chamber which had contained his books, hoping that, when the cause was removed, the effect might cease; and that they should pretend that an enchanter had carried room and all away. This was speedily executed; and two days after, when Don Quixote left his bed, the first thing that occurred to him was to visit his books; and, not finding the room, he went up and down looking for it; when, coming to the former situation of the door, he felt with his hands, and stared about on all sides without speaking a word for some time: at length he asked the housekeeper where the chamber was in which he kept his books. She, who was already well tutored what to answer, said to him, "What room, or what nothing, does your worship look for? There is neither room nor books in this house, for the devil himself has carried all away." "It was not the devil," said the niece, "but an enchanter, who came one night upon a cloud, after the day of your departure, and, alighting from a serpent on which he rode, entered the room: what he did there I know not; but, after some little time, out he came, flying through the roof, and left the house full of smoke; and when we went to see what he had been doing, we saw neither books nor room; only we very well remember, both I and Mistress Housekeeper here, that when the wicked old thief went away, he said with a loud voice that, from a secret enmity he bore to the owner of those books and of the room, he had done a mischief in this house which would soon be manifest: he told us also that he was called the sage Munniaton."

" Freston he meant to say," quoth Don Quixote. " I know not," answered the housekeeper, " whether his name be Freston or Friton ; all I know is that it ended in *ton*." " It doth so," replied Don Quixote. " He is a sage enchanter, a great enemy of mine, and bears me malice, because by his skill and learning he knows, that in process of time I shall engage in single combat with a knight whom he favours, and shall vanquish him, in spite of his protection. On this account he endeavours as much as he can to molest me : but let him know from me that he cannot withstand or avoid what is decreed by Heaven." " Who doubts of that ? " said the niece ; " but, dear uncle, what have you to do with these broils ? Would it not be better to stay quietly at home, and not ramble about the world seeking for better bread than wheaten, without considering that many go out for wool and return shorn ? " "O niece," answered Don Quixote, " how little dost thou know of the matter ! Before they shall shear me, I will pluck and tear off the beards of all those who dare think of touching the tip of a single hair of mine." Neither of them would make any further reply, for they saw his choler began to rise. Fifteen days he remained at home very tranquil, discovering no symptom of an inclination to repeat his late frolics, during which time much pleasant conversation passed between him and his two neighbours, the priest and the barber : he always affirming that the world stood in need of nothing so much as knights-errant and the revival of chivalry. The priest sometimes contradicted him, and at other times acquiesced ; for, had he not been thus cautious, there would have been no means left to bring him to reason.

In the meantime Don Quixote tampered with a labourer, a neighbour of his, and an honest man (if such an epithet can be given to one that is poor), but shallow-brained : in short, he said so much, used so many arguments, and made so many promises, that the poor fellow resolved to sally out with him and serve him in the capacity of a squire. Among other things, Don Quixote told him that he ought to be very glad to accompany him, for such an adventure might some time or the other occur, that by one stroke an island might be won, where he might leave him governor. With this and other promises Sancho Panza (for that was the labourer's name) left his wife and children, and engaged himself as squire to his neighbour. Don Quixote now set about raising money ; and, by selling one thing, pawning another, and losing by all, he collected a tolerable sum. He fitted himself likewise with a buckler, which he borrowed of a friend, and, patching up his broken helmet in the best manner he could, he acquainted his squire Sancho of the day and hour he intended to set out, that he might provide himself with what he thought would be most needful. Above all, he charged him not to forget a wallet, which Sancho assured him he would not neglect ; he said also that he thought of taking an ass with him, as he had a very good one, and he was not used to travel much on foot. With regard to the ass, Don Quixote paused a little, endeavouring to recollect whether any knight-errant had ever carried a squire mounted on ass-back, but no instance of the kind occurred to his memory. However, he consented that he should take his ass, resolving to accommodate him more honourably at the earliest opportunity, by dismounting the first discourteous knight he should meet. He provided himself also with shirts, and other things, conformably to the advice given him by the innkeeper.

All this being accomplished, Don Quixote and Sancho Panza, without taking leave, the one of his wife and children, or the other of his housekeeper and niece, one night sallied out of the village unperceived; and they travelled so hard that by break of day they believed themselves secure, even if search were made after them. Sancho Panza proceeded upon his ass like a patriarch, with his wallet and leathern bottle, and with a vehement desire to find himself governor of the island which his master had promised him. Don Quixote happened to take the same route as on his first expedition, over the plain of Montiel, which he passed with less inconvenience than before; for it was early in the morning, and the rays of the sun, darting on them horizontally, did not annoy them. Sancho Panza now said to his master, "I beseech your worship, good Sir Knight-errant, not to forget your promise concerning that same island; for I shall know how to govern it, be it ever so large." To which Don Quixote answered: "Thou must know, friend Sancho Panza, that it was a custom much in use among the knights-errant of old to make their squires governors of the islands or kingdoms they conquered; and I am determined that so laudable a custom shall not be lost through my neglect; on the contrary, I resolve to outdo them in it: for they, sometimes, and perhaps most times, waited till their squires were grown old; and when they were worn out in their service, and had endured many bad days and worse nights, they conferred on them some title, such as count, or at least marquis, of some valley or province of more or less account: but if you live and I live, before six days have passed I may probably win such a kingdom as may have others depending on it, just fit for thee to be crowned king of one of them. And do not think this any extraordinary matter; for things fall out to knights by such unforeseen and unexpected ways, that I may easily give thee more than I promise." "So, then," answered Sancho Panza, "if I were a king, by some of those miracles your worship mentions, Joan Gutierrez, my duck, would come to be a queen, and my children infantas!" "Who doubts it?" answered Don Quixote. "I doubt it," replied Sancho Panza; "for I am verily persuaded that, if God were to rain down kingdoms upon the earth, none of them would sit well upon the head of Mary Gutierrez; for you must know, sir, she is not worth two farthings for a queen. The title of countess would sit better upon her, with the help of Heaven and good friends." "Recommend her to God, Sancho," answered Don Quixote, "and He will do what is best for her; but do thou have a care not to debase thy mind so low as to content thyself with being less than a viceroy." "Sir, I will not," answered Sancho; "especially having so great a man for my master as your worship, who will know how to give me whatever is most fitting for me and what I am best able to bear."

CHAPTER VIII.

Of the valorous Don Quixote's success in the dreadful and never-before-imagined adventure of the windmills; with other events worthy to be recorded.

ENGAGED in this discourse, they came in sight of thirty or forty windmills, which are in that plain; and as soon as Don Quixote espied them, he said to his squire, "Fortune disposes our affairs better than we ourselves could have desired : look yonder, friend Sancho Panza, where thou mayest discover somewhat more than thirty monstrous giants, whom I intend to encounter and slay, and with their spoils we will begin to enrich ourselves; for it is lawful war, and doing God good service, to remove so wicked a generation from off the face of the earth." "What giants?" said Sancho Panza. "Those thou seest yonder," answered his master, "with their long arms; for some are wont to have them almost of the length of two leagues." "Look, sir," answered Sancho, "those which appear yonder are not giants, but windmills, and what seem to be arms are the sails, which, whirled about by the wind, make the mill-stone go." "It is very evident," answered Don Quixote, "that thou art not versed in the business of adventures. They are giants; and if thou art afraid, get thee aside and pray, whilst I engage with them in fierce and unequal combat." So saying, he clapped spurs to his steed, notwithstanding the cries his squire sent after him, assuring him that they were certainly windmills, and not giants. But he was so fully possessed that they were giants, that he neither heard the outcries of his squire Sancho, nor yet discerned what they were, though he was very near them, but went on crying out aloud, "Fly not, ye cowards and vile caitiffs ! for it is a single knight who assaults you." The wind now rising a little, the great sails began to move; upon which Don Quixote called out, "Although ye should have more arms than the giant Briareus, ye shall pay for it."

Then recommending himself devoutly to his lady Dulcinea, beseeching her to succour him in the present danger, being well covered with his buckler and setting his lance in the rest, he rushed on as fast as Rozinante could gallop, and attacked the first mill before him ; when, running his lance into the sail, the wind whirled it about with so much violence that it broke the lance to shivers, dragging horse and rider after it, and tumbling them over and over on the plain in very evil plight. Sancho Panza hastened to his assistance as fast as the ass could carry him ; and when he came up to his master he found him unable to stir, so violent was the blow which he and Rozinante had received in their fall. "God save me !" quoth Sancho, "did not I warn you to have a care of what you did, for that they were nothing but windmills ? And nobody could mistake them but one that had the like in his head." "Peace, friend Sancho," answered Don Quixote ; "for matters of war are, of all others, most subject to continual change. Now I verily believe, and it is most certainly the fact, that the sage Freston, who stole away my chamber and books, has metamorphosed these giants into windmills, on purpose to deprive me of the glory of vanquishing them, so great is the enmity he bears me! But his wicked arts will finally avail but little against the goodness of my sword." "God grant it!" answered Sancho Panza; then helping him to rise, he mounted him again upon his steed, which was almost disjointed.

Conversing upon the late adventure, they followed the road that led to the Pass of Lapice; because there, Don Quixote said, they could not fail to meet with many and various adventures, as it was much frequented. He was, however, concerned at the loss of his lance; and, speaking of it to his squire, he said, "I remember to have read that a certain Spanish knight, called Diego Perez de Vargas, having broken his sword in fight, tore off a huge branch or limb from an oak, and performed such wonders with it that day, and dashed out the brains of so many Moors, that he was surnamed Machuca;* and from that day forward he and his descendants bore the names of Vargas and Machuca. I now speak of this because from the first oak we meet I mean to tear a limb at least as good as that, with which I purpose and resolve to perform such feats that thou shalt deem thyself most fortunate in having been thought worthy to behold them, and to be an eye-witness of things which will scarcely be credited." "Heaven's will be done!" quoth Sancho; "I believe all just as you say, sir. But pray set yourself more upright in your saddle, for you seem to me to ride sidelong, owing, perhaps, to the bruises received by your fall." "It is certainly so," said Don Quixote; "and if I do not complain of pain, it is because knights-errant are not allowed to complain of any wound whatever, even though their entrails should issue from it." "If so, I have nothing more to say," quoth Sancho, "but I should be glad to hear your worship complain when anything ails you. As for myself, I must complain of the least pain I feel, unless this business of not complaining extend also to the squires of knights-errant." Don Quixote could not forbear smiling at the simplicity of his squire, and told him he might complain whenever and as much as he pleased, either with or without cause, having never yet read anything to the contrary in the laws of chivalry.

Sancho put him in mind that it was time to dine. His master answered that at present he had no need of food, but that he might eat whenever he thought proper. With this licence, Sancho adjusted himself as well as he could upon his beast; and, taking out the contents of his wallet, he jogged on behind his master very leisurely, eating, and ever and anon raising the bottle to his mouth with so much relish, that the best-fed victualler of Malaga might have envied him. And whilst he went on in this manner repeating his draughts, he thought no more of the promises his master had made him; nor did he think it any toil, but rather a recreation, to go in quest of adventures, however perilous they

---

* From *machucar,* to bruise or break.

might be. In fine, they passed that night under the shelter of some trees; and from one of them the knight tore a withered branch, to serve him in some sort as a lance, after fixing upon it the iron head of the one that had been broken. All that night Don Quixote slept not, but ruminated on his lady Dulcinea, conformably to the practice of knights-errant, who, as their histories told him, were wont to pass many successive nights in woods and deserts, without closing their eyes, indulging the sweet remembrance of their mistresses. Not so did Sancho spend the night; for, his stomach being full, and not of succory-water, he made but one sleep of it; and, had not his master roused him, neither

His stomach being full, and not of succory-water, he made but one sleep of it.

the beams of the sun that darted full in his face, nor the melody of the birds, which in great numbers cheerfully saluted the approach of the new day, could have awaked him. At his uprising he applied again to his bottle, and found it much lighter than the evening before; which grieved him to the heart, for he did not think they were in the way soon to remedy that defect. Don Quixote would not yet break his fast, resolving, as we have said, still to subsist upon savoury remembrances.

They now turned again into the road they had entered upon the day before, leading to the Pass of Lapice, which they discovered about three in the afternoon. "Here, friend Sancho," said Don Quixote, upon seeing it, "we may plunge our arms up to the elbows in what are termed adventures. But attend to this caution, that, even shouldst thou see me in the greatest peril in the world, thou must not lay hand to thy sword to defend me, unless thou perceivest that my assailants are vulgar and low people: in that case thou mayest assist me; but should they be knights, it is in nowise agreeable to the laws of chivalry that thou shouldst interfere, until thou art thyself dubbed a knight." "Your worship," answered Sancho, " shall be obeyed most punctually therein, and the rather as I am naturally very peaceable, and an enemy to thrusting myself into brawls and squabbles; but, for all that, as to what regards the defence of my own person, I shall make no great account of those same laws, since both divine and human law allows every man to defend himself against whoever would wrong him." " That I grant," answered Don Quixote ; " but with respect to giving me aid against knights, thou must refrain, and keep within bounds thy natural impetuosity." " I say, I will do so," answered Sancho; " and I will observe this precept as religiously as the Lord's day."

As they were thus discoursing, there appeared on the road two monks of the order of St. Benedict, apparently mounted upon dromedaries; for the mules whereon they rode were not much less. They wore travelling masks, and carried umbrellas. Behind them came a coach, accompanied by four or five men on horseback and two muleteers on foot. Within the coach, as it afterwards appeared, was a Biscayan lady on her way to join her husband at Seville, who was there waiting to embark for India, where he was appointed to a very honourable post. The monks were not in her company, but were only travelling the same road. Scarcely had Don Quixote espied them, when he said to his squire, " Either I am deceived, or this will prove the most famous adventure that ever happened ; for those black figures that appear yonder must undoubtedly be enchanters, who are carrying off in that coach some princess whom they have stolen, which wrong I am bound to use my utmost endeavours to redress." " This may prove a worse business than the windmills," said Sancho; " pray, sir, take notice that those are Benedictine monks, and the coach must belong to some travellers. Hearken to my advice, sir; have a care what you do, and let not the devil deceive you." " I have already told thee, Sancho," answered Don Quixote, " that thou knowest little concerning adventures: what I say is true, as thou wilt presently see." So saying, he advanced forward, and planted himself in the midst of the highway by which the monks were to pass ; and when they were so near that he supposed they could hear what he said, he cried out with a loud voice, " Diabolical and monstrous race ! either instantly release the high-born princesses whom ye are carrying away perforce in that coach, or prepare for instant death, as the just chastisement of your wicked deeds." The monks stopped their mules, and stood amazed, as much at the figure of Don Quixote as at his expressions: to which they answered, " Signor cavalier, we are neither diabolical nor monstrous, but monks of the Benedictine order, travelling on our own business, and entirely ignorant whether any princesses are carried away in that coach by force or not." " No fair speeches to me, for I know ye, treacherous scoundrels ! " and without waiting for a reply, he clapped spurs to Rozinante, and, with his lance couched, ran at the foremost monk with such fury and resolution that, if he had not slid down from his mule, he would certainly have been thrown to the ground, and wounded too, if not killed outright. The second monk, on observing how his comrade was treated, clapped spurs to the sides of his good mule, and began to scour along the plain lighter than the wind itself.

Sancho Panza, seeing the monk on the ground, leaped nimbly from his ass, and, running up to him, began to disrobe him. While he was thus employed, the two lacqueys came up, and asked him why he was stripping their master. Sancho told them that they were his lawful perquisites, being the spoils of the battle which his lord Don Quixote had just won. The lacqueys, who did not understand the jest, nor what was meant by spoils or battles, seeing that Don Quixote was at a distance speaking with those in the coach, fell upon Sancho, threw him down, and, besides leaving him not a hair in his beard, gave him a hearty kicking, and left him stretched on the ground, deprived of sense and motion. Without losing a moment, the monk now got upon his mule again, trembling, terrified, and as pale as death, and was no sooner mounted than he spurred after his companion, who stood at some distance to observe the issue of this strange encounter; but, being unable to wait, they pursued their way, crossing themselves oftener than if the devil had been at their heels. In the meantime Don Quixote, as it hath been already mentioned, addressing the lady in the coach, " Your beauteous ladyship may now," said he, " dispose of your person as pleaseth you best, for the pride of your ravishers lies humbled in the dust, overthrown by my invincible arm: and that you may be at no trouble to learn the name of your deliverer, know that I am called Don Quixote de la Mancha, knight-errant and adventurer, and captive to the peerless and beauteous Dulcinea del Toboso; and in requital of the benefit you have received at my hands, all I desire is, that you would return to Toboso, and in my name present yourselves before that lady, and tell her what I have done to obtain your liberty."

All that Don Quixote said was overheard by a certain squire who accompanied the coach, a Biscayan, who, finding he would not let it proceed, but talked of their immediately returning to Toboso, flew at Don Quixote, and, taking hold of his lance, addressed him, in bad Castilian and worse Biscayan, after this manner: " Cavalier, begone, and the devil go with thee! I swear by the Power that made me, if thou dost not quit the coach, thou forfeitest thy life, as I am a Biscayan." Don Quixote understood him very well, and with great calmness answered, " If thou wert a gentleman, as thou art not, I would before now have chastised thy folly and presumption, thou pitiful slave." " I am no gentleman!" said the Biscayan; " I swear by the great God thou liest, as I am a Christian. If thou wilt throw away thy lance, and draw thy sword, thou shalt see how soon the cat will get into the water.*

---

* " To carry the cat to the water " is a saying applied to one who is victorious in any contest; and it is taken from a game in which two cats are tied together by the tail, then carried near a pit or well (having the water between them), and the cat which first pulls the other in is declared conqueror.

Biscayan by land, gentleman by sea, gentleman for the devil, and thou liest! Now what hast thou to say?" "Thou shalt see that presently, as said Agrages," answered Don Quixote; then, throwing down his lance, he drew his sword, grasped his buckler, and set upon the Biscayan with a resolution to take his life. The Biscayan, seeing him come on in that manner, would fain have alighted, knowing that his mule, a wretched hack, was not to be trusted; but he had only time to draw his sword. Fortunately for him, he was so near the coach as to be able to snatch from it a cushion, that served him for a shield; whereupon they immediately fell to, as if they had been mortal enemies. The rest of the company would have made peace between them, but it was impossible; for the Biscayan swore, in his jargon, that if they would not let him finish the combat, he would murder his mistress, or whoever attempted to prevent him. The lady of the coach, amazed and affrighted at what she saw, ordered the coachman to remove a little out of the way, and sat at a distance beholding the fierce conflict; in the progress of which the Biscayan gave Don Quixote so mighty a stroke on one of his shoulders, and above his buckler, that, had it not been for his armour, he had cleft him down to the girdle. Don Quixote, feeling the weight of that unmeasurable blow, cried out aloud, saying, "O lady of my soul! Dulcinea, flower of all beauty! succour this thy knight, who, to satisfy thy great goodness, exposes himself to this perilous extremity!" This invocation, the drawing his sword, the covering himself well with his buckler, and rushing with fury on the Biscayan, was the work of an instant—resolving to venture all on the fortune of a single blow. The Biscayan perceiving his intention, resolved to do the same, and therefore waited for him, covering himself well with his cushion; but he was unable to turn his mule either to the right or left, for, being already jaded, and unaccustomed to such sport, the creature would not move a step.

Don Quixote, as we before said, now advanced towards the wary Biscayan, with his uplifted sword, fully determined to cleave him asunder; and the Biscayan awaited him with his sword also raised, and guarded by his cushion. All the bystanders were in fearful suspense as to the event of those prodigious blows with which they threatened each other; and the lady of the coach and her attendants were making a thousand vows and promises of offerings to all the images and places of devotion in Spain, that God might deliver them and their squire from this great peril. But the misfortune is, that the author of this history, at that very crisis, leaves the combat unfinished, pleading, in excuse, that he could find no more written of the exploits of Don Quixote than what he has already related. It is true, indeed, that the second undertaker of this work could not believe that so curious a history should have been consigned to oblivion, or that the wits of La Mancha should have so little curiosity as not to preserve in their archives, or cabinets, some memorials of this famous knight; and, under that persuasion, he did not despair of finding the conclusion of this delectable history; which through the favour of Heaven actually came to pass, and in the manner that shall be faithfully recounted in the following chapter.

BOOK II.

CHAPTER IX.

Wherein is concluded the stupendous battle between the gallant Biscayan and the valiant Manchegan.

Now, LET it not be forgotten, that in the preceding part of this history we left the valiant Biscayan and the renowned Don Quixote with their naked swords raised on high, ready to discharge two such furious and cleaving strokes as must, if they had lighted full, at least have divided the combatants from head to heel, and split them asunder like a pomegranate; but at that critical moment this relishing history stopped short, and was left imperfect, without having any notice from the author of where the remainder might be found. This grieved me extremely; and the pleasure afforded by the little I had read gave place to mortification when I considered the uncertainty there was of ever finding the portion that appeared to me yet wanting of this delightful story. It seemed impossible, and contrary to all praiseworthy custom, that so accomplished a knight should have no sage to record his unparalleled exploits; for none of those knights-errant who travelled in quest of adventures were ever without them; each having one or two sages, made as it were on purpose, not only to record their actions, but to describe their most minute and trifling thoughts, however secret. Surely, then, a knight of such worth could not be so unfortunate as to want that with which Platir, and others like him, abounded. Hence I could not be induced to believe that so gallant a history had been left maimed and imperfect; and I blamed the malignity of Time—that devourer and consumer of all things—for having either concealed or destroyed it. On the other hand, recollecting that some of his books were of so recent a date as the " Cure for Jealousy " and the " Nymphs and Shepherds of Henares," I thought his story also might be modern, and, if not yet written, might still be remembered by the people of his village, and those of the neighbouring places. This idea impressed me deeply, and made me anxious to be truly informed of the whole life and wonderful actions of our renowned Spaniard, Don Quixote de la Mancha, the light and mirror of Manchegan chivalry! the first who, in our age and in these calamitous times, took upon him the toil and exercise of arms-errant, to redress wrongs, succour widows, and relieve those damsels who, with whip and palfrey, and with all their sweetness about them, rambled up and down from mountain to mountain, and from valley to valley; for damsels there were, in days of yore, who (unless overpowered by some miscreant or low clown with hatchet and steel cap, or some prodigious giant), at the expiration of fourscore years, and without ever sleeping during all that time beneath a roof, went to the grave as spotless as the mothers that bore them. Now, I say, upon these and many other accounts, our gallant Don Quixote is worthy of immortal memory and praise. Nor ought some share to be denied even to me, for the labour and pains I have taken to discover the end of this delectable history; though I am very sensible that, if Heaven and fortune had not befriended me, the world would have still been without that diversion and pleasure which, for nearly two hours, an attentive reader of it cannot fail to enjoy. Now the manner of finding it was this :

As I was walking one day on the Exchange of Toledo, a boy offered for sale some bundles of old papers to a mercer; and as I am fond of reading, though it be only tattered papers thrown about the streets, led by this natural inclination, I took a parcel of those the boy was selling, and perceived them to be written in Arabic. But not understanding it myself, although I knew the letters, I immediately looked about for some Moorish rabbi who could read them to me; nor was it difficult to find such an interpreter; for had I sought one to explain some more ancient and better language, I should have found him there. In fine, my good fortune presented one to me, to whom I communicated my desire, and, putting the book into his hands, he opened it towards the middle, and having read a little, began to laugh. I asked him what he smiled at, and he said that "it was at something which he found written in the margin, by way of annotation." I desired him to say what it was; and, still laughing, he told me that there was written on the margin as follows : "This Dulcinea del Toboso, so often mentioned in this history, was said to have been the best hand at salting pork of any woman in all La Mancha." When I heard the name of Dulcinea del Toboso, I stood amazed and confounded; for it immediately occurred to me that those bundles of paper might contain the history of Don Quixote.

With this idea, I pressed him to read the beginning, which he did, and, rendering extempore the Arabic into Castilian, said that it began thus : "The History of Don Quixote de la Mancha, written by Cid Hamet Benengeli, Arabian historiographer." Much discretion was necessary to dissemble the joy I felt at hearing the title of the book ; and, snatching the other part out of the mercer's hands, I bought the whole bundle of papers of the boy for half a real ; who, if he had been cunning, and had perceived how eager I was to have them, might well have promised himself, and really carried off, more than six reals by the bargain. I retired immediately with the Morisco through the cloister of the great church, and requested him to translate for me those papers which treated of Don Quixote into the Castilian tongue, without omitting or adding anything ; offering him in payment whatever he

It would have gone hard with him had not the ladies entreated that he would spare the life of their squire.

should demand. He was satisfied with fifty pounds of raisins and two bushels of wheat, and promised to translate them faithfully and expeditiously. But, in order to facilitate the business, and also to make sure of so valuable a prize, I took him home to my own house, where, in little more than six weeks, he translated the whole exactly as will be found in the following pages.

In the first sheet was portrayed, in a most lively manner, Don Quixote's combat with the Biscayan, in the attitude already described; their swords raised, the one covered with his buckler, the other with his cushion, and the Biscayan mule described so correctly to the life, that you might discover it to be a hack jade at the distance of a bowshot. The Biscayan had a label at his feet, on which was written "Don Sancho de Azpetia," which, without doubt, must have been his name; and at the feet of Rozinante was another, on which was written "Don Quixote." Rozinante was admirably delineated: so long and lank, so lean and feeble, with so sharp a backbone, and so like one in a galloping consumption, that you might see plainly with what judgment and propriety the name of Rozinante had been given him. Close by him stood Sancho Panza, holding his ass by the halter; at whose feet was another scroll, whereon was written "Sancho Zancas;" and not without reason, if he was really, as the painting represented him, paunch-bellied, short of stature, and spindle-shanked, which, doubtless, gave him the names of Panza and Zancas; for the history calls him by each of these surnames. There were some other more minute particulars observable; but they are all of little importance, and contribute nothing to the faithful narration of the history, though none are to be despised, if true. But if any objection be alleged against the truth of this history, it can only be that the author was an Arabian, those of that nation being not a little addicted to lying; though as they are so much our enemies, it may be conjectured that he rather fell short of than exceeded the bounds of truth. And, in fact, so he seems to have done; for when he might and ought to have launched out in the praises of so excellent a knight, it appears as if he had been careful to pass over them in silence: an evil act and worse design, for historians ought to be precise, faithful, and unprejudiced, and neither interest nor fear, hatred nor affection, should make them swerve from the way of truth, whose mother is history, the rival of time, the depository of great actions, the witness of the past, example to the present, and monitor to the future. In this history you will certainly find the most entertaining things imaginable; and if wanting in anything, it must, without question, be owing to its infidel author, and not to any defect in the subject. In short, the second part, according to the translation, began in this manner:

The trenchant blades of the two valorous and enraged combatants, being brandished aloft, seemed to stand threatening heaven and earth and the deep abyss, such was the courage and gallantry of their deportment. The first who discharged his blow was the choleric Biscayan, which fell with such force and fury that, if the edge of his sword had not turned aslant by the way, that single blow had been enough to have put an end to this cruel conflict, and to all the adventures of our knight. But good fortune, preserving him for greater things, so turned his adversary's sword, that, though it alighted on the left shoulder, it did him no other hurt than to disarm that side, carrying off by the way a great part of his helmet, with half an ear; all which with hideous ruin fell to the ground, leaving him in a piteous plight.

Good Heaven! who is he that can worthily describe the rage that entered into the breast of our Manchegan at seeing himself thus treated! Let it suffice that it was such that, raising himself afresh in his stirrups, and grasping his sword faster in both hands, he discharged it with such fury upon the Biscayan, directly over the cushion and upon his head, which was unprotected, that, as if a mountain had fallen upon him, the blood began to gush out of his nostrils, his mouth, and his ears ; and he seemed as if he was just falling from his mule, which doubtless he must have done, had not he laid fast hold of his neck ; but, notwithstanding that, he lost his stirrups and then let go his hold; while the mule, frightened at the terrible stroke, began to run about the field, and at two or three plunges laid her master flat on the ground. Don Quixote stood looking on with great calmness ; and, seeing him fall, he leaped from his horse with much agility, ran up to him, and clapping the point of his sword to his eyes, bade him yield, or he would cut off his head. The Biscayan was so stunned that he could not answer a word ; and it would have gone hard with him (so blinded with rage was Don Quixote) had not the ladies of the coach, who till now had been witnessing the combat in great dismay, approached him, and earnestly entreated that he would do them the great kindness and favour to spare the life of their squire. Don Quixote answered, with much solemnity and gravity, "Assuredly, fair ladies, I am most willing to grant you your request, but it must be upon a certain condition and compact; which is, that this knight shall promise to repair to the town of Toboso, and present himself from me before the peerless Donna Dulcinea, that she may dispose of him according to her pleasure." The terrified and disconsolate lady, without considering what Don Quixote required or inquiring who Dulcinea was, promised him that her squire should perform whatever he commanded. "Then, on the faith of this promise," said Don Quixote, "I will do him no further hurt, though he well deserves it at my hands."

CHAPTER X.

Of the pleasant discourse which Don Quixote had with his good squire Sancho Panza.

BEFORE this time Sancho Panza had got upon his legs, somewhat roughly handled by the servants of the monks, and stood an attentive spectator during the combat of his master, Don Quixote, beseeching God, in his heart, that He would be pleased to give him the victory, and that he might hereby win some island of which he might make him governor, according to his promise. Now, seeing the conflict at an end, and that his master was ready to mount again upon Rozinante, he came up to hold his stirrup ; but before he had mounted, fell upon his knees before him, then taking hold of his hand and kissing it, said to him,

" Be pleased, my lord Don Quixote, to bestow upon me the government of that island which you have won in this dreadful battle; for, be it ever so big, I feel in myself ability sufficient to govern it as well as the best that ever governed island in the world." To which Don Quixote answered, " Consider, brother Sancho, that this adventure, and others of this nature, are not adventures of islands, but of cross-ways, in which nothing is to be gained but a broken head or the loss of an ear. Have patience ; for adventures will offer whereby I may not only make thee a governor, but something yet greater." Sancho returned him abundance of thanks ; and, kissing his hand again and the skirt of his armour, he helped him to get upon Rozinante ; then mounting his ass, he followed his master, who, going off at a round pace, without taking his leave or speaking to those in the coach, immediately entered into an adjoining wood.

Sancho followed him as fast his beast could trot ; but Rozinante made such speed that, seeing himself left behind, he was forced to call aloud to his master to stay for him. Don Quixote did so, checking Rozinante by the bridle until his weary squire overtook him ; who, as soon as he came near, said to him, " Methinks, sir, it would not be amiss to retire to some church ; for, considering in what condition you have left your adversary, I should not wonder if they give notice of the fact to the Holy Brotherhood, who may seize us ; and, in faith, if they do, before we get out of their clutches we may chance to sweat for it." " Peace," quoth Don Quixote ; " for where hast thou ever seen or heard of a knight-errant having been brought before a court of justice, however numerous the homicides he may have committed ? " " I know nothing of your Omecils," answered Sancho, " nor in my life ever cared about them ; only this I know, that the Holy Brotherhood have something to say to those who fight in the fields ; and as to the other matter, I shall have nothing to do with it." " Set thy heart at rest, friend," answered Don Quixote ; " for I would deliver thee out of the hands of the Chaldeans, much more out of those of the Holy Brotherhood. But tell me, on thy life, hast thou ever seen a more valorous knight than I upon the whole face of the earth ? Hast thou read in history of any one who has, or ever had, more spirit in attacking, more breath in holding out, more dexterity in wounding, or more address in overthrowing ? " " The truth is," answered Sancho, " that I never read any history at all, for I can neither read nor write ; but what I dare affirm is, that I have never served a bolder master than your worship in all the days of my life ; and pray God we may not be called to account for this boldness where I just now said. What I beg of your worship is, that you would let your wound be dressed, for a great deal of blood comes from that ear ; and I have some lint and a little white ointment here in my wallet." " All this would have been needless," answered Don Quixote, " had I recollected to make a phial of the balsam of Fierabras ; for with one single drop of that we might have saved both time and medicine." " What phial and what balsam is that ? " said Sancho Panza. " It is a balsam," answered Don Quixote, " the receipt of which I hold in memory; and he who possesses it need not fear death, nor apprehend that any wound will be fatal: therefore, when I shall have made it, and given it to thy care, all thou wilt have to do, when thou seest me in some battle cleft asunder (as it frequently happens), is, to take up fair and softly that part of my body which shall fall to the ground, and with the greatest nicety, before the blood is congealed, place it upon the other half that shall remain in the saddle, taking especial care to make them tally exactly. Then shalt thou give me two draughts only of the balsam aforesaid, and instantly thou wilt see me become sounder than an apple." "If this be so," said Sancho, "I renounce from henceforward the government of the promised island, and only desire, in pay-

Sancho took some lint and ointment out of his wallet.

ment of my many and good services, that your worship will give me the receipt of this extraordinary liquor; for I dare say it will anywhere fetch more than two reals an ounce, and I want no more to pass this life with credit and comfort. But I should be glad to know whether the making of it will cost much?" "For less than three reals thou mayest make nine pints," answered Don Quixote. "Sinner that I am!" exclaimed Sancho, "why does your worship delay making it?" "Peace, friend," answered Don Quixote; "for I intend to teach thee greater secrets, and to do thee greater kindnesses; but at present let us set about the cure, for my ear pains me more than I could wish."

Sancho took some lint and ointment out of his wallet; but, when Don Quixote perceived that his helmet was broken, he was ready to run stark mad; and, laying his hand on his sword and raising his eyes to heaven, he said, " I swear, by the Creator of all things, and by all that is contained in the four holy evangelists, to lead the life that the great Marquis of Mantua led, when he vowed to revenge the death of his nephew Valdovinos; which was, not to eat bread on a tablecloth, nor again go home to his wife, and other things, which though I do not now remember, I consider as here expressed, until I have taken entire vengeance on him who hath done me this outrage!" Sancho, hearing this, said to him: " Pray consider, Signor Don Quixote, that if the knight has performed what was enjoined upon him, namely, to go and present himself before my lady Dulcinea del Toboso, he will then have done his duty, and deserves no new punishment unless he commit a new crime." " Thou hast spoken and remarked very justly," answered Don Quixote, " and I annul the oath, so far as concerns the taking a fresh revenge; but I make it, and confirm it anew, as to leading the life I have mentioned, until I shall take by force from some knight another helmet equally good. And think not, Sancho, that I am making a smoke of straw; for I well know whose example I shall follow, since precisely the same thing happened with regard to Mambrino's helmet, which cost Sacripante so dear." " I wish your worship would send such oaths to the devil," said Sancho, " for they are very hurtful to the health and prejudicial to the conscience. Besides, pray tell me, if perchance for many days we should not light on a man armed with a helmet, what must we do then? Must the oath be kept in spite of so many difficulties and inconveniences, such as sleeping in your clothes, and not sleeping in any inhabited place, and a thousand other penances contained in the oath of that mad old fellow the Marquis of Mantua, which your worship would now revive? Consider, that none of these roads are frequented by armed men, but carriers and carters, who, so far from wearing helmets, perhaps never so much as heard of them in all their lives." " Thou art mistaken in this," said Don Quixote; " for before we shall have passed two hours in these cross-ways, we shall have seen more armed men than came to the Siege of Albraca to carry off Angelica the Fair." " Well, then, be it so," quoth Sancho; " and Heaven grant us good success, and that we may speedily get this island, which costs me so dear; no matter, then, how soon I die." " I have already told thee, Sancho, to give thyself no concern upon that account; for, if an island cannot be had, there is the kingdom of Denmark, or that of Sobradisa, which will fit thee like a ring to the finger. Besides, as they are upon *terra firma*, thou shouldst prefer them. But let us leave this to its own time, and see if thou hast anything for us to eat in thy wallet; we will then go in quest of some castle, where we may lodge this night, and make the balsam that I told thee of; for I declare that my ear pains me exceedingly." " I have here an onion and a piece of cheese, and I know not how many crusts of bread," said Sancho; " but they are not eatables fit for so valiant a knight as your worship." " How little dost thou understand of this matter!" answered Don Quixote. " I tell thee, Sancho, that it is honourable in knights-errant not to eat once in a month; and, if they do taste food, it must be what first offers: and this thou wouldst have known hadst thou read as many histories as I have done; for though I have perused many, I never yet found in them any account of knights-errant taking food, unless it were by chance and at certain sumptuous banquets prepared expressly for them; the rest of their days they lived, as it were, upon smelling. And though it is to be presumed they could not subsist without eating and satisfying all other wants—as, in fact, they were men—yet, since they passed most part of their lives in wandering through forests and deserts, and without a cook, their usual diet must have consisted of rustic viands, such as those which thou hast now offered me. Therefore, friend Sancho, let not that trouble thee which gives me pleasure, nor endeavour to make a new world or to throw knight-errantry off its hinges." "Pardon me, sir," said Sancho; "for, as I can neither read nor write, as I told you before, I am entirely unacquainted with the rules of the knightly profession; but henceforward I will furnish my wallet with all sorts of dried fruits for your worship, who are a knight, and for myself, who am none, I will supply it with poultry and other things of more substance." "I do not say, Sancho," replied Don Quixote, "that knights-errant are obliged to eat nothing but the dried fruits thou hast mentioned, but that such was their ordinary sustenance, together with certain herbs they found in the fields, which were to them well known, as they are also to me." "It is a good thing to know these same herbs," answered Sancho; "for I am inclined to think we shall one day have occasion to make use of that knowledge."

He now brought out what provisions he had, and they ate together in a very peaceable and friendly manner. But, being desirous to seek out some place wherein to rest that night, they soon finished their poor and dry meal, and then made what haste they could to reach some village before night; but both the sun and their hopes failed them near the huts of some goatherds. They determined, therefore, to take up their lodging with them: but if Sancho was grieved that they could not reach a village, his master was as much rejoiced to lie in the open air, conceiving that, every time this befell him, he was performing an act which confirmed his title to chivalry.

CHAPTER XI.

Of what befell Don Quixote with the goatherds.

No one could be more kindly received than was Don Quixote by the goatherds; and Sancho, having accommodated Rozinante and his ass in the best manner he was able, pursued the odour emitted by certain pieces of goat's flesh that were boiling in a kettle on the fire; and though he would willingly, at that instant, have tried whether they were ready to be transferred from the kettle to the stomach, he forbore doing so, as the goatherds themselves took them off the fire, and, spreading some sheepskins on the ground, very speedily served up their rural mess, and with much cordiality invited them both to partake of it. Six of them that belonged to the fold seated themselves round the skins, having first, with rustic compliments, requested Don Quixote to seat himself upon a trough with the bottom upwards placed on purpose for him. Don Quixote sat down, and Sancho remained standing to serve the cup, which was made of horn. His master, seeing him standing, said to him, " That thou mayest see the intrinsic worth of knight-errantry, and how speedily those who exercise any ministry whatsoever belonging to it may attain honour and estimation in the world, it is my will that thou be seated here by my side, in company with these good people, and become one and the same thing with me, who am thy master and natural lord ; that thou eat from off my plate, and drink of the same cup from which I drink ; for the same may be said of knight-errantry which is said of love, that it makes all things equal." " I give you a great many thanks, sir," said Sancho ; " but let me tell your worship that, provided I have victuals enough, I can eat as well, or better, standing and alone, than if I were seated close by an emperor. And further, to tell you the truth, what I eat in a corner, without compliments and ceremonies, though it were nothing but bread and an onion, relishes better than turkeys at other men's tables, where I am forced to chew leisurely, drink little, wipe my mouth often, neither sneeze nor cough when I have a mind, nor do other things which may be done when alone and at liberty. So that, good sir, let these honours which your worship is pleased to confer upon me, as a servant and adherent of knight-errantry (being squire to your worship), be exchanged for something of more use and profit to me ; for, though I place them to account as received in full, I renounce them from this time forward to the end of the world." " Notwithstanding this," said Don Quixote, " thou shalt sit down ; for whosoever humbleth himself, God doth exalt ; " and, pulling him by the arm, he forced him to sit down next him. The goatherds did not understand this jargon of squires and knights-errant, and therefore only ate, held their peace, and stared at their guests, who, with much satisfaction and appetite, swallowed down pieces as large as their fists. The service of flesh being finished, they spread upon the skins a great quantity of acorns, together with half a cheese, harder than if it had been made of mortar. The horn in the meantime stood not idle ; for it went round so often, now full, now empty, like the bucket of a well, that they presently emptied one of the two wine-bags that hung in view. After Don Quixote had satisfied his hunger, he took up a handful of acorns, and, looking on them attentively, gave utterance to expressions like these :

" Happy times, and happy ages, were those which the ancients termed the Golden Age ! not because gold, so prized in this our iron age, was to be obtained in that fortunate period without toil ; but because they who then lived were ignorant of those two words, *mine* and *thine*. In that blessed age all things were in common : to provide their ordinary sustenance, no other labour was necessary than to raise their hands and take it from the sturdy oaks, which stood liberally inviting them to taste their sweet and relishing fruit. The limpid fountains and running streams offered them, in magnificent abundance, their delicious and transparent waters. In the clefts of rocks, and in hollow trees, the industrious and provident bees formed their commonwealths, offering to every hand, without interest, the fertile produce of their most delicious toil. The stately cork trees, impelled by their own courtesy alone, divested themselves of their light and expanded bark, with which men began to cover their houses, supported by rough poles, only as a defence against the inclemency of the heavens. All then was peace, all amity, all concord. The heavy coulter of the crooked plough had not yet dared to force open and search into the tender bowels of our first mother, who, unconstrained, offered, from every part of her fertile and spacious bosom, whatever might feed, sustain, and delight those her children by whom she was then possessed. Then did the simple and beauteous young shepherdesses trip from dale to dale, and from hill to hill, their tresses sometimes plaited, sometimes loosely flowing, with no more clothing than was necessary modestly to cover what modesty has always required to be concealed : nor were their ornaments like those now in fashion, to which a value is given by the Tyrian purple and the silk so many ways martyred; but, adorned with green dock leaves and ivy interwoven, perhaps they appeared as splendidly and elegantly decked as our court ladies, with all those rare and foreign inventions which idle curiosity hath taught them. Then were the generous conceptions of the soul clothed in simple and sincere expressions, in the same way and manner they were conceived, without seeking artificial phrases to enhance their value. Nor had fraud, deceit, and malice intermixed with truth and plain-dealing. Justice maintained her proper bounds, undisturbed and unassailed by favour and interest, which now so much depreciate, molest, and persecute her. Law was not yet left to the interpretation of the judge; for then there was neither cause nor judge. Maidens and modesty, as I said before, went about alone, without fear of danger from the unbridled freedom and lewd designs of others ; and, if they were undone, it was entirely owing to their own natural inclination and will. But now, in these detestable ages of ours, no damsel is secure, though she were hidden and inclosed in another labyrinth like that of Crete; for even there, through some cranny, or through the air, by the zeal of evil importunity, the amorous pestilence finds entrance, and they are often wrecked in spite of all seclusion. Therefore, as times became worse, and wickedness increased, to defend maidens, to protect widows, and to relieve orphans and persons distressed, the order of knight-errantry was instituted. Of this order am I, brother goatherds, whom I thank for the good cheer and kind reception ye have given me and my squire; for though, by the law of nature, every one living is bound to favour knights-errant, yet as ye have received and regaled me without being aware of this obligation, it is but reasonable that I should return you my warmest acknowledgments."

Our knight made this long harangue (which might well have been spared) because the acorns they had put before him reminded him of the Golden Age, and led him to make that unprofitable discourse to the goatherds; who, in astonishment, listened to him without saying a word. Sancho also was silent, devouring the acorns, and making frequent visits to the second wine-bag, which was hanging upon a cork tree in order to keep the wine cool.

The musician was a youth of an agreeable mien, about two-and-twenty years of age.

Don Quixote spent more time in talking than in eating, and, supper being over, one of the goatherds said, "That your worship, Signor Knight-errant, may the more truly say that we entertain you with a ready good-will, one of our comrades, who will soon be here, shall sing for your pleasure and amusement. He is a very intelligent lad, and deeply in love; above all, he can read and write, and play upon the rebeck as well as heart can desire." The goatherd had scarcely said this when the sound of the rebeck reached their ears, and presently after came the musician, who was a youth of an agreeable mien, about two-and-twenty years age. His comrades asked him if he had supped, and he having answered in the affirmative, one of them said, "If so,

Antonio, you may let us have the pleasure of hearing you sing a little, that this gentleman, our guest, may see that even here, among woods and mountains, there are some who are skilled in music. We have told him of your great abilities, and wish you to show them, and prove the truth of what we have said; and therefore I entreat you to sit down and sing the ballad of your love, which your uncle the curate composed for you, and which was so well liked in our village." "With all my heart," replied the youth; and, without further entreaty, he sat down upon the trunk of an old oak, and, after tuning his rebeck, began to sing in a most agreeable manner, as follows:

ANTONIO.

Yes, lovely nymph, thou art my prize;
 I boast the conquest of thy heart,
Though nor the tongue nor speaking eyes
 Have yet revealed the latent smart.

Thy wit and sense assure my fate,
 In them my love's success I see;
Nor can he be unfortunate
 Who dares avow his flame for thee.

Yet sometimes hast thou frowned, alas!
 And given my hopes a cruel shock;
Then did thy soul seem formed of brass.
 Thy snowy bosom of the rock.

But in the midst of thy disdain,
 Thy sharp reproaches, cold delays,
Hope from behind, to ease my pain,
 The border of her robe displays.

Ah, lovely maid! in equal scale
 Weigh well thy shepherd's truth and love,
Which ne'er but with his breath can fail,
 Which neither frowns nor smiles can move.

If love, as shepherds wont to say,
 Be gentleness and courtesy,
So courteous is Olalia,
 My passion will rewarded be.

And if obsequious duty paid
 The grateful heart can ever move,
Mine, sure, my fair, may well persuade
 A due return, and claim thy love.

For, to seem pleasing in thy sight,
 I dress myself with studious care,
And, in my best apparel dight,
 My Sunday clothes on Monday wear.

And shepherds say I'm not to blame,
 For cleanly dress and spruce attire
Preserve alive love's wanton flame,
 And gently fan the dying fire.

To please my fair, in mazy ring
   I join the dance, and sportive play ;
And oft beneath thy window sing,
   When first the cock proclaims the day.

With rapture on each charm I dwell,
   And daily spread thy beauty's fame :
And still my tongue thy praise shall tell,
   Though envy swell, or malice blame.

Teresa of the Berrocal,
   When once I praised you, said in spite,
" Your mistress you an angel call,
   But a mere ape is your delight :

" Thanks to the bugle's artful glare,
   And all the graces counterfeit ;
Thanks to the false and curléd hair,
   Which wary Love himself might cheat."

I swore 't was false, and said she lied ;
   At that her anger fiercely rose ;
I boxed the clown that took her side,
   And how I boxed my fairest knows.

I court thee not, Olalia,
   To gratify a loose desire :
My love is chaste, without alloy
   Of wanton wish or lustful fire.

The Church hath silken cords, that tie
   Consenting hearts in mutual bands :
If thou, my fair, its yoke wilt try,
   Thy swain its ready captive stands.

If not, by all the saints I swear
   On these bleak mountains still to dwell,
Nor ever quit my toilsome care,
   But for the cloister and the cell.

Here ended the goatherd's song, and Don Quixote requested him to sing something else ; but Sancho Panza was of another mind, being more disposed to sleep than to hear ballads : he therefore said to his master, " Sir, you had better consider where you are to rest to-night ; for the labour which these honest men undergo all day will not suffer them to pass the night in singing." " I understand thee, Sancho," answered Don Quixote ; " for it is very evident that visits to the wine-bag require to be paid rather with sleep than music." " It relished well with us all, blessed be God," answered Sancho. " I do not deny it," replied Don Quixote. " Lay thyself down where thou wilt, but it is more becoming those of my profession to watch than to sleep. However, it would not be amiss, Sancho, if thou wouldst dress this ear again, for it pains me more than it ought." Sancho did as he was desired ; and one of the goatherds seeing the wound, bade him not be concerned about it, for he would apply such a remedy as should quickly heal it ; then taking some rosemary leaves, which abounded in that place, he chewed them, and mixed with them a little salt, and, laying them to the ear, bound them on very fast, assuring him that no other salve would be necessary, which indeed proved to be true.

CHAPTER XII.

What a certain goatherd related to those who were with Don Quixote.

SOON after this there arrived another young lad, laden with provisions from the village. " Comrades," said he, " do you know what is passing in the village ? " " How should we know ? " answered one of them. " Know, then," continued the youth, " that the famous shepherd and scholar, Chrysostom, died this morning ; and it is rumoured that it was for love of that saucy girl Marcela, daughter of William the rich ; she who rambles about these woods and fields in the dress of a shepherdess." " For Marcela, say you ? " quoth one. " For her, I say," answered the goatherd ; " and the best of it is, he has ordered in his will that they should bury him in the fields, like a Moor, at the foot of the rock, by the cork tree fountain, which, according to report, and as they say, he himself declared was the very place where he first saw her. He ordered also other things so extravagant that the clergy say they must not be performed ; nor is it fit that they should, for they seem to be heathenish. But his great friend Ambrosio, the student, who accompanied him, dressed also like a shepherd, declares that the whole of what Chrysostom enjoined shall be executed ; and upon this the village is all in an uproar : but by what I can learn, they will at last do what Ambrosio and all his friends require ; and to-morrow they come to inter him, with great solemnity, in the place I mentioned : and, in my opinion, it will be a sight well worth seeing ; at least, I shall not fail to go, although I were certain of not returning to-morrow to the village." " We will do the same," answered the goatherds ; " and let us cast lots who shall stay behind to look after the goats." " You say well, Pedro," quoth another ; " but it will be needless to make use of this expedient, for I will remain for you all : and do not attribute this to self-denial or want of curiosity in me, but to the thorn which stuck into my foot the other day, and hinders me from walking." " We thank you, nevertheless," answered Pedro.

Don Quixote requested Pedro to give him some account of the deceased man and the shepherdess. To which Pedro answered, " that all he knew was, that the deceased was a wealthy gentleman, and inhabitant of a village situate among these mountains, who had studied many years at Salamanca ; at the end of which time he returned home, with the character of a very learned and well-read person : particularly, it was said, he understood the science of the stars, and what the sun and moon are doing in the sky; for he told us punctually the clipse of the sun and moon." " Friend," quoth Don Quixote, " the obscuration of those two luminaries is called an *eclipse*, and not a *clipse.*" But Pedro, not regarding niceties, went on with his story, saying, " He also foretold when the year would be plentiful or starel." " *Sterile*, you would say, friend," quoth Don Quixote. " *Sterile* or *starel*," answered Pedro, " comes all to the same thing. And, as I was saying, his father and friends, who gave credit to his words, became very rich thereby; for they followed his advice in everything. This year he would say, ' Sow barley, and not wheat; in this you may sow vetches, and not barley; the next year there will be plenty of oil; the three following there will not be a drop.' " " This science they call astrology," said Don Quixote. " I know not how it is called," replied Pedro, " but I know that he knew all this, and more too. In short, not many months after he came from Salamanca, on a certain day he appeared dressed like a shepherd, with his crook and sheepskin jacket, having thrown aside his scholar's gown; and with an intimate friend of his, called Ambrosio, who had been his fellow-student, and who now put on likewise the apparel of a shepherd. I forgot to tell you how the deceased Chrysostom was a great man at making verses; insomuch that he made the carols for Christmas-eve, and the religious plays for Corpus Christi, which the boys of the village represented; and everybody said they were most excellent. When the people of the village saw the two scholars so suddenly habited like shepherds, they were amazed, and could not get at the cause that induced them to make that strange alteration in their dress. About this time the father of Chrysostom died, and he inherited a large estate, in lands and goods, flocks, herds, and money, of all which the youth remained absolute master; and, indeed, he deserved it all, for he was a very good companion, a charitable man, and a friend to those that were good, and had a face like any blessing. Afterwards it came to be known that he changed his habit for no other purpose but that he might wander about these desert places after that shepherdess Marcela, with whom, as our lad told you, he was in love. And I will now tell you (for it is fit you should know) who this young lass is; for, perhaps, and even without a perhaps, you may never have heard the like in all the days of your life, though you were as old as Sarna." " *Sarah*, you mean," replied Don Quixote, not being able to endure the goatherd's mistaking words. " Sarna will do," answered Pedro; " and, sir, if you must at every turn be correcting my words, we shall not have done this twelvemonth." " Pardon me, friend," said Don Quixote, " and go on with your story, for I will interrupt you no more."

" I say, then, dear sir of my soul," quoth the goatherd, " that in our village there was a farmer still richer than the father of Chrysostom, called William; on whom Providence bestowed, besides great wealth, a daughter, whose mother, the most respected woman in all our country, died in giving her birth—I think I see her now, with that goodly presence, looking as if she had the sun on one side of her and the moon on the other: and, above all, she was a notable housewife, and a friend to the poor; for which I believe her soul is at this very moment in heaven. Her husband William died for grief at the death of so good a wife, leaving his daughter Marcela, young and rich, under the care of an uncle, a priest and the curate of our village. The girl grew up with so much beauty that it put us in mind of her mother, who had a great share, yet it was thought that the daughter would surpass her; and so it fell out; for when she came to be fourteen or fifteen years of age, nobody beheld her without blessing God for making her so handsome, and most men were in love with and distracted for her. Her uncle kept her both carefully and close; nevertheless, the fame of her extraordinary beauty so spread itself that, partly for her person, partly for her great riches, her uncle was applied to, solicited, and importuned, not only by those of our own village, but by many others, and those of the better sort too, for several leagues round, to dispose of her in marriage. But he, who, to do him justice, is a good Christian, though he was desirous of disposing of her as soon as she was marriageable, yet would not do it without her consent. Not that he had an eye to any advantage he might make of the girl's estate by deferring her marriage; and, in good truth, this has been told in praise of the good priest in more companies than one in our village. For I would have you to know, Sir Errant, that, in these little places, everything is talked of and everything censured. And, take my word for it, that a clergyman, especially in country towns, must be over and above good who makes all his parishioners speak well of him."

"That is true," said Don Quixote: "but proceed, for the story is excellent, and you, honest Pedro, tell it with a good grace." "May the grace of the Lord never fail me! which is most to the purpose. And you must further know," quoth Pedro, "that, though the uncle made these proposals known to his niece, and acquainted her with the qualities of each one in particular of the many that sought her hand, advising her also to marry and choose to her liking, her only answer was that she was not so disposed at present, and that, being so young, she did not feel herself able to bear the burden of matrimony. Her uncle, satisfied with these seemingly just excuses, ceased to importune her, and waited till she was grown a little older, when she would know how to choose a companion to her taste. For, said he—and he said well—parents ought not to settle their children against their will. But, behold! when we least thought of it, on a certain day the coy Marcela appears as a shepherdess, and, without the consent of her uncle and against the entreaties of all the neighbours, would needs go into the fields, with the other country lasses, and tend her own flock. And now that she appeared in public, and her beauty was exposed to all beholders, it is impossible to tell you how many wealthy youths, gentlemen, and farmers have taken the shepherd's dress, and wander about these plains making their suit to her. One of whom, as you have already been told, was the deceased; and he, it is said, rather adored than loved her. But think not that, although Marcela has given herself up to this free and unconfined way of life, and with so little, or rather no reserve, she has given

Sancho took up his lodging between Rozinante and his ass.

the least colour of suspicion to the prejudice of her modesty and discretion. No: rather, so great and strict is the watch she keeps over her
honour, that of all those who serve and solicit her, no one has boasted,
or can boast with truth, that she has given him the least hope of
obtaining his wishes. For, though she does not fly or shun the company and conversation of the shepherds, but treats them in a courteous
and friendly manner, yet, when any one of them ventures to discover
his intention, though it be as just and holy as that of marriage, she
casts him from her as out of a stone-bow. And by this sort of behaviour
she does more mischief in this country than if she carried the plague
about with her: for her affability and beauty win the hearts of those
who converse with her, and incline them to serve and love her; but her
disdain and frank dealing drive them to despair; and so they know not
what to say to her, and can only exclaim against her, calling her cruel
and ungrateful, with such other titles as plainly denote her character;
and, were you to abide here, sir, awhile, you would hear these mountains
and valleys resound with the complaints of those rejected wretches that
yet follow her. There is a place not far hence, where about two dozen
of tall beeches grow, and not one of them is without the name of Marcela
written and engraved on its smooth bark; over some of them is carved

a crown, as if the lover would more clearly express that Marcela deserves and wears the crown of all human beauty. Here sighs one shepherd, there complains another; here are heard amorous sonnets, there despairing ditties. One will pass all the hours of the night seated at the foot of some rock or tree, where, without having closed his weeping eyes, wrapped up and lost in thought, the sun finds him in the morning; whilst another, giving no truce to his sighs, lies stretched on the burning sand in the midst of the most sultry noonday heat of summer, sending up his complaints to all-pitying Heaven. In the meantime, the beautiful Marcela, free and unconcerned, triumphs over them all. We who know her wait with impatience to see how all this will end, and who is to be the happy man that shall subdue so intractable a disposition and enjoy so incomparable a beauty. As all that I have related is certain truth, I can more readily believe what our companion told us concerning the cause of Chrysostom's death; and therefore I advise you, sir, not to fail being to-morrow at his funeral, which will be very well worth seeing: for Chrysostom had a great many friends; and it is not half a league hence to the place of interment appointed by himself."

"I will certainly be there," said Don Quixote, "and I thank you for the pleasure you have given me by the recital of so entertaining a story." "Oh," replied the goatherd, "I do not yet know half the adventures of Marcela's lovers; but to-morrow, perhaps, we shall meet by the way with some shepherd who may tell us more: at present it will not be amiss for you to go and sleep under some roof, for the cold dew of the night may do harm to your wound, though the salve I have put to it is such that you need not fear any trouble from it." Sancho Panza, who for his part had wished this long-winded tale of the goatherd at the devil, pressed his master to lay himself down to sleep in Pedro's hut. He did so, and passed the rest of the night thinking of his lady Dulcinea, in imitation of the lovers of Marcela. Sancho took up his lodging between Rozinante and his ass, where he slept, not like a discarded lover, but like a man who had been grievously kicked.

CHAPTER XIII.

The conclusion of the story of the shepherdess Marcela, with other incidents.

MORNING scarcely had dawned through the balconies of the east, when five of the six goatherds got up and went to awake Don Quixote, whom they asked whether he continued in his resolution of going to see the famous interment of Chrysostom, for, if so, they would bear him company. Don Quixote, who desired nothing more, arose, and ordered Sancho to saddle and pannel immediately, which he did with great expedition; and with the same dispatch they all set out on their journey.

They had not gone a quarter of a league, when, upon crossing a pathway, they saw six shepherds advancing towards them, clad in jackets of black sheepskin, with garlands of cypress and bitter rosemary on their heads; each of them having in his hand a thick holly club. There came also with them two gentlemen on horseback, well equipped for travelling, who were attended by three lacqueys on foot. When the two parties met, they courteously saluted each other, and finding upon inquiry that all were proceeding to the place of burial, they continued their journey together.

One of the horsemen, addressing his companion, said, " I think, Signor Vivaldo, we shall not repent having stayed to see this famous interment; for, without doubt, it will be an extraordinary sight, according to the strange accounts these shepherds have given us of the deceased shepherd and beautiful shepherdess." " I think so too," answered Vivaldo; " and so far from regretting the delay of one day, I would stay four to see it." Don Quixote asked them what they had heard of Marcela and Chrysostom? The traveller said they had met those shepherds early in the morning, and that, observing their mournful apparel, they had inquired the cause, and were informed of it by one of them, who told them of the beauty and singularity of a certain shepherdess called Marcela, and the loves of many that wooed her; with the death of Chrysostom, to whose burial they were going. In fine, he related all that Pedro had told Don Quixote.

The discourse ceased, and another began, by Vivaldo asking Don Quixote what might be the reason that induced him to go armed in that manner through a country so peaceable? To which Don Quixote answered, " The profession I follow will not allow or suffer me to go in any other manner. Revels, banquets, and repose were invented for effeminate courtiers; but toil, disquietude, and arms alone were designed for those whom the world calls knights-errant, of which number I, though unworthy, am the least." As soon as they heard this, they all perceived his derangement, but, in order to discover the nature of his madness, Vivaldo asked him what he meant by knights-errant. " Have you not read, sir," answered Don Quixote, " the annals and histories of England, wherein are recorded the famous exploits of King Arthur, whom, in our Castilian tongue, we perpetually call King Artus? of whom there exists an ancient tradition, universally received over the whole kingdom of Great Britain, that he did not die, but that, by magic art, he was transformed into a raven; and that, in process of time, he shall reign again, and recover his kingdom and sceptre; for which reason it cannot be proved that, from that time to this, any Englishman hath killed a raven. Now, in this good king's time was instituted that renowned order of chivalry entitled the Knights of the Round Table; and the amours related of Sir Lancelot du Lake with the Queen Guinevra passed exactly as they are recorded; that honourable duenna Quintaniana being their mediatrix and confidante: whence originated that well-known ballad, so much admired here in Spain, ' Never was knight by ladies so well served as was Sir Lancelot when he came from

Britain,' with the rest of that sweet and charming account of his amours and exploits. Now, from that time the order of chivalry has been extending and spreading itself through many and divers parts of the world; and among those of the profession distinguished and renowned for heroic deeds was the valiant Amadis de Gaul, with all his sons and grandsons to the fifth generation; the valorous Felixmarte of Hyrcania; and the never-enough-to-be-praised Tirante the White. Nay, even almost in our own times, we have seen, heard, and conversed with the invincible and valorous knight Don Belianis of Greece. This, gentlemen, it is to be a knight-errant; and the order of chivalry is what I have described. To this order, as I said before, I, though a sinner, have devoted myself; and the same which those knights profess do I profess also; therefore am I travelling through these solitudes and deserts in quest of adventures, with a determined resolution to oppose my arm and person to the most perilous that fortune may present, in aid of the weak and oppressed."

By this discourse the travellers were fully convinced of the disordered state of Don Quixote's mind; and the species of insanity with which they perceived him to be affected struck them with the same surprise that all felt upon first discovering it. Vivaldo, who was a man of discernment, and withal of a gay disposition, to enliven the remainder of their journey to the funeral mountain, resolved to give him an opportunity of pursuing his extravagant discourse. He therefore said to him, " In my opinion, Sir Knight-errant, you have engaged in one of the most austere professions upon earth; more rigid even than that of the Carthusian monks." " That order of monks may be as rigid," answered Don Quixote, " but that it is equally necessary to the world I am much inclined to doubt; for, to say the truth, the soldier who executes his captain's orders does no less than the captain himself, who gives him the orders. I would say that the religious order in peace and tranquillity implore Heaven for the good of the world; but we soldiers and knights really execute what they pray for, defending it with the strength of our arms and the edge of our swords; not under covert, but in open field, exposed to the intolerable beams of the summer's sun and the chilling frosts of winter. Thus we are Heaven's ministers upon earth, and the arms by which God executes His justice. And as the affairs of war, and those appertaining to it, cannot be put in execution without toil, pain, and labour, so they who profess it must, unquestionably, endure more than those who, in peace and repose, are employed in praying to Heaven to assist them, and who can do but little for themselves. I mean not to say, nor do I entertain such a thought, that the state of the knight-errant is as good as that of the religious recluse: I would only infer, from what I suffer, that it is, doubtless, more laborious, more bastinadoed, more hungry and thirsty, more wretched, more ragged, and more filthy; for there is no doubt but that the knights-errant of old suffered much in the course of their lives: if some of them were raised to empires by the valour of their arms, in good truth they paid dearly for it in blood and sweat: and, after all, had they been without the assistance of enchanters and sages, their hopes would have been frustrated and their wishes unattained."

"I am of the same opinion," replied the traveller: "but one thing, among many others which appear to me to be censurable in knights-errant, is that, when they are prepared to engage in some great and perilous adventure, to the manifest hazard of their lives, at the moment of attack they never think of commending themselves to God, as every Christian is bound to do at such a crisis, but rather commend themselves to their mistresses, and that with as much fervour and devotion as if they were really their god: a thing which to me savours of paganism."

"Signor," answered Don Quixote, "this can by no means be otherwise, and the knight-errant who should act in any other manner would digress much from his duty; for it is a received maxim and custom in chivalry, that the knight-errant who, on the point of engaging in some great feat of arms, has his lady before him, must turn his eyes fondly and lovingly towards her, as if imploring her favour and protection in the hazardous enterprise that awaits him; and, even if nobody hear him, he must pronounce some words between his teeth, by which he commends himself to her with his whole heart: and of this we have innumerable examples in history. Nor is it thence to be inferred that they neglect commending themselves to God; for there is time and opportunity enough to do it in the course of the action." "Notwithstanding all that," replied the traveller, "I have one scruple still remaining; for I have often read that, words rising between two knights-errant, and choler beginning to kindle in them both, they turn their horses round, and, taking a large compass about the field, immediately encounter at full speed, and, in the midst of their career, commend themselves to their mistresses: what commonly happens in the encounter is, that one of them tumbles back over his horse's crupper, pierced through and through by his adversary's lance; and if the other had not laid hold of his horse's mane he must have fallen to the ground. Now I cannot imagine what leisure the deceased had to commend himself to God in the course of so expeditious a work. Better had it been if the words he spent in commending himself to his lady, in the midst of the career, had been employed as the duties of a Christian require; particularly as I imagine that all knights-errant have not ladies to commend themselves to, because they are not all in love." "That cannot be," answered Don Quixote: "I say, there cannot be a knight-errant without a mistress; for it is as essential and as natural for them to be enamoured as for the sky to have stars: and, most certainly, no history exists in which a knight-errant is to be found without one; for, from the very circumstance of his being without, he would not be acknowledged as a legitimate knight, but as one who had entered the fortress of chivalry, not by the gate, but over the pales, like a thief and robber."

"Nevertheless," said the traveller, "if I am not mistaken, I remember having read that Don Galaor, brother to the valorous Amadis de Gaul, never had a particular mistress to whom he might commend himself; notwithstanding which, he was no less esteemed, and was a very valiant and famous knight." To which Don Quixote answered, " Signor, ' one swallow makes not a summer.' Moreover, I know that Don Galaor was in secret very deeply enamoured, besides the general love that he entertained towards all whom he thought handsome: a propensity natural to him, and which he was unable to control. But, in short, it is well ascertained that there was one whom he had made mistress of his devotion, and to whom he often commended himself, but very secretly; for upon this quality of secresy he especially valued himself."

" If it is essential that every knight-errant be a lover," said the traveller, " it may well be presumed that you are yourself one, being of the profession; and, if you do not pique yourself upon the same secresy as Don Galaor, I earnestly entreat you, in the name of all this good company and in my own, to tell us the name, country, quality, and beauty of your mistress, who cannot but account herself happy that all the world should know that she is loved and served by so worthy a knight." Here Don Quixote breathed a deep sigh, and said, " I cannot positively affirm whether that sweet enemy of mine is pleased or not that the world should know I am her servant: I can only say, in answer to what you so very courteously inquire of me, that her name is Dulcinea; her country Toboso, a town of la Mancha; her quality at least that of a princess, since she is my queen and sovereign lady; her beauty more than human, since in her all the impossible and chimerical attributes of beauty which the poets ascribe to their mistresses are realised; for her hair is gold, her forehead the Elysian Fields, her eyebrows rainbows, her eyes suns, her cheeks roses, her lips coral, her teeth pearls, her neck alabaster, her bosom marble, her hands ivory, her whiteness snow, and her whole person without parallel."

" We would fain know," replied Vivaldo, " her lineage, race, and family." To which Don Quixote answered, " She is not of the ancient Roman Curtii, Caii, or the Scipios; nor of the modern Colonnas or Orsinis; nor of the Moncadas and Requesenes of Catalonia; neither is she of the Rebellas and Villanovas of Valentia; the Palafoxes, Nuzas, Rocabertes, Corellas, Lunas, Alagones, Urreas, Foxes, and Gurreas of Arragon; the Cerdas, Manriques, Mendozas, and Guzmans of Castile; the Alencastros, Pallas, and Meneses of Portugal; but she is of those of Toboso de la Mancha: a lineage, though modern, yet such as may give a noble beginning to the most illustrious families of future ages: and in this let no one contradict me, unless it be on the conditions that Zerbino fixed under the arms of Orlando, where it said,

> ' That knight alone these arms shall move,
> Who dares Orlando's prowess prove.' "

" Although mine be of the Cachopines of Laredo," replied the traveller, " I dare not compare it with that of Toboso de la Mancha; though, to say the truth, no such appellation hath till now ever reached my ears." " Is it possible that you should never have heard it !" exclaimed Don Quixote. The whole party had listened with great attention to this dialogue; and even the goatherds and shepherds perceived the excessive distraction of our knight. Sancho Panza alone believed all that his master said to be true, knowing who he was, and having been acquainted with him from childhood; but he had some doubts as to that part which concerned the fair Dulcinea del Toboso, never having heard of such a name, or such a princess, although he lived so near Toboso.

Thus conversing, they proceeded on, when they discerned, through a cleft between two high mountains, about twenty shepherds coming down, all clad in jerkins of black wool, and crowned with garlands, some of which, as appeared afterwards, were of yew and some of cypress. Six of them carried a bier covered with various flowers and boughs. Upon which one of the goatherds said, "Those who come hither are bearing the corpse of Chrysostom, and at the foot of yonder mountain is the place where he desired to be interred." They made haste, therefore, to reach them, which they did just as the bier was set down upon the ground; and four of them, with sharp pickaxes, were making the grave by the side of a hard rock. After mutual salutations, Don Quixote and his company went to take a view of the bier, upon which they saw a dead body, strewed with flowers, in the dress of a shepherd, apparently about thirty years of age; and though dead, it was evident that his countenance had been beautiful and his figure elegant. Several books and a great number of papers, some open and some folded, lay round him on the bier. All that were present, spectators as well as those who were opening the grave, kept a marvellous silence, until one of those who had borne the deceased said to another, "Observe carefully, Ambrosio, whether this be the place which Chrysostom mentioned, since you wish to be so exact in executing his will." "It is here," answered Ambrosio; "for in this very place my unhappy friend often told me of his woe. Here it was, he told me, that he first beheld that mortal enemy of the human race; here it was that he declared to her his no less honourable than ardent passion; here it was that Marcela finally undeceived and treated him with such disdain that she put an end to the tragedy of his miserable life; and here, in memory of so many misfortunes, he desired to be deposited in the bowels of eternal oblivion."

Then, addressing himself to Don Quixote and the travellers, he thus continued: "This body, sirs, which you are regarding with compassionate eyes, was the receptacle of a soul upon which Heaven had bestowed an infinite portion of its treasures: this is the body of Chrysostom, who was a man of rare genius, matchless courtesy, and unbounded kindness; he was a phœnix in friendship, magnificent without ostentation, grave without arrogance, cheerful without meanness; in short, the first in all that was good, and second to none in all that was unfortunate. He loved, and was abhorred; he adored, and was scorned; he courted a savage; he solicited a statue; he pursued the wind; he called aloud to the desert; he was the slave of ingratitude, whose recompense was to leave him, in the middle of his career of life, a prey to death, inflicted by a certain shepherdess, whom he endeavoured to render immortal in the memories of men; as these papers you are looking at would sufficiently demonstrate, had he not ordered me to commit them to the flames at the same time that his body was deposited in the earth." "You would then be more rigorous and cruel to them," said Vivaldo, "than their master himself; for it is neither just nor wise to fulfil the will of him who commands what is utterly unreasonable. Augustus Cæsar deemed it wrong to consent to the execution of what the divine Mantuan commanded in his will; therefore, Signor Ambrosio, although you commit your friend's body to the earth, do not commit his writings also to oblivion; and if he has ordained like a man aggrieved, do not you fulfil like one without discretion, but rather preserve these papers, in order that the cruelty of Marcela may be still remembered, and serve for an example to those who shall live in times to come, that they may avoid falling down the like precipices; for I am acquainted, as well as my companions here, with the story of this your enamoured and despairing friend; we know also your friendship, and the occasion of his death, and what he ordered on his death-bed: from which lamentable history we may conclude how great has been the cruelty of Marcela, the love of Chrysostom, and the sincerity of your friendship; and also learn the end of those who run headlong in the path that delirious passion presents to their view. Last night we heard of Chrysostom's death, and that he was to be interred in this place: led, therefore, by curiosity and compassion, we turned out of our way, and determined to behold with our eyes what had interested us so much in the recital; and, in return for our pity, and our desire to give aid, had it been possible, we beseech you, O wise Ambrosio—at least I request it on my own behalf—that you will not burn the papers, but allow me to take some of them." Then, without waiting for the shepherd's reply, he stretched out his hand and took some of those that were nearest to him: upon which Ambrosio said, "Out of civility, signor, I will consent to your keeping those you have taken; but if you expect that I shall forbear burning those that remain, you are deceived." Vivaldo, desirous of seeing what the papers contained, immediately opened one of them, and found that it was entitled, "The Song of Despair." Ambrosio hearing it, said, "This is the last thing which the unhappy man wrote; and that all present may conceive, signor, to what a state of misery he was reduced, read it aloud, for you will have time enough while they are digging the grave." "That I will do with all my heart," said Vivaldo; and, as all the bystanders had the same desire, they assembled around him, and he read in an audible voice as follows.

CHAPTER XIV.

Wherein are rehearsed the despairing verses of the deceased shepherd with other unexpected events.

CHRYSOSTOM'S SONG.

I.

Since, cruel maid, you force me to proclaim
From clime to clime the triumphs of your scorn,
Let hell itself inspire my tortured breast
With mournful numbers, and untune my voice;
Whilst the sad pieces of my broken heart
Mix with the doleful accents of my tongue,
At once to tell my griefs and thy exploits.
Hear, then, and listen with attentive ear,
Not to harmonious sounds, but echoing groans,
Fetched from the bottom of my lab'ring breast,
To ease, in spite of thee, my raging smart.

II.

The lion's roar, the howl of midnight wolves,
The scaly serpent's hiss, the raven's croak,
The burst of fighting winds that vex the main,
The widowed owl and turtle's plaintive moan,
With all the din of hell's infernal crew,
From my grieved soul forth issue in one sound,
Leaving my senses all confused and lost;
For ah! no common language can express
The cruel pains that torture my sad heart.

III.

Yet let not Echo bear the mournful sounds
To where old Tagus rolls his yellow sands,
Or Betis, crowned with olives, pours his flood;
But here, 'midst rocks and precipices deep,
Or to obscure and silent vales removed,
On shores by human footsteps never trod,
Where the gay sun ne'er lifts his radiant orb,
Or with th' envenomed face of savage beasts
That range the howling wilderness for food,
Will I proclaim the story of my woes—
Poor privilege of grief!—whilst echoes hoarse
Catch the sad tale, and spread it round the world.

IV.

Disdain gives death; suspicions, true or false,
O'erturn th' impatient mind; with surer stroke
Fell jealousy destroys; the pangs of absence
No lover can support, nor firmest hope
Can dissipate the dread of cold neglect:
Yet I, strange fate! though jealous, though disdained,

Absent, and sure of cold neglect, still live,
And 'midst the various torments I endure,
No ray of hope e'er darted on my soul.
Nor would I hope : rather in deep despair
Will I sit down, and, brooding o'er my griefs,
Vow everlasting absence from her sight.

V.

Can hope and fear at once the soul possess,
Or hope subsist with surer cause of fear?
Shall I, to shut out frightful jealousy,
Close my sad eyes, when ev'ry pang I feel
Presents the hideous phantom to my view?
What wretch so credulous but must embrace
Distrust with open arms, when he beholds
Disdain avowed, suspicions realised,
And truth itself converted to a lie?
O cruel tyrant of the realm of Love,
Fierce Jealousy, arm with a sword this hand;
Or thou, Disdain, a twisted cord bestow.

VI.

Let me not blame my fate ; but, dying, think
The man most blest who loves, the soul most free
That love has most enthralled.   Still to my thoughts
Let fancy paint the tyrant of my heart
Beauteous in mind as face, and in myself
Still let me find the source of her disdain;
Content to suffer, since imperial Love
By lovers' woes maintains his sovereign state.
With this persuasion, and the fatal noose,
I hasten to the doom her scorn demands,
And, dying, offer up my breathless corse,
Uncrowned with garlands, to the whistling winds.

VII.

O thou whose unrelenting rigour's force
First drove me to despair, and now to death,
When the sad tale of my untimely fall
Shall reach thy ear, though it deserve a sigh,
Veil not the heaven of those bright eyes in grief,
Nor drop one pitying tear, to tell the world
At length my death has triumphed o'er thy scorn;
But dress thy face in smiles, and celebrate,
With laughter and each circumstance of joy,
The festival of my disastrous end.
Ah ! need I bid thee smile ? too well I know
My death's thy utmost glory and thy pride.

VIII.

Come, all ye phantoms of the dark abyss :
Bring, Tantalus, thy unextinguished thirst,
And, Sisyphus, thy still returning stone;
Come, Tityus, with the vulture at thy heart ;
And thou, Ixion, bring thy giddy wheel;
Nor let the toiling sisters stay behind.
Pour your united griefs into this breast,
And in low murmurs sing sad obsequies

(If a despairing wretch such rites may claim)
O'er my cold limbs, denied a winding-sheet;
And let the triple porter of the shades,
The sister Furies, and Chimeras dire,
With notes of woe the mournful chorus join.
Such funeral pomp alone befits the wretch
By beauty sent untimely to the grave.

IX.

And thou, my song, sad child of my despair,
Complain no more; but, since my wretched fate
Improves her happier lot who gave thee birth,
Be all thy sorrows buried in my tomb.

Chrysostom's song was much approved by those who heard it; but he who read it said it did not seem to agree with the account he had heard of the reserve and goodness of Marcela; for Chrysostom complains in it of jealousy, suspicion, and absence, all to the prejudice of her credit and good name. Ambrosio, being well acquainted with the most hidden thoughts of his friend, said in reply, " To satisfy you, signor, on this point, I must inform you that, when my unhappy friend wrote this song, he was absent from Marcela, from whom he had voluntarily banished himself, to try whether absence would have upon him its ordinary effect; and, as an absent lover is disturbed by every shadow, so was Chrysostom tormented with causeless jealousy and suspicions: thus the truth of all which fame reports of Marcela's goodness remains unimpeached; and, excepting that she is cruel, somewhat arrogant, and very disdainful, envy itself neither ought nor can charge her with any defect." " You are right," answered Vivaldo; who, as he was going to read another of the papers he had saved from the fire, was interrupted by a wonderful vision (for such it seemed) that suddenly presented itself to their sight; for on the top of the rock under which they were digging the grave appeared the shepherdess herself, so beautiful that her beauty even surpassed the fame of it. Those who had never seen her until that time beheld her in silence and admiration; and those who had been accustomed to the sight of her were now surprised at her appearance. But as soon as Ambrosio had espied her, he said with indignation, " Comest thou, O fierce basilisk of these mountains, to see whether the wounds of this wretch, whom thy cruelty has deprived of life, will bleed afresh at thy appearance? or comest thou to triumph in the cruel exploits of thy inhuman disposition, which from that eminence thou beholdest, as the merciless Nero gazed on the flames of burning Rome? or insolently to trample on this unhappy corse, as did the impious daughter on that of her father Tarquin?* Tell us quickly for what thou comest, or what thou wouldst have; for since I know that Chrysostom while living never disobeyed thee, I will take care that all those who call themselves his friends shall obey thee, although he is now no more."

---

* It should have been Servius Tullius, who was father of Tullia, not Tarquin.—(*Tit. Liv., lib.* i. *c.* 46.)

*On the top of the rock appeared the shepherdess, so beautiful that her beauty
even surpassed the fame of it.*

"I come not, O Ambrosio, for any of those purposes you have
mentioned," answered Marcela; "but to vindicate myself, and to declare
how unreasonable are those who blame me for their own sufferings, or
for the death of Chrysostom; and therefore I entreat you all to hear me
with attention, for I need not spend much time nor use many words to
convince persons of sense. Heaven, as you say, made me handsome,

and to such a degree that my beauty impels you involuntarily to love me; and, in return for this passion, you pretend that I am bound to love you. I know, by the understanding which God has given me, that whatever is beautiful is amiable; but I cannot conceive that the object beloved for its beauty is obliged to return love for love. Besides, it may happen that the lover is a deformed and ugly person; and being on that account an object of disgust, it would seem inconsistent to say, Because I love you for your beauty, you must love me although I am ugly. But supposing beauty to be equal, it does not follow that inclinations should be mutual; for all beauty does not inspire love: some pleases the sight without captivating the affections. If all beauties were to enamour and captivate, the hearts of mankind would be in a continual state of perplexity and confusion, without knowing where to fix; for beautiful objects being infinite, the sentiments they inspire must also be infinite. And I have heard say, true love cannot be divided, and must be voluntary and unconstrained. If so, why would you have me yield my heart by compulsion, urged only because you say you love me? For, pray tell me, if Heaven, instead of giving me beauty, had made me unsightly, would it have been just in me to have complained that you did not love me? Besides, you must consider that the beauty I possess is not my own choice; but, such as it is, Heaven bestowed it freely, unsolicited by me: and as the viper does not deserve blame for her sting, though she kills with it, because it is given her by nature, as little do I deserve reprehension for being handsome; for beauty in a modest woman is like fire on a sharp sword at a distance: neither doth the one burn, nor the other wound, those that come not too near them. Honour and virtue are ornaments of the soul, without which the body, though it be really beautiful, ought not to be thought so. Now, if modesty be one of the virtues which most adorns and beautifies both body and mind, why should she who is loved for being beautiful part with it to gratify the desires of him who, merely for his own pleasure, endeavours to destroy it? I was born free, and, that I might live free, I chose the solitude of these fields. The trees on these mountains are my companions; the clear waters of these brooks are my mirrors; to the trees and the waters I devote my meditations and my beauty. I am fire at a distance, and a sword afar off. Those whom my person has enamoured my words have undeceived; and if love be nourished by hopes, as I gave none to Chrysostom, nor gratified those of any one else, surely it may be said that his own obstinacy, rather than my cruelty, destroyed him. If it be objected to me that his intentions were honourable, and that therefore I ought to have complied with them, I answer that when, in this very place where his grave is now digging, he made known to me his favourable sentiments, I told him that it was my resolution to live in perpetual solitude, and that the earth alone should enjoy the fruit of my seclusion and the spoils of my beauty; and if he, notwithstanding all this frankness, would obstinately persevere against hope and sail against the wind, is it surprising that he should be overwhelmed in the gulf of his own folly? If I had held him in suspense, I had been false; if I had complied with him, I had acted contrary to my better purposes and resolutions. He persisted although undeceived; he despaired without being hated. Consider, now, whether it be reasonable to lay the blame of his sufferings upon me. Let him who is deceived complain; let him to whom faith is broken despair; let him whom I shall encourage presume; and let him vaunt whom I shall admit: but let me not be called cruel or murderous by those whom I never promise, deceive, encourage, nor admit. Heaven has not yet ordained that I should love by destiny, and from loving by choice I desire to be excused. Let every one of those who solicit me profit by this general declaration; and be it understood henceforward, that if any one dies for me, he dies not through jealousy or disdain; for she who loves none can make none jealous, and sincerity ought not to pass for disdain. Let him who calls me savage and a basilisk shun me as a mischievous and evil thing; let him who calls me ungrateful not serve me; him who thinks me cruel not follow me; for this savage, this basilisk, this ungrateful, this cruel thing, will never either seek, serve, or follow them. If Chrysostom's impatience and presumptuous passion killed him, why should my modest conduct and reserve be blamed? If I preserve my purity unspotted among these trees, why should he desire me to lose it among men? I possess, as you all know, wealth of my own, and do not covet more. My condition is free, and I am not inclined to subject myself to restraint. I neither love nor hate anybody. I neither deceive this man, nor lay snares for that. I neither cajole one, nor divert myself with another. The modest conversation of the shepherdesses of these villages, and the care of my goats, are my entertainment. My desires are bounded within these mountains, and if my thoughts extend beyond them, it is to contemplate the beauty of heaven—steps by which the soul ascends to its original abode."

Here she ceased, and, without waiting for a reply, retired into the most inaccessible part of the neighbouring mountain, leaving all who were present equally surprised at her beauty and good sense.

Some of those whom her bright eyes had wounded, heedless of her express declaration, seemed inclined to follow her; which Don Quixote perceiving, and thinking it a proper occasion to employ his chivalry in the relief of distressed damsels, he laid his hand on the hilt of his sword, and in a loud voice said, "Let no person, whatever be his rank or condition, presume to follow the beautiful Marcela, on pain of incurring my furious indignation. She has demonstrated, by clear and satisfactory arguments, how little she deserves censure on account of Chrysostom's death, and how averse she is to encourage any of her lovers; for which reason, instead of being followed and persecuted, she ought to be honoured and esteemed by all good men in the world, for being the only woman in it whose intentions are so virtuous." Now, whether it was owing to the menaces of Don Quixote, or to the request of Ambrosio, that they would finish the last offices due to his friend, none of the shepherds departed until, the grave being made and the papers burnt, the body of Chrysostom was interred, not without many tears from the spectators. They closed the sepulchre with a large fragment of a rock, until a tombstone was finished which Ambrosio said it was his intention to provide, and to inscribe upon it the following epitaph :

> The body of a wretched swain,
> Killed by a cruel maid's disdain,
> In this cold bed neglected lies.
> He lived, fond, hapless youth ! to prove
> Th' inhuman tyranny of love,
> Exerted in Marcela's eyes.

Then they strewed abundance of flowers and boughs on the grave, and, after expressions of condolence to his friend Ambrosio, they took their leave of him. Vivaldo and his companion did the same; and Don Quixote bade adieu to his hosts and the travellers, who entreated him to accompany them to Seville, being a place so favourable for adventures, that in every street and turning they were to be met with in greater abundance than in any other place. Don Quixote thanked them for their information and courtesy, but said that neither his inclination nor duty would admit of his going to Seville until he had cleared all those mountains of the robbers and assassins with which they were said to be infested. The travellers, hearing his good resolutions, would not importune him further; but, taking leave of him, pursued their journey, during which the history of Marcela and Chrysostom, as well as the frenzy of Don Quixote, supplied them with subjects of conversation. The knight, on his part, resolved to go in quest of the shepherdess Marcela, to make her an offer of his services; but things took a different course as will be related in the progress of this true history.

BOOK III.

CHAPTER XV.

*Wherein is related the unfortunate adventure which befell Don Quixote, in meeting with certain unmerciful Yanguesians.**

LEAVE having been taken, as the sage Cid Hamet Benengeli relates, by Don Quixote, of all those who were present at Chrysostom's funeral, he and his squire entered the same wood into which they had seen the shepherdess Marcela enter. And having ranged through it for above two hours in search of her without success, they stopped in a meadow full of fresh grass, near which ran a pleasant and refreshing brook, insomuch that it invited and compelled them to pass there the sultry hours of mid-day, which now became very oppressive. Don Quixote and Sancho alighted, and, leaving the ass and Rozinante at large to feed upon the abundant grass, they ransacked the wallet; and, without any ceremony, in friendly and social wise, master and man shared what it contained. Sancho had taken no care to fetter Rozinante, being well assured his disposition was so correct that all the mares of the pastures of Cordova would not provoke him to any indecorum. But fortune, or the devil, who is not always asleep, so ordered it that there were grazing in the same valley a number of Galician mares belonging to certain Yanguesian carriers, whose custom it is to pass the noon, with their drove, in places where there is grass and water; and that where Don Quixote then reposed suited their purpose. Now it so happened that Rozinante conceived a wish to pay his respects to the females, and, having them in the wind, he changed his natural and sober pace to a brisk trot, and without asking his master's leave departed to indulge in his inclination. But they being, as it seemed, more disposed to feed than anything else, received him with their heels and their teeth, in such a manner that in a little time his girths broke and he lost his saddle. But what must have affected him more sensibly was, that the carriers, having witnessed his intrusion, set upon him with their pack-staves, and so belaboured him that they laid him along on the ground in wretched plight.

By this time the knight and squire, having seen the drubbing of

---

* Carriers of Galicia, and inhabitants of the district of Yanguas in the Rioja.

Rozinante, came up in great haste; and Don Quixote said, "By what I see, friend Sancho, these are no knights, but low people of a scoundrel race. I tell thee this because thou art on that account justified in assisting me to take ample revenge for the outrage they have done to Rozinante before our eyes." "What the devil of revenge can we take," answered Sancho, "since they are about twenty, and we no more than two, and perhaps but one and a half?" "I am equal to a hundred!" replied Don Quixote; and, without saying more, he laid his hands on his sword, and flew at the Yanguesians; and Sancho did the same, incited by the example of his master. At the first blow, Don Quixote gave one of them a terrible wound on the shoulder, through a leathern doublet. The Yanguesians, seeing themselves assaulted in this manner by two men only, seized their staves, and, surrounding them, began to dispense their blows with great vehemence and animosity; and true it is that at the second blow they brought Sancho to the ground. The same fate befell Don Quixote, his courage and dexterity availing him nothing; and, as fate would have it, he fell just at Rozinante's feet, who had not yet been able to rise. Whence we may learn how unmercifully pack-staves will bruise, when put into rustic and wrathful hands. The Yanguesians, perceiving the mischief they had done, loaded their beasts with all speed, and pursued their journey, leaving the two adventurers in evil plight.

The first who came to his senses was Sancho Panza, who, finding himself close to his master, with a feeble and plaintive voice cried, "Signor Don Quixote! ah, Signor Don Quixote!" "What wouldst thou, brother Sancho?" answered the knight, in the same feeble and lamentable tone. "I could wish, if it were possible," said Sancho Panza, "your worship would give me two draughts of that drink of Feo Blass, if you have it here at hand. Perhaps it may do as well for broken bones as it does for wounds." "Unhappy I, that we have it not!" answered Don Quixote. "But I swear to thee, Sancho Panza, on the faith of a knight-errant, that, before two days pass (if fortune decree not otherwise), I will have it in my possession, or my hands shall fail me much." "But in how many days," said the squire, "does your worship think we shall recover the use of our feet?" "For my part," answered the battered knight, Don Quixote, "I cannot ascertain the precise term: but I alone am to blame, for having laid hand on my sword against men who are not knights like myself; and therefore I believe the God of battles has permitted this chastisement to fall upon me, as a punishment for having transgressed the laws of chivalry. On this account, brother Sancho, it is requisite thou shouldst be forewarned of what I shall now tell thee, for it highly concerns the welfare of us both; and it is this: that, when we are insulted by low people of this kind, do not stay still till I take up my sword against them, for I will by no means do it; but do thou draw thy sword and chastise them to thy satisfaction. If any knights shall come up to their assistance, I shall then know how to defend thee and offend them with all my might: for thou hast already had a thousand proofs how far the valour of this strong arm of mine extends;"—so arrogant was the poor gentleman become by his victory over the valiant Biscayan!

But Sancho Panza did not so entirely approve his master's instructions as to forbear saying, in reply, "Sir, I am a peaceable, tame, and quiet man, and can forgive any injury whatsoever; for I have a wife and children to maintain and bring up; so that, give me leave to tell your worship by way of hint, since it is not for me to command, that I will upon no account draw my sword, either against peasant or against knight; and that, from this time forward, in the presence of God, I forgive all injuries any one has done or shall do me, or that any person is now doing or may hereafter do me, whether he be high or low, rich or poor, gentle or simple, without excepting any state or condition whatever." Upon which his master said, "I wish I had breath to talk a little at my ease, and that the pain I feel in this rib would cease long enough for me to convince thee, Panza, of thy error. Hark ye, sinner: should the gale of fortune, now so adverse, change in our favour, filling the sails of our desires, so that we may securely and without opposition make the port of some one of those islands which I have promised thee, what would become of thee, if, when I had gained it and made thee lord thereof, thou shouldst render all ineffectual by not being a knight, nor desiring to be one, and by having neither valour nor resolution to revenge the injuries done thee, or to defend thy dominions? For thou must know that, in kingdoms and provinces newly conquered, the minds of the natives are at no time so quiet, nor so much in the interest of their new master, but there is still ground to fear that they will endeavour to effect a change of things, and once more, as they call it, try their fortune; therefore the new possessor ought to have understanding to know how to conduct himself, and courage to act offensively and defensively, on every occasion." "In this that hath now befallen us," answered Sancho, "I wish I had been furnished with that understanding and valour your lordship speaks of; but I swear, on the faith of a poor man, I am at this time more fit for plaisters than discourses. Try, sir, whether you are able to rise, and we will help up Rozinante, though he does not deserve it, for he was the principal cause of all this mauling. I never believed the like of Rozinante, whom I took to be chaste, and as peaceable as myself. But it is a true saying that ' much time is necessary to know people thoroughly ;' and that ' we are sure of nothing in this life.' Who could have thought that, after such swinging lashes as you gave that luckless adventurer, there should come post, as it were, in pursuit of you, this vast tempest of cudgel-strokes, which has discharged itself upon our shoulders?" "Thine, Sancho," replied Don Quixote, "should, one would think, be used to such storms; but mine, that were brought up between muslins and cambrics, must, of course, be more sensible to the pain of this unfortunate encounter. And were it not that I imagine—why do I say *imagine?*—did I not know for certain that all these inconveniences are inseparably annexed to the profession of arms, I would suffer myself to die here out of pure vexation." "Since these mishaps," said the squire, "are the natural fruits and harvest of chivalry, pray tell me whether they come often, or whether they have their set times in which they happen; for, to my thinking, two such harvests would disable us from ever reaping a third, if God of His infinite mercy does not succour us."

"Learn, friend Sancho," answered Don Quixote, "that the lives of knights-errant are subject to a thousand perils and disasters, but at the same time they are no less near becoming kings and emperors; as experience hath shown us in many and divers knights, with whose histories I am perfectly acquainted. I could tell thee now, if this pain would allow me, of some who, by the strength of their arm alone, have mounted to the exalted ranks I have mentioned; yet these very men were, before and after, involved in sundry calamities and misfortunes. The valorous Amadis de Gaul, for instance, was himself in the power of his mortal enemy, Archelaus the enchanter, of whom it it positively affirmed that, when he had him prisoner, he tied him to a pillar in his courtyard, and gave him above two hundred lashes with his horse's bridle. There is, moreover, a private author of no small credit, who tells us that the 'Knight of the Sun, being caught by a trap-door which sunk under his feet in a certain castle, found himself at the bottom of a deep dungeon under ground bound hand and foot, where they administered to him one of those things called a clyster of snow-water and sand, that almost dispatched him; and had he not been succoured in that great distress by a certain sage, his particular friend, it would have gone hard with the poor knight.' So that I may well submit to suffer among so many worthy persons who endured much greater affronts than those we have now experienced. For I would have thee know, Sancho, that wounds given with instruments that are accidentally in the hand are no affront: thus it is expressly written in the law of combat that, if a shoemaker strike a person with the last he has in his hand, though it be really of wood, it will not therefore be said that the person thus beaten with it was cudgelled. I say this that thou mayest not think, though we are bruised in this scuffle, we are disgraced; for the arms those men carried, and with which they assailed us, were no other than their staves; and none of them, as I remember, had either tuck, sword, or dagger."

"They gave me no leisure," answered Sancho, "to observe so narrowly; for scarcely had I laid hand on my weapon than my shoulders were crossed with their saplings, in such a manner that they deprived my eyes of sight and my feet of strength, laying me where I now lie, and where I am not so much concerned about whether the business of the thrashing be an affront or not, as I am at the pain of the blows, which will leave as deep an impression on my memory as on my shoulders." "Notwithstanding this, I tell thee, brother Panza," said Don Quixote, "that there is no remembrance which time does not obliterate, nor pain which death does not terminate." "But what greater misfortune can there be," replied Panza, "than that which waits for time to cure and for death to end? If this mischance of ours were of that sort which might be cured with a couple of plaisters, it would not be altogether so bad; but, for aught I see, all the plaisters of a hospital will not be sufficient to set us to rights again."

"Have done with this, and gather strength out of weakness, Sancho," said Don Quixote, "for so I purpose to do; and let us see how Rozinante does, for it seems to me that not the least part of our misfortune has fallen to the share of this poor animal." "That is not at all strange," answered Sancho, "since he also belongs to a knight-errant; but what I wonder at is that my ass should come off scot-free where we have paid so dear." "Fortune always leaves some door open in misfortune to admit a remedy," said Don Quixote: "this I say because thy beast may now supply the want of Rozinante, by carrying me hence to some castle, where I may be cured of my wounds. Nor do I account it dishonourable to be so mounted; for I remember to have read that the good old Silenus, governor and tutor of the merry god of laughter,

Sancho endeavoured to raise himself, but stopped half-way, bent like a Turkish bow.

when he made his entry into the city of the hundred gates, was mounted, much to his satisfaction, on a most beautiful ass." "It is likely he rode as your worship says," answered Sancho; "but there is a main difference between riding and lying athwart like a sack of rubbish." "The wounds received in battle," said Don Quixote, "rather give honour than take it away; therefore, friend Panza, answer me no more, but, as I said before, raise me up as well as thou canst, and place me as it may best please thee upon thy ass, that we may get hence before night overtakes us in this uninhabited place." "Yet I have heard your worship say," quoth Panza, "that it is usual for knights-errant to sleep on heaths and deserts most part of the year, and therein think themselves very fortunate." "That is," said Don Quixote, "when they cannot do otherwise, or are in love: and so true is this, that there have been knights who, unknown to their mistresses, have exposed themselves for two years together upon rocks to the sun and the shade, and to the inclemencies of heaven. One of these was Amadis, when, calling himself Beltenebros, he took up his lodging on the Poor Rock—whether for eight years or eight months I know not, for I am not perfect in his history; it is sufficient that there he was, doing penance for I know not what displeasure manifested towards him by the lady Oriana. But let us leave this, Sancho, and hasten before such another misfortune happens to thy beast as hath befallen Rozinante." "That would be the devil, indeed," quoth Sancho; and sending forth thirty "alases," and sixty sighs, and a hundred and twenty curses on those who had brought him into that situation, he endeavoured to raise himself, but stopped half-way, bent like a Turkish bow, being wholly unable to stand upright : notwithstanding this, he managed to saddle his ass, who had also taken advantage of that day's excessive liberty to go a little astray. He then heaved up Rozinante, who, had he had a tongue wherewithal to complain, most certainly would not have been outdone either by Sancho or his master. Sancho at length settled Don Quixote upon the ass, to whose tail he then tied Rozinante, and, taking hold of the halter of Dapple, he led them, now faster, now slower, towards the place where he thought the high-road might lie; and had scarcely gone a short league when fortune, that was conducting his affairs from good to better, discovered to him the road, where he also espied an inn; which, much to his sorrow and Don Quixote's joy, must needs be a castle. Sancho positively maintained it was an inn, and his master that it was a castle, and the dispute lasted so long that they arrived there before it was determined : and Sancho, without further expostulation, entered it with his string of cattle.

CHAPTER XVI.

Of what happened to Don Quixote in the inn which he imagined to be a castle.

Looking at Don Quixote laid across the ass, the innkeeper inquired of Sancho what ailed him. Sancho answered him that it was nothing but a fall from the rock, by which his ribs were somewhat bruised. The innkeeper had a wife of a disposition uncommon among those of the like occupation, for she was naturally charitable, and felt for the misfortunes of her neighbours; so that she immediately prepared to relieve Don Quixote, and made her daughter, a very comely young maiden, assist in the cure of her guest. There was also a servant at the inn, an Asturian wench, broad-faced, flat-headed, with a little nose, one eye squinting, and the other not much better. It is true, the elegance of her form made amends for other defects. She was not seven hands high; and her shoulders, which burdened her a little too much, made her look down to the ground more than she would willingly have done. This agreeable lass now assisted the damsel to prepare for Don Quixote a very sorry bed in a garret, which gave evident tokens of having formerly served many years as a hay-loft. In this room lodged also a carrier, whose bed was at a little distance from that of our knight; and though it was composed of pannels, and other trappings of his mules, it had much the advantage over that of Don Quixote, which consisted of four not very smooth boards upon two unequal tressels, and a mattress no thicker than a quilt, and full of knots, which from their hardness might have been taken for pebbles, had not the wool appeared through some fractures; with two sheets like the leather of an old target, and a rug, the threads of which you might count, if you chose, without losing one of the number.

In this wretched bed was Don Quixote laid; after which the hostess and her daughter plaistered him from head to foot, Maritornes (for so the Asturian wench was called) at the same time holding the light. And as the hostess was thus employed, perceiving Don Quixote to be mauled in every part, she said that his bruises seemed the effect of hard drubbing, rather than of a fall. "Not a drubbing," said Sancho, "but the knobs and sharp points of the rock, every one of which has left its mark. And now I think of it," added he, "pray contrive to spare a morsel of that tow, as somebody may find it useful—indeed, I suspect that my sides would be glad of a little of it." "What, you have had a fall too, have you?" said the hostess. "No," replied Sancho, "not a fall, but a fright, on seeing my master tumble, which so affected my whole body that I feel as if I had received a thousand blows myself." "That may very well be," said the damsel; "for I have often dreamed that I was falling down from some high tower, and could never come to the ground; and when I awoke, I have found myself as much bruised and battered as if I had really fallen." "But here is the point, mistress," answered Sancho Panza, "that I, without dreaming at all, and more awake than I am now, find myself with almost as many bruises as my master Don Quixote." "What do you say is the name of this gentleman?" quoth the Asturian. "Don Quixote de la Mancha," answered Sancho Panza: "he is a knight-errant, and one of the best and most valiant that has been seen for this long time in the world." "What is a knight-errant?" said the wench. "Are you such a novice as not to know that?" answered Sancho Panza. "You must know, then, that a knight-errant is a thing that, in two words, is cudgelled and made an emperor: to-day he is the most unfortunate wretch in the world, and to-morrow will have two or three crowns of kingdoms to give to his squire." "How comes it then to pass that you, being squire to this worthy gentleman," said the hostess, "have not yet, as it seems, got so much as an earldom?" "It is early days yet," answered Sancho, "for it is but a month since we set out in quest of adventures, and hitherto we have met with none that deserve the name. And sometimes we look for one thing and find another. But the truth is, if my master Don Quixote recovers of this wound or fall, and I am not disabled thereby, I would not truck my hopes for the best title in Spain."

To all this conversation Don Quixote had listened very attentively; and now, raising himself up in the bed as well as he could, and taking the hand of his hostess, he said to her, " Believe me, beauteous lady, you may esteem yourself fortunate in having entertained me in this your castle, being such a person that, if I say little of myself, it is because, as the proverb declares, self-praise depreciates; but my squire will inform you who I am. I only say that I shall retain the service you have done me eternally engraven on my memory, and be grateful to you as long as my life shall endure. And, had it pleased the high heavens that Love had not held me so enthralled and subject to his laws, and to the eyes of that beautiful ingrate whose name I silently pronounce, those of this lovely virgin had become enslavers of my liberty."

The hostess, her daughter, and the good Maritornes stood confounded at this harangue of our knight-errant, which they understood just as much as if he had spoken Greek, although they guessed that it all tended to compliments and offers of service; and not being accustomed to such kind of language, they gazed at him with surprise, and thought him another sort of man than those now in fashion; and, after thanking him in their inn-like phrase for his offers, they left him. The Asturian Maritornes doctored Sancho, who stood in no less need of plaisters than his master. The carrier and she, it appeared, had agreed to sup that night together; and she had given him her word that, when the guests were all quiet and her master and mistress asleep, she would repair to him. And it is said of the honest Maritornes that she never made a promise but she performed it, even though she had made it on a mountain, without any witness; for she valued herself upon her gentility, and thought it no disgrace to be employed in service at an inn, since misfortunes and unhappy accidents, as she affirmed, had brought her to that state.

Don Quixote's hard, scanty, beggarly, crazy bed, stood first in the middle of the cock-loft; and close by it Sancho had placed his own, which consisted only of a rush mat, and a rug that seemed to be rather of beaten hemp than of wool. Next to the squire's stood that of the carrier, made up, as hath been said, of pannels, and the whole furniture of two of his best mules; for he possessed twelve in number, sleek, fat, and stately—being one of the richest carriers of Arevalo, according to the author of this history, who makes particular mention of this carrier, for he knew him well: nay, some go so far as to say he was related to him. Besides, Cid Hamet Benengeli was a very minute and very accurate historian in all things; and this is very evident from the circumstances already related, which, though apparently mean and trivial, he would not pass over unnoticed. This may serve as an example to those grave historians who relate facts so briefly and succinctly that we have scarcely a taste of them: omitting, either through neglect, malice, or ignorance, things the most pithy and substantial. A thousand blessings upon the author of Tablante, of Ricamonte, and on him who wrote the exploits of the Count de Tomilas! With what punctuality do they describe everything!

I say, then, that after the carrier had visited his mules and given them their second course, he laid himself down upon his pannels, in expectation of his most punctual Maritornes. Sancho was already plaistered and in bed ; and, though he endeavoured to sleep, the pain of his ribs would not allow him ; and Don Quixote, from the same cause, kept his eyes as wide open as those of a hare. The whole inn was in profound silence, and contained no other light than what proceeded from a lamp which hung in the middle of the entry. This marvellous stillness, and the thoughts of our knight, which incessantly recurred to those adventures so common in the annals of chivalry, brought to his imagination one of the strangest whims that can well be conceived ; for he imagined that he was now in some famous castle, and that the daughter of its lord, captivated by his fine appearance, had become enamoured of him, and had promised to steal that night privately to him, and pass some time with him. Then, taking all this chimera formed by himself for reality, he began to feel some alarm, reflecting on the dangerous trial to which his fidelity was on the point of being exposed ; but resolved in his heart not to commit disloyalty against his lady Dulcinea del Toboso, though Queen Guinevra herself, with the Lady Quintaniana, should present themselves before him.

Whilst his thoughts were occupied by these extravagances, the hour —an unlucky one to him—arrived when the gentle Asturian, mindful of her promise, entered the room, and, with silent and cautious step, advanced towards the couch of the carrier. But scarcely had she passed the threshold of the door when Don Quixote heard her ; and, sitting up in his bed, in spite of plaisters and the pain of his ribs, stretched out his arms to receive his beauteous damsel, who, crouching, and holding her breath as she went, with hands extended feeling for her lover, encountered the arms of Don Quixote, who caught first hold of her by the wrist, and drawing her towards him (she not daring to speak a word), made her sit down on the bed. On touching her garment, though it was of canvas, it seemed to him to be of the finest and softest lawn ; the glass beads that encircled her wrists to his fancy were precious oriental pearls ; her hairs, not unlike those of a horse's mane, he took for threads of the brightest gold of Arabia, whose splendour obscures that of the sun itself ; and though her breath, doubtless, smelt powerfully of the last night's stale salt fish, he fancied himself inhaling a delicious and aromatic odour. In short, his imagination painted her to him in the very form and manner of some princess described in his books, who comes thus adorned to visit the wounded knight with whom she is in love ; and so great was the poor gentleman's infatuation, that neither the touch, nor the breath, nor other things she had about her, could undeceive him. So far from this, he imagined that he held the goddess of beauty in his arms ; and, clasping her fast, in a low and amorous voice he said to her, "Oh that I were in a state, beautiful and exalted lady, to return so vast a favour as this you confer upon me by your charming presence ! but fortune, never weary of persecuting the good, is pleased to lay me on this bed, so bruised and disabled that, how much soever I may be inclined to convince you of my devotion, it is impossible; to which is added another still greater impossibility—the plighted faith I have sworn to the peerless Dulcinea del Toboso, sole mistress of my most recondite thoughts! Had not these articles intervened, I should not have been so insensible a knight as to let slip the happy opportunity with which your great goodness has favoured me."

Maritornes was in the utmost vexation at being thus confined by Don Quixote; and, not hearing or attending to what he said, she struggled, without speaking a word, to release herself. The good carrier, whom busy thoughts had kept awake, having heard his fair one from the first moment she entered the door, listened attentively to all that Don Quixote said; and suspecting that the Asturian nymph had played false with him, he advanced towards Don Quixote's bed, and stood still, in order to discover the tendency of his discourse, which, however, he could not understand; but, seeing that she struggled to get from him, and that Don Quixote laboured to hold her, and also not liking the jest, he lifted up his arm, and discharged so terrible a blow on the lantern jaws of the enamoured knight, that his mouth was bathed in blood; and, not content with this, he mounted upon his ribs, and paced them somewhat above a trot from one end to the other. The bed, which was crazy, and its foundations none of the strongest, being unable to bear the additional weight of the carrier, came down to the ground with such a crash that the innkeeper awoke; and, having called aloud to Maritornes without receiving an answer, he immediately conjectured it was some affair in which she was concerned. With this suspicion he arose, and, lighting a candle, went to the place where he had heard the bustle. The Asturian, seeing her master coming, and knowing his furious disposition, retreated in terror to Sancho Panza's bed, who was now asleep, and there rolled herself into a ball. The innkeeper entered, calling out, "Where are you, Maritornes? for these are some of your doings." Sancho was now disturbed, and feeling such a mass upon him, fancied he had got the nightmare, and began to lay about him on every side; and not a few of his blows reached Maritornes, who, provoked by the smart, cast aside all decorum, and made Sancho such a return in kind that she effectually roused him from sleep, in spite of his drowsiness. The squire finding himself thus treated, and without knowing by whom, raised himself up as well as he could, and grappled with Maritornes; and there began between them the most obstinate and delightful skirmish in the world. The carrier, perceiving by the light of the host's candle how it fared with her, quitted Don Quixote, and ran to her assistance. The landlord followed him, but with a different intention; for it was to chastise the wench, concluding that she was the sole occasion of all this harmony. And so, as the proverb says, the cat to the rat, the rat to the rope, and the rope to the post: the carrier belaboured Sancho, Sancho Maritornes, Maritornes Sancho, and the innkeeper Maritornes; all redoubling their blows without intermission: and the best of it was, the landlord's candle went out;

when, being left in the dark, they indiscriminately thrashed each other, and with so little mercy that every blow left its mark.

It happened that there lodged that night at the inn, an officer belonging to the Holy Brotherhood of Toledo; who, hearing the strange noise of the scuffle, seized his wand and the tin box which held his commission, and entered the room in the dark, calling out, " Forbear, in the name of justice; forbear, in the name of the Holy Brotherhood." And the first he encountered was the battered Don Quixote, who lay senseless on his demolished bed, stretched upon his back; and, laying hold of his beard as he was groping about, he cried out repeatedly, " I charge you to aid and assist me; " but, finding that the person whom he held was motionless, he concluded that he was dead, and that the people in the room were his murderers. Upon which he raised his voice still louder, crying, " Shut the inn-door, and let none escape, for here is a man murdered ! " These words startled them all, and the conflict instantly ceased. The landlord withdrew to his chamber, the carrier to his pannels, and the lass to her straw: the unfortunate Don Quixote and Sancho alone were incapable of moving. The officer now let go the beard of Don Quixote, and, in order to search after and secure the delinquents, he went out for a light, but could find none, for the inn-keeper had purposely extinguished the lamp when he retired to his chamber; and therefore he was obliged to have recourse to the chimney, where, after much time and trouble, he lighted another lamp.

CHAPTER XVII.

Wherein are continued the innumerable disasters that befell the brave Don Quixote and his good squire Sancho Panza in the inn which he unhappily took for a castle.

Don Quixote by this time had come to himself, and, in the same dolorous tone in which the day before he had called to his squire, when he lay extended in the valley of pack-staves, he now again called to him, saying, " Sancho, friend, art thou asleep? art thou asleep, friend Sancho ? " " How should I sleep? woe is me ! " answered Sancho, full of trouble and vexation ; " for I think all the devils in hell have been with me to-night." " Well mayest thou believe so," answered Don Quixote; " for either I know nothing, or this castle is enchanted. Listen to me, Sancho—but what I am now going to disclose thou must swear to keep secret until after my death." " Yes, I swear," answered Sancho. " I require this," said Don Quixote, " because I would not injure the reputation of any one." " I tell you I do swear," replied Sancho, " and will keep it secret until your worship's death ; and Heaven grant I may discover it to-morrow." " Have I done thee so much evil,

Sancho," answered Don Quixote, "that thou shouldst wish for my decease so very soon?" "It is not for that," answered Sancho; "but I am an enemy to holding things long, and would not have them rot in my keeping." "Be it for what it will," said Don Quixote, "I confide in thy love and courtesy, and therefore I inform thee that this night a most extraordinary adventure has befallen me; and, to tell it briefly, thou must know that, a little while since, I was visited by the daughter of the lord of this castle, who is the most accomplished and beautiful damsel to be found over a great part of the habitable earth. How I could describe the graces of her person, the sprightliness of her wit, and the many other hidden charms which, from the respect I owe to my lady Dulcinea del Toboso, I shall pass over undescribed! All that I am permitted to say is that Heaven, jealous of the great happiness that fortune had put in my possession, or, what is more probable, this castle being enchanted, just as we were engaged in most sweet and delightful conversation, an invisible hand, affixed to the arm of some monstrous giant, gave me so violent a blow that my mouth was bathed in blood, and afterwards so bruised me that I am now in a worse state than that wherein the fury of the carriers left us yesterday, owing to the indiscretion of Rozinante. Whence I conjecture that the treasure of this damsel's beauty is guarded by some enchanted Moor, and therefore not to be approached by me." "Nor by me neither," answered Sancho; "for more than four hundred Moors have buffeted me in such a manner that the basting of the pack-staves was tarts and cheesecakes to it. But tell me, pray, sir, call you this an excellent and rare adventure, which has left us in such a pickle? Not that it was quite so bad with your worship, who had in your arms that incomparable beauty whom you speak of. As for me, what had I but the heaviest blows that I hope I shall ever feel in all my life? Woe is me, and the mother that bore me! for I am no knight-errant, nor ever mean to be one; yet, of all our mishaps, the greater part still falls to my share." "What! hast thou likewise been beaten?" said Don Quixote. "Have not I told you so? evil befall my lineage!" quoth Sancho. "Console thyself, my friend," said Don Quixote, "for I will now make that precious balsam which will cure us in the twinkling of an eye." At this moment the officer, having lighted his lamp, entered to examine the person whom he conceived to have been murdered; and Sancho, seeing him enter in his shirt, with a nightcap on his head, a lamp in his hand, and a countenance far from well-favoured, asked his master if it was the enchanted Moor coming to finish the correction he had bestowed upon them. "It cannot be the Moor," answered Don Quixote, "for the enchanted suffer not themselves to be visible." "If they do not choose to be seen, they will be felt," said Sancho: "witness my shoulders." "Mine might speak too," answered Don Quixote; "but this is not sufficient evidence to convince us that he whom we see is the enchanted Moor."

The officer, finding them communing in so calm a manner, stood in astonishment: although it is true that Don Quixote still lay flat on his

He took his simples, and made a compound of them, boiling them until he thought the mixture had arrived at the exact point.

back, unable to stir, from bruises and plaisters. The officer approached him, and said, "Well, my good fellow, how are you?" "I would speak more respectfully," answered Don Quixote, "were I in your place. Is it the fashion of this country, blockhead! thus to address knights-errant?" The officer, not disposed to bear this language from one of so scurvy an aspect, lifted up his lamp, and dashed it, with all its contents, at the head of Don Quixote, and then made his retreat in the dark. "Surely," quoth Sancho Panza, "this must be the enchanted Moor; and he reserves the treasure for others, and for us only fisti-cuffs and lamp-shots."* "It is even so," answered Don Quixote; "and it is to no purpose to regard these affairs of enchantments, or to be out of humour or angry with them; for, being invisible, and mere phantoms, all endeavours to seek revenge would be fruitless. Rise,

* In the original, *Candilazos*, a new-coined word.

Sancho, if thou canst, and call the governor of this fortress, and procure me some oil, wine, salt, and rosemary, to make the healing balsam; for in truth I want it much at this time, as the wound this phantom has given me bleeds very fast."

Sancho got up with aching bones; and, as he was proceeding in the dark towards the landlord's chamber, he met the officer, who was watching the movements of his enemy, and said to him, "Sir, whoever you are, do us the favour and kindness to help us to a little rosemary, oil, salt, and wine; for they are wanted to cure one of the best knights-errant in the world, who lies there sorely wounded by the hands of the enchanted Moor who is in this inn." The officer, hearing this, took him for a maniac; and, as the day now began to dawn, he opened the inn-door, and calling the host, told him what Sancho wanted. The innkeeper furnished him with what he desired, and Sancho carried them to Don Quixote, who lay with his hands on his head, complaining of the pain caused by the lamp, which, however, had done him no other hurt than raising a couple of tolerable large tumours; what he took for blood being only moisture, occasioned by the pelting of the storm which had just blown over. In fine, he took his simples, and made a compound of them, mixing them together, and boiling them some time, until he thought the mixture had arrived at the exact point. He then asked for a phial to hold it; but, as there was no such thing in the inn, he resolved to put it in a cruse, or tin oil-flask, of which the host made him a present. This being done, he pronounced over the cruse above four-score *paternosters,* and as many *Ave Marias, salves,* and *credos,* accompanying every word with a cross, by way of benediction; all which was performed in the presence of Sancho, the innkeeper, and the officer: as for the carrier, he had gone soberly about the business of tending his mules. Having completed the operation, Don Quixote resolved to make trial immediately of the virtue of that precious balsam, and therefore drank about a pint and a half of what remained in the pot wherein it was boiled after the cruse was filled; and scarcely had he swallowed the potion when it was rejected, and followed by so violent a retching that nothing was left on his stomach. To the pain and exertion of the vomit, a copious perspiration succeeding, he desired to be covered up warm, and left alone. They did so, and he continued asleep above three hours, when he awoke and found himself greatly relieved in his body, and his battered and bruised members so much restored that he considered himself as perfectly recovered, and was thoroughly persuaded that he was in possession of the true balsam of Fierabras; and consequently, with such a remedy, he might thenceforward encounter, without fear, all dangers, battles, and conflicts, however hazardous.

Sancho Panza, who likewise took his master's amendment for a miracle, desired he would give him what remained in the pot, which was no small quantity. This request being granted, he took it in both hands, and, with good faith and better will, swallowed down very little less than his master had done. Now the case was, that poor Sancho's stomach was not so delicate as that of his master; and therefore, before he could reject it, he endured such pangs and loathings, with such cold sweats and faintings, that he verily thought his last hour was come; and finding himself so afflicted and tormented, he cursed the balsam, and the thief that had given it to him. Don Quixote, seeing him in that condition, said, " I believe, Sancho, that all this mischief hath befallen thee because thou art not dubbed a knight; for I am of opinion this liquor can do good only to those who are of that order."

He sweated and sweated again, with such faintings and shivering-fits, that all present
thought he was expiring.

" If your worship knew that," replied Sancho, " evil betide me and all my generation! why did you suffer me to drink it?" By this time the beverage commenced its operation, and he sweated and sweated again, with such faintings and shivering-fits, that not only himself, but all present, thought he was expiring. These pangs lasted nearly two hours; and left him, not sound like his master, but so exhausted and shattered that he was unable to stand. Don Quixote, feeling, as we said before, quite renovated, was moved to take his departure imme-diately in quest of adventures, thinking that by every moment's delay he was depriving the world of his aid and protection; and more especially as he felt secure and confident in the virtues of the balsam. Thus stimulated, he saddled Rozinante with his own hands, and pannelled the ass of his squire, whom he also helped to dress, and afterwards to mount. He then mounted himself, and, having observed a pike in a corner of the inn-yard, he took possession of it to serve him for a lance. All the people in the inn, above twenty in number, stood gazing at him, and, among the rest, the host's daughter, while he on his part removed not his eyes from her, and ever and anon sent forth a sigh which seemed torn from the bottom of his bowels : all believing it to proceed from pain in his ribs—at least those who the night before had seen how he was plaistered.

Being now both mounted and at the door of the inn, he called to the host, and, in a grave and solemn tone of voice, said to him, " Many and great are the favours, Signor Governor, which in this your castle I have received, and I am bound to be grateful to you all the days of my life. If I can make you some compensation, by taking vengeance on any proud miscreant who hath insulted you, know that the duty of my profession is no other than to strengthen the weak, to revenge the injured, and to chastise the perfidious. Consider, and if your memory recalls anything of this nature to recommend to me, you need only declare it; for I promise you, by the order of knighthood I have received, to procure you satisfaction and amends to your heart's desire ! " The host answered with the same gravity, " Sir Knight, I have no need of your worship's avenging any wrong for me ; I know how to take the proper revenge when any injury is done me : all I desire of your worship is to pay me for what you have had in the inn, as well for the straw and barley for your two beasts, as for your supper and lodging." " What ! is this an inn ? " exclaimed Don Quixote. " Aye, and a very creditable one," answered the host. " Hitherto, then, I have been in an error," answered Don Quixote ; " for in truth, I took it for a castle ; but since it is indeed no castle, but an inn, all that you have now to do is to excuse the payment; for I cannot act contrary to the law of knights-errant, of whom I certainly know (having hitherto read nothing to the contrary) that they never paid for lodging, or anything else, in the inns where they reposed ; because every accommodation is legally and justly due to them in return for the insufferable hardships they endure while in quest of adventures, by night and by day, in winter and in summer, on foot and on horseback, with thirst and with hunger, with heat and with cold ; subject to all the inclemencies of heaven, and to all the inconveniences upon earth." " I see little to my purpose in all this," answered the host : " pay me what is my due, and let me have none of your stories and knight-errantries ; all I want is to get my own." " Thou art a blockhead, and a pitiful innkeeper ! " answered Don Quixote : so, clapping spurs to Rozinante and brandishing his lance, he sallied out of the inn without opposition, and never turning to see whether his squire followed him, was soon a good way off.

The host, seeing him go without paying, ran to seize on Sancho Panza, who said that, since his master would not pay, neither would he pay; for, being squire to a knight-errant, the same rule and reason held as good for him as for his master. The innkeeper, irritated on hearing this, threatened, if he did not pay him, he should repent his obstinacy. Sancho swore by the order of chivalry which his master had received, that he would not pay a single farthing, though it should cost him his life; for the laudable and ancient usage of knights-errant should not be lost for him, nor should the squires of future knights have cause to reproach him for not maintaining so just a right.

Poor Sancho's ill luck would have it, that among the people in the inn there were four cloth-workers of Segovia, three needle-makers from the fountain of Cordova, and two neighbours from the market-place of Seville, all merry, good-humoured, frolicksome fellows; who, instigated and moved, as it appeared, by the self-same spirit, came up to Sancho, and having dismounted him, one of them produced a blanket from the landlord's bed, into which he was immediately thrown; but, perceiving that the ceiling was too low, they determined to execute their purpose in the yard, which was bounded upwards only by the sky. Thither Sancho was carried; and, being placed in the middle of the blanket, they began to toss him aloft, and divert themselves with him as with a dog at Shrovetide. The cries which the poor blanketed squire sent forth were so many and so loud, that they reached his master's ears; who, stopping to listen attentively, believed that some new adventure was at hand, until he plainly recognised the voice of the squire: then turning the reins, he gallopped back to the inn-door, and finding it closed, he rode round in search of some other entrance; but had no sooner reached the yard-wall, which was not very high, when he perceived the wicked sport they were making with his squire. He saw him ascend and descend through the air with so much grace and agility that, if his indignation would have suffered him, he certainly would have laughed outright. He made an effort to get from his horse upon the pales, but was so maimed and bruised that he was unable to alight; and therefore, remaining on horseback, he proceeded to vent his rage, by uttering so many reproaches and invectives against those who were tossing Sancho, that it is impossible to commit them to writing. But they suspended neither their laughter nor their labour; nor did the flying Sancho cease to pour forth lamentations, mingled now with threats, now with entreaties; yet all were of no avail, and they desisted at last only from pure fatigue. They then brought him his ass, and, wrapping him in his cloak, mounted him thereon. The compassionate Maritornes, seeing him so exhausted, bethought of helping him to a jug of water, and that it might be the cooler, she fetched it from the well. Sancho took it, and as he was lifting it to his mouth, stopped on hearing the voice of his master, who called to him aloud, saying, "Son Sancho, drink not water; do not drink it, son; it will kill thee: behold here the most holy balsam," (showing him the cruse of liquor) "two drops of which will infallibly restore thee." At these words, Sancho, turning his eyes askance, said in a louder voice, "Perhaps you have forgot, sir, that I am no knight, or you would not have me vomit up what remains of my inside after last night's work. Keep your liquor, in the devil's name, and let me alone." He then instantly began to drink; but at the first sip, finding it was water, he could proceed no further, and besought Maritornes to bring him some wine: which she did willingly, and paid for it with her own money; for it is indeed said of her that, although in that station, she had some faint traces of a Christian. When Sancho had ceased drinking, he clapped heels to his ass; and, the inn-gate being thrown wide open, out he went, satisfied that he had paid nothing, and had carried his point, though at the expense of his usual pledge, namely, his back. The landlord, it is true, retained his wallets in payment of what was due to him; but Sancho never missed them in the hurry of his departure. The innkeeper would have fastened the door well after him as soon as he saw him out; but the blanketeers would not let him, being persons of that sort that, though Don Quixote had really been one of the knights of the Round Table, they would not have cared two farthings for him.

CHAPTER XVIII.

The discourse which Sancho Panza held with his master Don Quixote; with other adventures worth relating.

SANCHO came up to his master, so faint and dispirited that he was not able to urge his ass forward. Don Quixote, perceiving him in that condition, said, "Honest Sancho, that castle, or inn, I am now convinced, is enchanted; for they who so cruelly sported with thee, what could they be but phantoms and inhabitants of another world? And I am confirmed in this, from having found that, when I stood at the pales of the yard, beholding the acts of your sad tragedy, I could not possibly get over them, nor even alight from Rozinante; so that they must certainly have held me enchanted. for I swear to thee, by the faith of what I am, that, if I could have got over or alighted, I would have avenged thee in such a manner as would have made those poltroons and assassins remember the jest as long as they lived, even though I would have thereby transgressed the laws of chivalry; for, as I have often told thee, they do not allow a knight to lay hand on his sword against any one who is not so, unless it be in defence of his own life and person, and in cases of urgent and extreme necessity." "And I too," quoth Sancho, "would have revenged myself if I had been able, knight or no knight, but I could not, though, in my opinion, they who diverted themselves at my expense were no hobgoblins, but men of flesh and bones, as we are; and each of them, as I heard while they were tossing me, had his proper name: one was called Pedro Martinez, another Tenorio Hernandez; and the landlord's name is John Palomeque, the

left-handed : so that, sir, as to your not being able to leap over the pales
nor to alight from your horse, the fault lay not in enchantment, but in
something else. And what I gather clearly from all this is, that these
adventures we are in quest of will in the long run bring us into so
many misadventures that we shall not know which is our right foot.
So that, in my poor opinion, the better and surer way would be to
return to our village, now that it is reaping-time, and look after our
business ; nor go rambling from Ceca to Mecca, and out of the frying-
pan into the fire."

"How little dost thou know, Sancho," answered Don Quixote, " of
what appertains to chivalry ! Peace, and have patience, for the day
will come when thine eyes shall witness how honourable a thing it is
to follow this profession : for tell me, what greater satisfaction can the
world afford, or what pleasure can be compared with that of winning
a battle, and triumphing over an adversary ? Undoubtedly none."
"It may be so," answered Sancho, "though I do not know it. I only
know that, since we have been knights-errant, or since you have been
one, sir (for I have no right to reckon myself of that honourable
number), we have never won any battle, except that of the Biscayan ;
and even there your worship came off with half an ear and half a
helmet ; and from that day to this we have had nothing but drubbings
upon drubbings, cuffs upon cuffs, with my blanket-tossing into the
bargain, and that by persons enchanted, on whom I cannot revenge
myself, and thereby know what that pleasure of overcoming an enemy
is which your worship talks of." "That is what troubles me, and
ought to trouble thee also, Sancho," answered Don Quixote ; "but
henceforward I will endeavour to have ready at hand a sword made
with such art that no kind of enchantment can touch him that wears
it ; and perhaps fortune may put me in possession of that of Amadis,
when he called himself Knight of the Burning Sword, which was one
of the best weapons that ever was worn by knight ; for, besides the
virtue aforesaid, it cut like a razor ; and no armour, however strong or
enchanted, could withstand it." "Such is my luck," quoth Sancho,
"that though this were so, and your worship should find such a sword,
it would be of service only to those who are dubbed knights—like
the balsam : as for the poor squires, they may sing sorrow." "Fear
not, Sancho," said Don Quixote ; "Heaven will yet deal more kindly
by thee."

The knight and his squire went on conferring thus together, when
Don Quixote perceived in the road on which they were travelling a great
and thick cloud of dust coming towards them ; upon which he turned to
Sancho, and said, "This is the day, O Sancho, that shall manifest the
good that fortune hath in store for me. This is the day, I say, on
which shall be proved, as at all times, the valour of my arm, and on
which I shall perform exploits that will be recorded and written in the
book of fame, and there remain to all succeeding ages. Seest thou that
cloud of dust, Sancho ? It is raised by a prodigious army of divers and
innumerable nations, who are on the march this way." " If so, there

must be armies," said Sancho; "for here, on this side, arises just such another cloud of dust." Don Quixote turned, and seeing that it really was so, he rejoiced exceedingly, taking it for granted they were two armies coming to engage in the midst of that spacious plain; for at all hours and moments his imagination was full of the battles, enchantments, adventures, extravagances, amours, and challenges detailed in his favourite books; and in every thought, word, and action he reverted to them. Now, the cloud of dust he saw was raised by two great flocks of sheep going the same road from different parts, and, as the dust concealed them until they came near, and Don Quixote affirmed so positively that they were armies, Sancho began to believe it, and said, "Sir, what then must we do?" "What?" replied Don Quixote, "favour and assist the weaker side! Thou must know, Sancho, that the army which marches toward us in front is led and commanded by the great Emperor Alifanfaron, lord of the great island of Taprobana; this other, which marches behind us, is that of his enemy, the King of the Garamantes, Pentapolin of the Naked Arm, for he always enters into battle with his right arm bare." "But why do these two princes bear one another so much ill-will?" demanded Sancho. "They hate one another," answered Don Quixote, "because this Alifanfaron is a furious pagan, in love with the daughter of Pentapolin, who is a most beautiful and superlatively graceful lady, and also a Christian; but her father will not give her in marriage to the pagan king unless he will first renounce the religion of his false prophet Mahomet, and turn Christian." "By my beard," said Sancho, "Pentapolin is in the right; and I am resolved to assist him to the utmost of my power." "Therein thou wilt do thy duty, Sancho," said Don Quixote; "for in order to engage in such contests it is not necessary to be dubbed a knight." "I easily comprehend that," answered Sancho. "But where shall we dispose of this ass, that we may be sure to find him when the fray is over? for I believe it was never yet the fashion to go to battle on a beast of this kind." "Thou art in the right," said Don Quixote; "and thou mayest let him take his chance whether he be lost or not, for we shall have such choice of horses after the victory, that Rozinante himself will run a risk of being exchanged. But listen with attention whilst I give thee an account of the principal knights in the two approaching armies; and, that thou mayest observe them the better, let us retire to that rising ground, whence both armies may be distinctly seen." They did so, and placed themselves for that purpose on a hillock, from which the two flocks which Don Quixote mistook for armies might easily have been discerned, had not their view been obstructed by the clouds of dust. Seeing, however, in his imagination what did not exist, he began with a loud voice to say: "The knight thou seest yonder with the gilded armour, who bears on his shield a lion crowned, *couchant* at a damsel's feet, is the valorous Laurcalco, lord of the Silver Bridge. The other, with the armour flowered with gold, who bears the three crowns *argent* in a field *azure*, is the formidable Micocolembo, Grand Duke of Quiracia. The third, with gigantic limbs, who marches on his right, is the undaunted Brandabarbaran of Boliche, lord of the three Arabias. He is armed with a serpent's skin, and bears instead of a shield, a gate, which fame says is one of those belonging to the temple which Samson pulled down when with his death he avenged himself upon his enemies. But turn thine eyes on this other side, and there thou wilt see, in front of this other army, the ever-victorious and never-vanquished Timonel de Carcajona, Prince of the New Biscay, who comes clad in armour quartered *azure, vert, argent,* and *or* ; bearing on his shield a cat *or* in a field *gules,* with a scroll inscribed MIAU, being the beginning of his mistress's name ; who, it is reported, is the peerless Miaulina, daughter of Alphenniquen, Duke of Algarve. That other, who burdens and oppresses the back of yon powerful steed, whose armour is as white as snow, and his shield also white, without any device, he is a new knight, by birth a Frenchman, called Peter Papin, lord of the baronies of Utrique. The other whom thou seest, with his armed heels pricking the flanks of that fleet piebald courser, and his armour of pure azure, is the mighty Duke of Nerbia, Espartafilardo of the Wood, whose device is an asparagus-bed, with this motto in Castilian, ' *Rastrea mi suerte* ' (' Thus drags my fortune ')."

In this manner he went on naming sundry knights of each squadron, as his fancy dictated, and giving to each their arms, colours, devices, and mottoes extempore ; and, without pausing, he continued thus :— " That squadron in the front is formed and composed of people of different nations. Here stand those who drink the sweet waters of the famous Xanthus ; the mountaineers, who tread the Massilian fields ; those who sift the pure and fine gold-dust of Arabia Felix ; those who dwell along the famous and refreshing banks of the clear Thermodon ; those who drain, by divers and sundry ways, the golden veins of Pactolus ; the Numidians, unfaithful in their promises ; the Persians, famous for bows and arrows ; the Parthians and Medes, who fight flying ; the Arabians, perpetually changing their habitations ; the Scythians, as cruel as fair ; the broad-lipped Ethiopians ; and an infinity of other nations, whose countenances I see and know, although I cannot recollect their names. In that other squadron come those who drink the crystal streams of olive-bearing Betis ; those who brighten and polish their faces with the liquor of the ever rich and golden Tagus ; those who enjoy the beneficial waters of the divine Genil ; those who tread the Tartesian fields, abounding in pasture ; those who recreate themselves in the Elysian meads of Xereza ; the rich Manchegans, crowned with yellow ears of corn ; those clad in iron, the antique remains of the Gothic race ; those who bathe themselves in Pisuerga, famous for the gentleness of its current ; those who feed their flocks on the spacious pastures of the winding Guadiana, celebrated for its hidden source ; those who shiver on the cold brow of the woody Pyreneus, and the snowy tops of lofty Appeninus : in a word, all that Europe contains and includes."

Good heaven, how many provinces did he name ! how many nations did he enumerate ! giving to each, with wonderful readiness, its peculiar attributes. Sancho Panza stood confounded at his discourse, without speaking a word; and now and then he turned his head about to see whether he could discover the knights and giants his master named. But seeing none, he said, " Sir, the devil a man, or giant, or knight, of all you have named, can I see anywhere: perhaps all may be enchantment, like last night's goblins." "How sayest thou, Sancho?" answered Don Quixote. "Hearest thou not the neighing of the steeds, the sound of the trumpets, and the rattling of the drums?" "I hear nothing," answered Sancho, "but the bleating of sheep and lambs." And so it was, for now the two flocks were come very near them. " Thy fears, Sancho," said Don Quixote, " prevent thee from hearing or seeing aright; for one effect of fear is to disturb the senses, and make things not to appear what they really are: and if thou art so much afraid, retire and leave me alone; for with my single arm I shall insure victory to that side which I favour with my assistance:" then clapping spurs to Rozinante and setting his lance in rest, he darted down the hillock like lightning. Sancho cried out to him, "Hold, Signor Don Quixote, come back! As God shall save me, they are lambs and sheep you are going to encounter! Pray come back. Woe to the father that begot me! what madness is this? Look; there is neither giant nor knight, nor cats, nor arms, nor shields quartered nor entire, nor true azures nor bedevilled! Sinner that I am! what are you doing?" Notwithstanding all this, Don Quixote turned not again, but still went on, crying aloud, "Ho, knights! you that follow and fight under the banner of the valiant Emperor Pentapolin of the Naked Arm, follow me all, and you shall see with how much ease I revenge him on his enemy Alifanfaron of Taprobana." With these words he rushed into the midst of the squadron of sheep, and began to attack them with his lance as courageously and intrepidly as if in good earnest he was engaging his mortal enemies. The shepherds and herdsmen who came with the flocks called out to him to desist; but, seeing it was to no purpose, they unbuckled their slings, and began to salute his ears with a shower of stones. Don Quixote cared not for the stones; but, gallopping about on all sides, cried out, "Where art thou, proud Alifanfaron? Present thyself before me: I am a single knight, desirous to prove thy valour hand to hand, and to punish thee with the loss of life, for the wrong thou dost to the valiant Pentapolin Garamanta." At that instant a large stone struck him with such violence on the side, that it buried a couple of ribs in his body; insomuch that he believed himself either slain or sorely wounded: and therefore, remembering his balsam, he pulled out the cruse, and applying it to his mouth, began to swallow some of the liquor; but before he could take what he thought sufficient, another of those almonds hit him full on the hand, and dashed the cruse to pieces, carrying off three or four of his teeth by the way, and grievously bruising two of his fingers. Such was the first blow, and such the second, that the poor knight fell from his horse to the ground. The shepherds ran to him, and verily believed they had killed him: whereupon in all haste they

He rushed into the midst of the squadron of sheep, and began to attack them with his lance.

collected their flock, took up their dead, which were about seven, and marched off without further inquiry.

All this while Sancho stood upon the hillock, beholding his master's extravagances; tearing his beard, and cursing the unfortunate hour and moment that ever he knew him. But seeing him fallen to the ground, and the shepherds gone off, he descended from the hillock, and, running to him, found him in a very ill plight, though not quite bereaved of sense, and said to him, "Did I not beg you, Signor Don Quixote, to come back, for those you went to attack were a flock of sheep, and not an army of men?" "How easily," replied Don Quixote, "can that thief of an enchanter, my enemy, transform things or make them invisible! Thou must know, Sancho, that it is a very easy matter for such men to give things what semblance they please; and this malignant persecutor of mine, envious of the glory that he saw I should acquire in this battle, has transformed the hostile squadrons into flocks of sheep. However, do one thing, Sancho, for my sake, to undeceive thyself and see the truth of what I tell thee: mount thy ass, and follow them fairly and softly, and thou wilt find that, when they are got a little farther off, they will return to their first form, and, ceasing to be sheep, will become men, proper and tall as I described them at first. But do not go now, for I want thy assistance; come and see how many of my teeth are deficient, for it seems to me that I have not one left in my head." Sancho came so close to him that he almost thrust his eyes into his mouth; and being precisely at the time that the balsam began to work in Don Quixote's stomach, the contents thereof were at that instant discharged, with as much violence as if shot out of a demi-culverin, directly upon the beard of the compassionate squire. "Blessed Virgin!" quoth Sancho, "what has befallen me? This poor sinner must be mortally wounded, since he vomits blood at the mouth." But, reflecting a little, he found by the colour, savour, and smell, that it was not blood, but the balsam which he had seen him drink; and so great was the loathing he then felt, that his stomach turned, and he was grievously sick upon his master, so that they were both in a precious pickle. Sancho ran to his ass, to take something out of his wallets to cleanse himself and cure his master; but not finding them, he was very near running distracted. He cursed himself again, and resolved in his mind to leave his master, and return home, although he should lose his wages for the time past, and his hopes of the promised island.

Don Quixote now raised himself up, and placing his left hand on his mouth, to prevent the remainder of his teeth from falling out, with the other he laid hold on Rozinante's bridle, who had not stirred from his master's side—such was his fidelity—and went towards his squire, who stood leaning with his breast upon the ass, and his cheek reclining upon his hand, in the posture of a man overwhelmed with thought. Don Quixote seeing him thus, and to all appearance so melancholy, said to him, "Know, Sancho, that one man is no more than another, only inasmuch as he does more than another. All these storms that we have encountered are signs that the weather will soon clear up, and things will go smoothly; for it is impossible that either evil or good should be durable; and hence it follows that, the evil having lasted long, the good cannot be far off. So do not afflict thyself for the mischances that befall me, since thou hast no share in them." "How no share in them?" answered Sancho: "peradventure he they tossed in a blanket yesterday was not my father's son; and the wallets I have lost to-day, with all my moveables, belong to somebody else?" "What, are the wallets lost?" quoth Don Quixote. "Yes, they are," answered Sancho. "Then we have nothing to eat to-day," replied Don Quixote. "It would be so," answered Sancho, "if these fields did not produce those herbs which your worship says you know, and with which unlucky knights-errant like your worship are used to supply such wants." "Nevertheless," said Don Quixote, "at this time I would rather have a slice of bread and a couple of heads of salt pilchards than all the herbs described by Dioscorides, though commented upon by Doctor Laguna* himself. But,

---

* Andres de Laguna, born at Segovia, and physician to Pope Julio III.

"Reach hither thy hand, and feel how many teeth are wanting on the right side of my jaw."

good Sancho, get upon thy ass, and follow me; for God, who provides for all, will not desert us; more especially, being engaged, as we are, in His service: since He neglects neither the gnats of the air, the worms of the earth, nor the spawn of the waters; and so merciful is He, that He maketh His sun to shine upon the good and the bad, and causeth the rain to fall alike upon the just and unjust." "Your worship," said Sancho, "would make a better preacher than a knight-errant." "Sancho," said Don Quixote, "the knowledge of knights-errant must be universal: there have been knights-errant in times past, who would make sermons or harangues on the king's highway as successfully as if they had taken their degrees in the University of Paris: whence it may be inferred that the lance never blunted the pen, nor the pen the lance." "Well! be it as your worship says," answered Sancho; "but let us be gone hence, and endeavour to get a lodging to-night: and pray Heaven it be where there are neither blankets nor blanket-heavers, nor hobgoblins nor enchanted Moors; for if there be, the devil take both the flock and the fold."

"Pray to God, my son," said Don Quixote, "and lead me whither thou wilt; for this time I leave our lodging to thy choice. But reach hither thy hand, and feel how many teeth are wanting on the right side of my upper jaw; for there I feel the pain." Sancho put his finger into his mouth, and feeling about, said, "How many teeth had your worship on this side?" "Four," answered Don Quixote, "besides the eye-tooth, all perfect and sound." "Think well what you say, sir," answered Sancho. "I say four, if not five," answered Don Quixote; "for in my whole life I never had a tooth drawn, nor have I lost one by rheum or decay." "Well, then," said Sancho, "on this lower side your worship has but two teeth and a half; and in the upper, neither half nor whole: all is as smooth and even as the palm of my hand." "Unfortunate that I am!" said Don Quixote, hearing these sad tidings from his squire: "I had rather they had torn off an arm, provided it were not the sword-arm; for thou must know, Sancho, that a mouth without teeth is like a mill without a stone, and that a diamond is not so precious as a tooth. But to all this we who profess the strict order of chivalry are liable. Mount, friend Sancho, and lead on; for I will follow thee at what pace thou wilt." Sancho did so, and proceeded in a direction in which he thought it probable they might find a lodging, without going out of the high-road, which in that part was much frequented. As they slowly pursued their way, for the pain of Don Quixote's jaws gave him no ease, nor inclination to make haste, Sancho, wishing to amuse and divert him, began to converse, and said among other things what will be found in the following chapter.

CHAPTER XIX.

Of the sage discourse that passed between Sancho and his master, and the succeeding adventure of the dead body; with other famous occurrences.

"It is my opinion, sir, that all the misfortunes which have befallen us of late are doubtless in punishment of the sin committed by your worship against your own order of knighthood, in neglecting to perform the oath you took, not to eat bread on a tablecloth, nor solace yourself with the queen, with all the rest that you swore, until you had taken away the helmet of Malandrino—or how do you call the Moor? for I do not well remember." "Sancho, thou art in the right," said Don Quixote: "but, to confess the truth, it had wholly escaped my memory; and rely upon it, the affair of the blanket happened to thee as a punishment for not having reminded me sooner: but I will make compensation, for in the order of chivalry there are ways of compounding for everything." "Why, did I swear anything?" said Sancho. "That thou hast not sworn avails thee nothing," replied Don Quixote: "it is enough that I know thou art not free from the guilt of an accessory;

and, at all events, it will not be amiss to provide ourselves a remedy." "If that be the case," said Sancho, "take care, sir, you do not forget this too, as you did the oath: perhaps the goblins may again take a fancy to divert themselves with me, or with your worship, if they find you so obstinate."

While they were thus discoursing, night overtook them, and they were still in the high-road, without having found any place of reception; and the worst of it was, they were famished with hunger, for with their wallets they had lost their whole larder of provisions; and to complete their misfortunes an adventure now befell them which appeared indeed to be truly an adventure. The night came on rather dark; notwithstanding which they proceeded, as Sancho hoped that, being on the king's highway, they might very probably find an inn within a league or two. Thus situated, the night dark, the squire hungry, and the master well disposed to eat, they saw advancing towards them, on the same road, a great number of lights, resembling so many moving stars. Sancho stood aghast at the sight of them, nor was Don Quixote unmoved. The one checked his ass and the other his horse, and both stood looking before them with eager attention. They perceived that the lights were advancing towards them, and that as they approached nearer they appeared larger. Sancho trembled like quicksilver at the sight, and Don Quixote's hair bristled upon his head; but, somewhat recovering himself, he exclaimed, "Sancho, this must be a most perilous adventure, wherein it will be necessary for me to exert my whole might and valour." "Woe is me!" answered Sancho; "should this prove to be an adventure of goblins, as to me it seems to be, where shall I find ribs to endure?" "Whatsoever phantoms they may be," said Don Quixote, "I will not suffer them to touch a thread of thy garment; for, if they sported with thee before, it was because I could not get over the wall; but we are now upon even ground, where I can brandish my sword at pleasure." "But, if they should enchant and benumb you, as they did then," quoth Sancho, "what matters it whether we are in the open field or not?" "Notwithstanding that," replied Don Quixote, "I beseech thee, Sancho, to be of good courage, for experience shall give thee sufficient proof of mine." "I will, if it please God," answered Sancho; and, retiring a little on one side of the road, and again endeavouring to discover what those walking lights might be, they soon after perceived a great many persons clothed in white. This dreadful spectacle completely annihilated the courage of Sancho, whose teeth began to chatter, as if seized with a quartan ague; and his trembling and chattering increased as more of it appeared in view: for now they discovered about twenty persons in white robes, all on horseback, with lighted torches in their hands; and behind them came a litter covered with black, which was followed by six persons in deep mourning, the mules on which they were mounted being covered likewise with black down to their heels—for that they were mules, and not horses, was evident by the slowness of their pace. Those robed in white were muttering to themselves in a low and plaintive tone.

This strange vision, at such an hour, and in a place so uninhabited, might well strike terror into Sancho's heart, and even into that of his master; and so it would have done had he been any other than Don Quixote. As for Sancho, his whole stock of courage was now exhausted. But it was otherwise with his master, whose lively imagination instantly suggested to him that this must be truly a chivalrous adventure. He conceived that the litter was a bier, whereon was carried some knight sorely wounded or slain, whose revenge was reserved for him alone: he, therefore, without delay couched his spear, seated himself firmly in his saddle, and with grace and spirit advanced into the middle of the road by which the procession must pass; and when they were near, he raised his voice, and said, "Ho, knights! whoever ye are, halt, and give me an account to whom ye belong, whence ye come, whither ye are going, and what it is ye carry upon that bier; for in all appearance either ye have done some injury to others, or others to you; and it is expedient and necessary that I be informed of it, either to chastise ye for the evil ye have done, or to revenge ye of wrongs sustained." "We are in haste," answered one in the procession; "the inn is a great way off, and we cannot stay to give so long an account as you require:" then spurring his mule, he passed forward. Don Quixote, highly resenting this answer, laid hold of his bridle, and said, "Stand, and with more civility give me the account I demand; otherwise I challenge ye all to battle." The mule was timid, and started so much upon his touching the bridle, that, rising on her hind legs, she threw her rider over the crupper to the ground. A lacquey that came on foot, seeing the man in white fall, began to revile Don Quixote, whose choler being now raised, he couched his spear, and immediately attacking one of the mourners, laid him on the ground grievously wounded; then turning about to the rest, it was worth seeing with what agility he attacked and defeated them; and it seemed as if wings at that instant had sprung on Rozinante, so lightly and swiftly he moved! All the white-robed people, being timorous and unarmed, soon quitted the skirmish, and ran over the plain with their lighted torches, looking like so many masqueraders on a carnival or festival night. The mourners were so wrapped up and muffled in their long robes, that they could make no exertion; so that Don Quixote with entire safety assailed them all, and, sorely against their will, obliged them to quit the field; for they thought him no man, but the devil from hell broke loose upon them to seize the dead body they were conveying in the litter.

All this Sancho beheld with admiration at his master's intrepidity, and said to himself, "This master of mine is certainly as valiant and magnanimous as he pretends to be." A burning torch lay upon the ground near the first whom the mule had overthrown, by the light of which Don Quixote espied him, and going up to him, placed the point of his spear to his throat, commanding him to surrender on pain of death. To which the fallen man answered, "I am surrendered enough already, since I cannot stir; for one of my legs is broken. I beseech you, sir, if you are a Christian gentleman, do not kill me: you would

As for Sancho, his whole stock of courage was now exhausted.

commit a great sacrilege; for I am a licentiate, and have taken the lesser orders." "Who the devil, then," said Don Quixote, "brought you hither, being an ecclesiastic?" "Who, sir?" replied the fallen man; "my evil fortune." "A worse fate now threatens you," said Don Quixote, "unless you reply satisfactorily to all my first questions." "Your worship shall soon be satisfied," answered the licentiate; "and therefore you must know, sir, that though I told you before I was a licentiate, I am in fact only a bachelor of arts, and my name is Alonzo Lopez. I am a native of Alcovendas, and came from the city of Baeza, with eleven more ecclesiastics, the same who fled with the torches: we were attending the corpse in that litter to the city of Segovia. It is that of a gentleman who died in Baeza, where he was deposited till now that, as I said before, we are carrying his bones to their place of burial in Segovia, where he was born." "And who killed him?" demanded Don Quixote. "God," replied the bachelor, "by means of a pestilential fever." "Then," said Don Quixote, "our Lord hath saved me the labour of revenging his death, in case he had been slain by any other hand.

But, since he fell by the hand of Heaven, there is nothing expected from us but patience and a silent shrug; for just the same must I have done had it been His pleasure to pronounce the fatal sentence upon me. It is proper that your reverence should know that I am a knight of La Mancha, Don Quixote by name, and that it is my office and profession to go over the world, righting wrongs and redressing grievances." "I do not understand your way of righting wrongs," said the bachelor; "for from right you have set me wrong, having broken my leg, which will never be right again whilst I live; and the grievance you have redressed for me is to leave me so aggrieved that I shall never be otherwise; and to me it was a most unlucky adventure to meet you, who are seeking adventures." "All things," answered Don Quixote, "do not fall out the same way: the mischief, Master Bachelor Alonzo Lopez, was occasioned by your coming, as you did, by night, arrayed in those surplices, with lighted torches, chanting, and clad in doleful weeds, so that you really resembled something evil and of the other world. I was therefore bound to perform my duty by attacking you: which I certainly should have done although you had really been, as I imagined, devils from hell." "Since my fate ordained it so," said the bachelor, "I beseech you, Signor Knight-errant, who have done me such arrant mischief, to help me to get from under this mule, for my leg is held fast between the stirrup and the saddle." "I might have continued talking until to-morrow," said Don Quixote; "why did you delay acquainting me with your embarrassment?" He then called out to Sancho Panza to assist; but he did not choose to obey, being employed in ransacking a sumpter-mule, which those pious men had brought with them, well stored with eatables. Sancho made a bag of his cloak, and having crammed into it as much as it would hold, he loaded his beast; after which he attended to his master's call, and helped to disengage the bachelor from the oppression of his mule; and, having mounted him and given him the torch, Don Quixote bade him follow the track of his companions, and beg their pardon, in his name, for the injury which he could not avoid doing them; Sancho likewise said, "If perchance those gentlemen would know who is the champion that routed them, it is the famous Don Quixote de la Mancha, otherwise called the Knight of the Sorrowful Figure."

The bachelor being gone, Don Quixote asked Sancho what induced him to call him the Knight of the Sorrowful Figure at that time more than at any other. "I will tell you," answered Sancho: "it is because I have been viewing you by the light of the torch which that unfortunate man carried; and, in truth, your worship at present very nearly makes the most woeful figure I have ever seen; which must be owing, I suppose, either to the fatigue of this combat or the want of your teeth." "It is owing to neither," replied Don Quixote; "but the sage, who has the charge of writing the history of my achievements, has deemed it proper for me to assume an appellation like the knights of old; one of whom called himself the Knight of the Burning Sword; another of the Unicorn; this of the Damsels; that of the Phœnix; another the Knight of the Griffin; and another the Knight of Death; and by those names and ensigns they were known over the whole surface of the earth. And therefore I say that the sage I just now mentioned has put it into thy thoughts and into thy mouth to call me the Knight of the Sorrowful Figure, as I purpose to call myself from this day forward; and that this name may fit me the better, I determine, when an opportunity offers, to have a most sorrowful figure painted on my shield."

"You need not spend time and money in getting this figure made," said Sancho; "your worship need only show your own, and, without any other image or shield, they will immediately call you, 'him of the sorrowful figure.' And be assured I tell you the truth; for I promise you, sir, (mind, I speak not in jest,) that hunger and the loss of your grinders makes you look so ruefully that, as I said before, the sorrowful picture may very well be spared."

Don Quixote smiled at Sancho's pleasantry; nevertheless, he resolved to call himself by that name, and to have his shield or buckler painted accordingly; and he said, "I conceive, Sancho, that I am liable to excommunication for having laid violent hands on holy things, '*Juxta illud, Siquis suadente diabolo,*' &c.; although I know I did not lay my hands, but my spear, upon them. Besides, I did not know that I was engaging with priests, or things belonging to the Church, which I reverence and adore, like a good Catholic and faithful Christian as I am, but with phantoms and spectres of the other world. And even were it otherwise, I perfectly remember what befell the Cid Ruy Diaz, when he broke the chair of that king's ambassador in the presence of His Holiness the Pope, for which he was excommunicated; yet honest Roderigo de Vivar passed that day for an honourable and courageous knight."

The bachelor having departed, as hath been said, Don Quixote wished to examine whether the corpse in the hearse consisted only of bones or not; but Sancho would not consent, saying, "Sir, your worship has finished this perilous adventure at less expense than any I have seen; and though these folks are conquered and defeated, they may chance to reflect that they were beaten by one man, and, being ashamed thereat, may recover themselves and return in quest of us, and then we may have enough to do. The ass is properly furnished; the mountain is near; hunger presses, and we have nothing to do but decently to march off; and, as the saying is, 'To the grave with the dead, and the living to the bread.'" And, driving on his ass before him, he entreated his master to follow, who, thinking Sancho in the right, followed without replying. They had not gone far between two hills, when they found themselves in a retired and spacious valley, where they alighted. Sancho disburdened his beast; and, extended on the green grass, with hunger for sauce, they dispatched their breakfast, dinner, afternoon's luncheon, and supper, all at once: regaling their palates with more than one cold mess, which the ecclesiastics who attended the deceased (such gentlemen seldom failing in a provident attention to themselves) had brought with them on the sumpter-mule. But there was another misfortune, which Sancho accounted the worst of all; namely, they had no wine, nor even water, to drink, and were, moreover, parched with thirst. Sancho, however, perceiving the meadow they were in to be covered with green and fresh grass, said—what will be related in the following chapter.

CHAPTER XX

Of the unparalleled adventure achieved by the renowned Don Quixote, with less hazard than any was ever achieved by the most famous knight in the world.

"It is impossible, sir, but there must be some fountain or brook near, to make these herbs so fresh, and therefore, if we go a little farther on, we may meet with something to quench the terrible thirst that afflicts us, and which is more painful than even hunger itself." Don Quixote approved the counsel, and, taking Rozinante by the bridle, and Sancho his ass by the halter (after he had placed upon him the relics of the supper), they began to march forward through the meadow, feeling their way; for the night was so dark they could see nothing. But they had not gone two hundred paces when a great noise of water reached their ears, like that of some mighty cascade pouring down from a vast and steep rock. The sound rejoiced them exceedingly, and, stopping to listen whence it came, they heard on a sudden another dreadful noise, which abated the pleasure occasioned by that of the water; especially in Sancho, who was naturally faint-hearted. I say they heard a dreadful din of irons or rattling chains, accompanied with mighty strokes repeated in regular time and measure; which, together with the furious noise of the water, would have struck terror into any other heart but that of Don Quixote. The night, as we have before said, was dark, and they chanced to enter a grove of tall trees, whose leaves, agitated by the breeze, caused a kind of rustling noise, not loud, though fearful; so that the solitude, the situation, the darkness, and the sound of rushing water, with the agitated leaves, all concurred to produce surprise and horror, especially when they found that neither the blows ceased, nor the wind slept, nor the morning approached; and in addition to all this was their total ignorance of the place where they were in. But Don Quixote, supported by his intrepid heart, leaped upon Rozinante, and, bracing on his buckler, brandished his spear, and said, "Friend Sancho, know that, by the will of Heaven, I was born in this age of iron to revive in it that of gold, or, as it is usually termed, the Golden Age. I am he for whom dangers, great exploits, and valorous achievements are reserved: I am he, I say again, who am destined to revive the order of the Round Table, that of the twelve peers of France, and the nine worthies; and to obliterate the memory of the Platirs, the Tablantes, Olivantes, and Tirantes, Knights of the Sun, and the Belianises, with the whole tribe of the famous knights-errant of times past; performing, in this age, such stupendous deeds and feats of arms as are sufficient to obscure the brightest ever achieved by them.   Trusty and loyal squire, observe the darkness of this night, its strange silence, the confused sound of these trees, the fearful noise of that water which we came hither in search of, and which, one would think, precipitates itself head-long from the high mountains of the moon; that incessant striking and clashing which wound our ears: all these together, and even each sepa-rately, are sufficient to infuse terror, fear, and amazement into the breast of Mars himself; how much more into that of one unaccustomed to such adventures!   Yet all I have described serves but to rouse and awaken my courage, and my heart already bounds within my breast with eager desire to encounter this adventure, however difficult it may appear.   Therefore, tighten Rozinante's girth, and God be with thee! Stay for me here three days, and no more: if I return not in that time, thou mayest go back to our village; and thence, to oblige me, repair to Toboso, and inform my incomparable lady Dulcinea that her enthralled knight died in attempting things that might have made him worthy to be styled hers."

When Sancho heard these words of his master, he dissolved into tears, and said, " Sir, I cannot think why your worship should encounter this fearful adventure.   It is now night, and nobody sees us.   We may easily turn aside, and get out of danger, though we should not drink these three days; and, being unseen, we cannot be taxed with cowardice. Besides, I have heard the curate of our village, whom your worship knows very well, say in the pulpit that ' he who seeketh danger perisheth therein:' so that it is not good to tempt God by undertaking so extra-vagant an exploit, whence there is no escaping but by a miracle.   Let it suffice that Heaven saved you from being tossed in a blanket, as I was, and brought you off victorious, safe, and sound, from among so many enemies as accompanied the dead man.   And if all this be not sufficient to soften your stony heart, let this assurance move you, that, scarcely shall your worship be departed hence, when I, for very fear, shall give up my soul to whosoever shall be pleased to take it.   I left my country, and forsook my wife and children, to follow and serve your worship, believing I should be the better and not the worse for it: but, as cove-tousness burst the bag, so hath it rent my hopes; for when they were most alive, and I was just expecting to obtain that cursed and unlucky island, which you have so often promised me, I find myself, in lieu thereof, ready to be abandoned by your worship in a place remote from everything human.   For Heaven's sake, dear sir, do not be so cruel to me: and if your worship will not wholly give up this enterprise, at least defer it till daybreak, which, by what I learnt when a shepherd, cannot be above three hours; for the muzzle of the north bear* is at the top of the head, and makes midnight in the line of the left arm."   " How

---

* Literally, " the mouth of the hunting horn, or cornet."   So the " Ursa Minor " is called, from a fancied configuration of the stars of that constellation.

canst thou, Sancho," said Don Quixote, " see where this line is made, or where this muzzle or top of the head may be, since the night is so dark, that not a star appears in the whole sky?" "True," said Sancho ; " but fear has many eyes, and sees things beneath the earth, much more above the sky ; besides, it is reasonable to suppose that it does not want much of daybreak." "Want what it may," answered Don Quixote, " it shall never be said of me, now nor at any time, that tears or entreaties could dissuade me from performing the duty of a knight: therefore I pray thee, Sancho, be silent, for God, who has inspired me with courage to attempt this unparalleled and fearful adventure, will not fail to watch over my safety, and comfort thee in thy sadness. All thou hast to do is to girt Rozinante well, and remain here ; for I will quickly return alive or dead."

Sancho, now seeing his master's final resolution, and how little his tears, prayers, and counsel availed, determined to have recourse to stratagem, and compel him, if possible, to wait until day ; therefore, while he was tightening the horse's girths, softly and unperceived, with his halter he tied Rozinante's hinder feet together, so that when Don Quixote would fain have departed, the horse could move only by jumps. Sancho, perceiving the success of his contrivance, said, "Ah, sir ! behold how Heaven, moved by my tears and prayers, has ordained that Rozinante should be unable to stir ; and if you will obstinately persist to spur him, you will but provoke fortune, and, as they say, ' kick against the pricks.' " This made Don Quixote quite desperate, and the more he spurred his horse the less he could move him ; he therefore thought it best to be quiet, and wait until day appeared, or until Rozinante could proceed, never suspecting the artifice of Sancho, whom he thus addressed : " Since so it is, Sancho, that Rozinante cannot move, I consent to wait until the dawn smiles, although I weep in the interval." "You need not weep," answered Sancho, " for I will entertain you until day by telling you stories, if you had not rather alight and compose yourself to sleep a little upon the green grass, as knights-errant are wont to do, so that you may be less weary when the day and hour comes for engaging in that terrible adventure you wait for." " To whom dost thou talk of alighting or sleeping?" said Don Quixote : "am I one of those knights who take repose in time of danger? Sleep thou, who wert born to sleep, or do what thou wilt: I shall act as becomes my profession." " Pray, good sir, be not angry," answered Sancho, " I did not mean to offend you : " and, coming close to him, he laid hold of the saddle before and behind, and thus stood embracing his master's left thigh, without daring to stir from him a finger's breadth, so much was he afraid of the blows which still continued to sound in regular succession. Don Quixote bade him tell some story for his entertainment, as he had promised : Sancho replied that he would, if his dread of the noise would permit him. " I will endeavour," said he, " in spite of it, to tell a story, which, if I can hit upon it, and it slips not through my fingers, is the best of all stories ; and I beg your worship to be attentive, for now I begin

" What hath been, hath been; the good that shall befall be for us all, and evil to him that evil seeks. And pray, sir, take notice that the beginning which the ancients gave to their tales was not just what they pleased, but rather some sentence of Cato Zonzorinus the Roman, who says, ' And evil be to him that evil seeks;' which fits the present purpose like a ring to your finger, signifying that your worship should be quiet, and not go about searching after evil, but rather that we turn aside into some other road; for we are under no obligation to continue in this, where we are overtaken by so many fears." "Proceed with thy tale, Sancho," said Don Quixote, " and leave to my care the road we are to follow." " I say, then," continued Sancho, "that in a village in Estremadura, there was a shepherd—I mean a goatherd; which shepherd, or goatherd, as my story says, was called Lope Ruiz; and this Lope Ruiz was in love with a shepherdess called Torralva, which shepherdess called Torralva was daughter to a rich herdsman, and this rich herdsman—" " If this be thy manner of telling a story, Sancho," said Don Quixote, " repeating everything thou hast to say, thou wilt not have done these two days : tell it concisely, and like a man of sense, or else say no more." " I tell it in the same manner that they tell all stories in my country," answered Sancho ; " and I cannot tell it otherwise, nor ought your worship to require me to make new customs." " Tell it as thou wilt, then," said Don Quixote : " since it is the will of fate that I must hear thee, go on."

" And so, sir," continued Sancho, " as I said before, this shepherd was in love with the shepherdess Torralva, who was a jolly, strapping wench, somewhat scornful, and somewhat masculine, for she had certain small whiskers; and methinks I see her now." " What, didst thou know her ? " said Don Quixote. " I did not know her," answered Sancho ; " but he who told me this story said it was so certain and true, that I might, when I told it to another, affirm and swear that I had seen it all. And so, in process of time, the devil, who sleeps not, and troubles all things, brought it about, that the love which the shepherd bore to the shepherdess turned into mortal hatred; and the cause, according to evil tongues, was a certain quantity of little jealousies she gave him, so as to exceed all bounds : and so much did he hate her thenceforward, that, to shun the sight of her, he chose to absent himself from that country, and go where his eyes should never more behold her. Torralva, who found herself disdained by Lope, then began to love him better than ever she had loved him before." " It is a disposition natural in women," said Don Quixote, " to slight those who love them, and love those who hate them : but go on, Sancho."

" It fell out," proceeded Sancho, " that the shepherd put his design into execution; and, collecting together his goats, went over the plains of Estremadura, in order to pass over the kingdom of Portugal. Upon which, Torralva went after him, and followed him at a distance, on foot and bare-legged, with a pilgrim's staff in her hand, and a wallet about her neck, in which she carried, as is reported, a piece of looking-glass, the remains of a comb, and a kind of small gallipot of paint for the face. But whatever she carried (for I shall not now set myself to vouch what it was), I only tell you that, as they say, the shepherd came with his flock to pass over the river Guadiana, which at that time was swollen, and had almost overflowed its banks; and on the side he came to there was neither boat nor anybody to ferry him or his flock over to the other side, which grieved him mightily, for he saw that Torralva was at his heels, and would give him much disturbance by her entreaties and tears. He therefore looked about him until he espied a fisherman with a boat near him, but so small that it would hold only one person and one goat; however, he spoke to him, and agreed to carry over himself and his three hundred goats. The fisherman got into the boat, and carried over a goat; he returned, and carried over another; he came back again, and again carried over another. Pray, sir, keep an account of the goats that the fisherman is carrying over; for if you lose count of a single goat the story ends, and it will be impossible to tell a word more of it. I go on, then, and say that the landing-place on the opposite side was covered with mud, and slippery, and the fisherman was a great while coming and going. However, he returned for another goat, and another, and another." "Suppose them all carried over," said Don Quixote, "and do not be going and coming in this manner, or thou wilt not have finished carrying them over in a twelvemonth." "How many have passed already?" said Sancho. "How the devil should I know?" answered Don Quixote. "See there now! did I not tell thee to keep an exact account? Before Heaven, there is an end of the story: I can go no further." "How can this be?" answered Don Quixote. "Is it so essential to the story to know the exact number of goats that passed over, that, if one error be made, the story can proceed no further?" "No, sir, by no means," answered Sancho; "for when I desired your worship to tell me how many goats had passed, and you answered you did not know, at that very instant all that I had to say fled out of my memory; and, in faith, it was very edifying and satisfactory." "So, then," said Don Quixote, "the story is at an end?" "As sure as my mother is," quoth Sancho. "Verily," answered Don Quixote, "thou hast told one of the rarest tales, fables, or histories, imaginable; and thy mode of relating and concluding it is such as never was, nor ever will be, equalled; although I expected no less from thy good sense: however, I do not wonder at it, for this incessant din may have disturbed thy understanding." "All that may be," answered Sancho, "but, as to my story, I know there's no more to be told, for it ends just where the error begins in the account of carrying over the goats."* "Let it end where it will, in God's name," said Don Quixote, "and let us see whether Rozinante can stir himself." And he clapped spurs to him, and again the animal jumped, and then stood stock still, so effectually was he fettered.

---

* This tale was not the invention of Cervantes; for, though altered and improved by him, the idea is taken from the "Cento Nouvelle Antiche," which are given at the end of the "Cento Nouvelle Scelte," published at Venice in the year 1571.

Sancho kept close to his side, stretching out his neck, and looking between Rozinante's legs.

In this position they passed the night; and when Sancho perceived the dawn of morning, with much caution he unbound Rozinante, who, on being set at liberty, though naturally not over-mettlesome, seemed to feel himself alive, and began to paw the ground; but as for curvetting, (begging his pardon) he knew nothing about it. Don Quixote, perceiving that Rozinante began to be active, took it for a good omen, and a signal that he should forthwith attempt the tremendous adventure. The dawn now making the surrounding objects visible, Don Quixote perceived he was beneath some tall chestnut trees, which afforded a gloomy shade; but the cause of that striking, which yet continued, he was unable to discover : therefore, without further delay, he made Rozinante feel the spur, and again taking leave of Sancho, commanded him to wait there three days at the furthest, as he had said before, and that if he returned not by that time, he might conclude that it was God's will that he should end his days in that perilous adventure. He again also repeated the embassy and message he was to carry to his lady Dulcinea; and as to what concerned the reward of his service, he told him that he need be under no concern, since, before his departure from his village, he had made his will, wherein he would find himself satisfied regarding his wages, in proportion to the time he had served; but, if God should bring him off safe and sound from the impending danger, he might reckon himself infallibly secure of the promised island. Sancho wept afresh at hearing again the moving expressions of his good master, and resolved not to leave him till the last moment and termination of this affair. The author of this history concludes, from the tears and this honourable resolution of Sancho Panza, that he must have been well born, and at least an old Castilian. His master was somewhat moved by it : not that he betrayed any weakness; on the contrary, dissembling as well as he could, he advanced towards the place whence the noise of the water and of the strokes seemed to proceed. Sancho followed him on foot, leading his ass—that constant companion of his fortunes, good or bad. And having proceeded some distance among those shady chestnut trees, they came to a little green meadow, bounded by some steep rocks, down which a mighty torrent precipitated itself. At the foot of these rocks were several wretched huts, that seemed more like ruins than habitable dwellings; and it was from them, they now discovered, that the fearful din proceeded. Rozinante was startled at the noise, but Don Quixote, after quieting him, went slowly on towards the huts, recommending himself devoutly to his lady, and beseeching her to favour him in so terrific an enterprise; and by the way he also besought God not to forget him. Sancho kept close to his side, stretching out his neck, and looking between Rozinante's legs to see if he could discover the cause of his terrors. In this manner they advanced about a hundred yards farther, when, on doubling a point, the true and undoubted cause of that horrible noise which had held them all night in such suspense appeared plain and exposed to view. It was (kind reader, take it not in dudgeon !) six fulling-hammers, whose alternate strokes produced that hideous sound. Don Quixote, on beholding them, was struck dumb, and was in the utmost confusion. Sancho looked at him, and saw he hung down his head upon his breast with manifest indications of being abashed. Don Quixote looked also at Sancho, and seeing his cheeks swollen, and his mouth full of laughter, betraying evident signs of being ready to explode, notwithstanding his vexation he could not forbear laughing himself at the sight of his squire, who, thus encouraged by his master, broke forth in so violent a manner that he was forced to apply both hands to his sides to secure himself from bursting. Four times he ceased, and four times the fit returned, with the same impetuosity as at first. Upon which, Don Quixote now wished him at the devil, especially when he heard him say, ironically, " ' Thou must know, friend Sancho, that I was born, by the will of Heaven, in this our age of iron, to revive in it the golden, or that of gold. I am he for whom are reserved dangers, great exploits, and valorous achievements ! ' " And so he went on, repeating many of the expressions which Don Quixote used upon first hearing those dreadful sounds. Don Quixote, perceiving that Sancho made a jest of him, was so enraged that he lifted up his lance, and discharged two such blows on him that, had he received them on his head instead of his shoulders, the knight would have acquitted himself of the payment of his wages, unless it were to his heirs. Sancho, finding he paid so dearly for his jokes, and fearing lest his master should proceed further, with much humility said, "Pray, sir, be pacified: as heaven is my hope, I did but jest." "Though thou mayest jest, I do not," answered Don Quixote. "Come hither, merry sir: what thinkest thou? Supposing these mill-hammers had really been some perilous adventure, have I not given proof of the courage requisite to undertake and achieve it? Am I obliged, being a knight as I am, to distinguish sounds, and know which are, or are not, those of a fulling-mill, more especially if (which is indeed the truth) I had never seen any fulling-mills in my life, as thou hast—a pitiful rustic as thou art, who wert born and bred amongst them! But let these six fulling-hammers be transformed into six giants, and let them beard me one by one, or all together, and if I do not set them all on their heads, then make what jest thou wilt of me." "It is enough, good sir," replied Sancho; "I confess I have been a little too jocose: but pray tell me, now that there is peace between us, as God shall bring you out of all the adventures that shall happen to you safe and sound, as He has brought you out of this, was it not a thing to be laughed at, and worth telling, what a fearful taking we were in last night—I mean that I was in—for I know your worship is a stranger to fear?" "I do not deny," answered Don Quixote, "that what has befallen us may be risible, but it is not proper to be repeated; for all persons have not the sense to see things in the right point of view." "But," answered Sancho, "your worship knew how to point your lance aright when you pointed it at my head, and hit me on the shoulders—thanks be to Heaven and to my own agility in slipping aside. But let that pass: for I have heard say, 'he loves thee well who makes thee weep:' and besides, your people of condition, when they have given a servant a hard word, presently give him some old hose, though what is usually given after a beating I cannot tell, unless it be that your knights-errant, after bastinadoes, bestow islands or kingdoms on *terra firma.*" "The die may so run," quoth Don Quixote, "that all thou hast said may come to pass: excuse what is done, since thou art considerate; for know that first impulses are not under man's control; and, that thou mayest abstain from talking too much with me henceforth, I apprise thee of one thing, that in all the books of chivalry I ever read, numerous as they are, I recollect no example of a squire who conversed so much with his master as thou dost with thine. And, really, I account it a great fault both in thee and in myself: in thee, because thou payest me so little respect; in me, that I do not make myself respected more. There was Gandalin, squire to Amadis de Gaul, Earl of the Firm Island, of whom we read that he always spoke to his master cap in hand, his head inclined and body bent in the Turkish fashion. What shall we say of Gasabel, squire to Don Galaor, who was so silent that, to illustrate the excellence of his marvellous taciturnity, his name is mentioned but once in all that great and faithful history? From what I have said thou mayest infer, Sancho, that there ought to be a difference between master and man, between lord and lacquey, and between knight and squire; so that, from this day forward, we must be treated with more respect, for, howsoever thou mayest excite my anger, 'it will go ill with the pitcher.' The favours and benefits I promised thee will come in due time ; and if they do not come, the wages, at least, thou wilt not lose." "Your worship says very well," quoth Sancho; "but I would fain know (if perchance the time of the favours should not come, and it should be necessary to have recourse to the article of the wages) how much might the squire of a knight-errant get in those times? and whether they agreed by the month or by the day, like labourers?" "I do not believe," answered Don Quixote, "that those squires were retained at stated wages, but they relied on courtesy ; and if I have appointed thee any in the will I left sealed at home, it was in case of accidents; for I know not yet how chivalry may succeed in these calamitous times, and I would not have my soul suffer in the other world for trifles; for I would have thee know, Sancho, that there is no state more perilous than that of adventurers." "It is so, in truth," said Sancho, "since the noise of the hammers of a fulling-mill were sufficient to disturb and discompose the heart of so valorous a knight as your worship. But you may depend upon it that henceforward I shall not open my lips to make merry with your worship's concerns, but shall honour you as my master and natural lord." "By so doing," replied Don Quixote, "thy days shall be long in the land; for next to our parents we are bound to respect our masters."

CHAPTER XXI.

Which treats of the grand adventure and rich prize of Mambrino's helmet, with other things which befell our invincible knight.

ABOUT this time it began to rain a little, and Sancho proposed entering the fulling-mill; but Don Quixote had conceived such an abhorrence of them for the late jest, that he would by no means go in : turning, therefore, to the right hand, they struck into another road, like that they had travelled through the day before. Soon after Don Quixote discovered a man on horseback, who had on his head something which glittered as if it had been of gold; and scarcely had he seen it when, turning to Sancho, he said, "I am of opinion, Sancho, there is no proverb but what is true, because they are all sentences drawn from experience itself, the mother of all the sciences; especially that which says, 'Where one door is shut another is opened.' I say this because, if fortune last night shut the door against what we sought, deceiving us with the fulling-mills, it now opens wide another, for a better and more certain adventure; in which if I am deceived, the fault will be mine, without imputing it to my ignorance of fulling-mills or to the darkness of night. This I say because, if I mistake not, there comes one towards us who carries on his head Mambrino's helmet, concerning which thou mayest remember I swore the oath." "Take care, sir, what you say, and more what you do," said Sancho ; "for I would not wish for other fulling-mills, to finish the milling and mashing of our senses." "The devil take thee ! " replied Don Quixote : "what has a helmet to do with fulling-mills ?" "I know not," answered Sancho ; "but, in faith, if I might talk as much I used to do, perhaps I could give such reasons that your worship would see you are mistaken in what you say." "How can I be mistaken in what I say, thou scrupulous traitor ?" said Don Quixote. "Tell me, seest thou not yon knight coming towards us on a dapple-grey steed, with a helmet of gold on his head ?" "What I see and perceive," answered Sancho, "is only a man on a grey ass like mine, with something on his head that glitters." "Why, that is Mambrino's helmet," said Don Quixote. "Retire, and leave me alone to deal with him, and thou shalt see how, in order to save time, I shall conclude this adventure without speaking a word, and the helmet I have so much desired remain my own." "I shall take care to get out of the way," replied Sancho ; "but Heaven grant, I say again, it may not prove another fulling-mill adventure." "I have already told thee, Sancho, not to mention those fulling-mills, nor even think of them," said Don Quixote : "if thou dost — I say no more, but I vow to mill thy soul for thee ! " Sancho held his peace, fearing lest his master should perform his vow, which had struck him all of a heap.

Now the truth of the matter, concerning the helmet, the steed, and the knight which Don Quixote saw, was this. There were two villages in that neighbourhood, one of them so small that it had neither shop nor barber, but the other adjoining to it had both ; therefore the barber of the larger served also the less, wherein one customer now wanted to be let blood, and another to be shaved ; to perform which, the barber was now on his way, carrying with him his brass basin : and it so happened that while upon the road it began to rain, and to save his hat, which was a new one, he clapped the basin on his head, which being lately scoured was seen glittering at the distance of half a league ; and he rode on a grey ass, as Sancho had affirmed. Thus Don Quixote took the barber for a knight, his ass for a dapple-grey steed, and his basin for a golden helmet · for whatever he saw was quickly adapted to his knightly extravagances : and when the poor knight drew near, without staying to reason the case with him, he advanced at Rozinante's best speed, and couched his lance, intending to run him through and through ; but, when close upon him, without checking the fury of his career, he cried out, "Defend thyself, caitiff ! or instantly surrender what is justly my due." The barber, so unexpectedly seeing this phantom advancing upon him, had no other way to avoid the thrust of the lance than to slip down from the ass ; and no sooner had he touched the ground than, leaping up nimbler than a roebuck, he scampered over the plain with such speed that the wind could not overtake him. The basin he left on the ground ; with which Don Quixote was satisfied, observing that the pagan had acted discreetly, and in imitation of the beaver, which, when closely pursued by the hunters, tears off with his teeth that which it knows by instinct to be the object of pursuit. He ordered Sancho to take up the helmet : who, holding it in his hand, said, " Before Heaven, the basin is a special one, and is well worth a piece of eight, if it is worth a farthing." He then gave it to his master, who immediately placed it upon his head, turning it round in search of the vizor; but not finding it, he said, " Doubtless the pagan for whom this famous helmet was originally forged must have had a prodigious head—the worst of it is that one-half is wanting." When Sancho heard the basin called a helmet, he could not forbear laughing ; which, however, he instantly checked on recollecting his master's late choler. " What dost thou laugh at, Sancho ?" said Don Quixote. " I am laughing," answered he, " to think what a huge head the pagan had who owned that helmet, which is for all the world just like a barber's basin." " Knowest thou, Sancho, what I conceive to be the case ? This famous piece, this enchanted helmet, by some strange accident must have fallen into the possession of one who, ignorant of its true value as a helmet, and seeing it to be of the purest gold, hath inconsiderately melted down the one-half for lucre's sake, and of the other half made this, which, as thou sayest, doth indeed look like a barber's basin : but to me, who know what it really is, its transformation is of no importance, for I will have it so repaired in the first town where there is a smith, that it shall not be surpassed nor even equalled by that which the god of smiths himself made and forged for the god of battles. In the meantime I will wear it as I best can, for something is better than nothing, and it will be sufficient to defend me from stones." " It will so," said Sancho, " if they do not throw them with slings, as they did in the battle of the two armies, when they crossed your worship's chaps, and broke the cruse of that most blessed liquor which made me vomit up my inside." " The loss of that balsam gives me no concern," said Don Quixote ; " for knowest thou, Sancho, I have the recipe by heart ? " " So have I, too," answered Sancho; " but if ever I make or try it again while I live, may I be fixed and rooted to this place. Besides, I do not intend to put myself in the way of requiring it; for I mean to keep myself, with all my five senses, from being wounded, or from wounding anybody. As to being tossed again in a blanket, I say nothing, for it is difficult to prevent such mishaps; and if they do come, there is nothing to be done but wink, hold one's breath, and submit to go whither fortune and the blanket shall please." " Thou art no good Christian, Sancho," said Don Quixote " since thou dost not forget an injury once done thee : but know, it is inherent in generous and noble minds to disregard trifles. What leg of thine is lamed, or what rib or head broken, that thou canst not forget that jest ?—for, properly considered, it was a mere jest and pastime : otherwise, I should long ago have returned thither, and done more mischief in revenging thy quarrel than the Greeks did for the rape of Helen, who, had she lived in these times, or my Dulcinea in those, would never have been so famous for beauty as she is ! " and here he heaved a sigh, and sent it to

The barber had no other way to avoid the thrust of the lance than to slip down from the ass.

the clouds. "Let it pass, then, for a jest," said Sancho, "since it is not likely to be revenged in earnest: but I know of what kind the jests and the earnests were; and I know also they will no more slip out of my memory than off my shoulders. But, setting this aside, tell me, sir, what shall we do with this dapple-grey steed which looks so much like a grey ass, and which that caitiff whom your worship overthrew has left behind here to shift for itself? for, by his scouring off so hastily, he does not think of ever returning for him: and, by my beard, the beast is a special one." "It is not my custom," said Don Quixote, "to plunder those whom I overcome, nor is it the usage of chivalry to take from the vanquished their horses, and leave them on foot, unless the victor had lost his own in the conflict; in such a case it is lawful to take that of the enemy, as fairly won in battle. Therefore, Sancho, leave this horse, or ass, or whatever thou wilt have it to be; for when we are gone, his owner will return for him." "God knows whether it were best for me to take him," replied Sancho, "or at least to exchange him for mine, which, methinks, is not so good. Verily, the laws of chivalry are very strict if they do not even allow the swopping of one ass for another; but I would fain know whether I might exchange furniture, if I were so inclined?" "I am not very clear as to that point," answered Don Quixote; "and, being a doubtful case, until better information can be had, I think thou mayest make the exchange, if thou art in extreme want of them." "So extreme," replied Sancho, "that I could not want them more if they were for my own proper person." Thus authorised, he proceeded to an exchange of caparisons, and made his own beast three parts in four the better for his new furniture. This done, they breakfasted on the remains of the plunder from the sumpter-mule, and drank of the water belonging to the fulling-mills, but without turning their faces towards them—such was the abhorrence in which they were held, because of the effect they had produced. Being thus refreshed and comforted both in body and mind, they mounted; and, without determining upon what road to follow, according to the custom of knights-errant, they went on as Rozinante's will directed, which was a guide to his master and also to Dapple, who always followed, in love and good-fellowship, wherever he led the way. They soon, however, turned into the great road, which they followed at a venture, without forming any plan.

As they were thus sauntering on, Sancho said to his master, "Sir, will your worship be pleased to indulge me the liberty of a word or two? for since you imposed on me that harsh command of silence, sundry things have been rotting in my breast, and I have one just now at my tongue's end that I would not for anything should miscarry." "Speak, then," said Don Quixote, "and be brief in thy discourse; for what is prolix cannot be pleasing." "I say, then, sir," answered Sancho, "that for some days past I have been considering how little is gained by wandering about in quest of those adventures your worship is seeking through these deserts and cross-ways, where, though you should overcome and achieve the most perilous, there is nobody to see or know anything of them; so that they must remain in perpetual oblivion, to the prejudice of your worship's intention and their deserts. And therefore I think it would be more advisable for us, with submission to your better judgment, to serve some emperor or other great prince engaged in war, in whose service your worship may display your valour, great strength, and superior understanding; which being perceived by the lord we serve, he must of course reward each of us according to his merit: nor can you there fail of meeting with somebody to put your worship's exploits in writing, as a perpetual memorial. I say nothing of my own, because they must not exceed the squirely limits; though, I dare say, if it be the custom in chivalry to pen the deeds of squires, mine will not be forgotten."

"Thou sayest not amiss, Sancho," answered Don Quixote: "but, previous to this, it is necessary for a knight-errant to wander about the world seeking adventures by way of probation; where, by his achievements, he may acquire such fame and renown that, when he comes to the court of some great monarch, he shall be already known by his works; and scarcely shall the boys see him enter the gates of the city, when they shall all follow and surround him, crying aloud, 'This is the Knight of the Sun,' or of the Serpent, or of any other device under which he may have achieved great exploits. 'This is he,' they will say, 'who overthrew the huge giant Brocabruno, of mighty force, in single combat; he who disenchanted the great Mameluke of Persia from the long enchantment which held him confined almost nine hundred years;' and thus from mouth to mouth they shall go on blazoning his deeds. At length, attracted by the bustle made by the inhabitants, young and old, the king of that country shall appear at the windows of his royal palace; and, as soon as he espies the knight, whom he will recognise by his armour or by the device on his shield, he will of course say, 'Ho, there! Go forth, my knights, all that are at court, to receive the flower of chivalry, who is approaching.' At which command they all shall go forth, and the king himself, descending half-way down the great staircase, shall receive him with a close embrace, saluting and kissing him; then, taking him by the hand, he shall conduct him to the apartment of the queen, where the knight shall find her with the infanta her daughter, who is so beautiful and accomplished a damsel that her equal cannot easily be found in any part of the known world. It immediately follows that she casts her eyes on the knight, and he his eyes upon hers, each appearing to the other something rather divine than human; and, without knowing how or which way, they remain entangled in the inextricable net of love, and are in great perplexity of mind, not knowing how to converse and discover their amorous anguish to each other. He will then, no doubt, be conducted to some quarter of the palace richly furnished, where, having taken off his armour, they will clothe him in a rich scarlet mantle; and if he looked well in armour he must look still better in ermine. Night being arrived, he shall sup with the king, queen, and infanta; when he shall never take his eyes off the princess, viewing her by stealth, and she will do the same by him, with equal caution; for, as I said before, she is a very discreet damsel. The tables being removed, there shall enter unexpectedly at the hall door a little ill-favoured dwarf, followed by a beautiful matron between two giants, with the proposal of a certain adventure, so contrived by a most ancient sage, that he who shall accomplish it shall be esteemed the best knight in the world. The king shall immediately command all who are present to prove their skill, and none shall be able to accomplish it but the stranger knight, to the great advantage of his fame; at which the infanta will be delighted, and esteem herself happy in having placed her thoughts on so exalted an object. Fortunately, it happens that this king, or prince, or whatever he be, is carrying on a bloody war with another monarch as powerful as himself; and the stranger knight, after having been a few days at court, requests his majesty's permission to serve him in that war. The king shall readily grant his request, and the knight shall most courteously kiss his royal hands for the favour done him. On that night he shall take leave of his lady the infanta at the iron rails of a garden adjoining to her apartment, through which he has already conversed with her several times, by the mediation of a female confidante in whom the infanta greatly trusts. He sighs, she swoons; the damsel runs for cold water, and is very uneasy at the approach of the morning light, and would by no means her lady should be discovered, for the sake of her lady's honour. The infanta at length comes to herself, and gives her snowy hands to the knight through the rails, who kisses them a thousand and a thousand times over, bedewing them with his tears. They concert together how to communicate to each other their good or ill fortune, and the princess entreats him to be absent as short a time as possible; which he promises with many oaths: again he kisses her hands, and they part with so much emotion that he is nearly deprived of life. Thence he repairs to his chamber, throws himself on his bed, and cannot sleep for grief at the separation. He rises early in the morning, and goes to take leave of the king, queen, and infanta. Having taken his leave of the two former, he is told the princess is indisposed and cannot admit of a visit. The knight thinks it is for grief at his departure; his heart is pierced, and he is very near giving manifest indications of his passion. The damsel confidante is present, and observes what passes; she informs her lady, who receives the account with tears, and tells her that her chief concern is that she knows not the name nor country of her knight, and whether he be of royal descent or not: the damsel assures her he is, since so much courtesy, politeness, and valour as her knight is endowed with cannot exist but in a royal and exalted subject. The afflicted princess is then comforted, and endeavours to compose herself, that she may not give her parents cause of suspicion, and two days after she again appears in public. The knight is now gone to the war: he fights and vanquishes the king's enemy; takes many cities; wins several battles; returns to court; sees his lady at the usual place of interview; and it is agreed that he shall demand her in marriage of her father, in recompense of his services. The king does not consent to give her to him, not knowing who he is; notwithstanding which, either by carrying her off, or some other means, the infanta becomes his spouse: and her father afterwards finds it to be a piece of the greatest good fortune, having ascertained that the knight is son to a valorous king, of I know not what kingdom, nor is it, perhaps, to be found in the map. The father dies; the infanta inherits; and, in two words, the knight becomes a king. Then immediately follows the rewarding of his squire, and all those who assisted in his elevation to so exalted a state. He marries his squire to one of the infanta's maids of honour, who is doubtless the very confidante of his amour, and daughter to one of the chief dukes."

"This is what I would be at, and a clear stage," quoth Sancho: "this I stick to, for every tittle of this must happen precisely to your worship, being called the Knight of the Sorrowful Figure." "Doubt it not, Sancho," replied Don Quixote; "for, by those very means and those very steps which I have recounted, knights-errant do rise, and have risen, to be kings and emperors. All that remains to be done is to look out and find what king of the Christians or of the pagans is at war and has a beautiful daughter. But there is time enough to think of this; for, as I told thee, we must procure renown elsewhere before we repair to court. Besides, there is yet another difficulty; for, if a king were found who is at war and has a handsome daughter, and I had acquired incredible fame throughout the whole universe, I do not see how it can be made appear that I am of the lineage of kings, or even second cousin to an emperor: for the king will not give me his daughter to wife until he is first very well assured that I am such, however my renowned actions might deserve it. Through this defect, therefore, I am afraid I shall lose that which my arm has richly deserved. It is true, indeed, I am a gentleman of an ancient family, possessed of property and a title to the 'revenge of the five hundred sueldos;'* and perhaps the sage who writes my history may throw such light upon my kindred and genealogy that I may be found the fifth or sixth in descent from a king. For thou must know, Sancho, that there are two kinds of lineages in the world. Some there are who derive their pedigree from princes and monarchs, whom time has gradually reduced until they have ended in a point, like a pyramid; others have had a low origin, and have risen by degrees until they have become great lords. So that the difference is, that some have been what they now are not, and others are now what they were not before. And who knows but I may be one of the former, and that, upon examination, my origin may be found to have been great and glorious? with which the king, my future father-in-law, ought to be satisfied: and, if he should not be satisfied, the infanta is to be so in love with me that, in spite of her father, she is to receive me for her lord and husband, even though she knew me to be the son of a water-carrier; and, in case she should not, then is the time to take her away by force, and convey her whither I please, there to remain until time or death puts a period to the displeasure of her parents."

"Here," said Sancho, "comes in properly what some naughty people say, 'Never stand begging for that which you have the power to take:' though this other is nearer to the purpose: 'A leap from a hedge is better than the prayer of a bishop.' I say this because if my lord the king, your worship's father-in-law, should not vouchsafe to yield unto you my lady the infanta, there is no more to be done, as your worship says, but to steal and carry her off. But the mischief is, that while peace is making, and before you can enjoy the kingdom quietly, the poor squire may go whistle for his reward; unless the go-between damsel, who is to be his wife, goes off with the infanta, and he shares his misfortune with her until it shall please Heaven to ordain otherwise; for I believe his master may immediately give her to him for his lawful

---

* "The Spaniards of old paid a tribute of five hundred sueldos, or pieces of coin, to the Moors, until they were delivered from this imposition by the gallantry of the gentlemen, or people of rank: from which exploit a Castilian of family used to express the nobility and worth of his extraction by saying he was 'of the revenge of the sueldos.'"—SMOLLETT.

spouse." "On that thou mayest rely," said Don Quixote. "Since it is so," answered Sancho, "we have only to commend ourselves to God, and let things take their course." "Heaven grant it," answered Don Quixote, "as I desire and thou needest, and let him be wretched who thinks himself so." "Let him, in God's name," said Sancho; "for I am an old Christian, and that is enough to qualify me to be an earl." "Aye, and more than enough," said Don Quixote: "and even if thou wert not so, it would be immaterial; for I, being a king, can easily bestow nobility on thee, without either purchase or service on thy part; and, in creating thee an earl, thou art a gentleman of course. And say what they will, in good faith, they must style thee 'your lordship,' however unwillingly." "Do you think," quoth Sancho, "I should not know how to give authority to the indignity?" "*Dignity*, you should say, and not *indignity*," said his master. "So let it be," answered Sancho Panza. "I say, I should do well enough with it, for I assure you I was once beadle of a company, and the beadle's gown became me so well that I had a presence fit to be warden of the same company: what, then, will it be when I am arrayed in a duke's robe, all shining with gold and pearls, like a foreign count? I am of opinion folks will come a hundred leagues to see me." "Thou wilt make a goodly appearance, indeed," said Don Quixote; "but it will be necessary to trim thy beard a little oftener; for it is so rough and matted that, if thou shavest not every other day at least, what thou art will be seen at the distance of a bow-shot." "Why," said Sancho, "it is but taking a barber into the house, and giving him a salary: and, if there be occasion, I will make him follow me like a gentleman of the horse to a grandee." "How camest thou to know," demanded Don Quixote, "that grandees have their gentlemen of the horse to follow them?" "I will tell you," said Sancho: "some years ago I was near the court for a month, and I often saw a very little gentleman riding about, who, they said, was a very great lord; and behind him I noticed a man on horseback, turning about as he turned, so that one would have thought he had been his tail. I asked why that man did not ride by the side of the other, but kept always behind him? They answered me that it was his gentleman of the horse, and that it was the custom for noblemen to be followed by them; and from that day to this I have never forgotten it." "Thou art in the right," said Don Quixote, "and in the same manner thou mayest carry about thy barber; for all customs do not arise together, nor were they invented at once; and thou mayest be the first earl who carried about his barber after him: and, indeed, it is a higher trust to dress the beard than to saddle a horse." "Leave the business of the barber to me," said Sancho, "and let it be your worship's care to become a king, and to make me an earl." "So it shall be," answered Don Quixote: and raising his eyes, he saw—what will be told in the following chapter.

CHAPTER XXII.

How Don Quixote set at liberty several unfortunate persons, who, much against their will, were being conveyed where they had no wish to go.

CID HAMET BENENGELI, the Arabian and Manchegan author, relates, in this most grave, lofty, accurate, delightful, and ingenious history, that after the conversation which passed between the famous Don Quixote de la Mancha and Sancho Panza his squire, given at the end of the foregoing chapter, Don Quixote raised his eyes, and saw approaching in the same road about a dozen men on foot, strung like beads, by the necks, in a great iron chain, and all handcuffed. There came also with them two men on horseback and two on foot: those on horseback were armed with firelocks, and those on foot with pikes and swords. As soon as Sancho Panza saw them, he said, "This is a chain of galley-slaves, persons forced by the king to serve in the galleys." "How! *forced*, do you say?" quoth Don Quixote: "is it possible the king should force anybody?" "I said not so," answered Sancho; "but that they were persons who for their crimes are condemned by law to the galleys, where they are forced to serve the king." "In truth, then," replied Don Quixote, "these people are conveyed by force, and not voluntarily?" "So it is," said Sancho. "Then," said his master, "here the execution of my office begins, which is to defeat violence, and to succour and relieve the wretched." "Consider, sir," quoth Sancho, "that justice—which is the king himself—does no violence to such persons: he only punishes them for their crimes."

By this time the chain of galley-slaves had reached them, and Don Quixote in most courteous terms desired the guard to be pleased to inform him of the cause or causes for which they conducted those persons in that manner. One of the guards on horseback answered that they were slaves belonging to his majesty, and on their way to the galleys, which was all he had to say, nor was there anything more to know. "Nevertheless," replied Don Quixote, "I should be glad to be informed, by each of them individually, of the cause of his misfortune." To this he added such courteous expressions, entreating the information he desired, that the other horseman said, "Though we have here the record and certificate of each of these worthies, this is no time to produce and read them. Draw near, sir, and make your inquiry of themselves; they may inform you if they please, and no doubt they will, for they are such as take a pleasure in acting and relating rogueries." With this leave, which Don Quixote would have taken had it not been given, he went up to them, and demanded of the first for what offence he marched in such evil plight. He answered that it was for being in love. "For that alone?" replied Don Quixote: "if people are sent to the galleys for being in love, I might long since have been rowing in them myself." "It was not such love as your worship imagines," said the galley-slave. "Mine was a strong affection for a basket of fine linen, which I embraced so closely that, if justice had not taken it from me by force, I should not have parted with it by my own good-will even to this present day. I was taken in the fact, so there was no opportunity for the torture. The process was short: they accommodated my shoulders with a hundred lashes, and, as a further kindness, have sent me for three years to the Gurapas, and there is an end of it." "What are the Gurapas?" quoth Don Quixote. "The Gurapas are galleys," answered the convict, who was a young man about twenty-four years of age, born, as he said, at Piedrahita. Don Quixote put the same question to the second, who returned no answer, he was so melancholy and dejected; but the first answered for him, and said, "This gentleman goes for being a canary-bird—I mean, for being a musician and a singer." "How so?" replied Don Quixote; "are men sent to the galleys for being musicians and singers?" "Yes, sir," replied the slave, "for there is nothing worse than to sing in an agony." "Nay," said Don Quixote, "I have heard say, 'Who sings in grief, procures relief.'" "This is the very reverse," said the slave; "for here, he who sings once, weeps all his life after." "I do not understand that," said Don Quixote. One of the guards said to him, "Signor cavalier, to sing in an agony means, in the cant of these rogues, to confess upon the rack. This offender was put to the torture, and confessed his crime, which was that of being a Quatrero, that is, a stealer of cattle; and because he confessed he is sentenced for six years to the galleys, besides two hundred lashes he has already received on the shoulders. He is always pensive and sad, because all the other rogues abuse, vilify, flout, and despise him for confessing, and not having had the courage to say No; for, say they, *No* does not contain more letters than *Ay*; and think it lucky when it so happens that a man's life or death depends upon his own tongue, and not upon proofs and witnesses; and, for my part, I think they are in the right." "And so I think," answered Don Quixote: who, passing on to the third, interrogated him as he had done the others. He answered very readily, and with much indifference, "I am also going to their ladyships the Gurapas for five years, merely for want of ten ducats." "I will give twenty, with all my heart," said Don Quixote, "to redeem you from this misery." "That," said the convict, "is like having money at sea, where, though dying with hunger, nothing can be bought with it. I say this, because if I had been possessed in time of those twenty ducats you now offer me, I would have so greased the clerk's pen and sharpened my advocate's wit, that I would have been this day upon the market-place of Zocodover, in Toledo; and not upon this road, coupled and dragged like a hound: but God is great; patience and—that is enough."

Don Quixote passed on to the fourth, who was a man of venerable aspect, with a white beard reaching below his breast; who, being asked the cause of his coming, began to weep, and answered not a word; but

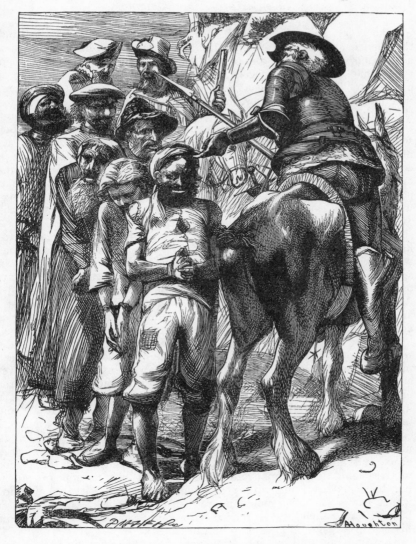

Don Quixote went up to them, and demanded of the first for what offence he marched in such evil plight?

the fifth lent him a tongue, and said, "This honest gentleman goes for four years to the galleys, after having appeared in the usual procession, pompously apparelled and mounted."* "That is, I suppose," said

---

* Such malefactors as in England were formerly set in the pillory, in Spain were carried about in a particular habit, mounted on an ass, with their faces to the tail; the crier going before and proclaiming their crime.

Sancho, " put to public shame ? "   " Right," replied the slave ; " and
the offence for which he suffered this punishment was his having been
a broker of the ear, yea, and even of the whole body.   In fact, I mean
to say that this gentleman goes for pimping, and exercising the trade of
a conjuror."   " Had it been merely for pimping," said Don Quixote,
" he had deserved not to row, but to be commander of the galleys ; for
the office of pimp is no light concern, but an avocation requiring discretion, and very necessary in a well-regulated commonwealth.   None but
such as are well born ought to exercise it ; in truth, it should have its
inspectors and comptrollers, as there are of other offices, limited to a
certain appointed number, like exchange-brokers ; by which means
many evils would be prevented which now happen because this office is
performed only by foolish and ignorant persons, such as silly waiting-
women, pages, and buffoons, without age or experience, who, in the
greatest exigency, and where there is occasion for the utmost address,
suffer the morsel to freeze between the fingers and the mouth, and scarce
know which is their right hand.   I could go on, and assign the reasons
why it would be expedient to make a proper choice in filling an office of
such importance to the state ; but this is not the place for it.   I may,
one day or other, lay this matter before those who can provide a remedy.
At present I only say that the concern I felt at seeing those grey hairs
and that venerable countenance in so much distress for pimping is
entirely removed by his additional character of a wizard ; though I well
know there are no sorceries in the world which can affect and force the
will, as some foolish people imagine ; for our will is free, and no herb
nor charm can compel it, though some silly women and crafty knaves
are wont, by certain mixtures and poisons, to turn the brain, under the
pretence that they have power to excite love ; but, as I said before, it is
impossible to force the will."   " Very true," said the old man ; " and
indeed, sir, as to being a wizard, I am not guilty : as for being a pimp, I
cannot deny it ; but I never thought there was any harm in it, for all
my intention was that the world should divert themselves, and live in
peace and quiet without quarrels or troubles.   But, alas ! these good
motives could not save me from going whence I have no hope of returning, burdened as I am with years, and so troubled with an affliction
which leaves me not a moment's repose."   Here he began to weep, as
before ; and Sancho was so moved with compassion, that he drew from
his bosom a real, and gave it to him in charity.

Don Quixote went on, and demanded of another what his offence was,
who answered, not with less, but much more alacrity than the former :
" I am going for making a little too free with two she cousins-german of
mine, and with two other cousins-german not mine.   In short, I carried
the jest so far with them all, that the result of it was the increasing of
kindred so intricately that no casuist can make it out.   The whole was
proved upon me, and I had neither friends nor money : my windpipe was
in the utmost danger ; I was sentenced to the galleys for six years.   I
submit—it is the punishment of my fault.   I am young ; life may last,
and time brings everything about.   If your worship has anything about

you to relieve us poor wretches, God will repay you in heaven, and we will make it the business of our prayers to beseech Him that your worship's life and health may be as long and prosperous as your goodly presence deserves." This convict was in the habit of a student, and one of the guards said he was a great speaker and a very pretty scholar.

Behind all these came a man about thirty years of age, of a goodly aspect, only that his eyes looked at each other. He was bound somewhat differently from the rest, for he had a chain to his leg, so long that it was fastened round his middle, and two collars about his neck, one of which was fastened to the chain, and the other, called a keep-friend, or friend's-foot, had two straight irons which came down from it to his waist, at the ends of which were fixed two manacles, wherein his hands were secured with a huge padlock; insomuch that he could neither lift his hands to his mouth, nor bend down his head to his hands. Don Quixote asked why this man was fettered so much more than the rest. The guard answered, because he alone had committed more crimes than all the rest together; and that he was so bold and desperate a villain that, although shackled in that manner, they were not secure of him, but were still afraid he would make his escape. "What kind of villanies has he committed," said Don Quixote, "that have deserved no greater punishment than being sent to the galleys?" "He goes for ten years," said the guard, "which is a kind of civil death. You need only to be told that this honest gentleman is the famous Gines de Passamonte, *alias* Ginesillo de Parapilla." "Fair and softly, Signor Commissary," interrupted the slave: "let us not now be spinning out names and surnames. Gines is my name, and not Ginesillo; and Passamonte is the name of my family, and not Parapilla, as you say. Let every one turn himself round, and look at home, and he will find enough to do." "Speak with less insolence, Sir Thief-above-measure," replied the commissary, "unless you would oblige me to silence you to your sorrow." "You may see," answered the slave, "that man goeth as God pleaseth: but somebody may learn one day whether my name is Ginesillo de Parapilla or no." "Are you not so called, lying rascal?" said the guard. "Yes," answered Gines; "but I will make them cease calling me so, or I will flea them where I care not at present to say. Signor Cavalier," continued he, "if you have anything to give us, let us have it now, and Heaven be with you, for you tire us with inquiring so much after other men's lives. If you would know mine, I am Gines de Passamonte, whose life is written by these very fingers." "He says true," said the commissary; "for he himself has written his own history as well as heart could wish, and has left the book in prison pawned for two hundred reals." "Aye, and I intend to redeem it," said Gines, "if it lay for two hundred ducats." "What! is it so good?" said Don Quixote. "So good," answered Gines, "that woe be to Lazarillo de Tormes, and to all that have written or shall write in that way. What I can affirm is that it relates truths, and truths so ingenious and entertaining that no fictions can equal them." "What is the title of your book?" demanded Don Quixote. "The 'Life of Gines de Passamonte,'" replied Gines himself. "And is it finished?" quoth Don Quixote. "How can it be finished?" answered he, "since my life is not yet finished? What is written relates everything from my cradle to the moment of being sent this last time to the galleys." "Then you have been there before?" said Don Quixote. "Four years, the other time," replied Gines, "to serve God and the king; and I know already the relish of the biscuit and lash: nor does it grieve me much to go to them again, since I shall there have an opportunity of finishing my book; for I have a great many things to say, and in the galleys of Spain there is leisure enough; though I shall not want much for what I have to write, because I have it by heart." "You seem to be an ingenious fellow," said Don Quixote. "And an unfortunate one too," answered Gines; "but misfortunes always persecute genius." "Persecute villany," said the commissary. "I have already desired you, Signor Commissary," answered Passamonte, "to go fair and softly; for your superiors did not give you that staff to misuse us poor wretches here, but to conduct us whither his Majesty commands. Now, by the life of —— ! I say no more; but the spots which were contracted in the inn may perhaps one day come out in the bucking; and let every one hold his tongue, live well, and speak better. Now let us march on, for we have had enough of this."

The commissary lifted up his staff to strike Passamonte in return for his threats; but Don Quixote interposed, and desired that he would not ill-treat him, since it was but fair that he who had his hands so tied up should have his tongue a little at liberty. Then turning about to the whole string, he said, "From all you have told me, dearest brethren! I clearly gather that, although it be only the punishment of your crimes, you do not much relish what you are to suffer, and that you go to it with ill-will, and much against your inclination; and that, probably, the pusillanimity of him who was put to the torture, this man's want of money, and the other's want of friends, and, in short, the biassed sentence of the judge, may have been the cause of your not meeting with that justice to which you have a right. Now, this being the case, as I am strongly persuaded it is, my mind prompts and even compels me to manifest in you the purpose for which Heaven cast me into the world, and ordained me to profess the order of chivalry, which I do profess, and the vow I thereby made to succour the needy and those oppressed by the powerful. Conscious, however, that it is the part of prudence not to do by force that which may be done by fair means, I will entreat these gentlemen, your guard and the commissary, that they will be pleased to loose and let you go in peace, since there are people enough to serve the king from better motives; for it seems to me a hard case to make slaves of those whom God and nature made free. Besides, gentlemen guards," added Don Quixote, "these poor men have committed no offence against you: let every one answer for his sins in the other world: there is a God in heaven who fails not to chastise the wicked and to reward the good; neither doth it become honourable men to be the executioners of others, when they have no interest in the matter. I request this of you in a calm and gentle manner, that I may have cause to thank you for your compliance; but, if you do it not willingly, this lance and this sword, with the vigour of my arm, shall compel you to it." "This is pleasant fooling," answered the commissary. "An admirable conceit he has hit upon at last! He would have us let the king's prisoners go—as if we had authority to set them free, or he to command us to do it! Go on your way, signor, and adjust the basin on your noddle, and do not go feeling about for three legs to a cat." "You are a cat, and a rat, and a rascal to boot!" answered Don Quixote: and thereupon, with a word and a blow, he attacked him so suddenly, that, before he could stand upon his defence, he threw him to the ground, much wounded with a thrust of the lance; and it happened, luckily for Don Quixote, that this was one of the two who carried fire-locks. The rest of the guards were astonished and confounded at the unexpected encounter; but, recovering themselves, he on horseback drew his sword, and those on foot took their javelins, and advanced upon Don Quixote, who waited for them with much calmness: and doubtless it had gone ill with him if the galley-slaves had not seized the opportunity now offered to them of recovering their liberty, by breaking the chain by which they were linked together. The confusion was such that the guards, now endeavouring to prevent the slaves from getting loose, and now engaging with Don Quixote, did nothing to any purpose. Sancho, for his part, assisted in releasing Gines de Passamonte, who was the first that leaped free and unfettered upon the plain; and, attacking the fallen commissary, he took away his sword and his gun, which, by levelling first at one and then at another, without discharging it, he cleared the field of all the guard, who fled no less from Passamonte's gun than from the shower of stones which the slaves, now at liberty, poured upon them.

Sancho was much grieved at what had happened, from an apprehension that the fugitives would give notice of the fact to the Holy Brotherhood, who, upon ring of bell, would sally out in quest of the delinquents. These fears he communicated to his master, and begged of him to be gone immediately, and take shelter among the trees and rocks of the neighbouring mountain. "It is well," said Don Quixote; "but I know what is the first expedient to be done." Then, having called all the slaves together, who were in disorder, after having stripped the commissary to his buff, they gathered around him to know his pleasure; when he thus addressed them: "To be grateful for benefits received is natural to persons well born; and one of the sins which most offend God is ingratitude. This I say, gentlemen, because you already know, by manifest experience, the benefit you have received at my hands; in return for which, it is my desire that, bearing with you this chain, which I have taken from your necks, you immediately go to the city of Toboso, and there present yourselves before the Lady Dulcinea del Toboso, and tell her that her Knight of the Sorrowful Figure sends you to present his service to her; and recount to her every circumstance of this memorable adventure, to the point of restoring you to your wished-for liberty: this done, you may go wherever good fortune may lead you."

Gines de Passamonte answered for them all, and said, "What your worship commands us, noble sir, and our deliverer, is of all impossibilities the most impossible to be complied with; for we dare not be seen together on the road, but must go separate, each man by himself, and endeavour to hide ourselves in the very bowels of the earth from the Holy Brotherhood, who will doubtless be out in quest of us. What your worship may and ought to do is to change this service and duty to the Lady Dulcinea del Toboso into a certain number of *Ave Marias* and *credos*, which we will say for your worship's success; and this is what we may do, by day or by night, flying or reposing, in peace or in war: but to think that we will now return to our chains, and put ourselves on our way to Toboso, is to imagine it already night, whereas it is not yet ten o'clock in the morning; and to expect this from us is to expect pears from an elm-tree." "I vow, then," quoth Don Quixote, in a rage, "Don Son of a Rogue, Don Ginesillo de Parapilla, or whatever you call yourself, that you alone shall go with your tail between your legs, and the whole chain upon your back!" Passamonte, who was not over-passive, seeing himself thus treated, and being aware that Don Quixote, from what he had just done, was not in his right senses, gave a signal to his comrades, upon which they all retired a few paces, and then began to rain such a shower of stones upon Don Quixote, that he could not contrive to cover himself with his buckler; and poor Rozinante cared no more for the spur than if he had been made of brass. Sancho got behind his ass, and thereby sheltered himself from the hail-storm that poured upon them both. Don Quixote could not screen himself sufficiently to avoid I know not how many stones, that came against him with such force that they brought him to the ground; when the student instantly fell upon him, and, taking the basin from off his head, gave him three or four blows with it over the shoulders, and then struck it as often against the ground, whereby he almost broke it to pieces. They stripped him of a jacket he wore over his armour, and would have taken his trousers too, if the greaves had not hindered them. They took Sancho's cloak, leaving him stripped; and, after dividing the spoils of the battle, they made the best of their way off, each taking a different course: more solicitous to escape the Holy Brotherhood than to drag their chain to Toboso, and present themselves before the Lady Dulcinea.

The ass and Rozinante, Sancho and Don Quixote, remained by themselves: the ass hanging his head and pensive, and now and then shaking his ears, thinking that the storm of stones was not yet over and still whizzing about his head; Rozinante having been brought to the ground, lay stretched by his master's side; Sancho stripped, and troubled with apprehensions of the Holy Brotherhood; and Don Quixote much chagrined at being so maltreated by those on whom he had conferred so great a benefit.

CHAPTER XXIII.

Of what befell the renowned Don Quixote in the Sierra Morena,* being one of the most uncommon adventures related in this faithful history.

DON QUIXOTE, finding himself thus ill-requited, said to his squire, "Sancho, I have always heard it said that to do good to the vulgar is to throw water into the sea. Had I believed what you said to me, I might have prevented this trouble : but it is done—I must have patience, and henceforth take warning." "Your worship will as much take warning," answered Sancho, "as I am a Turk : but since you say that, if you had believed me, the mischief would have been prevented, believe me now, and you will avoid what is still worse; for, let me tell you, there is no putting off the Holy Brotherhood with chivalries—they do not care two farthings for all the knights-errant in the world; and I fancy already that I hear their arrows whizzing about my ears." "Thou art naturally a coward, Sancho," said Don Quixote : "but, that thou mayest not say that I am obstinate and that I never do what thou advisest, I will for once take thy counsel, and retire from that fury of which thou art so much in fear; but upon this one condition—that, neither living nor dying, thou shalt ever say that I retired and withdrew myself from this peril out of fear, but that I did it out of mere compliance with thy entreaties. If thou sayest otherwise, it is a lie ; and, from this time to that, and from that time to this, I tell thee thou liest, and wilt lie, every time thou shalt either say or think it. Reply not, for the bare thought of withdrawing and retreating from any danger, and especially from this, which seems to carry some appearance of danger with it, inclines me to remain here and expect alone not that Holy Brotherhood only of whom thou speakest, but the brothers of the twelve tribes of Israel, and the seven Maccabees, and Castor and Pollux, and even all the brothers and brotherhoods in the world." "Sir," answered Sancho, "retreating is not running away, nor is staying wisdom when the danger overbalances the hope ; and it is the part of wise men to secure themselves to-day for to-morrow, and not to venture all upon one throw. And know that, although I am but a clown and a peasant, I yet have some smattering of what is called good conduct : therefore repent not of having taken my advice, but get upon Rozinante if you can, if not I will assist you, and follow me ; for my noddle tells me that for the present we have more need of heels than hands." Don Quixote mounted without replying a word more ; and, Sancho leading the way upon his ass, they entered on one side of the Sierra Morena, which was near ; and it was

---

* A mountain, or rather chain of mountains, dividing the kingdom of Castile from the province of Andalusia.

Sancho's intention to pass through it, and get out at Viso or Almodovar del Campo, and there hide themselves for some days among those craggy rocks in case the Holy Brotherhood should come in search of them. He was encouraged to this, by finding that the provisions carried by his ass had escaped safe from the skirmish with the galley-slaves, which he looked upon as a miracle, considering what the slaves took away and how narrowly they searched.

That night they got into the heart of the Sierra Morena, where Sancho thought it would be well to pass the remainder of the night, if not some days, or at least as long as their provisions lasted. Accordingly, there they took up their lodging, under the shelter of rocks overgrown with cork trees. But destiny, which, according to the opinion of those who have not the light of the true faith, guides and disposes all things its own way, so ordered it that Gines de Passamonte, the famous cheat and robber (whom the valour and frenzy of Don Quixote had delivered from the chain), being justly afraid of the Holy Brotherhood, took it into his head to hide himself among those very mountains, and in the very place where, by the same impulse, Don Quixote and Sancho Panza had taken refuge ; arriving just in time to distinguish who they were, although they had fallen asleep. Now, as the wicked are always ungrateful, and necessity urges desperate measures, and present convenience overbalances every consideration of the future, Gines, who had neither gratitude nor good-nature, resolved to steal Sancho Panza's ass —not caring for Rozinante, as a thing neither pawnable nor saleable. Sancho Panza slept : the varlet stole his ass, and before dawn of day was too far off to be recovered.

Aurora issued forth, giving joy to the earth, but grief to Sancho Panza, who, when he missed his Dapple, began to utter the most doleful lamentations, insomuch that Don Quixote awakened at his cries, and heard him say :—"O child of my bowels, born in my house, the joy of my children, the entertainment of my wife, the envy of my neighbours, the relief of my burdens, lastly, the half of my maintenance !— for with the six and twenty maravedis which I have earned every day by thy means have I half supported my family !" Don Quixote, on learning the cause of these lamentations, comforted Sancho in the best manner he could, and desired him to have patience, promising to give him a bill of exchange for three asses out of five which he had left at home. Sancho, comforted by this promise, wiped away his tears, moderated his sighs, and thanked his master for the kindness he showed him.

Don Quixote's heart gladdened upon entering among the mountains, being the kind of situation he thought likely to furnish those adventures he was in quest of. They recalled to his memory the marvellous events which had befallen knights-errant in such solitudes and deserts. He went on meditating on these things, and his mind was so absorbed in them that he thought of nothing else. Nor had Sancho any other concern, now that he thought himself out of danger, than to appease his hunger with what remained of the clerical spoils : and thus, sitting

The portmanteau contained four fine Holland shirts and other linen.

sideways, as women do, upon his beast,* he jogged after his master,
appeasing his hunger while emptying the bag ; and while so employed
he would not have given two maravedis for the rarest adventure that
could have happened.

While thus engaged, he raised his eyes, and observed that his master,
who had stopped, was endeavouring with the point of his lance to raise
something that lay upon the ground : upon which he hastened to assist
him, if necessary, and came up to him just as he had turned over with
his lance a saddle-cushion and a portmanteau fastened to it, half, or
rather quite, rotten and torn, but so heavy that Sancho was forced to

---

* It appears that Cervantes added subsequently in this chapter, and after he had
already written the two following ones, the theft of Sancho's ass by Gines de Passamonte.
In the first edition of "Don Quixote" he continued, after the relation of the theft, to
speak of the ass as though it had not ceased to be in Sancho's possession, and said in
this place, "Sancho followed his master, sitting sideways on his ass." In the second
edition he corrected this inadvertence, but incompletely, and allowed it to remain in
several places. The Spaniards have religiously preserved his text, even to the con-
tradictions made by his partial correction.

alight in order to take it up. His master ordered him to examine it. Sancho very readily obeyed, and although the portmanteau was secured with its chain and padlock, he could see through the chasms what it contained, which was, four fine Holland shirts, and other linen, no less curious than clean; and in a handkerchief he found a quantity of gold crowns, which he no sooner espied than he exclaimed, "Blessed be Heaven, which has presented us with one profitable adventure!" And, searching further, he found a little pocket-book, richly bound, which Don Quixote desired to have, bidding him take the money and keep it for himself. Sancho kissed his hands for the favour; and taking the linen out of the portmanteau, he put it in the provender-bag. All this was perceived by Don Quixote, who said, "I am of opinion, Sancho (nor can it possibly be otherwise), that some traveller must have lost his way in these mountains, and fallen into the hands of robbers, who have killed him, and brought him to this remote part to bury him." "It cannot be so," answered Sancho; "for, had they been robbers, they would not have left this money here." "Thou art in the right," said Don Quixote, "and I cannot conjecture what it should be: but stay; let us see whether this pocket-book has anything written in it that may lead to a discovery." He opened it, and the first thing he found was a rough copy of verses; and, being legible, he read aloud, that Sancho might hear it, the following sonnet:

> "Know'st thou, O Love, the pangs that I sustain,
> Or, cruel, dost thou view those pangs unmoved?
> Or has some hidden cause its influence proved,
> By all this sad variety of pain?
>
> "Love is a god: then surely he must know,
> And, knowing, pity wretchedness like mine;
> From other hands proceeds the fatal blow—
> Is then the deed, unpitying Chloe, thine?
>
> "Ah, no! a form so exquisitely fair
> A soul so merciless can ne'er enclose.
> From Heaven's high will my fate resistless flows,
> And I, submissive, must its vengeance bear.
> Nought but a miracle my life can save,
> And snatch its destined victim from the grave."

"From these verses," quoth Sancho, "nothing can be collected, unless from the clue there given you can come at the whole bottom." "What clue is here?" said Don Quixote. "I thought," said Sancho, "your worship made a clue." "No, I said *Chloe*," answered Don Quixote; "and doubtless that is the name of the lady of whom the author of this sonnet complains: and, in faith, either he is a tolerable poet, or I know but little of the art." "So, then," said Sancho, "your worship understands making verses too?" "Yes, and better than thou thinkest," answered Don Quixote; "and so thou shalt see, when thou bearest a letter to my lady Dulcinea del Toboso, written in verses from beginning to end: for know, Sancho, that all or most of the knights-errant of times past were great poets and great musicians; these two accomplishments, or rather graces, being annexed to lovers-errant. True it is that the couplets of former knights have more of passion than elegance in them." " Pray, sir, read on further," said Sancho : "perhaps you may find something to satisfy us." Don Quixote turned over the leaf, and said, "This is in prose, and seems to be a letter." " A letter of business, sir ? " demanded Sancho. " By the beginning, it seems rather to be one of love," answered Don Quixote. " Then pray, sir, read it aloud," said Sancho, " for I mightily relish these love-matters." " With all my heart," said Don Quixote : and reading aloud, as Sancho desired, he found it to this effect :

" Thy broken faith, and my certain misery, drives me to a place whence thou wilt sooner hear the news of my death than the cause of my complaint. Thou hast renounced me, O ungrateful maid, for one of larger possessions, but not of more worth, than myself. If virtue were a treasure now in esteem, I should have no reason to envy the good fortune of others, nor to bewail my own wretchedness. What thy beauty excited, thy conduct has erased : by the former I thought thee an angel, by the latter I know thou art a woman. Peace be to thee, fair cause of my disquiet ! and may Heaven grant that the perfidy of thy consort remain for ever unknown to thee, that thou mayest not repent of what thou hast done, and afford me that revenge which I do not desire."

The letter being read, Don Quixote said, " We can gather little more from this than from the verses. It is evident, however, that the writer of them is some slighted lover." Then, turning over other parts of the book, he found other verses and letters, some of which were legible, and some not ; but the purport was the same in all—their sole contents being reproaches, lamentations, suspicions, desires, dislikings, favours, and slights, interspersed with rapturous praises and mournful complaints. While Don Quixote was examining the book, Sancho examined the portmanteau, without leaving a corner either in that or in the saddle-cushion which he did not examine, scrutinise, and look into, nor seam which he did not rip, nor lock of wool which he did not carefully pick, that nothing might be lost from want of diligence or through care-lessness — such was the cupidity excited in him by the discovery of this golden treasure, consisting of more than a hundred crowns ! And, although he could find no more, he thought himself abundantly rewarded by those already in his possession for the tossings in the blanket, the vomitings of the balsam, the benedictions of the pack-staves, the cuffs of the carrier, the loss of the wallet, and the theft of his cloak ; together with all the hunger, thirst, and fatigue he had suffered in his good master's service.

The Knight of the Sorrowful Figure was extremely desirous to know who was the owner of the portmanteau ; for he concluded, from the sonnet and the letter, by the money in gold, and by the fineness of the linen, that it must doubtless belong to some lover of condition, whom the disdain and ill-treatment of his mistress had reduced to despair ; but, as no information could be expected in that rugged and uninhabitable place, he had only to proceed forward, taking whatever road Rozinante pleased (who invariably gave preference to that which he found the most passable), and still thinking that among the rocks he should certainly meet with some strange adventure.

As he went onwards impressed with this idea, he espied, on the top of a rising ground not far from him, a man springing from rock to rock with extraordinary agility. He seemed to be almost naked, his beard black and bushy, his hair long and tangled, his legs and feet bare : he had on breeches of sad-coloured velvet, but so ragged as scarcely to cover him : all which particulars, though he passed swiftly by, were observed by the knight. He endeavoured, but in vain, to follow him, for it was not given to Rozinante's feebleness to make way over those craggy places, especially as he was naturally slow-footed and phlegmatic. Don Quixote immediately conceived that this must be the owner of the saddle-cushion and portmanteau, and resolved therefore to go in search of him, even though it should prove a twelvemonth's labour in that wild region. He immediately commanded Sancho to cut short over one side of the mountain while he skirted the other, as they might possibly by this expedition find the man who had so suddenly vanished from their sight. "I cannot do it," answered Sancho, "for the moment I offer to stir from your worship fear is upon me, assaulting me with a thousand kind of terrors and apparitions : and let this serve to advertise you that henceforward I depart not a finger's breadth from your presence." "Be it so," said he of the Sorrowful Figure; "and I am well pleased that thou shouldst rely upon my courage, which shall never fail thee, though the very soul in thy body should desert thee. Follow me, therefore, step by step, or as thou canst, and make lanterns of thine eyes : we will go round this craggy hill, and perhaps we may encounter the man we saw, who, doubtless, is the owner of what we have found." To which Sancho replied, "It would be much more prudent not to look after him ; for if we should find him, and he, perchance, proves to be the owner of the money, it is plain I must restore it ; and therefore it would be better, without this unnecessary diligence, to preserve it faithfully, until, by some way less curious and officious, its true owner shall be found ; by which time, perhaps, I may have spent it, and then I am free by law." "Therein thou art mistaken, Sancho," answered Don Quixote; "for, since we have a vehement suspicion of who is the right owner, it is our duty to seek him, and to return it ; otherwise that suspicion makes us no less guilty than if he really were so. Do not then repine, friend Sancho, at this search, considering how much I shall be relieved by finding him." Then he pricked Rozinante on, and Sancho followed; when, having gone round part of the mountain, they found a dead mule lying in a brook, saddled and bridled, and half-devoured by dogs and crows ; which confirmed them in the opinion that he who fled from them was owner both of the mule and the bundle.

While they stood looking at the mule, they heard a whistle like that of a shepherd tending his flock; and presently, on their left appeared a number of goats, and behind them, higher up on the mountain, an old man, being the goatherd that kept them. Don Quixote called to him aloud, and beckoned him to come down to them. He as loudly answered, inquiring what had brought them to that desolate place, seldom or never trodden unless by the feet of goats, wolves, or other beasts that frequented those mountains. Sancho promised, in reply, that if he would come down, they would satisfy him in everything. The goatherd descended, and coming to the place where Don Quixote stood, he said, " I suppose, gentlemen, you are looking at the dead mule? In truth, it has now lain there these six months. Pray tell me, have you met with his master hereabouts?" "We have met with nothing," answered Don Quixote, " but a saddle-cushion and a small portmanteau, which we found not far hence." " I found it, too," answered the goatherd, " but would by no means take it up, nor come near it, for fear of some mischief, and of being charged with theft: for the devil is subtle, and lays stumbling-blocks in our way, over which we fall without knowing how." " So say I," answered Sancho; " for I also found it, and would not go within a stone's throw of it: there I left it, and there it may lie for me: for I will not have a dog with a bell." " Tell me, honest man," said Don Quixote, " do you know who is the owner of these goods?" " What I know," said the goatherd, " is that six months ago, more or less, there came to a shepherd's hut, about three leagues from this place, a genteel and comely youth, mounted on the very mule which lies dead there, and with the same saddle-cushion and portmanteau that you say you found and touched not. He inquired of us which part of these mountains was the most rude and unfrequented. We told him it was here where we now are; and so it is truly, for if you were to go on about half a league farther, perhaps you would never find the way out: and I wonder how you could get even hither, since there is no road nor path to lead you to it. The youth, then, I say, hearing our answer, turned about his mule and made towards the part we pointed out, leaving us all pleased with his goodly appearance, and wondering at his question and the haste he made to reach the mountain. From that time we saw him not again until some days after, when he issued out upon one of our shepherds, and, without saying a word, struck him and immediately fell upon our sumpter-ass, which he plundered of our bread and cheese, and then fled again to the rocks with wonderful swiftness. Some of us goatherds after this sought for him nearly two days through the most intricate part of these mountains, and at last found him lying in the hollow of a large cork tree. He came out to us with much gentleness, his garments torn, and his face so disfigured and scorched by the sun that we should scarcely have known him, but that his clothes, ragged as they were, convinced us he was the person we were in search after. He saluted us courteously, and in few but civil words bade us not be surprised to see him in that condition, which was necessary in order to perform a certain penance enjoined him for his manifold sins. We entreated him to tell us who he was, but could get no more from him. We also desired him to inform us where he might be found, because when he stood in need of food, without which he could not subsist, we would willingly bring some to him; and, if this did not please him, we begged that at least he would come and ask for it, and not take it away from the shepherds by force. He thanked us for our offers, begged pardon for his past violence, and promised thenceforth to ask it for God's sake, without molesting anybody. As to the place of his abode, he said he had no other than that which chance presented him wherever the night overtook him; and he ended his discourse with so many tears, that we who heard him must have been very stones not to have wept with him, considering what he was when we first saw him, and what he now appeared: for, as I before said, he was a very comely and graceful youth, and by his courteous behaviour showed himself to be well born; which was very evident even to country people like us. Suddenly he was silent, and, fixing his eyes on the ground, he remained in that posture for a long time, whilst we stood still in suspense, waiting to see what would be the end of his trance; for by his motionless position, and the furious look of his eyes, frowning and biting his lips, we judged that his mad fit was coming on; and indeed our suspicions were quickly confirmed, for he suddenly darted forward, and fell with great fury upon one that stood next him, whom he bit and struck with so much violence that, if we had not released him, he would have taken away his life. In the midst of his rage he frequently called out, ' Ah, traitor Fernando! now shalt thou pay for the wrong thou hast done me; these hands shall tear out that heart, the dark dwelling of deceit and villany!' and to these he added other expressions, all pointed at the same Fernando, and charging him with falsehood and treachery. We disengaged our companion from him at last, with no small difficulty; upon which he suddenly left us, and plunged into a thicket so entangled with bushes and briers that it was impossible to follow him. By this we guessed that his madness returned by fits, and that some person whose name is Fernando must have done him some injury of so grievous a nature as to reduce him to the wretched condition in which he appeared. And in that we have since been confirmed, as he has frequently come out into the road, sometimes begging food of the shepherds, and at other times taking it from them by force: for when the mad fit is upon him, though the shepherds offer it freely, he will not take it without coming to blows; but, when he is in his senses, he asks it with courtesy and receives it with thanks, and even with tears. In truth, gentlemen, I must tell you," continued the goatherd, "that yesterday I and four young men, two of them my servants and two my friends, resolved to go in search of him, and, having found him, either by persuasion or force carry him to the town of Almodovar, which is eight leagues off, there to get him cured, if his distemper be curable; or at least to learn who he is, and whether he has any relations to whom we may give notice of his misfortune. This, gentlemen, is all I can tell you in answer to your inquiry; by which you may understand that the owner of the goods you found is the same wretched person who passed you so quickly "—for Don Quixote had told him that he had seen a man leaping about the rocks.

Don Quixote was surprised at what he heard from the goatherd; and,

The tattered knight drew back a little, and, laying his hands on Don Quixote's shoulders, stood contemplating him, as if to ascertain whether he knew him.

being now still more desirous of knowing who the unfortunate madman was, he renewed his determination to search every part of the mountain, leaving neither corner nor cave unexplored until he should find him. But fortune managed better for him than he expected; for at that very instant the same youth appeared descending towards them, and muttering to himself something which was not intelligible. The rags he wore were such as have been described; but, when he drew near, Don Quixote perceived that his buff doublet, though torn to pieces, still retained the perfume of amber, whence he concluded that he could not possibly be of low condition. When the young man came up to them, he saluted them in a harsh and untuned voice, but with a civil air. Don Quixote politely returned the salute, and alighting from Rozinante, with graceful demeanour and address advanced to embrace him, and held him a considerable time clasped within his arms, as if they had been long acquainted. The other, whom we may truly call the tattered knight of the woeful, as Don Quixote was of the sorrowful, figure, having suffered himself to be embraced, drew back a little, and, laying his hands on Don Quixote's shoulders, stood contemplating him, as if to ascertain whether he knew him; and perhaps no less surprised at the aspect, demeanour, and habiliments of the knight than was Don Quixote at the sight of him. In short, the first who broke silence after this prelude was the ragged knight; and what he said shall be told in the next chapter.

CHAPTER XXIV.

A continuation of the adventure in the Sierra Morena.

The history informs us that great was the attention wherewith Don Quixote listened to the tattered knight of the mountain, who thus addressed himself to the knight: "Assuredly, signor, whoever you are, for I do not know you, I am obliged to you for the courtesy you have manifested towards me; and I wish it were in my power to serve you with more than my good-will, which is all that my fate allows me to offer in return for your civility." "So great is my desire to do you service," answered Don Quixote, "that I had determined not to quit these mountains until I found you and learned from yourself whether your affliction, which is evident by the strange life you lead, may admit of any remedy, and, if so, make every possible exertion to procure it; and, should your misfortune be of such a kind that every avenue to consolation is closed, I intended to join in your moans and lamentations —for sympathy is ever an alleviation to misery: and if you should think my intention merits any acknowledgment, I beseech you, sir, by the infinite courtesy I see you possess—I conjure you also by whatever in this life you have loved, or do love most—to tell me who you are, and what has brought you hither, to live and die like a brute beast, amidst these solitudes: an abode, if I may judge from your person and attire, so unsuitable to you. And I swear," added Don Quixote, "by the order of knighthood I have received, though unworthy and a sinner, and by the profession of a knight-errant, if you gratify me in this, to serve you with all the energy which it is my duty to exert, either in remedying your misfortune, if it admit of remedy, or in assisting you to bewail it, as I have already promised." The knight of the mountain, hearing him of the Sorrowful Figure talk thus, could only gaze upon him, viewing him from head to foot; and, after surveying him again and again, he said to him, "If you have anything to give me to eat, for Heaven's sake let me have it; and when I have eaten I will do all you desire, in return for the good wishes you have expressed towards me."

Sancho immediately took from his wallet, and the goatherd from his scrip, some provisions, wherewith the wretched wanderer satisfied his hunger, eating what they gave him like a distracted person, so raven-ously that he made no interval between one mouthful and another, for he rather devoured than ate; and during his repast neither he nor the bystanders spoke a word. When he had finished, he made signs to them to follow him, which they did ; and having conducted them a short distance to a little green plot, he there laid himself down, and the rest did the same. When the tattered knight had composed himself, he said : " If you desire, gentlemen, that I should tell you, in few words, the immensity of my misfortunes, you must promise not to interrupt, by questions or otherwise, the thread of my doleful history; for in the instant you do so my narrative will break off." These words brought to Don Quixote's memory the tale related by his squire, which, because he had not reckoned the number of goats that had passed the river, remained unfinished. " I give this caution," said the ragged mountaineer, " because I would pass briefly over the account of my misfortunes, for recalling them to my remembrance only adds to my woe; and the less I am questioned the sooner shall I have finished my story : yet will I not omit any material circumstance, as it is my wish entirely to satisfy you." Don Quixote, in the name of all the rest, promised not to interrupt him, and upon this assurance he began in the following manner:

" My name is Cardenio; the place of my birth, one of the best cities of Andalusia ; my family noble; my parents wealthy; my wretchedness so great, that it must have been deplored by my parents and felt by my relations, although not to be alleviated by all their wealth; for riches are of little avail in many of the calamities to which mankind are liable. In that city there existed a heaven, wherein love had placed all the joy I could desire ; such is the beauty of Lucinda, a damsel as well born and rich as myself, though more fortunate, and less constant than my honourable intentions deserved. This Lucinda I loved and adored from my childhood ; and she on her part loved me with that innocent affection proper to her age. Our parents were not unacquainted with our attachment, nor was it displeasing to them—foreseeing that it could only end in a union sanctioned, as it were, by the equality of our birth and circumstances. Our love increased with our years, insomuch that Lucinda's father thought it prudent to restrain my wonted freedom of access to his house : thus imitating the parents of the unfortunate Thisbe, so celebrated by the poets. This restraint served only to increase the ardour of our affection ; for though it was in their power to impose silence on our tongues, they could not do the same on our pens, which reveal the secrets of the soul more effectually than even the speech; for the presence of a beloved object often so bewilders and confounds its faculties, that the tongue cannot perform its office. Oh heavens, how many *billets-doux* did I write to her ! What charming, what modest answers did I receive ! How many sonnets did I pen ! How many love-verses indite, in which my soul unfolded all its passions described its ardour, cherished its remembrances, and indulged it, fancy ! At length my patience being exhausted, and my soul languishing to see her, I resolved at once to put into execution what seemed to

me the most likely means to obtain my desired and deserved reward :
that was, to demand her of her father for my lawful wife, which I immediately did.   In reply, he thanked me for the desire I expressed to
honour him by an alliance with his family; but that, as my father was
living, it belonged more properly to him to make this demand; for
without his entire concurrence the act would appear secret, and unworthy of his Lucinda.   I returned him thanks for the kindness of his
reception ; his scruples I thought were reasonable, and I made sure of
my father's ready acquiescence.   I went, therefore, directly to him, and
upon entering his apartment found him with a letter open in his hand,
which he gave me before I spoke a word, saying, ' By this letter you
will see, Cardenio, the inclination Duke Ricardo has to do you service.'
(Duke Ricardo, gentlemen, as you cannot but know, is a grandee of
Spain, whose estate lies in the best part of Andalusia.)   I read the letter,
which was so extremely kind, that I thought even myself it would be
wrong in my father not to comply with its request, which was that I
should be sent immediately to the duke, who was desirous of placing
me, not as a man-servant, but as a companion, to his eldest son ; which
honour should be accompanied by such preferment as should correspond
with the estimation in which he held me.   I was nevertheless much
perplexed by the letter, and quite confounded when I heard my father
say, ' Two days hence, Cardenio, you shall depart, in compliance with
the duke's desire : and give thanks to God for opening you a way to
that fortune I know you deserve ;' to which he added other paternal
admonitions.

"The time fixed for my departure came.   I conversed the night
before with my Lucinda, and told her all that had passed, and also
entreated her father to wait a few days, and not to dispose of her until
I knew what Duke Ricardo's pleasure was with me.   He promised me
all I desired, and she confirmed it with a thousand vows and a thousand
faintings.   I arrived, in short, at the residence of Duke Ricardo, who
received and treated me with so much kindness that envy soon became
active, by possessing his old servants with an opinion that every favour
the duke conferred upon me was prejudicial to their interest.   But the
person most pleased at my arrival was a second son of the duke, called
Fernando, a sprightly young gentleman, of a most gallant, liberal, and
amorous disposition, who in a very short time contracted so intimate a
friendship with me that it became the subject of general conversation;
and though I was treated with much favour by his elder brother, it was
not equal to the kindness and affection of Don Fernando.

" Now, as unbounded confidence is always the effect of such intimacy,
and my friendship for Don Fernando being most sincere, he revealed to
me all his thoughts, and particularly an amour which gave him some
disquiet.   He loved a country girl, the daughter of one of his father's
vassals.   Her parents were rich, and she herself was so beautiful, discreet, and modest, that no one could determine which of these qualities
she most excelled in.   Don Fernando's passion for this lovely maiden
was so excessive that, in order to overcome the difficulties opposed by

her virtue, he resolved to promise her marriage; knowing that she was to be conquered by no other means. Prompted by friendship, I employed the best arguments I could suggest to divert him from such a purpose; but, finding it was all in vain, I resolved to acquaint his father the duke with the affair. Don Fernando, being artful and shrewd, suspected and feared no less; knowing that I could not, as a faithful servant, conceal from my lord and master a concern so prejudicial to his honour; and therefore, to amuse and deceive me, he said that he knew no better remedy for effacing the remembrance of the beauty that had so captivated him than to absent himself for some months: this, he said, might be effected by our going together to my father's house, under pretence, as he would tell the duke, of purchasing horses in our town, which is remarkable for producing the best in the world. No sooner had he made this proposal than, prompted by my own love, I expressed my approbation of it, as the best that possibly could be devised; and should have done so even had it been less plausible, since it afforded me so good an opportunity of returning to see my dear Lucinda. Thus influenced, I seconded his design, and desired him to put it in execution without delay; since absence, I assured him, would certainly have its effect in spite of the strongest inclination. At the very time he made this proposal to me he had already, as appeared afterwards, possessed the maiden under the title of a husband, and only waited for a convenient season to divulge it with safety to himself, being afraid of what the duke his father might do when he should hear of his folly. Now, as love in young men is, for the most part, nothing but appetite, and pleasure its ultimate end, it expires with the attainment of its object; and what seems to be love vanishes, because it has nothing of the durable nature of true affection. In short, Don Fernando having obtained his desire, his fondness abated; and that absence which he proposed as a remedy for his passion, he only chose to avoid what was now no longer agreeable to him. The duke consented to his proposal, and ordered me to bear him company. We reached our city, and my father received him according to his quality. I immediately visited Lucinda: my passion revived (though, in truth, it had been neither dead nor asleep), and, unfortunately for me, I revealed it to Don Fernando; thinking that, by the laws of friendship, nothing should be concealed from him. I expatiated so much on the beauty, grace, and discretion of Lucinda, that my praises excited in him a desire of seeing a damsel endowed with such accomplishments. Unhappily, I consented to gratify him, and showed her to him one night by the light of a taper at a window, where we were accustomed to converse together. He beheld her, and every beauty he had hitherto seen was cast into oblivion. He was struck dumb: he lost all sense: he was entranced: in short, he became deeply enamoured, as will appear by the sequel of my unfortunate story. And, the more to inflame his passion, which he concealed from me, he saw by chance a letter which she had written to me, expressing a wish that I would again urge her father's consent to our marriage, in terms so sensible, so modest, and so full of tenderness, that when he had read it he declared to me that he thought in Lucinda alone were united all the beauty, good sense, and excellent qualities which were dispersed and divided among the rest of her sex. True it is, I confess, that although I knew what just cause Don Fernando had to admire Lucinda, I was grieved to hear commendations from his mouth. From that time I began to fear and suspect him; for he was every moment talking of Lucinda, and would begin the subject himself, however abruptly, which awakened in me I know not what jealousy; and though I feared no change in the goodness and fidelity of Lucinda, yet I could not but dread the very thing against which they seemed to secure me. He also constantly importuned me to show him the letters I wrote to Lucinda, as well as her answers, pretending to be extremely delighted with both.

"Now, it happened that Lucinda, having desired me to lend her a book of chivalry, of which she was very fond, entitled 'Amadis de Gaul' ——" Scarcely had Don Quixote heard him mention a book or chivalry than he said, " Had you told me, sir, at the beginning of your history, that the Lady Lucinda was fond of reading books of chivalry, no more would have been necessary to convince me of the sublimity or her understanding; for it could never have been so excellent as you have described it had she wanted a relish for such savoury reading; so that, with respect to me, it is needless to waste more words in displaying her beauty, worth, and understanding, since, from only knowing her taste, I pronounce her to be the most beautiful and the most ingenious woman in the world. And I wish, sir, that, together with ' Amadis de Gaul,' you had sent her the good ' Don Rugel of Greece ;' for I know that the Lady Lucinda will be highly delighted with Daraida and Garaya, and the wit of the shepherd Darinal; also with those admirable verses of his *Bucolics* which he sung and repeated with so much grace, wit, and freedom. But this fault may be amended, and reparation made, as soon as ever you will be pleased, sir, to come with me to our town, where I can furnish you with more than three hundred books that are the delight of my soul and the entertainment of my life. Yet it now occurs to me that I have not one of them left—thanks to the malice of wicked and envious enchanters ! Pardon me, sir, for having broken my promise by this interruption; but when I hear of matters appertaining to knights-errant and chivalry, I can as well forbear talking of them as the beams of the sun can cease to give heat, or those of the moon to moisten. Pray, therefore, excuse me, and proceed; for that is of most importance to us at present."

While Don Quixote was saying all this, Cardenio hung down his head upon his breast, apparently in profound thought; and although Don Quixote twice desired him to continue his story, he neither lifted up his head nor answered a word. But after some time he raised it, and said, " I cannot get it out of my mind, nor can any one persuade me—indeed he must be a blockhead who understands or believes otherwise—but that Master Elisabat, that wicked rogue, lay with Queen Madasima." " It is false, I swear !" answered Don Quixote, in great wrath; " it is extreme malice, or rather villany, to say so.   Queen Madasima was a very noble lady, and it is not to be presumed that so high a princess should associate with a quack; and whoever asserts that she did, lies like a very rascal: and I will make him know it, on foot or on horseback, armed or unarmed, by night or by day, or how he pleases.''   Cardenio sat looking at him very attentively, and, the mad fit being now upon him, he was in no condition to prosecute his story, neither would Don Quixote have heard him, so much was he irritated by what he had heard of Madasima; and strange it was to see him take her part with as much earnestness as if she had been his true and natural mistress—such was the effect of those cursed books!

The replies and rejoinders ended in taking each other by the beard, and coming to blows.

Cardenio, being now mad, and hearing himself called liar and villain, with other opprobrious names, did not like the jest; and, catching at a stone that lay close by him, he threw it with such violence at Don Quixote's breast that it threw him on his back.   Sancho Panza, seeing his master treated in this manner, attacked the madman with his clenched fist; and the ragged knight received him in such sort, that with one blow he laid him at his feet, and then trampled him to his heart's content.   The goatherd, who endeavoured to defend him, fared little better; and when the madman had sufficiently vented his fury upon them all he left them, and quietly retired to his rocky haunts among the mountains.   Sancho got up in a rage to find himself so roughly handled, and so undeservedly withal, and was proceeding to take revenge on the goatherd, telling him the fault was his, for not having given them warning that this man was subject to these mad fits;

for had they known it they might have been upon their guard. The goatherd answered that he had given them notice of it, and that, if they had not attended to it, the fault was not his. Sancho Panza replied, the goatherd rejoined; and the replies and rejoinders ended in taking each other by the beard, and coming to such blows that, if Don Quixote had not interposed, they would have demolished each other. But Sancho still kept fast hold of the goatherd, and said, "Let me alone, Sir Knight of the Sorrowful Figure, for this fellow being a bumpkin like myself, and not a knight, I may very safely revenge myself by fighting with him hand to hand, like a man of honour." "True," said Don Quixote, "but I know that he is not to blame for what has happened." Hereupon they were pacified; and Don Quixote again inquired of the goatherd whether it were possible to find out Cardenio; for he had a vehement desire to learn the end of his story. The goatherd told him, as before, that he did not exactly know his haunts, but that, if he waited some time about that part, he would not fail to meet him, either in or out of his senses.

CHAPTER XXV.

Which treats of the strange things that befell the valiant knight of La Mancha in the Sierra Morena; and how he imitated the penance of Beltenebros.

DON QUIXOTE took his leave of the goatherd, and, mounting Rozinante, commanded Sancho to follow him; which he did very unwillingly. They proceeded slowly on, making their way in the most difficult recesses of the mountain. In the meantime Sancho was dying to converse with his master, but would fain have had him begin the discourse, that he might not disobey his orders. Being, however, unable to hold out any longer, he said to him, "Signor Don Quixote, be pleased to give me your worship's blessing and my dismission; for I will get home to my wife and children, with whom I shall at least have the privilege of talking and speaking my mind; for, to desire me to bear your worship company through these solitudes night and day, without suffering me to talk when I list, is to bury me alive. If fate had ordered it that beasts should talk now, as they did in the days of Guisopete, it would not have been quite so bad, since I might then have communed with my ass as I pleased, and so have forgotten my ill fortune; for it is very hard, and not to be borne with patience, for a man to ramble about all his life in quest of adventures, and to meet with nothing but kicks and cuffs, tossings in a blanket, and bangs with stones, and, with all this, to have his mouth sewed up, not daring to utter what he has in his heart, as if he were dumb." "I understand thee, Sancho," answered Don Quixote: "thou art impatient until I take off the embargo I have laid on thy tongue. Suppose it then removed, and thou art permitted to say what thou wilt, upon condition that this revocation is to last no longer than whilst we are wandering amongst these mountains." " Be it so," said Sancho; " let me talk now, for God knows what will be hereafter. And now, taking the benefit of this licence, I ask, what had your worship to do with standing up so warmly for that same Queen Magimasa, or what's her name? or what was it to the purpose whether that abbot * was her gallant or not? for, had you let that pass, as you were not his judge, I verily believe the madman would have gone on with his story, and you would have escaped the thump with the stone, the kicks, and above half a dozen buffets."

" In faith, Sancho," answered Don Quixote, " if thou didst but know, as I do, how honourable and excellent a lady Queen Madasima was, I am certain thou wouldst acknowledge that I had a great deal of patience in forbearing to dash to pieces that mouth out of which such blasphemies issued; for it is a monstrous impiety to say, or even to think, that a queen should be paramour to a barber-surgeon. The truth of the story is, that Master Elisabat, of whom the madman spoke, was a most prudent man, of sound judgment, and served as tutor and physician to the queen; but, to suppose that she was his mistress is an absurdity deserving of severe punishment : and to prove that Cardenio knew not what he spoke, thou mayest remember that, when he said it, he was not in his senses." " That is what I say," quoth Sancho; "and therefore no account should have been made of his words; for, if good fortune had not befriended your worship, and directed the flint stone at your breast instead of your head, we had been in a fine condition for standing up in defence of that dear lady, whom Heaven confound; and Cardenio would have come off unpunished, being insane." " Against the sane and insane," answered Don Quixote, " it is the duty of a knight-errant to defend the honour of women, particularly that of a queen of such exalted worth as Queen Madasima, for whom I have a particular affection, on account of her excellent qualities; for, besides being extremely beautiful, she was very prudent, and very patient in her afflictions, which were numerous; and the counsels and company of Master Elisabat were of great use and comfort to her, enabling her to bear her sufferings with prudence and patience. Hence the ignorant and evil-minded vulgar took occasion to say that she was his paramour; and I say again they lie, and will lie two hundred times more, all who say or think it." " I neither say nor think so," answered Sancho. " Let those who say it eat the lie, and swallow it with their bread : whether they were guilty or no, they have given account to God before now. I come from my vineyard; I know nothing. I am no friend to inquiring into other men's lives; for he that buys and lies shall find the lie left in his purse behind. Besides, naked was I born, and naked I remain; I neither win nor lose : if they were guilty, what is that to me?

---

* *Abad.* Sancho, remembering only the latter part of Master Elisabat's name, pleasantly calls him an abbot.

Many think to find bacon, when there is not so much as a pin to hang it on; but who can hedge in the cuckoo—especially as God himself is not spared?" "Heaven defend me!" said Don Quixote; "what a string of nonsense! What has our subject to do with all these proverbs? Prithee, Sancho, peace; and henceforward attend to thy ass, and forbear any interference with what does not concern thee. Be convinced, by thy five senses, that whatever I have done, do, or shall do, is highly reasonable and exactly conformable to the rules of chivalry, which I am better acquainted with than all the knights whoever professed it in the world." " Sir," replied Sancho, " is it a good rule of chivalry for us to go wandering through these mountains, without either path or road, in quest of a madman who, perhaps, when he is found, will be inclined to finish what he began—not his story, but the breaking of your worship's head and my ribs?"

" Peace, Sancho, I repeat," said Don Quixote; "for know that it is not only the desire of finding the madman that brings me to these parts, but an intention to perform in them an exploit whereby I shall acquire perpetual fame and renown over the face of the whole earth; and it shall be such a one as shall set the seal to make an accomplished knight-errant." "And is this exploit a very dangerous one?" quoth Sancho. " No," answered the knight; " although the die may chance to run unfortunately for us, yet the whole will depend upon thy diligence." "Upon my diligence!" exclaimed Sancho. " Yes," said Don Quixote; " for if thy return be speedy from the place whither I intend to send thee, my pain will soon be over, and my glory forthwith commence: and that thou mayest no longer be in suspense with regard to the tendency of my words, I inform thee, Sancho, that the famous Amadis de Gaul was one of the most perfect of knights-errant—I should not say *one*, for he was the sole, the principal, the unique—in short, the prince of all his contemporaries. A fig for Don Belianis, and all those who say that he equalled Amadis in anything! for I swear they are mistaken. I say, moreover, that if a painter would be famous in his art, he must endeavour to copy after the originals of the most excellent masters; the same rule is also applicable to all the other arts and sciences which adorn the commonwealth: thus, whoever aspires to a reputation for prudence and patience must imitate Ulysses, in whose person and toils Homer draws a lively picture of those qualities; so also Virgil, in the character of Æneas, delineates filial piety, courage, and martial skill, being representations of not what they really were, but of what they ought to be, in order to serve as models of virtue to succeeding generations. Thus was Amadis the polar, the morning star, and the sun of all valiant and enamoured knights, and whom all we who militate under the banners of love and chivalry ought to follow. This being the case, friend Sancho, that knight-errant who best imitates him will be most certain of arriving at pre-eminence in chivalry. And an occasion upon which the knight particularly displayed his prudence, worth, courage, patience, constancy, and love, was his retiring, when disdained by the Lady Oriana, to do penance on the sterile rock, changing his name to that of Beltenebros—a name most certainly significant and proper for the life he had voluntarily chosen. Now, it is easier for me to imitate him in this than in cleaving of giants, beheading serpents, slaying dragons, routing armies, shattering fleets, and dissolving enchantments; and, since this place is so well adapted for the purpose, I ought not to neglect the opportunity which is now so commodiously offered to me."

"What is it your worship really intends to do in so remote a place as this?" demanded Sancho. "Have I not told thee," answered Don Quixote, "that I design to imitate Amadis, acting here the desperate, raving, and furious lover? at the same time following the example of the valiant Don Orlando, when he found by the side of a fountain some indications that Angelica the Fair had dishonoured herself with Medoro; at grief whereof he ran mad, tore up trees by the roots, disturbed the waters of the crystal springs, slew shepherds, destroyed flocks, fired cottages, demolished houses, dragged mares along the ground, and committed a hundred thousand other extravagances worthy of eternal record. And although it is not my design to imitate Roldan, or Orlando, or Rotolando (for he is called by all these names), in every point and in all his frantic actions, words, and thoughts, yet I will give as good a sketch as I can of those which I deem most essential. Or I may, perhaps, be content to imitate only Amadis, who, without committing any mischievous excesses, by tears and lamentations alone attained as much fame as all of them." "It seems to me," quoth Sancho, "that the knights who acted in such manner were provoked to it, and had a reason for these follies and penances; but pray, what cause has your worship to run mad? What lady has disdained you? or what tokens have you discovered to convince you that the Lady Dulcinea del Toboso has committed folly either with Moor or Christian?" "There lies the point," answered Don Quixote, "and in this consists the refinement of my plan. A knight-errant who runs mad with just cause deserves no thanks; but to do so without reason is the point—giving my lady to understand what I should perform in the wet if I do this in the dry. Besides, I have cause enough given me by so long an absence from my ever-honoured lady Dulcinea del Toboso; for as thou heardst that shepherd, Ambrosio, say, 'The absent feel and fear every ill.' Therefore, friend Sancho, counsel me not to refrain from so rare, so happy, and so unparalleled an imitation. Mad I am, and mad I must be until thy return with an answer to a letter I intend to send by thee to my lady Dulcinea; and if it proves such as my fidelity deserves, my madness and my penance will terminate. But if the contrary, I shall be mad indeed; and, being so, shall become insensible to everything: so that, whatever answer she returns, I shall be relieved of the conflict and pain wherein thou leavest me; for if good, I shall enjoy it in my right senses; if otherwise, I shall be mad, and consequently insensible of my misfortune.

"But, tell me, Sancho, hast thou taken care of Mambrino's helmet? for I saw thee take it from the ground, when that ungrateful wretch proved the excellence of its quality, by vainly endeavouring to break it to pieces." To which Sancho answered, " As God liveth, Sir Knight of the Sorrowful Figure, I cannot bear with patience some things your worship says: they are enough to make me think that all you tell me of chivalry, and of winning kingdoms and empires, of bestowing islands, and doing other favours and mighty things, according to the custom of knights-errant, must be matter of mere smoke, and all friction, or fiction, or how do you call it ? For, to hear you say that a barber's basin is Mambrino's helmet, and to persist in that error for near about four days, what can one think, but that he who says and affirms such a thing must be crack-brained ? I have the basin in my wallet, all battered ; and I shall take it home to get it mended, for the use of my beard, if Heaven be so gracious as to restore me one time or other to my wife and children." " Now I swear by the same oath," said Don Quixote, " that thou hast the shallowest brain that any squire has, or ever had, in the world. Is it possible that, notwithstanding all the time thou hast travelled with me, thou dost not perceive that all affairs in which knights-errant are concerned appear chimeras, follies, and extravagances, and seem all done by the rule of contraries ? Not that they are in reality so, but because there is a crew of enchanters always about us, who metamorphose and disguise all our concerns, and turn them according to their own pleasure, or according as they are inclined to favour or ruin us. Hence it is that the thing which to thee appears a barber's basin, appears to me the helmet of Mambrino, and to another will appear something else : and it was a singular foresight of the sage, my friend, to make that appear to others a basin which really and truly is Mambrino's helmet ; because, being of such high value, all the world would persecute me in order to obtain it ; but now, thinking it nothing but a barber's basin, they give themselves no trouble about it, as was evident in him who, after endeavouring to break it, cast it from him ; which, in faith, he would never have done had he known what it was. Take care of it, friend ; since I must strip off all my armour, and remain as naked as I was born, if I should determine upon imitating Orlando in my penance, instead of Amadis."

While they were thus discoursing, they arrived at the foot of a high mountain, which stood separated from several others that surrounded it, as if it had been hewn out from them. Near its base ran a gentle stream, that watered a verdant and luxuriant vale, adorned with many wide-spreading trees, plants, and wild flowers of various hues. This was the spot in which the Knight of the Sorrowful Figure chose to perform his penance ; and, while contemplating the scene, he thus broke forth in a loud voice: " This is the place, O ye heavens ! which I select and appoint for bewailing the misfortune in which ye have involved me. This is the spot where my flowing tears shall increase the waters of this crystal stream, and my sighs, continual and deep, shall incessantly move the foliage of these lofty trees, in testimony and token of the pain my persecuted heart endures. O ye rural deities, whoever ye be, that inhabit these remote deserts, give ear to the complaints of an unhappy lover, whom long absence and some pangs of jealousy have driven to bewail himself among these rugged heights, and to complain of the cruelty of that ungrateful fair, the utmost extent and ultimate perfection of all human beauty! O ye wood nymphs and dryads, who are accustomed to inhabit the dark recesses of the mountain groves (so may the nimble and lascivious satyrs, by whom ye are wooed in vain, never disturb your sweet repose), assist me to lament my hard fate, or at least be not weary of hearing my groans! O my Dulcinea del Toboso, light of my darkness, glory of my pain, the north-star of my travels, and overruling planet of my fortunes! (so may Heaven listen to all thy petitions) consider, I beseech thee, to what a condition thy absence hath reduced me, and reward me as my fidelity deserves! O ye solitary trees, who henceforth are to be the companions of my retirement, wave gently your branches, to indicate that my presence does not offend you! And, O thou my squire, agreeable companion in my prosperous and adverse fortune, carefully imprint on thy memory what thou shalt see me here perform, that thou mayest recount and recite it to her who is the sole cause of all!" Thus saying, he alighted from Rozinante, and in an instant took off his bridle and saddle, and, clapping him on the hinder parts, said to him, "O steed, as excellent for thy performance as unfortunate in thy fate! he gives thee liberty who is himself deprived of it. Go whither thou wilt; for thou hast it written on thy forehead that neither Astolpho's Hippogriff, nor the famous Frontino, which cost Bradamante so dear, could match thee in speed."

Sancho, observing all this, said, "Heaven's peace be with him who saved us the trouble of unharnessing Dapple; for, in faith, he should have wanted neither slaps nor speeches in his praise. Yet if he were here, I would not consent to his being unpannelled, there being no occasion for it, for he had nothing to do with love or despair, any more than I, who was once his master, when it so pleased God. And truly, Sir Knight of the Sorrowful Figure, if it be so that my departure and your madness take place in earnest, it will be well to saddle Rozinante again, that he may supply the loss of my Dapple, and save me time in going and coming; for if I walk, I know not how I shall be able either to go or return, being in truth but a sorry traveller on foot." "Be that as thou wilt," answered Don Quixote, "for I do not disapprove thy proposal: and I say thou shalt depart within three days, during which time I intend thee to bear witness of what I do for her sake, that thou mayest report it accordingly." "What have I more to see," quoth Sancho, "than what I have already seen?" "So far thou art well prepared," answered Don Quixote; "but I have now to rend my garments, scatter my arms about, and dash my head against these rocks; with other things of the like sort, which will strike thee with admiration." "For the love of Heaven," said Sancho, "beware how you give yourself those blows, for you may chance to touch upon some unlucky point of rock, that may at once put an end to this new project of penance. I should think, since your worship is of opinion that knocks of the head are necessary, and that this work cannot be done without them, you might content yourself, since all is a fiction, a counterfeit, and a sham—I say, you might content yourself with running your head against water, or some soft thing, such as cotton; and leave it to me to tell my lady that you dashed your head against the point of a rock harder than a diamond." "I thank thee for thy good intentions, friend Sancho," answered Don Quixote; "but I would have thee to know, that all these actions of mine are no mockery, but done very much in earnest; for to act otherwise would be an infraction of the rules of chivalry, which enjoin us to utter no falsehood, on pain of being punished as apostates; and the doing one thing for another is the same as lying: therefore, blows must be real and substantial, without artifice or evasion. However, it will be necessary to leave me some lint for my wounds, since it was the will of fortune that we should lose the balsam." "It was worse to lose the ass," answered Sancho; "for with him we lost lint and everything else. And I beseech your worship not to put me in mind of that cursed drench; for at barely hearing it mentioned, my very soul, as well as my stomach, is turned inside out. As for the three days allowed me for seeing your mad pranks, I beseech you to reckon them as already passed, for I take all for granted, and will tell wonders to my lady. Do you write the letter and dispatch me quickly, for I long to come back and release your worship from this purgatory in which I leave you." "Purgatory, dost thou call it, Sancho?" said Don Quixote. "Call it rather hell, or worse, if anything can be worse." "I have heard say," quoth Sancho, "that 'from hell there is no retention.'" "I know not," said Don Quixote, "what *retention* means." "Retention," answered Sancho, "means that he who is once in hell never does, nor ever can, get out again. But it will be quite the reverse with your worship, or it shall go hard with my heels, if I have but spurs to enliven Rozinante. Let me but once get to Toboso, and into the presence of my lady Dulcinea, and I will tell her such a story of the foolish, mad things (for they are all no better) which your worship has done and is still doing, that I shall bring her to be as supple as a glove, though I find her harder than a cork tree; and with her answer, all sweetness and honey, will I return through the air, like a witch, and fetch your worship out of this purgatory, which, though it seems so, is no hell, because, as I said, your worship may hope to get out of it."

"That is true," answered the Knight of the Sorrowful Figure: "but how shall we contrive to write the letter?" "And the ass-colt bill?" added Sancho. "Nothing shall be omitted," said Don Quixote; "and since we have no paper, we shall do well to write it as the ancients did, on the leaves of trees, or on tablets of wax; though it will be as difficult at present to meet with these as with paper. But, now I recollect, it may be as well, or indeed better, to write it in Cardenio's pocket-book, and you will take care to get it fairly transcribed upon paper in the first town you reach where there is a schoolmaster; or, if there be none, any parish clerk will transcribe it for you: but be sure you give it to no hackney writer of the law; for the devil himself will never be able to read their confounded law-hand." "But what must we do about the signing it with your own hand?" said Sancho. "The letters of Amadis were never subscribed," answered Don Quixote. "Very well," replied Sancho: "but the order for the colts must needs be signed by yourself; for if that be copied they will say it is a false signature, and I shall be forced to go without the colts." "The order shall be signed in the same pocket-book, and at sight of it my niece will make no difficulty in complying with it. As to the love-letter, let it be subscribed thus: 'Yours until death, the Knight of the Sorrowful Figure.' And it is of little importance whether it be written in another hand; for I remember Dulcinea can neither write nor read, nor has she ever seen a letter or writing of mine in her whole life; for our loves have always been of the Platonic kind, extending no further than to modest glances at each other; and even those so very rarely that I can truly swear that, during the twelve years that I have loved her more than the light of those eyes which the earth must one day consume, I have not seen her four times; and perhaps of these four times she may not have once perceived that I looked upon her—such is the reserve and seclusion in which she is brought up by her father, Lorenzo Corchuelo, and her mother, Aldonza Nogales!"

"Heyday!" exclaimed Sancho, "what, the daughter of Lorenzo Corchuelo! Is she the Lady Dulcinea del Toboso, otherwise called Aldonza Lorenzo?" "It is even she," said Don Quixote, "and she deserves to be mistress of the universe." "I know her well," quoth Sancho; "and I can assure you she will pitch the bar with the lustiest swain in the parish. Long live the giver! Why, she is a lass of mettle, tall, straight, and vigorous, and I warrant can make her part good with any knight-errant that shall have her for a mistress. Oh, the jade, what a pair of lungs and a voice she has! I remember she got out one day upon the bell-tower of the church, to call some young ploughmen who were in a field of her father's; and though they were half a league off, they heard her as plainly as if they had stood at the foot of the tower. And the best of her is, that she is not at all coy, but as bold as a court lady, and makes a jest and a may-game of everybody. I say, then, Sir Knight of the Sorrowful Figure, that you not only may and ought to run mad for her, but also you may justly despair and hang yourself; and nobody that hears it but will say you did extremely well, though the devil should carry you away. I would fain begone, if it is only to see her; for I have not seen her this many a day, and by this time she must needs be altered; for it mightily spoils women's faces to be always abroad in the field, exposed to the sun and weather. I confess to your worship, Signor Don Quixote, that hitherto I have been hugely mistaken, for I thought for certain that the Lady Dulcinea was some great princess, with whom you were in love, or at least some person of such great quality as to deserve the rich presents you have sent her, as well of the Biscainer as of the galley-slaves; and many others from the victories your worship must have gained before I came to be your squire. But, all things considered, what good can it do the Lady

Aldonza Lorenzo—I mean the Lady Dulcinea del Toboso—to have the vanquished whom your worship sends, or may send, falling upon their knees before her? For perhaps at the time they arrive she may be carding flax, or threshing in the barn, and they may be confounded at the sight of her, and she may laugh and care little for the present." "I have often told thee, Sancho," said Don Quixote, "that thou art an eternal babbler, and, though void of wit, thy bluntness often stings : but to convince thee at once of thy folly and my discretion, I will tell thee a short tale.

"Know, then, that a certain widow, handsome, young, gay, and rich, and withal no prude, fell in love with a lay-brother, young, well-made, and vigorous. His superior heard of it, and one day took occasion to speak to the good widow, in the way of brotherly reprehension. ' I wonder, madam,' said he, ' and not without great reason, that a woman of your quality, so beautiful and so rich, should fall in love with such a despicable, mean, silly fellow, when there are, in this house, so many graduates, dignataries, and divines, among whom you might pick and choose, and say, This I like and this I leave, as you would among pears.' But she answered him with great frankness and gaiety, ' You are much mistaken, worthy sir, and your sentiments are very antiquated, if you imagine that I have made an ill choice in that fellow, silly as he may appear ; since, for aught that I desire of him, he knows as much of philosophy as Aristotle himself, if not more.' In like manner, Sancho, Dulcinea del Toboso, for the purpose I intend her, deserves as highly as the greatest princess on earth. For of those poets who have celebrated the praises of ladies under fictitious names, many had no such mistresses. Thinkest thou that the Amaryllises, the Phyllises, the Silvias, the Dianas, the Galateas, the Alidas, and the like, famous in books, ballads, barbers' shops, and stage-plays, were really ladies of flesh and blood, and beloved by those who have celebrated them? Certainly not : they are mostly feigned, to supply subjects for verse, and to make the authors pass for men of gallantry. It is, therefore, sufficient that I think and believe that the good Aldonza Lorenzo is beautiful and chaste; and as to her lineage, it matters not; for no inquiry concerning it is requisite; and to me it is unnecessary, as I regard her as the greatest princess in the world. For thou must know, Sancho, if thou knowest it not already, that two things, above all others, incite to love, namely, beauty and a good name. Now both these are to be found in perfection in Dulcinea ; for in beauty none can be compared to her, and for purity of reputation few can equal her. In fine, I conceive she is exactly what I have described, and everything that I can desire, both as to beauty and quality—unequalled by Helen, or by Lucretia, or any other of the famous women of antiquity, whether Grecian, Roman, or Goth : and I care not what be said; since, if upon this account I am blamed by the ignorant, I shall be acquitted by the wise." "Your worship," replied Sancho, "is always in the right, and I am an ass—why do I mention an ass ?—one should not talk of halters in the house of the hanged. But I am off—give me the letter, sir, and God be with you.'

Don Quixote took out the pocket-book, and, stepping aside, began with much composure to write the letter; and having finished, he called Sancho, and said he would read it to him, that he might have it by heart, lest he might perchance lose it by the way, for everything was to be feared from his evil destiny. To which Sancho answered, "Write it, sir, two or three times in the book, and give it me, and I will take good care of it; but to suppose that I can carry it in my memory is a folly, for mine is so bad that I often forget my own name. Your worship, however, may read it to me: I shall be glad to hear it, for it must needs be very much to the purpose." "Listen, then," said Don Quixote: "this is what I have written:

" Don Quixote's letter to Dulcinea del Toboso.

"'High and sovereign lady,—He who is stabbed by the point of absence, and pierced by the arrows of love, O sweetest Dulcinea del Toboso, greets thee with wishes for that health which he enjoys not himself. If thy beauty despise me, if thy worth favour me not, and if thy disdain still pursue me, although inured to suffering, I shall ill support an affliction which is not only severe but lasting. My good squire Sancho will tell thee, O ungrateful fair, and most beloved foe, to what a state I am reduced on thy account. If it be thy pleasure to relieve me, I am thine; if not, do what seemeth good to thee: for by my death I shall at once appease thy cruelty and my own passion.— Until death thine,

"'THE KNIGHT OF THE SORROWFUL FIGURE.'"

"By the life of my father," quoth Sancho, after hearing the letter, "it is the finest thing I ever heard. Odds boddikins! how choicely your worship expresses whatever you please! and how well you close all with 'the Knight of the Sorrowful Figure!' Verily, your worship is the devil himself—there is nothing but what you know." "The profession which I have embraced," answered Don Quixote, "requires a knowledge of everything." "Well, then," said Sancho, "pray clap on the other side of the leaf, the order for the three ass-colts, and sign it very plain, that people may know your hand at first sight." "With all my heart," said the knight; and having written it, he read as follows:

"Dear niece,—At sight of this my first bill of ass-colts, give order that three out of the five I left at home in your custody, be delivered to Sancho Panza, my squire: which three colts I order to be delivered and paid for the like number received of him here in tale; and this, with his acquittance, shall be your discharge. Done in the heart of the Sierra Morena, the twenty-second of August, this present year ——."

"It is mighty well," said Sancho; "now you have only to sign it." "It wants no signing," said Don Quixote; "I need only put my cypher to it, which is the same thing, and is sufficient not only for three, but for three hundred asses." " I rely upon your worship," answered Sancho; " let me go and saddle Rozinante, and prepare to give me your blessing, for I intend to depart immediately, without staying to see the mad frolics you are about to commit; and I will tell quite enough to satisfy her." " At least, Sancho," said Don Quixote, " I wish, nay, it is necessary, and I will have thee see me naked, and perform a dozen or two frantic actions; for I shall dispatch them in less than half an hour: and having seen these with thine own eyes, thou mayest safely swear to those thou shalt add; for be assured thou wilt not relate so many as I intend to perform." " For the love of Heaven, dear sir," quoth Sancho, " let me not see your worship naked, for it will move my pity so much that I shall not be able to forbear weeping; and my head is so bad, after the tears I shed last night for the loss of poor Dapple, that I am in no condition at present to begin new lamentations. So, if your worship will have me an eye-witness to any of your antics, pray do them clothed, and with all speed, and let them be such as will stand you in most stead: though, indeed, there is no need of them—as I said before, it is only delaying my return with the news your worship so much desires and deserves. So let the Lady Dulcinea look to it; for if she does not answer as she should do, I solemnly protest I will fetch it out of her by dint of kicks and buffets; for it is a shame that so famous a knight-errant as your worship should run mad, without why or wherefore, for a ——: let not madam provoke me to speak out; or, before Heaven, I shall blab, and out with all by wholesale, though it spoil the market. I am pretty good at this sport: she does not know me; if she did, by my faith, we should be of one mind." " In truth, Sancho," said Don Quixote, " to all appearance thou art as mad as myself." " Not so," answered Sancho, " only a little more choleric. But, setting that aside, what has your worship to eat until my return? Are you to go upon the highway, to rob the shepherds, like Cardenio?" " Trouble not thyself about that," answered Don Quixote; " for were I otherwise provided, I should eat nothing but the herbs and fruits which here grow wild; for abstinence and other austerities are essential in this affair." " Now I think of it, sir," said Sancho, " how shall I be able to find my way back again to this bye-place?" " Observe and mark well the spot, and I will endeavour to remain near it," said Don Quixote; " and will, moreover, ascend some of the highest ridges to discover thee upon thy return. But the surest way not to miss me or lose thyself, will be to cut down some of the broom that abounds here, and scatter it here and there on the way to the plain, to serve as marks and tokens to guide thee on thy return, in imitation of Theseus' clue to the labyrinth."

Sancho Panza followed this counsel; and having provided himself with branches, he begged his master's blessing, and, not without many tears on both sides, took his leave of him; and mounting upon Rozinante, with especial charge from Don Quixote to regard him as he would his own proper person, he rode towards the plain, strewing the

Sancho Panza begged his master's blessing, and, not without many tears on both sides, took his leave of him.

boughs at intervals, as his master directed him. Thus he departed, although Don Quixote still importuned him to stay and see him perform if it were but a couple of his gambols. He had not gone above a hundred paces when he turned back and said, "Your worship, sir, said right that, to enable me to swear with a safe conscience, it would be proper I should at least see one of your mad tricks; though, in plain truth, I have seen enough in seeing you stay here." "Did I not tell thee so?" quoth Don Quixote: "stay but a moment, Sancho—I will dispatch them as quickly as you can say a *credo*." Then stripping off his clothes in all haste, without more ado he cut a couple of capers in the air, and as many tumbles heels over head. Sancho turned Rozinante about, fully satisfied that he might swear his master was stark mad: we will therefore leave him pursuing his journey until his return, which was speedy.

CHAPTER XXVI.

A continuation of the refinements practised by Don Quixote, as a lover, in the Sierra Morena.

THE history then recounting what the Knight of the Sorrowful Figure did when he found himself alone, informs us that, having finished his gambols, half-naked, and perceiving that Sancho was gone without caring to be witness of any more of his pranks, he mounted the top of a high rock, and there began to deliberate on a subject that he had often considered before, without coming to any resolution; and that was, which of the two was the best and most proper model for his imitation, Orlando in his furious fits, or Amadis in his melancholy moods: and thus he argued with himself: If Orlando was as good and valiant a knight as he is universally allowed to have been, where is the wonder? since, in fact, he was enchanted, and could only be slain by having a needle thrust into the sole of his foot; and therefore he always wore shoes with seven soles of iron. This contrivance, however, availed him nothing against Bernardo del Carpio, who knew the secret, and pressed him to death between his arms at Roncesvalles. But setting aside his valour, let us consider his madness, which was certainly occasioned by the discovery he made at the fountain, and by the intelligence given him by the shepherd that Angelica had proved faithless with Medoro, a little curly-pated Moor, page to Agramante. And if he knew this, and was convinced of his lady's infidelity, it was no wonder that he ran mad. But how can I imitate him in his frenzy without a similar cause? My Dulcinea del Toboso, I dare swear, never in all her life beheld a real and acknowledged Moor, and that she is this day as the mother that bore her; and I should do her a manifest wrong, if, suspecting otherwise, I should be seized with the same species of frenzy as that of Orlando Furioso. On the other side, I see that Amadis de Gaul, without losing his senses or having any raving fits, acquired a reputation equally high as a lover, since, finding himself disdained by the Lady Oriana, who commanded him not to appear in her presence until it was her pleasure, he only retired to the sterile rock, accompanied by a hermit, and there wept abundantly until Heaven succoured him in his great tribulation. Now, this being the case, why should I take the pains to strip myself naked, or molest these trees that never did me harm? Or wherefore should I disturb the water of these crystal streams, which are to furnish me with drink when I want it? All honour, then, to the memory of Amadis! and let him be the model of Don Quixote de la Mancha, of whom shall be said, what was said of another, that, if he did not achieve great things, he at least died in attempting them;

and though neither rejected nor disdained by my Dulcinea, it is sufficient that I am absent from her. Now, then, to the work. Come to my memory, ye deeds of Amadis, and instruct me where to begin the task of imitation! It now occurs to me that he prayed much—that will I also do." Whereupon he strung some large galls of a cork tree, which served him for a rosary; but he regretted exceedingly that there was no hermit to hear his confession and administer consolation to him. He thus passed the time, walking about, and writing, and graving on the barks of trees, or tracing in the fine sand, many verses of a plaintive kind, or in praise of his Dulcinea. Amongst those discovered afterwards, only the following were entire and legible:

> Ye lofty trees, with spreading arms,
>   The pride and shelter of the plain;
> Ye humbler shrubs and flowery charms,
>   Which here in springing glory reign!
> If my complaints may pity move,
> Hear the sad story of my love!
>   While with me here you pass your hours,
> Should you grow faded with my cares,
>   I 'll bribe you with refreshing showers;
> You shall be watered with my tears.
>   Distant, though present in idea
>   I mourn my absent Dulcinea
>   Del Toboso.
>
> Love's truest slave, despairing, chose
>   This lonely wild, this desert plain,
> This silent witness of the woes
>   Which he, though guiltless, must sustain.
> Unknowing why these pains he bears,
> He groans, he raves, and he despairs.
>   With lingering fires love racks my soul:
> In vain I grieve, in vain lament;
>   Like tortured fiends I weep, I howl,
> And burn, yet never can repent.
>   Distant, though present in idea,
>   I mourn my absent Dulcinea
>   Del Toboso.
>
> While I through honour's thorny ways
>   In search of distant glory rove,
> Malignant fate my toil repays
>   With endless woes and hopeless love.
> Thus I on barren rocks despair,
> And curse my stars, yet bless my fair.
>   Love, armed with snakes, has left his dart,
> And now does like a fury rave,
>   And scourge and sting on every part,
> And into madness lash his slave.
>   Distant, though present in idea,
>   I mourn my absent Dulcinea
>   Del Toboso.

The whimsical addition at the end of each stanza occasioned no small amusement to those who found the verses; for they concluded that Don

Quixote had thought that, unless to the name of "Dulcinea" he added "Del Toboso," the object of his praise would not be known—and they were right, as he afterwards confessed. He wrote many others, but only these three stanzas could be clearly made out. In such tender and melancholy occupations, sighing, or invoking the sylvan deities, the nymphs of the mountain streams, and the mournful echo, to listen and answer to his moan, he passed the time; and sometimes in gathering herbs to sustain himself until Sancho's return; who, if he had tarried three weeks instead of three days, the Knight of the Sorrowful Figure would have been so disfigured that he would not have been recognised by his own mother. Here, however, it will be proper to leave him, wrapped up in poetry and grief, to relate what happened to the squire during his embassy.

As soon as Sancho had gained the high-road, he directed his course immediately to Toboso, and the next day he came within sight of the inn where the misfortune of the blanket had befallen him, and, fancying himself again flying in the air, he felt no disposition to enter it, although it was then the hour of dinner, and he longed for something warm—all having been cold-treat with him for many days past. This inclination, nevertheless, drew him forcibly towards the inn; and, as he stood doubtful whether or not to enter, two persons came out, who immediately recognised him. "Pray, Signor Licentiate," said one to the other, "is not that Sancho Panza yonder on horseback, who, as our friend's housekeeper told us, accompanied her master as his squire?" "Truly it is," said the licentiate; "and that is our Don Quixote's horse." No wonder they knew him so well, for they were the priest and barber of his village, and the very persons who had tried and passed sentence of execution on the mischievous books. Being now certain it was Sancho Panza and Rozinante, and hoping to hear some tidings of Don Quixote, the priest went up to him, and calling him by his name, "Friend Sancho Panza," said he, "where have you left your master?" Sancho immediately knew them, and resolved to conceal the circumstances and place of Don Quixote's retreat; he therefore told them that his master was very busy in a certain place, about a certain affair of the greatest importance to himself, which he durst not discover for the eyes in his head. "No, no, Sancho," quoth the barber, "that story will not pass. If you do not tell us where he is, we shall conclude, as we suspect already, that you have murdered and robbed him, since you come thus upon his horse. See, then, that you produce the owner of that horse, or woe be to you!" "There is no reason why you should threaten me," quoth Sancho; "for I am not a man to rob or murder anybody. Let every man's fate kill him, or God who made him. My master is doing a certain penance much to his liking in the midst of yon mountains." He then, very freely and without hesitation, related to them in what state he had left him, the adventures that had befallen them, and how he was then carrying a letter to the Lady Dulcinea del Toboso—the daughter of Lorenzo Corchuelo, with whom his master was up to the ears in love.

They were both astonished at Sancho's report; and, though they already knew the nature of Don Quixote's derangement, yet every fresh instance of it was to them a new source of wonder. They begged of Sancho Panza to show them the letter he was carrying to the Lady Dulcinea del Toboso. He said it was written in a pocket-book, and that his master had ordered him to get it copied out upon paper at the first town he should arrive it. The priest said, if he would show it to him he would transcribe it in a very fair character. Sancho Panza put his hand into his bosom to take out the book, but found it not; nor could he have found it had he searched until this time, for it remained with Don Quixote, who had forgotten to give it to him. When Sancho found he had no book, he turned as pale as death; and, having felt again all over his body in great perturbation without success, he laid hold of his beard with both hands, and tore away half of it; and then gave himself sundry cuffs on the nose and mouth, bathing them all in blood. The priest and barber seeing this, asked him wherefore he treated himself so roughly. "Wherefore?" answered Sancho, "but that I have let slip through my fingers three ass-colts, each of them a castle!" "How so?" returned the barber. "I have lost the pocket-book," answered Sancho, "that contained the letter to Dulcinea, and a bill signed by my master, in which he ordered his niece to deliver to me three colts out of four or five he had at home." This led him to mention his loss of Dapple; but the priest bid him be of good cheer, telling him that when he saw his master he would engage him to renew the order upon paper in a regular way; for that one written in a pocket-book would not be accepted. Sancho was comforted by this assurance, and said that he did not care for the loss of the letter to Dulcinea, as he could almost say it by heart, so that they might write it down, where and when they pleased. "Repeat it, then, Sancho," quoth the barber, "and we will write it afterwards." Sancho then began to scratch his head, in order to fetch the letter to his remembrance: now he stood upon one foot, and then upon the other; sometimes he looked down upon the ground, and sometimes up to the sky: then, after biting off half a nail of one finger, and keeping his hearers long in expectation, he said, "The devil take all I remember of the letter; though at the beginning I believe it said, 'High and subterrane lady.'" "No," said the barber, "not *subterrane*, but superhumane, or sovereign lady." "Aye, so it was," said Sancho. "Then, if I do not mistake, it went on, 'the stabbed, and the waking, and the pierced, kisses your honour's hands, ungrateful and most regardless fair;' and then it said I know not what of 'health and sickness that he sent;' and so he went on, until at last he ended with 'thine till death, the Knight of the Sorrowful Figure.'"

They were both not a little diverted at Sancho's excellent memory, and commended it much, desiring him to repeat the letter twice more, that they also might get it by heart, in order to write it down in due time. Thrice Sancho repeated it, and thrice he added three thousand other extravagances: relating to them also many other things concerning his master, but not a word of the blanket. He informed them likewise how his lord, upon his return with a kind despatch from his lady Dulcinea del Toboso, was to set about endeavouring to become an emperor, or at least a king (for so it was concerted between them)— a thing that would be very easily done, considering the valour and strength of his arm; and when this was accomplished, his master was to marry him (as by that time he should, no doubt, be a widower), and give him to wife one of the empress's maids of honour, heiress to a large and rich territory on the mainland; for, as to islands, he was quite out of conceit with them. Sancho said all this with so much gravity, ever and anon wiping his nose, that they were amazed at the potency of Don Quixote's malady, which had borne along with it the senses also of this poor fellow. They would not themselves take the trouble to convince him of his folly, as it was of a harmless nature, and afforded them amusement; they therefore told him he should pray for his lord's health, since it was very possible and very practicable for him in process of time to become an emperor, as he said, or at least an archbishop, or something else of equal dignity. To which Sancho answered, " Gentlemen, if fortune should so order it that my master should take it into his head not to be an emperor, but an archbishop, I would fain know what archbishops-errant usually give to their squires? " " They usually give them," answered the priest, " some benefice or cure, or vergership, which brings them in a good penny rent, besides the perquisites of the altar, usually valued at as much more." " For this it will be necessary," replied Sancho, " that the squire be unmarried, and that he know, at least, the responses to the mass; and if so, woe is me! for I am married, and do not know my ABC. What will become of me if my master should have a mind to be an archbishop, and not an emperor, like other knights-errant? " " Be not uneasy, friend Sancho," said the barber, " for we will admonish and entreat your master, even to make it a case of conscience, to become an emperor, and not an archbishop;—indeed, it will suit him better, as he is more of a soldier than a scholar." " So I think," answered Sancho, " though I can affirm that he has a head-piece for everything; but for my part, I will pray Heaven to direct him to that which is best for him, and will enable him to do the most for me." " You talk like a wise man," said the priest, " and a good Christian: but we must now contrive to relieve your master from this unprofitable penance; and, therefore, let us go in to concert proper measures, and also to get our dinner, which by this time is ready." Sancho said they might go in, but that he should choose to stay without —he would tell them why another time; he begged them, however, to bring him out something warm to eat, and also some barley for Rozinante. Accordingly they left him and entered the inn, and soon after the barber returned to him with some food.

The curate and barber having deliberated together on the best means of accomplishing their purpose, a device occurred to the priest, exactly fitted to Don Quixote's humour, and likely to effect what they desired: which was, that he should perform himself the part of a damsel-errant, and the barber equip himself as her squire; in which disguise they should repair to Don Quixote; and the curate presenting himself as an afflicted and distressed lady, should beg a boon of him, which he, as a valorous knight-errant, could not do otherwise than grant; and this should be a request that he would accompany her whither she should lead him, to redress an injury done her by a discourteous knight; entreating him, at the same time, not to desire her to remove her mask, nor make any further inquiries concerning her, until he had done her justice on that wicked knight. He made no doubt but that Don Quixote would consent to any such terms, and they might thus get him away from that place and carry him home, where they would endeavour to find some remedy for his extraordinary malady.

CHAPTER XXVII.

How the priest and the barber put their design in execution, with other matters worthy to be recited in this history.

THE barber liked the priest's contrivance so well that they immediately began to carry it into execution. They borrowed a petticoat and head-dress from the landlady, leaving in pawn for them a new cassock belonging to the priest; and the barber made himself a huge beard of the tail of a pied ox, in which the innkeeper used to hang his comb. The hostess having asked them for what purpose they wanted those things, the priest gave her a brief account of Don Quixote's insanity, and the necessity of that disguise to draw him from his present retreat. The host and hostess immediately conjectured that this was the same person who had once been their guest, the maker of the balsam and the master of the blanketed squire; and they related to the priest what had passed between them, without omitting what Sancho had been so careful to conceal. In the meantime the landlady equipped the priest to admiration : she put him on a cloth petticoat, laid thick with stripes of black velvet, each the breadth of a span, all pinked and slashed; and a corset of green velvet, bordered with white satin, which, together with the petticoat, must have been made in the days of King Bamba. The priest would not consent to wear a woman's head-dress, but put on a little white quilted cap which he used as a nightcap, and bound one of his garters of black taffeta about his head, and with the other made a kind of veil, which covered his face and beard very well. He then pulled his hat over his face, which was so large that it served him for an umbrella, and, wrapping his cloak around him, he got upon his mule sideways like a woman. The barber mounted also, with a beard that reached to his girdle, of a colour between sorrel and white, being, as before said, made of the tail of a pied ox. They took leave of all, not excepting the good Maritornes, who promised, though a sinner, to pray over an entire rosary that Heaven might give them good success in so arduous and Christian a business as that which they had undertaken.

But scarcely had they got out of the inn, when the curate began to think he had done amiss, and that it was indecent for a priest to be so accoutred, although for so good a purpose; and acquainting the barber with his scruples, he begged him to exchange apparel, as it would better become him to personate the distressed damsel, and he would himself act the squire, as being a less profanation of his dignity; and, if he would not consent, he was determined to proceed no farther, though the devil should run away with Don Quixote. They were now joined by Sancho, who was highly diverted at their appearance. The barber consented to the proposed exchange; upon which the priest began to instruct him how to act his part, and what expressions to use to Don Quixote, in order to prevail upon him to accompany them, and leave the place of his penance. The barber assured him that, without his instructions, he would undertake to manage that point to a tittle. The dress, however, he would not put on until they came near to the place of Don Quixote's retreat. The priest then adjusted his beard, and they proceeded forward, guided by Sancho Panza, who on the way related to them their adventure with the madman whom they had encountered in the mountain, but said not a word about the portmanteau and its contents; for, with all his folly and simplicity, the rogue was somewhat covetous.

The next day they arrived at the place where Sancho had strewed the branches to ascertain the place where he had left his master; and, upon seeing them, he gave notice that they had entered the mountain pass, and would therefore do well to put on their disguise, if that had any concern with the delivery of his master. They had before told him that their disguise was of the utmost importance towards disengaging his master from the miserable life he had chosen, and that he must by no means tell him who they were: and if he should inquire, as no doubt he would, whether he had delivered the letter to Dulcinea, he should say he had; and that she, not being able to read or write, had answered by word of mouth, and commanded the knight, on pain of her displeasure, to repair to her immediately upon an affair of much importance: for with this, and what they intended to say themselves, they should certainly reconcile him to a better mode of life, and put him in the way of soon becoming an emperor or a king; as to an archbishop, he had nothing to fear on that subject. Sancho listened to all this, and imprinted it well on his memory, and gave them many thanks for promising to advise his lord to be an emperor, and not an archbishop; for he was persuaded that, in rewarding their squires, emperors could do more than archbishops-errant. He told them also it would be proper he should go before, to find him and deliver his lady's answer; for, perhaps, that alone would be sufficient to bring him out of that place, without further trouble. They agreed with Sancho, and determined to wait for his return with intelligence of his master. Sancho entered the mountain pass, and left them in a pleasant spot refreshed by a streamlet of clear water and shaded by rocks and overhanging foliage.

It was in the month of August, when in those parts the heats are

They borrowed a petticoat and head-dress from the landlady, and the barber made himself a huge beard of the tail of a pied ox.

violent, about three o'clock in the afternoon; on which account they found the situation very agreeable, and consented the more readily to wait there till Sancho's return. While they were reposing in the shade, a voice reached their ears, which, although unaccompanied by any instrument, sounded sweet and melodious. They were much surprised, since that was not a place where they might expect to hear fine singing: for, although it is common to tell of shepherds with melodious voices warbling over hills and dales, yet this is rather poetical fancy than plain truth. Besides, the verses they heard were not those of a rustic muse, but of refined and courtly invention, as will appear by the following stanzas:

> What causes all my grief and pain?
>   Cruel disdain.
> What aggravates my misery?
>   Accursed jealousy.
> How has my soul its patience lost?
>   By tedious absence crossed.

Alas! no balsam can be found
To heal the grief of such a wound,
When absence, jealousy, and scorn,
Have left me hopeless and forlorn.

What in my breast this grief could move?
     Neglected love.
What doth my fond desires withstand?
     Fate's cruel hand.
And what confirms my misery?
     Heaven's fixed decree.
Ah me! my boding fears portend
This strange disease my life will end:
For die I must, when three such foes,
Heav'n, fate, and love, my bliss oppose.

My peace of mind what can restore?
     Death's welcome hour.
What gains love's joys most readily?
     Fickle inconstancy.
Its pains what medicine can assuage?
     Wild frenzy's rage.
'T is therefore little wisdom, sure,
For such a grief to seek a cure,
That knows no better remedy
Than frenzy, death, inconstancy.

The hour, the season, the solitude, the voice, and the skill of the singer, all conspired to impress the auditors with wonder and delight, and they remained for some time motionless, in expectation of hearing more; but finding the silence continue, they resolved to see who it was who had sung so agreeably; and were again detained by the same voice, regaling their ears with this sonnet:

Friendship, thou hast with nimble flight
Exulting gained th' empyrean height,
In heaven to dwell, whilst here below
Thy semblance reigns in mimic show:
From thence to earth, at thy behest,
Descends fair peace, celestial guest!
Beneath whose veil of shining hue
Deceit oft lurks, concealed from view.
     Leave, friendship! leave thy heavenly seat,
Or strip thy livery off the cheat.
If still he wears thy borrowed smiles,
And still unwary truth beguiles,
Soon must this dark terrestrial ball
Into its first confusion fall.

The song ended with a deep sigh, and they again listened very attentively, in hopes of hearing more; but the music being changed into sobs and lamentations, they went in search of the unhappy person whose voice was no less excellent than his complaints were mournful. They had not gone far, when, turning the point of a rock, they perceived a man of the same stature and appearance that Sancho had described

Cardenio to them. The man expressed no surprise at the sight of them, but stood still, inclining his head upon his breast in a pensive posture, without again raising his eyes from the ground. The priest, who was a well-spoken man, being already acquainted with his misfortune, went up to him, and in few but very impressive words entreated him to forsake that miserable kind of life, and not hazard so great a misfortune as to lose it in that inhospitable place. Cardenio was then perfectly tranquil, and free from those outrageous fits with which he was so often seized; he likewise appeared to be sensible that the persons who now accosted him were unlike the inhabitants of those mountains: he was still more surprised to hear them speak of his concerns; and he replied, 'It is very evident to me, gentlemen, whoever you are, that Heaven, which succours the good, and often even the wicked, unworthy as I am, sends to me in this solitude, so remote from the commerce of human kind, persons who, representing to me by various and forcible arguments how irrational is my mode of life, endeavour to divert me from it; but not knowing as I do that by flying from this misery I shall be plunged into worse, they doubtless take me for a fool or a madman; and no wonder, for I am myself aware that, so intense and overwhelming is the sense of my misery, that I sometimes become like a stone, void of all knowledge and sensation. I know this to be true, by the traces I leave of my frenzy; but I can only lament in vain, curse my fortune, and seek an excuse for my extravagance by imparting the cause to all who will listen to me, since none who are acquainted with my situation could fail to pardon my conduct and compassionate my sufferings. And, gentlemen, if you come with the same intention that others have done, before you proceed any further in your prudent counsel, I beseech you to hear my sad story; for then you will probably spare yourselves the trouble of endeavouring to find consolation for an evil which has no remedy."

The two friends being desirous of hearing his own account of himself, entreated him to indulge them, assuring him they would do nothing but what was agreeable to him, either in the way of remedy or advice. The unhappy young man began his melancholy story almost in the same words in which he had related it to Don Quixote and the goatherd some few days before, when, on account of Master Elisabat, and Don Quixote's zeal in defending the honour of knight-errantry, the tale was abruptly suspended; but Cardenio's sane interval now enabled him to conclude it quietly. On coming to the circumstance of the love-letter which Don Fernando found between the leaves of the book of Amadis de Gaul, he said he remembered it perfectly well, and that it was as follows:

" 'Each day I discover in you qualities which raise you in my esteem; and, therefore, if you would put it in my power to discharge my obligations to you without prejudice to my honour, you may easily do it. I have a father who knows you, and has an affection for me; who will never force my inclinations, and will comply with whatever you can justly desire, if you really have that value for me which you profess, and which I trust you have.'

"This letter made me resolve to demand Lucinda in marriage, as I have already related, and was one of those which pleased Don Fernando so much. It was this letter, also, which made him determine upon my ruin before my design could be effected. I told Don Fernando that Lucinda's father expected that the proposal should come from mine, but that I durst not mention it to him, lest he should refuse his consent: not that he was ignorant of Lucinda's exalted merits, which might ennoble any family of Spain, but because I had understood from him that he was desirous I should not marry until it should be seen what Duke Ricardo would do for me. In short, I told him that I had not courage to speak to my father about it, being full of vague apprehensions and sad forebodings. In reply to all this, Don Fernando engaged to induce my father to propose me to the father of Lucinda. O ambitious Marius! cruel Catiline! wicked Scylla! crafty Galalon! perfidious Vellido! vindictive Julian! O covetous Judas! Cruel, wicked, and crafty traitor! what injury had been done thee by a poor wretch who so frankly disclosed to thee the secrets of his heart? Wherein had I offended thee? Have I not ever sought the advancement of thy interest and honour? But why do I complain?—miserable wretch that I am! For when the stars are adverse, what is human power? Who could have thought that Don Fernando, noble and generous, obliged by my services, and secure of success wherever his amorous inclinations led him, should take such cruel pains to deprive me of my single ewe-lamb? But no more of these unavailing reflections: I will now resume the broken thread of my sad story.

"Don Fernando, thinking my presence an obstacle to the execution of his treacherous design, resolved to send me to his elder brother for money to pay for six horses, which he bought merely for a pretence to get me out of the way, that he might the more conveniently execute his diabolical purpose. Could I foresee such treachery? Could I even suspect it? Surely not: on the contrary, well satisfied with his purchase, I cheerfully consented to depart immediately. That night I had an interview with Lucinda, and told her what had been agreed upon between Don Fernando and myself, assuring her of my hopes of a successful result. She, equally unsuspicious of Don Fernando, desired me to return speedily, since she believed the completion of our wishes was only deferred until proposals should be made to her father by mine. I know not whence it was, but, as she spoke, her eyes filled with tears, and some sudden obstruction in her throat prevented her articulating another word. I was surprised at her unusual emotion, for we generally conversed together with pleasure, unalloyed by tears, sighs, jealousy, suspicion, or alarms—I expatiating upon my good fortune in possessing such a mistress; and she kindly commending in me what she thought worthy of commendation. We amused each other also by the little concerns of our neighbours and acquaintance; and my presumption never extended further than to seize, by force, one of her snowy hands, and press it to my lips as well as the narrowness of the iron gate between us would permit. But the night preceding the doleful day of my departure she wept, sighed, and abruptly withdrew, leaving me full of surprise and trepidation at witnessing such uncommon indications of grief and tenderness in my Lucinda. Still I cherished my hopes, and ascribed all to the excess of her tenderness for me, and the sorrow natural in lovers upon separation. I set out upon my journey sad and pensive, my soul full of gloomy thoughts and fears—manifest presages of the sad fate in store for me.

" I executed my commission to Don Fernando's brother, by whom I was well received, but not soon dismissed; for, to my grief, he ordered me to wait eight days, and to keep out of his father's sight, because his brother had desired that a certain sum of money might be sent to him without the duke's knowledge. All this was a contrivance of the false Fernando; and I felt disposed to resist the injunction, as it seemed to me impossible to support life so many days absent from Lucinda, especially having left her in such a state of dejection. Nevertheless, I did obey, like a good servant, although at the expense of my health. But four days after my arrival a man came in quest of me with a letter, which by the superscription I knew to be from Lucinda. I opened it with alarm, convinced it must be something extraordinary that had induced her to write. Before I read it I made some inquiries of the messenger. He told me that passing accidentally through a street in the town, a very beautiful lady, with tears in her eyes, called to him from a window, and said to him, in great agitation, ' Friend, if you are a Christian, I beg of you, for the love of Heaven, to carry this letter with all expedition to the place and person to whom it is directed : in so doing you will perform an act of charity; and to supply you with the necessary expense, take what is tied up in this handkerchief.' So saying, she threw the handkerchief out of the window, which contained a hundred reals, and this gold ring, with the letter I have given you. She saw me take up the letter and the handkerchief, and assure her by signs that I would do what she commanded, and she then quitted the window. Finding myself so well paid for the trouble, and knowing by the superscription it was for you, sir; induced, moreover, by the tears of that beautiful lady, I resolved to trust no other person, but deliver it with my own hands : and within sixteen hours I have performed the journey, which you know is eighteen leagues.' While the grateful messenger thus spoke, I hung upon his words, my legs trembling so that I could scarcely stand. At length I opened the letter, which contained these words :

" ' The promise Don Fernando gave you to intercede with your father he has fulfilled, more for his own gratification than your interest. Know, sir, that he has demanded me to wife ; and my father, allured by the advantage he thinks Don Fernando possesses over you, has accepted this proposal so eagerly that the marriage is to be solemnized two days hence, and with so much privacy that, except Heaven, a few of our own family are alone to witness it. Conceive my situation ! and think whether you ought not to return. Whether I love you or not the event will prove. Heaven grant this may come to your hand before mine be compelled to join his who breaks his promised faith !'

" I set out immediately, without waiting for any other answer or the money; for now I plainly saw it was not the purchase of horses, but the indulgence of his pleasure, that had induced Don Fernando to send me to his brother. My rage against Don Fernando, and the fear of losing the rich reward of my long service and affection, gave wings to my speed; and the next day I reached our town, at the moment favourable for an interview with Lucinda. I went privately, having left my mule with the honest man who brought me the letter: and fortune was just then so propitious that I found Lucinda at the gate, the constant witness of our loves. We saw each other—but how? Who is there in the world that can boast of having fathomed and thoroughly penetrated the intricate and ever-changing nature of woman? Certainly none. As soon as Lucinda saw me she said, 'Cardenio, I am in my bridal habit: they are now waiting for me in the hall—the treacherous Don Fernando and my covetous father, with some others, who shall sooner be witnesses of my death than of my nuptials. Be not afflicted, my friend; but endeavour to be present at this sacrifice, which, if my arguments cannot avert, I carry a dagger about me, which can oppose a more effectual resistance, by putting an end to my life, and will give you a convincing proof of the affection I have ever borne you.' I answered with confusion and precipitation, 'Let your actions, madam, prove the truth of your words. If you carry a dagger to secure your honour, I carry a sword to defend you, or kill myself, if fortune proves adverse.' I do not believe she heard all I said, being hastily called away, for the bridegroom waited for her. Here the night of my sorrow closed in upon me! here set the sun of my happiness! My eyes were clouded in darkness, and my brain was disordered. I was irresolute whether to enter her house, and seemed bereaved of the power to move; but, recollecting how important my presence might be on that occasion, I exerted myself, and hastened thither. Being perfectly acquainted with all the avenues, and the whole household engaged, I escaped observation, and concealed myself in the recess of a window in the hall, behind the hangings, where two pieces of tapestry met, whence I could see all that passed. Who can describe the flutterings of my heart, and my various sensations, as I stood there? The bridegroom entered the hall, in his usual dress, accompanied by a cousin of Lucinda; and no other person was present, except the servants of the house. Soon after, from a dressing-room, came forth Lucinda, accompanied by her mother and two of her own maids, adorned in the extreme of courtly splendour. The agony and distraction I endured allowed me not to observe the particulars of her dress: I remarked only the colours, which were carnation and white, and the precious stones that glittered on every part of her attire—surpassed, however, by the singular beauty of her fair and golden tresses, in the splendour of which the brilliance of her jewels and the blaze of the surrounding lights seemed to be lost. O memory, thou mortal enemy of my repose! wherefore now recall to me the incomparable beauty of that adored enemy of mine! Were it not better, thou cruel faculty! to represent to my imagination her conduct at that period —that, moved by so flagrant an injury, I may strive, if not to avenge it, at least to end this life of pain! Be not weary, gentlemen, of these digressions; for my misfortunes are not such as can be related briefly and methodically, since every circumstance appears to me of importance."

The priest assured him that, far from being tired of listening to him, they took great pleasure in his minutest details, which merited no less attention than the principal parts of his story.

" I say, then," continued Cardenio, "that, being all assembled in the hall, the priest entered, and having taken them both by the hand, in order to perform what is necessary on such occasions, when he came to these words—'Will you, Signora Lucinda, take Signor Don Fernando, who is here present, for your lawful husband, as our holy mother the Church commands?'—I thrust out my head and neck through the tapestry, and with attentive ears and distracted soul awaited Lucinda's reply, as the sentence of my death or the confirmation of my life. Oh that I had then dared to venture forth, and to have cried aloud, ' Ah, Lucinda, Lucinda! beware what you do; consider what you owe to me! Remember that you are mine, and cannot belong to another! Be assured that in pronouncing *Yes*, you will instantly destroy me! Ah, traitor Don Fernando! ravisher of my glory, death of my life! what is it thou wouldst have? to what dost thou pretend? Reflect, that as a Christian thou canst not accomplish thy purpose; for Lucinda is my wife, and I am her husband.' Ah, fool that I am! now I am absent, I can say what I ought to have said, but did not! Now that I have suffered myself to be robbed of my soul's treasure, I am cursing the thief, on whom I might have revenged myself if I had been then as prompt to act as I am now to complain! I was then a coward and a fool; no wonder, therefore, if I now die ashamed, repentant, and mad.

" The priest stood expecting Lucinda's answer, who paused for a long time; and when I thought she would draw forth the dagger in defence of her honour, or make some declaration which might redound to my advantage, I heard her say in a low and faint voice, ' I will.' Don Fernando said the same, and the ring being put on, they remained tied in an indissoluble band. The bridegroom approached to embrace his bride; and she, laying her hand on her heart, fainted in the arms of her mother. Imagine my condition after that fatal *Yes*, by which my hopes were frustrated, Lucinda's vows and promises broken, and I for ever deprived of all chance of happiness. I was totally confounded—I thought myself abandoned by heaven and earth; the air denying me breath for my sighs, and the water moisture for my tears : fire alone supplied me with rage and jealousy. On Lucinda's fainting, all were in confusion; and her mother, unlacing her bosom to give her air, discovered in it a folded paper, which Don Fernando instantly seized, and read it by one of the flambeaux; after which he sat himself down in a chair, apparently full of thought, and without attending to the exertions made to recover his bride.

" During this general consternation, I departed, indifferent whether I was seen or not; but determined, if seen, to act so desperate a part that all the world should know the just indignation of my breast, by the chastisement of the false Don Fernando, and of the fickle though swooning traitress. But my fate, to reserve me for greater evils, if greater can possibly exist, ordained that at that juncture I had the use of my understanding, which has since failed me; and instead of seizing the opportunity to revenge myself on my cruel enemies, I condemned myself to a more severe fate than I could have inflicted on them; for what is sudden death, to a protracted life of anguish? In short, I quitted the house; and returning to the place where I had left the mule, I mounted and rode out of the town, not daring, like another Lot, to look behind me; and when I found myself alone on the plain, concealed by the darkness of the night, the silence inviting my lamentations, I gave vent to a thousand execrations on Lucinda and Don Fernando, as if that, alas! would afford me any satisfaction for the wrongs I had sustained. I called her cruel, false, and ungrateful; and, above all, mercenary, since the wealth of my enemy had seduced her affections from me. But, amidst all these reproaches, I sought to find excuses for her submission to parents whom she had ever been accustomed implicitly to obey; especially as they offered her a husband with such powerful attractions. Then, again, I considered that she need not have been ashamed of avowing her engagement to me, since, had it not been for Don Fernando's proposals, her parents could not have desired a more suitable connexion; and I thought how easily she could have declared herself mine when on the point of giving her hand to my rival. In fine, I concluded that her love had been less than her ambition, and she had thus forgotten those promises by which she had beguiled my hopes and cherished my passion.

"In the utmost perturbation of mind, I journeyed on the rest of the night, and at daybreak reached these mountains, over which I wandered three days more, without road or path, until I came to a valley not far hence; and inquiring of some shepherds for the most rude and solitary part, they directed me to this place, where I instantly came, determined to pass here the remainder of my life. Among these crags, my mule fell down dead through weariness and hunger, or, what is more probable, to be relieved of so useless a burden; and thus was I left, extended on the ground, famished and exhausted, neither hoping nor caring for relief. How long I continued in this state I know not; but at length I got up, without the sensation of hunger, and found near me some goatherds, who had undoubtedly relieved my wants. They told me of the condition in which they found me, and of many wild and extravagant things that I had uttered, clearly proving the derangement of my intellect; and I am conscious that since then I have not been always quite right, but have committed a thousand extravagances, tearing my garments, howling aloud through these solitudes, cursing my fortune, and repeating in vain the name of my beloved. When my senses return, I find myself so weary and bruised that I can scarcely move. My usual abode is in the hollow of a cork tree, large enough to enclose this wretched body. The goatherds charitably supply me with food, laying it on the rocks, and in places where they think I may find it. At other times, as they have informed me in my lucid intervals, I come into the road, and take from the shepherds by force those provisions which they would freely give me. Thus I pass my miserable life, waiting until it shall please Heaven to bring it to a period, or erase from my memory the beauty and treachery of Lucinda and the perfidy of Don Fernando; otherwise, Heaven have mercy on me! for I feel no power to change my mode of life.

"This, gentlemen, is my melancholy tale. Trouble not yourselves, I beseech you, to counsel or persuade me; for it will be of no more avail than to prescribe medicines to the patient who rejects them. I will have no health without Lucinda; and since she has pleased to give herself to another when she was or ought to have been mine, let me have the pleasure of indulging myself in unhappiness, since I might have been happy if I had pleased. She, by her mutability, would have irretrievably undone me; I, by endeavouring to destroy myself, would satisfy her will, and I shall stand an example to posterity of having been the only unfortunate person whom the possibility of receiving consolation could not comfort, but plunged in still greater afflictions and misfortunes; for I verily believe they will not have an end even in death itself."

Here Cardenio terminated the long recital of his story, no less full of misfortunes than of love; and just as the priest was preparing to say something to him by way of consolation, he was prevented by a voice which in mournful accents said what will be related in the fourth book of this history, for at this point the wise and judicious historian Cid Hamet Benengeli puts an end to the third.

BOOK IV.

CHAPTER XXVIII.

Which treats of the new and agreeable adventure which befell the priest and the barber in the Sierra Morena.

How HAPPY and fortunate was that age in which the most daring knight Don Quixote de la Mancha was ushered into the world! since, in consequence of his honourable resolution to revive the long-neglected and almost extinguished order of knight-errantry, we are regaled in these our times, so barren of entertainment, not only by his own delightful history, but also by the tales and episodes contained in it, which are scarcely less agreeable, ingenious, and true than the narration itself; the thread of which, being already carded, twisted, and reeled, may now be resumed.

As narrated in the last chapter, the priest was preparing to say something consolatory to Cardenio, when he was prevented by a voice uttering these mournful accents :

"O heavens! have I then at last found a place which may afford a secret grave for this wretched body? Yes—if the silence of this rocky desert deceive me not, here I may die in peace. Ah, woe is me! Here at least I may freely pour forth my lamentations to Heaven, and shall be less wretched than among men, from whom I should in vain seek counsel, redress, or consolation."

These words being distinctly heard by the curate and his companions, they rose up to seek the mourner, who they knew by the voice to be near them; and they had not gone many paces when they espied a youth dressed like a peasant sitting under an ash tree at the foot of a rock. They could not at first see his face, as he was stooping to bathe his feet in a rivulet which ran by. They drew near so silently that he did not hear them; and while he continued thus employed, they stood in admiration at the beauty and whiteness of his feet, which looked like pure crystal among the pebbles of the brook, and did not seem formed for breaking clods or following the plough, as might have been expected from the apparel of the youth. The curate, who went foremost, made a sign to the others to crouch down and conceal themselves behind some fragments of a rock, whence they might watch his motions. He was clad in a drab-coloured jerkin, girded closely round his body with a piece of white linen; his breeches, gaiters, and his cap were all of the

The lovely maiden looked up on hearing them approach, and with both her hands putting her hair from before her eyes, she saw the intruders.

same colour. His gaiters being now pulled up, exposed his legs, which in colour resembled alabaster. After bathing his lovely feet, he wiped them with a handkerchief which he drew from under his cap; and in doing this he displayed a face of such exquisite beauty, that Cardenio said to the priest, in a low voice, " Since it is not Lucinda, this can be no human creature." The youth then took off his cap, and shaking his head, a profusion of hair that Apollo himself might envy fell over his shoulders—and betrayed the woman, and the most beautiful one that two of the party had ever beheld. Cardenio declared that Lucinda alone could be compared to her. Her long and golden tresses covered not only her shoulders, but nearly her whole body; and her snowy fingers served her for a comb. Her beauty made the three spectators impatient to find out who she was, and they now determined to accost her. The lovely maiden looked up on hearing them approach, and with both her hands putting her hair from before her eyes, she saw the intruders; upon which she hastily rose, and snatched up a bundle, apparently of clothes, which lay near her; and without staying to put on her shoes or bind up her hair, she fled with precipitation and alarm; but had scarcely gone six paces, when, her tender feet being unable to bear the sharp stones, she fell to the ground. The priest now addressed himself to her. " Do not fly, madam, I entreat you; for we only desire to serve you; indeed, there is no reason why you should attempt so inconvenient a flight." Surprised and confounded, she made no reply. The priest then, taking her hand, proceeded to say, " Your hair reveals to us, madam, what your habit would conceal; and it is manifest that no slight cause has induced you to disguise your beauty in such unworthy attire, and brought you to a solitude like this, where it has been our good fortune to find you; and I hope, dear madam, or, if you please, dear sir, that you will dismiss every alarm on our account, and give us an opportunity of rendering you some assistance."

When the priest thus addressed her, the disguised maiden stood like one stupefied, her eyes fixed on them, without answering one word—like a country clown when he is suddenly surprised by some new sight. At length, after the priest had said more to the same purpose, she heaved a deep sigh, and breaking the silence, said, " Since even these retired mountains have failed to conceal me, and my hair has betrayed me, I can no longer attempt to disguise myself. Indeed, gentlemen, I feel very grateful for your kind offers to serve me, but such is my unfortunate situation that commiseration is all I can expect; nevertheless, that I may not suffer in your opinion from the strange circumstances under which you have discovered me, I will tell you the cause without reserve, whatever pain it may give me." She spoke with so much grace, and in so sweet a voice, that they were still more charmed with her, and repeated their kind offers and solicitations for her confidence. Having first modestly put on her shoes and stockings, and gathered up her hair, she seated herself upon a flat stone, her three auditors placing themselves around her; and after some efforts to restrain her tears, she began her story in this manner :

" There is a town in the province of Andalusia, from which a duke takes his title, that makes him a grandee of Spain. This duke has two sons : the elder heir to his estate, and apparently to his virtues ; the younger heir to I know not what, unless it be to the treachery of Vellido and the deceitfulness of Galalon. My parents are vassals to this nobleman, and are very rich, though of humble birth, otherwise I should not be in this wretched state; for their want of rank is probably the cause of all my misfortunes. Not, indeed, that there is anything disgraceful in the condition of my family—they are farmers, simple, honest people, and such as are called old rusty Christians,* of that class which by their wealth and handsome way of living are by degrees acquiring the name of gentlemen.

" But what they prized above rank or riches was their daughter, sole

---

* That is, original Spaniards, without mixture of Moorish or Jewish blood for several generations; such only being qualified for titles of honour.

heiress of their fortune; and I was always treated by them with the utmost indulgence and affection. I was the light of their eyes, the staff of their old age, and, under Heaven, the sole object of all their hopes. And, as I was mistress of their affections, so was I of all they possessed. To me they entrusted the management of the household: through my hands passed the accounts of all that was sown and reaped: the oil-mills, the wine-presses, the numerous herds, flocks, and the bee-hives—everything, in short, was entrusted to my care. I was both steward and mistress, and always performed my duties to their satisfaction. The leisure hours that remained I passed in sewing, spinning, or making lace, and sometimes in reading good books; or, if my spirits required the relief of music, I had recourse to my gittern. Such was the life I led in my father's house: and I have not been so particular in describing it out of ostentation, but that you may know how undeservedly I have been cast from that happy state into my present misery. Thus I passed my time, constantly occupied and in retirement, seen only, as I imagined, by our own servants; for when I went to mass it was early in the morning, accompanied by my mother, and so closely veiled that my eyes saw no more ground than the space which my foot covered. Yet the eyes of love, or rather of idleness, which are like those of a lynx, discovered me. Don Fernando, the younger son of the duke, whom I mentioned to you"—she had no sooner named Don Fernando, than Cardenio's colour changed, and he was so violently agitated that the priest and the barber were afraid that he would be seized with one of those paroxysms of frenzy to which he was subject. But he remained quiet, fixing his eyes attentively on the country maid, well conjecturing who she was; while she, not observing the emotions of Cardenio, continued her story, saying: "No sooner had he seen me, than (as he afterwards declared) he conceived for me a violent affection—but, to shorten the account of my misfortunes, I pass over in silence the devices Don Fernando employed to make his passion known to me. He bribed all our servants: he offered presents to my relations: every day was a festival in our streets; and at night nobody could sleep for serenades. Infinite were the *billets-doux* that came, I knew not how, to my hands, filled with amorous declarations and expressions of kindness, containing more promises and oaths than letters. All these efforts I resisted: not that the gallantry and solicitations of Don Fernando were displeasing to me; for I confess that I felt flattered and gratified by the attentions of a gentleman of his high rank; besides, women are always pleased to be admired. However, I was supported by a sense of virtue, and the good advice of my parents, who told me that they relied on my virtue and prudence, and at the same time begged me to consider the inequality between myself and Don Fernando, and to suspect, whatever he might say to the contrary, that it was his own pleasure, not my happiness, that he had in view; and if I would consent to raise a barrier against his unworthy projects, they would engage immediately to find a suitable match for me. Thus cautioned, I maintained the utmost reserve towards Don Fernando, and never gave him the least encouragement either by

look or word; but my behaviour only increased his brutal passion—
love I cannot call it; for had he truly loved me, you would have been
spared this sad tale.

"Don Fernando, having discovered my parents' intentions for my
security, was determined to defeat them; and one night, as I was in my
chamber, the door fast locked, and only my maid present, he suddenly
stood before me. Terrified at his unexpected appearance, I was deprived
of the power of utterance, and, all my strength failing me, he caught
me in his arms. The traitor then pleaded by sighs and tears, and with
such an appearance of truth, that I, a poor simple creature, without
experience, began to give some credit to him, though I was far from
being moved to any criminal compassion. When I was sufficiently
recovered to speak, I exerted myself, and said to him, 'If my life
depended on the sacrifice of my honour, I would not preserve it on
such terms; and though within your grasp, you have no power over
my mind. I am your vassal—not your slave. Your rank does not give
you the privilege to insult me, who have an equal claim to self-respect
with yourself. I despise your riches, and distrust your words; neither
am I to be moved by your sighs and tears. Had I been thus solicited
by one who had obtained the sanction of my parents, and honourably
demanded my hand, I might have listened to proposals—but to no others
than those of a lawful husband.'

"'If that be all, beautiful Dorothea!' said the treacherous man,
'here I pledge to you my hand; and let all-seeing Heaven and that
image of our Lady witness the agreement!'"

When Cardenio heard her call herself Dorothea, he was confirmed in
his conjecture; but he would not interrupt the story, being desirous to
hear the event of what in part he knew already; and he only said,
"What, madam! is your name Dorothea? I have heard of one of
that name whose misfortunes much resemble yours. But proceed;
another time I may tell you things that will equally excite your wonder
and compassion." Dorothea, struck by Cardenio's words, and by his
strange and tattered dress, entreated him, if he knew anything of her
affairs, to tell her without delay; for fortune had still left her courage
to bear any disaster that might befall her, being certain that nothing
could increase her misery. "I should be sorry to say anything that
would do so, madam," replied Cardenio; "nor is it necessary for me to
speak at present."

Dorothea proceeded: "Don Fernando then took up the holy image,
and called upon it to witness our espousals: pledging himself by the
most solemn vows to become my husband, notwithstanding my entreaties
that he would consider the displeasure of his family, and other dis-
advantages that might result from so unequal an union. All that I
urged was of no avail, since it cost him nothing to make promises
which he never meant to perform. Being in some degree moved by
his perseverance, I began to consider that I should not be the first of
lowly birth who had been elevated by her beauty to rank, and that such
good fortune should not be lightly rejected. I reflected also that my

reputation would infallibly suffer by this visit, in spite of my innocence; and, alas! above all I was moved by his insinuating manners and tender protestations, which might well have softened a harder heart than mine. I called my maid to bear testimony to his plighted faith — again he repeated the most solemn vows, attesting new saints to hear them, and thus he finally succeeded in becoming a perjured traitor.

"On the morning that followed that fatal night, Don Fernando quitted me without reluctance: he assured me, indeed, of his truth and honour, but not with the warmth and vehemence of the preceding night; and at parting he drew a valuable ring from his finger, and put it upon mine. Whatever his sensations might have been, I remained confused and almost distracted. I knew not whether good or harm had befallen me, and was uncertain whether I should chide my maid for her treachery in admitting Don Fernando to my chamber. That perfidious man visited me but once more, although access was free to him, as I had become his wife. Months passed away, and in vain I watched for his coming; yet he was in the town, and every day amusing himself with hunting. What melancholy days and hours were those to me! for I began to doubt his fidelity. Then my damsel heard those reproofs for her presumption which she had before escaped. I long strove to hide my tears, and so to guard my looks that my parents might not see and inquire into the cause of my wretchedness; but suddenly my forbearance was at an end, with all regard to delicacy and fame, upon the intelligence reaching me that Don Fernando was married, in a neighbouring village, to a beautiful young lady, of some rank and fortune, named Lucinda."—Cardenio heard the name of Lucinda, at first, only with signs of indignation, but soon after a flood of tears burst from his eyes. Dorothea, however, pursued her story, saying, "When this sad news reached my ears, my heart, instead of being chilled by it, was so incensed and inflamed with rage, that I could scarcely forbear rushing into the streets and proclaiming the baseness and treachery I had experienced. But I became more tranquil after forming a project, which I executed the same night. I borrowed this apparel of a shepherd swain in my father's service, whom I entrusted with my secret, and begged him to attend me in my pursuit of Don Fernando. He assured me it was a rash undertaking; but finding me resolute, he said he would go with me to the end of the world. Immediately I packed up some of my own clothes, with money and jewels, and at night secretly left the house, attended only by my servant and a thousand anxious thoughts, and travelled on foot to the town where I expected to find my husband; impatient to arrive, if not in time to prevent his perfidy, to reproach him for it.

"I inquired where the parents of Lucinda lived; and the first person to whom I addressed myself told me more than I desired to hear. He directed me to the house, and gave me an account of all that had happened at the young lady's marriage. He told me also that on the night Don Fernando was married to Lucinda, after she had pronounced the fatal *Yes*, she fell into a swoon; and the bridegroom, in unclasping her bosom to give her air, found a paper written by herself, in which she affirmed that she could not be wife to Don Fernando because she was already betrothed to Cardenio (who, as the man told me, was a gentlemen of the same town), and that she had pronounced her assent to Don Fernando merely in obedience to her parents. The paper also revealed her intention to kill herself as soon as the ceremony was over, which was confirmed by a poniard they found concealed upon her. Don Fernando was so enraged to find himself thus mocked and slighted, that he seized hold of the same poniard, and would certainly have stabbed her, had he not been prevented by those present; whereupon he immediately quitted the place. When Lucinda revived, she confessed to her parents the engagement she had formed with Cardenio, who, it was suspected, had witnessed the ceremony, and had hastened from the city in despair; for he left a paper expressing his sense of the wrong he had suffered, and declaring his resolution to fly from mankind for ever.

" All this was publicly known, and the general subject of conversation; especially when it appeared that Lucinda also was missing from her father's house—a circumstance that overwhelmed her family with grief, but revived my hopes; for I flattered myself that Heaven had thus interposed to prevent the completion of Don Fernando's second marriage, in order to touch his conscience and to restore him to a sense of duty and honour. These illusive hopes enabled me to endure a life which is now become insupportable to me.

" In this situation, undecided what course to take, I heard myself proclaimed by the public crier, offering a great reward for discovering me, and describing my person and dress. It was also reported that I had eloped from my father's house with the lad that attended me. I was stung to the soul to find how very low I had fallen in public opinion; and, urged by the fear of discovery, I instantly left the city, and at night took refuge among these mountains. But it is truly said one evil produces another, and misfortunes never come singly; for my servant, hitherto so faithful, took advantage of this solitary place, and, dismissing all regard either to God or his mistress, began to make love to me; and, on my answering him as he deserved, he would have used force, but merciful Heaven favoured me, and endued me with strength to push him down a precipice, where I left him, whether dead or alive I know not, for, in spite of terror and fatigue, I fled from the spot with the utmost speed. After this I engaged myself in the service of a shepherd, and have lived for some months among these wilds, always endeavouring to be abroad, lest I should betray myself. Yet all my care was to no purpose, for my master at length discovered that I was not a man, and the same evil thoughts sprang up in his breast that had possessed my servant. Lest I might not find the same means at hand to free myself from violence, I sought for security in flight, and have endeavoured to hide myself among these rocks. Here, with incessant sighs and tears, I implore Heaven to have pity on me, and either alleviate my misery or put an end to my life in this desert, that no traces may remain of so wretched a creature."

CHAPTER XXIX.

Which treats of the beautiful Dorothea's discretion; with other very ingenious and entertaining particulars.

"This, gentlemen," added Dorothea, "is my tragical story: think whether the sighs and tears which you have witnessed have not been more than justified. My misfortunes, as you will confess, are incapable of a remedy; and all I desire of you is to advise me how to live without the continual dread of being discovered: for although I am certain of a kind reception from my parents, so overwhelmed am I with shame that I choose rather to banish myself for ever from their sight than appear before them the object of such hateful suspicions."

Here she was silent, while her blushes and confusion sufficiently manifested the shame and agony of her soul. Her auditors were much affected by her tale, and the curate was just going to address her, when Cardenio interrupted him, saying, "You, madam, then, are the beautiful Dorothea, only daughter of the rich Clenardo?" Dorothea stared at hearing her father named by such a miserable-looking object, and she asked him who he was, since he knew her father. "I am that hapless Cardenio," he replied, "who also suffers from the base author of your misfortunes, reduced, as you now behold, to nakedness and misery— deprived even of reason! Yes, Dorothea, I heard that fatal *Yes* pronounced by Lucinda, and, unable to bear my anguish, I fled precipitately from her house. Amidst these mountains I thought to have terminated my wretched existence; but the account you have just given has inspired me with hopes that Heaven may still have happiness in store for us. Lucinda has avowed herself to be mine, and therefore cannot wed another; Don Fernando, being yours, cannot have Lucinda. Let us, then, my dear lady, indulge the hope that we may both yet recover our own, since it is not absolutely lost. Indeed, I swear to you that, although I leave it to Heaven to avenge my own injuries, your claims will I assert; nor will I leave you until I have obliged Don Fernando, either by argument or my sword, to do you justice."

Dorothea would have thrown herself at the feet of Cardenio, to express her gratitude to him, had he not prevented her. The licentiate too commended his generous determination, and entreated them both to accompany him to his village, where they might consult on the most proper measures to be adopted in the present state of their affairs; a proposal to which they thankfully acceded. The barber, who had hitherto been silent, now joined in expressing his good wishes to them; he also briefly related the circumstances which had brought them to that place; and when he mentioned the extraordinary insanity of Don

Quixote, Cardenio had an indistinct recollection of having had some altercation with the knight, but could not remember whence it arose.

They were now interrupted by the voice of Sancho Panza, who, not finding them where he left them, began to call out loudly : they went instantly to meet him, and were eager in their inquiries after Don Quixote. He told them that he had found him naked to his shirt, feeble, wan, and half dead with hunger, sighing for his lady Dulcinea ; and though he had informed him that it was her express desire that he should leave that place and repair to Toboso, where she expected him, his answer was that he positively would not appear before her beauty until he had performed exploits that might render him worthy of her favour : if his master, he added, persisted in that humour, he would run a risk of never becoming an emperor, as in honour bound ; nor even an archbishop, which was the least he could be : so they must consider what was to be done to get him away. The licentiate begged him not to give himself any uneasiness on that account, for they should certainly contrive to get him out of his present retreat.

The priest then informed Cardenio and Dorothea of their plan for Don Quixote's cure, or at least for decoying him to his own house. Upon which Dorothea said she would undertake to act the distressed damsel better than the barber, especially as she had apparel with which she could perform it to the life ; and they might have reliance upon her, as she had read many works of chivalry, and was well acquainted with the style in which distressed damsels were wont to beg their boons of knights-errant. " Let us, then, hasten to put our design into execution," exclaimed the curate, " since fortune seems to favour all our views." Dorothea immediately took from her bundle a petticoat of very rich stuff, and a mantle of fine green silk ; and out of a casket a necklace and other jewels, with which she quickly adorned herself, in such a manner that she had all the appearance of a rich and noble lady. They were charmed with her beauty, grace, and elegance, and agreed that Don Fernando must be a man of little taste, since he could slight so much excellence. But her greatest admirer was Sancho Panza, who thought that in all his life he had never seen so beautiful a creature ; and he earnestly desired the priest to tell him who this beautiful lady was, and what she was looking for in those parts. " This beautiful lady, friend Sancho," answered the priest, " is, to say the least of her, heiress, in the direct male line, of the great kingdom of Micomicon ; and she comes in quest of your master, to beg a boon of him, which is, to redress a wrong or injury done her by a wicked giant : for it is the fame of your master's prowess, which is spread over all Guinea, that has brought this princess to seek him." " Now, a happy seeking and a happy finding ! " quoth Sancho Panza ; " especially if my master is so fortunate as to redress that injury, and right that wrong, by killing the rascally giant you mention : and kill him he certainly will, if he encounters him, unless he be a goblin ; for my master has no power at all over goblins. But one thing I must again beg of your worship, Signor Licentiate, and that is, to prevent my master from taking it into his head to be an archbishop, and advise him to marry this princess out of hand; for then, not being qualified to receive archiepiscopal orders, he will come with ease to his kingdom, and I to the end of my wishes: for I have considered the matter well, and find by my account it will not suit me for my master to be an archbishop, as I am unfit for the Church, being a married man; and for me to be now going about to procure dispensations for holding Church living, having, as I have, a wife and children, would be an endless piece of work. So that, sir, the whole business rests upon my master's marrying this lady out of hand—not knowing her grace, I cannot call her by name." "The Princess Micomi-conia is her name," said the priest; "for as her kingdom is named Micomicon, of course she must be called so." "To be sure," answered Sancho; "for I have known many take their title and surname from their birthplace, as Pedro de Alcala, John de Ubeda, Diego de Valla-dolid; and, for aught I know, it may be the custom in Guinea for queens to take the names of their kingdoms." "It is certainly so," said the priest; "and as to your master's marrying this princess, I will promote it to the utmost of my power." With which assurance Sancho was no less satisfied than the priest was amazed at his simplicity in thus entering into the extravagant fancies of his master.

Dorothea having now mounted the priest's mule, and the barber fitted on the ox-tail beard, they desired Sancho to conduct them to Don Quixote, cautioning him not to say that he knew the licentiate or the barber, since on that depended all his fortune. Neither the priest nor Cardenio would go with them: the latter, that he might not remind Don Quixote of the dispute which he had had with him; and the priest, because his presence was not then necessary: so the others, therefore, went on before, while they followed slowly on foot. The priest would have instructed Dorothea in her part; but she would not trouble him, assuring him that she would perform it precisely according to the rules and precepts of chivalry.

Having proceeded about three-quarters of a league, they discovered Don Quixote in a wild, rocky recess, at that time clothed, but not armed. Dorothea now whipped on her palfrey, attended by the well-bearded squire; and having approached the knight, the squire leaped from his mule to assist his lady, who, lightly dismounting, went and threw herself at Don Quixote's feet, where, in spite of his efforts to raise her, she remained kneeling, as she thus addressed him:

"I will never arise from this place, O valorous and redoubted knight, until your goodness and courtesy vouchsafe me a boon, which will redound to the honour and glory of your person, and to the lasting benefit of the most disconsolate and aggrieved damsel the sun has ever beheld. And if the valour of your puissant arm correspond with the report of your immortal fame, you are bound to protect an unhappy wight, who, attracted by the odour of your renown, is come from distant regions to seek at your hands a remedy for her misfortunes."

"It is impossible for me to answer you, fair lady," said Don Quixote, "while you remain in that posture." "I will not arise, signor," answered the afflicted damsel, "until your courtesy shall vouchsafe the boon I ask." "I do vouchsafe and grant it to you," answered Don Quixote, "provided my compliance be of no detriment to my king, my country, or to her who keeps the key of my heart and liberty." "It will not be to the prejudice of either of these, dear sir," replied the afflicted damsel. Sancho, now approaching his master, whispered softly in his ear, "Your worship may very safely grant the boon she asks, for it is a mere trifle—only to kill a great lubberly giant; and she who begs it is the mighty Princess Micomiconia, Queen of the great kingdom of Micomicon, in Ethiopia." "Whosoever the lady may be," answered Don Quixote, "I shall act as my duty and my conscience dictate, in conformity to the rules of my profession:" then addressing himself to the damsel, he said, "Fairest lady, arise; for I vouchsafe you whatever boon you ask." "My request, then, is," said the damsel, "that your magnanimity will go whither I shall conduct you, and that you will promise not to engage in any other adventure until you have avenged me on a traitor who, against all right, human and divine, has usurped my kingdom." "I grant your request," answered Don Quixote; "and therefore, lady, dispel that melancholy which oppresses you, and let your fainting hopes recover fresh life and strength; for, by the help of Heaven and my powerful arm, you shall soon be restored to your kingdom, and seated on the throne of your ancient and high estate, in despite of all the miscreants who would oppose it; and therefore we will instantly proceed to action, for there is always danger in delay." The distressed damsel would fain have kissed his hands; but Don Quixote, who was in every respect a most gallant and courteous knight, would by no means consent to it, but, making her arise, embraced her with much politeness and respect, and ordered Sancho to look after Rozinante's girths, and to assist him to arm. Sancho took down the armour from a tree, where it hung like a trophy; and having got Rozinante ready, quickly armed his master, who then cried, "In God's name, let us hasten to succour this great lady."

The barber was still upon his knees, and under much difficulty to forbear laughing, and keep his beard from falling—an accident which might have occasioned the miscarriage of their ingenious stratagem; but seeing that the boon was already granted, and that Don Quixote prepared to fulfil his engagement, he got up and took his lady by the other hand, when they both assisted to place her upon the mule, and then mounted themselves. Sancho alone remained on foot, which renewed his grief for the loss of his Dapple: but he bore it cheerfully; reflecting that his master was now in the right road, and just upon the point of becoming an emperor; for he made no doubt but that he was to marry that princess, and be at least King of Micomicon. One thing only troubled him, which was, that his kingdom being in the land of negroes, his subjects would all be blacks; but presently recollecting a special remedy, he said to himself, "What care I, if my subjects be blacks?—what have I to do but to ship them off to Spain, where I may sell them for ready money, with which money I may buy some title or

*" Happy is this meeting, O thou mirror of chivalry." Having thus spoken, he embraced
Don Quixote by the knee of his left leg.*

office, on which I may live at ease all the days of my life? See whether
I have not brains enough to manage matters, and sell thirty or ten
thousand slaves in the turn of a hand! Before Heaven, I will make
them fly, little and big; and let them be ever so black, I will turn them
into white and yellow boys. Let me alone to lick my own fingers."
After these reflections, he went on in such good spirits that he forgot
the fatigue of travelling on foot.

Cardenio and the priest, concealed among the bushes, had observed
all that passed, and being now desirous to join them, the priest, who
had a ready invention, soon hit upon an expedient; for with a pair of
scissors which he carried in a case he quickly cut off Cardenio's beard;
then put on him a grey capouch, and gave him his own black cloak
(himself remaining in his breeches and doublet), which so changed
Cardenio's appearance, that had he looked in a mirror he would not
have known himself. Although the others had in the meantime been
proceeding onward, they easily gained the high-road first, because the
narrow passes between the rocks were more difficult to horse than to

foot travellers. They waited in the plain until Don Quixote and his party came up; whereupon the curate, after gazing for some time earnestly at him, at last ran towards him with open arms, exclaiming aloud, " Happy is this meeting, O thou mirror of chivalry, my noble countryman, Don Quixote de la Mancha! the flower and cream of gentility,—the protector of suffering mankind,—the quintessence of knight-errantry!" Having thus spoken, he embraced Don Quixote by the knee of his left leg.

The knight was surprised at this address; but after attentively survey-ing the features of the speaker, he recognised him, and would imme-diately have alighted; but the priest would not suffer it. " You must permit me to alight, Signor Licentiate," answered Don Quixote; " for it would be very improper that I should remain on horseback while so reverend a person as you were travelling on foot." " I will by no means consent to your dismounting," replied the priest, " since on horseback you have achieved the greatest exploits this age has witnessed. As for myself, an unworthy priest, I shall be satisfied if one of these gentlemen of your company will allow me to mount behind him; and I shall then fancy myself mounted on Pegasus, or on a zebra, or on the sprightly courser bestrode by the famous Moor Muzarque, who lies to this day enchanted in the great mountain Zulema, not far distant from the grand Compluto."* " I did not think of that, dear Signor Licentiate," said Don Quixote; " and I know her highness the princess will for my sake order her squire to accommodate you with the saddle of his mule; and he may ride behind, if the beast will carry double." " I believe she will," answered the princess; " and I know it is unnecessary for me to lay my commands upon my squire, for he is too courteous and well-bred to suffer an ecclesiastic to go on foot when he may ride." "Most certainly," answered the barber; and, alighting in an instant, he com-plimented the priest with the saddle, which he accepted without much persuasion. But it unluckily happened that, as the barber was getting upon the crupper, the animal, which was a hackney, and consequently a vicious jade, threw up her hind legs twice or thrice into the air, and had they met with Master Nicholas's breast or head, he would have wished his rambling after Don Quixote at the devil. He was, however, thrown to the ground, and so suddenly that he forgot to take due care of his beard, which fell off; and all he could do was to cover his face with both hands, and cry out that his jaw-bone was broken. Don Quixote seeing such a mass of beard without jaws and without blood, lying at some distance from the face of the fallen squire, exclaimed, " Heavens! what a miracle! His beard has fallen as clean from his face as if he had been shaven!" The priest, seeing the danger they were in of discovery, instantly seized the beard, and ran to Master Nicholas, who was still moaning on the ground; and going up close to him, with one twitch replaced it, muttering over him some words which he said were a specific charm for fixing on beards, as they should soon

---

* A university of Spain, now called Alcala de Henares.

see; and when it was adjusted the squire remained as well bearded and as whole as before. Don Quixote was amazed at what he saw, and begged the priest to teach him that charm; for he was of opinion that its virtue could not be confined to the refixing of beards, because it was clear that where the beard was torn off the flesh must be left wounded and bloody, and, since it wrought a perfect cure, it must be valuable upon other occasions. The priest said that his surmise was just, and promised to take the first opportunity of teaching him the art. They now agreed that the priest should mount first, and that all three should ride by turns until they came to the inn, which was distant about two leagues.

Don Quixote, the princess, and the priest, being thus mounted, attended by Cardenio, the barber, and Sancho Panza on foot, Don Quixote said to the damsel, "Your highness will now be pleased to lead on, in whatever direction you choose." Before she could reply, the licentiate, interposing, said, "Whither would your ladyship go? To the kingdom of Micomicon, I presume, or I am much mistaken." She, being aware that she was to answer in the affirmative, said, "Yes, signor, that kingdom is indeed the place of my destination." "If so," said the priest, "we must pass through my native village; and thence you must go straight to Carthagena, where you may embark; and if you have a fair wind, a smooth sea, and no storms, in somewhat less than nine years you will get within view of the great Lake of Meona— I mean Meotis—which is not more than a hundred days' journey from your highness's territories." "You are mistaken, good sir," said she; "for it is not two years since I left it; and although I had very bad weather during the whole passage, here I am, and I have beheld what so ardently I desired to see—Signor Don Quixote de la Mancha; the fame of whose valour reached my ears the moment I set foot in Spain, and determined me upon seeking him, that I might appeal to his courtesy, and commit the justice of my cause to the valour of his invincible arm." "Cease, I pray, these encomiums," said Don Quixote; "for I am an enemy to every species of flattery; and even this, if it be not such, still are my chaste ears offended at this kind of discourse. All that I can say, dear madam, is that my powers, such as they are, shall be employed in your service, even at the forfeit of my life. But waiving these matters for the present, I beg the Signor Licentiate to tell me what has brought him into these parts alone, unattended, and so lightly apparelled." "I can soon satisfy your worship," answered the priest: "our friend, Master Nicholas, and I were going to Seville, to receive a legacy left me by a relation in India, and no inconsiderable sum, being sixty thousand crowns; and on our road, yesterday, we were attacked by four highway robbers, who stripped us of all we had, to our very beards, and in such a manner that the barber thought it expedient to put on a false one; and for this youth here" (pointing to Cardenio) "you see how they have treated him. It is publicly reported here that those who robbed us were galley-slaves, set at liberty near this very place by a man so valiant that, in spite of the commissary and his guards, he released them all : but he certainly must have been out of his senses, or as great a rogue as any of them, since he could let loose wolves among sheep, foxes among poultry, and wasps among the honey ; for he has defrauded justice of her due, and has set himself up against his king and natural lord, by acting against his lawful authority. He has, I say, disabled the galleys of their hands, and disturbed the many years' repose of the Holy Brotherhood ; in a word, he has done a deed by which his body may suffer, and his soul be for ever lost."

Sancho had communicated the adventure of the galley-slaves, so gloriously achieved by his master ; and the priest laid it on thus heavily to see what effect it would have upon Don Quixote, whose colour changed at every word, and he dared not confess that he had been the deliverer of those worthy gentlemen. "These," said the priest, "were the persons that robbed us ; and God of His mercy pardon him who prevented the punishment they so richly deserved."

CHAPTER XXX.

Which treats of the pleasant and ingenious method pursued to withdraw our enamoured knight from the rigorous penance which he had imposed on himself.

LAUGHING in his sleeve, Sancho said, as soon as the priest had done speaking, "By my truth, Signor Licentiate, it was my master who did that feat : not but that I gave him fair warning, and advised him to mind what he was about, and that it was a sin to set them at liberty, for that they were all going to the galleys for being most notorious villains." "Blockhead!" said Don Quixote, "knights-errant are not bound to inquire whether the afflicted, fettered, and oppressed whom they meet upon the road, are brought to that situation by their faults or their misfortunes. It is their part to assist them under oppression, and to regard their sufferings, not their crimes. I encountered a bead-roll and string of miserable wretches, and acted towards them as my profession required of me. As for the rest, I care not ; and whoever takes it amiss, saving the holy dignity of signor the licentiate, and his reverend person, I say he knows but little of the principles of chivalry, and lies in his throat ; and this I will maintain with the edge of my sword !" So saying, he fixed himself firmly in his stirrups and lowered his vizor ; for Mambrino's helmet, as he called it, hung useless at his saddle-bow, until it could be repaired of the damage it had received from the galley-slaves.

Dorothea was possessed of too much humour and sprightly wit not to join with the rest in their diversion at Don Quixote's expense ; and perceiving his wrath, she said, "Sir Knight, be pleased to remember the boon you have promised me, and that you are thereby bound not to engage in any other adventure, however urgent; therefore assuage your wrath; for had signor the licentiate known that the galley-slaves were freed by that invincible arm, he would sooner have sewed up his mouth with three stitches, and thrice have bitten his tongue, than he would have said a word that might redound to the disparagement of your worship." "By my faith I would," exclaimed the priest; "or even have plucked off one of my mustachios." "I will say no more, madam," said Don Quixote; "and I will repress that just indignation raised within my breast, and quietly proceed until I have accomplished the promised boon. But in requital, I beseech you to inform me of the particulars of your grievance, as well as the number and quality of the persons on whom I must take due, satisfactory, and complete revenge." "That I will do most willingly," answered Dorothea, "if a detail of my afflictions will not be wearisome to you." "Not in the least, my dear madam," replied the knight. "Well, then," said Dorothea, "you have only to favour me with your attention." Cardenio and the barber now walked by her side, curious to hear what kind of story she would invent. Sancho, who was as much deceived as his master, did the same; and after a hem or two, and other preparatory airs, with much grace she thus began her story:

"In the first place, you must know, gentlemen, that my name is—" here she stopped short, having forgotten the name the priest had given her; but he came to her aid, saying, "I am not at all surprised at your highness's emotion upon this recurrence to your misfortunes; for affliction too often deprives us of the faculty of memory: even now, your highness seems to forget that you are the great Princess Micomiconia." "True, indeed!" answered Dorothea; "but I will command my distracted thoughts, and proceed in my true tale of sorrow.

"My father, Tinacrio the Wise, was very learned in the magic art, and foresaw by it that my mother, the Queen Xaramilla, would die before him; that he must soon after depart this life, and that I should be thus left an orphan. But this, he said, did not trouble him so much as the foreknowledge he had that a monstrous giant, lord of a great island bordering upon our kingdom, called Pandafilando of the Gloomy Aspect—for it is averred that although his eyes stand in their proper place, he always looks askew, as if he squinted; and this he does of pure malignity, to scare and frighten those he looks at—my father foresaw, as I said before, that this giant would take advantage of my orphan state, invade my kingdom with a mighty force, and take it all from me, without leaving me the smallest village wherein to hide my head; but that it was in my power to avoid all this ruin and misery by marrying him, although he could not imagine that I would consent to the match —and he was in the right, for I could never think of marrying this nor any other giant, however huge and monstrous. My father's advice was that when, upon his decease, Pandafilando invaded my kingdom, I should not make any defence, for that would be my ruin: but, to avoid death and the total destruction of my faithful and loyal subjects, my best way was voluntarily to quit the kingdom, since it would be impossible for me to defend myself against the terrible power of the giant, and immediately set out, with a few attendants, for Spain, where I should find a remedy for my distress, in a knight-errant whose fame about that time would extend all over that kingdom; and whose name, if I remember right, was to be Don Axote, or Don Gigsote." "Don Quixote, you mean, madam," quoth Sancho Panza, "or otherwise called the Knight of the Sorrowful Figure." "You are right," said Dorothea. "He said further, that he was to be tall and thin-visaged; and on his right side, under the left shoulder, or thereabouts, he was to have a grey mole, with hair like bristles."

Don Quixote, hearing this, said to his squire, "Come hither, Sancho; help me to strip, that I may know whether I am the knight alluded to in the prophecy of that sage king." "You need not strip," said Sancho; "I know you have exactly such a mole on the ridge of your back—a sure sign of strength." "That is sufficient," said Dorothea; "for we must not stand upon trifles. It matters not whether it be on the shoulder or on the back-bone—there is a mole, and it is all the same flesh. And doubtless I am perfectly right in recommending myself to Signor Don Quixote; for he must be the knight whom my father meant, since it is proved, both by his person and his extraordinary fame, not only in Spain, but over all La Mancha: for I was hardly landed in Ossuna before I heard of so many of his exploits that I felt immediately assured that he must be the very person whom I came to seek." "But, dear madam, how came you to land at Ossuna," said Don Quixote, "since that is not a seaport town?" Before Dorothea could reply, the priest, interposing, said, "Doubtless the princess would say that, after she had landed at Malaga, the first place where she heard news of your worship was Ossuna." "That is what I meant to say," said Dorothea. "Nothing can be more clear," rejoined the priest. "Please your Majesty to proceed." "I have little more to add," replied Dorothea, "but that, having now had the good fortune to meet with Signor Don Quixote, I already look upon myself as queen and mistress of my whole kingdom, since he out of his courtesy and generosity has promised, in compliance with my request, to go with me wherever I please to conduct him; which shall be only into the presence of Pandafilando of the Gloomy Aspect, that he may slay him, and restore to me that which has been so unjustly usurped. Nor is there the smallest reason to doubt but that all this will come to pass according to the prophecy of the wise Tinacrio, my good father; who, moreover, left an order, written either in Chaldean or Greek (for I cannot read them), that if this knight in his prophecy, after cutting off the giant's head, should desire to marry me, I must immediately submit to be his lawful wife, and with my person give him also possession of my kingdom."

"Now what thinkest thou, friend Sancho?" quoth Don Quixote. "Dost thou hear that? Did not I tell thee so? See whether we have not now a kingdom to command, and a queen to marry!" "Odds my life! so it is," cried Sancho; "and plague take him for a son of a rascal who will not marry as soon as Signor Pandafilando's wizen is cut. About it, then : her Majesty is a dainty bit : I wish all the fleas in my bed were no worse." And so saying, he cut a couple of capers, and exhibited other tokens of delight. Then laying hold of the reins of Dorothea's mule, and making her stop, he fell down upon his knees before her, beseeching her to give him her hand to kiss, in token that he acknowledged her for his queen and mistress. With difficulty could the rest of the party restrain their laughter at the madness of the master and the simplicity of the man. Dorothea held out her hand to him, and promised to make him a great lord in her kingdom, when Heaven should be so propitious as to put her again in possession of it. Sancho returned her thanks in expressions which served to increase their mirth.

"This, gentlemen," continued Dorothea, "is my history. I have only to add, that of all the attendants I brought with me from my kingdom, I have none left but this well-bearded squire ; for the rest were all drowned in a violent storm which overtook us in sight of the port. He and I got ashore on a couple of planks, as it were by a miracle ; and, indeed, the whole progress of my life is a miracle and mystery, as you may have observed. And if I have exaggerated, or not been so exact as I ought to have been, ascribe it, I entreat you, to what the reverend gentleman said at the beginning of my narrative, that continual and extraordinary troubles deprive the sufferer even of memory." "Mine shall never fail me, O most worthy and exalted lady!" cried Don Quixote, "whatever I may be called upon to endure in your service. And again I confirm my engagement, and swear to accompany you to the remotest regions of the earth until I shall meet and grapple with that fierce enemy of yours, whose proud head, by the help of Heaven and this my strong arm, I will cut off with the edge of this (I will not say good) sword—thanks be to Gines de Passamonte, who carried off my own." These last words he uttered in a lower tone ; then, again raising his voice, he proceeded to say, "Having severed it from his body, and replaced you in peaceable possession of your dominions, the disposal of your person will be at your own discretion, since, while my memory is engrossed, my heart enthralled, and my mind subjected to her who—I say no more—it is impossible I should prevail upon myself even to think of marrying, although it were a phœnix."

Don Quixote's last declaration was so displeasing to Sancho, that, in a great fury, he exclaimed, "I vow and swear, Signor Don Quixote, your worship cannot be in your right senses! How else is it possible you should scruple to marry so great a princess? Do you think that fortune is to offer you at every turn such good luck as this? Is my lady Dulcinea more beautiful? No, indeed, not by half! nay, I could almost say she is not worthy to tie this lady's shoe-string. I am like, indeed, to get the earldom, if your worship stands fishing for mushrooms at the bottom of the sea! Marry, marry at once, in the devil's name, and take this kingdom that drops into your hand ; and when you are a king, make me a marquis or a lord-lieutenant, and then the devil take the rest!" Don Quixote, unable to endure such blasphemies against his lady Dulcinea, raised his lance, and, without word or warning, let it fall with such violence upon Sancho that he was laid flat on the ground; and had not Dorothea called out entreating him to forbear, the squire had doubtless been killed on the spot. "Thinkest thou," said Don Quixote to him, after a short pause, "base varlet! that I am always to stand with my arms folded, and that there is to be nothing but transgression on thy side, and forgiveness on mine? Expect it not, excommunicated wretch! for so thou surely art, having presumed to speak ill of the peerless Dulcinea. Knowest thou not, rustic, slave, beggar! that were it not for the power she infuses into my arm, I should not have enough to kill a flea? Tell me, envenomed scoffer! what, thinkest thou, has gained this kingdom, and cut off the head of this giant, and made thee a marquis (all of which I look upon as done), but the valour of Dulcinea, employing my arm as the instrument of her exploits? She fights, she vanquishes in me; in her I live and breathe, and of her I hold my life and being. O base-born villain! what ingratitude, when thou seest thyself exalted from the dust of the earth to the title of a lord, to make so base a return as to speak contemptuously of the hand that raised thee!"

Sancho was not so much hurt but that he heard all his master said to him; and getting up nimbly, he ran behind Dorothea's palfrey; and thus sheltered, he said to him, "Pray, sir, tell me—for if you are resolved not to marry this princess, it is plain the kingdom will not be yours—what favours then will you be able to bestow on me? That is what I complain of. Marry this queen, sir, once for all, now we have her, as it were, rained down upon us from heaven, and afterwards you may turn to my lady Dulcinea: for there have been kings who have had mistresses. As to the matter of beauty, I have nothing to say to that; but if I must speak the truth, I really think them both very well to pass, though I never saw the Lady Dulcinea." "How! never saw her, blasphemous traitor!" said Don Quixote; "hast thou not just brought me a message from her?" "I say, I did not see her so leisurely," said Sancho, "as to take particular notice of her features piece by piece; but, take her altogether, she looks well enough." "Now I pardon thee," said Don Quixote; "and do thou excuse my wrath towards thee; for first emotions are not in our power." "So I find," answered Sancho; "and in me the desire of talking is always a first motion, and I cannot forbear uttering at once whatever comes to my tongue's end." "Nevertheless," quoth Don Quixote, "take heed, Sancho, what thou utterest; for 'the pitcher that goes often to the well'—I say no more." "Well, then," answered Sancho, "God is in heaven, who sees all guile, and shall be judge of which does most harm, I in not speaking well, or your worship in not doing well." "Let there be no more of this," said Dorothea: "go, Sancho, and kiss your master's hand, and ask his pardon. Henceforward be more cautious in your praises and dispraises; and speak no ill of that Lady Toboso, of whom I know no more than that I am her humble servant. Put your

Sancho ran to his Dapple, and embracing him, said, "How hast thou done, my dearest Dapple?"

trust in Heaven, for you shall not want an estate to live upon like a prince." Sancho went with his head hanging down, and begged his master's hand, who presented it to him with much gravity; and when he had kissed it, Don Quixote gave him his blessing: he then begged that he would walk on before with him, as he wished to put some questions to him, and to have some conversation on affairs of great importance. Having both advanced a little distance before the rest, Don Quixote said, "Since thy return I have had no opportunity to inquire after many particulars concerning thy embassy, and the answer thou broughtest back; and now that fortune presents a favourable occasion, deny me not the gratification which thou art able to bestow by such agreeable communications." "Ask me what questions you please, sir," answered Sancho: "I warrant I shall get out as well as I got in; but I beseech your worship not to be so revengeful for the future." "What dost thou mean, Sancho?" quoth Don Quixote. "I say so," replied Sancho, "because the blows you were pleased to bestow on me just now were rather on account of the quarrel the devil raised between us the other night than for what I said against my lady Dulcinea, whom I love and reverence like any relic, though she is one only inasmuch as she belongs to your worship." "No more of that.

Sancho, at thy peril," said Don Quixote, "for it much offends me : I forgave thee before, and thou knowest the saying—' For a new sin a new penance.'" At this time they saw a man coming towards them mounted upon an ass, and as he drew near he had the appearance of a gipsy. But Sancho Panza, who, whenever he saw an ass, followed it with eyes and heart, had no sooner got a glimpse of the man, than he recognised Gines de Passamonte, and, by the same clue, was directed to his lost ass ; it being really Dapple himself on which Gines was mounted : for in order to escape discovery and sell the animal, he had disguised himself like a gipsy, as he could speak their language, among many others, as readily as his native tongue. Sancho immediately called out aloud to him, " Ah, rogue Ginesillo ! leave my darling, let go my life, rob me not of my comfort, quit my sweetheart, leave my delight !—fly, rapscallion, fly !—get you gone, thief ! and give up what is not your own." So much railing was not necessary ; for at the first word Gines dismounted in a trice, and taking to his heels, was out of sight in an instant. Sancho ran to his Dapple, and embracing him, said, " How hast thou done, my dearest Dapple, delight of my eyes, my sweet companion ? " Then he kissed and caressed him, as if he had been a human creature. The ass held his peace, and suffered himself to be thus kissed and caressed by Sancho without answering him one word. They all came up, and wished him joy on the restoration of his Dapple ; especially Don Quixote, who at the same time assured him that he should not on that account revoke his order for the three colts ; for which he had Sancho's hearty thanks.

In the meantime the priest commended Dorothea for her ingenuity in the contrivance of her story, for its conciseness, and its resemblance to the narrations in books of chivalry. She said she had often amused herself with such kind of books, but that she did not know much of geography, and therefore had said at a venture that she landed at Ossuna. " So I conjectured," said the priest ; " and therefore I corrected your mistake. But is it not strange to see how readily this unhappy gentleman believes all these fictions, only because they resemble the style and manner of his absurd books ? " " It is indeed extraordinary," said Cardenio ; " and so unprecedented that I much question whether any one could be found possessed of ingenuity enough to invent and fabricate such a character." " There is another thing remarkable," said the priest ; " which is, that except on that particular subject, this good gentleman can discourse very rationally, and seems to have a clear judgment and an excellent understanding."

CHAPTER XXXI.

Of the relishing conversation which passed between Don Quixote and his squire Sancho Panza; with other incidents.

They were thus pursuing their conversation while Don Quixote proceeded in his with Sancho. "Let us forget, friend Panza, what is past; and tell me now, all rancour and animosity apart, where, how, and when didst thou find Dulcinea? What was she doing? What didst thou say to her? What answer did she return? How did she look when she read my letter? Who transcribed it for thee? Tell me all that is worth knowing, inquiring, or answering. Inform me of all, without adding or diminishing aught to deprive me of any satisfaction." "Sir," answered Sancho, "to say the truth, nobody transcribed the letter for me, for I carried no letter at all." "Thou sayest true," quoth Don Quixote, "for I found the pocket-book in which I wrote it two days after thy departure, which troubled me exceedingly; and I thought thou wouldst return for it." "So I should have done," answered Sancho, "had I not got it by heart when your worship read it to me; and so perfectly, that I repeated it to a parish clerk, who wrote it down so exactly, that he said, though he had read many letters of excommunication, he had never in all his life seen or read so pretty a letter." "And hast thou it still by heart, Sancho?" said Don Quixote. "No, sir," answered Sancho; "for after I had delivered it, seeing it was to be of no further use, I forgot it on purpose. If I remember anything, it is 'subterrane,' I mean 'sovereign lady,' and the conclusion, 'thine until death, the Knight of the Sorrowful Figure;' and between these two things I put above three hundred souls, and lives, and dear eyes."

"This is very well—proceed," said Don Quixote. "On thy arrival, what was that queen of beauty doing? I suppose thou foundest her stringing pearls, or embroidering some device with threads of gold for this her captive knight." "No, faith!" answered Sancho; "I found her winnowing two bushels of wheat in a back yard of her house." "Then be assured," said Don Quixote, "that the grains of that wheat were so many grains of pearl, when touched by her hands. And didst thou observe, friend, whether the wheat was fine, or of the ordinary sort?" "It was neither," answered Sancho, "but of the reddish kind." "Rely upon it, however," quoth Don Quixote, "that, when winnowed by her hands, it made the finest manchet bread. But go on. When thou gavest her my letter, did she kiss it? Did she put it upon her head? Did she use any ceremony worthy of such a letter?—or what did she do?" "When I was going to give it to her," answered Sancho, "she was so busy winnowing a good sieve-full of the wheat, that she said to me, ' Lay the letter, friend, upon that sack ; for I cannot read it until I have done what I am about.' " " Discreet lady ! " said Don Quixote ; " this was assuredly that she might read and enjoy it at leisure. Proceed, Sancho : while thus employed, what discourse had she with thee ?—what did she inquire concerning me ? And what didst thou answer ? Tell me all ; omit not the slightest circumstance." " She asked me nothing," said Sancho ; " but I told her how your worship was doing penance, for her service, among these rocks, naked from the waist upwards, just like a savage ; sleeping on the ground, not eating bread on a napkin, nor combing your beard, weeping, and cursing your fortune." " In saying that I cursed my fortune, thou saidst wrong," quoth Don Quixote : " I rather bless it, and shall bless it all the days of my life, for having made me worthy to love so high a lady as Dulcinea del Toboso." " So high, indeed," answered Sancho, " that in good faith she is a hand taller than I am." " Why, how ! Sancho," said Don Quixote, " hast thou measured with her ?" " Yes," answered Sancho ; " for as I was helping her to put a sack of wheat upon an ass, we came so close together that I noticed she was taller than I by more than a full span." " True," replied Don Quixote ; " and is not this uncommon stature adorned by millions of intellectual graces ? One thing, Sancho, thou canst not deny : when near her, thou must have perceived a Sabæan odour, an aromatic fragrance, a something sweet, for which I cannot find a name—a scent, a perfume—as if thou wert in the shop of some curious glover." " All I can say is," quoth Sancho, " that I perceived somewhat of a strong smell, which must have been owing to the sweat she was in with hard work." " Impossible ! " cried Don Quixote ; " that smell must have proceeded from thyself : for well I know the scent of that lovely rose among thorns, that lily of the valley, that liquid amber." " Very likely," answered Sancho ; " for the very same smell often comes from me which methought then came from my lady Dulcinea : but where 's the wonder that one devil should be like another ? " " Well, then," continued Don Quixote, " she has now done winnowing, and the corn is sent to the mill. What did she do when she had read the letter ? " " The letter," quoth Sancho, " she did not read ; for she said that she could neither read nor write ; so she tore it to pieces, saying she would not give it to anybody to read, that her secrets might not be known all over the village ; and that what I had told her by word of mouth concerning your worship's love, and all you were doing for her sake, was enough ; and she bid me tell your worship that she kissed your hands, and that she would rather see you than write to you : so begged and commanded you, at sight hereof, to quit these brakes and bushes, and leave off these foolish pranks, and set out immediately for Toboso, if business of more consequence did not prevent you ; for she wished mightily to see your worship. She laughed heartily when I told her how you called yourself the Knight of the Sorrowful Figure. I asked her whether the Biscayan had been there with her ; she told me he had, and that he was a very good kind of fellow. I asked her also after the galley-slaves, but she had not yet seen any of them." "All this is well," said Don Quixote; "but, tell me, what jewel did she present thee with at thy departure, in return for the tidings thou hadst brought her? for it is an ancient and universal custom among knights and ladies-errant to bestow some rich jewel on the squires, damsels, or dwarfs who bring them news of their mistresses or knights, as a reward or acknowledgment for their welcome intelligence." "Very likely," quoth Sancho, "and a very good custom it was; but it must have been in days of yore, for now-a-days the custom is to give only a piece of bread and cheese, for that was what my lady Dulcinea gave me, over the pales of the yard, when she dismissed me; and, by the way, the cheese was made of sheep's-milk." "She is extremely generous," said Don Quixote; "and if she did not give thee a jewel, it must have been because she had none about her; but gifts are good after Easter.* I shall see her, and all will then be rectified.

"But I marvel at one thing, Sancho, which is, that thou must have gone and returned through the air; for thou hast been little more than three days in performing this journey, although the distance between this place and Toboso is more than thirty leagues; whence I conclude that the sage enchanter who has the superintendence of my affairs (for such an one there is, or I should be no true knight-errant)—I say, this same enchanter must have expedited thy journey; for there are sages who will take up a knight-errant sleeping in his bed, and, without his knowing anything of the matter, he awakes the next day above a thousand leagues from the place where he fell asleep. Indeed, were it otherwise it would be impossible for knights-errant to succour each other, as they often do, in the critical moment of danger. A knight, for instance, happens to be fighting in the mountains of Armenia with some dreadful monster, or fierce goblin, or doughty knight; he has the worst of the combat, and is just on the point of being killed, when suddenly another knight, his friend, who perhaps a moment before was in England, comes upon a cloud, or in a fiery chariot, and rescues him from death; and on the same evening he finds himself in his own chamber, with a good appetite for supper, after a journey of two or three thousand leagues. And all this is effected by the diligence and skill of those sage enchanters. So that, friend Sancho, I make no difficulty in believing that thou hast really performed the journey in that short time; having, doubtless, been borne unconsciously through the air by some friendly power." "It may be so," quoth Sancho; "for, in good faith, Rozinante went like any Bohemian's ass with quicksilver in his ears." † "With quicksilver!" said Don Quixote; "aye, and with a legion of devils to boot—a sort of cattle that travel and make others travel as fast as they please without being tired. But, waiving this subject for the present, what

---

* A proverbial expression, signifying that a good thing is always seasonable.

† In allusion to a trick practised by the Bohemian horse-dealers, who, to give pace to the most stupid mule, or to the idlest ass, were in the habit of pouring a small quantity of quicksilver into its ears.

thinkest thou I should do respecting my lady's orders that I should wait upon her? I am bound to obey her commands; yet how is it possible, on account of the boon I have promised to the princess? The laws of chivalry oblige me to consider my honour rather than my pleasure. On the one hand, I am torn with impatience to see my lady; on the other, I am incited by glory to the accomplishment of this enterprise. My best plan, I believe, will be to travel with all possible expedition, cut off the giant's head, replace the princess on her throne, and then instantly return to that sun which illumines my senses, who will pardon a delay which was only to augment her fame and glory; since all my victories past, present, and to come, are but emanations from her favour."

"Alack!" cried Sancho, "your worship must needs be downright crazy! Tell me, pray, do you mean to take this journey for nothing? And will you let slip such a match as this, when the dowry is a kingdom which, they say, is above twenty thousand leagues round, and abounding in all things necessary for the support of life, and bigger than Portugal and Castile together? For the love of Heaven, talk no more in this manner, but follow my advice, and be married out of hand at the first place where there is a priest: our licentiate here will do it very cleverly. And please to recollect, I am old enough to give advice, and what I now give is as fit as if it were cast in a mould for you: for a sparrow in the hand is worth more than a bustard on the wing; and he that will not when he may, when he would he shall have nay." "Hear me, Sancho," replied Don Quixote: "if thou advisest me to marry, only that I may have it in my power to reward thee, be assured that I can gratify thy desire without taking such a measure: before the battle I will make an agreement to possess part of the kingdom without marrying the princess; and when I have it, to whom dost thou think I shall give it but to thyself?" "No doubt," answered Sancho; "but pray, sir, take care to choose it towards the sea, that, if I should not like living there, I may ship off my black subjects, and dispose of them, as I said before. I would not have your worship trouble yourself now about seeing my lady Dulcinea, but go and kill the giant, and let us make an end of this business; for, before Heaven, I verily believe it will bring us much honour and profit." "Thou art in the right, Sancho," said Don Quixote, "and I shall follow thy counsel, and accompany the princess before I visit my lady Dulcinea. But I beg thou wilt say nothing on the subject of our conference, not even to our companions: for since Dulcinea is so reserved that she would not have her thoughts known, it would be improper in me or in any other person to reveal them." "If so," quoth Sancho, "why does your worship send all those you conquer by your mighty arm, to present themselves before my lady Dulcinea? for this is giving it under your hand that you are in love with her." "How dull and simple thou art!" said Don Quixote. "Seest thou not, Sancho, that all this redounds the more to her exaltation? For thou must know that, in this our style of chivalry, it is to the honour of a lady to have many knights-errant, who serve her merely for her own sake, without indulging a hope of any other reward for their zeal than the honour of being admitted among the number of her knights." "I have heard it preached," quoth Sancho, "that God is to be loved with this kind of love, for Himself alone, without our being moved to it by hope of reward or fear of punishment; though, for my part, I am inclined to love and serve Him for what He is able to do for me." "The devil take thee for a bumpkin," said Don Quixote; "thou sayest ever and anon such apt things that one would almost think thee a scholar." "And yet, by my faith," quoth Sancho, "I cannot so much as read."

While they were thus talking, Master Nicholas called aloud to them to stop, as they wished to quench their thirst at a small spring near the road. Don Quixote halted, much to the satisfaction of Sancho, who began to be tired of telling so many lies, and was afraid his master should at last catch him tripping: for although he knew Dulcinea was a peasant-girl of Toboso, he had never seen her in his life. Meanwhile, Cardenio had put on the clothes worn by Dorothea in her disguise, being better than his own. They alighted at the fountain, and with the provisions which the curate had brought from the inn they all appeased their hunger.

While they were thus employed, a lad happened to pass that way, who, after looking earnestly at the party, ran up to Don Quixote, and, embracing his knees, began to weep, saying, "Ah, dear sir! does not your worship know me? Look at me well: I am Andres, the lad whom you delivered from the oak to which I was tied." Don Quixote recollected him, and, taking him by the hand, he thus addressed the company: "To convince you of the importance of knights-errant in the world, in order to redress the wrongs and injuries committed by insolent and wicked men, know that some time since, as I was passing a wood, I heard certain cries, and the voice of some person in affliction and distress. Prompted by my duty, I hastened towards the place whence the voice seemed to come, and I found, tied to an oak, this lad whom you see here. I am rejoiced to my soul that he is present, for he will attest the truth of what I tell you. He was bound, I say, to an oak tree, naked from the waist upward, and a country-fellow, whom I afterwards found to be his master, was lashing him with a bridle. I immediately demanded the reason of so severe a chastisement. The clown answered that he was his servant, whom he was punishing for neglect, proceeding rather from knavery than simplicity. 'Sir,' said the boy, 'he whips me only because I ask him for my wages.' The master, in reply, made many speeches and excuses, which I heard indeed, but did not admit. In short, I compelled him to unbind the youth, and made him swear to take him home, and pay every real, perfumed into the bargain. Is not all this true, son Andres? Didst thou not observe with what authority I commanded, and with what humility he promised to do whatever I enjoined, notified, and required of him? Answer boldly: relate to this company what passed, that they may see the benefits resulting from the vocation of knights-errant."

" All that your worship has said is very true," answered the lad; " but the business ended quite contrary to what your worship supposes." " How contrary ? " replied Don Quixote : " did not the rustic instantly pay thee ? " " He not only did not pay me," answered the boy, " but as soon as your worship was out of the wood and we were left alone, he tied me again to the same tree, and gave me so many fresh lashes that I was flayed like any Saint Bartholomew; and at every stroke he said something by way of scoff or jest upon your worship, which, if I had not felt so much pain, would have made me laugh. In short, he laid on in such a manner that I have been ever since in a hospital, to get cured of the bruises that cruel fellow then gave me : for all which your worship is to blame; for had you gone on your way, and not come when you were not called, nor meddled with other folks' business, my master would have been satisfied with giving me a dozen or two of lashes, and then would have loosed me and paid me my due. But, as your worship abused him so unmercifully, and called him so many bad names, his wrath was kindled; and, not having it in his power to be revenged on you, no sooner had you left him than he discharged such a tempest upon me that I shall never be a man again while I live."

" The mischief," said Don Quixote, " was in my departing before I had seen you paid; for I should have known, by long experience, that no rustic will keep his word if he finds it his interest to break it. But thou mayest remember, Andres, that I swore if he paid thee not I would hunt him out although he were concealed in a whale's belly." " That is true," quoth Andres; " but it signified nothing." " Thou shalt see that," said Don Quixote : and so saying, he started up, and ordered Sancho to bridle Rozinante, who was grazing. Dorothea asked him what he intended to do. He told her that he was going in search of the rustic, to chastise him for his base conduct, and make him pay Andres to the last farthing, in spite and defiance of all the rustics in the world. She desired he would recollect that, according to the promised boon, he could not engage in any other adventure until hers had been accomplished; and, as no one could be more sensible of this than himself, she entreated him to curb his resentment until his return from her kingdom. " You are right," answered Don Quixote; " and Andres must, as you say, madam, have patience until my return; and I again swear not to rest until he is revenged and paid." " I do not think much of these oaths," said Andres; " I would rather have wherewithal to carry me to Seville than all the revenges in the world. If you have anything to give me to eat, let me have it, and Heaven be with your worship, and with all knights-errant, and may they prove as lucky errants to themselves as they have been to me." Sancho pulled out a piece of bread and cheese, and, giving it to the lad, said to him, " Here, brother Andres, we have all a share in your misfortune." " Why, what share have you in it ? " said Andres. " This piece of bread and cheese which I give you," answered Sancho, " God knows whether I may not want it myself; for I would have you know, friend, that we squires to knights-errant are subject to much hunger and ill-luck, and other things too, which are better felt than told." Andres took the bread and cheese, and, seeing that nobody else gave him anything, he made his bow and marched off. It is true, he said at parting to Don Quixote, " For the love of Heaven, Signor Knight-errant, if you ever meet me again, though you see me beaten to pieces, do not come with your help, but leave me to my fate, which cannot be so bad but that it will be made worse by your worship, whom God confound, together with all the knights-errant that ever were born ! " So saying, he ran off with so much speed that nobody attempted to follow him. Don Quixote was much abashed at this affair of Andres, and his companions endeavoured to restrain their inclination to laugh, that they might not put him quite out of countenance.

CHAPTER XXXII.

Which treats of what befell Don Quixote and his company at the inn.

LEAVING the fountain, after having made a hearty repast, they forthwith mounted, and without encountering any adventure worth relating, arrived the next day at the inn so much the dread and terror of Sancho Panza, who now, much against his will, was obliged to enter it. The hostess, the host, their daughter, and Maritornes, seeing Don Quixote and his squire, went out to meet and welcome them. The knight received them with a grave but approving countenance, desiring them to prepare a better bed than they had given him before ; to which the hostess answered, that provided he would pay better than he did before, she would get him a bed for a prince. Don Quixote having satisfied them by his promises, they provided him with a tolerable bed, in the same apartment which he had before occupied ; and, being so much shattered both in body and brains, he immediately threw himself down upon it. He was no sooner shut into his chamber, than the hostess fell upon the barber, and, taking him by the beard, said, " By my faith, you shall use my tail no longer for a beard : give me my tail again, for my husband's comb is so thrown about that it is a shame." The barber would not part with it for all her tugging, until the priest told him that he might give it to her ; for as there was no further need of that artifice, he might now appear in his own shape, and tell Don Quixote that, being robbed by the galley-slaves, he had fled to this inn ; and if he should ask for the princess's squire, they should say she had dispatched him before, with intelligence to her subjects of her approach with their common deliverer. Upon which the barber willingly surrendered the tail to the hostess, together with the other articles she had lent them in order to effect Don Quixote's enlargement. All the people at the inn were struck with the beauty of Dorothea and the comely person of Cardenio. The priest ordered them to get ready what the house afforded, and the host, hoping to be well paid, quickly served up a

"By my faith, you shall use my tail no longer for a beard: give me my tail again."

decent supper. Don Quixote still continued asleep, and they agreed not to awake him; for at that time he had more occasion for sleep than food.

During the supper, at which the host and his family were present, as well as the strangers who happened to be then at the inn, the discourse turned upon the extraordinary derangement of Don Quixote, and the state in which he had been found in the mountain. The hostess seeing that Sancho was not present, related to them his adventure with the carrier, and also the whole story of the blanket, at which they were not a little diverted. The priest happening to remark that the books of chivalry which Don Quixote had read had turned his brain, the inn-keeper said, "I cannot conceive how that can be; for, really, in my opinion, there is no choicer reading in the world. I have three or four of them by me, with some manuscripts, which in good truth have kept me alive, and many others: for, in harvest time, among the reapers who take shelter here during the noon-day heat, there is always some one able to read, who will take up one of these books; and above thirty of us place ourselves around him, and listen to him with so much pleasure that it keeps away a thousand grey hairs: at least, I can say for myself that when I hear of those furious and terrible blows which the knights-errant lay on, I long to be doing as much, and could sit and hear them day and night." "I wish you did," quoth the hostess; "for I never have a quiet moment in my house but when you are listening to the reading; for you are then so besotted that you forget to scold." "Yes, indeed," said Maritornes; "and in good faith I too like much to hear those things; for they are very fine, especially when they tell us how such a lady and her knight lie embracing each other under an orange tree, and how a duenna stands upon the watch, dying with envy, and her heart going pit-a-pat. I say all this is pure honey." "And pray, young damsel, what is your opinion of these matters?" said the priest, addressing himself to the innkeeper's daughter. "I do not know, indeed, sir," answered the girl: "I listen too; and though I do not understand, I take some pleasure in hearing. Yet truly these blows and slashes, which please my father so much, are not to my mind. I like the complaints the knights make when they are absent from their mistresses; and really sometimes they make me weep for pity."

"Then you would soon afford them relief, young gentlewoman," said Dorothea, "if they wept for you?" "I do not know what I should do," answered the girl: "I only know that some of those ladies are so cruel that their knights call them tigers and lions, and a thousand other ugly names. And, Jesu! I cannot imagine what kind of folks they must be who are so hard-hearted and unconscionable that, rather than bestow a kind look on an honest gentleman, they will let him die or run mad. For my part, I cannot see any reason for so much coyness: if they would behave like honest women, let them marry them; for that is what the gentlemen would be at." "Hold your tongue, hussey," said the hostess: "methinks you know a great deal of these matters; it does not become young maidens to know or talk so much." "When this gentleman asked me a civil question," replied the girl, "I could do no less, sure, than answer him." "Well, well," said the priest; "but pray, landlord, let us see those books." "With all my heart," answered the host; and going into his chamber, he brought out an old trunk, with a padlock and chain to it, and opening it, he took out three large volumes, and some manuscript papers written in a very fair character. The first book which he opened he found to be "Don Cirongilio of Thrace," the next, "Felixmarte of Hyrcania," and the third the "History of the Grand Captain Gonzalo Hernandez of Cordova," with the "Life of Diego Garcia de Paredes." When the priest had read the titles of the two first, he turned to the barber and said, "We want here our friend's house-keeper and niece." "Not at all," replied the barber; "for I myself can carry them to the yard, or to the chimney, where there is a very good fire." "What, sir! would you burn my books?" said the inn-keeper. "Only these two," said the priest, "'Don Cirongilio' and 'Felixmarte.'" "What, then, are my books heretical or phlegmatical, that you want to burn them?" "*Schismatical*, you would say, my friend," said the barber, "and not *phlegmatical*." "Yes, yes," replied the innkeeper; "but if you intend to burn any, let it be this of the great captain and ' Diego de Garcia ; ' for I will sooner let you burn one of my children than either of the others." " Brother," said the priest, " these two books are full of extravagant fictions and absurd conceits ; whereas the ' History of the Great Captain' is matter of fact, and contains the exploits of Gonzalo Hernandez of Cordova, who for his numerous brave actions acquired all over the world the title of the Great Captain — a name renowned and illustrious, and merited by him alone. As for Diego Garcia de Paredes, he was a distinguished gentleman, born in the town of Truxillo in Estremadura ; a brave soldier, and of so much bodily strength that he could stop a mill-wheel in its most rapid motion with a single finger. Being once posted with a two-handed sword at the entrance to a bridge, he repelled a prodigious army, and prevented their passage over it. There are other exploits of the same kind, which, if instead of being related by himself with the modesty of a cavalier who is his own historian, they had been recorded by some other dispassionate and unprejudiced author, would have eclipsed the actions of the Hectors, Achilleses, and Orlandos." " Persuade my grandmother to that," quoth the innkeeper ; " do but see what it is he wonders at—the stopping of a mill-wheel ! Before Heaven, your worship should read what I have read, concerning Felixmarte of Hyrcania, who with one back-stroke cut asunder five giants through the middle, as if they had been so many bean-cods of which the children make puppet friars. At another time he encountered a great and powerful army, consisting of about a million six hundred thousand soldiers, all armed from head to foot, and routed them as if they had been a flock of sheep. But what will you say of the good Don Cirongilio of Thrace ? who was so stout and valiant, as you may there read in the book, that once as he was sailing on a river, seeing a fiery serpent rise to the surface of the water, he immediately threw himself upon it, and getting astride its scaly shoulders, squeezed its throat with both his hands with so much force that the serpent, finding itself in danger of being choked, had no other remedy but to plunge to the bottom of the river, carrying with him the knight, who would not quit his hold ; and when they reached the bottom, he found himself in such a fine palace and beautiful gardens, that it was wonderful ; and presently the serpent turned into an old man, who said so many things to him that the like was never heard ! Therefore pray say no more, sir ; for if you were but to hear all this, you would run mad with pleasure. A fig for the Grand Captain and your Diego Garcia ! "

Dorothea, here whispering to Cardenio, said, " Our landlord wants but little to make the second part of Don Quixote." " I think so too," answered Cardenio ; " for he evidently takes all that is related in these books for gospel, and the barefooted friars themselves could not make him believe otherwise." " Look you, brother," said the priest, " there never was in the world such a man as Felixmarte of Hyrcania, nor Don Cirongilio of Thrace, nor any other knights mentioned in the books of chivalry ; for all is the invention of idle wits, who composed them for the purpose of that amusement which you say your readers find in them.

The innkeeper was carrying away the books, when the priest said to him, "Pray stop till I have looked at those papers which are written in so fair a character."

I swear to you there never were such knights in the world, nor were such feats and extravagances ever performed." "To another dog with that bone," answered the host: "what, then! I do not know how many make five, nor where my own shoe pinches? Do not think, sir, that I am now to be fed with pap; for, before Heaven, I am no suckling. A fine jest, indeed, that your worship should endeavour to make me believe that the contents of these good books, printed with the license of the king's privy council, are all extravagant fables; as if they would allow the printing of a pack of lies!" "I have already told you, friend," replied the priest, "that it is done for the amusement of our idle thoughts; and as in all well-instituted commonwealths the games of chess, tennis, and billiards are permitted for the entertainment of those who have nothing to do, and who ought not or cannot work, for the same reason they permit such books to be published; presuming, as they well may, that nobody can be so ignorant as to take them for truth : and if this had been a seasonable time, I could lay down such rules for the composing books of chivalry as should, perhaps, make them not only agreeable but even useful; however, I hope an opportunity may offer for me to communicate my ideas to those who have the power to turn them to account. Here, landlord, take your books; and if you will not trust my word, you must settle the point of their truth or fiction as you please. Much good may they do you; and Heaven grant you halt not on the same foot as your guest, Don Quixote." "Not so," answered the innkeeper : "I shall not be so mad as to turn knight-errant; for I know very well that times are altered since those famous knights wandered about the world."

Sancho entered during this conversation, and was much confounded at hearing that knights-errant were not now in fashion, and that all books of chivalry were mere lies and fooleries; he therefore secretly resolved to wait the event of his master's present expedition, determined, if it was not successful, to leave him, and return home to his wife and children, and to his accustomed labour.

The innkeeper was carrying away the books, when the priest said to him, "Pray stop till I have looked at those papers which are written in so fair a character." The host took them out, and having given them to him, he found about eight sheets in manuscript, with a large title-page, on which was written, "The Novel of the Curious Impertinent." The priest having read three or four lines to himself, said, "In truth, I do not dislike the title of this novel, and I feel disposed to read the whole." "Your reverence will do well," answered the innkeeper; "for I assure you that some of my guests who have read it liked it mightily, and earnestly begged it of me; but I would not give it them, meaning to restore it to the person who left behind him the portmanteau with these books and papers. Perhaps their owner may come this way again some time or other; and though I shall feel the loss of the books, I will faithfully restore them; for though I am an innkeeper, thank Heaven I am a Christian." "You are much in the right, friend," said the priest; "nevertheless, if the novel pleases me, you must give me leave to take a copy of it." "With all my heart," answered the innkeeper. In the meantime Cardenio had taken up the novel, and being likewise pleased with what he saw, he requested the priest to read it aloud. "I will," said the priest, "unless you think we had better spend our time in sleeping." "I would rather listen to some tale," said Dorothea; "for my spirits are not so tranquil as to allow me to sleep." Master Nicholas and Sancho expressed the same inclination. "Well, then," said the priest, "I will read it; for I myself feel a little curiosity, and possibly it may yield us some amusement. So listen to me, good people, for thus it begins."

CHAPTER XXXIII.

In which is recited the novel of " The Curious Impertinent."

In Florence, a rich and famous city of Italy, in the province called Tuscany, lived Anselmo and Lothario, two gentlemen of rank and fortune, and so united in friendship, that by all who knew them they were distinguished by the appellation of The Two Friends. They were both unmarried, and of similar age and disposition. Anselmo was indeed somewhat more inclined to amorous pleasures than Lothario, who gave the preference to country sports; but each would occasionally neglect his own favourite pursuits to follow those of his friend: thus were their inclinations as harmoniously regulated as the motions of a clock. It so happened that Anselmo fell desperately in love with a beautiful young lady of condition in the same city, named Camilla; and he resolved, with the approbation of his friend Lothario, without which he did nothing, to demand her in marriage of her father. He employed Lothario in the affair, who managed it much to his satisfaction, for in a short time he found himself in possession of the object of his affection; and Lothario received the warmest acknowledgments from both for his friendly mediation.

For some days after the marriage—days usually dedicated to festivity —Lothario frequented as usual his friend Anselmo's house; but the nuptial season being passed, and compliments of congratulation over, Lothario began to remit the frequency of his visits to Anselmo; discreetly thinking it improper to visit friends when married as often as in their bachelor state: for although true friendship is not suspicious, yet so nice is the honour of a husband that it is liable to suffer even by a relative, much more by a friend. Anselmo observed Lothario's remissness, and complained of it; telling him that he would never have married had he suspected that it would occasion any abatement in their friendly intercourse; and he entreated him to resume his visits on their former terms of familiarity, assuring him that his wife's sentiments and wishes on the subject entirely corresponded with his own. Lothario replied with much prudence to the friendly importunities of Anselmo, and at length induced him to rest satisfied by a promise that he would dine with him twice a week, and on holidays. Lothario, however, resolved to observe this agreement no further than he should find consistent with the honour of his friend, whose reputation was no less dear to him than his own. He justly thought that a man on whom Heaven has bestowed a beautiful wife should be as cautious respecting the friends he introduces at home as to her female acquaintance abroad; for what cannot be concerted at the market-place, at church, or at public assemblies, may be easily effected by the assistance of some female relative or confidential friend. At the same time, he acknowledged that a husband often required the admonition or interference of a friend, in case of any inadvertency or want of prudence in a wife, which his own affection might cause him to overlook. But where was Anselmo to find such an adviser, so discreet, so faithful, and so sincere, unless it were in Lothario himself? — who, with the utmost diligence and attention, watched over the honour of his friend, and contrived to retrench, cut short, and abridge the number of appointed visiting days, lest the idle and malicious should censure the free access of a young, rich, and accomplished cavalier like himself to the house of a beautiful woman like Camilla. And though his known integrity and worth might bridle the tongues of the censorious, yet he was unwilling that his own honour or that of his friend should be in the least suspected. Most of the days, therefore, on which he had agreed to visit him he employed in concerns which he pretended were indispensable; and thus gave occasion for friendly complaints on one side, and excuses on the other.

One day, as they were walking in the fields together, Anselmo said to his friend, " I am sensible, Lothario, that I can never be sufficiently grateful to God for the blessings he has bestowed on me in giving me such excellent parents, and the goods of nature and fortune in abundance, and especially in having blessed me with such a friend as yourself, and such a wife as Camilla—treasures which I feel to be inestimable. Yet, notwithstanding all these advantages, I am the most uneasy and dissatisfied man living; having been for some time past harassed by a desire so strange and singular, that I am surprised and irritated at my own folly, and have endeavoured with all my power to repress it; but I find it impossible. On your friendly breast, then, I would fain repose my care, and trust by your assiduity to be restored to tranquillity and happiness."

Lothario was surprised at this long preamble, and could not possibly conjecture to what it tended. He told Anselmo that he was bound in friendship to repose implicit confidence in him, and that he might rely on all the assistance in his power.

" With this assurance, my friend," answered Anselmo, " I will confess, then, to you, that the cause of my solicitude is a desire to ascertain whether my wife be as good and perfect as I think she is. Of this I cannot be assured, unless she pass an ordeal, as gold does that of fire: for how, my friend, can a woman prove her virtue if she be not tried? She only is chaste who has resisted all the various solicitations of an importunate lover. What merit can a woman claim for being virtuous, if nobody persuades her to be otherwise? What is there extraordinary in a woman's prudence, if no opportunity is given her to go astray, or if she be only restrained by the fear of a husband's vengeance? She therefore, who is correct out of fear, or from want of opportunity, does not deserve to be held in the same degree of estimation as one who resists importunity. For these reasons, and others that I could assign, my desire is that Camilla should pass through the fiery ordeal of temptation; and if she comes out triumphant, as I believe she will, I shall account myself supremely happy, and can then say that I have attained the summit of good fortune, since the virtuous woman has fallen to my lot of whom the wise man says, 'Who can find her?' But should the event prove otherwise, the satisfaction of having proved the truth will enable me to bear the affliction occasioned by so costly an experiment. And, since nothing can divert me from it, I request you, my friend Lothario, to be my instrument in this business, for which I will afford you every facility, and you shall want nothing that I can think necessary to gain upon a modest, virtuous, reserved, and disinterested woman. Among other reasons which induce me to trust this nice affair to you is my confidence that, if Camilla should be overcome, you will not push the victory to the last extremity; so that I shall be wronged only in the intention, and the injury will remain by you buried in silence, which, as it regards me, will most certainly be eternal as that of death. Therefore, if you would have me enjoy my existence, you must immediately engage in this amorous combat, not languidly and lazily, but with all the fervour and diligence my design requires, and with the secresy which I expect from your friendship."

Lothario had listened to Anselmo with the utmost attention, and without once interrupting him; even after he had ceased speaking he continued for some time gazing at him in silence and surprise. "Surely, my friend Anselmo," he at length exclaimed, "you have been saying all this in jest! Could I think you in earnest, I should doubt the evidence of my senses, and question whether you were really Anselmo, and I Lothario. Certainly you are not the Anselmo you were wont to be, or you would not have made such a request of your Lothario; for men may prove and use their friends, as the poet expresses it, *usque ad aras;* meaning that a friend should not be required to act contrary to the law of God. If such was the precept of a heathen, surely it would be unbecoming a Christian to transgress it : if an infraction ever admitted of excuse, it could only be when the honour and life of a friend were at stake. But tell me, I pray, which of these are now in danger, that I should venture to gratify you by committing so detestable an action? On the contrary, if I understand you rightly, instead of preserving, you would have me deprive both you and myself of honour and life; for in robbing you of honour I should take your life, since a man dishonoured is worse than dead; and if I become the instrument of this evil, shall I not incur the same fate? Hear me patiently, my friend, and answer not until you have heard all my arguments against your strange proposal." "With all my heart," said Anselmo: "say what you please."

"It seems to me, Anselmo," resumed Lothario, "that it is now with you as it always is with the Moors, who never can be convinced of the errors of their sect by the evidence of Holy Scripture, nor by arguments drawn from reason or founded upon articles of faith; but you must give them proofs that are plain, intelligible, undeniable, and, in short, mathematically demonstrated; such as, 'If from equal parts we take equal parts, those that remain are also equal.' And if they do not comprehend this by words—and indeed they do not—you must show it to them with your hands, and set it before their very eyes; and after all, perhaps nothing can convince them of the truths of our holy religion. Thus it is with you; and so hopeless is the task of contending by argument against such preposterous folly, that only my friendship for you prevents me from leaving you at once to the punishment that will attend it. You desire me, Anselmo, to assail her who is modest and prudent—to seduce her who is virtuous. As you thus acknowledge that your wife possesses these qualities, what is it you would have? Being convinced of what is doubtless the fact—that her virtue is impregnable, how can she be raised higher in your estimation? for she cannot be more than perfect. If, in reality, you have not that favourable opinion of her which you profess to have, wherefore put her to such a test? Treat her rather as you think she deserves. But if, on the contrary, you believe in her chastity and truth, it is absurd to make an impertinent experiment, which cannot enhance the intrinsic worth of those qualities. To attempt voluntarily that which must be productive of evil rather than good, is madness and folly. Difficult works are undertaken for the sake of Heaven, of the world, or of both: the first are those performed by the saints, while they endeavour to live a life of angels in their human frames; such as are performed for love of the world are encountered by those who navigate the boundless ocean, traverse distant countries and various climates, to acquire what are called the goods of fortune. Those who assail hazardous enterprises for the sake of both God and man are brave soldiers, who no sooner perceive in the enemy's wall a breach made by a single cannon-ball, than, regardless of danger, and full of zeal in the defence of their faith, their country, and their king, they rush where death in a thousand shapes awaits them. These are difficulties commonly attempted; and though perilous, they are glorious and profitable. But your enterprise will neither acquire you glory from above, the goods of fortune, nor reputation among men; for, supposing the event to be satisfactory, you will be no gainer; if it should be otherwise, your situation will be wretched beyond conception, and it can afford you but little satisfaction, under the consciousness of such a misfortune, to think that it is unknown to others. For, as that celebrated poet Luis Tansilo says, in his 'Tears of St. Peter,'—

> " ' Shame, grief, remorse, in Peter's breast increase,
> Soon as the blushing morn his crime betrays:
> When most unseen, then most himself he sees,
> And with due horror all his soul surveys.

> " ' For a great spirit needs no censuring eyes
> To wound his soul, when conscious of a fault;
> But, self-condemned, and e'en self-punished, lies,
> And dreads no witness like upbraiding Thought.'

" Expect not, therefore, by concealment to banish sorrow ; for, even though you weep not openly, tears of blood will flow from your heart. So wept that simple doctor, who, according to the poet, would venture to make a trial of the cup which the more prudent Rinaldo wisely declined doing ; and although this be a poetical fiction, there is a concealed moral in it worthy to be observed and followed. But I have yet something more to say upon this subject, which, I hope, will fully convince you of the folly of your project.

" Tell me, Anselmo, if you were so fortunate as to possess a superlatively fine diamond, the value of which was acknowledged by jewellers, who all unanimously declared that, in weight, goodness, and beauty, it was most excellent of its kind, would it. be reasonable to insist on this diamond being laid on an anvil to try by the hammer whether it were really so hard and so fine as it was pronounced to be? If the stone bear the proof, it could not thereby acquire additional value ; and, should it break, would not all be lost? Yes, certainly, and its owner pass for a fool ! Consider, then, my friend Anselmo, that Camilla is a precious gem, both in your own estimation and in that of the world, and that it is absurd to expose her to danger, since though she should remain entire, she cannot rise in value; and should she fail, reflect what will be your loss as well as your self-reproaches for having caused both her ruin and your own ! There is no jewel in the world so valuable as a chaste and virtuous woman. The honour of women consists in the good opinion of the world ; and since that of your wife is eminently good, why would you have it questioned? Woman, my friend, is an imperfect creature ; and, instead of laying stumbling-blocks in her way, we should clear the path before her, that she may readily attain that virtue which is essential in her. Naturalists inform us that the ermine is a little creature with extremely white fur, and that when the hunters are in pursuit of it they spread with mire all the passes leading to its haunts, to which they then drive it, knowing that it will submit to be taken rather than defile itself. The virtuous and modest woman is an ermine, and her character whiter than snow ; and in order to preserve it, a very different method must be taken from that which is used with the ermine : she must not be driven into mire, that is, the foul addresses of lovers ; since she may not have sufficient virtue and strength to extricate herself from the snare. Instead of exposing her to such danger, you should present to her view the beauty of virtue and fair fame. The reputation of a woman may also be compared to a mirror of crystal, shining and bright, but liable to be sullied by every breath that comes near it. The virtuous woman must be treated like a relic—adored, but not handled ; she should be guarded and prized, like a fine flower-garden, the beauty and fragrance of which the owner allows others to enjoy only at a distance, and through iron rails. I will also repeat to you some verses, applicable to the present subject, which I remember to have heard in a modern comedy. A prudent old man advises the father of a young maiden to look well after her, and lock her up. Among others, he gives the following reasons :

> " ' If woman's glass, why should we try
> Whether she can be broke or no?
> Great hazards in the trial lie,
> Because, perchance, she may be so.
>
> " ' Who that is wise, such brittle ware
> Would careless dash upon the floor,
> Which, broken, nothing can repair,
> Nor solder to its form restore?
>
> " ' In this opinion all are found,
> And reason vouches what I say:
> Wherever Danaës abound,
> There golden showers will make their way.'

" All that I have hitherto said, Anselmo, relates to you. It is now proper I should say something concerning myself; and pardon me if I am prolix, for I am compelled to be so, in order to extricate you from the labyrinth into which you have strayed. You look upon me as your friend, and yet, against all rules of friendship, would have me forfeit my own honour, as well as deprive you of yours. That mine would be lost is plain; for when Camilla heard of my professions of love, she would certainly regard me as the basest of men, for entertaining views so derogatory to myself and my friend. And that your honour would suffer is equally certain; for she would naturally think that I had discovered some levity in her, which encouraged me to declare a guilty passion, and would consequently regard herself as dishonoured; and in her dishonour, you, as her husband, must participate. For the husband of an adulteress, though not accessory, nor even privy, to her transgressions, is nevertheless universally branded by an opprobrious and vilifying name, and regarded with contempt rather than pity: yet if you will listen to me with patience, I will explain to you why it is just that the husband should suffer this odium. We are informed by the Holy Scriptures that woman was formed from the rib of our first parent Adam, and thence pronounced to be one flesh. At the same time, the holy sacrament of marriage was ordained, with ties that death alone can dissolve. The husband, therefore, being of the same flesh as his wife, must needs be affected by whatever affects her, as the head feels the smart of the ankle, and pain in any one of the members is communicated to the whole body. Thus, however guiltless the man, he must participate in the woman's dishonour, and her shame is his disgrace. Think, then, Anselmo, on the danger to which you expose yourself in seeking to disturb the repose of your virtuous consort. Consider from what vain and impertinent curiosity you would stir up the passions now dormant in the breast of your chaste spouse. Reflect what an immense risk you incur for a trifling gratification. But if all I have said be not sufficient to dissuade you from your preposterous design, you must seek another instrument to effect your disgrace and misery; for I am resolved not to act this part, though I should lose your friendship, which is the greatest loss I can conceive."

Here the virtuous and discreet Lothario ceased; and Anselmo was perplexed for some time how to answer him; at length he said, "I have listened to you, my friend, with attention; and your arguments prove the sincerity of your friendship, as well as your good sense. I am well aware that in adhering to my project and rejecting your counsel, I am acting unwisely; but my dear Lothario, you must look upon my folly as a disease, and grant it some indulgence. Satisfy me by just making an attempt, even though it be but a cold one, upon Camilla, who surely will not surrender at the first onset; and with this act of friendship on your part I promise to rest contented. You will thereby restore me to the enjoyment of existence, and preserve my honour, which would otherwise be endangered by your forcing me to apply to another person; for determined I still am to make this experiment. Do not be concerned at the temporary loss of Camilla's good opinion; for after her integrity has been proved, you may disclose our plot to her, whereupon she will immediately restore you to favour. I entreat you, then, not to decline the task, since you may so easily gratify me; and again I promise to be satisfied by your first essay."

Lothario finding Anselmo determined in his purpose, and being unable to suggest any other dissuasive arguments, affected to yield to his request, lest he should expose his folly to some other person. Anselmo embraced him with great tenderness and affection, and thanked him as much for his compliance as if he had done him some great favour. It was agreed between them that he should begin operations the very next day, when Anselmo would give him an opportunity to converse alone with Camilla, and supply him also with money and jewels for presents to her. He advised him to serenade her, and write verses in her praise, and, if he thought it too much trouble, he would himself compose them for him. Lothario consented to everything, but with an intention very different from what his friend imagined. This arrangement being made, they returned to Anselmo's house, where they found Camilla anxiously waiting the return of her spouse, who that day was later than usual. Lothario after some time retired to his own house, leaving his friend no less happy than he was himself perplexed at the impertinent business in which he had engaged. However, he devised a plan by which he might deceive Anselmo and avoid giving offence to his wife. The next day he went to dine with his friend, and was kindly received by Camilla, who indeed always treated him with much cordiality, on account of the friendship her husband entertained for him. Dinner being finished, and the cloth removed, Anselmo desired Lothario to stay with Camilla while he went upon an urgent affair, which he should dispatch in about an hour and a half. Camilla entreated him not to go, and Lothario offered to accompany him; but it was all to no purpose: he importuned Lothario to wait for him, saying he wished particularly to speak with him on his return; at the same time he desired Camilla to entertain his friend during his absence, for which he made a very plausible excuse.

Anselmo departed, and Camilla and Lothario remained together, the rest of the family being engaged at dinner. Thus Lothario perceived that he had entered the lists, as his friend desired, with an enemy before him sufficiently powerful to conquer, by her beauty alone, a squadron of armed cavaliers: think, then, whether Lothario had not cause to fear. However, the first thing that he did was to lean his elbow on the arm of the chair, and his cheek on his hand; and begging Camilla to pardon his ill-manners, he said he was inclined for a little repose. Camilla answered that he would be more at ease on the couch than in the chair, and therefore begged that he would lie down upon it. Lothario declined the offer, and remained sleeping in his chair until Anselmo returned, who, finding Camilla retired to her chamber, and Lothario asleep, concluded, as his absence had been long, that there had been time enough for them both to talk and to sleep; and he thought Lothario would never awake, so great was his impatience to learn his success. Lothario at length awakening, they walked out together, when, in answer to the inquiries of Anselmo, he said that he did not think it proper to open too far the first time, and therefore all that he had done was to tell her she was very handsome, and that the whole city talked of her wit and beauty; and this he thought a good introduction, as he should thus insinuate himself into her good-will, and dispose her to listen to him the next time with pleasure: employing the same artifice as the devil, who, when he would entrap a cautious person, assumes an angel form till he carries his point, when the cloven foot appears. Anselmo was extremely well satisfied, and said he would give him the same opportunity every day, without leaving home, for that he could find some employment to account for his withdrawing himself.

Many days now passed, and Lothario, still preserving his respect to Camilla, assured Anselmo that he had assailed her, but that she never betrayed the least symptom of weakness, nor gave him a shadow of hope; on the contrary, that she threatened to inform her husband if he did not relinquish his base design. " So far, all is well," said Anselmo; "hitherto Camilla has resisted words; we must now attack her another way. To-morrow I will give you two thousand crowns in gold to present to her, and as many more to purchase jewels, by way of lure, for women are pleased with finery; and if she resists this temptation I will be satisfied, and give you no further trouble." Lothario promised that, since he had begun, he would go through with this affair, although his defeat was certain. The next day he received the four thousand crowns, and with them four thousand perplexities as to the new lies he must invent; he resolved, however, to tell him that Camilla was quite as inflexible to presents and promises as to words, so that he need not trouble himself further, since it was all time lost.

Unfortunately, however, Anselmo was seized with an inclination one day, after leaving Lothario and his wife alone as usual, to listen at the door and peep through the keyhole, when, after waiting above half an hour, he heard not a single word pass between them—in truth, if he had waited all day it would have been to no purpose. He now concluded that his friend had deceived him; but to ascertain it he called him aside, and inquired how matters were going on. Lothario said in reply that

Anselmo was seized with an inclination one day to listen at the door.

he could not persevere any longer, for she rebuked him so sharply, that he could not presume to open his lips to her again upon the subject. "Ah, Lothario, Lothario!" cried Anselmo, "is this your return for my confidence? Is it thus you fulfil your engagement to me? I have been watching you a long time at the door, and find that you have not spoken a word to Camilla; from which I must infer that you have never yet spoken to her. If so, why is it you deceive me, and prevent me from applying to others who would gratify my desire?" Anselmo said no more. Lothario was abashed and confounded; and, thinking his honour touched by being detected in a lie, swore to Anselmo that from that moment he engaged to satisfy him, and would deceive him no more, as he should find if he had the curiosity to watch him: he might, however, save himself the trouble, for he was determined to make such exertions for his satisfaction, that there should be no room left for suspicion. Anselmo believed him; and, to give him an opportunity less liable to interruption, he resolved to absent himself from home for eight days, and to visit a friend who lived in a neighbouring village, from whom he managed to get a pressing invitation in order to account for his departure to Camilla. Rash, foolish Anselmo! what art thou doing? Plotting thine own dishonour, contriving thine own ruin! Thou art in tranquil possession of a virtuous wife, the sole object of her affections, and, under Heaven, her only guide! Thus blessed by the treasures of honour, beauty, and virtue, why do you madly endanger them? Consider that he who seeks after what is impossible, ought in justice to be denied what is possible; as a certain poet has better expressed it in these verses:

> " In death alone I life would find,
>   And health in racking pain;
> Fair honour in a traitor's mind,
>   Or freedom in a chain.

> " But since I ask what ne'er can be,
>   The Fates, alas! decide,
> What they would else have granted me
>   Shall ever be denied."

Anselmo, on leaving home, told Camilla that Lothario would take charge of the house during his absence, and he desired she would treat him as his own person. The discreet and virtuous wife did not approve this arrangement, and represented to him the impropriety of another man taking his place at table when he was absent; and she assured him that, if he would intrust the charge of the household to her, he would find her fully competent to the charge. Anselmo, however, still persisted in his orders, and Camilla was compelled to yield to them, though with great reluctance.

The day after Anselmo's departure, Lothario went to his house, where he met with a kind but modest reception from Camilla, who, to avoid being left alone with him, was constantly attended by her servants, especially a female one, named Leonela, to whom she had been attached from her infancy. Three days passed, and Lothario had not begun his enterprise, though he was not without opportunities during the necessary absence of the servants at their dinner-time. Leonela, indeed, was desired by her mistress to dine first, so that she might never quit her side; but she had her own engagements, and often left them alone, notwithstanding the orders of her mistress. However, the modest demeanour of Camilla and the propriety of her conduct restrained Lothario's tongue; but the influence of her virtue in imposing this silence proved but the more dangerous; for if his tongue was at rest his thoughts were in motion, and he had leisure to contemplate all the perfections of her mind and person, which could not have failed to move even a heart of marble. This silent but dangerous contemplation gradually undermined his fidelity to Anselmo; yet a thousand times he thought of retiring from the city, and absenting himself for ever both from Camilla and his friend; but the pleasure he experienced in her presence still detained him. Many were the internal struggles he had to resist the delight he felt in gazing on her; and still, when alone, he reproached himself for being so false a friend and so bad a Christian; yet, on considering the conduct of Anselmo, whose folly he thought exceeded his own perfidy, he only wished he could stand as excusable before God as before men. In fine, the beauty and goodness of Camilla, together with the opportunity which the inconsiderate husband had forced upon him, quite overcame Lothario's integrity; and after maintaining a hard conflict with his passion during three days, he became regardless of everything but its gratification. At their next meeting, therefore, he began to address Camilla with so much warmth of expression, that she was astonished, and without making any reply rose from her seat, and retired to her chamber. But her frigidity did not discourage her lover, for hope is ever born with love: he only grew more ardent. In the meantime Camilla, thinking it improper to give him another opportunity of addressing her, dispatched a messenger the same night to Anselmo with the following letter.

CHAPTER XXXIV.

In which is continued the novel of " The Curious Impertinent."

"CAMILLA TO ANSELMO.

"CASTLES should not be left without governors, nor armies without generals; but it is worse for a young wife to be left without her husband. I find it so impossible to endure your absence any longer, that if you do not return immediately I must retreat to my father's house, though I leave yours unguarded; for he whom you left as a protector is, I believe, more intent upon his own pleasure than your interests. You are prudent, so I need say no more."

Anselmo received this letter, and understood by it that Lothario had begun the attack, and that Camilla must have received it according to his wish. Overjoyed at this good news, he sent Camilla a verbal message, desiring her not to remove from her house upon any account, for he would return very speedily. Camilla was surprised at this answer, which only increased her perplexity; for now she was equally afraid to remain in her own house and to retire to that of her parents, since by staying her virtue was endangered, and by departing she would act contrary to her husband's positive commands. Her final determination proved the worst, which was to stay and not shun Lothario, lest it might excite the observation of the servants; and she now regretted having written to her husband, lest he should suspect that some impropriety in her conduct had encouraged Lothario to treat her with disrespect. But conscious of her own integrity, she trusted in God and her own virtue, resolving by her silence to discourage Lothario, without communicating any more on the subject to her husband, lest it should involve him in a quarrel. She even began to consider how she might excuse Lothario to Anselmo when he should inquire into the meaning of her letter.

With this determination, more honourable than prudent, the next day she quietly heard what Lothario had to say; and he pleaded with so much energy that the firmness of Camilla began to waver, and her virtue could hardly prevent her eyes from showing some indications of amorous compassion. This was not lost upon him, and it only tended to increase the ardour of his passion. He resolved to press the siege while time and opportunity served; and he employed against her the powerful engine of flattery, thus assailing her in the most vulnerable part of woman—her vanity. In fact, he undermined the fortress of her virtue, and directed against it so irresistible a force that had she been made of brass she must have fallen. He wept, entreated, flattered, and solicited with such vehemence of passion, that he gradually overcame her reserve, and finally obtained a triumph. She surrendered—yes, even Camilla surrendered!—No wonder, when Lothario's friendship could not stand its ground! A clear proof that the passion of love is to be conquered by flight alone; that it is vain to contend with a power which, though human, requires more than human strength to subdue it.

Leonela alone was privy to her lady's frailty, for it was impossible to have concealed it from her. Lothario never told Camilla of her husband's project, and of his having purposely afforded him the opportunity of addressing her, lest she should doubt his sincerity, or set less value on his passion.

After some days, Anselmo returned, little thinking he had lost a treasure which, though least guarded, he most valued. He repaired instantly to Lothario, and embracing him, inquired for the news which was to decide his fate. "The news I have for you, O friend Anselmo," said Lothario, "is that you have a wife worthy to be the model and crown of all good women. My words were thrown to the wind: my offers have been despised, my presents refused, and the tears I feigned treated with ridicule. In short, as Camilla is the sum of all beauty, so is she of goodness, modesty, and every virtue which can make a woman praiseworthy and happy. Therefore, friend, take back your money. Here it is: I had no occasion to use it, for Camilla's integrity is not to be shaken by anything so base. Be satisfied, Anselmo; and since you have safely passed the gulf of suspicion, do not hazard fresh trials on the dangerous ocean, but rest securely in harbour until you are required to pay that tribute from which no human being is exempted."

Anselmo was entirely satisfied with Lothario's report, to which he gave as much credit as if it had been delivered by an oracle. Nevertheless, he desired him not entirely to give up the pursuit, were it only out of curiosity and amusement; though it would not be necessary to ply her so closely as before. All that he now desired of him was to write verses in her praise, under the name of Chloris; and he would give Camilla to understand that he was in love with a lady to whom he had given that name, that he might celebrate her without offending her modesty. He even engaged to write the verses himself, if Lothario was unwilling to take that trouble. " There will be no need of that," said Lothario; " for the Muses are not so unpropitious to me but that now and then they make me a visit. Tell Camilla of my counterfeit passion, and leave the verses to me, which, if not so good as the subject deserves, shall at least be the best I can make." This agreement being concluded between the curious husband and the treacherous friend, the former returned home, and inquired of Camilla, as she had expected, the occasion of her writing the letter which she sent him. Camilla answered that she then fancied Lothario treated her with rather more freedom than when he was at home, but that she now believed it to have been merely imaginary on her part; for, indeed, of late he had avoided seeing and being alone with her. Anselmo replied that she might dismiss all suspicion; for, to his knowledge, Lothario was in love with a young lady of condition in the city, whom he celebrated under the name of Chloris; and, even were it not so, she had nothing to fear, considering Lothario's virtue and the great friendship that subsisted between them. Had not Camilla been advertised by Lothario that this story of his love for Chloris was all a fiction, which he had invented merely to obtain an opportunity of indulging in praises of herself, she would doubtless have been seized with a fit of jealousy; but, having been thus prepared, she felt no uneasiness on the subject.

The next day, as they were at table together, Anselmo desired Lothario to recite some of the verses he had composed on his beloved Chloris; for, since she was unknown to Camilla, he need not scruple to repeat them.

" Even were she not unknown," answered Lothario, " I would not conceal the praises which are her due; for when a lover complains of his mistress, while he extols her perfections, he casts no reproach upon her good name. I will, therefore, without scruple read to you this sonnet, which I composed yesterday, on the ingratitude of Chloris:

SONNET.

In the dead silence of the peaceful night,
 When others' cares are hushed in soft repose,
 The sad account of my neglected woes
To conscious heaven and Chloris I recite.
And when the sun, with his returning light,
 Forth from the east his radiant journey goes,
 With accents such as sorrow only knows
My griefs to tell is all my poor delight.
And when bright Phœbus from his starry throne
 Sends rays direct upon the parchéd soil,
  Still in the mournful tale I persevere;
  Returning night renews my sorrow's toil;
And though from morn to night I weep and moan,
 Nor Heaven nor Chloris my complainings hear."

Camilla was very well pleased with the sonnet, and Anselmo was lavish in his commendation, declaring that the lady was too cruel not to reward so much truth. "What, then!" replied Camilla, "are we to take all that the enamoured poets tell us for truth?" "Whatever they may say as poets," answered Lothario, "certainly as lovers they speak the truth, and express still less than they feel." "Undoubtedly," said Anselmo, who was ready to confirm all Lothario said, to advance his credit with Camilla; but this complacency in her husband she did not observe, being engrossed by her passion for Lothario. And, taking pleasure in hearing his verses (especially as she was conscious of being herself the Chloris to whom they were addressed), she requested him, if he could recollect any others, to repeat them. "I do recollect another," replied Lothario, "but I fear it is even worse than the one you have just heard; however, you shall judge for yourself.

SONNET.

"Believe me, nymph, I feel th' impending blow,
   And glory in the near approach of death;
   For, when thou seest my corse devoid of breath,
My constancy and truth thou sure wilt know.
Welcome to me oblivion's shade obscure!
   Welcome the loss of fortune, life, and fame!
   But thy loved features, and thy honoured name,
Deep graven on my heart, shall still endure.
And these, as sacred relics, will I keep
   Till that sad moment when to endless night
   My long-tormented soul shall take her flight.
Alas for him who on the darkened deep
   Floats idly, sport of the tempestuous tide,
   No port to shield him, and no star to guide!"

Anselmo commended this second sonnet as much as he had done the first; and thus he went on labouring to secure his own shame and adding fresh links to the chain of his infamy; and the more the lover triumphed, the more he assured the husband of his unblemished honour. Thus, the lower Camilla sunk into the abyss of infamy, the higher she rose, in her husband's opinion, towards the pinnacle of virtue and honour.

One day, when Camilla was alone with her maid, she said to her, "I am ashamed, Leonela, to think how little value I placed upon myself in allowing Lothario so soon to gain the entire possession of my heart. I fear he will look upon my easy surrender as the effect of levity, without reflecting on his own resistless power." "Dear madam," answered Leonela, "let not this trouble you, for there is nothing in it. A gift, if it be worth anything, is not worse for being soon given; and therefore they say, He who gives quickly gives twice." "But they say also," returned Camilla, "That which is lightly gained is little valued." "This does not affect your case," answered Leonela; "for love, as I have heard say, sometimes flies and sometimes walks—runs with one person, and goes leisurely with another: some he warms, and some he burns; some he wounds, and others he kills: in one and the same instant he forms and accomplishes his projects. He often in the morning lays siege to a fortress which in the evening surrenders to him ; for no force is able to resist him. What then are you afraid of, if this was the case with Lothario? My master's absence was instrumental to love's success; and no time was to be lost, for love has no better minister than opportunity. This I am well acquainted with, from experience rather than hearsay ; and one day or other, madam, I may let you see that I also am a girl of flesh and blood. Besides, madam, you did not yield before you had seen, in his eyes, in his sighs, in his expressions, in his promises and his presents, the whole soul of Lothario, and how worthy he was of your love. Then let not these scruples and niceties disturb you, but be assured Lothario esteems you no less than you do him , and rest satisfied that, since you have fallen into the snare of love, it is with a person of worth and character, and one who possesses not only the four S's*, which they say all true lovers ought to have, but the whole alphabet. Do but hear me, and you shall see how I have it by heart. He is, if I am not mistaken, amiable, bountiful, constant, daring, enamoured, faithful, gallant, honourable, illustrious, kind, loyal, mild, noble, obliging, prudent, quiet, rich, and the S's, as they say ; lastly, true, valiant, and wise. The X suits him not, because it is a harsh letter ; the Y, he is young; the Z, zealous of your honour."

Camilla smiled at this alphabet of her maid, whom she found to be more conversant in love matters than she had hitherto owned ; and, indeed, she now confessed to her that she had an affair with a young gentleman of the same city. At this Camilla was much disturbed, fearing lest from that quarter her own honour might be in danger. She therefore inquired whether her amour had gone further than words. Leonela, with the utmost assurance, owned that it had ; for it is certain that the slips of the mistress take all shame from the maid, who, when her mistress makes a false step, thinks nothing of downright halting, and takes no trouble to conceal it. Camilla could only entreat Leonela to say nothing of the affair to her lover, and to manage her own concerns with such secrecy that it might not come to the knowledge of Anselmo or Lothario. Leonela promised to be careful. Nevertheless, Camilla's fears were verified ; for the shameless girl, when she found that her mistress's conduct was not what it had been, made bold to introduce and conceal her lover in the house, presuming that her lady would not dare to complain if she should discover it. For this inconvenience, among others, attends the misconduct of mistresses : they become slaves to their own servants, whose dishonesty and lewdness they are compelled to conceal. Thus it was with Camilla ; for though she frequently saw that Leonela entertained her gallant in the house, so far from daring to chide her, she gave her opportunities of secreting him, and did all she could to prevent him being seen by her husband. Yet, notwithstanding her precautions, Lothario once discovered him retreating from the house at break of day. At first he thought it must be some vision of his fancy ; but when he saw him steal off, muffling himself up and endea-

---

* *Sabio, solo, solícito y secreto.*

vouring to conceal himself, suspicions succeeded which would have been the ruin of them all had it not been averted by Camilla. It never occurred to Lothario that the man whom he had seen coming out of Anselmo's house at so unseasonable an hour might have gone thither upon Leonela's account; he did not even remember that there was such a person in the world; but he thought that Camilla, as she had been easy and complying to him, was not less so to another; for a woman always loses with her virtue the confidence even of the man to whose entreaties and solicitations she surrendered her honour; and he is ready to believe, upon the slightest grounds, that she yields to others even with greater facility.

All Lothario's good sense and prudence seemed to have failed him upon this occasion; for, without a moment's rational reflection, blinded with jealous rage, and furious to be revenged on Camilla, who had offended him in nothing, he hastened to Anselmo. " My friend," he said, " I can no longer forbear communicating to you what for some days past I have been struggling to conceal. Your wife, Anselmo, submits to my will and pleasure. One of my motives for delaying to tell you was my uncertainty whether she was really culpable, or only meant to try whether the love I professed was with your connivance or in earnest, in which case she would have informed you of my attempts upon her; but finding she has been silent to you on the subject, I must conclude that she is serious in her promises to grant me an interview in the wardrobe the next time you are absent from home. However, as the fault is committed only in thought, do not rashly seek to revenge yourself; for before the appointed time Camilla may change her mind and repent. If you will follow my advice, you shall have an opportunity of ascertaining the truth without the possibility of being mistaken; and you can then act as you may think proper. Let your wife imagine that you have left home for some days, and conceal yourself behind the tapestry in the wardrobe, where you may be convinced by your own eyes of Camilla's real sentiments; and if they are evil, you may then secretly and quietly avenge your wrongs."

Anselmo was struck aghast at Lothario's intelligence; for already he looked upon her victory as complete, and began to enjoy the glory of her triumph. For some time he remained with his eyes fixed motionless on the ground. At length he said, " Lothario, you have acted the friendly part I required of you : I will now be guided by your advice in everything—do what you will, only be cautious to preserve secrecy." Lothario satisfied him by his promises; but scarcely had he quitted him when he began to be sensible of the folly of his conduct, and to regret that he had taken so cruel and unmanly a way to revenge himself on Camilla. He cursed his senseless impetuosity, and felt quite at a loss how to act in such a dilemma. Finally he resolved to confess all to Camilla; and on the same day contrived to see her alone. " Ah, my dear Lothario," she exclaimed, immediately on his entrance, " I am overwhelmed with anxiety; for Leonela's impudence is now carried to such a height that she entertains her gallant every night in the house,

For some time Anselmo remained with his eyes fixed motionless on the ground.

and he stays with her until daylight, to the imminent danger of my
reputation, which is exposed to the suspicions of those who may chance
to see him leave the house at such unseasonable hours; and what grieves
me is this, that I cannot chastise nor even reprimand her, for though I
am alarmed at her conduct, I am compelled to bear it in silence, as she
is in our confidence."

Lothario at first suspected that this was all artifice in Camilla to
deceive him, in case he had seen the man going out of the house; but
he was soon convinced of her sincerity, and felt ashamed and full of
remorse at his unjust suspicions. However, he endeavoured to tran-
quilise Camilla, and promised to curb Leonela's insolence. He then
confessed to her the furious fit of jealousy that had taken possession of
him, and what had passed between Anselmo and himself while he was
under its influence. He entreated her to pardon his madness, and to
devise some means of averting the mischief in which his rashness had
involved them both. Camilla was surprised on hearing Lothario's confession, and expressed no little resentment towards him for having

harboured such unworthy suspicions of her, as well as for the rash and inconsiderate step he had taken. But she instantly thought of an expedient to repair the state of their affairs, which at present seemed so desperate; for women have naturally a ready invention, either for good or evil, though they are not equally successful in their premeditated schemes. She desired Lothario to introduce her husband to the appointed place of concealment the following day, in pursuance of a plan by which she proposed to facilitate their future intercourse; and, without letting him into the whole of her design, she only desired him, after Anselmo was posted, to be ready at Leonela's call, and to answer whatever she should say to him, just as he would do if he were unconscious that Anselmo was listening. Lothario pressed her to explain to him her whole design, that he might be the better prepared. "No other preparation is necessary," replied Camilla; "you have only to give me direct answers." She was unwilling to impart to him the whole design, lest he should find objections to it.

Lothario then left her; and the next day Anselmo, under pretence of going to his friend's villa, went from home, but immediately returned to his hiding-place, where he remained in a state of violent perturbation, as may readily be imagined, since he thought himself on the point of witnessing his own dishonour and losing that treasure which he had fancied he possessed in his beloved Camilla. The mistress and maid having ascertained that Anselmo was behind the hangings, entered the wardrobe together, when Camilla, heaving a deep sigh, said, "Ah, my Leonela, would it not be better you should plunge Anselmo's sword into this infamous bosom? But no!—why should I alone be punished for another's fault? I will first know what the insolent Lothario saw in me to encourage him to make so wicked an attempt against my honour and that of his friend. Go to the window, Leonela, and call him; for I doubt not but that he is waiting in the street, in expectation of succeeding in his atrocious design—but my purpose shall sooner be executed." "Ah, dear madam!" cried the artful Leonela, "what do you mean to do with that dagger? Is it to be used against yourself or Lothario? In either case both your reputation and mine will suffer. Bear the insult he has offered you, rather than let this wicked man into the house now that we are alone. Consider, madam, we are helpless women, and he is a strong man, bent upon a villanous purpose; and before you could effect yours, he might do worse than deprive you of life. A mischief take my master Anselmo for giving this impudent fellow such an ascendency in his house! But pray, madam, if you kill him—which I suppose is your intention—what shall we do with his body?" "What, my friend!" answered Camilla, "why leave him here for Anselmo to inter; for it is but just he should have the satisfaction of burying his own infamy. Call him immediately; for every moment's delay of my revenge is an offence against that loyalty I owe to my husband."

To all this Anselmo listened, and every word spoken by Camilla had the intended effect upon him; and when she talked of killing Lothario he was on the point of coming forth to prevent it, but was withheld by the strong desire he had to see the end of so gallant and virtuous a resolution; intending, however, to appear in time to prevent mischief. Camilla was in the next place taken with a strong fainting-fit; and, throwing herself upon a couch, Leonela began to weep bitterly, exclaiming, "Ah, woe is me! that the flower of virtue, the crown of good women, the pattern of chastity, should die here in my arms!" with other such expressions, which might well have made her pass with whoever heard them for the most virtuous and faithful damsel in the universe, and her lady for another persecuted Penelope. Camilla, having recovered from her swoon, said, "Why do you not go, Leonela, and call the most faithless friend that ever existed? Be quick, run, fly—let not the fire of my rage evaporate by delay, and my just vengeance be spent in empty threats and curses!" "I am going to call him," said Leonela; "but, dear madam, you must first give me that dagger, lest, when I am gone, you should give those who love you cause to weep all their lives." "Go, dear Leonela, and fear not," said Camilla: "I will not do it; for though I am resolute in defending my honour, I shall not act like Lucretia, who is said to have killed herself without having committed any fault, and without first taking his life who was the cause of her misfortune. Yes, I will die—die I must; but it shall be after I have satiated my revenge on him who has insulted me without provocation."

After much entreaty, Leonela obeyed; and while she was away, Camilla indulged in soliloquy. "Good heavens!" she cried, "would it not have been more advisable to have repulsed Lothario, as formerly, rather than give him reason to think injuriously of me by delaying to undeceive him? Surely it would; but then I should go unrevenged, nor would my husband's honour be satisfied if he were to escape with impunity. No! let the traitor pay for his insolence with his life! and if ever the affair be known, Camilla shall be vindicated to the world. It might, indeed, have been better to have disclosed all to Anselmo; but he disregarded my hints—his own confiding nature would not admit of a thought prejudicial to his friend. Scarcely could I trust my own senses when he first declared himself. But wherefore do I talk thus? My resolution is taken. Yes, vengeance on the traitor! Let him die! Unspotted my husband received me to his arms, and unspotted I will leave him, though bathed in my own blood and that of the falsest of friends." She now paced about the room with the drawn dagger in her hand, taking such irregular and huge strides, and with such gestures, that her brain seemed disordered, and she was more like a desperate ruffian than a delicate woman.

All this Anselmo observed with amazement from behind the arras, and thinking that what he had witnessed was sufficient to dispel doubts still greater than those he had entertained, he began to wish that Lothario might not come, for fear of some fatal accident, and was upon the point of rushing out to clasp his wife in his arms, when he was prevented by the return of Leonela, accompanied by Lothario; upon whose entrance Camilla drew with the dagger a long line between them, and said : " Observe, Lothario, if you dare to pass that line, I will instantly pierce my breast with this dagger. But listen to what I have to say to you. In the first place, tell me, Lothario, do you know Anselmo, my husband, and in what estimation do you hold him? Tell me also whether you know me? Answer me at once—for these are simple questions." Lothario easily comprehended her design, and accordingly humoured it, so that they managed the whole scene admirably together. " I did not imagine, fair Camilla," he replied, " that you called me to answer to things so foreign to the purpose for which I came hither. If it be to delay the promised favour, why not have adjourned it to a still further day ?—for the nearer the prospect of possession, the more eager we are for the enjoyment. In answer to your questions, I say that I have known your husband Anselmo from infancy : of our friendship I will say nothing, that I may not be witness against myself of the wrong which love—that powerful excuse for greater faults—compels me to commit against him. You, too, I know and adore—for less excellence I should not have transgressed the laws of friendship, which are now violated by its potent adversary, love." " If you acknowledge so much," replied Camilla, " thou mortal enemy of all deserving love ! how dare you appear before me—the beloved of Anselmo, whom without provocation you injure ? But, alas ! unhappy creature that I am ! perhaps unconsciously I may have encouraged your presumption, not by immodesty, but through some inadvertency into which a woman may innocently fall when she conceives no reserve to be necessary. But say, perfidious man, did I ever, by a single expression, encourage you to hope? Was not your flattery always repulsed with indignation, and your presents rejected with scorn? Still I take blame to myself for having moved you to so criminal an attempt, and I cannot acquit myself of indiscretion, since you have nourished hope; I will, therefore, suffer the punishment due to your offence, and have brought you hither to witness the sacrifice I intend to make to the wounded honour of my worthy husband, who by you has been so deliberately injured ; and, alas ! by me also, through negligence—the thought of which is so agonizing to me that I am impatient to become my own executioner. Yes, I will die ! but not without revenging myself on him who has reduced me to this state of desperation ! "

At these words she flew upon Lothario with the drawn dagger, with such incredible force and velocity, and apparently so determined to stab him to the heart, that he was almost in doubt himself whether her efforts were feigned or real, and he was obliged to exert all his dexterity to escape a wound : indeed, she acted so much to the life that she actually shed her own blood. Finding, or rather feigning, that she was unable to stab Lothario, she exclaimed, " Though fate denies me complete satisfaction, it shall not disappoint me of one part of my revenge!" Then, forcibly releasing her dagger-hand from the grasp of Lothario, she directed the point against herself (being, however, careful in her choice of the part) ; and having wounded herself on the left side, near the shoulder, she fell, as if fainting, to the ground. Leonela and

She flew upon Lothario with the drawn dagger, with such force that he was obliged to exert all his dexterity to escape a wound.

Lothario stood in amazement at this action, and knew not what to think when they saw Camilla lying on the floor bathed in her own blood. Lothario ran up to her, terrified and breathless, to draw out the dagger; but on perceiving the slightness of the wound, his fears vanished, and he admired the sagacity, prudence, and ingenuity of the fair Camilla. And now he took up his part, and began to make a most pathetic lamentation over the body of Camilla, as if she were dead ; imprecating heavy curses, not only on himself, but on him who had been the cause of this disaster: his grief, in short, appeared so inconsolable, that he seemed an object even of greater compassion than Camilla herself. Leonela took her lady in her arms, and laid her on the couch, beseeching Lothario secretly to procure medical aid. She also desired his advice as to what they should say to Anselmo, if he should return before the wound was healed. He answered that they might say what they pleased, for he was not in a condition to give advice; all he desired was that she would endeavour to stanch the blood : as for himself, he would go where he should never be seen more. Then, with every demonstration of sorrow, he left the house; and when he found himself alone and out of sight, he never ceased crossing himself in amazement at the ingenuity of Camilla and the art of Leonela. He amused himself, too, in thinking of Anselmo's happy certainty of possessing in his wife a second Portia, and was impatient to be with him, that they might rejoice at the most complete imposture that ever was practised.

Leonela stanched her mistress's blood, of which there was just enough to give effect to her stratagem ; and washing the wound with a little wine, she bound it up as well as she could. In the meantime her expressions were such as might alone have convinced Anselmo that in Camilla he possessed a model of chastity; and Camilla too now uttered some words reproaching herself for a deficiency of courage and spirit in having failed in ridding herself of a life she so much abhorred. She asked her maid's advice, whether or not she should relate what had happened to her beloved spouse. Leonela persuaded her to say nothing about it, since it would oblige him to take revenge on Lothario, which he could not do without great danger to himself; and that it was the duty of a good wife to avoid every occasion of involving her husband in a quarrel. Camilla approved her advice, and said she would follow it ; but that they must consider what to say to Anselmo about the wound, which he could not fail to observe. To which Leonela answered, that for her part she could not tell a lie even in jest. " How then can I ? " said Camilla, " who neither could invent nor persist in one, if it were to save my life. If a good excuse cannot be contrived, it will be better to tell him the naked truth than be caught in a falsehood." " Do not be uneasy, madam," answered Leonela ; " for between this and to-morrow morning I will consider of something to tell him ; and perhaps you may be able to conceal the wound from his sight, and Heaven will befriend us. Compose yourself, good madam ; endeavour to quiet your spirits, that my master may not find you in such agitation; and leave the rest to my care, and to Heaven, which always favours the honest purpose."

Anselmo stood an attentive spectator of this tragedy, representing the death of his honour; in which the actors performed with so much expression and pathos that they seemed transformed into the very characters they personated. He longed for night, that he might have an opportunity of slipping out of his house to see his dear friend Lothario, and rejoice with him on finding so precious a jewel, by the happy development of his wife's virtue. They both took care to give him an opportunity to retreat, of which he instantly availed himself, to hasten in search of Lothario ; and on their meeting, his embraces were innumerable and his praises of Camilla unbounded. All which Lothario listened to without being able to testify any joy ; for he could not but reflect how much his friend was deceived, and how ungenerously he was treated. Anselmo perceived that Lothario did not express any pleasure, but he ascribed it to Camilla's wound, of which he had been the occasion. He therefore desired him not to be unhappy about Camilla, as the wound must be slight, since she and her maid had agreed to hide it from him : he might then be assured that there was no cause for alarm, but much for joy ; for that by his friendly exertions he was elevated to the highest summit of human felicity ; and he desired no better amusement than to write verses in praise of Camilla, to perpetuate her memory to all future ages. Lothario commended his resolution, and promised his assistance in the execution of so meritorious a work.

Thus Anselmo remained the most agreeably deceived man that ever existed. He led home under his arm the instrument, as he thought, of his glory, but, in truth, his bane ; who was received by Camilla with a frowning aspect, but a joyful heart. This imposture lasted for a few months, when Fortune turning her wheel, the iniquity hitherto so artfully concealed came to light, and Anselmo's impertinent curiosity cost him his life.

CHAPTER XXXV.

The dreadful battle which Don Quixote fought with the wine-bags, and the conclusion of the novel of "The Curious Impertinent."

The novel was nearly finished, when Sancho Panza, full of dismay, came running out of Don Quixote's chamber, crying aloud, "Run, gentlemen, quickly! and succour my master, who is over head and ears in the toughest battle my eyes ever beheld! As God shall save me, he has given the giant, that enemy of the Princess Micomiconia, such a stroke that he has cut his head as clean off his shoulders as if it had been a turnip!" "What say you, brother?" quoth the priest, laying aside the novel. "Are you in your senses, Sancho? How can this possibly be, since the giant is two thousand leagues off?" At that instant they heard a great noise in the room, and Don Quixote calling aloud, "Stay, cowardly thief! robber! rogue! Here I have you, and your scimitar shall avail you nothing!" Then followed the sound of strokes and slashes against the walls. "Do not stand listening," quoth Sancho, "but go in and end the fray, or help my master; though by this time there will be no occasion, as I daresay the giant is dead, and giving an account to God of his past wicked life; for I saw the blood run about the floor, and the head cut off, lying on one side, and as big as a wine-skin." "I will be hanged," exclaimed the inn-keeper, "if Don Quixote, or Don Devil, has not gashed some of the wine-skins that hung at his bed's head, and the wine he has spilt this fellow takes for blood." So saying, he rushed into the room, followed by the whole company: and they found Don Quixote in the strangest situation imaginable. He was in his shirt, and on his head a little greasy red cap which belonged to the innkeeper. About his left arm he had twisted the bed-blanket (to which Sancho owed a grudge—he well knew why), and in his right hand he held his drawn sword, with which he was laying about him on all sides, calling out as if in actual combat; his eyes were shut, being still asleep, and dreaming that he was engaged in battle with the giant; for his mind was so full of the adventure which he had undertaken that he dreamt that, having reached the kingdom of Micomicon and engaged in combat with his enemy, he was cleaving the giant down with a stroke that also proved fatal to the wine-skins, and set the whole room afloat with wine. The innkeeper seeing this, was in such a rage, that with his clenched fists he fell so furiously upon Don Quixote, that if Cardenio and the priest had not taken him off he would have put an end to the war of the giant. The barber, seeing that the poor gentleman was not awake, brought up a large bucket of cold water, with which he soused him all over; and even that ablution did not restore him so entirely as to make him sensible of his situation. Dorothea, perceiving how scantily he was arrayed, would not

He was cleaving the giant down with a stroke that also proved fatal to the wine-skins.

stay to see the fight between her champion and his adversary. Sancho searched about the floor for the head of the giant, and not finding it, he said, "Well, I see plainly that everything about this house is enchantment; for the last time I was here I had thumps and blows given me in this very same place by an invisible hand; and now the head is vanished, which I saw cut off with my own eyes, and the blood spouting from the body like any fountain." "What blood, and what fountain, thou enemy to God and his saints?" said the innkeeper: "dost thou not see, fellow, that the blood and the fountain are nothing but these skins ripped open, and the red wine floating about the room? Perdition catch his soul that pierced them!" "So much the worse for me," said Sancho; "for want of this head I shall see my earldom melt away like salt in water." Thus Sancho awake was as wise as Don Quixote asleep, his head being quite turned by his master's promises. The innkeeper lost all patience at the indifference of the squire and the mischievous havoc of the knight; and he swore they should not escape, as they did before, without paying; and that the privileges of his chivalry should not exempt him this time from discharging both reckonings, even to the patching of the wine-skins.

Don Quixote (whose hands were held by the priest) now conceiving the adventure to be finished, and that he was in the presence of the

Princess Micomiconia, fell on his knees before the priest, and said, "High and renownd lady, your highness may henceforward live secure of harm from that ill-born wretch. I have now discharged the promise I gave you, since, by the assistance of Heaven, and through the favour of her by whom I live and breathe, I have so happily accomplished the enterprise." "Did not I tell you so?" quoth Sancho, hearing this: "you see I was not drunk—look if my master has not already put the giant in pickle! Here are the bulls!* my earldom is cock-sure." Who could help laughing at the absurdities of both master and man? They were all diverted except the innkeeper, who swore like a trooper. At length the barber, Cardenio, and the priest, with much difficulty got Don Quixote upon his bed again, where, exhausted with his labour, he slept soundly. They left him to his repose, and went out to the inndoor, trying to comfort Sancho for his disappointment in not finding the giant's head; but they had most trouble in pacifying the innkeeper, who was in despair at the untimely death of his wine-skins. The hostess grumbled too, muttering to herself, "In an evil hour this knight-errant came into my house! Oh that I had never set my eyes on him, for he has been a dear guest to me! The last time he went away without paying his night's reckoning for supper, bed, straw, and barley, for himself, squire, his horse and ass; telling us, forsooth, that he was a knight-adventurer—evil befall him, and all the adventurers in the world! —and so he was not obliged to pay anything, according to the rules of knight-errantry. It was on his account, too, that this other gentleman carries off my tail, which he returns me damaged and good for nothing: and, after all, to rip open my skins, and let out my wine—would it were his blood! But he shall not escape again; for, by the bones of my father and the soul of my mother, they shall pay me down upon the nail every farthing, or I am not my father's daughter!" Thus the hostess went on in great wrath; and honest Maritornes agreed with her mistress. The daughter held her peace, but now and then smiled. The priest endeavoured to quiet all of them; promising to make the best reparation in his power for the skins as well as the wine; and especially for the damage done to the tail which they valued so much. Dorothea comforted Sancho Panza, telling him that if it should really appear that his master had cut off the giant's head, she would, when peaceably seated on her throne, bestow on him the best earldom in her dominions. With this promise Sancho was comforted, and he assured the princess that she might depend upon it he had seen the giant's head, and that it had a beard which reached down to the girdle; and if it could not be found it was owing to the witchcraft in that house, of which he had seen and felt enough the last time they lodged there. Dorothea agreed with him, but assured him that all would end well and to his heart's desire. Tranquillity being now restored, the priest was requested by Cardenio, Dorothea, and the rest, to read the remainder of the novel; and to please them, as well as himself, he continued as follows:

---

* In allusion to the joy of the mob in Spain when they see the bulls coming.

Anselmo now lived perfectly happy and free from care, being convinced of Camilla's virtue. She affected to treat Lothario with coldness, to deceive her husband, and Lothario entreated him to excuse his visits to the house, since it was plain that the sight of him was disagreeable to his wife. But the duped Anselmo would by no means comply with his request; and thus by a thousand different ways he administered to his own dishonour. As for Leonela, she was so pleased to find herself thus at liberty that, regardless of everything, she abandoned herself to her pleasures without the least restraint, being certain of her lady's connivance and help.

In short, one night Anselmo heard steps in Leonela's chamber; and on his attempting to go in to see who it was, he found the door held against him, which made him only more determined to be satisfied; he therefore burst open the door, and, just as he entered, saw a man leap down from the window into the street. He would immediately have pursued him, but was prevented by Leonela, who clung about him, crying, " Dear sir, be calm; do not be angry, nor pursue the man who leaped out; he belongs to me—in fact, he is my husband." Anselmo would not believe Leonela, but drew his poniard in a great fury, and threatened to stab her if she did not tell him the whole truth. In her fright, not knowing what she said, she cried out, " Do not kill me, sir, and I will tell you things of greater importance than you can imagine." " Tell me them quickly," said Anselmo, " or you are a dead woman ! " " At present it is impossible," said Leonela, " I am in such confusion; let me alone until to-morrow morning, and then you shall hear what will astonish you : in the meantime be assured that the person who jumped out at the window is a young man of the city who has given me a promise of marriage." Anselmo was now appeased, and consented to wait till next morning for an explanation; never dreaming that he should hear anything against Camilla. But he locked Leonela into her room, telling her that she should not stir thence until he had heard what she had to communicate. He went immediately to Camilla, and related to her all that had passed with her waiting-woman, and the promise she had given to impart to him things of the utmost importance. It is needless to say whether Camilla was alarmed or not : so great was her consternation that, never doubting of Leonela's intention to tell Anselmo all she knew of her infidelity, she had not the courage to wait until she saw whether her fears were well or ill-grounded. But that same night, when Anselmo was asleep, she collected her jewels, with some money, and privately leaving her house, went to Lothario, to whom she communicated what had passed; desiring him to conduct her to a place of safety, or to accompany her to some retreat where they might live secure from Anselmo. Lothario was so confounded that he knew not what to say or how to act. At length he proposed to conduct her to a convent of which his sister was the prioress. Camilla consented, and Lothario immediately conveyed her to the monastery, where he left her. He likewise absented himself from the city.

At daybreak Anselmo arose, without observing Camilla's absence, and, impatient for Leonela's communication, he hastened to the chamber in which he had confined her. He opened the door and went in, but found no Leonela there: he only found the sheets tied to the window, by means of which it appeared she had slid down and made her escape. He returned, much disappointed, to inform Camilla of the circumstance, and not finding her in her bed, nor in any part of the house, he was all astonished. He inquired of the servants for her, and no one could give him any tidings. But when he found her jewels gone, he began to suspect the fatal truth. Full of grief and consternation, he ran half-dressed to the house of his friend Lothario, to tell him of his disaster; and being informed by his servants that their master had gone away in the night with all the money he had by him, he became nearly frantic. To complete his misery, on his return home he found his house entirely deserted, every servant, male and female, having quitted it. He was unable either to think, speak, or act, and his senses gradually began to fail him. In an instant he found himself forsaken by his wife, his friend, and even his servants—robbed of honour, abandoned by Heaven! He at last resolved to leave the city and go to the friend he had visited before. Having locked up his house, he mounted on horseback, and set out, oppressed with sorrow; but before he had reached half-way, over-whelmed with the thoughts of his misfortune, he was unable to proceed: he therefore alighted and tied his horse to a tree, at the foot of which he sank down and gave vent to the most bitter and mournful lamentations. There he remained till the evening, when a man on horseback happening to pass that way, he saluted him, and inquired what news there was in Florence. "Very strange news, indeed," said the man; "for it is publicly reported that last night Lothario, the rich Anselmo's particular friend, carried off Camilla, wife to Anselmo; and that he also is missing. All this was told by Camilla's maid-servant, whom the governor caught in the night letting herself down by a sheet from a window of Anselmo's house. However, I do not know all the particulars; I only know that the whole town is in astonishment at this event, for no one could have expected any such thing, considering the great friendship of the gentlemen, which was so remarkable that they were styled The Two Friends." "Is it known," said Anselmo, "what road Lothario and Camilla have taken?" "It is not," replied the citizen, "although the governor has ordered diligent search to be made after them." "Heaven be with you!" said Anselmo. "And with you also," said the man, who proceeded on his way.

This dismal news almost bereaved Anselmo both of his senses and his life. With difficulty he mounted his horse again, and reached the house of his friend, who had not yet heard of his misfortune, but, seeing him pale, spiritless, and faint, he concluded that he had met with some heavy affliction. Anselmo begged he would lead him to a chamber, and give him pen, ink, and paper. They complied with his request, leaving him alone on the bed. So acute was now the sense of his misery, that he felt it was impossible for him to survive it, and he wished to leave behind some memorial of the cause of his death; but before he could write all he intended, his breath failed him, and he expired—a victim to that grief which he had brought upon himself by his impertinent curiosity.

The master of the house, after some time, went to Anselmo's chamber to inquire after him, when he found him lying upon his face, his body half in bed, and half resting on the table, upon which lay a written paper—the pen was still in his hand. His friend spoke to him, and approaching him, took hold of his hand, but he found him cold and breathless. Surprised and grieved, he called his family to witness the disastrous end of Anselmo. On the paper he then read the following lines, which he knew to be in Anselmo's handwriting:

He therefore alighted and tied his horse to a tree, at the foot of which he sank down and gave vent to the most bitter and mournful lamentations.

"A foolish and impertinent desire has deprived me of life. If Camilla hear of my death, let her know that I forgive her; for she was not obliged to perform miracles, nor ought I to have required them of her: and since I was the contriver of my own dishonour, there is no reason why ——."

Thus far had Anselmo written, unable, as it appeared, to finish the sentence. On the following day his friend sent to inform his relations of the sad event. They already knew of his disgrace and the retreat of his wife. Camilla, indeed, was on the point of quitting life at the same time as her husband—not for grief at his fate, but at her lover's absence. Although now a widow, she would neither leave the convent nor take the veil until some time after, when intelligence reached her that Lothario had been slain in a battle fought between Monsieur de Lautrec and that great commander, Gonzalo Hernandez of Cordova, in the kingdom of Naples, whither the too-late repentant friend had retreated. She then took the religious habit, and died shortly after, a prey to sorrow. Such was the fatal catastrophe of a drama which commenced in folly.

"I like this novel very well," said the priest, "but I cannot persuade myself that it is true; and if it be a fiction, the author has erred against probability; for it is impossible to conceive that any husband would be so absurd as to venture upon so dangerous an experiment as that made by Anselmo. Had this case been supposed between a gallant and his mistress, it might pass; but between husband and wife it is perfectly incredible. However, the story is not ill told."

CHAPTER XXXVI.

Which treats of other uncommon incidents which happened at the inn.

"Ен! by our Lady!" suddenly exclaimed the host, who was standing at the inn-door, "here comes a goodly company of guests! If they stop here we shall sing 'Oh be joyful!'" "What are they?" said Cardenio. "Four men," answered the host, "on horseback, *à la* Gineta,* with lances and targets, and black masks† on their faces; and there is a woman with them, on a side-saddle, dressed in white, and her face likewise covered; besides these, there are two lads on foot." "Are they near?" said the priest. "So near," replied the innkeeper, "that they are already at the door." Dorothea, hearing this, veiled her face, and Cardenio retired to Don Quixote's chamber. When the persons mentioned by the host entered the yard, the four horsemen (who appeared to be gentlemen) having alighted, went to assist the lady to dismount; and one of them, taking her in his arms, placed her in a chair near the door of the chamber to which Cardenio had retired. During all this time not one of the party had taken off their masks or spoken a word. The lady, when seated in a chair, heaved a deep sigh, and her arms hung listlessly down, as if she were in a weak and fainting state. When the servants took the horses to the stable, the priest followed and questioned one of them, being curious to know who these people were. "In truth, signor," replied the servant, "I cannot tell you who they are; but they must be people of quality, especially he who took the lady in his arms, because all the rest pay him such respect, and do nothing but what he orders and directs." "And the lady, pray

---

* A mode of riding with short stirrups, which the Spaniards took from the Arabs.
† A piece of thin black silk worn before the face in travelling; not for disguise, but to keep off the dust and sun.

who is she?" asked the priest. "Neither can I tell that," replied the lacquey; "for I have not once seen her face during the whole journey. I often, indeed, hear her sigh, and utter such groans that any one of them was enough to break her heart; but it is no wonder that we cannot tell you any more, as my comrade and I have been only two days in their service; for having met us upon the road, they persuaded us to go as far as Andalusia, and promised to pay us well." "Have you heard any of their names?" said the priest. "No, indeed," answered the lad; "for they all travel in so much silence, we hear nothing but the sighs and the sobs of the poor lady, which move our pity; and wheresoever she is going, we suspect it is against her will. From her habit she must be a nun, or perhaps going to be made one, and not from her own choice, which makes her so sorrowful." "Very likely," quoth the priest; and then leaving them, he returned to the room where he had left Dorothea, whose compassion being excited by the sighs of the masked lady, she approached her and said, "You seem in distress, dear madam; if it be in the power of woman to render you any service, most willingly I offer you mine." The afflicted lady returned no answer; and although Dorothea renewed her offers, she persisted in her silence until the cavalier in the mask, who seemed to be the superior of the party, came up and said to Dorothea, "Trouble not yourself, madam, to offer anything to this woman, for she is very ungrateful; nor endeavour to get an answer from her, unless you wish to hear some falsehood." "No," said the lady, who had hitherto been silent: "on the contrary, it is from my aversion to falsehood that I am thus wretched; for it is my truth alone which makes you act so false and treacherous a part."

These words were distinctly heard by Cardenio, who was very near to the speaker, being separated only by the door of Don Quixote's chamber; and, on hearing them, he cried aloud, "Good Heaven! what do I hear? What voice is that which has reached my ears?" The lady, in much surprise, turned her head at these exclamations; and, not seeing who uttered them, she started up, and was going into the room, when the cavalier detained her, and would not suffer her to move a step. In this sudden commotion her mask fell off, and discovered a face of incomparable beauty, although pale and full of terror; for she looked wildly around her, examining every place with so much eagerness that she seemed distracted, and excited the sympathy of Dorothea and others of the party, who could not conjecture the cause of her agitation. The cavalier held her fast by the shoulders, and his hands being thus engaged, he could not keep on his mask, which at length fell to the ground; and Dorothea, who also had her arms round the lady, raising her eyes, discovered in the stranger—her husband, Don Fernando! when instantly, with a long and dismal "Oh!" she fell backward in a swoon; and had not the barber, who stood close by, caught her in his arms, she would have fallen to the ground. The priest then hastily removed her veil to throw water in her face, upon which Don Fernando recognized her, and seemed petrified at the sight. Nevertheless, he still kept his hold of Lucinda, who was the lady that was endeavouring to release herself from him; for she knew Cardenio's voice, and he well recollected hers. The groan of Dorothea when she fainted was also heard by Cardenio, who believing it came from his Lucinda, rushed into the room, and the first object he saw was Don Fernando holding Lucinda in his arms. They all gazed upon each other in silence, for none seemed able to utter a word. Lucinda was the first to recover the power of speech, and she thus addressed Don Fernando: "Let me go, my lord. I entreat you, as you are a gentleman, that you will suffer me to fly to the protection of him from whom in vain you have endeavoured to separate me. See how mysteriously Heaven has conducted me into the presence of my true husband! You well know, by a thousand proofs, that nothing can shake the faith I have pledged to him. Cease, therefore, your fruitless persecution, or let your love be converted into rage, and destroy me; for then at least I shall die in the presence of my beloved, who by my death will be convinced of my inviolable fidelity."

Dorothea in the meantime had recovered her senses, and hearing what Lucinda said, she conjectured who she was. Seeing that Don Fernando still held her, she approached him, and threw herself at his feet, her lovely face bathed in tears. "Ah, my lord!" said she, "were you not dazzled by that beauty now in your arms, you would see the unhappy Dorothea, who is prostrate at your feet. I am that humble country girl whom you vouchsafed to call yours: she who lived a happy and modest life, until, seduced by your importunities and the apparent sincerity of your affection, she resigned her liberty to you. How you requited her is now too manifest! But do not think that I have followed the path of dishonour: grief and misery alone have attended my steps since your cruel desertion. When I was persuaded to bind myself to you, it was with ties that, changed as your sentiments may be, can never be dissolved. Ah, my lord! will not my tenderness compensate for the beauty and rank of her for whom you abandon me? Recollect that you are mine, and that Lucinda belongs to Cardenio: surely it will be easier for you to revive your own love towards her who adores you, than to inspire with love her who hates you. You were not ignorant of my condition when I consented to become yours on honourable terms: then, as you are a Christian and a gentleman, I claim the fulfilment of your promise, for I am your true and lawful wife! Still, if you refuse to acknowledge me, protect me as your slave, and I will submit; but do not abandon me to the world—do not afflict the declining years of my parents, who have ever been your faithful vassals. Think not of their meanness, for rank is not essential in a wife; besides, true nobility consists in virtue, and if you forfeit that by wronging me, you degrade yourself below me. But however you may please to act towards me, my lord, I am still your wife—witness your words, witness your letters, and witness Heaven, whom you called upon to sanctify our mutual vows! Lastly, I appeal to your conscience, which will embitter with self-reproach every enjoyment of your life, if you fail to listen to its dictates."

The afflicted Dorothea urged these and other arguments in so affecting a manner that she excited the most lively interest in all present. Don Fernando listened in silence to her words, which were followed by such bursts of overwhelming grief that no human heart could witness it without emotion. Lucinda longed to comfort her and condole with her, but she was still detained. Don Fernando at length suddenly disengaged his arms from her, after having gazed awhile on Dorothea. "You have conquered, fair Dorothea!" he exclaimed: "you have conquered. There is no resisting you!"

Lucinda was so faint, when released from Don Fernando's embrace, that she was just falling to the ground; but Cardenio hastened to her support. "These arms," said he, "shall protect thee, my beloved, my faithful mistress! Heaven grant you may now find repose!" Lucinda looked up, to be assured that it was indeed her Cardenio; and on seeing his beloved face, regardless of forms, she threw her arms around his neck, and embraced him with the utmost tenderness. "O Cardenio! you are my true lord! Whatever the fates may condemn me to suffer, I am for ever yours!"

This was an affecting scene to all present. Dorothea watched Don Fernando, and fearing that he meditated revenge on Cardenio, as he looked agitated, and put his hand to his sword, she clung around him, embracing his knees, and said to him, "What means my love, my only refuge? Behold your true wife at your feet! Lucinda is in the arms of her husband, and even in your presence bedews his bosom with tears of love: how, then, can you think of uniting yourself to her? For Heaven's sake, and the honour of your name, let their declarations of mutual affection, instead of moving your wrath, induce you to leave them unmolested, to pass their lives happily together. You will thus show to the world that you are not governed by your passions, but have a noble and generous mind."

While Dorothea spoke, Cardenio kept his eyes fixed on Don Fernando, and was prepared to defend himself if assaulted by him. But that nobleman was now surrounded by the whole party, not excepting honest Sancho, who all interceded for Dorothea; and the priest represented to him that so singular a meeting must not be ascribed to chance, but to the special providence of Heaven. He begged him also to consider how vain would be the attempt to separate Cardenio and Lucinda, who would be happy even to die proving each other's faith; and how prudent as well as noble it would be in him to triumph over his passion, and freely leave the two lovers to enjoy the happiness of mutual affection; that he should turn to the lovely Dorothea, who had such strong claims upon him, not only on account of her extreme tenderness for him, but the promises he had made to her, which, as a Christian and a man of honour, he was bound to perform: adding to these arguments, that it would be no derogation to his rank to elevate beauty adorned with virtue.

These truths, so forcibly urged, were not lost upon the mind of Don Fernando, who embraced Dorothea, saying, "Rise, my dear lady, for that is not a posture for the mistress of my soul; and if I have offended against you, surely it has been by the will of Heaven, that I might know your true value by such proofs of your constancy and affection. I only entreat that you will not reproach me for my involuntary offence, but look at the now happy Lucinda, and her eyes will plead my excuse. May she enjoy long years of happiness with her Cardenio, and Heaven grant me the same with my Dorothea!" Again he pressed her to his heart, and could scarcely forbear showing his emotions of tenderness and repentance by tears : indeed, all the company present were so much affected, that their tears of sympathy might have been mistaken for those of sorrow. Even Sancho Panza wept; though he owned afterwards that it was only because Dorothea turned out not to be the Queen Micomicona who was to have made his fortune. Cardenio and Lucinda expressed their acknowledgments to Don Fernando for his present conduct in so feeling a manner that he was too much moved to find words to reply to them.

Dorothea being now questioned by Don Fernando as to the circumstances which had brought her to that place, she gave a brief detail of what she had before related to Cardenio; and so interesting was her narrative to Don Fernando and his party, and so graceful her delivery, that they even regretted when the story of her misfortunes was ended. Don Fernando then related what he had done after finding in Lucinda's bosom the paper declaring herself the wife of Cardenio. He confessed that his first impulse was to take her life, and he should actually have done so had he not been prevented by her parents; upon which he immediately quitted the house, full of shame and fury, determined to seize the first opportunity of revenge. On the following day he heard that she had left her father's house, concealing the place of her retreat; but after some months he discovered that she had retired to a convent, whither he immediately pursued her, accompanied by the three gentlemen then present. He then watched an opportunity when the convent gate was open to make his entrance, leaving two of his companions to secure the gate; and having found Lucinda walking in the cloisters, attended only by a nun, they seized her, and bore her away to a place where they had prepared every accommodation necessary for their project. Lucinda, he said, had fainted on seeing herself in his power; and when her senses returned she wept and sighed, but never spoke a single word. Thus, in silence and sorrow, they had reached that inn, which he trusted was the goal of all their earthly misfortunes.

CHAPTER XXXVII.

Wherein is continued the history of the famous Infanta Micomiconia, with other pleasant adventures.

SANCHO experienced no small grief of mind on thus seeing all his hopes of preferment fast disappearing and vanishing into smoke, by the transformation of the fair Princess Micomiconia into Dorothea, and the giant into Don Fernando; while his master, unconscious of what was passing, lay wrapped in profound sleep. Dorothea could not be certain whether the happiness she enjoyed was not a dream; and Cardenio and Lucinda entertained the same doubts. Don Fernando gave thanks to Heaven for having delivered him from a perilous situation, in which his honour as well as his soul were in imminent danger. In short, all were pleased at the happy conclusion of such intricate and hopeless affairs. The priest, like a man of sense, placed everything in its true light, and congratulated each upon their share of the good fortune that had befallen them. But the landlady was more delighted than all, as Cardenio and the priest had promised to pay her with interest for every loss she had sustained upon Don Quixote's account.

Sancho alone was afflicted, unhappy, and full of sorrow; and, with dismal looks, he went in to his master, just then awake, to whom he said, "Your worship may sleep on, Signor Sorrowful Figure, without troubling yourself about killing any giant or restoring the princess to her kingdom, for that is already done and over." "I verily believe it," answered Don Quixote, "for I have had the most monstrous and dreadful battle with the giant that ever I expect to have in the whole course of my life. With one back stroke I tumbled his head to the ground; and so great was the quantity of blood that rushed from it, that the stream ran along the ground like a torrent of water." "Like red wine, your worship might better say," answered Sancho; "for I can tell you, if you do not know it already, that the dead giant is a pierced wine-skin, and the blood eighteen gallons of red wine contained in the belly; and may the devil take all for me!" "What sayest thou, fool?" replied Don Quixote: "art thou in thy senses?" "Pray get up, sir," quoth Sancho, "and you will see what a fine day's work you have made, and what a reckoning we have to pay; and you will see, too, the queen converted into a private lady called Dorothea, with other matters which, if you take them rightly, will astonish you." "I shall wonder at nothing," replied Don Quixote; "for thou mayest remember, the last time we were here, I told thee that all things in this place went by enchantment; and there can be nothing surprising in it if this were the case again." "I should believe soo too," answered Sancho, "if my being tossed in the blanket had been a matter of this nature · but it was downright real and true. And I saw the very same innkeeper hold a corner of the blanket, and cant me towards heaven with notable alacrity, laughing, too, all the time; and where it happens that we know persons, in my opinion (simple and a sinner as I am) there is no enchantment at all, but much misusage and much mishap." "Well, Heaven will remedy it," quoth Don Quixote. "Give me my clothes, that I may go and see the events and transformations thou hast mentioned."

Sancho reached him his apparel; and while he was dressing, the priest gave Don Fernando and his companions an account of Don Quixote's madness, and of the artifice they had used to get him from the barren mountain to which he imagined himself banished through his lady's disdain. He related also most of the adventures which Sancho had communicated to them, to their great diversion and astonishment; for they, like others, considered it as the most singular species of insanity that ever took possession of the imagination. The priest said further, that since the Lady Dorothea's good fortune would not permit her to prosecute their design, it was necessary to contrive some other expedient to get him home. Cardenio offered his assistance, and proposed that Lucinda should personate Dorothea. "No," said Don Fernando, "it must not be so, for I will have Dorothea herself proceed in her part; and as this good gentleman's village is not far distant, I shall be glad to contribute to his cure." "It is not above two days' journey," said the priest. "If it were farther," said Don Fernando, "I would undertake it with pleasure for so good a purpose."

Don Quixote now came forth, clad in all his armour; Mambrino's helmet, though bruised and battered, on his head; his target braced, and resting on his sapling or lance. His strange appearance greatly surprised Don Fernando and his company, who failed not to observe his long and withered visage of sallow hue, his ill-matched armour, and measured pace. They paused, in silent expectation of hearing him speak, when with much gravity and solemnity, fixing his eyes upon the fair Dorothea, he said, "I am informed, fair lady, by this my squire, that your grandeur is annihilated, and your very being demolished; and that from a queen you are metamorphosed into a private maiden. If this has been done by order of the necromantic king your father, fearing lest I should not afford you the necessary aid, I say he knew not one half of his art, and that he was but little versed in histories of knight-errantry; for had he read them as attentively as I have read and considered them, he would have known that other knights, of less fame than myself, have achieved still greater difficulties, it being no such mighty business to kill a pitiful giant, arrogant as he may be; for not many hours are passed since I was engaged with one myself, and—I say no more, lest I should be suspected of falsehood; but time, the revealer of all things, will declare it when least expected." "It was with a couple of wine-skins, and not a giant," quoth the innkeeper. Here he was interrupted by Don Fernando, who commanded him to hold his peace, and in no wise to interrupt Don Quixote's discourse; who went on, saying, "I assure you, therefore, high and disinherited lady, that if

"Give me my clothes, that I may go and see the events and transformations thou hast mentioned."

for the cause I have mentioned your father has made this metamorphose in your person, it is perfectly needless; for there is no danger upon earth through which my sword shall not force a way; and, by bringing down the head of your enemy to the ground, shortly place upon your own the crown of your kingdom."

Here Don Quixote ceased, and waited the answer of the princess, who, knowing it to be Don Fernando's desire that she should carry on the deception until Don Quixote's return home, with much dignity and grace replied: " Whosoever told you, valorous Knight of the Sorrowful Figure, that I was changed and altered from what I was, spoke not the truth; for I am the same to-day that I was yesterday. It is true, indeed, that certain events, fortunate beyond my hopes, have befallen me since then, yet I do not cease to be what I was before, and to entertain the same thoughts I have ever indulged of availing myself of the valour of your valiant and invincible arm. Therefore, dear sir, with your accustomed goodness, do justice to the honour of my father, and acknowledge his wisdom and prudence, since by his skill he found out so easy and certain a way to remedy my misfortunes; for I verily believe had it not been for you, sir, I should never have enjoyed my present happiness; and in this I speak the exact truth, as most of these gentlemen, I am sure, will testify. Let us, then, proceed on our journey tomorrow (for to-day it is too late); and to Heaven and your prowess I trust for a successful issue."

Thus spoke the discreet Dorothea; whereupon Don Quixote, turning to Sancho, said to him, "I tell thee, Sancho, thou art the greatest rascal in Spain. Say, vagabond! didst thou not tell me just now that this princess was transformed into a damsel called Dorothea, with other absurdities which were enough to confound me? I vow"—(and here he looked up to heaven and gnashed his teeth)—"I have a great inclination to make such an example of thee as shall put sense into the brains of all the lying squires of future times!" "Pray, sir, be pacified," answered Sancho; "for I may have been mistaken as to the change of my lady the Princess Micomicona; but as to the giant's head, or at least the piercing of the skins, and the blood being red wine, I am not deceived, as God liveth; for there are the skins at your worship's bed-head, cut and slashed, and the red wine has made a pond of the room; and you will find I speak true when our host demands damages. As for the rest, I rejoice in my heart that my lady-queen is as she was; for I have my share in it, like every neighbour's child." "I tell thee, Sancho," said Don Quixote, "thou art an ass. Excuse me, that's enough." "It is enough," said Don Fernando, "and let no more be said on the subject; and since the princess hath declared that we are to set forward in the morning, it being too late to-day, let us pass this night in agreeable conversation, and to-morrow we will all accompany Signor Don Quixote; for we desire to be eye-witnesses of the valorous and unheard-of deeds which he is to perform in the accomplishment of this great enterprise." "It is my part to serve and attend you," answered Don Quixote; "and much am I indebted to you for your good opinion, which it shall be my endeavour not to disappoint, even at the expense of my life, or even more, if more were possible."

Many were the compliments and polite offers of service passing between Don Quixote and Don Fernando, when they were interrupted by the arrival of two other persons at the inn. The one was a man, who by his garb seemed to be a Christian lately come from among the Moors; for he had on a blue cloth coat, with short skirts, half sleeves, and no collar. His breeches also were of blue cloth, and his cap of the same colour. He had on a pair of date-coloured buskins, and a Moorish scimitar hung in a shoulder-belt across his breast. He was accompanied by a female in a Moorish dress, mounted on an ass, her face veiled, a brocade turban on her head, and covered with a mantle from her shoulders to her feet. The man was of a robust and agreeable figure, rather above forty years of age, of a dark complexion, with large mustachios and a well-set beard; in short, his deportment, had he been well dressed, would have marked him for a gentleman. Upon his entrance he asked for a room, and seemed disconcerted on hearing that there was not one unoccupied; nevertheless, he assisted his female companion, who was evidently a Moor, to alight. The other ladies, as well as the landlady, her daughter, and maid, all surrounded the stranger, attracted by the novelty of her appearance; and Dorothea, who was always obliging and considerate, perceiving they were disappointed at not having an apartment, accosted her, saying, " Do not be distressed, my dear madam, at an inconvenience which must be expected in places of this kind; but if you will please to share with us" (pointing to Lucinda) "such accommodation as we have, you may perhaps have found worse in the course of your journey." The veiled lady returned her no answer; but, rising from her seat, and laying her hands across her breast, bowed her head and body in token that she thanked her. By her silence they conjectured that she could not speak their language, and were confirmed in their opinion of her being a Moor.

Her companion, who had been engaged out of the room, now entered, and seeing that she was addressed by some of the company, he said : " Ladies, this young person understands scarcely anything of the Spanish language, and is therefore unable to converse with you." " We have only been requesting her to favour us with her company, and share our accommodations," said Lucinda; " and we will show her all the attention due to strangers who need it, especially those of our own sex." " My dear madam," he replied, " I return you a thousand thanks both for this lady and myself, and am fully sensible of the extent of the favour you offer us." " Allow me to ask you, signor, whether the lady is a Christian or a Moor ? " " By birth she is a Moor," replied the stranger, " but in heart she is a Christian, having an ardent wish to become one." " She is not yet baptized, then ? " inquired Lucinda. " There has not yet been an opportunity," answered the stranger, " since she left Algiers, her native country; and she has not hitherto been in such imminent danger of death as to make it necessary to have her baptized before she be instructed in all the ceremonies enjoined by our Church; but, if it please Heaven, she will be soon baptized in a manner becoming her rank, which is beyond what either her appearance or mine indicate."

These strangers excited the curiosity of the whole party, who refrained, however, from importuning them with questions, conceiving they would be more inclined to take repose than to satisfy them. Dorothea now took the lady's hand, and, leading her to a seat, placed herself by her, and then requested her to unveil; upon which she gave an inquiring look at her companion; and he having interpreted what had been said to her in Arabic, she removed her veil, and discovered a face so exquisitely beautiful that Dorothea thought she exceeded Lucinda, who on her part thought her handsomer than Dorothea; while their admirers all seemed to confess that if either of them could have a rival in beauty it was in this Moorish lady; and, as it is the privilege of beauty to conciliate and attract good-will, they were all eager to show her attention. Don Fernando inquired her name of her companion. " Lela

Zoraida," he replied; when she interposed in a sweet earnest manner —" No, not Zoraida Maria, Maria:" giving them to understand that her name was Maria, not Zoraida. These words were pronounced in so touching a voice that they were all affected, especially the ladies, who were naturally tender-hearted. Lucinda embraced her most affectionately, saying, " Yes, yes; Maria, Maria;" who answered, " Yes, Maria; *Zoraida macange*"—meaning not Zoraida.

It being now night, supper was served up (in providing which the landlord had, by Don Fernando's order, exerted himself to the utmost). They seated themselves at a long table, like those in halls; for there was no other, either round or square, in the house. They insisted on Don Quixote's taking the head of the table, though he would have declined it; the Princess Micomiconia he placed next to him, being her champion; Lucinda and Zoraida seated themselves beside her; opposite them sat Don Fernando and Cardenio; the curate and barber sat next to the ladies, and the rest of the gentlemen opposite to them; and thus they banqueted much to their satisfaction. Don Quixote added to their amusement; for being moved by the same spirit which had inspired him with eloquence at the goatherd's supper, instead of eating, he now harangued as follows :

" It must certainly be confessed that great and wonderful are the occurrences which befall those who profess the order of knight-errantry. What man existing who should now enter at this castle-gate, and see us thus seated, could imagine us to be the persons we really are? Who should say that this lady here seated by my side is that great queen we all know her to be, and I that Knight of the Sorrowful Figure so blazoned abroad by the mouth of fame? There no longer remains a doubt that this art and profession exceeds all that have ever been followed by man; and that it is the more honourable inasmuch as it is exposed to more danger. Away with those who say that letters have advantage over arms! Whoever they may be, I will maintain that they know not what they say; for the reason they usually give, and upon which they usually lay the greatest stress, is that the labours of the brain exceed those of the body, and that arms is simply a corporeal exercise; as if it were the business of porters alone, for which mere strength is required, or as if the profession of arms did not call for that fortitude which depends on a vigorous understanding, or as if the mental powers of the warrior who has an army or the defence of a besieged city committed to his charge, are not called into exertion as well as those of his body! Let it be shown how, by mere corporeal strength, he can penetrate the designs of the enemy, form stratagems, overcome diffi- culties, and avert threatened dangers! No, these are all the efforts of the understanding, in which the body has no share. Since, then, arms exercise the mind as well as letters, let us now see whose mind is most exerted, the scholar's or the soldier's. This may be determined by the ultimate object of each; for that pursuit deserves the most esteem which has the noblest aim in view. Now, the end and design of letters —I speak not of theology, the aim of which is to guide and elevate the soul of man to heaven, for with that none can be compared—but I speak of human learning, whose end, I say, is to regulate distributive justice, and give to every man his due; to know good laws, and cause them to be strictly observed : an object most certainly generous and exalted, and worthy of high commendation, but not equal to that which is annexed to the profession of arms, whose end and purpose is peace—the greatest blessing man can enjoy in this life; for the first glad tidings the world received was what the angels brought on that night which was our day, when they sang in the clouds, ' Glory to God on high, and on earth peace and good-will towards men ! ' And the salutation which the Master of earth and of heaven taught His disciples was, that when they entered any house they should say, ' Peace be to this house ; ' and many times He said, ' My peace I give unto you; my peace I leave with you ; peace be amongst you.' It is, indeed, a treasure without which there can be no true happiness. To obtain this peace is the legitimate object of war—by war and arms I mean the same thing. Peace, then, being the object of war, it must be granted that in its ultimate aim it is superior to the pursuit of letters. We will now compare the corporeal labours of the soldier and the scholar."

Don Quixote thus pursued his discourse so rationally, that his auditors could scarcely think him insane; on the contrary, most of them being gentlemen, to whom the exercise of arms properly appertains, they listened to him with particular pleasure while he thus continued :

" Among the hardships of the scholar we may, in the first place, name poverty (not that all are poor—but let us suppose the worst) ; and when I have said that he endures poverty, no more need be said of his misery, for he who is poor is destitute of every good thing : he endures misery in all shapes, in hunger and in cold, sometimes in nakedness, and sometimes in a combination of all. Still, however, he gets something to eat, either from the rich man's leavings or the sops of the convent—that last miserable resource of the poor scholar ; nor are they without some neighbour's fireside or chimney-corner to keep them at least from extreme cold; and at night they can generally sleep under cover. I will not enlarge upon other trifling inconveniences to which they are exposed, such as scarcity of linen, want of shoes, threadbare coats, and the surfeits they are liable to when good fortune sets a plentiful table in their way. This is the hard and rugged path they tread, sometimes falling, then rising and falling again, till they reach the eminence they have had in view; and after passing these Scyllas and Charybdises, we have seen them from a chair command and govern the world, their hunger converted into satiety, their pinching cold into refreshing coolness, their nakedness into embroidery, and their slumbers on a mat to repose on holland and damask—a reward justly merited by their virtue. But their hardships fall far short of those of the warrior, as I shall soon convince you."

CHAPTER XXXVIII.

The continuation of Don Quixote's curious oration upon arms and letters.

Don Quixote, after a short pause, continued his discourse thus: " Since, in speaking of the scholar, we began with his poverty and its several branches, let us see whether the soldier be richer. We shall find that poverty itself is not more poor; for he depends on his wretched pay, which comes late, and sometimes never; or upon what he can pillage, at the imminent risk of his life and conscience. Such often is his nakedness that his slashed buff-doublet serves him both for finery and shirt; and in the midst of winter, on the open plain, he has nothing to warm him but the breath of his mouth, which, issuing from an empty place, must needs be cold. But let us wait, and see whether night will make amends for these inconveniences: if his bed be too narrow it is his own fault, for he may measure out as many feet of earth as he pleases, and roll himself thereon at pleasure without fear of rumpling the sheets. Suppose the moment arrived of taking his degree—I mean, suppose the day of battle come: his doctoral cap may then be of lint, to cover some gun-shot wound, which, perhaps, has gone through his temples, or deprived him of an arm or a leg. And even suppose that Heaven in its mercy should preserve him alive and unhurt, he will probably remain as poor as ever; for he must be engaged and victorious in many battles before he can expect high promotion; and such good fortune happens only by a miracle: for you will allow, gentlemen, that few are the number of those that have reaped the reward of their services, compared with those who have perished in war. The dead are countless; whereas those who survive to be rewarded may be numbered with three figures. Not so with scholars, who by their salaries (I will not say their perquisites) are generally handsomely provided for. Thus the labours of the soldier are greater, although his reward is less. It may be said in answer to this, that it is easier to reward two thousand scholars than thirty thousand soldiers; for scholars are rewarded by employments which must of course be given to men of their profession; whereas the soldier can only be rewarded by the property of the master whom he serves; and this defence serves to strengthen my argument.

" But, waiving this point, let us consider the comparative claims to pre-eminence; for the partizans of each can bring powerful arguments in support of their own cause. It is said in favour of letters that without them arms could not subsist; for war must have its laws, and laws come within the province of the learned. But it may be alleged in reply, that arms are necessary to the maintenance of law: by arms the public roads are protected, cities guarded, states defended, kingdoms preserved, and the seas cleared of corsairs and pirates. In short, without arms there would be no safety for cities, commonwealths, or kingdoms. Besides, it is just to estimate a pursuit in proportion to the cost of its attainment. Now it is true that eminence in learning is purchased by time, watching, hunger, nakedness, vertigo, indigestion, and many other inconveniences already mentioned; but a man who rises gradually to be a good soldier endures all these, and far more. What is the hunger and poverty which menace the man of letters compared to the situation of the soldier, who, besieged in some fortress, and placed as sentinel in some ravelin or cavalier, perceives that the enemy is mining towards the place where he stands, and yet must on no account stir from his post or shun the imminent danger that threatens him? All that he can do in such a case is to give notice to his officer of what passes, that he may endeavour to counteract it; in the meantime he must stand his ground, in momentary expectation of being mounted to the clouds without wings, and then dashed headlong to the earth. And if this be thought but a trifling danger, let us see whether it be equalled or exceeded by the encounter of two galleys, prow to prow, in the midst of the white sea, locked and grappled together, so that there is no more room left for the soldier than the two-foot plank at the beak-head; and though he sees as many threatening ministers of death before him as there are pieces of artillery pointed at him from the opposite side, not the length of a lance from his body; though he knows that the first slip of his foot sends him to the bottom of the sea; yet, with an undaunted heart, inspired by honour, he exposes himself as a mark to all their fire, and endeavours by that narrow pass to force his way into the enemy's vessel! And, what is most worthy of admiration, no sooner is one fallen, never to rise again in this world, than another takes his place; and if he also fall into the sea, which lies in wait to devour him, another and another succeeds without intermission! In all the extremities of war there is no example of courage and intrepidity to exceed this. Happy those ages which knew not the dreadful fury of artillery!—those instruments of hell (where, I verily believe, the inventor is now receiving the reward of his diabolical ingenuity), by means of which the cowardly and the base can deprive the bravest soldier of life. While a gallant spirit animated with heroic ardour is pressing to glory, comes a chance ball, sent by one who perhaps fled in alarm at the flash of his own accursed weapon, and in an instant cuts short the life of him who deserved to live for ages! When I consider this, I could almost repent having undertaken this profession of knight-errantry in so detestable an age; for though no danger can daunt me, still it gives me some concern to think that powder and lead may suddenly cut short my career of glory. But Heaven's will be done! I have this satisfaction, that I shall acquire the greater fame if I succeed, inasmuch as the perils by which I am beset are greater than those to which the knights-errant of past ages were exposed."

Don Quixote made this long harangue while the rest were eating, forgetting to raise a morsel to his mouth, though Sancho Panza ever and anon reminded him of his supper, telling him he would have time enough afterwards to talk as much as he pleased. His other auditors were concerned that a man who seemed to possess so good an understanding should, on a particular point, be so egregiously in want of it. The priest told him there was great reason in all that he had said in favour of arms, and although himself a scholar and a graduate, he acquiesced in his opinion.

The collation being over, the cloth was removed; and while the hostess and her damsels were preparing the chamber which Don Quixote had occupied for the ladies, Don Fernando requested the stranger to gratify them by relating his adventures; since, from the appearance of the lady who accompanied him, he was certain they must be both interesting and extraordinary. The stranger said that he would willingly comply with their request, though he was afraid his history would not afford them much amusement. The priest and rest of the party thanked him; and, seeing them all prepared to listen to him with attention, he began his narrative in a modest and agreeable manner, as follows.

CHAPTER XXXIX.

Wherein the captive relates his life and adventures.

" In a village among the mountains of Leon my family had its origin; and, although more favoured by nature than fortune, in that humble region my father was considered wealthy, and might really have been so, had he known the art of economising rather than squandering his estate. This disposition to profusion proceeded from his having been a soldier in his younger days, for the army is a school in which the miser becomes generous, and the generous prodigal: miserly soldiers are, like monsters, but very rarely seen. Liberality may be carried too far in those who have children to inherit their name and rank; and this was my father's failing. He had three sons, and being himself aware of his propensity to extravagance, and of his inability to restrain it, he determined to dispose of his property, and by that means effectually deprive himself of the power of lavishing it. He therefore called us one day together, and thus addressed us:

" ' My sons, I need not say I love you, for you are my children; and yet you may well doubt my love, since I have not refrained from dissipating your inheritance. But to prove to you that I am not an unnatural father, I have finally resolved upon the execution of a plan which is the result of mature deliberation. You are now of an age to establish yourselves in the world, or at least to choose some employment from which you may hereafter reap honour and profit. I intend to divide my property into four parts, three of which you shall equally share, and the fourth I will reserve to subsist upon for the remaining days it may please Heaven to allot me: it is my wish, however, that each, when in possession of his share, should follow the path that I shall direct.   We have a proverb in Spain, in my opinion a very true one, as most proverbs are, being maxims drawn from experience: it is this: "The Church, the sea, or the court;" meaning that whoever would prosper should either get into the Church, engage in commerce, or serve the king in his court; for it is also said, that "the king's morsel is better than the lord's bounty."   It would, therefore, give me great satisfaction if one of you would follow letters, another merchandise, and the third serve the king in the army, for it is difficult to get admission into his household; and though a military career is not favourable to the acquirement of wealth, it seldom fails to confer honour.   Within eight days I will give you each your share in money.   And now tell me whether you are disposed to follow my advice.'

"As I was the eldest, he desired me to answer first.   Upon which I entreated him not to part with his estate, but to spend as much as he pleased, for that we were young enough to labour for ourselves; and I concluded by assuring him that I would do as he desired, and enter the army, to serve God and my king.   My second brother complied likewise, and chose to go to the Indies, turning his portion into merchandise. The youngest, and I believe the wisest, said he would take to the Church, and for that purpose finish his studies at Salamanca.

" Having determined upon our several professions, my father embraced us, and insisted upon our taking each his share of the estate, which an uncle of ours purchased, that it might not be alienated from the family. The portion of each, I remember, amounted to three thousand ducats. We all took our leave of our good father on the same day; and, thinking it inhuman to leave him at his advanced age with so reduced an income, I prevailed on him to take back two thousand ducats from my share; the remainder being sufficient to equip me with what was necessary for a soldier.   My two brothers followed my example, and returned him each a thousand ducats, so that my father now had four thousand in ready money, and the value of three thousand more, which was his share of the land.   In short, we separated, not without much grief on all sides, and mutual promises of correspondence; one of my brothers taking the road to Salamanca, the other to Seville, and I to Alicant.   It is now two-and-twenty years since I left my father, and in all that time I have heard nothing either of him or of my brothers, although I have sent them many letters.   But I shall now briefly relate to you what has befallen me during that period.

" On my arrival at Alicant, finding a vessel bound to Genoa with a cargo of wool, I embarked, and had a good passage to that city. Thence I proceeded to Milan, where I furnished myself with arms and military finery, intending at that time to enter the service of Piedmont; but hearing, on my journey to Alexandria de la Paglia, that the Duke of Alva was entering Flanders with an army, I changed my mind, and joined the duke, whom I continued to serve in all his battles, and was present at the death of the Counts d'Egmont and Horn.   I procured an ensign's commission in the company of the celebrated captain of

Guadalajara, named Diego de Urbina. Soon after my arrival in Flanders, news came of the league concluded between Pope Pius V., of happy memory, and Spain, against the common enemy, the Turk; who about the same time had taken the island of Cyprus from the Venetians, a serious loss to that republic. Don John of Austria, natural brother of our good King Philip, was appointed generalissimo of this alliance, and such great preparations for war were everywhere talked of, that I conceived an ardent desire to be present in the expected engagement; therefore, in spite of the assurances I had received of being promoted, I relinquished all, and resolved to go into Italy; and fortunately for my design, Don John passed through Genoa, on his way to Naples, to join the Venetian fleet. In the glorious action which followed I was engaged; and, more from good hap than merit, was already advanced to the honourable post of captain. But on that day, so happy for Christendom, by showing the fallacy of the prevailing opinion that the Turks were invincible at sea—on that day, so humiliating to Ottoman pride, I alone remained unfortunate; for surely more happy were the Christians who died on that occasion than the survivors! Instead of receiving a naval crown for my services, I found myself the following night loaded with chains.

" My misfortune was occasioned in this way: Uchali, King of Algiers, a bold and successful corsair, having boarded and taken the captain-galley of Malta, in which three knights only were left alive, and those desperately wounded, the captain-galley of John Andrea d'Oria came up to her relief, on board of which I was with my company; and acting as my duty enjoined upon this occasion, I leaped into the enemy's galley, expecting to be followed by my men; but the two vessels separating, I was left alone among enemies too numerous for me to resist, and carried off prisoner, after receiving many wounds. Thus Uchali escaped, and I remained his captive—the only mourner on a day of joy—a slave at the moment when so many were set free!—for fifteen thousand Christians from the Turkish galleys were on that day restored to liberty. I was carried to Constantinople, where the Grand Signor Selim appointed my master general of the sea for his bravery, and for having brought off the flag of the Order of Malta.

" The following year, which was 'seventy-two, I was at Navarino, rowing in the captain-galley of the *Three Lanthorns;* and there I observed the opportunity that was then lost of taking the whole Turkish fleet in port; for all the Levantines and Janizaries on board took it for granted that they should be attacked in the very harbour, and had their baggage and *passamaquas* in readiness for making their escape on shore, without intending to resist—such was the terror which our navy had inspired. But it was ordered otherwise—not through any fault in our general, but for the sins of Christendom, and because God ordains that there should always be some scourge to chastise us. In short, Uchali got into Modon, an island near Navarino; and putting his men on shore, he fortified the entrance of the port, and remained quiet until the season forced Don John to return home. In this campaign the galley called the

I remained captive—the only mourner on a day of joy—a slave at the moment when so many were set free.

Prize, whose captain was a son of the famous corsair Barbarossa, was taken by the *She-wolf*, of Naples, commanded by that thunderbolt of war, the fortunate and invincible Captain Don Alvara de Bazan, Marquis of Santa Cruz. I cannot forbear relating what happened at the taking of this vessel. The son of Barbarossa was so cruel, and treated his slaves so ill, that as soon as the rowers saw that the *She-wolf* was ready to board them, they all at once let fall their oars, and seizing their captain, who stood near the poop, they tossed him along from bank to bank, and from the poop to the prow, giving him such blows, that before his body had passed the mainmast his soul was gone to Hades; so great was the hatred his cruelty had inspired!

"We returned to Constantinople, where the year following we received intelligence that Don John had taken the city of Tunis from the Turks, and put Muley Hamet in possession of it; thus cutting off the hopes of Muley Hamida, who was one of the bravest but most cruel of Moors. The Grand Turk felt this loss very sensibly; and with that sagacity which is inherent in the Ottoman family, he made peace with the Venetians (to whom it was very acceptable); and the next year he attacked the fortress of Goleta, as well as the fort which Don John had left half finished near Tunis. During all these transactions I was still at the oar, without any hope of redemption, being determined not to let my father know of my captivity. The Goleta and the fort were both lost, having been attacked by the Turks with an army of seventy-five thousand men, besides above four hundred thousand Moors and Arabs; which vast multitudes were furnished with immense quantities of ammunition and warlike stores, together with so many pioneers, that each man bringing only a handful of earth might have covered both the Goleta and the fort. Although the Goleta was until then supposed to be impregnable, no blame attached to the defenders; for it was found that, water being no longer near the surface as formerly, the besiegers were enabled to raise mounds of sand that commanded the fortifications; and thus attacking them by a cavalier, it was impossible to make any defence. It has been ignorantly asserted that our troops ought not to have shut themselves up in the Goleta, but have met the enemy at the place of disembarkment: as if so small a number, being scarcely seven thousand men, could have at once defended the works and taken the field against such an overwhelming force! But many were of opinion, and myself among the rest, that the destruction of that place was a providential circumstance for Spain; for it was the forge of iniquity, the sponge, the devourer of countless sums, idly expended for no other reason than because it was a conquest of the invincible Charles the Fifth: as if his immortal fame depended upon the preservation of those ramparts! The fort was also so obstinately defended, that above five-and-twenty thousand of the enemy were destroyed in twenty-two general assaults; and of three hundred that were left alive, not one was taken unwounded — an evident proof of their unconquerable spirit. A little fort also, in the middle of the lake, commanded by Don John Zanoguera, of Valencia, yielded upon terms. Don Pedro Portocarrero, general of Goleta, was made prisoner, and died on his way to Constantinople, broken-hearted for the loss of the fortress which he had so bravely defended. They also took the commander of the fort, Gabrio Cerbellon, a Milanese gentlemen, a great engineer and a brave soldier. Several persons of distinction lost their lives in these two garrisons; among whom was Pagan d'Oria, Knight of Malta, a gentleman well known for his exalted liberality to his brother, the famous John Andrea d'Oria; and his fate was the more lamented, having been put to death by some African Arabs, who, upon seeing that the fort was lost, offered to convey him disguised as a Moor to Tabarca, a small haven or settlement which the Genoese have on that coast for the coral-fishing. These Arabs cut off his head, and carried it to the general of the Turkish fleet, who made good our Castilian proverb, that 'though we love the treason, we hate the traitor;' for the general ordered those who delivered him the present to be instantly hanged, because they had not brought him alive. Among the Christians taken in the fort was an ensign, whose name was Don Pedro d'Aguilar, an Andalusian, who was a good soldier, as well as a poet. I mention this because it was our fate to be slaves to the same master: we served in the same galley, and worked at the same oar. He composed two sonnets, by way of epitaph—one upon Goleta, and the other upon the fort, which I will endeavour to repeat, for I think they will please you."

When the captive named Don Pedro d'Aguilar, Don Fernando looked and smiled at one of his companions; who, when he mentioned the sonnets, said, "I beseech you, sir, before you proceed, tell me what became of that same Don Pedro d'Aguilar." "All I know concerning him," answered the captive, "is, that after he had been two years at Constantinople, he escaped, disguised as an Arnaut,* with a Greek; and I believe he succeeded in recovering his liberty, but am not certain; for though I saw the Greek about a year after in Constantinople, I had not an opportunity of asking him the success of their journey." "That Don Pedro," replied the gentleman, "is my brother: he returned to Spain, and is now married and settled in his native city: he has three children, and is blessed with both health and affluence." "Thanks be to Heaven!" exclaimed the captive; "for what transport in life can equal that which a man feels on the restoration of his liberty?" "I well remember those sonnets which you mention," added the gentleman. "Then, pray, sir, repeat them," said the captive; "for you will do it better than I can." The gentleman willingly complied: that upon the Goleta was as follows:

SONNET.

"'O happy souls, by death at length set free
From the dark prison of mortality,
By glorious deeds, whose memory never dies—
From earth's dim spot exalted to the skies!
What fury stood in every eye confessed!
What generous ardour fired each manly breast,
Whilst slaughtered heaps distained the sandy shore,
And the tinged ocean blushed with hostile gore!
O'erpowered by numbers, gloriously ye fell:
Death only could such matchless courage quell.
Whilst dying thus, ye triumph o'er your foes—
Its fame the world, its glory Heaven, bestows!'"

"You have it correctly," said the captive. "This," said the gentleman, "if I remember rightly, was the one written on the fort:

SONNET.

"'From 'midst these walls, whose ruins spread around,
And scattered clods that heap th' ensanguined ground
Three thousand souls of warriors, dead in fight,
To better regions took their happy flight.
Long with unconquered souls they bravely stood
And fearless shed their unavailing blood;
Till, to superior force compelled to yield,
Their lives they quitted in the well-fought field.
This fatal soil has ever been the tomb
Of slaughtered heroes, buried in its womb;
Yet braver bodies did it ne'er sustain,
Nor send more glorious souls the skies to gain.'"

---

* A native of Albania.

CHAPTER XL.

In which is continued the history of the captive.

AFTER the company had expressed their approbation of the sonnets, the captive pursued his story.

"When the Turks had got possession of Goleta, they gave orders for its demolition; and to lessen their labour, they undermined it in three different places: the new works, erected by the engineer Fratin, came easily down; but the old walls, though apparently the weakest part, they could not raze. The fleet returned in triumph to Constantinople, and within a few months, Uchali, whose slave I had become, died; he was called Uchali Fartax, or The Leprous Renegado, being so nicknamed according to the custom of the Turks, who have but four family surnames, and these descend from the Ottoman race; the rest of the people are named either from their incidental blemishes, or peculiarities of body or mind. This leper had been fourteen years a slave to the Grand Signor; and when he was about four-and-thirty years of age, being irritated by a blow he received from a Turk while he was at the oar, he renounced his religion that he might have it in his power to be revenged on him. He rose by bravery alone, and not by the base intrigues of court; and became King of Algiers, and afterwards general of the sea, which is the third command in the empire. He was a native of Calabria, a man of good morals, and treated his slaves with humanity. He had three thousand of them, and in his will he left one-half of them among his renegadoes, the other to the Grand Signor, who is always joint-heir with the heirs of all his subjects. I fell to the lot of a Venetian, who had been cabin-boy in a vessel taken by Uchali, with whom he became a great favourite. His name was Hassan Aga, and one of the most cruel of that apostate class: he was afterwards King of Algiers; and with him I left Constantinople, pleased at the idea of being nearer to Spain: not that I intended to inform my family of my wretched situation, but I hoped to find another place more favourable to my schemes of escape, which hitherto I had attempted in vain. In Algiers I purposed to renew my efforts; for notwithstanding my numerous disappointments, the hope of recovering my liberty never abandoned me: no sooner did one expedient fail than I grasped at another, which still preserved my hopes alive.

"By these means I supported existence, shut up in a prison which the Turks call a bath,* where they confine their Christian captives—not only those which belong to the king, but the captives of private individuals. In this place there is also another class, who serve the

---

* The baths of the Christian captives are large courtyards, the interiors of which are surrounded by small chambers. Within these the captives who are not under strict confinement are enclosed at night; the others are confined in dungeons.

city in its public works, and in other offices : they are called the slaves of the Almazen ; and as they belong to the public, having no particular master, they find it very difficult to regain their liberty ; for even when they might procure money, there are none with whom they can negotiate their ransom. The king's slaves do not work with the rest, unless their ransom is slow in coming, in which case they are put upon toilsome labour, to hasten its arrival. As they knew my rank to be that of a captain, in spite of my assurances that I had neither interest nor money, they would place me among those who expected to be redeemed ; and the chain I wore was rather as a sign of ransom than to secure my person.

" Thus I passed years of captivity, with other gentlemen of condition from whom ransom was expected. We suffered much both from hunger and nakedness ; but these were less painful to endure than the sight of those unparalleled and excessive cruelties which our tyrant inflicted upon his Christian slaves : not a day passed on which one of these unfortunate men was not either hanged, impaled, or mutilated, and often without the least provocation. Even the Turks acknowledged that he acted thus merely for the gratification of his murderous and inhuman disposition.

" One Spanish soldier only, whose name was something de Saavedra,* happened to be in his good graces ; and although his enterprises to effect an escape were such as will long be remembered there, he never gave him a blow, nor ordered one to be given him, nor even rebuked him : yet, for the least of many things he did, we all feared he would be impaled alive ; so indeed he feared himself, more than once. Did the time allow I could tell you of some things done by this soldier which would surprise you more than my own narrative.

" But to return. The courtyard of our place of confinement was overlooked by the windows of a house belonging to a Moor of distinction, which, as is usual there, were rather peep-holes than windows, and even these had thick and close lattices. It happened that one day, as I was upon a terrace belonging to our prison with three of my companions, trying by way of pastime who could leap farthest with his chains, I accidentally looked up, and observed a cane held out from one of the windows above us ; a handkerchief was fastened to the end of it, which waving, seemed to invite us to take hold of it. One of my comrades seeing it, placed himself under the cane, expecting it would be dropped ; but as he approached the cane was drawn back again. Upon his retiring the cane was again lowered as before. Another of our party then went towards it, but was rejected in the same manner. The third then tried it, but without any better success. Upon which I determined to try my fortune ; and I had no sooner placed myself under the cane, than it fell at my feet. I immediately untied the handkerchief, and in a knot at

---

* The Saavedra here mentioned is Miguel de Cervantes himself, who in this passage only speaks expressly of himself ; the hero of the captive's tale being Captain Viedma, who was a fellow-sufferer with him under the tyranny of Hassan Aga.

one corner found ten zianyis—a sort of base gold coin used by the Moors, each piece worth about ten reals of our money. You will conceive that I felt no less pleasure than surprise at this singular circumstance, especially as it was so obvious that the favour was intended exclusively for me. I took my money, returned to the terrace, looked again to the window, and perceived a very white hand hastily open and close it. Thence we conjectured that it must be some woman residing in that house who had been thus charitable; and to express our thanks we made our reverences after the Moorish fashion, inclining the head, bending the body, and laying the hands on the breast.

" Soon after, a small cross made of cane was held out of the window, and then drawn in again. On this signal we concluded that it must be some Christian woman who was a captive in that house ; but the whiteness of the hand, and the bracelet on the wrist, seemed to oppose this idea. Then again we imagined it might be a Christian renegade, whom their masters often marry ; for they value them more than the women of their own nation. But our reasonings and conjectures were wide of the truth. From this time we continued to gaze at the window with great anxiety, as to our polar star; but fifteen days elapsed without our having once seen either the hand or any other signal; and though in this interval we had anxiously endeavoured to procure information as to the inhabitants of that house, we never could learn more than that the house belonged to a rich Moor, named Agi-Morato, who had been Alcaid of the port of Bata—an office among them of great authority. At length the cane and handkerchief again appeared, with a still larger knot, and at a time when, as before, all the other captives were absent except myself and three companions. We repeated our former trial, each of my three companions going before me ; but the cane was not let down until I approached. The knot, I found, contained Spanish crowns in gold, and a paper written in Arabic, which was marked with a large cross. I kissed the cross, took the crowns, and returned to the terrace, where we all made our reverences. Again the hand appeared : I made signs that I would read the paper, and the window closed.

" We were very impatient to know the contents of the paper, but none of us understood Arabic, and it was difficult to find an interpreter. I determined at length to confide in a renegado, a native of Murcia, who had professed himself friendly towards me, and whom, from an interchange of confidence, I could safely trust: for it is usual with these men, when they wish to return to Christendom, to procure certificates from captives of distinction, attesting their character as good Christians. These certificates are, however, sometimes employed for artful purposes. For instance, if on their piratical excursions they happen to be shipwrecked or taken, they produce their written characters, pretending that they had only joined the pirates to effect their escape into a Christian country, and by this means live unmolested until they have an opportunity of returning to Barbary to resume their former course of life. But my friend was not of this number. With a good design he had obtained certificates, in which we had spoken of him in the highest terms; and, had the Moors found these papers upon him, they would certainly have burnt him alive. I knew that this man was well acquainted with the Arabic language; but before I intrusted to him the whole affair, I desired him to read the paper, which I pretended to have found by chance in a hole in my cell. He opened it, and stood for some time studying and translating it to himself. I asked him if he understood it. 'Perfectly,' he said, 'and if I would provide him with a pen and ink, he would give me an exact translation.' We instantly supplied him with what he required, and he wrote down a literal translation of the Moorish paper, observing to us that the words *Lela Marien* signified our Lady the Virgin Mary. We read the paper, which was nearly in these words:

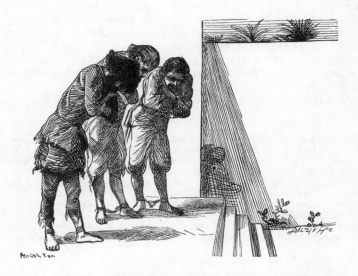

To express our thanks we made our reverences after the Moorish fashion.

"'When I was a child, my father had a woman slave who instructed me in the Christian worship, and told me many things of Lela Marien. This Christian died, and I know she did not go to the fire, but to Allah; for I saw her twice afterwards, and she bid me go to the country of the Christians to see Lela Marien, who loved me very much. I know not how it is, though I have seen many Christians from this window, none has looked like a gentleman but thyself. I am very beautiful, and young, and have a great deal of money to carry away with me. Try if thou canst find means for us to get away, and thou shalt be my husband, if it please thee; and if otherwise, I shall not care, for Lela Marien will provide me a husband. I write this myself: be careful who reads it. Trust not any Moor, for they are all treacherous. I am full of tears, and would not have thee trust anybody; for if my father hears of it he will immediately throw me into a well, and cover me with stones. I will fasten a thread to the cane: tie thy answer to it; and if thou hast nobody that can write Arabic, tell me by signs—Lela Marien will enable me to understand them. Both she and Allah protect thee! and this cross too, which I often kiss; for so the captive instructed me.'

"Conceive, gentlemen, our emotion at the contents of this paper! Being indeed so manifest, the renegado clearly perceived that it could not have been found by accident, but was actually written to one of us; and he therefore entreated us, if his conjectures were true, to confide in him, for he would venture his life for our liberty. As he spoke, he drew from his bosom a crucifix of brass, and with tears swore by the Deity that image represented, in whom, though a sinner, he firmly believed, that he would faithfully keep secret whatever we should reveal to him; for he hoped that through the same means by which we regained our liberty he should be restored to the bosom of our Holy Church, from which, like a rotten member, he had been separated through his ignorance and sin. This was spoken with such evident marks of sincerity that we agreed to tell him the truth; and therefore communicated to him the whole affair, without reserve. We showed him the window out of which the cane had appeared, and he determined to find out the owner of the house. Having considered that it would be proper to answer the lady's billet, the renagado instantly wrote what I dictated to him, which I can repeat correctly to you; for not one of the material circumstances which befell me in this adventure has yet escaped my memory, nor ever will, as long as I live. My answer to the Moor was this:

"'The true Allah preserve thee, dear lady, and that blessed Marien, the true Mother of God! who, because she loves thee, has inspired thee with a desire to go into the land of Christians. Pray that she will instruct thee how to obey her commands, and she is so good that she will not deny thee. As for myself and the Christians with me, we are ready to hazard our lives to serve thee. Fail not to write and inform me of thy resolution, and I will always answer thee; for, thanks to the great Allah! we have a Christian captive who is well acquainted with thy language; and thou mayest, without fear, communicate anything to us. I promise thee, on the word of a good Christian, to make thee my wife, as soon as we reach a Christian country; and be assured the Christians perform their promises. Allah, and Marien his mother, protect thee, dear lady!'

"My letter being thus prepared, I waited for two days, when an opportunity again offered of being alone on the terrace; and the cane soon made its appearance, though I could not see by whom it was held. I found the thread already attached to the end of it to receive my letter, which I immediately fastened to it. Shortly afterwards the handkerchief was dropped, in which I now found gold and silver coin to the amount of fifty crowns—a joyful sight, when regarded as the means of obtaining liberty. On the same evening we were told by our renegado that this house was inhabited by a very rich Moor, named Agi-Morato; and that he had an only daughter, heiress to his whole property, who was considered the most beautiful woman in all Barbary; and that several of the viceroys who had been sent thither had sought her in marriage, but that she had rejected them. He also learned that he had a Christian woman-slave, who died some time before: all which agreed perfectly with the contents of the paper. We then consulted with the renegado on what measures we should take to carry off the Moorish lady, and make our escape into Christendom: and it was finally agreed that we should wait for a second letter from Zoraida (the name of her who now desires to be called Maria); for it was obvious that she was in possession of the surest means of effecting our design. During the four following days the bath was constantly full of people; but the first time it was vacant, the cane again appeared with the prolific handkerchief. The billet I then received contained these words:

"'I do not know, dear signor, how we are to get to Spain, nor has Lela Marien informed me, although I have asked her. The only means I can think of is to convey to thee through this window a large sum of money, with which thou mayest redeem thyself and friends; one of whom may then procure a bark from the land of the Christians, and return to the rest. I will be ready in my father's garden, at the Babazon Gate, close to the sea-side—thou mayest safely convey me thence to the bark; but remember thou art to be my husband; otherwise I will pray to Marien to punish thee. If thou canst trust nobody to go for the bark, ransom thyself and go; for I shall be secure of thy return, as thou art a gentleman and a Christian. Take care not to mistake the garden: when I see thee walking there I shall conclude thou art alone, and will furnish thee with money. Allah preserve thee, dear signor!'

"On hearing the proposal contained in this letter, each offered himself to be the ransomed person, promising faithfully to return with the boat. But the renegado would not trust any of us; for he said he well knew, by experience, how seldom promises made in slavery are remembered after a release from bondage. Many captives of distinction, he said, had tried this expedient: ransoming one, to send with money to Valencia or Majorca, in order to procure a vessel for the conveyance of others; but none ever returned to fulfil his engagement; for the dread of again falling into captivity effaces from the memory every other obligation. In confirmation of what he said, he related to us many extraordinary instances of the kind; and he concluded with saying that the best way would be to give the money intended for the ransom of a Christian to him, that he might purchase a vessel there, in Algiers, under pretence of turning merchant, and trading to Tetuan and along the coast; that when master of the vessel he could easily contrive means to get us from the bath, and put us on board, especially if the Moor would furnish money enough to redeem us all. The greatest difficulty, he said, was that the Moors do not allow a renegado to have any but large vessels fitted for piratical uses, as they suspect their real motives, if they purchase small ones; but he thought this objection might be removed by taking in a Tagarin Moor as a partner in his pretended mercantile concern. Having once got a vessel at their command, he assured us we might consider everything as accomplished.

"Although my companions and myself would have preferred sending for the vessel to Majorca, as the Moorish lady proposed, yet we dared not contradict him, lest he should betray our project, and, by discovering the clandestine correspondence of Zoraida, endanger her life, for whom we would willingly have sacrificed our own: we therefore resolved to commit ourselves into the hands of God, and trust the renegado. He instantly wrote my answer to Zoraida, saying that we would do all she advised, for she had directed as well as if Lela Marien herself had inspired her; that the delay or immediate execution of the plan depended solely upon herself; and I repeated my promise to become her husband. The next day, therefore, when the bath was clear, she at various times, with the help of the cane and handkerchief, gave us two thousand crowns in gold, and a paper informing me that on the first Juma, that is, Friday, she was to go to her father's garden, and that before she went she would give us more money; desiring us to tell her if it was not sufficient, as she could give us any sum, having such abundance under her care that her father would never miss it.

" We immediately gave five hundred crowns to the renegado, to buy the vessel. With eight hundred I ransomed myself, and deposited the money with a merchant of Valencia then at Algiers, who redeemed me from the king; passing his word for me that by the first ship from Valencia my ransom should be paid; for had he paid him then it would have made the king suspect that it had lain some time in his hands, and that he had employed it to his own use. Indeed, it would have been by no means safe, with a master of such a disposition as mine, to have paid the money immediately. The Thursday preceding the Friday on which the fair Zoraida was to go to the garden, she gave us a thousand crowns more, with a billet entreating me when I was ransomed to seek her father's garden, and take every opportunity of seeing her. I promised her in a few words that I would not fail, and begged that she would recommend us in her prayers to Lela Marien. We now concerted the means for redeeming our three companions, lest if I were ransomed without them they might feel uneasy, and be tempted by the devil to do something to the prejudice of Zoraida: I therefore ransomed them in the same way, and placed the whole amount in the hands of the merchant, that he might have no fear in becoming responsible for us; although we did not admit him into our confidence.

CHAPTER XLI.

Wherein the captive continues his story.

" Our renegado about fifteen days afterwards purchased a very good bark, large enough to hold thirty persons; and to prevent suspicion he made a short voyage to a place called Sargel, thirty leagues from Algiers, towards Oran—a place of great trade for dried figs. Two or three times he made this trip, accompanied by his Tagarin partner. The Moors of Arragon are in Barbary called *Tagarins*, and those of Granada, *Mudajeres*; and in the kingdom of Fez the *Mudajeres* are called *Elches*, who are principally employed by the king in military service. Each time that he arrived with his bark, he cast anchor in a little creek very near to the garden where Zoraida waited for us; and there he either performed the *zala* with his Moorish rowers, or contrived some way of practising

Our renegado purchased a very good bark, large enough to hold thirty persons.

in jest their future project, in order to elude suspicion. He would also occasionally visit Zoraida's garden, and beg some fruit, which her father often gave him, without knowing who he was. His object was to speak to Zoraida, and tell her that he was the person whom I had intrusted to convey her to Christendom, and that she might feel in perfect security. But this was impossible, as the Moorish women never suffer themselves to be seen either by Moor or Turk, unless by the command of their husbands or fathers: though Christian slaves, it is true, are allowed to converse with them, and perhaps even with too much freedom. I should have been sorry if he had spoken to her, as she might have been alarmed at the affair having been intrusted to a renegado; but he had no opportunity of effecting his design. Finding that he could now safely go to and from Sargel, and anchor where he pleased, and that the Tagarin, his partner, was wholly subservient to him—in short, that nothing was wanting but some Christians to assist at the oar—he desired me to determine on our party, and be ready on the following Friday. I immediately engaged twelve Spaniards, all able rowers, whom just at that time it was no easy matter to procure; for there were twenty corsairs out on pirating excursions, and they had taken almost all the rowers with them. All I said to them was, that they must steal privately out of the town on the following Friday, in the dusk of the evening, and wait for me near Agi-Morato's garden; and with this caution, which I gave to each separately, that if they should see any other Christians there, they had only to say I had ordered them to stay for me in that place.

"After these steps were taken, one thing was yet wanting, and that the most essential of all, namely, to apprise Zoraida of our intended movements, that she might not be alarmed if we rushed upon her without previous warning. I went, therefore, myself, on the day preceding our departure, to the garden, under pretence of gathering herbs. The first person I met was her father, who addressed me in a jargon which is used over all Barbary, and even at Constantinople, among the captives and Moors. It is neither Morisco nor Castilian, nor the language of any other nation, but a medley of several, and is very generally understood. He asked me what I sought for in that garden, and to whom I belonged? I told him that I was a slave of Arnaute Mami, his friend, and that I came to request herbs for his table. He then asked me if I was upon ransom? At this moment the fair Zoraida, having observed me in the garden, had quitted the house, and came towards us. Her father seeing her slowly approach, called her to him. It would be in vain for me to attempt to describe the beautiful creature who then appeared before my eyes. More jewels hung about her lovely neck, and were suspended from her ears, or scattered over her tresses, than she had hairs on her head. Her ankles were, according to custom, bare, and encircled by *carcaxes*, or foot-bracelets, of the purest gold, and so studded with diamonds that, as she told me since, her father valued them at ten thousand pistoles; and those she wore on her arms were of equal value. Pearls of the finest quality were strewed about her in profusion: those precious gems, indeed, form one of the principal embellishments of the Moorish ladies, and are, therefore, in great request among the natives. Zoraida's father was said to have possessed them in abundance, and other wealth to the amount of two hundred thousand crowns: of all which she who is now mine was once sole mistress. Whether or not she then appeared beautiful thus adorned, and in the days of her prosperity, may well be conjectured by what remains after so many fatigues; for it is well known that beauty is often at the mercy of accidents, as well as liable to be improved or impaired by the passions. In short, I gazed upon her as the most lovely object my eyes had ever beheld. Indeed, when I considered my obligations to her, I could only regard her as an angel descended from heaven for my deliverance.

"When she had come up to us, her father told her, in his own language, that I was a captive belonging to his friend Arnaute Mami. She then asked me, in that medley speech which I mentioned to you, whether I was a gentleman, and why I did not ransom myself. I told her that I was already ransomed, and by the sum which was to be paid she might judge how my master ranked me, whose demand had been fifteen hundred pieces of eight. 'Truly,' said she, 'had you belonged to my father, he should not have parted with you for twice that sum; for you Christians always deceive in the account you give of yourselves, pretending to be poor, in order to cheat the Moors.' 'It may be so, signora,' answered I; 'but, in truth, I dealt sincerely with my master, and shall ever do the same by everybody.' 'And when do you go away?' said Zoraida. 'I believe to-morrow,' said I; 'for there is a French vessel which is expected to sail then, and I intend to go in her.' 'Would it not be better,' replied Zoraida, 'to stay until some ships come from Spain, and go with one of them, rather than with the French, who are not your friends?' 'I think not, signora,' replied I; 'but should the late intelligence of the arrival of a Spanish ship prove true, I would perhaps stay a short time longer: it is, however, more probable that I shall depart to-morrow; for I so ardently desire to be in my own country, and with the persons I love, that I am impatient of any delay.' 'You are, perhaps, married,' said Zoraida, 'and therefore anxious to return, and be at home with your wife?' 'No, indeed,' I replied, 'but I am under an engagement to marry as soon as I return.' 'And is the lady to whom you are engaged beautiful?' said Zoraida. 'So beautiful,' answered I, 'that to compliment her, and say the truth, she is very like yourself.' Her father laughed heartily at this, and said, 'By the Prophet, Christian, she must be beautiful indeed, if she resembles my daughter, who is the handsomest woman in this kingdom! Observe her well, and you will see that I speak the truth.' Zoraida's father was our interpreter in most of this conversation, being better acquainted than she was with the language; for, although she knew something of it, she expressed her meaning more by signs than words.

"While we were thus engaged, a Moor came running to us, crying aloud that four Turks had leaped over the wall of the garden, and were gathering the fruit, though it was not yet ripe. The old man, as well as Zoraida, was much alarmed; for the Moors are afraid of the Turks, especially their soldiers, whose conduct towards them is insolent and imperious, even more so than to their slaves. Zoraida's father therefore said to her, 'Daughter, make haste into the house, and lock yourself in, while I go and speak to these dogs; and you, Christian, gather your herbs, and begone in peace, and Allah send you safe to your own country.' I made my obeisance, and he went after the Turks. Zoraida also retired, but as soon as her father was out of sight she returned to me, and said, with her eyes full of tears, '*Tamexi, Christiano? Tamexi?*' that is, 'Art thou going away, Christian? Art thou going?' 'Yes, dearest lady,' said I, 'but not without you. Expect me the next Juma, and be not alarmed when you see us; for we will convey you safely to a Christian land.' She understood all that I said; and, throwing her arm about my neck, she began with faltering steps to move towards the house; when, unfortunately as it might have proved, her father returned and saw us in that attitude. We were aware that he had seen us, and Zoraida had the presence of mind not to take her arm from my neck, but rather held me closer; and letting her head fall upon my breast, and bending her knees, she pretended to be fainting : so that I appeared to be under the necessity of supporting her. Her father came running to us, and seeing his daughter in that situation, inquired the cause. But as she made no reply, he said, ' These dogs have certainly terrified her;' and taking her from me, he supported her in his arms; and she, heaving a deep sigh, with her eyes still full of tears, said, ' *Amexi, Christiano, amexi!*' (' Begone, Christian, begone!') Her father said, ' There is no occasion, child, for the Christian to go away : he has done you no harm, and the Turks are gone off. Be not alarmed, for there is no danger.' ' They have indeed frightened her very much,' said I, ' and as she desires me to go, I will not disobey; but, with your leave, I will come again to this garden for herbs. Peace be with you.' ' Come whenever you please,' said Agi-Morato; ' for my daughter does not say this as having been offended by you or any other Christian.' I now took my leave of them both; and she, looking as if her soul had been rent from her, went away with her father, while I, under pretence of gathering herbs, carefully surveyed the whole garden, examining all the inlets and outlets, the strength of the house, and whatever might tend to facilitate our business.

" Having finished my observations, I communicated to the renegado and my companions all that had passed, anxiously wishing for the hour when I might securely enjoy the happiness which fortune presented to me in the company of the beautiful Zoraida.

"The appointed day at length arrived; and, strictly following the rules and directions we had previously settled, everything proceeded with the fairest prospect of success. The day following my interview with Zoraida, our renegado, at the close of the evening, cast anchor almost opposite her residence; and the Christians who were to be employed at the oar were ready, and concealed about the neighbourhood, anxiously waiting for me, and eager to surprise the bark, which was lying within view; for they knew nothing of our plan, but thought they were to regain their liberty by force and by killing the Moors who were on board the vessel: they joined us, therefore, the moment we made our appearance. The critical time was now arrived, the city gates being shut, and not a person to be seen abroad; we therefore deliberated whether it would be better to go first to Zoraida, or secure the Moors who rowed the vessel. In the meantime our renegado came to us, asking us why we delayed, for that now was the time, all his Moors being thoughtless of danger, and most of them asleep. When we told him what we were consulting about, he assured us that it was necessary first to seize the vessel, which might be done with the utmost ease and safety; and then we might go for Zoraida. We all approved his counsel, and guided by him, immediately proceeded to the vessel; when he, leaping in first, drew his cutlass, and said in Morisco, ' Let not one man of you stir, or he shall instantly die.' All the Christians quickly followed their leader; and the Moors, who were cowardly fellows, in great alarm and without making any resistance (for indeed they had few or no arms), quietly suffered themselves to be bound, which was done in a moment; the Christians still threatening that if they made the least noise they would instantly put them all to death.

" This being done, and half our number left on board to guard them, the remainder, led on by the renegado, went to Agi-Morato's garden. Fortunately the door opened as easily to us as if it had not been locked, and we came up to the house in profound silence. The lovely Zoraida was waiting for us at a window, and hearing us approach, she asked in a low voice whether we were *Nazareni*—that is, Christians. I answered in the affirmative, and desired her to come down. She knew my voice, and instantly obeyed the summons, appearing to us beautiful beyond description, and in the richest attire. I took her hand, and kissed it, the renegado and the rest of our party following my example, thinking that I only meant to express our thanks and acknowledgments to her as the instrument of our deliverance. The renegado asked her in Morisco whether her father was in the house. She said that he was, but that he was asleep. ' Then we must awake him,' replied the renegado, ' and carry him and all his treasures with us.' ' No,' said she, ' my father shall not be touched; and there is nothing of much value but what I have with me, which is sufficient to satisfy and enrich you all : wait a moment and you shall see.' She then went in again, promising to return quickly, and entreating us to be silent. The renegado having told me what had passed, I insisted that she should be obeyed in every-thing. Zoraida soon returned with a little trunk so full of gold crowns that she could scarcely carry it.

" In the meantime the father of Zoraida unfortunately awoke, and hearing a noise in the garden, looked out at the window and saw the Christians. Upon which he cried out as loud as he could in Arabic, ' Christians, Christians ! thieves, thieves ! ' His outcry threw us all into the utmost consternation. The renegado, perceiving our danger and the necessity of prompt exertion, rushed up with several others to the chamber of Agi-Morato, while I remained below, not daring to quit Zoraida, who had fainted in my arms. They acquitted themselves so well that in a moment they came down with their prisoner, his hands tied, and his mouth stopped with a handkerchief, and threatening, if he made the least noise, that it would cost him his life. When Zoraida saw her father she covered her eyes, to avoid the sight of him; and he was astonished to see her with us, but little thought how willingly she had put herself into our hands. We hastened with all possible speed to the bark, where our comrades were waiting for us with impatience; and scarcely two hours of the night had passed when we were all safely on board. We now untied the hands of Zoraida's father, and took the handkerchief out of his mouth; but the renegado again warned him, at peril of his life, not to speak a word. When he saw his daughter he began to sigh piteously; especially when he observed that I held her closely embraced, without resistance or complaint on her part; nevertheless he remained silent, lest we should put the renegado's threat into execution.

" When Zoraida saw that we were on the point of leaving the coast, she begged the renegado to communicate to me her wish that I would unbind the Moors, and set her father at liberty, for that she would sooner throw herself into the sea than behold a parent who loved her so tenderly carried away captive before her eyes, and upon her account. The renegado told me her request, and I desired that she might be gratified; but he refused to comply, saying that if they were put on shore at that place they would immediately raise the country and dispatch armed vessels to pursue us; and, thus beset by sea and land, it would be impossible for us to escape: all, therefore, that could be done was to give them their liberty at the first Christian country we should touch at. In this opinion we all concurred; and Zoraida was herself satisfied on hearing our determination, with the reasons why we could not then grant her request. With glad silence and cheerful diligence our brave rowers now handled their oars; and recommending ourselves to God with all our hearts, we began to make towards the island of Majorca, which is the nearest Christian land. But the north wind beginning to blow freshly, and the sea being somewhat rough, it was found impossible to steer our course to Majorca, and we were compelled to keep along shore towards Oran, though not without great apprehensions of being discovered from the town of Sargel, which lies on that coast, about sixty miles from Algiers. We were afraid, likewise, of meeting in our passage with some of the galiots which bring merchandise from Tetuan; though, unless it were a cruizer, we trusted we should be able to defend ourselves, if not capture some vessel wherein we might more securely pursue our voyage. During this time Zoraida kept her head constantly upon my breast, that she might not look at her father; and I could hear her calling upon Lela Marien to assist us.

"We had rowed about thirty miles when morning dawned, and we found ourselves near a shore which seemed to be quite a desert, and no human creature to be seen. However, by labouring hard at the oars, we got a little out to sea, which had now become more calm; and having made about two leagues, we ordered the rowers to rest by turns, in order to recruit themselves with the food, of which we had abundance; but they refused to quit their oars, saying that it was not a time to repose, but that they could eat and row at the same time, if those who were unemployed would supply them. This was done; but soon the wind began to blow a brisk gale, which compelled us to lay aside our oars; therefore, hoisting sail, we steered directly to Oran, as it was impossible to hold any other course; and we proceeded with great rapidity, without any other fear than that of meeting some corsair. We gave provisions to the Moorish prisoners, comforting them with the assurance that they were not slaves, but should have their liberty the first opportunity; and we promised the same to Zoraida's father. 'I might hope for much,' he replied, 'from your liberality and generous treatment, O Christians; but I am not so simple as to expect my liberty, or that you would expose yourselves to danger in robbing me of it, without some view to my ransom; however, you have only to name the sum you require for myself and this my unhappy daughter, who is the

better part of my soul.'   He then wept so bitterly that we were moved
to compassion; and Zoraida looking up, and seeing her father in tears,
left me to throw herself into his arms.   Nothing could be more affecting than the scene.   The father now observing her rich attire, said,
' How is this, daughter ?—last night I saw you dressed as usual, and
now you are adorned in your gayest apparel ! '   She answered not a
word.   The renegado interpreted to us what the Moor had said, for he
had spoken in his own language.   He then noticed the casket in which
his daughter kept her jewels, and being still more perplexed, he asked
how it had come into our hands, and what it contained.   The renegado
now interposed, saying, ' Do not trouble yourself with so many questions,
signor; for in a word I can answer all—your daughter is a Christian,
and has been the means of filing off our chains and restoring us to
liberty.   She is here with her own consent, and, I believe, well pleased :
like one who goes out of darkness into light, from death to life, and from
suffering to glory.'   ' Is this true, daughter ?' said the Moor.   ' It is,'
answered Zoraida.   ' You are, then, become a Christian,' replied the old
man, ' and have thrown your father into the power of his enemies ? '
To which Zoraida answered, ' I am indeed a Christian, but I never
thought of doing you harm; I only wished to do myself good.'   ' And
what good have you done yourself, my daughter ? '   ' Ask that,' answered
she, ' of Lela Marien, who can tell you better than I can.'   On hearing his daughter speak thus, the Moor with sudden impetuosity threw
himself headlong into the sea, and would certainly have been drowned
had not the wide and cumbrous garments he wore kept him a short
time above water.   Zoraida called out to us to save him, and we all
hastened to his assistance, and dragged him out half-drowned and senseless, a sight which so much affected Zoraida that she lamented over him
as if he were dead.   We placed him so that he might disgorge the
water he had swallowed, and in about two hours he recovered his senses.
In the meantime, the wind changing, we were obliged to ply our oars to
avoid running upon the shore; and by good fortune we came to a creek
by the side of a small promontory, which by the Moors is called the
Cape of Cava Rumia, meaning in our language ' The wicked Christian
woman;' for the Moors have a tradition that Cava,* who occasioned the
loss of Spain, lies buried there.   Although they reckon it an ill omen to
be forced to anchor at this place, it proved a safe harbour to us, considering how high the sea ran.   We placed sentinels on shore, and never
dropped our oars; and after partaking of the refreshments which the
renegado had provided, we prayed devoutly to God and to our Lady for
assistance and protection in the happy accomplishment of our enterprise.
Order was given, at Zoraida's entreaty, to set her father on shore,
and also the rest of the Moors, who until now had been fast bound;
for her tender heart could not endure to see her father and countrymen
under confinement.   We promised her it should be done when we put to
sea again, since we ran no risk in leaving them in so desolate a place.

---

* The daughter of Count Julian, who was the cause of bringing the Moors into Spain.

Our prayers were not in vain; for the wind presently changed in our favour, and the sea was calm, inviting us to prosecute our voyage.

"We now unbound the Moors, and sent them one by one on shore, to their great surprise; but when we came to Zoraida's father, who was then perfectly in his senses, he said, 'Why, Christians, is this wicked woman desirous of my being set at liberty? Think you it is out of filial piety? No, certainly: it is because my presence would disturb her in the indulgence of her evil inclinations. Nor think she is moved to change her religion because she thinks it better than ours; no, but because she knows there is more licentiousness in your country.' Then, turning to Zoraida, while we held him fast, lest he should do her any violence, he said, 'Thou ill-advised, thou infamous girl! whither art thou blindly going with these dogs, our natural enemies? Cursed be the hour wherein I begat thee, and cursed the indulgence and luxury in which I brought thee up!' Finding him not disposed to be soon silent, I hurried him ashore, where he continued his execrations and wailings, praying to Mahomet that he would beseech Heaven to destroy, confound, and annihilate us; and when we had got too far off to hear his words, we could see him tearing his beard, plucking off his hair, and rolling himself on the ground: so high he once raised his voice that these words reached us: 'Come back, beloved daughter! come back, and I will forgive thee all! Let those men keep the money they have, but do thou come back and comfort thy wretched father, who must perish in this desert land if thou forsakest him!' All this Zoraida heard—all this she felt and bewailed; but could only say in reply, 'May it please Allah, my dearest father, that Lela Marien, who has been the cause of my turning Christian, may comfort you in your affliction! Allah well knows that I could not do otherwise than I have done, and that these Christians owe me no thanks for any favour to them, since my mind would never have had rest until I had performed this work, which to me seems as good as you, my dearest father, think it bad.' But her father could no longer see or hear her. I said all I could to console her as we proceeded on our voyage, and happily the wind was so favourable that we made no doubt of being next morning upon the coast of Spain.

"But as good seldom or never comes unmixed with evil, it happened unfortunately, or perhaps through the curses the Moor bestowed on his daughter (for a father's curse is always to be dreaded, whatever he may be)—I say it happened that, about the third hour of the night, when we were far out at sea, and under full sail, we discovered by the light of the moon a vessel with all her sails out, a little ahead of us, but so near that to avoid running foul of her we were forced to strike sail, and they also put the helm hard up, to enable us to pass. The men had posted themselves on the quarter-deck, to ask who we were, whither we were going, and whence we came; but as their inquiries were in French, our renegado said, 'Let no one answer, for these are certainly French corsairs, who plunder everything that falls in their way.' Upon this caution all were silent, and we continued our course, their vessel being to the windward; but we had not proceeded far when they suddenly fired two guns, and both, as it appeared, with chain-shots, for one cut our mast through the middle, which together with the sail fell into the sea, and the other at the same instant came through the middle of our bark, laying it quite open, though without wounding any of us. But finding ourselves sinking, we began to cry aloud for help, and entreated them to save us from drowning. They then struck their sails, and sent out a boat, with twelve Frenchmen on board, well armed with muskets, and their matches lighted; but seeing how few we were, and that our vessel was sinking, they took us in, and told us that we had suffered for our incivility in returning them no answer. Our renegado took the trunk containing Zoraida's treasure, and unperceived threw it into the

We could see him tearing his beard, plucking off his hair, and rolling himself on the ground.

sea. In short, we all passed into the French ship, where, having gained from us all the information they wanted, they proceeded to treat us as enemies, stripping us of everything, even of the gold bracelets which Zoraida wore upon her ankles. But I suffered most from apprehensions lest they should rob her of the most precious jewel of all. But the desires of these kind of men seldom extend further than to money, in the pursuit of which they are insatiable. They would have taken away even the clothes we wore as slaves, had they thought them of the smallest value. Some of them proposed throwing us all overboard, wrapped up in a sail: for their object was to trade in some of the Spanish ports, pretending to be of Brittany; and should they carry us with them, they would there be seized and punished for the robbery. But the captain, who had plundered my dear Zoraida, said he was contented with what he had already got, and that he would not touch at any part of Spain, but pass the Straits of Gibraltar by night, and make the best of his way for Rochelle, whence he came; and therefore they finally agreed to provide us with a boat and what was necessary for so short a voyage as we had to make. This they did on the following day, when in view of the Spanish coast, at the sight of which all our troubles were forgotten—so great is the delight of regaining liberty! It was about noon when they dismissed us, with two barrels of water and some biscuit. The captain was even so far moved by compassion as to give Zoraida about forty crowns in gold, at the same time forbidding his soldiers to strip her of her clothes—the same which she now wears.

"We expressed to them more gratitude for what they refrained from doing than resentment for what we had suffered from them; and thus we separated, they steering towards the Straits, and we towards the land before us, rowing so hard that we hoped to reach it before morning. Some of our party thought it unsafe to land at dark upon a coast with which we were unacquainted; while others were so impatient, that they were for making the attempt even though among rocks, rather than be exposed to the corsairs of Tetuan, who are often at night in Barbary and the next morning on the coast of Spain, where they usually make some prize, and return to sleep at their own homes. It was agreed at last that we should row gently towards the shore, and, if the sea proved calm, land where we could; and before midnight we found ourselves close to a large and high mountain, at the foot of which there was a convenient landing-place. We ran our boat into the sand, leaped on shore, and kissed the ground, thanking God with tears of joy for the happy termination of our perilous voyage. We dragged our boat on shore, and then climbed the mountain, scarcely crediting that we were really upon Christian ground. We were anxious for daybreak; but having at length gained the top of the mountain, whence we had hoped to discover some village or shepherd's hut, we could see no indications of human abode; we therefore proceeded farther into the country, trusting we should soon meet with some person to inform us where we were. But what most troubled me was to see Zoraida travel on foot through those craggy places; for though I sometimes carried her in my arms, she was more distressed than relieved by my labour. I therefore led her by the hand, and she bore the fatigue with the utmost patience and cheerfulness.

"Thus we proceeded for about a quarter of a league, when the sound of a little bell reached our ears, which was a signal that flocks were near; and eagerly looking around us, we perceived a young shepherd at the foot of a cork tree, quietly shaping a stick with his knife. We called out to him, upon which he raised his head and hastily got up; and, the first who presented themselves to his sight being the renegado and Zoraida, in Moorish habits, he thought all the Moors in Barbary were upon him: making, therefore, towards the wood with incredible speed, he cried out, as loud as he could, 'Moors! the Moors are landed! Moors, Moors! arm, arm!' We were perplexed at first how to act; but considering that he would certainly alarm the country, and that the

Others were so impatient, that they were for making the attempt even though among rocks.

militia of the coast would soon be out to see what was the matter, we agreed that the renegado should strip off his Turkish habit, and put on a jerkin, or slave's cassock, which one of our party immediately gave him, leaving himself only in his shirt. Then recommending ourselves to Heaven, we pursued the same road that the shepherd had taken, expecting every moment that the coast-guard would be upon us. Nor were we deceived in our apprehensions; for not long afterwards, when we were descending into the plain, we discovered above fifty horsemen advancing at a half-gallop; upon which we stood still to await their approach: but as they drew near, and found, instead of the Moors they had expected, a party of poor Christian captives, they were not a little surprised; and one of them asked us whether we had been the cause of the alarm spread in the country. I told him that I believed so, and was proceeding to inform him whence we came and who we were, when one of our party recognized the horseman who had questioned us; and interrupting me, he exclaimed, 'God be praised for bringing us to this part of the country! for if I am not mistaken, the ground we stand upon is the territory of Velez Malaga; and if long captivity has not impaired my memory, you, sir, who now question us, are Pedro de Bustamante, my uncle.' Scarcely had the Christian captive ceased speaking, when the horseman threw himself from his horse, and ran to embrace the young man, saying to him, 'Dear nephew of my soul, I well remember you! How often have I bewailed your loss, with your mother and kindred, who are still living to enjoy the pleasure of seeing you again! We knew you were living in Algiers; and by your dress, and that of your companions, I conjecture that you must have recovered your liberty in some miraculous manner.' 'It is so, indeed,' answered the young man, 'and when an opportunity offers you shall know the whole story.' As soon as the horsemen understood that we were Christian captives, they alighted, and each of them invited us to accept of his horse to carry us to the city of Velez Malaga, which was a league and a half distant. Some of them went back to convey the boat to the town, on being informed where we had left it; others took us up behind them, and Zoraida rode behind our captive's uncle. The news of our coming having reached the town before us, multitudes came out to greet us. They were not much surprised by the sight of liberated captives, or of Moors made slaves, for the people of that coast are accustomed to both; but they were struck by the beauty of Zoraida, which then appeared in perfection; for the exercise of walking, and the delight of being safe in Christendom, produced such a complexion that, if my affection did not deceive me, the world never saw a more beautiful creature.

" We went directly to the church, to return thanks for the mercy of our deliverance; and Zoraida, upon first entering, said the images there were very like that of Lela Marien. The renegado told her that she was right, and explained to her as well as he could what they signified, that she might adore them as the representations of that very Lela Marien who had spoken to her; nor was she slow in comprehending him, for she had good sense and a ready apprehension. After this they accommodated us in different houses of the town; and the Christian, our companion, took the renegado, Zoraida, and myself to the house of his parents, who treated us with the same kindness they showed towards their own son. We stayed in Velez six days, when the renegado, having gained all necessary information on the subject, repaired to the city of Granada, there to be re-admitted, by means of the Holy Inquisition, into the bosom of our Church. The rest of the freed captives each went their own way, leaving Zoraida and myself to pursue ours, with no other worldly wealth than the crowns which the courtesy of the Frenchman had bestowed on her, some of which proved useful in purchasing the animal on which she rides. I have hitherto attended her as a father and esquire, not as a husband; and we are going to see if my father be yet alive, or whether my brothers have been more fortunate than myself; though, since Heaven has given me Zoraida, I cannot conceive that any better fortune could have befallen me. The patience with which she bears the inconvenience attendant on poverty, and the fervour of her piety, excites my warmest admiration; and I consider myself bound to serve her all the days of my life: yet the delight I feel in knowing her to be mine is sometimes disturbed by an uncertainty whether I shall find any corner in my own country wherein to shelter her; and also whether time or death may not have made such alterations in my family that I shall find none left to acknowledge me.

"This, gentlemen, is my story: whether it has been entertaining or uncommon, you are the best judges. I can only say, for my own part, that I would willingly have been more brief; and, indeed, I have omitted many circumstances, lest you should think me tedious."

CHAPTER XLII.

Which treats of other occurrences at the inn, and of various things worthy to be known.

As soon as the captive ceased speaking, "Truly, captain," said Don Fernando, "your narrative has been so interesting to us, both from the extraordinary nature of the events themselves and your manner of relating them, that we should not have been wearied had it lasted till to-morrow." The whole party now offered their services with such expressions of kindness and sincerity that the captain felt highly gratified. Don Fernando, in particular, offered, if he would return with him, to prevail with the marquis his brother to stand godfather at Zoraida's baptism; and promised on his own part to afford him all the assistance necessary for his appearance in his own country with the dignity and distinction due to his person. The captive thanked him most courteously, but declined his generous offers.

Night was now advanced, and a coach arrived at the inn, with some horsemen. The travellers wanted lodging for the night; but the hostess told them that there was not an inch of room disengaged in the whole inn. "Notwithstanding that," said one of the men on horseback, "there must be room made for my lord judge here in the coach." On hearing this, the hostess was disturbed, and said, "Sir, the truth is, I have no bed; but if his worship, my lord judge, brings one with him, let him enter, in Heaven's name; for I and my husband will quit our own chamber to accommodate his honour."

"Be it so," quoth the squire; and by this time a person had alighted from the coach, whose garb immediately showed the nature and dignity of his station; for his long gown and tucked-up sleeves denoted him to be a judge, as his servant had said. He led by the hand a young lady, apparently about sixteen years of age, in a riding-dress, so lovely and elegant in her person, that all were struck with so much admiration, that had they not seen Dorothea, Lucinda, and Zoraida, they would never have believed that there was such another beautiful damsel in existence. Don Quixote was present at their entrance, and he thus addressed them: "Your worship may securely enter, and range this castle; for however confined and inconvenient it may be, place will always be found for arms and letters, especially when, like your worship, they appear under the patronage of beauty; for to this fair maiden not only castles should throw open wide their gates, but rocks divide and separate, and mountains bow their lofty heads in salutation. Enter, sir, into this paradise; for here you will finds suns and stars worthy of that lovely heaven you bring with you. Here you will find arms in their zenith, and beauty in perfection!" The judge marvelled greatly at this speech, and he earnestly surveyed the knight, no less astonished by his appearance than his discourse, and was considering what to say in reply, when the other ladies made their appearance, attracted by the account the hostess had given of the beauty of the young lady. Don Fernando, Cardenio, and the priest paid their compliments in a more intelligible manner than Don Quixote, and all the ladies of the castle welcomed the fair stranger. In short, the judge easily perceived that he was in the company of persons of distinction; but the mien, visage, and behaviour of Don Quixote confounded him. After mutual courtesies and inquiries as to what accommodation the inn afforded, the arrangements previously made were adopted; namely, that all the women should lodge in the large chamber, and the men remain without as their guard. The judge was content that the young lady, who was his daughter, should accompany the other ladies, and she herself readily consented. Thus, with part of the innkeeper's narrow bed, together with that which the judge had brought with him, they accommodated themselves during the night better than they had expected.

The captive, from the moment he saw the judge, felt his heart beat, from an impression that this gentleman was his brother. He therefore inquired his name and country of one of the servants, who told him that he was the licentiate John Perez de Viedma, and he had heard that his native place was in a town in the mountains of Leon. This account confirmed him in the opinion that this was indeed that brother, who, by the advice of his father, had applied himself to letters. Agitated and overjoyed, he called aside Don Fernando, Cardenio, and the priest, and communicated to them his discovery. The servant had also told him that he was going to the Indies, as judge of the courts of Mexico, and that the young lady was his daughter, whose mother had died in giving her birth, but had left her a rich inheritance. He asked them how they thought he had best make himself known, or how he could ascertain whether his brother, seeing him so poor, would not be ashamed to own him, or receive him to his bosom with affection. "Leave me to make that experiment," said the priest; "not that I make any doubt, Signor Captain, of your meeting with a kind reception; for there is an appearance of worth and good sense in your brother which neither implies arrogance nor inability to appreciate duly the accidents of fortune." "Nevertheless," said the captain, "I would rather not discover myself abruptly to him." "Leave all to me," answered the priest, "and I will manage the affair to your satisfaction."

A collation being now ready, they all sat down to table, except the captain, to partake of it, and also the ladies, who remained in their own chamber. The priest took this opportunity of speaking to the judge. "My lord, I had a comrade of your name in Constantinople, where I was a slave some years. He was a captain, and one of the bravest soldiers in the Spanish infantry; but he was as unfortunate as brave." "Pray, what was this captain's name?" said the judge. "He was called," answered the priest, "Ruy Perez de Viedma, and was born in a village in the mountains of Leon. He related to me a circumstance which, from a person of less veracity than himself, I should have taken for a tale such as old women tell by a winter's fireside. He told me that his father had divided his estate equally between himself and his three sons, and after giving them certain precepts better than those of Cato, he proposed to them the choice of three professions. My friend adopted that of arms; and I can assure you that he was so successful that in a few years, without any other aid than his own bravery and merit, he rose to the rank of a captain of foot, and was in the high-road to preferment, when fortune proved adverse, and he lost her favours together with his liberty, in that glorious action which gave freedom to so many—I mean the battle of Lepanto. I was myself taken in Goleta; and afterwards, by different adventures, we became comrades in Constantinople. He was afterwards sent to Algiers, where he met with one of the strangest adventures in the world." The priest then briefly related to him what had passed between his brother and Zoraida. He was listened to by the judge with extreme attention; but he proceeded no further than to that point where the Christians were plundered by the French, and his comrade and the beautiful Moor left in poverty; pretending that he knew not what became of them afterwards, whether they ever reached Spain or were carried by their captors to France.

The captain stood listening at some distance, and watching all the emotions of his brother, who, when the priest had finished his story, sighed profoundly, and, with tears in his eyes, said, "Oh, sir, you know not how nearly I am affected by what you have communicated! That gallant captain you mention is my elder brother, who, having entertained more elevated thoughts than my younger brother or myself, chose the honourable profession of arms, which was one of the three pursuits proposed to us by our father. I applied myself to letters, which, by the blessing of Heaven and my own exertions, has raised me to my present rank. My younger brother is in Peru, abounding in riches, and has amply repaid the sum he took out with him. He has enabled my father to indulge his liberal disposition, and supplied me with the means of prosecuting my studies with every advantage until I attained the rank which at present I enjoy. My father is still living, and continually prays to God that his eyes may not be closed in death before he has once again beheld his first-born son. It surprises me that he never communicated his situation to his family; for had either of us known of it, he need not have waited for the miracle of the cane to have obtained his ransom. My anxiety is now about the treatment he may have met with from those Frenchmen: this uncertainty as to his fate will render my voyage most sad and melancholy.   O my brother! if I knew but where to find thee, I would deliver thee at any risk.   Ah, who shall bear the news to our aged father that thou art living?   Wert thou buried in the deepest dungeon of Barbary, his wealth and that of thy brothers should redeem thee!   O lovely and bountiful Zoraida! who can repay thy kindness to my brother?   Who shall be so happy as to witness thy regeneration by baptism, and be present at thy nuptials, which would give us all so much delight?"   The judge affected all his auditors by these and other demonstrations of sorrow and fraternal affection.

The priest, finding he had gained his point according to the captain's wish, would no longer protract their pain, and, rising from table, he went into the adjoining chamber, and led out Zoraida, who was followed by the other ladies.   He also took the hand of the captain, and introduced them both to the judge, saying, " My lord, cease your lamentations, for here is your brother and good sister-in-law, Captain Viedma and the beautiful Moor, to whom he owes so much.   They have been reduced to poverty by the French, only to have an opportunity of proving a brother's liberality."   The captain ran towards his brother, who first held back to look at him; then, recognizing him, he pressed him to his heart, while his eyes overflowed with tears of joy.   The meeting was indeed affecting beyond description.   From time to time their mutual inquiries were suspended by renewed demonstrations of fraternal love. Often the judge embraced Zoraida, and as often returned her to the caresses of his daughter; and a most pleasing sight it was to see the mutual embraces of the fair Christian and the lovely Moor.

Don Quixote was all this time a silent but attentive observer, satisfied at the correspondence of these singular events with the annals of chivalry. It was agreed that the captain and Zoraida should go with their brother to Seville, and acquaint their father of his return, so that the old man might be present at the baptism and nuptials of Zoraida, as it was impossible for the judge to defer his journey beyond a month.   The night being now far advanced, they proposed retiring to repose during the remainder, Don Quixote offering his service to guard the castle, lest some giant, or other miscreant errant, tempted by the treasure of beauty there enclosed, should presume to make an attack upon it.   His friends thanked him, and took occasion to amuse the judge with an account of his strange frenzy.   Sancho Panza alone was out of all patience at sitting up so late.   However, he was better accommodated than any of them, upon the accoutrements of his ass, for which he dearly paid, as shall be hereafter related.   The ladies having retired to their chamber, and the rest accommodated as well as could be, Don Quixote, according to promise, sallied out of the inn to take his post at the castle-gate.

CHAPTER XLIII.

Which treats of the agreeable history of the young muleteer; with other strange incidents that happened at the inn.

JUST before daybreak, a voice reached the ears of the ladies, so sweet and melodious that it forcibly arrested their attention, especially that of Dorothea, by whose side slept Donna Clara de Viedma, the daughter of the judge. The voice was unaccompanied by any instrument, and they were surprised at the skill of the singer. Sometimes they fancied that the sound proceeded from the yard, and at other times from the stable. While they were in this uncertainty, Cardenio came to the chamber-door, and said, "If you are not asleep, pray listen, and you will hear one of the muleteers singing enchantingly." Dorothea told him that they had heard him; upon which Cardenio retired. Then listening with much attention, Dorothea plainly distinguished the following words:

> " Tossed in a sea of doubts and fears,
>   Love's hapless mariner, I sail
> Where no inviting port appears,
>   To screen me from the stormy gale.
>
> " At distance viewed, a cheering star
>   Conducts me through the swelling tide;
> A brighter luminary far
>   Than Palinurus e'er descried.
>
> " My soul, attracted by its blaze,
>   Still follows where it points the way,
> And, while attentively I gaze,
>   Considers not how far I stray.
>
> " But female pride, reserved and shy,
>   Like clouds that deepen on the day,
> Oft shrouds it from my longing eye,
>   When most I need the guiding ray.
>
> "O lovely star, so pure and bright!
>   Whose splendour feeds my vital fire,
> The moment thou deny'st thy light,
>   Thy lost adorer will expire."

Dorothea thought it was a great loss to Donna Clara not to hear such excellent singing; she therefore gave her a gentle shake and awoke her. " Excuse me, my dear, for disturbing you," she said, " since it is only that you may have the pleasure of hearing the sweetest voice which perhaps you ever heard in your life." Clara, half awake, was obliged to ask Dorothea to repeat what she had said to her; after which she endeavoured to command her attention, but had no sooner heard a few words of the song than she was seized with a fit of trembling as violent as the attack of a quartan ague; and, clinging round Dorothea, she cried, " Ah, my dear lady ! why did you wake me ? The greatest service that could be done me would be for ever to close both my eyes and ears, that I might neither see nor hear that unhappy musician." " What do you say, my dear ? " answered Dorothea. " Is it not a muleteer who is singing ? " " Oh no," replied Clara; " he is a young gentleman of large possessions, and so much master of my heart that, if he reject me not, it shall be his eternally." Dorothea was surprised at the passionate expressions of the girl, which she would not have expected from one of her tender years. She therefore said to her, " Your words surprise me, Signora Clara : explain yourself further. What is this you say of hearts and possessions ? and who is this musician whose voice affects you so much ? But stay—do not speak just yet : he seems to be preparing to sing again, and I must not lose the pleasure of hearing him." Clara, however, stopped her own ears with both her hands, to Dorothea's great surprise, who listened very attentively to the following

SONG.

" Unconquered hope, thou bane of fear,
　And last deserter of the brave,
Thou soothing ease of mortal care,
　Thou traveller beyond the grave ;
Thou soul of patience, airy food,
Bold warrant of a distant good,
　Reviving cordial, kind decoy ;
Though fortune frowns and friends depart,
　Though Silvia flies me, flattering joy,
Nor thou nor love shall leave my doting heart.

" No slave, to lazy ease resigned,
　E'er triumphed over noble foes :
The monarch Fortune most is kind
　To him who bravely dares oppose.
They say, Love rates his blessings high,
　But who would prize an easy joy ?
My scornful fair then I'll pursue,
　Though the coy beauty still denies ;
I grovel now on earth, 'tis true,
　But, raised by her, the humble slave may rise."

Here the musician ceased to sing, and Donna Clara again began to sigh, both of whom excited Dorothea's curiosity, and she pressed her to explain what she had just before said. Clara embraced her, and putting her face close to her ear, she whispered, lest she should be overheard by Lucinda, " That singer, my dear madam," said she, " is the son of an Arragonian gentleman who is lord of two towns, and when at court lives opposite to my father. Although my father kept his windows covered with canvas in the winter and lattices in summer, it happened by some chance that this young gentleman saw me—whether at church, or where it was, I know not; but, in truth, he fell in love with me, and expressed his passion from the window of the house by so many sighs and so many tears, that I was forced to believe him, and even to love him too. Among other signs, he often joined one hand with the other, signifying his desire to marry me; and, though I should have been very glad if it might have been so, yet being alone, and having no mother, I knew not whom to speak to on the subject, and therefore let it rest, without granting him any other favour than, when his father and mine were abroad, to lift up the lattice of my window, just to show myself, at which he seemed so delighted that you would have thought him mad. When the time of my father's departure drew near, he heard of it, though not from me, for I never had an opportunity to speak to him; and soon after he fell sick, as I was told, for grief; so that on the day we came away I could not see him to say farewell, though it were only with my eyes. But after we had travelled two days, on entering a village about a day's journey hence, I saw him at the door of an inn, in the habit of a muleteer, so disguised that, had not his image been deeply imprinted in my heart, I could not have known him. I was surprised and overjoyed at the sight of him; and he stole looks at me, unobserved by my father, whom he carefully avoids when he passes either on the road or at the inns. When I think who he is, and how he travels on foot, bearing so much fatigue for love of me, I am ready to die with pity, and cannot help following him with my eyes. I cannot imagine what his intentions are, or how he could leave his father, who loves him passionately, having no other heir, and also because he is so very deserving, as you will perceive when you see him. I can assure you, besides, that all he sings is of his own composing; for I have heard that he is a great scholar and a poet. Every time I see him, or hear him sing, I tremble all over with fright lest my father should recollect him, and discover our inclinations. Although I never spoke a word to him in my life, yet I love him so well that I can never live without him. This, dear madam, is all I can tell you about him whose voice has pleased you so much. By that alone you may easily perceive that he is no muleteer, but master of hearts and towns, as I have already told you."

"Enough, my dear Clara," said Dorothea, kissing her a thousand times; "you need not say more: compose yourself till morning, for I hope to be able to manage your affair so that the conclusion may be as happy as the beginning is innocent." "Ah, signora!" said Donna Clara, "what conclusion can be expected, since his father is of such high rank and fortune that I am not worthy to be his servant, much less his wife? As to marrying without my father's knowledge, I would not do it for all the world. I only wish this young man would go back, and leave me: absence, perhaps, may lessen the pain I now feel, though I fear it will not have much effect. What a strange sorcery this love is! I know not how it came to possess me, so young as I am—in truth, I believe we are both of the same age, and I am not yet sixteen, nor shall I be, as my father says, until next Michaelmas." Dorothea could not forbear smiling at Donna Clara's childish simplicity; however, she entreated her again to sleep the remainder of the night, and to hope for everything in the morning.

Profound silence now reigned over the whole house, all being asleep except the innkeeper's daughter and her maid Maritornes, who, knowing Don Quixote's weak points, determined to amuse themselves by playing him some trick while he was keeping guard without doors. There was no window on that side of the house which overlooked the field, except a small opening to the straw-loft, where the straw was thrown out. At this hole the pair of damsels planted themselves, whence they commanded a view of the knight on horseback, leaning on his lance, and could hear him ever and anon heaving such deep and mournful sighs that they seemed torn from the very bottom of his soul. They could also distinguish words, uttered in a soft, soothing, amorous tone, such as "O my Lady Dulcinea del Toboso! perfection of all beauty, quintessence of discretion, treasury of wit, and pledge of modesty! what may now be thy sweet employment? Art thou, peradventure, thinking of thy captive knight, who voluntarily exposes himself to so many perils for thy sake? O thou triformed luminary, bring me swift tidings of her! Perhaps thou art now gazing at her, envious of her beauty, as she walks through some gallery of her sumptuous palace, or leans over some balcony, considering how she may, without offence to her virtue or dignity, assuage the torment which this poor afflicted heart of mine endures for her! or meditating on what glory she shall bestow on my sufferings, what solace to my cares, or recompense to my long services! And thou, O sun! who must now be preparing to harness thy steeds, to come forth and visit my adorable lady, salute her, I entreat thee, in my name; but beware thou dost not kiss her face, for I shall be more jealous of thee than thou wert of that swift ingrate who made thee sweat and run over the plains of Thessaly, or along the banks of Peneus —I do not exactly remember over which it was thou rann'st so jealous and so enamoured!"

Thus far Don Quixote had proceeded in his soliloquy, when the innkeeper's daughter softly called to him, saying, "Pray, sir, come a little this way." Don Quixote turned his head, and perceiving by the light of the moon, which then shone bright, that some person beckoned him towards the spike-hole, which to his fancy was a window with gilded bars, suitable to the rich castle he conceived the inn to be; and his former visions again recurring, he concluded that the fair damsel of the castle, irresistibly enamoured of him, had now come to repeat her visit. Unwilling, therefore, to appear discourteous or ungrateful, he approached the aperture, and replied, "I lament, fair lady, that you should have placed your affections where it is impossible for you to meet with that return which your great merit and beauty deserve; yet ought you not to blame an unfortunate knight whom love has already enthralled. Pardon me, dear lady; retire, and do not by any further disclosure of your sentiments make me appear yet more ungrateful; but if I can repay you by any other way than a return of passion, I entreat that you will command me; and I swear, by that sweet absent enemy of mine, to gratify you immediately, though you should require a lock of Medusa's hair, which was composed of snakes, or the sunbeams enclosed in a phial." "Sir," quoth Maritornes, "my lady wants none of these."

Thus he remained standing upright on Rozinante, tied by the wrist, and in the utmost alarm lest Rozinante should move on either side, and leave him suspended.

"What then doth your lady require, discreet duenna?" answered Don Quixote. "Only one of your beautiful hands," quoth Maritornes, "whereby partly to satisfy that longing which brought her to this window, so much to the peril of her honour, that if her lord and father should know of it he would whip off at least one of her ears." "Let him dare to do it!" cried Don Quixote; "fatal should be his punishment for presuming to lay violent hands on the delicate members of an enamoured daughter." Maritornes, not doubting that he would grant the lady's request, hastened down into the stable, and brought back the halter belonging to Sancho's Dapple, just as Don Quixote had got upon Rozinante's saddle to reach the gilded window at which the enamoured damsel stood; and, giving her his hand, he said, "Accept, madam, this hand, or rather this scourge of the wicked: accept, I say, this hand, which that of woman never before touched, not even hers who has the entire right of my whole person. I offer it not to be kissed, but that you may behold the contexture of its nerves, the firm knitting of its muscles, the largeness and spaciousness of its veins, whence you may infer what must be the strength of that arm which belongs to such a hand." "We shall soon see that," quoth Maritornes. Then, making a running-knot in the halter, she fixed it on his wrist, and tied the other end of it fast to the staple of the hay-loft door. Don Quixote, feeling the harsh rope about his wrist, said, "You seem rather to rasp than grasp my hand : pray do not treat it so roughly, since it is not to blame for my adverse inclination ; nor is it just to vent your displeasure thus : indeed, this kind of revenge is very unworthy of a lover." But his expostulations were unheard ; for as soon as Maritornes had tied the knot, they both went laughing away, having fastened it in such a manner that it was impossible for him to get loose.

Thus he remained standing upright on Rozinante, his hand close to the hole, and tied by the wrist to the bolt of the door, and in the utmost alarm lest Rozinante should move on either side, and leave him suspended. He durst not, therefore, make the least motion ; though, indeed, he might well have expected, from the sobriety and patience of Rozinante, that he would remain in that position an entire century. In short, Don Quixote, finding himself thus situated and the ladies gone, concluded that it was an affair of enchantment, like others which had formerly happened to him in the same castle. He then cursed his own indiscretion for having entered it a second time, since he might have learnt from his chivalry that when a knight was unsuccessful in an adventure, it was a sign that its accomplishment was reserved for another, and that second trials were always fruitless. He made many attempts to release himself, though he was afraid of making any great exertion, lest Rozinante should stir ; but his efforts were all in vain, and he was compelled either to remain standing on the saddle or to tear off his hand. Now he wished for Amadis's sword, against which no enchantment had power, and now he cursed his fortune. Sometimes he expatiated on the loss the world would sustain during the period of his enchantment ; other moments were devoted to his beloved Dulcinea del Toboso ; and some to his good squire Sancho Panza, who, stretched on his ass's pannel and buried in sleep, was dreaming of no such misfortune ; nor did he fail to invoke the aid of the sages Lirgandeo and Alquife, and call upon his special friend Urganda. Thus the morning found him, roaring like a bull with despair ; for he expected no relief with the dawn, fearing his enchantment was eternal ; and he was the more induced to believe it, as Rozinante made not the least motion ; and he verily thought himself and his horse must remain in the same posture, without eating, drinking, or sleeping, until the evil influence of the stars had passed over, or some more powerful sage should disenchant him.

But he was mistaken ; for it was scarcely daylight, when four men on horseback stopped at the inn, well appointed and accoutred, with carbines hanging on their saddle-bows. Not finding the inn-door open, they called aloud and knocked very hard, upon which Don Quixote called out from the place where he stood sentinel, in an arrogant and loud voice, "Knights, or squires, or whoever ye are, desist from knocking at the gate of this castle ; for at this early hour its inmates are doubtless sleeping — at least they are not accustomed to open the gates of their fortress until the sun has spread his beams over the whole horizon. Retire until brighter daylight shall inform us whether it be proper to admit you or not." "What the devil of a fortress or castle is this," quoth one of them, "that we are obliged to observe all this ceremony? If you are the innkeeper, make somebody open the door, for we are travellers, and only want to bait our horses and go on, as we are in haste." "What say ye, sirs!—do I look like an innkeeper?" said Don Quixote. "I know not what you look like," answered the other; "but I am sure you talk preposterously to call this inn a castle." "A castle it is," replied Don Quixote, "and one of the best in the whole province; and at this moment contains within its walls persons who have had crowns on their heads and sceptres in their hands." "You had better have said the reverse," quoth the traveller; "the sceptre on the head, and the crown in the hand. But perhaps some company of strolling players are here, who frequently wear such things: this is not a place for any other sort of crowned heads." "Your ignorance must be great," replied Don Quixote, "if you know not that such events are very common in chivalry." The other horseman, impatient at the dialogue, repeated his knocks with so much violence that he roused not only the host, but all the company in the house.

Just at that time it happened that the horse of one of the travellers was seized with an inclination to smell at Rozinante, who, sad and spiritless, was then supporting his distended lord; but, being in fact a horse of flesh, although he seemed to be one of stone, he could not be insensible to the compliment, nor refuse to return it with equal kindness. But scarcely had he stirred a step, when Don Quixote's feet slipped from the saddle, and he remained suspended by the arm, in so much torture that he fancied his wrist or his arm was tearing from his body. He stretched and strained with all his might to reach the ground; like those who are tortured by the strappado, and who, being placed in the same dilemma, aggravate their sufferings by their fruitless efforts to stretch themselves.

CHAPTER XLIV.

A continuation of the extraordinary adventures that happened in the inn.

EXERTING his lungs to the utmost, Don Quixote roared so loudly that the host opened the inn-door, in great alarm, to discover the cause of the outcry. Maritornes, being awakened by the noise, and guessing the cause, went to the straw-loft and privately untied the halter which held up Don Quixote, who immediately came to the ground. Without answering a word to the many inquiries that were made to him by the innkeeper and travellers, he slipped the rope from off his wrist, and springing from the earth, mounted Rozinante, braced his target, couched his lance, and taking a good compass about the field, came up at a half gallop, saying, "Whoever shall dare to affirm that I was fairly enchanted, I say he lies; and provided my sovereign lady, the Princess Micomiconia, gives me leave, I challenge him to single combat." The new comers were amazed at Don Quixote's words, till the innkeeper explained the wonder, by telling them that he was disordered in his senses. They then inquired of the host whether there were not in the house a youth about fifteen years old, habited like a muleteer—in short, describing Donna Clara's lover. The host said that there were so many people in the inn, that he had not observed such a person as they described. But one of them just then seeing the judge's coach, said, "He must certainly be here, for there is the coach which he is said to have followed. Let one of us remain here, and the rest go in search of him; and it would not be amiss for one of us to ride round the house, in case he should attempt to escape over the pales of the yard." All this they immediately did, much to the innkeeper's surprise, who could not guess the meaning of so much activity.

It was now full daylight, and most of the company in the house were rising: among the first were Donna Clara and Dorothea, who had slept but indifferently; the one from concern at being so near her lover, and the other from a desire of seeing him. Don Quixote, finding that the four travellers regarded neither him nor his challenge, was furious with rage; and, could he have found a precedent among the ordinances of chivalry for engaging in a new adventure after he had pledged his word to forbear until the first had been accomplished, he would now have fiercely attacked them all, and compelled them to reply: but reflecting that he was bound in honour first to reinstate the princess on her throne, he endeavoured to tranquillize himself. In the meantime the men pursued their search after the youth, and at last found him peacefully sleeping by the side of a muleteer. One of them, pulling him by the arm, said, "Upon my word, Signor Don Louis, your dress is very becoming a gentleman like you, and the bed you lie on is very suitable to the tenderness with which your mother brought you up!" The youth was roused from his sleep, and looking earnestly at the man who held him, he soon recollected him to be one of his father's servants, and was so confounded that he could not say a word. "Signor Don Louis," continued the servant, "you must instantly return home, unless you would cause the death of my lord your father, he is in such grief at your absence." "Why, how did my father know," said Don Louis, "that I came this road, and in this dress?" "He was informed by a student, to whom you mentioned your project, and who was induced to disclose it from compassion at your father's distress. There are four of us here at your service, and we shall be rejoiced to restore you to your family." "That will be as I shall please, or as Heaven may ordain," answered Don Louis. "What, signor, should you please to do, but return home?" rejoined the servant: "indeed, you cannot do otherwise."

The muleteer who had been Don Louis's companion hearing this contest, went to acquaint Don Fernando and the rest of the company with what was passing, telling them that the man had called the young lad *Don*, and wanted him to return to his father's house, but that he refused to go. They all recollected his fine voice, and being eager to know who he was, and to assist him if any violence were offered to him, they repaired to the place where he was contending with his servants. Dorothea now came out of her chamber, with Donna Clara; and, calling Cardenio aside, she related to him in a few words the history of the musician and Donna Clara. He then told her of the search that had been made after the young man by the servants; and although he whispered, he was overheard by Donna Clara, who was thrown into such an agony by the intelligence, that she would have fallen to the ground if Dorothea had not supported her. Cardenio advised her to retire with Donna Clara, while he endeavoured to make some arrangement in their behalf. Don Louis was now surrounded by all the four servants, entreating that he would immediately return to comfort his father. He answered that he could not possibly do so until he had accomplished that on which his life, his honour, and his soul depended. The servants still urged him, saying that they would certainly not go back without him, and that they must compel him to return if he refused. " That you shall not do," replied Don Louis; " at least you shall not take me living." This contest had now drawn together most of the people in the house, Don Fernando, Cardenio, the judge, the priest, the barber; and even Don Quixote had quitted his post of castle guard. Cardenio, already knowing the young man's story, asked the men why they would take away the youth against his will. " To save his father's life," replied one of them; " which is in danger from distress of mind." " There is no occasion to give an account of my affairs here," said Don Louis : " I am free, and will go back if I please; otherwise, none of you shall force me." " But reason will prevail with you," answered the servant; " and if not, we must do our duty." " Hold ! " said the judge; " let us know the whole of this affair." The man (who recollected him) answered, " Does not your worship know this gentleman ? He is your neighbour's son, and has absented himself from his father's house, in a garb very unbecoming his quality, as your worship may see." The judge, after looking at him with attention, recognized him, and accosted him in a friendly manner. " What childish frolic is this, Signor Don Louis," said he, " or what powerful motive has induced you to disguise yourself in a manner so unbecoming your rank ? " The eyes of the youth were filled with tears, and he could not say a word. The judge desired the servants to be quiet, promising that all should be well ; and, taking Don Louis by the hand, he led him aside and questioned him.

In the meantime a great uproar was heard at the inn-door, which was occasioned by two guests who had lodged there that night, and who, seeing everybody engaged, had attempted to go off without paying their reckoning; but the host, being more attentive to his own business than to that of other people, laid hold of them as they were going out of the door, and demanded his money, giving them such hard words for their evil intention, that they were provoked to return him an answer with their fists, and so much to the purpose that the poor innkeeper was forced to call for help. The hostess and her daughter seeing none more proper to give him succour than Don Quixote, applied to him. "Sir Knight," said the daughter, "I beseech you, by the valour which God has given you, to come and help my poor father, whom a couple of wicked fellows are beating without mercy." Don Quixote, very leisurely and with much courtesy, replied, "Fair maiden, your petition cannot be granted at present, because I am incapacitated from engaging in any other adventure until I have accomplished one for which my word is already plighted; all that I can do in your service is to advise you to go and desire your father to maintain the fight as well as he can, and by no means allow himself to be vanquished; in the meantime I will request permission of the Princess Micomicona to relieve him in his distress, the which if she grant me, rest assured I will forthwith deliver him." "As I am a sinner," quoth Maritornes, who was present, "before your worship can do all that, my master may be gone into the other world." "Suffer me, madam, to obtain that permission," answered Don Quixote; "and if I procure it, it matters not though he be in the other world; for thence would I liberate him, in spite of the other world itself—or at least I will take such ample revenge on those who sent him thither, that you shall be entirely satisfied." Then, without saying another word, he approached Dorothea, and throwing himself on his knees before her, in chivalrous terms he entreated that her grandeur would vouchsafe to give him leave to succour the governor of the castle, who was in grievous distress. The princess very graciously consented; when, bracing on his target and drawing his sword, he proceeded to the inn-door, where the two guests were still maltreating the poor host; but before he came there, he suddenly stopped short and stood irresolute, though Maritornes and the hostess asked him why he delayed helping their master. "I delay," said Don Quixote, "because it is not lawful for me to draw my sword against plebeians; but call hither my squire, Sancho Panza, for to him doth this matter more properly belong." In the meantime the conflict at the door of the inn continued without intermission, very much to the disadvantage of the innkeeper, and the rage of Maritornes, the hostess, and her daughter, who were ready to run distracted to see the cowardice of Don Quixote, and the injury done to their lord and master.

But here we must leave him; for somebody will no doubt come to his relief; if, not, let him suffer for being so foolhardy as to engage in such an unequal contest: and let us remove some fifty paces off, to hear what Don Louis replied to the judge, whom we left questioning him as to the cause of his travelling on foot so meanly apparelled. The youth clasping his hands, as if some great affliction wrung his heart, and shedding tears in abundance, said in answer, "I can only say, dear sir, that from the moment Heaven was pleased by means of our vicinity to give me a sight of Donna Clara, your daughter she became sovereign mistress of my affections; and if you, my true lord and father, do not oppose it, this very day she shall be my wife. For her I left my father's house, and for her I assumed this garb, to follow her wheresoever she might go. She herself knows no more of my passion than what she may have perceived by occasionally seeing, at a distance, my eyes full of tenderness and tears. You know, my lord, the wealth and rank of my family, of whom I am the sole heir : if these circumstances can plead in my favour, receive me immediately for your son ; for though my father, influenced by other views of his own, should not approve my choice, time may reconcile him to it." Here the enamoured youth was silent, and the judge remained in suspense, no less surprised by the ingenious confession of Don Louis than perplexed how to act in the affair : in reply, therefore, he only desired him to be calm for the present, and not let his servants return that day, that there might be time to consider what was most expedient to be done. Don Louis kissed his hands with vehemence, bathing them with tears, that might have softened a heart of marble, much more that of the judge, who, being a man of sense, was aware how advantageous this match would be for his daughter. Nevertheless, he would rather, if possible, that it should take place with the consent of Don Louis's father, who he knew had pretensions to a title for his son.

By this time the innkeeper and his guests had made peace, more through the persuasions and arguments of Don Quixote than his threats ; and the reckoning was paid. And now the devil, who never sleeps, so ordered it that at this time the very barber entered the inn who had been deprived of Mambrino's helmet by Don Quixote, and of the trappings of his ass by Sancho Panza ; and as he was leading his beast to the stable he espied Sancho Panza, who at that moment was repairing something about the selfsame pannel. He instantly fell upon him with fury. " Ah, thief ! " said he, " have I got you at last ? Give me my basin and my pannel, with all the furniture you stole from me ! " Sancho finding himself thus suddenly attacked and abused, secured the pannel with one hand, and with the other made the barber such a return that his mouth was bathed in blood. Nevertheless, the barber would not let go his hold, but raised his voice so high that he drew everybody around him, while he called out, " Justice, in the king's name ! This rogue and highway robber here would murder me for endeavouring to recover my own goods." " You lie ! " answered Sancho : " I am no highway robber ; my master, Don Quixote, won these spoils in fair war." Don Quixote was now present, and not a little pleased to see how well his squire acted both on the offensive and defensive ; and regarding him thenceforward as a man of mettle, he resolved in his mind to dub him a knight the first opportunity that offered, thinking the order of chivalry would be well bestowed upon him.

During this contest the barber made many protestations. " Gentlemen," said he, " this pannel is as certainly mine as the death I owe to God : I know it as well as if it were made by myself ; and yonder stands my ass in the stable, who will not suffer me to lie—pray do but try it, and if it does not fit him to a hair, let me be infamous : and moreover, the very day they took this from me, they robbed me likewise of a new

"I swear that this very helmet is the same which I took from him."

brass basin, never hanselled, that cost me a crown." Here Don Quixote could not forbear interposing; and separating the two combatants, he made them lay down the pannel on the ground to public view, until the truth should be decided. "The error of this honest squire," said he, "is manifest, in calling that a basin which was, is, and ever shall be, Mambrino's helmet—that helmet which I won in fair war, and am therefore its right and lawful possessor. With regard to the pannel, I decline any interference; all I can say is, that my squire Sancho asked my permission to take the trappings belonging to the horse of this conquered coward, to adorn his own withal. I gave him leave—he took them, and if from horse trappings they are metamorphosed into an ass's pannel, I have no other reasons to give than that these transformations are frequent in affairs of chivalry. In confirmation of what I say, go, Sancho, and bring hither the helmet which this honest man terms a basin." "In faith, sir," quoth Sancho, "if we have no better proof than that your worship speaks of, Mambrino's helmet will prove as errant a basin as the honest man's trappings are a pack-saddle." "Do what I command," replied Don Quixote; "for surely all things in this castle cannot be governed by enchantment." Sancho went for the basin, and returning with it, he gave it to Don Quixote. "Only behold, gentlemen!" said he: "how can this squire have the face to declare that this is a basin, and not the helmet which I have described to you? By the order of knighthood which I profess, I swear that this very helmet is the same which I took from him, without addition or diminution." "There is no doubt of that," quoth Sancho; "for from the time my master won it, until now, he has fought but one battle in it, which was when he freed those unlucky galley-slaves; and had it not been for that same basin-helmet he would not have got off so well from the showers of stones which rained upon him in that skirmish."

CHAPTER XLV.

In which the dispute concerning Mambrino's helmet and the pannel is decided; with other adventures that really and truly happened.

"Good sirs," quoth the barber, "hear what these gentlefolks say! They will have it that this is no basin, but a helmet!" "Aye," said Don Quixote, "and whoever shall affirm the contrary, I will convince him, if he be a knight, that he lies; and if a squire, that he lies and lies again, a thousand times." Our barber, Master Nicholas, who was present, wishing to carry on the jest for the amusement of the company, addressed himself to the other barber, and said, "Signor Barber, or whoever you are, know that I also am of your profession, and have had my certificate of examination above these twenty years, and am well acquainted with all the instruments of barber-surgery, without exception. I have likewise been a soldier in my youth, and therefore know what a helmet is, and what a morion or cap of steel is, as well as a casque with its beaver, and other matters relating to soldiery—I mean to the arms commonly used by soldiers. And I say, with submission always to better judgments, that the piece before us, which that gentleman holds in his hand, not only is not a barber's basin, but is as far from being so as white is from black, and truth from falsehood. At the same time, I say that, although it be a helmet, it is not a complete helmet." "Certainly not," said Don Quixote; "for one-half of it is wanting, namely, the beaver." "Undoubtedly," said the priest, who perceived his friend the barber's design; and Cardenio, Don Fernando, and his companions all confirmed the same; even the judge, had not his thoughts been engrossed by the affair of Don Louis, would have taken some share in the jest; but in the perplexed state of his mind he could attend but little to these pleasantries.

"Mercy on me!" quoth the astonished barber, "how is it possible that so many honourable gentlemen should maintain that this is not a basin, but a helmet? This would be enough to astonish a whole university, be it ever so wise. Well, if the basin be a helmet, then the pannel must needs be a horse's furniture, as the gentleman has said." "To me, indeed, it seems to be a pannel," said Don Quixote; "but I have already told you I will not interfere on that subject," "Whether it be the pannel of an ass, or the caparison of a horse," said the priest, "must be left to the decision of Signor Don Quixote; for in matters of chivalry all these gentlemen and myself submit to his judgment." "By all that is holy! gentlemen," said Don Quixote, "such extraordinary things have befallen me in this castle, that I dare not vouch for the certainty of anything that it may contain; for I very believe that all is conducted by the powers of enchantment. During my first visit, I was tormented by an enchanted Moor, while Sancho fared no better among some of his followers; and this night I have been suspended for nearly two hours by my arm, without knowing either the means or the cause of my persecution: it would be rash in me, therefore, to give my opinion in an affair of so much perplexity. As to the question whether this be a basin or a helmet, I have already answered; but with regard to the pannel, gentlemen, not daring myself to pronounce a definitive sentence, I refer it to your wisdom to decide. Perhaps, as you are not knights-errant, the enchantments of this place may not have the same power over you; and, your understandings remaining free, you may judge of things as they really are, and not as they appear to me." "There is no doubt," answered Don Fernando, "that Signor Don Quixote is right in leaving the decision of this case to us; and that we may proceed in it upon solid grounds, I will take the votes of these gentlemen in secret, and then give you a clear and full account of the result."

To those acquainted with Don Quixote, all this was choice entertainment; while to others it seemed the height of folly, among whom were Don Louis, his servants, and three other guests, troopers of the Holy Brotherhood, who just then arrived at the inn. As for the barber, he was quite raving to see his basin converted into Mambrino's helmet before his eyes, and he made no doubt that his pannel would undergo a like transformation. It was diverting to see Don Fernando walking round and taking the opinion of each person at his ear, whether that precious object of contention was a pannel or caparison; and after he had taken the votes of all those who knew Don Quixote, he said aloud to the barber, "In truth, honest friend, I am weary of collecting votes; for I propose the question to nobody who does not say in reply, that it is quite ridiculous to assert that this is an ass's pannel, and not the caparison of a horse, and even of a well-bred horse; and as you have given us no proofs to the contrary, you must have patience and submit; for in spite of both you and your ass, this is no pannel." "Let me never enjoy a place in heaven!" exclaimed the barber, "if your worships are not all mistaken; and so may my soul appear in heaven as this appears to me a pannel, and not a caparison: but so go the laws. I say no more; and verily I am not drunk, for I am as yet fasting from everything but sin."

The barber's simplicity caused no less merriment than the vagaries of the knight, who now said, "As sentence is passed, let each take his own; and him to whom God giveth, may St. Peter bless." One of Don Louis's four servants now interposed. "How is it possible," said he, " that men of common understanding should say that this is not a basin nor that a pannel? But since you do actually affirm it, I suspect that there must be some mystery in obstinately maintaining a thing so contrary to the plain truth ; for by—" (and out he rapped a round oath) " all the votes in the world shall never persuade me that this is not a barber's basin and that a jackass's pannel." " May it not be that of a she-ass ? " quoth the priest. " That is all one," said the servant ; " the question is only whether it be or be not a pannel." One of the officers of the Holy Brotherhood, who had overheard the dispute, cried out, full of indignation, " It is as surely a pannel as my father is my father ; and whoever says, or shall say, to the contrary, must be drunk." " You lie like a pitiful scoundrel ! " answered Don Quixote ; and lifting up his lance, which was still in his hand, he aimed such a blow at the trooper, that had he not slipped aside he would have been levelled to the ground. The lance came down with such fury that it was shivered to pieces. " Help ! help the Holy Brotherhood ! " cried out the other officers. The innkeeper, being himself one of that body, ran instantly for his wand and sword, to support his comrades. Don Louis's servants surrounded their master, lest he should escape during the confusion. The barber perceiving the house turned topsy-turvy, laid hold again of his pannel, and Sancho did the same. Don Quixote drew his sword, and fell upon the troopers ; and Don Louis called out to his servants to leave him, that they might assist Don Quixote, Cardenio, and Don Fernando, who both took part with the knight. The priest cried out, the hostess shrieked, her daughter wept, Maritornes roared, Dorothea was alarmed, Lucinda stood amazed, and Donna Clara fainted away. The barber cuffed Sancho, and Sancho pummelled the barber. Don Louis gave one of his servants, who had presumed to hold him by the arm lest he should escape, such a blow with his fists that his mouth was bathed in blood ; which caused the judge to interpose in his defence. Don Fernando got one of the troopers down, and laid on his blows most unmercifully ; while the innkeeper bawled aloud for help to the Holy Brotherhood : thus was the whole inn filled with cries, wailings, and shrieks, dismay, confusion, and terror, kicks, cudgellings, and effusion of blood. In the midst of this chaos and hurly-burly Don Quixote suddenly conceived that he was involved over head and ears in the discord of King Agramante's camp, and he called out in a voice which made the whole inn shake, " Hold, all of you ! Put up your swords ! Be pacified, and listen all to me, if ye would live ! " His vehemence made them desist, and he went on, saying, " Did I not tell you, sirs, that this castle was enchanted, and that some legion of devils must inhabit it? Behold the confirmation of what I said ! Mark with your own eyes how the discord of Agramante's camp is transferred hither amongst us !—there they fight for the sword, here for the horse, yonder for the eagle, here again for the helmet : we all fight, and no one under- stands another. Let, then, my lord judge and his reverence the priest come forward, the one as King Agramante, the other as King Sobrino, and restore us to peace ; for by the powers divine it were most disgraceful and iniquitous that so many gentlemen of our rank should slay each other for such trivial matters." The troopers not understanding Don Quixote's language, and finding themselves still roughly handled by Don Fernando, Cardenio, and their companions, would not be pacified; but the barber submitted, for both his beard and his pannel were demolished in the scuffle; and Sancho, like a dutiful servant, obeyed the least word of his master. Don Louis's four servants were also quiet, seeing how unprofitable it was to interfere. The innkeeper, still refractory, insisted that the insolence of that madman ought to be chastised, who was continually turning his house upside down. At length the tumult subsided: the pannel was to remain a caparison, and the basin a helmet, and the inn a castle, at least in Don Quixote's imagination, until the Day of Judgment.

Amity and peace being now restored by the interposition of the judge and the priest, the servants of Don Louis renewed their solicitations for his return. The judge having in the meantime informed Don Fernando, Cardenio, and the priest, of what had passed between himself and the young man, he consulted with them on the affair, and it was finally agreed that Don Fernando should make himself known to Don Louis's servants, and inform them that it was his desire that the young gentleman should accompany him to Andalusia, where he would be treated by the marquis his brother in a manner suitable to his quality; for his determination was at all events not to return just at that time into his father's presence. The servants being apprised of Don Fernando's rank, and finding Don Louis resolute, agreed among themselves that three of them should return to give his father an account of what had passed, and that the other should stay to attend Don Louis, and not leave him until he knew his lord's pleasure. Thus was this complicated tumult appeased by the authority of Agramante and the prudence of Sobrino.

But the enemy of peace and concord, finding himself foiled and disappointed in the scanty produce of so promising a field, resolved to try his fortune once more, by contriving new frays and disturbances. The officers of the Holy Brotherhood, on hearing the quality of their opponents, retreated from the fray, thinking that, whatever might be the issue, they were likely to be losers. But one of this body, who had been severely handled by Don Fernando, happened to recollect that among other warrants in his possession he had one against Don Quixote, whom his superiors had ordered to be taken into custody for releasing galley-slaves: thus confirming Sancho's just apprehensions. In order to examine whether the person of Don Quixote answered the description, he drew forth a parchment scroll from his doublet, and began to read it slowly (for he was not much of a scholar), ever and anon as he proceeded fixing his eyes on Don Quixote, comparing the marks in his warrant with the lines of his physiognomy. Finding them exactly to correspond, and being convinced that he was the very person therein described, he held out the warrant in his left hand, while with his right he seized Don Quixote by the collar, with so powerful a grasp as almost to strangle him, at the same time crying aloud, "Help the Holy

Brotherhood! and that you may see I require it in earnest, read this warrant, wherein it is expressly ordered that this highway robber should be apprehended." The priest took the warrant, and found what the trooper said was true, the description exactly corresponding with the person of Don Quixote. The knight, finding himself so rudely handled by this scoundrel, was exasperated to the highest pitch, and, trembling with rage, caught the trooper by the throat with both hands; and had he not been immediately rescued by his comrades, he would certainly have been strangled before Don Quixote had loosed his hold. The innkeeper, who was bound to aid his brother in office, ran instantly to help him. The hostess, seeing her husband again engaged in battle, again exalted her voice; her daughter and Maritornes added their pipes to the same tune, calling upon Heaven and all around them for assistance. "As God shall save me!" exclaimed Sancho, "what my master says is true about the enchantments of this castle; for it is impossible to live an hour quietly in it." Don Fernando at length parted the officer and Don Quixote; and, to the satisfaction of both, unlocked their hands from the doublet collar of the one and from the windpipe of the other. Nevertheless, the troopers persisted in claiming their prisoner; declaring that the king's service and that of the Holy Brotherhood required it; and in whose name they again demanded help and assistance in apprehending that common robber and highway thief. Don Quixote smiled at these expressions, and with great calmness said, "Come hither, base and ill-born crew: call ye it robbing on the highway to loosen the chains of the captive, to set the prisoner free, to succour the oppressed, to raise the fallen, and relieve the needy and wretched? Ah, scoundrel race! undeserving, by the meanness and baseness of your understandings, that Heaven should reveal to you the worth inherent in knight-errantry, or make you sensible of your own sin and ignorance in not revering the shadow—much more the presence—of any knight-errant! Tell me, ye rogues in a troop!—not troopers, but highway marauders under license of the Holy Brotherhood—tell me, who was the blockhead that signed the warrant for apprehending such a knight as I am? Who was he that knew not that knights-errant are exempt from all judicial authority; that their sword is their law, valour their privilege, and their own will their edicts? Who was the madman, I say again, who knew not that there is no patent of gentility which contains so many privileges and exemptions as are required by the knight-errant on the day he devotes himself to the rigorous exercise of chivalry? What knight-errant ever paid custom, poll-tax, subsidy, quit-rent, porterage, or ferry-boat? What tailor ever brought in a bill for making his clothes? What governor that lodged him in his castle ever made him pay for his entertainment? What king did not seat him at his table? What damsel was not enamoured of him, and did not yield herself up entirely to his will and pleasure? Finally, what knight-errant ever did or shall exist, who has not courage, with his single arm, to bestow a hundred bastinadoes on any four hundred troopers of the Holy Brotherhood who shall dare to oppose him?"

CHAPTER XLVI.

In which is finished the notable adventure of the Holy Brotherhood; with an account of the ferocity of our good knight Don Quixote.

THUS eloquently did Don Quixote harangue the officers, while at the same time the priest endeavoured to persuade them that since the knight, as they might easily perceive, was deranged in his mind, it was useless for them to proceed further in the affair; for if they were to apprehend him, he would soon be released as insane. But the trooper only said in answer that it was not his business to judge of the state of Don Quixote's intellects, but to obey the order of his superiors; and that when he had once secured him, they might set him free as often as they pleased. "Indeed," said the priest, "you must forbear this once; nor do I think that he will suffer himself to be taken." In fact, the priest said so much, and Don Quixote acted so extravagantly, that the officers would have been more crazy than himself had they not desisted after such evidence of his infirmity. They judged it best, therefore, to be quiet, and endeavour to make peace between the barber and Sancho Panza, who still continued their scuffle with great rancour. As officers of justice, therefore, they compounded the matter, and pronounced such a decision that, if both parties were not perfectly contented, at least they were in some degree satisfied; it being settled that they should exchange pannels, but neither girths nor halters. As for Mambrino's helmet, the priest, unknown to Don Quixote, paid the barber eight reals, for which he received a discharge in full, acquitting him of all fraud thenceforth and for evermore.

Thus were these important contests decided, and fortune seemed to smile on all the heroes and heroines of the inn; even the face of Donna Clara betrayed the joy of her heart, as the servants of Don Louis had acquiesced in his wishes. Zoraida, although she could not understand everything, looked sad or gay in conformity with the expressions she observed in their several countenances, especially that of her Spaniard, on whom not only her eyes but her soul rested. The innkeeper, observing the recompense the priest had made the barber, claimed also the payment of his demands upon Don Quixote, with ample satisfaction for the damage done to his skins and the loss of his wine; and swore that neither Rozinante nor the ass should stir out of the inn until he had been paid the uttermost farthing. The priest, however, endeavoured to soothe him; and, what was more, Don Fernando settled the knight's account, although the judge would fain have taken the debt upon himself. Peace was, therefore, entirely restored; and the inn no longer displayed the confusion of Agramante's camp, as Don Quixote had called it, but rather the tranquillity of the days of Octavius Cæsar—thanks to the mediation and eloquence of the priest and the liberality of Don Fernando.

Don Quixote, now finding himself disengaged, thought it was time to pursue his journey, and accomplish the grand enterprise for which he had been elected. Accordingly, he approached the princess, and threw himself upon his knees before her; but she would not listen to him in that posture; and therefore, in obedience to her, he arose, and thus addressed her: "It is a common adage, fair lady, that ' diligence is the mother of success;' and experience constantly verifies its truth. The active solicitor brings the doubtful suit to a happy issue. But this truth is never more obvious than in military operations, where expedition and dispatch anticipate the designs of the enemy, and victory is secured before he is prepared for defence. I am induced to make these remarks, most exalted lady, because our abode in this castle seems no longer necessary, and may, indeed, be prejudicial; for who knows but your enemy the giant may, by secret spies, get intelligence of my approach, and thus gain time to fortify himself in some impregnable fortress, against which my vigilance and the force of my indefatigable arm may be ineffectual? Therefore, sovereign lady, that his designs may be prevented by our diligence, let us depart quickly, in the name of that good fortune which will be yours the moment I come face to face with your enemy." Here Don Quixote was silent, and with dignified composure awaited the answer of the beautiful infanta, who, with an air of majesty, and in a style corresponding with that of her knight, thus replied: "I am obliged to you, Sir Knight, for the zeal you testify in my cause, so worthy of a true knight whose office and employment it is to succour the orphan and distressed; and Heaven grant that our desires may be soon accomplished, that you may see that all women are not ungrateful. As to my departure, let it be instantly; for I have no other will but yours. Dispose of me entirely at your pleasure; for she who has committed the defence of her person and the restoration of her dominions into your hands must not oppose what your wisdom shall direct." "By Heaven!" exclaimed Don Quixote, "I will not lose the opportunity of exalting a lady who thus humbleth herself. I will replace her on the throne of her ancestors. Let us depart immediately, for the ardour of my zeal makes me impatient; nor hath Heaven created nor earth seen aught of danger that can daunt or affright me. Sancho, let Rozinante be saddled; get ready thine own beast, and also her majesty's palfrey: and let us take our leave of the governor of the castle and these nobles, that we may set forth instantly."

Sancho, who had been present all the time, shook his head, saying, "Ah, master of mine! there are more tricks in the town than are dreamt of; with all respect be it spoken." "What tricks can there be to my prejudice in any town or city in the world, thou bumpkin?" said Don Quixote. "If your worship puts yourself into a passion," answered Sancho, "I will hold my tongue, and not say what I am bound to say as a faithful squire and a dutiful servant." "Say what thou wilt," replied Don Quixote; "but think not to intimidate me: for it is thy nature to be faint-hearted—mine to be proof against all fear." "As I am a sinner to Heaven," answered Sancho, "I mean nothing of

all this ; I mean only that I am sure and positively certain this lady,
who calls herself queen of the great kingdom of Micomicon, is no more
a queen than my mother ; for if she were so she would not be nuzzling
at every turn and in every corner with a certain person in the company."
Dorothea's colour rose at Sancho's remark ; for it was indeed true that
her spouse, Don Fernando, now and then by stealth had snatched with
his lips an earnest of that reward which his affections deserved ; and
Sancho, having observed it, thought this freedom very unbecoming the
queen of so vast a kingdom. As Dorothea could not contradict Sancho,
she remained silent, and suffered him to continue his remarks. " I say
this, sir, because, supposing after we have travelled through thick and
thin, and passed many bad nights and worse days, one who is now
enjoying himself in this inn should chance to reap the fruit of our
labours, there would be no use in my hastening to saddle Rozinante, or
to get ready the ass and the palfrey ; therefore we had better be quiet.
Let every drab mind her spinning, and let us to dinner." Good heaven !
how great was the indignation of Don Quixote on hearing his squire
speak in terms so disrespectful ! It was so great that, with a faltering
voice and stammering tongue, while living fire darted from his eyes, he
cried, " Scoundrel ! unmannerly, ignorant, ill-spoken, foul-mouthed,
impudent, murmuring, and back-biting villain ! how darest thou utter
such words in my presence, and in the presence of these illustrious
ladies ? How darest thou to entertain such rude and insolent thoughts
in thy confused imagination ? Avoid my presence, monster of nature,
treasury of lies, magazine of deceit, storehouse of rogueries, inventor of
mischiefs, publisher of absurdities, and foe to all the honour due to
royalty ! Begone ! appear not before me on pain of my severest indignation ! " And as he spoke he arched his eyebrows, swelled his cheeks,
stared around him, and gave a violent stamp with his right foot on the
ground ; plainly indicating the fury that raged in his breast. Poor
Sancho was so terrified by this storm of passion, that he would have
been glad if the earth had opened that instant and swallowed him up.
He knew not what to say or do ; so he turned his back, and hastened
out of the presence of his furious master.

But the discreet Dorothea, perfectly understanding Don Quixote, in
order to pacify his wrath, said, " Be not offended, Sir Knight of the
Sorrowful Figure, at the impertinence of your good squire, for perhaps
he has not spoken without some foundation ; nor can it be suspected,
considering his good sense and Christian conscience, that he would bear
false witness against anybody : it is possible that since, as you affirm
yourself, Sir Knight, the powers of enchantment prevail in this castle,
Sancho may, by the same diabolical illusion, have seen what he has
affirmed so much to the prejudice of my honour." " By the Omnipotent
I swear," quoth Don Quixote, " your highness has hit the mark !—
some evil apparition must have appeared to this sinner, and represented
to him what it was impossible for him to see any other way ; for I am
perfectly assured of the simplicity and innocence of the unhappy wretch,
and that he is incapable of slandering any person living." " So it is,

and so it shall be," said Don Fernando: "therefore, Signor Don Quixote, you ought to pardon him and restore him to your favour, *sicut erat in principio*, before these illusions turned his brain." Don Quixote having promised his forgiveness, the priest went for Sancho, who came in with much humility, and on his knees begged his master's hand, which was given to him; and after he had allowed him to kiss it, he gave him his blessing, adding, "Thou wilt now, son Sancho, be thoroughly convinced of what I have often told thee, that all things in this castle are conducted by enchantment." "I believe so too," quoth Sancho, "except the business of the blanket, which really fell out in the ordinary way." "Believe not so," answered Don Quixote; "for in that case I would have revenged thee at the time, and even now; but neither could I then, nor can I now, find on whom to resent the injury." To gratify the curiosity which this remark had excited, the innkeeper gave a very circumstantial account of Sancho Panza's excursion in the air, which, though it entertained the rest, would have distressed the feelings of the squire, if his master had not given him fresh assurances that it was all a matter of enchantment. However, Sancho's faith was never so strong but that he shrewdly suspected it to be a downright fact, and no illusion at all, that he had been tossed in a blanket by persons of flesh and blood, and by no visionary phantoms.

This illustrious company had now passed two whole days in the inn; and thinking it time to depart, they considered how the priest and barber might convey the knight to his home without troubling Dorothea and Don Fernando to accompany them; and for that purpose, having first engaged a waggoner who happened to pass by with his team of oxen, they proceeded in the following manner: They formed a kind of cage, with poles grate-wise, large enough to contain Don Quixote at his ease; then, by the direction of the priest, Don Fernando and his companions, with Don Louis's servants, the officers of the Holy Brotherhood, and the innkeeper, covered their faces, and disguised themselves so as not to be recognized by Don Quixote. This done, they silently entered the room where the knight lay fast asleep, reposing after his late exertions, and secured him with cords; so that when he awoke he stared about in amazement at the strange visages that surrounded him, but found himself totally unable to move. His disordered imagination operating as usual, immediately suggested to him that these were goblins of the enchanted castle, and that he was entangled in its charms, since he felt himself unable to stir in his own defence—a surmise which the curate, who projected the stratagem, had anticipated. Sancho alone was in his own proper figure; and though he wanted but little of being infected with his master's infirmity, yet he was not ignorant who all these counterfeit goblins were; but he thought it best to be quiet until he saw what was intended by this seizure and imprisonment of his master. Neither did the knight utter a word, but submissively waited the issue of his misfortune. Having brought the cage into the chamber, they placed him within it, and secured it so that it was impossible he could make his escape. In this situation he was conveyed out of the house ; and on leaving the chamber a voice was heard, as dreadful as the barber could form (not he of the pannel, but the other), saying, "O Knight of the Sorrowful Figure ! let not thy present confinement afflict thee, since it is essential to the speedy accomplishment of the adventure in which thy great valour hath engaged thee, which shall be finished when the furious Manchegan lion shall be coupled with the white Tobosian dove, after having submitted their stately necks to the soft matrimonial yoke ; from which wonderful conjunction shall spring into the light of the world brave whelps, who shall emulate the ravaging claws of their valorous sire. And this shall come to pass before the pursuer of the fugitive nymph shall have made two circuits to visit the bright constellations, in his rapid and natural course. And thou, O the most noble and obedient squire that ever had sword in belt, beard on face, and smell in nostrils, be not dismayed nor afflicted to see the flower of knight-errantry carried thus away before thine eyes ; for ere long, if it so please the great Artificer of the world, thou shalt see thyself so exalted and sublimated as not to know thyself ; and thus will the promises of thy valorous lord be fulfilled. Be assured, moreover, in the name of the sage Mentironiana,* that thy wages shall be punctually paid thee. Follow, therefore, the valorous and enchanted knight, for it is expedient for thee to go where ye both may find repose. More I am not permitted to say. Heaven protect thee ! I now go—I well know whither ! " As he delivered this solemn prediction, the prophet first raised his voice high, then gradually lowered it to so pathetic a tone, that even those who were in the plot were not unmoved.

Don Quixote was much comforted by this prophecy, quickly comprehending the whole signification thereof ; for he saw that it promised him the felicity of being joined in holy wedlock with his beloved Dulcinea del Toboso, from whom should issue the whelps his sons, to the everlasting honour of La Mancha. Upon the strength of this conviction, he exclaimed, with a deep sigh, "O thou, whoever thou art, who hast prognosticated me so much good, I beseech thee to intercede in my behalf with the sage enchanter who hath the charge of my affairs, that he suffer me not to perish in the prison wherein I am now enclosed, before these promises of joyful and heavenly import are fulfilled. Let them but come to pass, and I shall glory in the pains of my imprisonment, enjoy the chains with which I am bound, and imagine this hard couch whereon I lie a soft bridal bed of down. On the affectionate attachment of my squire, Sancho Panza, I have too much reliance to think that he will desert me, whatever be my fortunes : and though it should even happen, through his or my evil destiny, that I were unable to give him the island, or something equivalent, according to my promise, at least he shall not lose his salary ; for in my will, which is already made, I have settled that point ; not, indeed, proportionate to his many and good services, but according to my own ability." Sancho Panza bowed with great respect, and kissed both his master's hands ;

---

* A word framed from *mentira,* a lie.

for one alone he could not, as they were both tied together. The goblins then took the cage on their shoulders, and placed it on the waggon.

CHAPTER XLVII.

Of the strange and wonderful manner in which Don Quixote de la Mancha was enchanted; with other remarkable occurrences.

" LEARNED and very grave historians of knights-errant have I read," said Don Quixote, on finding himself thus cooped up and carted; " but I never read, saw, nor heard of enchanted knights being transported in this manner, and so slowly as these lazy heavy animals seem to proceed; for they were usually conveyed through the air with wonderful speed, enveloped in some thick and dark cloud, or on some fiery chariot, or mounted upon a hippogriff, or some such animal. But to be carried upon a team drawn by oxen—before Heaven, it overwhelms me with confusion! Perhaps, however, the enchantments of these our times may differ from those of the ancients; and it is also possible that as I am a new knight in the world, and the first who revived the long-forgotten exercise of knight-errantry, new modes may have been invented. What thinkest thou of this, son Sancho?" "I do not know what to think," answered Sancho, "not being so well read as your worship in scriptures-errant; yet I dare affirm and swear that these hobgoblins here about us are not altogether Catholic." "Catholic my father!" answered Don Quixote: "how can they be Catholic, being devils who have assumed fantastic shapes to effect their purpose, and throw me into this state? To convince thyself of this, try to touch and feel them, and thou wilt find their bodies have no substance, but are of air, existing only to the sight." " 'Fore Heaven, sir!" replied Sancho, " I have already touched them; and this devil, who is so very busy here about us, is as plump as a partridge, and has another property very different from what your devils are wont to have—for it is said, they all smell of brimstone, and other bad scents; but this spark smells of amber at half a league's distance." Sancho spoke of Don Fernando, who, being a cavalier of rank, must have been perfumed as Sancho described. "Wonder not at this, friend Sancho," answered Don Quixote, " for thou must know that devils are cunning; and although they may carry perfumes about them, they have no scent themselves, being spirits; or, if they do smell, it can be of nothing but what is foul and offensive, since wherever they are they carry hell about them, and have no respite from their torments. Now, perfumes being pleasing and delicious, it is quite impossible that they should have such an odour; or if, to thy sense, one smelleth of amber, either you deceivest thyself, or he would mislead thee, that thou mightest not know him for a fiend."

Thus were the knight and squire discoursing together when Don

Fernando and Cardenio, fearing lest Sancho should see into the whole of their plot, being already not far from it, resolved to hasten their departure; and, calling the innkeeper aside, they ordered him to saddle Rozinante and pannel the ass, which he did with great expedition. In the meanwhile the priest engaged to pay the troopers of the Holy Brotherhood to accompany Don Quixote home to his village. Cardenio fastened the buckler on one side of the pommel of Rozinante's saddle, and the basin on the other; then, after placing the two troopers with their carbines on each side of the waggon, he made signs to Sancho to mount his ass, and lead Rozinante by the bridle. But before the car moved forward, the hostess, her daughter, and Maritornes came out to take their leave of Don Quixote, pretending to shed tears for grief at his misfortune. "Weep not, my good ladies," said the knight, "for disasters of this kind are incident to those of my profession; and if such calamities did not befall me, I should not account myself a distinguished knight-errant; for these events never occur to the ignoble, but to those whose valour and virtue excite the envy of princes and knights, who seek by evil machinations to defame whatever is praiseworthy and good. Notwithstanding which, so powerful is virtue, that of herself alone, in spite of all the necromantic skill of the first enchanter, Zoroaster, she will come off victorious in every attack, and spread her lustre over the world, as the sun illumines the heavens. Pardon me, fair ladies, if I have through inadvertence given you any offence—for intentionally I never offended any person; and I beseech you to pray Heaven for my deliverance from my present thraldom; and if ever I find myself at liberty, I shall not forget the favours you have done me in this castle, but shall acknowledge and requite them as they deserve."

While this passed between the ladies of the castle and Don Quixote, the priest and the barber took their leave of Don Fernando and his companions, the captain, and of all the ladies, now supremely happy. Don Fernando requested the priest to give him intelligence of Don Quixote, assuring him that nothing would afford him more satisfaction than to hear of his future proceedings; and he promised, on his part, to inform him of whatever might amuse or please him respecting his own marriage, the baptism of Zoraida, and the return of Lucinda to her parents, and also the issue of Don Louis's amour. The priest engaged to perform all that was desired of him with the utmost punctuality; after which they separated, with many expressions of mutual cordiality and good-will. Just before the priest left the house, the innkeeper brought him some papers which he said he had found in the lining of the wallet that contained the novel of "The Curious Impertinent;" and since the owner had never returned to claim them, and he could not read himself, he might take them away with him. The priest thanked him; and opening the papers, found them to be a novel, entitled "Rinconete and Cortadillo;"* and, concluding that it was by the same author as that of "The Curious Impertinent," was inclined to judge

---

* Written by Cervantes.

*The hostess, her daughter, and Maritornes came out to take their leave of Don Quixote,
pretending to shed tears for grief at his misfortune.*

favourably of it: he therefore accepted the manuscript, intending to
peruse it the first opportunity that offered. He and the barber then
joined the cavalcade, which was arranged in the following order: In
front was the car, guided by the owner, and on each side the troopers
with their matchlocks; then came Sancho upon his ass, leading Rozinante by the bridle; and in the rear the priest and his friend Nicholas,

mounted on their stately mules; and thus the whole moved on with great solemnity, regulated by the slow pace of the oxen. Don Quixote sat in the cage, with his hands tied and his legs stretched out, leaning against the bars as silently and patiently as if he had been not a man of flesh and blood, but a statue of stone. In this manner they travelled about two leagues, when they came to a valley which the waggoner thought a convenient place for resting and baiting his cattle; but on his proposing it, the barber recommended that they should travel a little farther, as beyond the next rising ground there was a vale that afforded much better pasture; and this advice was followed.

The priest, happening about this time to look back, perceived behind them six or seven horsemen, well mounted and accoutred, who soon came up with them; for they were not travelling with the phlegmatic pace of the oxen, but like persons mounted on good ecclesiastical mules, and eager to reach a place of shelter against the mid-day sun. The speedy overtook the slow, and each party courteously saluted the other. One of the travellers, who was a canon of Toledo, and master to those who accompanied him, observing the orderly procession of the waggon, the troopers, Sancho, Rozinante, the priest, and the barber, and especially Don Quixote caged up and imprisoned, could not forbear making some inquiries; though, on observing the badges of the Holy Brotherhood, he concluded that they were conveying some notorious robber, or other criminal, whose punishment belonged to that fraternity. "Why the gentleman is carried in this manner," replied one of the troopers who was questioned, "he must tell you himself; for we know nothing about the matter." Upon which Don Quixote (having overheard what passed) said, "If, perchance, gentlemen, you are conversant in the affairs of chivalry, I will acquaint you with my misfortunes; but if not, I will spare myself that trouble." The priest and the barber perceiving that the travellers were speaking with Don Quixote, rode up to them, lest anything should pass that might frustrate their plot. The canon, in answer to Don Quixote, said, "In truth, brother, I am more conversant in books of chivalry than in Villalpando's Summaries; you may, therefore, freely communicate to me whatever you please." "With Heaven's permission, then," replied Don Quixote, "be it known to you, Signor Cavalier, that I am enchanted in this cage through the envy and fraud of wicked necromancers; for virtue is more persecuted by the wicked than beloved by the good. A knight-errant am I: not one of those whose names fame has forgotten to eternize, but one who, in despite of envy itself, and of all the magicians of Persia, the Brahmins of India, and the gymnosophists of Ethiopia, shall enroll his name in the temple of immortality, to serve as a model and mirror to future ages, whereby knights-errant may see the track they are to follow, if they are ambitious of reaching the honourable summit and pinnacle of true glory." "Signor Don Quixote de la Mancha says the truth," said the priest; "for he is conveyed in that enchanted state not through his own fault or demerit, but by the malice of those to whom virtue is odious and courage obnoxious. This, sir, is the Knight of the Sorrowful Figure, whose valorous exploits and heroic deeds shall be recorded on solid brass and everlasting marble, in despite of all the efforts of envy and malice to conceal and obscure them." The canon, upon hearing not only the imprisoned but the free man talk in such a style, crossed himself in amazement, nor were his followers less surprised; and Sancho now coming up, to mend the matter, said, "Look ye, gentlemen, let it be well or ill taken, I will out with it: the truth of the case is, my master, Don Quixote, is just as much enchanted as my mother; he is in his perfect senses—he eats, drinks, and does everything else like other men, and as he did yesterday, before they cooped him up. This being so, will you persuade me he is enchanted? The enchanted, I have heard say, neither eat, nor sleep, nor speak; but my master here, if nobody stops him, will talk ye more than thirty barristers." Then, turning to the priest, he went on saying, "Ah, Master Priest, Master Priest, do I not know you? And think you I cannot guess what these new enchantments drive at? Let me tell you I know you, though you do hide your face, and understand you too, sly as you may be. But the good cannot abide where envy rules, nor is generosity found in a beggarly breast. Evil befall the devil! Had it not been for your reverence, before this time his worship had been married to the Princess Micomicona, and I had been an earl at least; for I could expect no less from my master's bounty and the greatness of my services. But I find the proverb true, that ' the wheel of fortune turns swifter than a mill-wheel,' and ' they who were yesterday at the top are to-day at the bottom.' I am grieved for my poor wife and children; for when they might reasonably expect to see their father come home a governor or viceroy of some island or kingdom, they will now see him return a pitiful groom. All this I say, Master Priest, only to make your paternity feel some compunction in regard to what you are doing with my master : take heed that you are not called to account in the next life for this imprisonment of my lord, and all the good he might have done during this time of his confinement be required at your hands." "Snuff me these candles!" quoth the barber, interrupting the squire: "what! art thou, Sancho, of thy master's fraternity? As Heaven shall save me, I begin to think thou art likely to keep him company in the cage, for thy share of his humour and his chivalry. In an evil hour wert thou puffed up by his promises, and thy head filled with islands." "I am not puffed up at all," answered Sancho, "nor am I a man to suffer myself to become so by the promises of the best king that may be : and though I am a poor man, I am an old Christian, and owe nobody anything ; and if I covet islands, there are others who covet worse things ; and every one is the son of his own works : and being a man, I may come to be pope, and much more easily governor of an island ; especially since my master may win so many, that he may be at a loss where to bestow them. Take heed, Master Barber, what you say ; for shaving beards is not all, and there is some difference between Pedro and Pedro. I say this because we know one another, and there is no putting false dice upon me. As for my master's enchantment, Heaven knows the truth, and let that rest—it is the worse for stirring." The barber would not answer Sancho, lest his simplicity should betray them; and for the same reason the priest desired the canon to go on a little before, saying he would let him into the mystery of the imprisonment, with other particulars that would amuse him.

The canon and his servants then rode on before with the priest, who entertained him with a circumstantial account of Don Quixote, from the first symptoms of his derangement to his present situation in the cage. The canon was surprised at what he heard. "Truly," said he to the curate, "those tales of chivalry are very prejudicial to the common weal. And though, led away by an idle and false taste, I have read in part almost all that are printed, I could never get through the whole of any one of them—they are all so much alike. In my opinion, this kind of writing and composition falls under the head of what are called Milesian fables, which are extravagant stories calculated merely to amuse, and very unlike those moral tales which are no less instructive than entertaining; and though the principal object of such books is to please, I know not how they can attain that end by such monstrous absurdities; for the mind receives pleasure from the beauty and consistency of what is presented to the imagination, not from that which is incongruous and unnatural. Where is the sense or consistency of a tale in which a youth of sixteen hews down a giant as tall as a steeple, and splits him in two as if he were made of paste? Or how are we to be interested in the detail of a battle, when we are told that the hero contends alone against a million of adversaries, and obtains the victory by his single arm? Then what shall we say to the facility with which a queen or empress throws herself into the arms of an errant and unknown knight? What mind, not wholly barbarous and uncultivated, can feel satisfied in reading that a vast tower, full of knights, is launched upon the ocean, and sailing like a ship before the wind, is to-night in Lombardy, and to-morrow morning in the country of Prester John, in the Indies, or in some other that Ptolemy never discovered, or Marco Polo never saw? It may be said that these, being professedly works of invention, should not be criticised for inaccuracy: but I say that fiction should be probable, and that in proportion as it is so, it is pleasing. Fables should not be composed to outrage the understanding; but by making the wonderful appear possible, and creating in the mind a pleasing interest, they may both surprise and entertain, which cannot be effected where no regard is paid to probability. I have never yet found a regular, well-connected fable in any of our books of chivalry—they are all inconsistent and monstrous; the style is generally bad; and they abound with incredible exploits, lascivious amours, absurd sentiments, and miraculous adventures: in short, they should be banished every Christian country."

The priest listened attentively to these observations of the canon, which he thought were perfectly just; and he told him that he also had such enmity to those tales of chivalry that he had destroyed all that Don Quixote had possessed, which were not a few in number; and he amused the canon very much by his account of the formal trial and condemnation through which they had passed. "Notwithstanding all that I have said against this kind of books," said the canon, " I think they certainly have the advantage of affording an ample field for the exercise of genius : there is such scope for descriptive powers in storms, shipwrecks, and battles; and also for the delineation of character — for instance, in the military hero—his foresight in anticipating the stratagems of his foe, his eloquence in encouraging or restraining his followers, his wisdom in council, his promptitude in action.   Now the author paints a sad and tragical event, and now one that is joyful; sometimes he expatiates on a valiant and courteous knight, at others on a rude and lawless barbarian; now on a warlike and affable prince, then a good and loyal vassal.   He may show himself to be an excellent astronomer or geographer, a musician or a statesman ; and, if he please, he may even dilate on the wonders of necromancy.   He may describe the subtlety of Ulysses, the piety of Æneas, the bravery of Achilles, the misfortunes of Hector, the treachery of Sinon, the friendship of Euryalus, the liberality of Alexander, the valour of Cæsar, the clemency and probity of Trajan, the fidelity of Zopyrus, the wisdom of Cato, and finally, all those qualities which constitute the perfect hero; either uniting them in a single person or distributing them among many : and if all this be done in a natural and pleasing style, a web of various and beautiful contexture might surely be wrought that would be equally delightful and instructive.   The freedom, indeed, of this kind of composition is alike favourable to the author, whether he would display his powers in epic (for there may be epic in prose as well as verse) or in lyric, in tragedy or comedy—in short, in every department of the delicious arts of poetry and oratory."

CHAPTER XLVIII.

In which the canon continues his discourse on books of chivalry; with other subjects worthy of his genius.

" VERY true—it is exactly as you say, sir," said the priest to the canon ; " and therefore, those who have hitherto composed such books are the more deserving of censure for their entire disregard to good sense and every rule by which they might have become the rivals in prose of the two princes of Greek and Latin poetry."   " I have myself made an attempt to write a book of knight-errantry on a better plan," said the canon; " and, to confess the truth, I have not written less than a hundred sheets, which I have shown to some learned and judicious friends, as well as to others less cultivated and more likely to be pleased with extravagance ; and from all I met with encouragement.   Notwithstanding this, I have never proceeded in the work, partly from an idea that it was foreign to my profession, and partly from the consideration of what a great majority of fools there are in the world ; and, although I know that the approbation of the judicious few should far outweigh the censure of the ignorant, yet I feel averse to exposing myself to vulgar criticism. I was discouraged, too, whenever I reflected on the present state of the drama, and the absurdity and incoherence of most of our modern comedies, whether fictitious or historical; for the actor and author both say that they must please the people, and not produce compositions which can only be appreciated by a half-score of men of sense; and that they would rather gain subsistence by the many than reputation by the few. What other fate, then, could I expect but that, after racking my brains to produce a reasonable work, I should get nothing but my labour for my pains? I have occasionally endeavoured to persuade theatrical managers that they would not only gain more credit, but eventually find it much more advantageous to produce better dramas; but they will not listen to reason. Conversing one day with a fellow of this kind, I said, 'Do you not remember that, a few years since, three tragedies were produced which were universally admired; that delighted both the ignorant and the wise, the vulgar as well as the cultivated; and that by those three pieces the players gained more than by thirty of the best which have since been represented?' 'I suppose you mean the "Isabella," "Phyllis," and "Alexandra,"' he replied. 'The same,' said I; 'and pray recollect, that although they were written in strict conformity to the rules of art, they were successful: the whole blame, therefore, is not to be ascribed to the taste of the vulgar. There is nothing absurd, for instance, in the play of "Ingratitude Revenged," nor in the "Numantia," nor in the "Merchant Lover," much less in the "Favourable Enemy," or in some others composed by ingenious poets, to their own renown and the profit of those who acted them.' To these I added other arguments, which I thought in some degree perplexed him, but were not so convincing as to make him reform his erroneous practice."

"Signor Canon," said the priest, "you have touched upon a subject which has revived in me an old grudge I have borne against our modern plays, scarcely less than that I feel towards books of chivalry; for though the drama, according to Cicero, ought to be the mirror of human life, an exemplar of manners, and an image of truth, those which are now produced are mirrors of inconsistency, patterns of folly, and images of licentiousness. What, for instance, can be more absurd than the introduction in the first scene of the first act of a child in swaddling-clothes, that in the second makes his appearance as a bearded man? Or to represent an old man valiant, a young man cowardly, a footman a rhetorician, a page a privy-councillor, a king a water-carrier, and a princess a scullion? Nor are they more observant of place than of time. I have seen a comedy, the first act of which was laid in Europe, the second in Asia, and the third in Africa; and had there been four acts, the fourth would doubtless have been in America. If truth of imitation be an important requisite in dramatic writing, how can any one with a decent share of understanding bear to see an action which passed in the reign of King Pepin or Charlemagne ascribed to the Emperor Heraclius, who is introduced carrying the cross into Jerusalem, or recovering the holy sepulchre, like Godfrey of Boulogne, though numberless years had elapsed between these actions? and, when the piece is founded on fiction, to see historical events mingled with facts relating to different persons and times?—and all this without any appearance of probability, but, on the contrary, full of the grossest absurdity? And yet there are people who think all this perfection, and call everything else mere pedantry. The sacred dramas too—how they are made to abound with false and incomprehensible events, frequently confounding the miracles of one saint with those of another; indeed, they are often introduced in plays on profane subjects merely to please the people. Thus is our natural taste degraded in the opinion of cultivated nations, who, judging by the extravagance and absurdity of our productions, conceive us to be in a state of ignorance and barbarism. It is not a sufficient excuse to say that the object in permitting theatrical exhibitions being chiefly to provide innocent recreation for the people, it is unnecessary to limit and restrain the dramatic author within strict rules of composition; for I affirm that the same object is, beyond all comparison, more effectually attained by legitimate works. The spectator of a good drama is amused, admonished, and improved by what is diverting, affecting, and moral in the representation: he is cautioned against deceit, corrected by example, incensed against vice, stimulated to the love of virtue. Such are the effects produced by dramatic excellence; but they are not to be expected on our present stage, although we have many authors perfectly aware of the prevailing defects, but who justify themselves by saying that, in order to make their works saleable, they must write what the theatre will purchase. We have a proof of this even in the happiest genius of our country, who has written an infinite number of dramatic works with such vivacity and elegance of style, such loftiness of sentiment, and richness of elocution, that his fame has spread over the world; nevertheless, in conforming occasionally to the bad taste of the present day, his productions are not all equally excellent. Besides the errors of taste, some authors have indulged in public and private scandal, insomuch that the actors have been obliged to abscond. These and every other inconvenience would be obviated if some intelligent and judicious person of the court were appointed to examine all plays before they are acted, and without whose approbation none should be performed. Thus guarded, the comedian might act without personal risk, and the author would write with more circumspection; and by such a regulation works of merit might be more frequent, to the benefit and honour of the country. And, in truth, were the same or some other person appointed to examine all future books of chivalry, we might hope to see some more perfect productions of this kind to enrich our language, and which, superseding the old romances, would afford rational amusement not to the idle alone, but to the active; for the bow cannot remain always bent, and relaxation both of body and mind is indispensable to all."

The canon and the priest were now interrupted in their dialogue by the barber, who, coming up to them, said, "This is the spot where I proposed we should rest ourselves; and the cattle will find here plenty of grass." The canon hearing this, determined to halt likewise, induced by the beauty of the place and the pleasure he found in the priest's conversation; besides, he was curious to see and hear more of Don Quixote. He ordered some of his attendants to go to the nearest inn and bring provisions for the whole party; but he was told by one of them that their sumpter-mule, which had gone forward, carried abundance of refreshment, and that they should want nothing from the inn but barley; upon which he dispatched them in haste for the mule.

During the foregoing conversation between the canon and the curate, Sancho perceiving that he might speak to his master without the continual presence of the priest and the barber, whom he looked upon with suspicion, came up to his master's cage, and said to him, "Sir, to disburden my conscience, I must tell you something about this enchantment of yours; and it is this, that those who are riding along with us, with their faces covered, are the priest and the barber of our town; and I fancy they have played you this trick and are carrying you in this manner out of pure envy of your worship for surpassing them in famous achievements. Now, supposing this to be true, it is plain that you are not enchanted, but cheated and fooled; for proof whereof I would ask you one thing, and if you answer me as I believe you must, you shall lay your finger upon this cheat, and find that it is just as I say." "Ask what thou wilt, son Sancho," answered Don Quixote; "for I will satisfy thee to the full without reserve. But as to thy assertion that those persons who accompany us are the priest and the barber, our townsmen and acquaintance—however they may appear to thee, thou must in nowise believe it. Of this thou mayest be assured, that if they appear to be such, they have only assumed their semblance; for enchanters can easily take what forms they please, and they may have selected those of our two friends in order to mislead and involve thee in such a labyrinth of fancies that even the clue of Theseus could not extricate thee. Besides, they may have also done it to make me waver in my judgment, and prevent me from suspecting from what quarter this injury comes. For if, on the one hand, thou sayest that the priest and barber of our village are our companions, and on the other I find myself locked up in a cage, and am conscious that supernatural force alone would have power to imprison me, what can I say or think but that the manner of my enchantment is more extraordinary than any that I have ever read of in history? Rest assured, therefore, that these are no more the persons thou sayest than I am a Turk. As to thy queries—make them; for I will answer thee, though thou shouldst continue asking until to-morrow morning." "Blessed Virgin!" answered Sancho, raising his voice, "is your worship indeed so thick-skulled and devoid of brains that you do not see what I tell you to be the very truth, and that there is more roguery than enchantment in this mishap of yours, as I will clearly prove? Now tell me, as Heaven shall deliver you from this trouble, and as you hope to find yourself in my lady

"Cease conjuring me," said Don Quixote, "and ask what questions thou wilt."

Dulcinea's arms when you least think of it——" "Cease conjuring me," said Don Quixote, "and ask what questions thou wilt, for I have already told thee that I will answer them with the utmost precision." "That is what I want," replied Sancho; "and all I crave is that you would tell me, without adding or diminishing a tittle, and with that truth which is expected from all who exercise the profession of arms, as your worship does, under the title of knights-errant——" "I tell thee I will lie in nothing," answered Don Quixote: "therefore speak; for in truth, Sancho, I am wearied with so many salvos, postulatums, and preparatives." "I say," replied Sancho, "that I am fully satisfied of the goodness and veracity of my master; and therefore, it being quite to the purpose in our affair, I ask (with respect be it spoken) whether since you have been cooped up, or as you call it enchanted, in this cage, your worship has had any natural inclinations?" "I do not understand thee, Sancho," said Don Quixote; "explain thyself, if thou wouldst have me give thee a direct answer." "Is it possible," quoth Sancho, "your worship should not understand that phrase, when the very children at school are weaned with it? You must know, then, it means whether you have not had an inclination to lighten your stomach of exhausted matters?" "Ay, now I comprehend thee, Sancho," said Don Quixote; "and in truth I have often had such inclination."

CHAPTER XLIX.

*Of the ingenious conference between Sancho Panza and his master
Don Quixote.*

"Ah!" quoth Sancho, "now I have caught you: this is what I longed to know with all my heart and soul. Come on, sir; can you deny what is in everybody's mouth, when a person is in the dumps? It is always then said, 'I know not what such a one ails — he neither eats, nor drinks, nor sleeps, nor answers to the purpose, like other men— surely he is enchanted.' Wherefore it is clear that such, and such only, are enchanted who neither eat, nor drink, nor sleep, and not they who eat and drink when they can get it, and answer properly to all that is asked them." "Thou art right, Sancho," answered Don Quixote; "but I have already told thee there are sundry sorts of enchantments, and it is probable that in process of time they may have changed, and that now it may be usual for those who are enchanted to do as I do, though it was formerly otherwise. It is impossible to argue or draw conclusions from the varying customs of different periods. I know and am verily persuaded that I am enchanted; and that is sufficient for my conscience, which would be heavily burdened if I thought I was not so, but suffered myself to lie in this cage like a coward, defrauding the necessitous and oppressed of succour, when perhaps at this very moment they may be in extreme want of my aid and protection." "But for all that," replied Sancho, "I say, for your greater and more abundant satisfaction, that your worship will do well to endeavour to get out of this prison; and I will undertake to help you with all my might. You may then once more mount your trusty Rozinante, who seems as if he were enchanted too, he looks so melancholy and dejected; and we may again try our fortune in search of adventures; and if matters turn out not quite to our hearts' content, we can come back to the cage; and I promise you, on the faith of a good and loyal squire, to shut myself up in it with your worship." "I am content to follow thy advice, brother Sancho," replied Don Quixote, "and when thou seest an opportunity for effecting my deliverance, I will be guided entirely by thee; but be assured, Sancho, thou wilt find thyself mistaken as to the nature of my misfortune."

In such conversation the knight-errant and the evil-errant squire were engaged until they came to the place where the priest, the canon, and the barber were already alighted and waiting for them. The waggoner then unyoked the oxen from his team, and turned them loose upon that green and delicious spot, the freshness of which was inviting, not only to those who were enchanted like Don Quixote, but to discreet and enlightened persons like his squire, who besought the priest to permit his master to come out of the cage for a short time, otherwise that prison would not be quite so clean as decency required in the accommodation of such a knight as his master. The priest understood him, and said that he would readily consent to his request; but he feared lest his master, finding himself at liberty, should play his old pranks, and be gone where he might never be seen more. "I will be security for his not running away," replied Sancho. "And I also," said the canon, "if he will give his parole of honour." "I give it," said Don Quixote; "especially as those who like myself are enchanted have no power over their own persons, for their persecutors may render them motionless during three centuries: you may, therefore, safely release me." He then intimated further that his removal might prove more agreeable to all the party on another account. The canon took him by the hand, though he was still manacled; and, upon his faith and word, they uncaged him, to his great satisfaction. The first thing he did was to stretch himself; after that, he went up to Rozinante, and giving him a couple of slaps on the hinder parts with the palm of his hand, he said, "I yet trust in Heaven, O thou flower and pattern of steeds! that we shall both soon see ourselves in that state which is the desire of our hearts—thou with thy lord on thy back, and I mounted upon thee, exercising the function for which Heaven destined me!" The knight then, attended by Sancho, retired to some little distance, whence he came back much relieved, and still more eager to put in execution what his squire had projected. The canon contemplated him with surprise; for he displayed in conversation a very good understanding, and seemed, as it hath been before observed, only to lose his stirrups on the theme of chivalry; and while they were waiting for the return of the sumpter-mule, he was induced, out of compassion to his infirmity, to address him on the subject.

"Is it possible, worthy sir," said the canon, "that the disgusting and idle study of books of chivalry should so powerfully have affected your brain as to make you believe that you are now enchanted, with other fancies of the same kind, as far from truth as falsehood itself? Is it possible that human reason can credit the existence of all that infinite tribe of knights—the Amadises, the Emperors of Trapisonda, Felixmartes of Hyrcania, all the palfreys, damsels-errant, serpents, dragons, giants; all the wonderful adventures, enchantments, battles, furious encounters; enamoured princesses, ennobled squires, witty dwarfs, *billets-doux*, amours, Amazonian ladies—in short, all the absurdities which books of chivalry contain? For my own part, I confess, when I read them without reflecting on their falsehood and folly, they gave me some amusement; but when I consider what they are, I dash them against

th₃ wall, and even commit them to the flames when I am near a fire, as
well deserving such a fate, for their want of common sense and their
injurious tendency in misleading the uninformed. Nay, they may even
disturb the intellects of sensible and well-born gentlemen, as is manifest
by the effect they have had on your worship, who is reduced by them to
such a state that you are forced to be shut up in a cage, and carried on
a team from place to place, like some lion or tiger exhibited for money.
Ah, Signor Don Quixote! have pity on yourself: shake off this folly,
and employ the talents with which Heaven has blessed you in the cultivation of literature more subservient to your honour, as well as profitable
to your mind. If a strong natural impulse still leads you to books
containing the exploits of heroes, read in the holy Scriptures the Book
of Judges, where you will meet with wonderful truths, and achievements
no less heroic than true. Portugal had a Viriatus, Rome a Cæsar,
Carthage a Hannibal, Greece an Alexander, Castile a Count Fernando
Gonzalez, Valencia a Cid, Andalusia a Gonzalo Fernandez, Estremadura
a Diego Garcia de Paredes, Xerez a Garcia Perez de Vargas, Toledo a
Garcilaso, and Seville a Don Manuel de Leon; the memoirs of whose
heroic deeds afford a rational source of amusement and pleasure. This,
indeed, would be a study worthy of your understanding, my dear sir, by
which you would become well instructed in history, enamoured of virtue,
familiar with goodness, improved in morals; and would acquire valour
without rashness and caution without cowardice; which would at the same
time redound to the glory of God, your own profit, and the fame of La
Mancha, whence I have been informed you derive your birth and origin."

Don Quixote listened with great attention to the canon till he had
ceased speaking, and then, looking steadfastly in his face, he replied, "I
conceive, sir, that you mean to insinuate that there never were knights-
errant in the world; that all books of chivalry are false, mischievous,
and unprofitable to the commonwealth; and that I have done ill in
reading, worse in believing, and still worse in imitating them by following the rigorous profession of knight-errantry, as by them exemplified;
and also that you deny that there ever existed the Amadises either of
Gaul or of Greece, or any of those celebrated knights?" "I mean
precisely what you say," replied the canon. "You also were pleased to
add, I believe," continued Don Quixote, "that those books had done
me much prejudice, having injured my brain, and occasioned my imprisonment in a cage; and that it would be better for me to change my
course of study by reading other books more true, more pleasant, and
more instructive?" "Just so," quoth the canon. "Why, then," said
Don Quixote, "in my opinion, sir, it is yourself who are deranged and
enchanted, since you have dared to blaspheme an order so universally
acknowledged in the world, and its existence so authenticated that he
who denies it merits that punishment you are pleased to say you inflict
on certain books. To assert that there never was an Amadis in the
world, nor any other of the knights-adventurers of whom so many
records remain, is to say that the sun does not enlighten, the frost
produce cold, nor the earth yield sustenance. What human ingenuity

can make us doubt the truth of that affair between the Infanta Floripes and Guy of Burgundy? and that of Fierabras at the bridge of Mantible, which occurred in the time of Charlemagne? I vow to God, they are as true as that it is now daylight! If these are fictions, it must be denied also that there ever was a Hector or an Achilles, or a Trojan war, or the twelve peers of France, or King Arthur of England, who is still wandering about transformed into a raven, and is every moment expected in his kingdom. They will even dare to affirm that the history of Guarino Mezquino and that of the acquisition of the Santo Graal are lies, and that the amour of Sir Tristram and the Queen Iseo, as well as those of Guinevra and Lancelot, are also apocryphal; although there are persons who almost remember to have seen the duenna Quintoniana, who was the best wine-skinner in Great Britain. And this is so certain, that I remember my grandmother by my father's side, when she saw any duenna reverently coifed, would say to me, 'That woman, grandson, looks like the duenna Quintoniana,' whence I infer that she must either have known her, or at least seen some true effigy of her. Then who can deny the truth of the history of Peter of Provence and the fair Magalona? since even to this day you may see in the king's armoury the very peg wherewith the valiant Peter steered the wooden horse that bore him through the air; which peg is somewhat larger than the pole of a coach; and near it lies the saddle of Babieca. In Roncesvalles, too, there may be seen Orlando's horn, the size of a great beam. It is, therefore, evident that there were the twelve peers, the Peters, the Cids, and all those knights commonly termed adventurers: and if that be doubted, it will be said, too, that the valiant Portuguese, John de Merlo, was no knight-errant; he who went to Burgundy, and in the city of Ras fought the famous lord of Charni, Monseigneur Pierre, and afterwards, in the city of Basil, Monseigneur Enrique of Remestan, coming off conquerer in both engagements. They will deny also the challenges and feats performed in Burgundy by the valiant Spaniards, Pedro Barba and Gutierre Quixada (from whom I am lineally descended), who vanquished the sons of the Count San Polo. Let them deny, likewise, that Don Fernando de Guevara travelled into Germany in quest of adventures, where he fought with Messire George, a knight of the Duke of Austria's court. Let them say that the jousts of Suero de Quinones of the Pass were all mockery; and the enterprises of Monseigneur Louis de Falces against Don Gonzalo de Guzman, a Castilian knight, with many other exploits performed by Christian knights of these and other kingdoms—all so authentic and true, that I say again, whoever denies them must be wholly destitute of sense and reason."

The canon was astonished at Don Quixote's medley of truth and fiction, as well as at the extent of his knowledge on affairs of chivalry; and he replied, "I cannot deny, Signor Don Quixote, that there is some truth in what you say, especially with regard to the knights-errant of Spain. I grant also that there were the twelve peers of France; but I can never believe that they performed all the deeds ascribed to them by Archbishop Turpin. The truth is, they were knights chosen by the kings of France, and called peers from being all equal in quality and prowess—at least, it was intended that they should be so; and in this respect they were similar to the religious order of Saint Jago or Calatrava, all the professors of which, it is presumed, are noble, valiant, and virtuous, and were called Knights of St. John, or of Alcantara, just as those of the ancient order were termed Knights of the Twelve Peers. That there was a Cid no one will deny, and likewise a Bernardo del Carpio; but that they performed all the exploits ascribed to them I believe there is great reason to doubt. As to Peter of Provence's peg, and its standing near Babieca's saddle in the king's armoury, I confess my sin in being so ignorant or short-sighted that, though I have seen the saddle, I never could discover the peg—large as it is, according to your description." "Yet, unquestionably, there it is," replied Don Quixote; "and they say, moreover, that it is kept in a leathern case to prevent rust." "It may be so," answered the canon; "but by the holy orders I have received, I do not remember to have seen it! Yet, even granting it, I am not therefore bound to believe all the stories of so many Amadises and the whole tribe of knights-errant; and it is extraordinary that a gentleman possessed of your understanding and talents should give credit to such extravagance and absurdity."

CHAPTER L.

Of the ingenious contest between Don Quixote and the canon; with other incidents.

"Vastly fine!—a good jest, truly," said Don Quixote, "that books printed with the license of kings and the approbation of the examiners, read with general pleasure, and applauded by great and small, poor and rich, learned and ignorant, nobles and plebeians — in short, by people of every state and condition, should be all lies, and at the same time appear so much like truth! For do they not tell us the parentage, the country, the kindred, the age, with a particular detail of every action of this or that knight? Good sir, be silent, and utter not such blasphemies; and believe me serious when I advise you to think on this subject more like a man of sense: only peruse these memoirs, and they will abundantly repay your trouble. What more delightful than to have, as it were, before our eyes a vast lake of boiling pitch, with a prodigious number of serpents, snakes, crocodiles, and divers other kinds of fierce and dreadful creatures, floating in it; and from the midst of the lake to hear a most dreadful voice saying, ' O knight, whosoever thou art, now surveying this tremendous lake, if thou wouldst possess the treasure that lies concealed beneath these sable waters, show the valour of thy undaunted breast, and plunge thyself headlong into the midst of the black and burning liquid; if not, thou wilt be unworthy to see the mighty

" Vastly fine !—a good jest, truly," said Don Quixote, " that books printed with the license of kings, and applauded by great and small, should be all lies."

wonders enclosed therein, and contained in the seven castles of the seven enchanted nymphs who dwell beneath this horrid blackness.' And scarcely has the knight heard these terrific words when, without further consideration or reflection upon the danger to which he exposes himself, and even without putting off his cumbrous armour, he commends himself to Heaven and his mistress, and plunges headlong into the boiling pool; when unexpectedly he finds himself in the midst of flowery fields, with which those of Elysium can bear no comparison, where the sky seems far more clear and the sun shines with greater brightness. Beyond it appears a forest of beautiful and shady trees, whose verdure regales the sight, whilst the ears are entertained with the sweet and artless notes of an infinite number of little birds of various hues, hopping among the intricate branches. Here he discovers a little brook, whose clear waters, resembling liquid crystal, run murmuring over the fine sands and snowy pebbles, which rival sifted gold and purest pearl. There he sees an artificial fountain of variegated jasper and polished marble; here he beholds another of rustic composition, in which the minute shells of the mussel, with the white and yellow wreathed houses of the snail, arranged in orderly confusion, interspersed with pieces of glittering crystal and pellucid emeralds, compose a work of such variety that art, imitating nature, seems here to surpass her. Then suddenly he descries a strong castle or stately palace, the walls of which are massy gold, the battlements composed of diamonds, and the gates of hyacinths; in short, the structure is so admirable that, though the materials whereof it is framed are no less than diamonds, carbuncles, rubies, pearls, gold, and emeralds, yet the workmanship is still more precious. And after this, can anything be more charming than to behold, sallying forth at the castle-gate, a goodly troop of damsels, in such rich and gorgeous attire, that were I to attempt the minute description that is given in history, the task would be endless; and then she who appears to be the principal takes by the hand the daring knight who threw himself into the burning lake, and silently leads him into the rich palace or castle; and stripping him as naked as when he first came into the world, bathes him in temperate water, and then anoints him with odoriferous essences, and puts on him a shirt of the finest lawn, all sweet-scented and perfumed. Then comes another damsel, and throws over his shoulders a mantle worth a city at least. He is afterwards led into another hall, where he is struck with wonder and admiration at the sight of tables spread in beautiful order. Then to see him wash his hands in water distilled from amber and sweet-scented flowers! To see him seated in a chair of ivory! To behold the damsels waiting upon him, all preserving a marvellous silence! Then to see such a variety of delicious viands, so savourily dressed that the appetite is at a loss where to direct the hand! To hear soft music while he is eating, without knowing whence the sounds proceed! And when the repast is finished, and the tables removed, the knight reclines on his seat, and perhaps is picking his teeth, when suddenly the door of the saloon opens, and lo! a damsel more beautiful than any of the former enters, who, seating herself by the knight's side, begins to give him an account of that castle, and to inform him how she is enchanted in it, with sundry other matters which amaze the knight and all those who read his history. I will enlarge on this no further; for you must be convinced, from what I have said, that every part of every history of a knight-errant must yield wonder and delight. Study well these books, signor; for, believe me, you will find that they will exhilarate and improve your mind. Of myself I can say, that since I have been a knight-errant I am become valiant, polite, liberal, well-bred, generous, courteous, daring, affable, patient, a sufferer of toils, imprisonments, and enchantment; and although so lately enclosed within a cage, like a maniac, yet do I hope, through the valour of my arm and the favour of Heaven, to see myself in a short time king of some kingdom, when I may display the gratitude and liberality enclosed in this breast of mine; for upon my faith, sir, the poor man is unable to exercise the virtue of liberality; and the gratitude which consists only in inclination is a dead thing, even as faith without works is dead. I shall, therefore, rejoice when fortune presents me with an opportunity of exalting myself, that I may show my heart in conferring benefits on my friends, especially on poor Sancho Panza here, my squire, who is one of the best men in the world; and I would fain bestow on him an earldom, as I have long since promised; although I am somewhat in doubt of his ability in the government of his estate."

Sancho, overhearing his master's last words, said, "Take you the trouble, Signor Don Quixote, to procure me that same earldom, which your worship has so often promised, and I have been so long waiting for, and you shall see that I shall not want ability to govern it. But even if I should, there are people, I have heard say, who farm these lordships; and, paying the owners so much a year, take upon themselves the government of the whole, while his lordship lolls at his ease, enjoying his estate, without concerning himself any further about it. Just so will I do, and give myself no more trouble than needs must, but enjoy myself like any duke, and let the world rub." "This, brother Sancho," said the canon, "may be done, as far as regards the management of your revenue; but the administration of justice must be attended to by the lord himself; and requires capacity, judgment, and, above all, an upright intention, without which nothing prospers: for Heaven assists the good intent of the simple, and disappoints the evil designs of the cunning." "I do not understand these philosophies," answered Sancho; "all that I know is, that I wish I may as surely have the earldom as I should know how to govern it: for I have as large a soul as another, and as large a body as the best of them; and I should be as mucl king of my own dominion as any other king: and, being so, I would do what I pleased; and, doing what I pleased, I should have my will; and, having my will, I should be contented; and, being content, there is no more to be desired; and when there is no more to desire, there is an end of it, and let the estate come; so Heaven be with ye, and let us see it, as one blind man said to another." "These are no bad philosophies, as you say, Sancho," quoth the canon: "nevertheless, there is a great deal more to be said upon the subject of earldoms." "That may be," observed Don Quixote; "but I am guided by the numerous examples offered on this subject by knights of my own profession; who, in compensation for the loyal and signal services they had received from their squires, conferred upon them extraordinary favours, making them absolute lords of cities and islands: indeed, there was one whose services were so great that he had the presumption to accept of a kingdom. But why should I say more, when before me is the bright example of the great Amadis de Gaul, who made his squire knight of the Firm Island? Surely I may, therefore, without scruple of conscience, make an earl of Sancho Panza, who is one of the best squires that ever served knight-errant." With all this methodical raving the canon was no less amused than astonished.

The servants who went to the inn for the sumpter-mule had now returned; and, having spread a carpet over the green grass, the party seated themselves under the shade of some trees, and there enjoyed their repast, while the cattle luxuriated on the fresh pasture. As they were thus employed, they suddenly heard a noise and a sound of a little bell from a thicket near them; at the same instant a beautiful she-goat, speckled with black, white, and grey, ran out of the thicket, followed by a goatherd, calling to her aloud, in the usual language, to stop and come back to the fold. The fugitive animal, trembling and affrighted, ran to the company, claiming, as it were, their protection; but the goatherd pursued her, and seizing her by the horns, addressed her as a rational creature. "Ah, wanton spotted thing! how hast thou strayed of late! What wolves have frightened thee, child? Wilt thou tell me, pretty one, what this means? But what else can it mean, but that thou art a female, and therefore canst not be quiet! A plague on thy humours, and all theirs whom thou resemblest! Turn back, my love, turn back; for though not content, at least thou wilt be more safe in thine own fold and among thy companions; for if thou, who shouldst protect and guide them, go astray, what must become of them?"

The party were very much amused by the goatherd's remonstrances, and the canon said, "I entreat you, brother, not to be in such haste to force back this goat to her fold; for, since she is a female, she will follow her natural inclination in spite of all your oppositon. Come, do not be angry, but eat and drink with us, and let the wayward creature rest herself." At the same time he offered him the hinder quarter of a cold rabbit on the point of a fork. The goatherd thanked him and accepted his offer, and being then in a better temper, he said, "Do not think me a fool, gentlemen, for talking so seriously to this animal, for, in truth, my words were not without a meaning; and though I am a rustic, I know the difference between conversing with men and beasts." "I doubt it not," said the priest; "indeed, it is well known that the mountains breed learned men, and the huts of shepherds contain philosophers." "At least, sir," replied the goatherd, "they contain men who have some knowledge gained from experience; and if I shall not be intruding, I will tell a circumstance which confirms it."

"Since this affair," said Don Quixote, "bears somewhat the semblance of an adventure, for my own part, friend, I shall listen to you most willingly: I can answer also for these gentlemen, who are persons of sense, and will relish the curious, the entertaining, and the marvellous, which, I doubt not, your story contains. I entreat you, friend, to begin it immediately." "I shall take myself away to the side of yonder brook," said Sancho, "with this pasty, of which I mean to lay in enough to last three days at least: for I have heard my master, Don Quixote, say that the squire of a knight-errant should eat when he can, and as long as he can, because he may lose his way for six days together in a wood; and then, if a man has not his stomach well lined or his wallet well provided, there he may stay till he is turned into a mummy." "Thou art in the right, Sancho," said Don Quixote; "go where thou wilt, and eat what thou canst : my appetite is already satisfied, and my mind only needs refreshment, which the tale of this good man will doubtless afford." The goatherd being now requested by the others of the company to begin his tale, he patted his goat, which he still held by the horns, saying, " Lie thee down by me, speckled fool ; for we shall have time enough to return to our fold." The goat seemed to understand him ; for as soon as her master was seated, she laid herself quietly down by him, and, looking up into his face, seemed to listen to his story, which he began as follows.

CHAPTER LI.

The goatherd's narrative.

" THREE leagues from this valley there is a town which, though small, is one of the richest in these parts ; and among its inhabitants was a farmer of such an excellent character that, though riches generally gain esteem, he was more respected for his good qualities than for his wealth ; and his happiness was completed in possessing a daughter of extraordinary beauty, discretion, and virtue. When a child, she was lovely, but at the age of sixteen she was perfectly beautiful, and her fame extended over all the neighbouring villages—villages, do I say ?— it spread itself to the remotest cities, even into the palaces of kings ! People came from every part to see her, as some relic or wonderworking image. Her father guarded her and she guarded herself ; for no padlocks, bolts, or bars secure a maiden so well as her own reserve. The wealth of the father, and the beauty of the daughter, induced many to seek her hand, insomuch that he whose right it was to dispose of so precious a jewel was perplexed, and knew not whom to select among her importunate suitors. I was one of the number, and had indulged fond hopes of success, being known to her father, born in the same village, untainted in blood, in the flower of my age, rich, and of no mean understanding. Another of our village, of equal pretensions with myself, solicited her also ; and her father being equally satisfied with both of us, was perplexed which to prefer, and therefore determined to leave the choice to Leandra herself—for so the maiden is called : an example worthy the imitation of all parents. I do not say they should give them their choice of what is improper ; but they should propose to them what is good, and leave them to select thence according to their taste. I know not which of us Leandra preferred ; this only I know, that her father put us both off by pleading the tender age of his daughter, and with such general expressions as neither bound himself nor disobliged us My rival's name is Anselmo, mine Eugenio ; for you ought to know the names of the persons concerned in this tragedy, the catastrophe of which, though still suspended, will surely be disastrous.

" About that time there came to our village one Vincent de la Rosa, the son of a poor farmer in the same place. This Vincent had returned from Italy and other countries, where he had served in the wars, having been carried away from our town at twelve years of age by a captain who happened to march that way with his company; and now, at the end of twelve more, he came back in a soldier's garb, bedizened with a variety of colours, and covered with a thousand trinkets and glittering chains. To-day he put on one piece of finery, to-morrow another, but all slight and counterfeit, of little or no value. The country-folks (who are naturally envious, and, if they chance to have leisure, are malice itself) observed and reckoned up all his trappings and gewgaws, and found that he had three suits of apparel, of different colours, with hose and garters to them; but those he disguised in so many different ways, and with so much contrivance, that had they not been counted, one would have sworn that he had above ten suits, and twenty plumes of feathers. Do not look upon this description of dress as impertinent or superfluous, for it is an important part of the story. He used to seat himself on a stone bench, under a great poplar tree in our market-place, and there he would hold us all gaping and listening to the history of his exploits. There was no country on the whole globe that he had not seen, nor battle in which he had not been engaged. He had slain more Moors than are in Morocco and Tunis, and fought more single combats, according to his own account, than Gante, Luna, Diego Garcia de Paredes, and a thousand others, from which he always came off victorious, and without losing a drop of blood; at the same time he would show us marks of wounds which, though they were not to be discerned, he assured us were so many musket-shots received in different actions. With the utmost arrogance he would 'thee' and 'thou' his equals and acquaintance, and boast that his arm was his father, his deeds his pedigree, and that under the title of soldier he owed the king himself nothing. In addition to this boasting, he pretended to be somewhat of a musician, and scratched a little upon the guitar, which some people admired. But his accomplishments did not end here; for he was likewise something of a poet, and would compose a ballad, a league and a half in length, on every trifling incident that happened in the village.

"Now, this soldier whom I have described, this Vincent de la Rosa, this hero, this gallant, this musician, this poet, was often seen and admired by Leandra, from a window of her house which faced the market-place. She was struck with the tinsel of his gaudy apparel; his ballads enchanted her; for he gave at least twenty copies about of all he composed. The exploits he related of himself reached her ears— and, as the devil would have it, she fell downright in love with him, before he had entertained the presumption of courting her. In short, as in affairs of love none are so easily accomplished as those which are favoured by the inclination of the lady, Leandra and Vincent soon came to a mutual understanding; and before any of her numerous suitors had the least suspicion of her design, she had already accomplished it, and left the house of her affectionate father (she had no mother), and quitted the town with the soldier, who came off in this enterprise more triumphantly than in any of those of which he had so arrogantly boasted.

This event excited great astonishment. Anselmo and I were utterly confounded, her father grieved, her kindred ashamed, justice alarmed, and the troopers of the Holy Brotherhood in full activity. They beset the highways, and searched the woods, leaving no place unexplored; and at the end of three days they found the poor giddy Leandra in the cave of a mountain, stripped of all her clothes and the money and jewels which she had carried away from home. They brought her back to her disconsolate father; and on being questioned, she freely confessed that Vincent de la Rosa had deceived her, and upon a promise of marriage had persuaded her to leave her father's house, telling her he would carry her to Naples, the richest and most delicious city in the whole world. The imprudent and credulous girl said, that having believed him, she had robbed her father, and given the whole to him on the night of her elopement; and that he had carried her among the mountains, and left her shut up in that cave, after plundering her of everything but her honour. It was no easy matter to persuade us of the young man's forbearance, but she affirmed it so positively, that her father was much comforted with the idea that she had not sustained an irreparable loss.

" The same day that Leandra returned, she disappeared from our eyes, as her father placed her in the monastery of a neighbouring town, in hopes that time might efface the blemish which her reputation had suffered. Her tender years were some excuse for her fault, especially with those who were indifferent as to whether she were good or bad, but those who know how much sense and understanding she possesses could only ascribe her fault to levity and the foibles natural to womankind. When Leandra was gone, Anselmo and myself were blind to everything —at least no object could give us pleasure. We cursed the soldier's finery, and reprobated her father's want of vigilance; nor had time any effect in diminishing our regret. At length we agreed to quit the town, and retire to this valley, where we pass our lives tending our flocks, and indulging our passion by praises, lamentations, or reproaches, and sometimes in solitary sighs and groans. Our example has been followed by many other admirers of Leandra, who have joined us in the same employment : indeed, we are so numerous that this place seems converted into the pastoral Arcadia; nor is there a part of it where the name of our beautiful mistress is not heard. One utters execrations against her, calling her fond, fickle, and immodest; another condemns her forwardness and levity : some excuse and pardon her; others arraign and condemn her : one praises her beauty, another rails at her disposition : in truth, all blame and all adore her—nay, such is the general frenzy, that some complain of her disdain who never had spoken to her, and some there are who bemoan themselves and affect to feel the raging disease of jealousy, though, as I have said before, her fault was known before her inclinations were suspected. There is no hollow of a rock, nor margin of a rivulet, nor shade of a tree, that is not occupied by some shepherd lamenting to the winds. Wherever there is an echo, it is continually heard repeating the name of Leandra; the mountains resound Leandra; the brooks murmur Leandra : in short, Leandra holds us all in a state of delirium and enchantment, hoping without hope, and dreading we know not what. He who shows the least, though he has the most sense, among us madmen, is my rival Anselmo, for he complains only of absence; and to the sound of a rebec, which he touches to admiration, pours forth his complaint in verses of wonderful ingenuity. I follow a better course, and inveigh against the levity of women, their inconstancy and double-dealing, their vain promises and broken faith, their absurd and misplaced affections.

" This, gentlemen, gave rise to the expressions I used to the goat; for being a female, I despise her, though she is the best of all my flock. I have now finished my story, which I fear you have thought tedious; but I shall be glad to make you amends by regaling you at my cottage, which is near, and where you will find new milk, good cheese, and abundance of fruit."

CHAPTER LII.

Of the quarrel between Don Quixote and the goatherd; with the rare adventure of the disciplinants, which he happily accomplished with the sweat of his brow.

Looking and speaking, as he did, more like a gentleman and a scholar than an unpolished goatherd, Eugenio's tale amused all his auditors; especially the canon, who was struck by his manner of telling it; and he was convinced that the priest was perfectly right when he affirmed that men of letters were often produced among mountains. They all offered their services to Eugenio; but the most liberal in his offers was Don Quixte, who said to him, " In truth, brother goatherd, were I in a situation to undertake any new adventure, I would immediately engage myself in your service, and release your lady from the nunnery in spite of the abbess and all opposers, then deliver her into your hands, to be disposed of at your pleasure, so far as is consistent with the laws of chivalry, which enjoin that no kind of outrage be offered to damsels. I trust, however, in Heaven, that the power of one malicious enchanter shall not be so prevalent over another but that a better disposed one may triumph; and then I promise you my aid and protection, according to the duty of my profession, which is no other than to favour the weak and necessitous."

The goatherd stared at Don Quixote, and observing his sad plight and scurvy appearance, he whispered to the barber, who sat next to him, " Pray, sir, who is that man that looks and talks so strangely?" " Who should he be," answered the barber, " but the famous Don Quixote de la Mancha, the redresser of injuries, the righter of wrongs, the protector of maidens, the dread of giants, and the conqueror of battles?" " Why, this is like what we hear in the stories of knights-errant," said the goatherd; " but I take it either your worship is in jest, or the apartments in this gentleman's skull are unfurnished."

" You are a very great rascal ! " exclaimed the knight : " it is yourself who are empty-skulled and shallow-brained ; for mine is fuller than was ever the head of any of your vile generation ! " and as he spoke, he snatched up a loaf and threw it at the goatherd's face with so much fury that he laid his nose flat. The goatherd did not much relish the jest; so without any respect to the table-cloth or the company present, he leaped upon Don Quixote, and seizing him by the throat with both hands, would doubtless have strangled him, had not Sancho Panza, who came up at that moment, taken him by the shoulders and thrown him back on the table-cloth, demolishing dishes and platters, and spilling and overturning all that was upon it. Don Quixote, finding himself free, turned upon the goatherd, who, being kicked and trampled upon by Sancho, was feeling about, upon all-fours, for some knife or weapon to take a bloody revenge withal; but the canon and the priest prevented him. The barber, however, maliciously contrived that the goatherd should get Don Quixote under him, whom he buffeted so unmercifully that he had ample retaliation for his own sufferings.

This ludicrous encounter overcame the gravity of both the churchmen, while the troopers of the Holy Brotherhood, enjoying the conflict, stood urging on the combatants, as if it had been a dog-fight. Sancho struggled in vain to release himself from one of the canon's servants, who prevented him from going to assist his master. In the midst of this sport a trumpet was suddenly heard sounding so dismally that every face was instantly turned in the direction whence the sound proceeded. Don Quixote's attention was particularly excited, though he still lay under the goatherd in a bruised and battered condition. " Thou devil ! " he said to him, " for a devil thou must be to have such power over me, I beg that thou wilt grant a truce for one hour, as the solemn sound of that trumpet seems to call me to some new adventure." The goatherd, whose revenge was by this time sated, immediately let him go, and Don Quixote, having got upon his legs again, presently saw several people descending from a rising ground, arrayed in white, after the manner of disciplinants.*

That year the heavens having failed to refresh the earth with seasonable showers, throughout all the villages of that district processions, disciplines, and public prayers were ordered, beseeching Heaven to show its mercy by sending them rain. For this purpose the people of a neighbouring village were coming in procession to a holy hermitage built upon the side of a hill not far from that spot. The strange attire of the disciplinants struck Don Quixote, who, not recollecting what he must often have seen before, imagined it to be some adventure which, as a knight-errant, was reserved for him alone; and he was confirmed in his opinion on seeing an image clothed in black, that they carried with them, and which, he doubted not, was some illustrious lady forcibly borne away by ruffians and miscreants. With all the expedition in his

---

* Persons, either volunteers or hirelings, who march in processions, whipping themselves by way of public penance.

power, he therefore went up to Rozinante, and taking the bridle and buckler from the pommel of the saddle, he bridled him in a trice, and calling to Sancho for his sword, he mounted, braced his target, and in a loud voice said to all that were present, " Now, my worthy companions, ye shall see how important to the world is the profession of chivalry ! now shall ye see, in the restoration of that captive lady to liberty, whether knights-errant are to be valued or not ! "

So saying, he clapped heels to Rozinante (for spurs he had none), and on a hand-gallop (for we nowhere read, in all this faithful history, that Rozinante ever went full speed), he advanced to encounter the disciplinants. The priest, the canon, and the barber in vain endeavoured to stop him ; and in vain did Sancho cry out, " Whither go ye, Signor Don Quixote ? What devils drive you to assault the Catholic faith ? Evil befall me ! do but look—it is a procession of disciplinants, and the lady carried upon the bier is the blessed image of our Holy Virgin : take heed, for this once I am sure you know not what you are about." Sancho wearied himself to no purpose ; for his master was so bent upon an encounter, that he heard not a word ; nor would he have turned back though the king himself had commanded him.

Having reached the procession, he checked Rozinante, who already wanted to rest a little, and in a hoarse and agitated voice cried out, " Stop there, ye who cover your faces—for an evil purpose, I doubt not— stop and listen to me." The bearers of the image stood still, and one of the four ecclesiastics, who sung the litanies, observing the strange figure of Don Quixote, the leanness of Rozinante, and other ludicrous circumstances attending the knight, replied, " Friend, if you have anything to say to us, say it quickly ; for these our brethren are scourging their flesh, and we cannot stay to hear anything that may not be said in two words." " I will say it in one," replied Don Quixote : " you must immediately release that fair lady, whose tears and sorrowful countenance clearly prove that she is carried away against her will, and that you have done her some atrocious injury. I, who was born to redress such wrongs, command you, therefore, not to proceed one step farther until you have given her the liberty she desires and deserves." By these expressions they concluded that Don Quixote must be some whimsical madman, and only laughed at him, which enraged him to such a degree that, without saying another word, he drew his sword and attacked the bearers ; one of whom leaving the burden to his comrades, stepped forward, brandishing the pole on which the bier had been supported ; but it was quickly broken in two by a powerful stroke aimed by the knight, who, however, received instantly such a blow on the shoulder of his sword-arm, that, his buckler being of no avail against rustic strength, he was felled to the ground. Sancho, who had followed him, now called out to the man not to strike again, for he was a poor enchanted knight, who had never done anybody harm in all his life. The peasant forbore, it is true, though not on account of Sancho's appeal, but because he saw his opponent without motion ; and, thinking he had killed him, he hastily tucked up his vest under his girdle, and fled like a deer over the field.

He clapped heels to Rozinante (for spurs he had none), and advanced to encounter the disciplinants.

By this time all Don Quixote's party had come up; and those in the procession, seeing among them troopers of the Holy Brotherhood armed with their cross-bows, began to be alarmed, and drew up in a circle round the image; then lifting up their hoods,* and grasping their whips, and the ecclesiastics their tapers, they waited the assault, determined to defend themselves, or, if possible, offend their aggressors, while Sancho threw himself upon the body of his master, and believing him to be really dead, poured forth the most dolorous lamentations. The alarm of both squadrons was speedily dissipated, as our curate was recognized by one of the ecclesiastics in the procession: and, on hearing from him who Don Quixote was, they all hastened to see whether the poor knight had really suffered a mortal injury or not; when they heard Sancho Panza, with streaming eyes, exclaim, " O flower of chivalry, who by one single stroke hast finished the career of thy well-spent life ! O glory of

---

* The disciplinants wear hoods, that they may not be known, but which they can see through.

thy race, credit and renown of La Mancha, yea, of the whole world, which, by wanting thee, will be overrun with evil-doers, who will no longer fear chastisement for their iniquities! O liberal above all Alexanders, since for eight months' service only thou hast given me the best island that sea doth compass or surround! O thou that wert humble with the haughty and arrogant with the humble, undertaker of dangers, sufferer of affronts, in love without cause, imitator of the good, scourge of the wicked, enemy of the base; in a word, knight-errant— which is all in all!'" Sancho's cries roused Don Quixote, who faintly said, "He who lives absent from thee, sweetest Dulcinea, endures far greater miseries than this! Help, friend Sancho, to place me upon the enchanted car: I am no longer in a condition to press the saddle of Rozinante, for this shoulder is broken to pieces." "That I will do with all my heart, dear sir," answered Sancho; "and let us return to our homes with these gentlemen, who wish you well; and there we can prepare for another sally, that may turn out more profitable." "Thou sayest well, Sancho," answered Don Quixote, "and it will be highly prudent in us to wait until the evil influence of the star which now reigns is passed over." The canon, the priest, and the barber told him they approved his resolution: and the knight being now placed in the waggon, as before, they prepared to depart.

The goatherd took his leave; and the troopers, not being disposed to attend them farther, were discharged. The canon also separated from them, having first obtained a promise from the priest that he would acquaint him with the future fate of Don Quixote. Thus the party now consisted only of the priest, the barber, Don Quixote, and Sancho, with good Rozinante, who bore all accidents as patiently as his master. The waggoner yoked his oxen, and, having accommodated Don Quixote with a truss of hay, they jogged on in the way the priest directed, and at the end of six days reached Don Quixote's village. It was about noon when they made their entrance; and, it being Sunday, all the people were standing about the market-place, through which the waggon passed. Everybody ran to see who was in it, and were not a little surprised when they recognized their townsman; and a boy ran off at full speed with tidings to the housekeeper that he was coming home, lean and pale, stretched out at length in a waggon drawn by oxen. On hearing this, the two good women made the most pathetic lamentations, and renewed their curses against books of chivalry; especially when they saw the poor knight entering the gate.

Upon the news of Don Quixote's arrival, Sancho Panza's wife repaired thither, and on meeting him, her first inquiry was whether the ass had come home well. Sancho told her that he was in a better condition than his master. "The Lord be praised," replied she, "for so great a mercy to me. But tell me, husband, what good have you got by your squireship? Have you brought a petticoat home for me, and shoes for your children?" "I have brought you nothing of that sort, dear wife," quoth Sancho; "but I have got other things of greater consequence." "I am very glad of that," answered the wife: "pray show me your things of greater consequence, friend, for I would fain see them, to gladden my heart, which has been so sad all the long time you have been away." "You shall see them at home, wife," quoth Sancho, " and be satisfied at present; for if it please God that we make another sally in quest of adventures, you will soon see me an earl or governor of an island, and no common one either, but one of the best that is to be had." " Heaven grant it may be so, husband," quoth the wife, " for we have need enough of it. But pray tell me what you mean by islands, for I do not understand you." "Honey is not for the mouth of an ass," answered Sancho : " in good time, wife, you shall see, yea, and admire to hear yourself styled ' ladyship ' by all your vassals." " What do you mean, Sancho, by ladyship, islands, and vassals ? " answered Teresa Panza, for that was the name of Sancho's wife, though they were not of kin, but because it was the custom of La Mancha for the wife to take the husband's name. " Do not be in so much haste, Teresa," said Sancho ; " it is enough that I tell you what is true, so lock up your mouth ; only take this by the way, that there is nothing in the world so pleasant as to be an honourable esquire to a knight-errant and seeker of adventures. To be sure, most of them are not so much to a man's mind as he could wish ; for, as I know by experience, ninety-nine out of a hundred fall out cross and unlucky ; especially when one happens to be tossed in a blanket, or well cudgelled ; yet, for all that, it is a fine thing to go about in expectation of accidents, traversing mountains, searching woods, marching over rocks, visiting castles, lodging in inns, all at pleasure, and the devil a farthing to pay."

While this discourse was passing between Sancho Panza and his wife Teresa, the housekeeper and the niece received Don Quixote, and, after undressing him, they laid him in his old bed, whence he looked at them with eyes askance, not knowing perfectly where he was. Often did the women raise their voices in abuse of all books of chivalry, over-whelming their authors with the bitterest maledictions. His niece was charged by the priest to take great care of him, and to keep a watchful eye that he did not again make his escape, after taking so much pains to get him home. Yet they were full of apprehensions lest they should lose him again as soon as he found himself a little better ; and indeed the event proved that their fears were not groundless.

But the author of this history, though he applied himself with the utmost curiosity and diligence to trace the exploits which Don Quixote performed in his third sally, could get no account of them, at least from any authentic writings ; fame has only left a tradition in La Mancha that Don Quixote, the third time he sallied from home, went to Sara-gossa, and was present at a famous tournament in that city, where he performed deeds worthy of himself. Nor would he have learned any-thing concerning his death, had he not fortunately become acquainted with an aged physician, who had in his custody a leaden box, found, as he said, under the ruins of an ancient hermitage ; in which box was discovered a manuscript, written on parchment, in Gothic characters, but in Castilian verse, containing many of his exploits, and describing the beauty of Dulcinea del Toboso, the form of Rozinante, the fidelity of Sancho Panza, and the burial of Don Quixote himself, with several epitaphs and eulogies on his life and habits. All that could be read, and perfectly made out, are here inserted by the faithful author of this most extraordinary history, who desires no other recompense for the vast labour he has bestowed in searching into the archives of La Mancha, than that this work may find equal favour with other books of knight-errantry: with this he will be quite satisfied, and moreover encouraged to seek after others that may be quite as entertaining, though not so true. The first stanzas written on the parchment which was found in the leaden box were the following:

The Academicians of Argamasilla,
A Town of La Mancha,
On the Life and Death of the Valorous
Don Quixote de la Mancha,
Hoc scripserunt.

MONICONGO, ACADEMICIAN OF ARGAMASILLA, ON THE SEPULTURE
OF DON QUIXOTE.

EPITAPH.

La Mancha's thunberbolt of war,
　　The sharpest wit and loftiest muse,
The arm which from Gaëta far
　　To Catai did its force diffuse;
He who, through love and valour's fire,
　　Outstript great Amadis's fame,
Bid warlike Galaor retire,
　　And silenced Belianis' name:
He who, with helmet, sword, and shield,
　　On Rozinante, steed well known,
Adventures fought in many a field,
　　Lies underneath this frozen stone.

PANIAGUADO, ACADEMICIAN OF ARGAMASILLA, IN PRAISE OF
DULCINEA DEL TOBOSO.

SONNET.

She whom you see, the plump and lusty dame,
　　With high erected chest and vigorous mien,
Was erst th' enamoured knight Don Quixote's flame,
　　The fair Dulcinea, of Toboso queen.

For her, armed cap-à-pie with sword and shield,
　　He trod the sable mountain o'er and o'er;
For her he traversed Montiel's well-known field,
　　And in her service toils unnumbered bore.
Hard fate! that death should crop so fine a flower!
And love o'er such a knight exert his tyrant power!

CAPRICHOSO, A MOST INGENIOUS ACADEMICIAN OF ARGAMASILLA, IN PRAISE OF
DON QUIXOTE'S HORSE ROZINANTE.

SONNET.

On the aspiring adamantine trunk
Of a huge tree, whose root, with slaughter drunk,
Sends forth a scent of war, La Mancha's knight,
Frantic with valour, and returned from fight,
His bloody standard trembling in the air,
Hangs up his glittering armour, beaming fair
With that fine-tempered steel whose edge o'erthrows,
Hacks, hews, confounds, and routs opposing foes.
Unheard-of prowess ! and unheard-of verse !
But art new strains invents, new glories to rehearse.
   If Amadis to Grecia gives renown,
Much more her chief does fierce Bellona crown,
Prizing La Mancha more than Gaul or Greece,
As Quixote triumphs over Amadis.
Oblivion ne'er shall shroud his glorious name,
Whose very horse stands up to challenge fame.
Illustrious Rozinante, wond'rous steed !
Not with more generous pride or mettled speed,
His rider erst Rinaldo's Bayard bore,
Or his mad lord, Orlando's Brilladore.

BURLADOR, THE LITTLE ACADEMICIAN OF ARGAMASILLA, ON
SANCHO PANZA.

SONNET.

See Sancho Panza, view him well,
And let this verse his praises tell.
His body was but small, 't is true,
Yet had a soul as large as two.
No guile he knew, like some before him,
But simple as his mother bore him.
This gentle squire on gentle ass
Went gentle Rozinante's pace,
Following his lord from place to place.
To be an earl he did aspire,
And reason good for such desire ;
But worth, in these ungrateful times,
To envied honour seldom climbs.
Vain mortals ! give your wishes o'er,
And trust the flatterer Hope no more,
Whose promises, whate'er they seem,
End in a shadow or a dream.

CACHIDIABLO, ACADEMICIAN OF ARGAMASILLA, ON THE SEPULTURE
OF DON QUIXOTE.

EPITAPH.

Here lies an evil-errant knight,
  Well bruised in many a fray,
Whose courser, Rozinante hight,
  Long bore him many a way

Close by his loving master's side
Lies booby Sancho Panza,
A trusty squire of courage tried,
And true as ever man saw.

———

TIQUITOC, ACADEMICIAN OF ARGAMASILLA, ON THE SEPULTURE OF
DULCINEA DEL TOBOSO.

Dulcinea, fat and fleshy, lies
Beneath this frozen stone,
But since to frightful death a prize,
Reduced to skin and bone.

Of goodly parentage she came,
And had the lady in her;
She was the great Don Quixote's flame,
But only death could win her.

These were all the verses that were legible; the remainder, being much defaced and worm-eaten, were put into the hands of one of the Academicians, that he might discover their meaning by conjecture, which, after much thought and labour, we are informed he has actually done, and that he intends to publish them, in the hope of Don Quixote's third sally.

Forse altro cantarà con miglior plectro.

PREFACE TO PART II.

——◆——

VERILY, reader, gentle or simple—whatever thou art, with what impatience must thou now be waiting for this Preface!—doubtless prepared to find it full of resentment, railing, and invective against the author of the second Don Quixote—him I mean who, the world says, was begotten in Tordesillas and born in Tarragona. But, in truth, it is not my intention to give thee that satisfaction; for, though injuries are apt to awaken choler in the humblest breast, yet in mine this rule must admit of an exception. Perhaps thou wouldst have me call him ass, madman, and coxcomb: but no; be his own folly his punishment.

There is one thing, however, which I cannot pass over in silence. I am guilty, it seems, of being old; and it is also proved upon me that I have lost my hand! as if I had the power to arrest the progress of time; and that this maim was the effect of some tavern brawl, and not received on the noblest occasion * that past or present times have witnessed, or the future can ever hope to see! If my wounds be disregarded by those who simply look on them, they will be honoured by those who know how they were gained; for a soldier makes a nobler figure dead on the field of battle than alive flying from his enemy; and so firmly fixed am I in this opinion that, could the impossibility be overcome, and I had the power to choose, I would rather be again present in that stupendous action than whole and sound without sharing in its glory. The scars on the front of a brave soldier are stars that direct others to the haven of honour, and create in them a noble emulation. Let it be remembered, too, that books are not composed by the hand, but by the understanding, which is ripened by experience and length of years.

I have also heard that this author calls me envious; and, moreover, in consideration of my ignorance, kindly describes to me what envy is!

---

* The famous sea-fight of Lepanto.

In truth, the only envy of which I am conscious is a noble, virtuous, and holy emulation, which would never dispose me to inveigh against an ecclesiastic; especially against one who holds a dignified rank in the Inquisition; and if he has been influenced by his zeal for the person* to whom he seems to allude, he is utterly mistaken in my sentiments; for I revere that gentleman's genius, and admire his works and his virtuous activity. Nevertheless, I cannot refuse my acknowledgment to this worthy author for his commendation of my novels, which, he says, are good, although more satirical than moral; but how they happen to be good, yet deficient in morality, it would be difficult to show.

Methinks, reader, thou wilt confess that I proceed with much forbearance and modesty, from a feeling that we should not add to the sufferings of the afflicted; and that this gentleman's case must be lamentable, is evident from his not daring to appear in open day: concealing his name and his country, as if some treason or other crime were upon his conscience. But shouldst thou by chance fall into his company, tell him from me that I do not think myself aggrieved; for I well know what the temptations of the devil are, and that one of the greatest is the persuading a man that he can write a book by which he will surely gain both wealth and fame; and, to illustrate the truth of this, pray tell him, in thy pleasant way, the following story:

"A madman once, in Seville, was seized with as whimsical a conceit as ever entered into a madman's brain. He provided himself with a hollow cane, pointed at one end, and whenever he met with a dog in the street or elsewhere, he laid hold of him, set his foot on one of his hinder legs, and seizing the other in his hand, dexterously applied the pointed end of the cane to the dog's posteriors, and blew him up as round as a ball; then giving his inflated body a slap or two with the palm of his hand, he let him go, saying to the bystanders, who were always numerous, 'Well, gentlemen, I suppose you think it an easy matter to blow up a dog?' And you, sir, perhaps, may think it an easy matter to write a book." If this story should not happen to hit his fancy, pray, kind reader, tell him this other, which is likewise of a madman and a dog:

"In the city of Cordova lived a maniac, whose custom was to walk about the streets with a large stone upon his head, of no inconsiderable weight; and wherever he met with any careless cur, he edged

---

* Lope de Vega.

slily towards him, and when quite close let the stone fall plump upon his body; whereupon the dog, in great wrath, limped away, barking and howling, for more than three streets' length, without once looking behind him. Now it happened that, among other dogs, he met with one that belonged to a cap-maker, who valued him mightily : down went the stone, and hit him exactly on the head ; the poor animal cried out ; his master, seeing the act, was enraged, and, catching up his measuring-yard, fell upon the madman, and left him with scarcely a whole bone in his skin : at every blow venting his fury in reproaches, saying, ' Dog ! rogue ! rascal ! What ! maltreat my dog ! a spaniel ! Did you not see, barbarian ! that my dog was a spaniel ? ' and after repeating the word ' spaniel ' very often, he dismissed the culprit, beaten to a jelly. The madman took his correction in silence, and walked off; nor did he show himself again in the market-place till more than a month afterwards, when he returned to his former amusement, with a still greater stone upon his head. It was observed, however, that on coming up to a dog, he first carefully surveyed it from head to tail, and not daring to let the stone fall, he said, ' 'Ware spaniel !—this won't do.' In short, whatever dog he met with — terrier, mastiff, or hound — they were all spaniels ; and so great was his dread of committing another mistake, that he never ventured to let fall his slab again." Thus warned, perhaps, our historian may think it necessary, before he again lets fall the ponderous weight of his wit, to look and examine where it is likely to drop.

Tell him also, that as to his threatening, by his counterfeit wares, to deprive me of my expected gain, I value it not a rush, and will only answer him from the famous interlude of Parendenga—" Long live my lord and master, and Heaven be with us all ! " Long live the great Count de Lemos ; whose well-known liberality supports me under all the strokes of adverse fortune ; and all honour and praise to the eminent bounty of his grace the Archbishop of Toledo, Bernardo de Sandoval ! and let them write against me as many books as there are letters in the rhymes of Mingo Rebulgo. These two nobles, unsought by adulation on my part, but merely of their own goodness, have taken upon them to patronise and favour me ; wherefore I esteem myself happier and richer than if fortune, by her ordinary means, had placed me on her highest pinnacle. Such honour the meritorious, not the vicious, may aspire to, although oppressed by poverty. The noble mind may be clouded by adversity, but cannot be wholly concealed ; for true merit shines by a light of its own, and, glimmering through the rents and crannies of indigence, is perceived, respected, and honoured by the generous and the great.

More than this, reader, thou needst not say to him; nor will I say more to thee, except merely observing for thy information, that this Second Part of Don Quixote, here offered to thee, is cut by the same hand, and out of the same piece, as the First Part; and that herein I present thee with Don Quixote whole and entire; having placed him in his grave at full length, and fairly dead, that no one may presume to expose him to new adventures, since he has achieved enough already. It is sufficient that his ingenious follies have been recorded by a writer of credit, who has resolved to take up the subject no more, for we may be surfeited by too much of what is good, and scarcity gives a relish to what is only indifferent.

I had forgotten to tell thee that thou mayest soon expect the "Persiles," which I have nearly complete, and also the second part of the "Galatea."

SECOND PART.

BOOK I.

CHAPTER 1.

Of what passed between the priest, the barber, and Don Quixote, concerning his indisposition.

CID HAMET BENENGELI relates in the Second Part of this history, containing the third sally of Don Quixote, that the priest and the barber refrained during a whole month from seeing him, lest they should revive in his mind the remembrance of things past. However, they paid frequent visits to the niece and housekeeper, charging them to take great care of him, and to give him good nourishing diet, as that would be salutary to his heart and his brain, whence all the mischief proceeded. The good women assured them of their continual care of the patient, and said they occasionally observed in him symptoms of returning reason. The priest and the barber were greatly pleased to hear this, and congratulated themselves on the success of the scheme they had adopted of bringing him home enchanted in the ox-waggon, as it is related in the last chapter of the First Part of this no less great than accurate history. They resolved, therefore, to visit him and make trial of his amendment: at the same time, thinking it scarcely possible that his cure could be complete, they agreed not to touch upon the subject of knight-errantry, lest they might open a wound which must yet be so tender.

They found him sitting on his bed, clad in a waistcoat of green baize, with a red Toledo cap on his head, and so lean and shrivelled that he looked like a mummy. He received them with much politeness, and when they inquired after his health, he answered them in a very sensible manner, and with much elegance of expression. In the course of their conversation they touched upon matters of state and forms of government, correcting this abuse and condemning that, reforming one custom and exploding another; each of the three setting himself up for a perfect legislator, a modern Lycurgus, or a spick-and-span-new Solon; and, by their joint efforts, they seemed to have clapped the commonwealth into a forge, and hammered it into quite a new shape. Don Quixote delivered himself with so much good sense upon every subject they had touched upon, that the two examiners were inclined to think that he was now really in full possession of all his mental faculties. The niece and the housekeeper were present at the conversation, and hearing from their master such proofs of a sound mind, thought they could never sufficiently thank Heaven. The priest, changing his former purpose of not touching upon matters of chivalry, was now resolved to put the question of his amendment fairly to the test: he therefore mentioned, among other things, some intelligence lately brought from court, that the Turk was advancing with a powerful fleet, and that, his object being unknown, it was impossible to say where the storm would burst; that all Christendom was in great alarm, and that the king had already provided for the security of Naples, Sicily, and the island of Malta. To this Don Quixote replied, " His majesty has acted with great prudence in providing in time for the defence of his dominions, that he may not be taken by surprise; but, if my counsel might be taken, I would advise him to a measure which probably never yet entered into his majesty's mind." On hearing this, the priest said within himself, " Heaven defend thee, poor Don Quixote! for methinks thou art about to fall from the summit of thy madness into the depth of folly!" The barber, who had made the same reflection, now asked Don Quixote what the measure was which he thought would be so advantageous; though, in all probability, it was like the impertinent advice usually given to princes. " Mine, Mr. Shaver," answered Don Quixote, "shall not be impertinent, but to the purpose." " I mean no offence," replied the barber; " only experience has shown that all or most of the projects so offered to his majesty are either impracticable, absurd, or prejudicial to himself or his kingdom." " True," answered Don Quixote; " but mine is neither impracticable nor absurd; but the most easy, the most just, and also the most reasonable and expeditious that ever entered the mind of a projector." " Signor Don Quixote," quoth the priest, " you keep us too long in suspense." " I do not choose," replied Don Quixote, "that it should be told here now, that another may carry it by daybreak to the lords of the privy-council, and thereby intercept the reward which is due only to me." " I give you my word," said the barber, " here and before Heaven, that I will not reveal what your worship shall say, either to king, or to rook, or to any mortal man —an oath which I learned from the romance of " The Priest," where he gives the king information of the thief that robbed him of the hundred pistoles and his ambling mule." " I know not the history," said Don Quixote; " but I presume the oath is a good one, because I am persuaded Master Barber is an honest man." " Though he were not," said the priest, " I will pledge myself for him, and engage, under any penalty you please, that he shall be as silent as the dumb on this affair." " And who will be bound for your reverence, Master Priest?" said Don Quixote. " My profession," answered the priest, "which enjoins secresy as an indispensable duty." " Body of me!" cried Don Quixote; " has his majesty anything to do but to issue a proclamation ordering all the knights-errant who are now wandering about Spain, to repair on an

They resolved to visit him, and make trial of his amendment. He received them with much politeness.

appointed day to court? If not more than half a dozen came, there might be one of that number able, with his single arm, to destroy the whole power of the Turk. Pray, gentlemen, be attentive, and listen to me. Is it anything new for a single knight-errant to defeat an army of two hundred thousand men, as if they had all but one throat or were made of pastry? How many examples of such prowess does history supply! If, in an evil hour for me (I will not say for any other), the famous Don Belianis, or some one of the numerous race of Amadis de Gaul, were in being at this day to confront the Turk, in good faith I would not farm his winnings! But God will protect His people, and provide some one, if not as strong as the knights-errant of old, at least not inferior to them in courage. Heaven knows my meaning. I say no more!" "Alas!" exclaimed the niece at this instant; "may I perish if my uncle has not a mind to turn knight-errant again!" Whereupon Don Quixote said, "A knight-errant I will live and die; and let the Turk come, down or up, when he pleases, and with all the forces he can raise—once more I say, Heaven knows my meaning!" "Gentlemen," said the barber, "give me leave to tell you a short story of what happened once in Seville; for it comes so pat to the purpose that I cannot help giving it to you." Don Quixote and the priest signified their consent, and the others being willing to hear, he began thus:

"A certain man being deranged in his intellects, was placed by his relations in the madhouse of Seville. He had taken his degrees in the canon law at Ossuna; but, had it been at Salamanca, many are of opinion he would nevertheless have been mad. This graduate, after some years' confinement, took it into his head that he was quite in his right senses, and therefore wrote to the archbishop, beseeching him, with great earnestness and apparently with much reason, that he would be pleased to deliver him from that miserable state of confinement in which he lived, since, through the mercy of God, he had regained his senses; adding that his relations, in order to enjoy part of his estate, kept him still there, and, in spite of the clearest evidence, would insist upon his being mad as long as he lived. The archbishop, prevailed upon by the many sensible epistles he received from him, sent one of his chaplains to the keeper of the madhouse to inquire into the truth of what the licentiate had alleged, and also to talk with him, and if it appeared that he was in his senses, to set him at liberty. The chaplain accordingly went to the rector, who assured him that the man was still insane; for though he sometimes talked very sensibly, it was seldom for any length of time without betraying his derangement, as he would certainly find on conversing with him. The chaplain determined to make the trial, and, during the conversation of more than an hour, could perceive no symptom of incoherence in his discourse; on the contrary, he spoke with so much sedateness and judgment that the chaplain could not entertain a doubt of the sanity of his intellects. Among other things, he assured him that the keeper was bribed by his relations to persist in reporting him to be deranged; so that his large estate was his great misfortune, to enjoy which his enemies had recourse to fraud, and pretended to doubt of the mercy of Heaven in restoring him from the condition of a brute to that of a man. In short, he talked so plausibly that he made the rector appear venal and corrupt, his relations unnatural, and himself so discreet that the chaplain determined to take him immediately to the archbishop, that he might be satisfied he had done right. With this resolution the good chaplain desired the keeper of the house to restore to him the clothes which he wore when he was first put under his care. The keeper again desired him to beware what he did, since he might be assured that the licentiate was still insane; but the chaplain was not to be moved either by his cautions or entreaties; and as he acted by order of the archbishop, the keeper was compelled to obey him. The licentiate put on his new clothes, and now finding himself rid of his lunatic attire, and habited like a rational

"I, who am the thundering Jove, and grasp in my hands the flaming bolts with which I might instantly destroy the world!"

creature, he entreated the chaplain, for charity's sake, to permit him to take leave of his late companions in affliction. Being desirous of seeing the lunatics who were confined in that house, the chaplain, with several other persons, followed him upstairs, and heard him accost a man who lay stretched in a cell, outrageously mad, though just then composed and quiet. 'Brother,' said he to him, 'have you any commands for me? for I am going to return to my own house, God having been pleased, of His infinite goodness and mercy, without any desert of mine, to restore me to my senses. I am now sound and well, for with God nothing is impossible: put your whole trust and confidence in Him, and He will doubtless restore you also. I will take care to send you some choice food; and fail not to eat it, for I have reason to believe, from my own experience, that all our distraction proceeds from empty stomachs and brains filled with wind. Take heart, then, my friend, take heart;

for despondence under misfortune impairs our health and hastens our death.' This discourse was overheard by another madman, the tenant of an opposite cell, who, rising from an old mat, whereon he had been lying stark naked, asked who it was that talked of going away restored to his senses. 'It is I, brother, that am going,' answered the licentiate; 'for, thanks to Heaven, my stay here is no longer necessary.' 'Take heed, friend, what you say,' replied the maniac; 'let not the devil delude you: stir not a foot, but keep where you are, and you will spare yourself the trouble of being brought back.' 'I know,' answered the other, 'that I am perfectly well, and shall have no more occasion to visit the station-churches.'* 'You well, truly?' said the madman; 'we shall soon see that. Farewell! but I swear by Jupiter, whose majesty I represent on earth, that for this single offence of setting thee at large, and pronouncing thee to be in thy sound senses, I am determined to inflict such a signal punishment on this city, that the memory thereof shall endure for ever and ever. And knowest thou not, pitiful fellow, that I have the power to do it? I, who am the thundering Jove, and grasp in my hands the flaming bolts with which I might instantly destroy the world!—but, remitting that punishment, I will chastise their folly by closing the flood-gates of heaven, so that no rain shall fall upon this city or the surrounding country for three years, reckoning from this very day and hour on which my vengeance is denounced. You at liberty!—you recovered, and in your right senses, and I here a madman, distempered, and in bonds!—I will no more rain than I will hang myself.' This rhapsody was heard by all present; and our licentiate, turning to the chaplain, 'My good sir,' said he, seizing both his hands, 'regard not his foolish threats, but be perfectly easy; for should he, being Jupiter, withhold his rain, I, who am Neptune, the god of water, can dispense as much as I please, and whenever there shall be occasion.' To which the chaplain answered, 'Nevertheless, Signor Neptune, it would not be well at present to provoke Signor Jupiter; therefore, I beseech you, remain where you are, and when we have more leisure and a better opportunity, we will return for you.' The rector and the rest of the party laughed, and put the chaplain quite out of countenance. In short, the licentiate was immediately disrobed, and he remained in confinement; and there is an end of my story."

"This, then, Master Barber," said Don Quixote, "is the story which was so much to the purpose that you could not forbear telling it? Ah, Signor Cut-beard! Signor Cut-beard! he must be blind indeed who cannot see through a sieve! Is it possible you should be ignorant that comparisons of all kinds, whether as to sense, courage, beauty, or rank, are always offensive? I, Master Barber, am not Neptune, god of the waters, nor do I set myself up for a wise man; all I aim at is to convince the world of its error in not reviving those happy times when the order of knight-errantry flourished. But this our degenerate age deserves not

---

* Certain churches with indulgences, appointed to be visited either for pardon of sins or for procuring blessings.

to enjoy so great a blessing as that which was the boast of former ages, when knights-errant took upon themselves the defence of kingdoms, the protection of orphans, the relief of damsels, the chastisement of the haughty, and the reward of the humble. The knights of these times rustle in damask and brocade, rather than in coats of mail. Where is the knight now who will lie in the open field, exposed to the rigour of the heavens, in complete armour from head to foot? or, leaning on his lance, take a short nap without quitting his stirrups, like the knights-errant of old times? You have no one now who, issuing out of a forest, ascends some mountain, and thence traverses a barren and desert shore of the sea, commonly stormy and tempestuous; and, finding on the beach a small skiff, without oars, sail, mast, or tackle of any kind, he boldly throws himself into it, committing himself to the implacable billows of the deep ocean, which now mount him up to the skies, and then cast him down to the abyss; and he, opposing his courage to the irresistible hurricane, suddenly finds himself above three thousand leagues from the place where he embarked; and, leaping on the remote and unknown shore, encounters accidents worthy to be recorded, not on parchment, but on brass. But in these days sloth triumphs over activity, idleness over labour, vice over virtue, arrogance over bravery, and the theory over the practice of arms, which only existed and flourished with knights-errant in those ages of gold. For, tell me, I pray, where was there so much valour and virtue to be found as in Amadis de Gaul? Who was more discreet than Palmerin of England? Who more affable and obliging than Tirante the White? Who more gallant than Lisuarte of Greece? Who gave or received more cuts and slashes than Don Belianis? Who was more intrepid than Perion of Gaul? Who more enterprising than Felixmarte of Hyrcania? Who more sincere than Esplandian? Who more daring than Don Cirongilio of Thrace? Who more brave than Rodamonte? Who more prudent than King Sobrino? Who more intrepid than Rinaldo? Who more invincible than Orlando? And who more gallant and courteous than Ruggierio, from whom, according to Turpin's Cosmography, the present dukes of Ferrara are descended? All these and others that I could name, Master Priest, were knights-errant, and the light of chivalry; and such as these are the men I would advise his majesty to employ. He then would be well served, a vast expense would be spared, and the Turk might go tear his beard for very madness. So now I will stay at home, since the chaplain does not fetch me out; and, if Jupiter is determined to withhold his rain, here am I, who will rain whenever I think proper—Goodman Basin will see that I understand him."

"In truth, Signor Don Quixote," said the barber, "I meant no harm in what I said; therefore your worship ought not to take it amiss." "Whether I ought or not," said Don Quixote, "is best known to myself." "Well," said the priest, "though I have yet scarcely spoken, I should be very glad to relieve my conscience of a scruple which has been started by what Signor Don Quixote just now said." "You may command me, Signor Curate, in such matters," answered Don

Quixote; " out, then, with your scruple, for there can be no peace with a scrupulous conscience." " With this license, then," said the curate, " I must tell you that I can by no means persuade myself that the multitude of knights-errant your worship has mentioned were really and truly persons of flesh and blood existing in the world; on the contrary, I imagine that the accounts given of them are all fictions and dreams, invented by men awake, or, to speak more properly, half asleep." " This is a common mistake," answered Don Quixote, " which I have, upon sundry occasions and in many companies, endeavoured to correct. Sometimes I have failed in my attempts, at other times succeeded, being founded on the basis of truth; for I can almost say these eyes have seen Amadis de Gaul, who was tall of stature, of a fair complexion, with a well-set beard, though black; his aspect between mild and stern; a man of few words, not easily provoked, and soon pacified. And as I have described Amadis, so, methinks, I could paint and delineate every knight-errant recorded in all the histories in the world. For I feel such confidence in the accuracy of their historians, that I find it easy, from their exploits and character, to form a good philosophical guess at their features, their complexions, and their stature." " Pray, Signor Don Quixote," quoth the barber, " what size do you think the giant Morgante might have been?" " As to the matter of giants," answered Don Quixote, " though it has been a controverted point whether they really existed or not, the Holy Scriptures, which cannot deviate a tittle from truth, prove their reality in the history of that huge Philistine Goliath, who was seven cubits and a half high—a prodigious stature! Besides, in the island of Sicily there have been found thigh and shoulder-bones so large that it is evident those to whom they belonged were giants, tall as lofty steeples, which may be ascertained beyond all doubt by the rules of geometry. Nevertheless, I cannot precisely tell you what were the dimensions of Morgante, although I am inclined to believe that he was not extremely tall; because I find in the history wherein his achievements are particularly mentioned, that he often slept under a roof; and since he found a house which could contain him, it is plain he was not himself of an immeasurable size." " That is true," quoth the priest, who, being amused with his solemn extravagance, asked his opinion of the persons of Rinaldo of Montalvan, Orlando, and the rest of the twelve peers of France, since they were all knights-errant. " Of Rinaldo," answered Don Quixote, " I dare boldly affirm, he was broad-faced, of a ruddy complexion, rolling and somewhat prominent eyes; punctilious, choleric to an excess, and a friend to robbers and profligates. Of Roldan, or Rotolando, or Orlando (for history gives him all these names), I believe, and will maintain, that he was of middle stature, broad-shouldered, rather bandy-legged, brown-complexioned, carroty-bearded, hairy-bodied, threatening in aspect, sparing in speech, yet courteous and well-bred." " If Orlando," replied the priest, " was not more comely than you have described him, no wonder that my lady Angelica the Fair disdained and forsook him for the grace, sprightliness, and gallantry of the smooth-faced little Moor; and she was discreet in preferring the softness of Medora to the roughness of Orlando." "That Angelica, Master Curate," replied Don Quixote, "was a light, wanton, and capricious damsel, and left the world as full of the fame of her folly as of her beauty. She slighted a thousand noble cavaliers, a thousand valiant and wise admirers, and took up with a paltry beardless page, without estate, and with no other reputation than what he acquired from his grateful fidelity to his friend. Even the great extoller of her beauty, the famous Ariosto, either not daring or not caring to celebrate what befell this lady after her low intrigue, the subject not being over-delicate, left her with these verses:

> " ' Another bard may sing in better strain,
> How she Cataya's sceptre did obtain.'

Poets are called *vates*, that is to say, ' diviners;' and certainly these lines were prophetic; for since that time a famous Andalusian poet * has bewailed and sung her tears, and her beauty has been celebrated by a Castilian poet † of extraordinary merit." "And pray tell me, Signor Don Quixote," said the barber, "among many who have sung her praises, has no poet written a satire upon this Lady Angelica?" "I verily believe," answered Don Quixote, "that if Orlando or Sacripante had been poets, they would long ago have settled that account; for it is not uncommon with poets, disdained or rejected by their mistresses, to retaliate by satires and lampoons—a species of revenge certainly unworthy a generous spirit. But hitherto I have not met with any defamatory verses against the Lady Angelica, although she was the author of so much mischief in the world." "Marvellous, indeed!" said the priest. At this moment they were interrupted by a noise in the courtyard; and hearing the niece and housekeeper vociferating aloud, they hastened to learn the cause.

CHAPTER II.

Which treats of the notable quarrel between Sancho Panza and Don Quixote's niece and housekeeper; with other pleasant occurrences.

LOOKING out of the window, Don Quixote, the priest, and the barber saw the niece and housekeeper engaged in defending the door against Sancho Panza, who had come to pay his master a visit. "Fellow, get home!" said one of them, "what have you to do here? It is by you our master is led astray, and carried rambling about the country like a vagabond." "Thou devilish housekeeper!" retorted Sancho, "it is I that am led astray, and carried rambling up and down the highways; and it was your master that led me this dance—so there you are quite

---

* Louis Barahona de Soto.　　　† Lope de Vega.

mistaken. He tempted me from home with promises of an island, which I still hope for." "May the cursed islands choke thee, wretch!" answered the niece; "and pray, what are islands? Are they anything eatable?—glutton, cormorant, as thou art!" "They are not to be eaten," replied Sancho, "but governed; and are better things than any four cities, or four justiceships at court." "For all that," said the housekeeper, "you shall not come in here, you bag of mischief and bundle of roguery! Get you home, and govern there; go, plough and cart, and do not trouble your silly pate about islands!" The priest and the barber were highly diverted at this dialogue; but Don Quixote, fearing lest Sancho should blunder out something unseasonably, and touch upon certain points not advantageous to his reputation, ordered the women to hold their peace, and let him in. Sancho entered, and the priest and the barber took their leave of Don Quixote, now quite despairing of his cure, seeing that he was more intoxicated than ever with knight-errantry. "You will see, neighbour," said the curate, as they walked away, "our friend will soon take another flight." "No doubt of it," said the barber; "yet I think the credulity of the squire still more extraordinary: it seems impossible to drive that same island out of his head." "Heaven help them!" cried the priest. "However, let us watch their motions: the knight and the squire seem both to be cast in the same mould, and the madness of the one without the folly of the other would not be worth a rush." "I should like to know what they are now conferring about," said the barber. "We shall soon hear that from the niece or housekeeper," replied the priest; "for, I lay my life, they will not refrain from listening."

Don Quixote having shut himself up in his chamber with Sancho, he said to him, "It concerns me much, Sancho, that thou wilt persist in saying that I enticed thee from thy home. How! did we not both leave our homes together, journey together, and were both exposed to the same fortune? If thou wert once tossed in a blanket, I have only had the advantage of thee, in being a hundred times exposed to hard blows." "That is but reasonable," answered Sancho; "for, as your worship says, 'misfortunes belong more properly to knights-errant than to their squires.'" "Thou art mistaken, Sancho," said Don Quixote; "for, according to the saying, *Quando caput dolet,* &c." "I understand no other language than my own," replied Sancho. "I mean," said Don Quixote, "that when the head aches, all the members ache also; and therefore I, being thy lord and master, am thy head, and thou, being my servant, art a portion of me; and therefore, whatever evil I suffer must be felt by thee, as thy sufferings likewise affect me." "And so it should be," quoth Sancho; "but when I, as a member, suffered in the blanket, my head stood on t' other side of the pales, seeing me tossed in the air, without taking the smallest share in my pain, though, as the members are bound to grieve at the ills of the head, the head should have done the like for them." "Wouldst thou then insinuate, Sancho," replied Don Quixote, "that I was not grieved when I saw thee tossed in the air? If that be thy meaning, be assured

"For all that," said the housekeeper, "you shall not come in here, you bag of mischief and bundle of roguery!"

thou art deceived; for I felt more at that time in my mind than thou didst in thy body. But let us dismiss this subject at present; for a time will come when we may set this matter to rights. And now tell me, friend Sancho, what do they say of me in the village? What opinion do the common people entertain of me? What think the gentlemen and the cavaliers? What is said of my prowess, of my exploits, and of my courteous demeanour? What say they to the design I have formed of reviving the long-forgotten order of chivalry? In short, Sancho, I would have thee tell me whatever thou hast heard concerning these matters; and this thou must do without adding to the good or omitting the evil, for it is the part of faithful vassals to tell their lords the truth in its native simplicity, neither embellished by adulation nor withheld out of any idle delicacy. And let me tell thee, Sancho, that if the naked truth could reach the ears of princes without the disguise of flattery, we should see happier days, and former ages would be deemed as iron in comparison with ours, which would then be truly termed the Golden Age. Now remember this, Sancho, and give me an ingenuous and faithful account of what thou knowest concerning these matters."

"That I will, with all my heart, sir," answered Sancho, "on condition that your worship be not angry at what I say, since you desire to have the truth just as it came to me." " I will in nowise be angry," replied Don Quixote; "speak, then, freely, Sancho, and without any circumlocution."

"First ana foremost, then," said Sancho, "the common people take your worship for a downright madman, and me for no less a fool. The gentry say that, not content to keep to your own proper rank of a gentleman, you call yourself Don, and set up for a knight, with no more than a paltry vineyard and a couple of acres of land. The cavaliers say they do not choose to be vied with by those country squires who clout their shoes, and take up the fallen stitches of their black stockings with green silk." " That," said Don Quixote, " is no reflection upon me; for I always go well clad, and my apparel is never patched; a little torn it may be, but more by the fretting of my armour than by time." " As to your valour, courtesy, achievements, and undertakings," continued Sancho, "there are many different opinions. Some say you are mad, but humourous; others, valiant, but unfortunate; others, courteous, but absurd; and thus they pull us to pieces, till they leave neither your worship nor me a single feather upon our backs." " Take notice, Sancho," said Don Quixote, " that, wherever virtue exists in any eminent degree, it is always persecuted. Few or none of the famous men of antiquity escaped the calumny of their malicious contemporaries. Julius Cæsar, a most courageous, prudent, and valiant general, was charged with being too ambitious, and also with want of personal cleanliness. Alexander, whose exploits gained him the surname of Great, is said to have been addicted to drunkenness. Hercules, who performed so many labours, is accused of being lascivious and effeminate. Don Galaor, brother of Amadis de Gaul, was taxed with being quarrelsome, and his brother with being a whimperer. Amidst so many aspersions cast on the worthy, mine, O Sancho, may very well pass, if they are no more than thou hast mentioned." " Body of my father! there's the rub, sir," exclaimed Sancho. " What, then, is there more yet behind?" said Don Quixote. " Why, all the things I have told you are tarts and cheesecakes to what remains behind," replied Sancho; " but if your worship would have all, to the very dregs, I will bring one hither presently who can tell you everything, without missing a tittle; for last night the son of Bartholomew Carrasco returned from his studies at Salamanca, where he has taken his bachelor's degree; and when I went to bid him welcome home, he told me that the history of your worship was already printed in books, under the title of 'Don Quixote de la Mancha;' and he says it mentions me too by my very name of Sancho Panza, and also the Lady Dulcinea del Toboso, and several other private matters which passed between us two only; insomuch that I crossed myself out of pure amazement, to think how the historian who wrote it should come to know them." " Depend upon it, Sancho," said Don Quixote, " that the author of this our history must be some sage enchanter; for nothing is concealed from them." " A sage, and an enchanter?" quoth Sancho: " why, the bachelor Sampson

Carrasco says the author of this story is called Cid Hamet Berengena."*
"That is a Moorish name," answered Don Quixote. "It may be so,"
replied Sancho; "for I have heard that your Moors, for the most part,
are lovers of berengenas." "Sancho," said Don Quixote, "thou must
be mistaken in the surname of that same Cid, which, in Arabic,
signifies 'a lord.'" "That may be," answered Sancho, "but if your
worship would like to see him, I will run and fetch him." "Thou wilt
give me singular pleasure, friend," said Don Quixote; "for I am
surprised at what thou hast told me, and shall be impatient till I am
informed of every particular." "I will go for him directly," said
Sancho; then, leaving his master, he went to seek the bachelor, with
whom he soon returned, and a most delectable conversation then passed
between them.

CHAPTER III.

*Of the pleasant conversation which passed between Don Quixote, Sancho
Panza, and the bachelor Sampson Carrasco.*

Don Quixote, full of thought, was impatient for the return of
Sancho and the bachelor Carrasco, anxious to hear about the printed
accounts of himself, yet scarcely believing that such a history could
really be published, since the blood of the enemies he had slain was
still reeking on his sword-blade; indeed, he did not see how it was
possible that his high feats of arms should be already in print. However, he finally concluded that some sage, either friend or enemy, by
art-magic, had sent them to the press: if a friend, to proclaim and
extol them above the most signal achievements of knights-errant; if an
enemy, to annihilate and sink them below the meanest that ever were
written even of a squire: though again he recollected that the feats of
squires were never recorded. At any rate he was certain, if it should
prove the fact that such a history was really extant, being that of a
knight-errant, it could not be otherwise than lofty, illustrious, magnificent, and true. This thought afforded him some comfort, but he lost it
again on considering that the author was a Moor, as it appeared from
the name of Cid, and that no truth could be expected from Moors, who
are all impostors, liars, and visionaries. He also felt much inquietude
lest the author might have treated his passion with indelicacy, and
thereby offend the immaculate purity of his lady Dulcinea del Toboso:
he hoped, however, he might find a faithful delineation of his own
constancy and the decorum he had ever inviolably preserved towards
her; slighting, for her sake, queens, empresses, and damsels of all
degrees, and resisting the most violent temptations. While he was
agitated by these and a thousand other fancies, Sancho returned,

---

* Sancho mistakes berengena, a species of fruit, for Benengeli.

accompanied by the bachelor, who was received with all possible courtesy

This bachelor, though Sampson by name, was no giant in person, but a little mirth-loving man, with a good understanding; about twenty-four years of age, of a pale complexion, round-faced, flat-nosed, and wide-mouthed : all indicating humour and native relish for jocularity, which, indeed, showed itself when, on approaching Don Quixote, he threw himself upon his knees, and said to him, " Signor Don Quixote de la Mancha, allow me the honour of kissing your illustrious hand, for by the habit of St. Peter, which I wear—though I have yet taken only the four first degrees towards holy orders—your worship is one of the most famous knights-errant that hath ever been or shall be upon the whole circumference of the earth ! A blessing light on Cid Hamet Benengeli, who has recorded the history of your mighty deeds ! and blessings upon blessings light on that ingenious scribe whose laudable curiosity was the cause of its being translated out of Arabic into our vulgar Castilian, for the profit and amusement of all mankind ! " Don Quixote, having raised him from the ground, said to him, " It is true, then, that my history is really published to the world, and that it was written by a Moor and a sage ? " " So true it is, sir," said Sampson, " that I verily believe there are, at this very day, above twelve thousand copies published of that history : witness Portugal, Barcelona, and Valencia, where they were printed ; and it is said to be now printing at Antwerp—indeed, I prophesy that no nation or language will be without a translation of it." " There cannot be a more legitimate source of gratification to a virtuous and distinguished man," said Don Quixote, " than to have his good name celebrated during his lifetime, and circulated over different nations : I say his good name, for if it were otherwise than good, death, in any shape, would be preferable." " As to high reputation and a good name," said the bachelor, " your worship bears the palm over all past knights-errant ; for the Moor in the Arabian language, and the Castilian in his translation, have both taken care to paint to the life that gallant deportment which distinguishes you, that greatness of soul in confronting dangers, that patience in adversity, that fortitude in suffering, that modesty and continence in love, so truly Platonic, as that subsisting between you and my lady Donna Dulcinea del Toboso."

Sancho here interposed, saying, " I never heard my lady Dulcinea called Donna before, but only plain Dulcinea del Toboso ; so that here the history is already mistaken." " That objection is of no importance," answered Carrasco. " No, certainly," replied Don Quixote ; " but pray tell me, Signor Bachelor, on which of my exploits do they lay the greatest stress in that same history ? " " As to that matter," said the bachelor, " opinions vary according to the difference of tastes. Some are for the adventure of the windmills, which your worship took for so many Briareuses and giants ; others prefer that of the fulling-mills : one cries up for the two armies which turned out to be flocks of sheep ; another for the dead body carrying for interment to Segovia. Some maintain that the affair of the galley-slaves is the flower of all; while others will have it that none can be compared to that of the two Benedictine giants, and the combat with the valorous Biscayan." "Pray tell me, Signor Bachelor," quoth Sancho, "has it got, among the rest, the affair of the Yanguesian carriers, when our good Rozinante was tempted to go astray?" "The sage," answered Sampson, "has omitted nothing—he minutely details everything, even to the capers Sancho cut in the blanket." "I cut no capers in the blanket," answered Sancho; "in the air I own I did, and not much to my liking." "There is no history of human affairs, I conceive," said Don Quixote, "which is not full of reverses, and none more than those of chivalry." "Nevertheless," replied the bachelor, "some who have read the history say they should have been better pleased if the authors of it had forborne to enumerate all the buffetings endured by Signor Don Quixote in his different encounters." "Therein," quoth Sancho, "consists the truth of the history." "They might, indeed, as well have omitted them," said Don Quixote, "since there is no necessity for recording actions which are prejudicial to the hero without being essential to the history. It is not to be supposed that Æneas was in all his actions so pure as Virgil represents him, nor Ulysses so uniformly prudent as he is described by Homer." "True," replied Sampson; "but it is one thing to write as a poet, and another to write as a historian. The poet may say or sing, not as things were, but as they ought to have been; but the historian must pen them, not as they ought to have been, but as they really were, without adding to or diminishing aught from the truth." "Well, then," said Sancho, "if this Signor Moor is so fond of telling the truth, and my master's rib-roastings are all set down, I suppose mine are not forgotten; for they never took measure of his worship's shoulders, but at the same time they contrived to get the length and breadth of my whole body. But why should I wonder at that, since, as this same master of mine says, the members must share the fate of the head?" "Sancho, thou art an arch rogue," replied Don Quixote, "and, in faith, upon some occasions, hast no want of memory." "Though I wanted ever so much to forget what my poor body has suffered," quoth Sancho, "the tokens that are still fresh on my ribs would not let me." "Peace, Sancho," said Don Quixote, "and let Signor Bachelor proceed, that I may know what is further said of me in the history." "And of me too," quoth Sancho, "for I hear that I am one of the principal parsons in it." "*Persons*, not parsons, friend Sancho," quoth Sampson. "What, have we another corrector of words?" quoth Sancho: "if we are to go on at this rate, we shall make but slow work of it." "As sure as I live, Sancho," answered the bachelor, "you are the second person of the history: nay, there are those who had rather hear you talk than the finest fellow of them all; though there are also some who charge you with being too credulous in expecting the government of that island promised you by Signor Don Quixote, here present." "There is still sunshine on the wall," quoth Don Quixote; "and when Sancho is more advanced in age, with the experience that years bestow, he will be better qualified to be a governor than he is at present." " 'Fore Gad! sir," quoth Sancho, " if I am not fit to govern an island at these years, I shall be no better able at the age of Methusalem. The mischief of it is, that the said island sticks somewhere else, and not in my want of a head-piece to govern it." " Recommend the matter to God, Sancho," said Don Quixote, " and all will be well—perhaps better than thou mayest think; for not a leaf stirs on the tree without His permission." " That is very true," quoth Sampson; " and if it please God, Sancho will not want a thousand islands to govern, much less one." " I have seen governors ere now," quoth Sancho, " who, in my opinion, do not come up to the sole of my shoe ; and yet they are called ' your lordship,' and eat their victuals upon plate." " Those are not governors of islands," replied Sampson, " but of other governments more manageable ; for those who govern islands must at least understand grammar." " Gramercy for that !" quoth Sancho; " it is all Greek to me, for I know nothing of the matter; so let us leave the business of governments in the hands of God, and let Him dispose of me in the way that I may best serve Him. But I am mightily pleased, Signor Bachelor Sampson Carrasco, that the author of the history has not spoken ill of me ; for, upon the faith of a trusty squire, had he said anything of me unbecoming an old Christian, as I am, the deaf should have heard it." " That would be working miracles," answered Sampson. " Miracles or no miracles," quoth Sancho, " people should take heed what they say and write of other folks, and not set anything down that comes uppermost."

" One of the faults found with this history," said the bachelor, " is that the author has inserted in it a novel called ' The Curious Impertinent;' not because the tale is bad in itself, or ill written, but they say that it is out of place, having nothing to do with the story of his worship Signor Don Quixote." " I will lay a wager," replied Sancho, " that the rascally author has made a fine hotch-potch of it, jumbling fish and flesh together." " I aver, then," said Don Quixote, " that the author of my history could not be a sage, but some ignorant pretender, who has engaged in the work without deliberation, and written down anything, just at random : like Orbeneja, the painter of Ubeda, who, being asked what he was painting, answered, ' As it may happen;' and who, when he had painted a cock, to prevent impertinent mistakes, wrote under it, ' This is a cock.' Thus, perhaps, it has fared with my history, which may require a comment to make it intelligible." " Not at all," answered Sampson ; " for it is so plain, so easy to be understood, that children thumb it, boys read it, men understand it, and old folks commend it ; in short, it is so tossed about, so conned, and so thoroughly known by all sorts of people, that no sooner is a lean horse seen than they cry, ' Yonder goes Rozinante.' But none are so much addicted to reading it as your pages : in every nobleman's antechamber you will be sure to find a 'Don Quixote.' If one lays it down, another takes it up; one asks for it, another snatches it : in short, this history is the most pleasing and least prejudicial work that was ever published ; for it contains

not one indecent expression, nor a thought that is not purely Catholic."
" To write otherwise of me," said Don Quixote, " had not been to write
truths, but lies; and historians who propagate falsehoods should be
condemned to the stake, like coiners of base money. Why the author
was induced to mix novels, or narratives of other persons, with my
history, which is itself so rich in matter, I know not; but some writers
think, as the proverb says, ' With hay or with straw, it is all the same.'
Verily, had he confined himself to the publication of my thoughts, my
sighs, my groans, my laudable intentions, or my actual achievements, he
might, with these alone, have compiled a volume as large, or larger,
than all the works of Tostatus.* But in truth, Signor Bachelor, much
knowledge and a mature understanding are requisite for a historian, or,
indeed, for a good writer of any kind; and wit and humour belong to
genius alone. There is no character in comedy which requires so much
ingenuity as that of the fool; for he must not in reality be what he
appears. History is like sacred writing, because truth is essential to it;
and where there is truth, the Deity Himself is present: nevertheless,
there are many who think that books may be written and tossed out
into the world like fritters."

" There is no book so bad," said the bachelor, " but that something
good may be found in it." " Undoubtedly," said Don Quixote; " I
have known many, too, that have enjoyed considerable reputation for
their talents in writing, until, by publishing, they have either injured
or entirely lost their fame." " The reason of this is," said Sampson,
" that as printed works may be read leisurely, their defects are more
easily seen, and they are scrutinised more or less strictly in proportion
to the celebrity of the author. Men of great talents, whether poets or
historians, seldom escape the attacks of those who, without ever favouring the world with any production of their own, take delight in criti-
cising the works of others." " Nor can we wonder at that," said Don
Quixote, " when we observe the same practice among divines, who,
though dull enough in the pulpit themselves, are wonderfully sharp-
sighted in discovering the defects of other preachers." " True, indeed,
Signor Don Quixote," said Carrasco. " I wish critics would be less
fastidious, nor dwell so much upon the motes which may be discerned
even in the brightest works; for, though *aliquando bonus dormitat
Homerus*, they ought to consider how much he was awake to produce a
work with so much light and so little shade; nay, perhaps even his
seeming blemishes are like moles, which are sometimes thought to be
rather an improvement to beauty. But it cannot be denied that whoever publishes a book to the world exposes himself to imminent peril,
since, of all things, nothing is more impossible than to satisfy everybody." " My history must please but very few, I fear," said Don
Quixote. " On the contrary," replied the bachelor, " as, *stultorum
infinitus est numerus*, so infinite is the number of those who have been
delighted with that history. Though some, it is true, have taxed the

---

* This author's works consists of twenty-four volumes, folio.

author with having a treacherous memory, since he never explained who it was that stole Sancho's Dapple : it only appears that he was stolen, yet soon after we find him mounted upon the same beast, without being told how it was recovered.　They complain also, that he has omitted to inform us what Sancho did with the hundred crowns which he found in the portmanteau in the Sierra Morena; for he never mentions them again, to the great disappointment of many curious persons, who reckon it one of the most material defects in the work."　"Master Sampson," replied Sancho, "I am not in the mind now to come to accounts or reckonings, for I have a qualm come over my stomach, and shall not be easy till I have rectified it with a couple of draughts of old stingo; I have the darling at home, and my duck looks for me.　When I have had my feed, and my girths are tightened, I shall be with you straight, and will satisfy you and all the world in whatever they are pleased to ask me, both touching the loss of Dapple and the laying out of the hundred crowns."　Then, without waiting for an answer, or saying another word, he set off home.　The bachelor, being pressed by Don Quixote to stay and do penance with him, he accepted the invitation, and a couple of pigeons were added to the usual fare : chivalry was the subject at table, and Carrasco carried it on with the proper humour and spirit.　Their banquet over, they slept during the heat of the day ; after which Sancho returned, and the former conversation was renewed.

CHAPTER IV.

Wherein Sancho Panza answers the bachelor Sampson Carrasco's doubts and questions ; with other incidents worthy of being known and recited.

SANCHO returned to Don Quixote's house ; and, reviving the late subject of discourse, which he had so abruptly quitted, he said, " Well, Master Sampson Carrasco, now you want to know when and how my Dapple was stolen, and who was the thief ?　You must know, then, that on the very night that we marched off to avoid the officers of the Holy Brotherhood, after the unlucky affair of the galley-slaves, having made our way into the Sierra Morena, my master and I got into a thicket, where he, leaning upon his lance, and I, sitting upon Dapple, mauled and tired by our late skirmishes, we both fell as fast asleep as if we had been stretched upon four feather beds.　For my own part, I slept so soundly that the thief, whoever he was, had leisure enough to prop me up on four stakes, which he planted under the four corners of the pannel, and then drawing Dapple from under me, he left me fairly mounted, without ever dreaming of my loss."　"That is an easy matter, and no new device," said Don Quixote ; "for it is recorded that, at the siege of Albraca, the famous robber Brunelo by the very same stratagem stole the horse of Sacripante from between his legs "　" At day-break," continued Sancho, " when I awoke and began to stretch myself, the

"When I awoke and began to stretch myself, the stakes gave way, and down I came, with a confounded squelch, to the ground."

stakes gave way, and down I came, with a confounded squelch, to the ground. I looked about me, but could see no Dapple; tears came into my eyes, and I made such a lamentation that if the author of our history has not set it down, he has surely omitted an excellent thing. After some days—I cannot exactly say how many—as I was following the Princess Micomicona, I saw my ass again, and who should be mounted on him but that cunning rogue and notorious malefactor Gines de Passamonte, whom my master and I freed from the galley-chain!" "The mistake does not lie there," said Sampson, "but in the author making Sancho ride upon the same beast before he is said to have recovered him." "All this," said Sancho, "I know nothing about: it might be a mistake of the historian, or perhaps a blunder of his printer." "No doubt it was so," quoth Sampson: "but what became of the hundred crowns? for there we are in the dark." "I laid them out," replied Sancho, "for the benefit of my own person and that of my wife and children, and they have been the cause of her bearing quietly my rambles from home in the service of my master Don Quixote; for had I returned after so long a time ass-less and penniless, I must have looked for a scurvy greeting. And if you want to know anything more of me, here I am, ready to answer the king himself in person; though it is nothing to anybody whether I bought or bought not, whether I spent or spent not; for if the cuffs and blows that have been given me in our travels were to be paid for in ready money, and rated only at four maravedis apiece, another hundred crowns would not pay for half of them : so let every man lay his hand on his heart, and not take white for black, nor black for white ; for we are all as God made us, and oftentimes a great deal worse."

" I will take care," said Carrasco, " to warn the author of the history not to forget, in his next edition, what honest Sancho has told us, which will make the book as good again." " Are there any other explanations wanting in the work, Signor Bachelor ? " quoth Don Quixote. " There may be others," answered Carrasco, " but none of equal importance with those already mentioned." " Peradventure," said Don Quixote, " the author promises a second part ? " " He does," answered Sampson, " but says he has not yet been able to find out the possessor of it; and therefore we are in doubt whether or not it will ever make its appearance. Besides, some people say that second parts are never good for anything ; and others, that there is enough of Don Quixote already : though it is true there are some merry souls who cry, ' Let us have more Quixotades ; let but Don Quixote encounter, and Sancho Panza talk, and go the world as it may ! ' " " But pray, how stands the editor affected ? " inquired Don Quixote. " How ? " said Sampson ; " why, as soon as he can find this history, which he is diligently searching for, he will immediately send it to press, more on account of the profit than the praise which he hopes to derive from it." " What ! then," said Sancho, " the author wants to get money by it ? If so, it will be a wonder indeed if it is well done ; for he will stitch away at it like a tailor on Easter-eve, and your hasty works are never good for anything. This same Signor Moor would do well to consider a little what he is about ; for I and my master will furnish him so abundantly with lime and mortar in matter of adventures that he may not only compile a second, but a hundred parts. The good man thinks, without doubt, that we lie sleeping here in straw, but let him hold up the limping foot, and he will see why it halts. All that I can say is, that if my master had taken my advice, we might have been now in the field, redressing grievances and righting wrongs, according to the usage of good knights-errant." At this moment, while Sancho was yet speaking, the neighing of Rozinante reached their ears ; which Don Quixote took for a most happy omen, and resolved, without delay, to resume his functions, and again sally forth into the world. He therefore consulted the bachelor as to what course he should take, and was advised by him to go straight to the kingdom of Arragon and the city of Saragossa, where, in a few days, a most solemn tournament was to be held in honour of the festival of Saint George ; and where, by vanquishing the Arragonian knights, he would acquire the ascendency over all the knights in the world. He commended his resolution as most honourable and brave, at the same time cautioning him to be more wary in encountering great and needless perils, because his life was not his own, but belonged to those who stood in need of his aid and protection. "That is just what I say, Signor Sampson," quoth Sancho; "for my master makes no more of attacking a hundred armed men than a greedy boy would do half a dozen melons. Body of me, Signor Bachelor! yes, there must be a time to attack, and a time to retreat, and it must not be always, 'Saint Jago, and charge, Spain!' * And further, I have heard it said (and, if I remember right, by my master himself) that true valour lies in the middle between cowardice and rashness; and, if so, I would not have him either fall on or fly, without good reason for it. But, above all, I would let my master know that, if he takes me with him, it must be upon condition that he shall battle it all himself, and that I shall only have to tend his person —I mean, look after his clothes and food; all which I will do with a hearty good-will; but if he expects I will lay hand to my sword, though it be only against beggarly wood-cutters with hooks and hatchets, he is very much mistaken. I, Signor Sampson, do not set up for being the most valiant, but the best and most faithful squire that ever served knight-errant; and if my lord Don Quixote, in consideration of my many and good services, shall please to bestow on me some one of the many islands his worship says he shall light upon, I shall be much beholden to him for the favour; and if he give me none, here I am, and it is better to trust God than each other; and mayhap my government bread might not go down so sweet as that which I should eat without it: and how do I know but the devil, in one of these governments, might set up a stumbling-block in my way, ever which I might fall, and dash out my grinders? Sancho I was born, and Sancho I expect to die: yet for all that, if, fairly and squarely, without much care or much risk, Heaven should chance to throw an island, or some such thing, in my way, I am not such a fool neither as to refuse it; for, as the saying is, 'When they give you a heifer, be ready with the rope,' and 'When good fortune knocks, make haste to let her in.'"

"Brother Sancho," quoth the bachelor, "you have spoken like any professor; nevertheless, trust in Heaven and Signor Don Quixote, and then you may get not only an island, but even a kingdom." "One as likely as the other," answered Sancho; "though I could tell Signor Carrasco that my master will not throw the kingdom he gives me into a rotten sack; for I have felt my pulse, and find myself strong enough to rule kingdoms and govern islands, and so much I have signified, before now, to my master." "Take heed, Sancho," quoth the bachelor, "for honours change manners; and it may come to pass, when you are a governor, that you may not know even your own mother." "That," answered Sancho, "may be the case with those that are born among the mallows, but not with one whose soul, like mine, is covered four inches thick with the grace of an old Christian. No, no, I am not one

---

* "*Santiago y cierra Espana!*" is the cry of the Spaniards at the onset in battle.

of the ungrateful sort." "Heaven grant it," said Don Quixote; "but we shall see when the government comes; and methinks I have it already in my eye."

The knight now requested Sampson Carrasco, if he were a poet, to do him the favour to compose some verses for him, as a farewell to his lady, and to place a letter of her name at the beginning of each verse, so that the initials joined together might make *Dulcinea del Toboso.* The bachelor said that, though he was not one of the great poets of Spain, who were said to be three and a half in number, he would endeavour to comply with his request; at the same time, he foresaw that it would be no easy task, as the name consisted of seventeen letters; for if he made four stanzas of four verses each, there would be a letter too much, and if he made them of five, which are called Decimas or Redondillas, there would be three letters wanting: however, he said that he would endeavour to sink a letter as well as he could, so that the name of Dulcinea del Toboso should be included in the four stanzas. "Let it be so by all means," said Don Quixote; "for, when the name is not quite plain and manifest, the lady is always doubtful whether the verses be really composed for her." On this point they agreed, and also that they should set out within eight days from that time. Don Quixote enjoined the bachelor to keep his intention secret, especially from the priest and Master Nicholas, as well as his niece and housekeeper, lest they might endeavour to obstruct his honourable purpose. Carrasco promised to attend to his caution, and took his leave, after obtaining a promise on his part to send him tidings of his progress whenever an opportunity offered. Sancho also went home to prepare for the intended expedition.

CHAPTER V.

Of the discreet and pleasant conversation which passed between Sancho Panza and his wife Teresa.

ENTERING on the present chapter, the translator of this history says that he takes it to be apocryphal, because Sancho therein expresses himself in a style very different from what might be expected from his shallow understanding, and speaks with an acuteness that seems wholly above his capacity; nevertheless, he would not omit the translation of it, in compliance with the duty of his office, and therefore proceeded as follows.

Sancho went home in such high spirits that his wife observed his gaiety a bow-shot off, insomuch that she could not help saying, "What makes you look so blithe, friend Sancho?" To which he answered, "Would to Heaven, dear wife, I were not so well pleased as I seem to be!" "I know not what you mean, husband," replied she, "by saying you wish you were not so much pleased; now, silly as I am, I cannot guess how any one can desire not to be pleased." "Look you, Teresa," answered Sancho, "I am thus merry because I am about to return to the service of my master Don Quixote, who is going again in search after adventures, and I am to accompany him, for so my fate wills it. Besides, I am merry with the hopes of finding another hundred crowns like those we have spent; though it grieves me to part from you and my children; and if Heaven would be pleased to give me bread, dry-shod and at home, without dragging me over crags and cross-paths, it is plain that my joy would be better grounded, since it is now mingled with sorrow for leaving you: so that I was right in saying that I should be glad if it pleased Heaven I were not so well pleased." "Look you, Sancho," replied Teresa, "ever since you have been a knight-errant man, you talk in such a roundabout manner that nobody can understand you." "It is enough, wife," said Sancho, "that God understands me, for He is the understander of all things; and so much for that. And do you hear, wife, it behoves you to take special care of Dapple for these three or four days to come, that he may be in a condition to bear arms; so double his allowance, and get the pack-saddle in order, and the rest of his tackling; for we are not going to a wedding, but to roam about the world, and to give and take with giants, fiery dragons, and goblins, and to hear hissings, roarings, bellowings, and bleatings; all which would be but flowers of lavender, if we had not to do with Yangueses and enchanted Moors." "I believe, indeed, husband," replied Teresa, "that your squires-errant do not eat their bread for nothing, and therefore I shall not fail to beseech Heaven to deliver you speedily from so much evil hap." "I tell you, wife," answered Sancho, "that, did I not expect, ere long, to see myself governor of an island, I vow I should drop down dead upon the spot." "Not so, good husband," quoth Teresa: "let the hen live, though it be with the pip. Do you live, and the devil take all the governments in the world. Without a government you came into the world, without a government you have lived till now, and without it you can be carried to your grave, whenever it shall please God. How many folks are there in the world that have no government? and yet they live, and are reckoned among the people. The best sauce in the world is hunger, and as that is never wanting to the poor, they always eat with a relish. But if, perchance, Sancho, you should get a government, do not forget me and your children. Consider that your son Sancho is just fifteen years old, and it is fit he should go to school, if his uncle the abbot means to breed him up to the Church. Consider also that Mary Sancha your daughter will not break her heart if we marry her; for I am mistaken if she has not as much mind to a husband as you have to a government: and verily, say I, better a daughter but humbly married than highly kept." "In good faith, dear wife," said Sancho, "if Heaven be so good to me that I get anything like a government, I will match Mary Sancha so highly that there will be no coming near her without calling her 'your ladyship.'" "Not so, Sancho," answered Teresa; "the best way is to marry her to her equal; for if you lift her from clouted shoes to high heels, and, instead of her russet coat of fourpenny stuff, give her a farthingale and petticoats of silk ; and instead of plain Molly and ' thou,' she be called ' madam ' and ' your ladyship,' the girl will not know where she is, and will fall into a thousand mistakes at every step, showing her homespun country stuff." " Peace, fool ! " quoth Sancho ; " she has only to practise two or three years, and the gravity will set upon her as if it were made for her ; and if not, what matters it ?   Let her be a lady, and come of it what will." " Measure yourself by your condition, Sancho," answered Teresa ; " and do not seek to raise yourself higher, but remember the proverb, ' Wipe your neighbour's son's nose, and take him into your house.'   It would be a pretty business, truly, to marry our Mary to some great count or knight, who, when the fancy takes him, would look upon her as some strange thing, and be calling her ' country-wench,' ' clod-breaker's brat,' and I know not what else.   No, not while I live, husband : I have not brought up my child to be so used.   Do you provide money, Sancho, and leave the matching of her to my care ; for there is Lope Tocho, John Tocho's son, a lusty, hale young man, whom we know, and I am sure he has a sneaking kindness for the girl : to him she will be very well married, considering he is our equal, and will be always under our eye ; and we shall be all as one, parents and children, grandsons and sons-in-law, and so the peace and blessing of Heaven will be among us all : and do not you be for marrying her at your courts and great palaces, where they will neither understand her, nor she understand herself."   " Hark you, beast, and wife for Barabbas ! " replied Sancho ; " why would you now, without rhyme or reason, hinder me from marrying my daughter with one who may bring me grandchildren that may be styled ' your lordships ' ?   Look you, Teresa, I have always heard my betters say, ' He that will not when he may, when he will he shall have nay ; ' and it would be wrong, now that fortune is knocking at our door, not to open it and bid her welcome.   ' Let us spread our sail to the favourable gale, now that it blows.' "

It was this language from Sancho, and more of the same kind which followed, that made the translator suspect the present chapter to be apocryphal.

" Do you not think, animal ! " continued Sancho, " that it would be well for me to get hold of some good rich government that may lift us out of the dirt, so that I may wed Mary Sancha to any one I please ? You will then see how people will call you Donna Teresa Panza, and you will sit in the church with velvet cushions, carpets, and tapestries, in spite of the best gentlewomen of the parish.   No, no, stay as you are, and be always the same thing, like a figure in the hangings, without being ever higher or lower.   But no more of this : little Sancha shall be a countess in spite of your teeth."   " Take care what you say, husband," answered Teresa ; " for I am afraid this countess-ship will be my daughter's undoing.   But you must do as you please—make her a duchess or a princess ; but it shall never be with my consent.   I always like to see things suited like to like, and cannot abide to see folks take upon them when they should not.   Plain Teresa was I

"I would not have people cry out, 'Look how stately Madam Hog-feeder struts it! Yesterday she went to mass with the tail of her petticoat over her head, for lack of a veil.'"

christened, and my name was never made to be 'dizened either with Dons or Donnas. My father's name was Cascajo, and I, being your wife, am called Teresa Panza, though indeed, by good right, I should be called Teresa Cascajo; but the laws follow the prince's will. I am content with that name as it is, without being burdened with Donna, to make it so heavy that I should not be able to carry it; and I would not have people cry out, when they see me decked out like any countess or governess, 'Look how stately Madam Hog-feeder struts it! Yesterday she toiled at her distaff from morning to night, and went to mass with the tail of her petticoat over her head, for lack of a veil; and to-day, forsooth, she goes with her farthingale, her embroideries, and all so lofty as if we did not know her!' Heaven keep me in my seven, or my five senses, or as many as I have; for I have no mind to expose myself after this manner. Go you, husband, to your governing and islanding, and puff yourself up as you please; as for my girl and me, by the life of my father! we will neither of us stir a step from our own town; for the proverb says,

> " ' The wife that expects to have a good name
> Is always at home, as if she were lame ;
> And the maid that is honest, her chiefest delight
> Is still to be doing from morning to night.'

Go you, with your Don Quixote, to your adventures, and leave us to
our ill fortunes ; God will better them for us, if we deserve it : though,
truly, I cannot guess who made him a Don, for neither his father nor his
grandfather had any such title." "Out of all question," quoth Sancho,
" some evil spirit must have got into that body of thine ! Heaven bless
thee, woman ! what a heap of stuff hast thou been twisting together,
without either head or tail ! What has Cascajo, embroideries, or the
proverbs, to do with what I am saying? Why, thou foolish ignorant
prater (for so I may well call thee, since thou canst neither understand
what I say, nor see what is for thy own good), had I told thee that
our daughter was to throw herself headlong from some high steeple,
or go gipsying about the world as did the Infanta Donna Urraca, thou
wouldst have been right in not coming into my mind ; but if, in two
turns of a hand, and less than the twinkling of an eye, I can equip her
with a Don and ' your ladyship,' and raise thee from the straw to sit
under a canopy of state, and upon a sofa with more velvet cushions
than all the Almohadas * of Morocco had Moors in their lineage, why
wilt thou not consent, and desire what I desire ? " " Would you know
why, husband ? " answered Teresa. "It is because of the proverb, which
says, ' He that covers thee discovers thee.' The poor man is scarcely
looked at, while every eye is turned upon the rich ; and if the poor man
grows rich and great, then I warrant you there is work enough for your
grumblers and backbiters, who swarm everywhere like bees."

" Hearken to me, Teresa," answered Sancho, " and listen to what I
am going to say ; mayhap thou hast never heard it before in all thy
life : and I do not speak now of my own head, but from the speeches
of that good father the preacher, who held forth to us last Lent in this
village, who, if I remember right, said that the things which are present
before our eyes take a stronger hold on our minds than things past."

All this parade of reasoning, so out of character in Sancho, tended to
confirm the opinion of the translator that this chapter could not possibly
be genuine. "That being the case," continued Sancho, " when we see
any person finely dressed, and set off with rich apparel and with a train
of servants, we are moved to show him respect ; for, though we cannot
but remember certain scurvy matters, either of poverty or parentage,
that formerly belonged to him, but which being long gone by are almost
forgotten, we only think of what we see before our eyes. And if, as the
preacher said, the person so raised by good luck, from nothing, as it
were, to the tip-top of prosperity, be well-behaved, generous, and civil,
and gives himself no ridiculous airs, pretending to vie with the old
nobility, take my word for it, Teresa, nobody will twit him with what

---

* A play on the word *almohada*, which signifies a cushion, and is also the name of a
famous tribe of Arabs in Africa.

he was, but will respect him for what he is; except, indeed, the envious, who hate every man's good luck." "I don't understand you, husband," replied Teresa: "do what you think fit, and do not crack my brains any more with your speeches and flourishes; but if you are revolved to do as you say—" "*Resolved*, you should say, wife," quoth Sancho, "and not revolved." "Do not trouble yourself to mend my words," answered Teresa; "I speak as it pleases God, and meddle not with your fine notions. I say, if you hold still in the same mind of being a governor, take your son Sancho with you, and train him up to your calling, for it is fit that sons should learn their fathers' trade." "When I have a government," quoth Sancho, "I will send for him by the post; and also money to you, which I shall have in abundance, for people are always ready enough to lend their money to governors; and mind you clothe the boy so that he may look, not like what he is, but what he will be." "Send you the money," quoth Teresa, "and I will make him as fine as a palm branch." "We are agreed, then," quoth Sancho, "that our daughter is to be a countess?" "The day that I see her a countess," answered Teresa, "I shall reckon I am laying her in her grave: but I say again, you must do as you please, for to this burden women are born —they must obey their husbands if they are ever such blockheads." And then she began to weep as bitterly as if she already saw little Sancha dead and buried. Sancho comforted her, and promised that, though he must make her a countess, he would put it off as long as possible. Thus ended their dialogue, and Sancho went to pay his master another visit, in order to confer on the subject of their departure.

CHAPTER VI.

Of what passed between Don Quixote, his niece, and housekeeper; which is one of the most important chapters in the whole history.

THE niece and housekeeper of Don Quixote, during the conversation of Sancho Panza and his wife Teresa Cascajo, were not idle; for they were led to suspect, from a thousand symptoms, that he was inclined to break loose a third time, and return to the exercise of his unlucky knight-errantry; and therefore endeavoured, by all possible means, to divert him from his unhappy purpose; but it was all preaching in the desert, and hammering on cold iron. Among the many dialogues which passed between them on the subject, the housekeeper said to him, "Indeed, sir, if you will not tarry quietly at home, and leave off rambling over hills and dales like a troubled spirit in quest of those same adventures, which I call misadventures, I am fully resolved to pray to Heaven and the king to put a stop to it." To which Don Quixote replied, "Mistress Housekeeper, what answer Heaven will return to your complaints I know not, any more than what his majesty will give you; I only know that, if I were king, I would excuse myself from answering the infinite number of impertinent memorials which are daily presented to him. Indeed, one of the greatest fatigues to which monarchs are subject is the hearing and answering of every person who chooses to address them; and therefore I should be sorry if he were troubled with my concerns." "Pray, sir," said the housekeeper, "are there no knights in his majesty's court?" "Yes, many," replied Don Quixote; "and highly necessary they are to keep up the state and dignity of princes." "Would it not, then, be better," replied she, "that your worship should be one of them, so that you might quietly serve your king and lord at court?" "Look you, friend," answered Don Quixote, "all knights cannot be courtiers, neither can, nor ought, all courtiers to be knights-errant. There must be some of every station in the world, and though we are all knights, there is a great difference between us; for the courtier-knight traverses the globe only on a map, without expense or fatigue, suffering neither heat nor cold, hunger nor thirst; whereas the true knight-errant, exposed to all the vicissitudes of the atmosphere, by night and by day, on foot and on horseback, explores every quarter of the habitable world. Nor do we know our enemies in picture only, but in their proper persons, and attack them upon every occasion, without standing upon trifles, or upon the laws of duelling, such as whether our adversary bears a shorter or longer lance or sword —whether he is protected by holy relics, or wears any secret coat of mail, or whether the sun be duly divided or not—with other ceremonies of the same stamp, used in single combats between man and man, which thou dost not understand, but I do. And thou must know, further, that the true knight-errant, though he should espy ten giants, whose heads not only touch, but overtop, the clouds, and though each of them stalk on two prodigious towers instead of legs, and hath arms like the mainmasts of huge and mighty ships of war, and each eye like a great mill-wheel, and glowing like a fiery furnace; yet must he in nowise be affrighted, but, on the contrary, with gentle demeanour and an undaunted heart, encounter, assail, and, if possible, in an instant vanquish and rout them, although they should come defended by the impenetrable coat of a certain shell-fish, harder than diamond, and, instead of swords, armed with dreadful sabres of Damascus steel, or, as I have seen more than once, huge maces pointed with the same metal. All this I have said, Mistress Housekeeper, that thou mayest understand the difference between one species of knight and another; and it were to be wished that all princes could duly appreciate this last, or rather first order—I mean the knights-errant, who were, in times past, the bulwark not only of one, but of many kingdoms."

"Ah, dear uncle!" said the niece, "be assured all the stories you tell us of knights-errant are fables and lies; and their histories deserve to be burnt, or at least to be marked by a *sanbenito*,* or some badge,

---

* A coat of black canvas painted over with flames and devils. It is worn by heretics when going to be burnt by order of the Inquisition.

that their wickedness may be known." "Now, by the God in whom I live!" said Don Quixote, "were you not my own sister's daughter, I would make such an example of you, for the blasphemy you have uttered, that the whole world should resound it. What! a young baggage who scarcely knows how to manage a dozen of bobbins, presume to raise her voice in censure of the histories of knights-errant! What would Sir Amadis have said to this? — though he, indeed, I believe, would have pardoned thee; for he was the most humble and most courteous knight of his time, and, moreover, a great protector of damsels. But thy profanity might have reached the ears of others, from whose indignation thou wouldst not have escaped so easily; for all are not equally gentle and courteous. Neither are all those who call themselves knights really so; for some are not sterling gold, but base counterfeit stuff, which, though deceiving the sight, cannot stand the test of truth. There are low fellows, who strain and swell even to bursting to appear great; and others you will see, of exalted rank, who seem desirous only to emulate the base. While the one class rises by ambition or virtue, the other sinks by meanness or vice: yet is it often difficult to distinguish between these varieties, so alike in name, and so different in their actions." "Bless me, uncle!" quoth the niece, "that you should be so knowing, that, if need were, you might mount a pulpit and hold forth in the streets, and yet so infatuated as to imagine yourself valiant at your time of life, and strong, when, alas! you are so infirm; and pretend to make crooked things straight, though bent yourself under the weight of years: and, above all, set up for a knight, when you are no such thing! — some gentry may indeed pretend to that honour, but those who are poor must not look so high."

"Thou art right, niece," answered Don Quixote; "and I could tell thee such things concerning lineages as would surprise thee; but, not choosing to mix sacred with profane subjects, I forbear. You must know, my friends, that all the genealogies in the world may be reduced to four kinds. The first are those families who from a low beginning have raised and extended themselves until they have reached the highest pinnacle of human greatness; the second are those of high extraction who have preserved their original dignity; the third sort are those who, from a great foundation, have gradually dwindled, until, like a pyramid, they terminate in a small point. The last, which are the most numerous class, are those who have begun and continued low, and who must end the same: such are the great mass of the people. Of the first kind we have an example in the Ottoman family, whose founder, from the lowly rank of a shepherd, has attained its present height. Of the second order, examples may be adduced from sundry hereditary princes, who peaceably govern within the limits of their own dominions, without seeking to enlarge or contract them. Of those who began great, and have ended in a point, there are thousands of instances; for all the Pharaohs and Ptolemies of Egypt, the Cæsars of Rome, with all that infinite herd (if I may so call them) of princes, monarchs, and lords, the Medes,

Assyrians, Greeks, Persians, and barbarians—I say, all these families and states, as well as their founders, have ended in a point—that is, in nothing; for it is impossible now to find any of their descendants, and, if they were in existence, it would be in some low and abject station. Of the lower race I have nothing to say, only that they serve to swell the number of the living, without deserving any other fame or eulogy. From all that I have said you must clearly see, my good simpletons, that genealogies are involved in endless confusion, and that those only are illustrious and great who are distinguished by their virtue and liberality, as well as their riches; for the great man who is vicious is only a great sinner, and the rich man who wants liberality is but a miserly pauper. The gratification which wealth can bestow is not in mere possession, nor in lavishing it with prodigality, but in the wise application of it. The poor knight can only manifest his rank by his virtues and general conduct. He must be well-bred, courteous, kind, and obliging; not proud nor arrogant; no murmurer: above all, he must be charitable; and by two maravedis given cheerfully to the poor he shall display as much generosity as the rich man who bestows large alms by sound of bell. Of such a man no one will doubt his honourable descent, and general applause will be the sure reward of his virtue. There are two roads, my daughters, by which men may attain riches and honour: the one by letters, the others by arms. I have more in me of the soldier than of the scholar; and it is evident, from my propensity to arms, that I was born under the influence of the planet Mars; so that I am, as it were, forced into that track, and must follow it in spite of the whole world. Your endeavours, therefore, will be fruitless in dissuading me from that which Heaven wills, fate ordains, reason demands, and above all, that to which my inclinations irresistibly impel me. Well I know the innumerable toils of knight-errantry; but I know also its honour and reward. The path of virtue is narrow, while that of vice is easy and broad; and equally different are the points to which they lead: the one to life eternal, the other to ignominy and death. I know, as our great Castilian poet expresses it, that

> " ' Through these rough paths, to gain a glorious name,
> We climb the steep ascent that leads to fame;
> They miss the road who quit the rugged way,
> And in the smoother tracks of pleasure stray.'

"Ah, woe is me!" quoth the niece; "my uncle a poet too! He knows everything; nothing comes amiss to him! I will lay a wager that, if he had a mind to turn mason, he could build a house with as much ease as a birdcage!" "I assure thee, niece," answered Don Quixote, "that were not my whole soul engrossed by the arduous duties of chivalry, I would engage to do anything:—there is not a curious art which I would not acquire; especially that of making birdcages and toothpicks."

A knocking at the door was now heard, and finding, upon inquiry, that it was Sancho Panza, the housekeeper, to avoid the sight of him whom she abhorred, ran to hide herself while the niece let him in. His master Don Quixote received him with open arms, and, being closeted together, a conversation ensued, not inferior to the former.

CHAPTER VII.

Of what passed between Don Quixote and his squire; with other remarkable occurrences.

As soon as the housekeeper saw that Sancho and her master were shut up together, she suspected the drift of their conference; and doubting not but that another unfortunate expedition would be the result, she put on her veil and set off, full of trouble and anxiety, to seek the bachelor Sampson Carrasco; thinking that as he was a well-spoken person, and a new acquaintance of her master, he might be able to dissuade him from so extravagant a project. She found him walking to and fro in the courtyard of his house, and she immediately fell down on her knees before him. The bachelor seeing her in this situation, and that she was apparently suffering under some heavy affliction, said to her, "What is the matter, Mistress Housekeeper? What has befallen you, that you seem ready to give up the ghost?" "Nothing at all, dear sir," quoth she, "only that my master is most certainly breaking forth." "How breaking forth, mistress?" demanded Sampson; "has he burst in any part of his body?" "No, but he is breaking forth into his old madness, Signor Bachelor," she replied: "he is surely in the mind to be strolling again about the wide world for the third time, in search of adventures, as he calls them. The first time, he was brought home to us laid athwart an ass, all battered and bruised. The second time he returned in an ox-waggon, locked up in a cage, and so changed, poor soul! that his own mother would not have known him; so feeble, wan, and withered, and his eyes sunk into the farthest corner of his brains, insomuch that it took me above six hundred eggs to get him a little up again, as Heaven and the world is my witness, and my hens, that will not let me lie." "I can easily believe that," answered the bachelor; "for your hens are too well bred and fed to say one thing and mean another. Then these apprehensions for your master are the whole and sole cause of your trouble, are they, Mrs. Housekeeper?" "Yes, sir," answered she. "Be in no pain, then," replied the bachelor, "but go home, in Heaven's name, and get me something warm for breakfast, and on your way repeat the prayer of St. Apollonia, if you know it. I will be with you instantly, and you shall see wonders." "Bless me!" replied the housekeeper, "the prayer of St. Apollonia, say you? that might do something if my master's distemper laid in his gums; but alas! it is all in his brain." "I know what I say, Mistress Housekeeper," replied Sampson; "get you home, and do not stand disputing with me; for you know I am a Salamancan bachelor of arts, and there is no bachelorising beyond that." Then away went the housekeeper home, while the bachelor repaired to the priest, with whom he held a consultation, the issue of which will come out in due time.

During the interview between Don Quixote and Sancho, some conversation took place, which the history relates at large with great accuracy and truth. "I have now, sir," quoth Sancho to his master, "reluced my wife to consent that I should go with your worship wherever you please to carry me." "*Reduced*, thou shouldst say, Sancho," said Don Quixote, "and not 'reluced.'" "Once or twice already," answered

She found him walking to and fro in the courtyard of his house, and she immediately fell down on her knees before him.

Sancho, "I have besought your worship not to mind my words, when you know my meaning; and when you do not, say, Sancho, or devil, I understand thee not; and then if I do not explain myself, you may correct me, for I am so focile." "I do not understand thee now, Sancho," said Don Quixote, "for I know not the meaning of 'focile.'" "So focile," answered Sancho, "means, I am so much so." "I understand thee still less now," replied Don Quixote. "Why, if you do not understand me," answered Sancho, "I cannot help it; I know no more, so Heaven help me!" "Oh! now I have it," answered Don Quixote: "thou wilt say that thou art so *docile*, so pliant, and so tractable, that thou wilt readily comprehend whatever I say, and wilt learn whatever I shall teach thee." "I will lay a wager," quoth Sancho, "you took me from the first, only you had a mind to puzzle me, that you might hear some more of my blunders." "Perhaps thou mayest be right there,"

answered Don Quixote; " but tell me, what says Teresa?" "Teresa,"
quoth Sancho, " says that 'fast bind, fast find,' and that we must have
less talking, and more doing; for ' he who shuffles is not he who cuts,'
and, ' a bird in the hand is worth two in the bush.' And I say, though
there is but little in woman's advice, yet he that won't take it is not
over-wise." " I say so too," replied Don Quixote; " proceed, Sancho,
for thou talkest admirably to-day." " The case is this," replied Sancho,
" that, as your worship very well knows, we are all mortal—here to-day
and gone to-morrow; that the lamb goes to the spit as soon as the
sheep; and that nobody can promise himself longer life than God pleases;
for when death knocks at the door, he turns a deaf ear to all excuses—
nothing can stay him, neither force, nor entreaties, nor sceptres, nor
mitres; for so it is said both in the street and in the pulpit." " All this
is true," said Don Quixote, " but I do not perceive what thou wouldst
be at." " What I would be at," quoth Sancho, " is that your worship
would be pleased to allow me wages—so much a month—as long as I
shall serve you, and that, in case of need, the same may be paid out of
your estate; for I have no mind to trust to rewards, which may come
late or never. Heaven help me with my own, which I would be glad to
know, be it little or much: for ' the hen sits, if it be but upon one egg;'
and ' many littles make a mickle,' and ' while something is getting, nothing is losing.' In good truth, should it fall out that your worship
should give me that same island you have promised me (but which I am
afraid will never come), I would not wish to make a hard bargain, but
am willing that my wages shall be deducted from the rent of such island
fairly, cantity for cantity." " Is not ' quantity ' as good as ' cantity,'
friend Sancho?" answered Don Quixote. " I understand you," quoth
Sancho; " I suppose, now, I should have said ' quantity,' and not
' cantity,' but that signifies nothing, since your worship knew my meaning." " Yes, and to the very bottom of it," returned Don Quixote.
" I plainly see the mark at which thou art levelling all thy proverbs;
but hear me, Sancho: I should have no objection to appoint thee wages
had I ever met with any example among the histories of knights-errant
that showed the least glimmering of any such monthly or yearly stipend.
I have read all, or most of those histories, and do not remember ever to
have read that any knight-errant allowed his squire fixed wages; on the
contrary, they all served upon courtesy: and when least expecting it, if
their masters were fortunate, they were rewarded with an island, or
something equal to it; at all events they were certain of title and rank.
If, Sancho, upon the strength of these expectations, thou art willing to
return to my service, in Heaven's name do so; but thou art mistaken
if thou hast any hope that I shall act in opposition to the ancient usages
of chivalry. Return home, therefore, Sancho, and inform thy wife of
my determination; and if she is willing and thou art disposed to stay
with me upon the terms I mentioned—*bene quidem*; if not, we will at
least part friends; for ' if the dove-house wants not bait, it will never
want pigeons;' and take notice, son, that ' a good reversion is better than
a bad possession,' and ' a good claim better than bad pay.' I talk thus,

Sancho, to show thee that I also can discharge a volley of proverbs. But, to be plain with thee, if thou art not disposed to accompany me upon courtesy, and follow my fortunes, the Lord have thee in His keeping, and make thee a saint; for I shall never want squires more obedient, more diligent, and at the same time less talkative and selfish than thou art."

On hearing this fixed resolution, the hopes of Sancho were over-clouded, and his heart sank within him; for hitherto he had never supposed it possible that his master would go without him for the world's worth: and as he was standing thoughtful and dejected, Samp-son Carrasco entered the chamber, followed by the niece and house-keeper, who were curious to hear what arguments he would use to dissuade the knight from his threatened expedition. The waggish bachelor approached him with great respect, and after embracing him, said, in an elevated tone, " O flower of knight-errantry ! O resplendent light of arms ! O mirror and glory of the Spanish nation ! May it please Heaven that all those who shall seek to prevent or impede your third sally be lost in the labyrinth of their own wiles, nor ever accom-plish their evil desire ! " Then turning to the housekeeper, he said, " Now, Mistress Housekeeper, you may save yourself the trouble of saying the prayer of St. Apollonia; for I know that it is the positive determination of the stars that Signor Don Quixote shall resume his glorious career, and I should greatly burden my conscience did I not give intimation thereof, and persuade this knight no longer to restrain the force of his valorous arm, nor check the virtuous ardour of his soul, since by delay he defrauds the injured world of redress, orphans of protection, damsels of deliverance, widows of relief, and matrons of support, with other matters of this nature dependent on knight-errantry. Go on, then, dear Signor Don Quixote, my brave and gallant knight ! lose no time, but set forward rather to-day than to-morrow; and if any-thing be wanting to hasten the execution of your design, here am I, ready to assist you with my life and fortune. If your excellency stand in need of a squire, I shall esteem myself singularly fortunate in having the honour to serve you in that capacity." " Did I not tell thee," said Don Quixote, turning to Sancho, " that I should be in no want of squires? Behold who now offers himself! The renowned bachelor Sampson Carrasco, the darling and delight of the Salamancan schools ! sound and active of body, patient of heat and cold, of hunger and thirst, no prater—in short, possessing all the qualifications requisite in the squire of a knight-errant. But Heaven forbid that, to gratify my own private inclination, I should endanger this pillar of literature, this urn of genius, and lop off so flourishing a branch of the noble and liberal arts. No, let our new Sampson abide in his country, and do honour to the grey hairs of his venerable parents, by becoming its ornament. I will be content with any squire, since Sancho deigns not to accompany me." " I do deign," quoth Sancho, with eyes swimming in tears ; " it shall never be said of me, dear master, ' the bread eaten, the company broke up.' I am not come of an ungrateful stock : for all the world knows, especially our village, who the Panzas were that have gone before me. Besides, I know, by many good works and better words, your worship's inclination to do me a kindness; and if I have said too much upon the article of wages, it was to please my wife, who, when once she sets about persuading one to a thing, no mallet drives the hoops of a tub as she does to get her will: but a man must be a man, and a woman a woman; and since I am a man elsewhere, I will also be one in my own house, in spite of anybody. So your worship has nothing to do but to look after your will and its codicil in such manner as it cannot be rebuked; and let us set out immediately, that the soul of Signor Sampson may be at rest, as he is obliged in conscience, he says, to persuade your worship to make a third sally; and I again offer myself to serve your worship faithfully and loyally, as well and better than all the squires that ever served knight-errant in past or present times."

The bachelor listened in admiration to Sancho; for though he had read the first part of the history, he hardly conceived it possible that he should really be so pleasant a fellow as he is therein described; but now he could believe all that had been said of him: in short, he set down both the master and man as the most extraordinary couple the world had ever yet produced. Don Quixote and Sancho being now perfectly reconciled, they agreed, with the approbation of the great Carrasco, their oracle, to depart within three days, in which time they might have leisure to provide what was necessary for the expedition, and especially a complete helmet, which Don Quixote declared to be indispensable. Sampson engaged to procure one from a friend, who he was sure would not refuse it; though he confessed the brightness of the steel was not a little obscured by tarnish and rust. The niece and the housekeeper, on hearing this determination, made a woful outcry, inveighing bitterly against Carrasco, who had been acting agreeably to a plan previously concerted with the priest and barber. They tore their hair, scratched and disfigured their faces, like the funeral mourners * of former times, and lamented the approaching departure of their master as if it were his death.

Three days were now employed in preparation, at the end of which time, Sancho having appeased his wife, and Don Quixote his niece and housekeeper, they issued forth in the evening, unobserved by any except the bachelor, who insisted on bearing them company half a league from the village. The knight was mounted on his good Rozinante, and the squire on his trusty Dapple, his wallets stored with food and his purse with money, providentially supplied by his master in case of need. When Sampson took his leave, he expressed an earnest desire to have advice of his good or ill fortune, that he might rejoice or condole with him, as the laws of friendship required. Don Quixote having promised to comply with this request, the bachelor returned to the village, and the knight and squire pursued their way towards the great city of Toboso.

---

* It was formerly the custom to hire these mourners, or bewailers, to lament over the body of the deceased.

CHAPTER VIII.

Wherein is related what befell Don Quixote as he was going to visit his lady Dulcinea del Toboso.

"Blessed be the mighty Allah!" exclaims Cid Hamet Benengeli, at the beginning of this eighth chapter, "blessed be Allah!" thrice uttering these pious ejaculations upon seeing Don Quixote and Sancho again take field; and he adds that from this point the readers of this delightful history may reckon that the exploits and pleasantries of the knight and his squire will recommence; and he entreats them to fix their attention only on the future achievements of the great adventurer, which now begin upon the road to Toboso, as did the former in the plain of Montiel. Nor, indeed, is this any very unreasonable request, considering what great things he promises. And thus he proceeds:

Don Quixote and Sancho were now left together; and scarcely had Sampson quitted them, when Rozinante began to neigh and Dapple to bray, which both knight and squire regarded as a good omen. It must be confessed that the snorting and braying of Dapple exceeded the neighings of the steed, whence Sancho gathered that his good luck was to rise above and exceed that of his master. But whether he drew this inference from any skill in judicial astrology is not known, as the history is silent in that particular : certainly he had been heard to say, when he happened to fall or stumble, that he wished he had not gone out that day, for nothing was to be got by stumbling or falling but a torn shoe or a broken rib · wherein, although a simpleton, he was not far out of the way.

"Friend Sancho," said Don Quixote to his squire, "the night comes on apace, and it will be dark before we reach Toboso, whither I am resolved to go before I undertake any other adventure. There will I receive the farewell benediction of the peerless Dulcinea, by which I shall secure the happy accomplishment of every perilous enterprise; for nothing in this life inspires a knight-errant with so much valour as the favour of his mistress." "I believe it," answered Sancho; "but I am of opinion it will be difficult for your worship to speak with her alone— at least in any place where you may receive her benediction—unless she tosses it over the pales of the yard where I saw her last, when I carried her the letter that gave an account of the pranks your worship was playing on the mountain." "Didst thou conceive those to be pales, Sancho," quoth Don Quixote, "over which thou didst behold that paragon of gentility and beauty? Impossible! Thou must mean galleries, arcades, or cloisters of some rich and royal palace." "All that may be," answered Sancho; "but, if I do not forget, to me they seemed pales, or I have a very shallow memory." "However, let us go thither, Sancho," said Don Quixote; " for, so I but gaze on her, be it through pales, the chinks of a hut, or lattice window, the smallest ray from the bright sun of her beauty will soon enlighten my understanding and fortify my heart, that I shall remain without a rival either in prudence or valour." "In truth, sir," answered Sancho, "when I saw this sun of the Lady Dulcinea del Toboso, it was not bright enough to cast forth any beams, owing, I take it, to the dust from the grain which I told you her ladyship was winnowing, and which overcast her face like a cloud." "What, Sancho!" said Don Quixote, " dost thou persist in saying and believing that my lady Dulcinea was winnowing wheat—an employment so unsuitable to persons of distinction, who are devoted to other exercises and amusements more becoming their elevated station? It seems thou dost not remember, Sancho, our poet's verses, in which he describes the labours of the four nymphs in their crystal mansions, when they raised their heads above the delightful Tagus, and seated themselves on the verdant mead to work those rich stuffs which, as described by the ingenious bard, were all embroidered with gold, silk, and pearls. And thus my lady must have been employed when thou sawest her; but the envy of some wicked enchanter changes and transforms everything that should give me pleasure; and therefore, should the author of that history of me which is said to be published be some enemy of mine, he may, I fear, have been very inaccurate, mingling a thousand lies with a single truth, and digressing into idle tales unworthy of true and genuine history. O envy! thou root of infinite evils, and canker-worm of virtues! There is no other vice, Sancho, which has not some object of pleasure to excuse it; but envy is attended only with nothing but disgust, malice, and rancour." " That is what I say too," replied Sancho; " and I take it for granted, in that same legend or history which the bachelor Carrasco tells us he has seen, my reputation is tossed about like a tennis-ball. Now, as I am an honest man, I never spoke ill of any enchanter, nor have I wealth enough to be envied. It may be true, indeed, what they say, that I am somewhat sly, and a little inclined to roguish tricks; but then I was always reckoned more simple than knavish. Besides, these same historians ought to spare me a little, if I had nothing else in me but my religion, for I am a true Catholic, and have a mortal hatred to the Jews. But let them say what they will: naked I came, and naked must go. I neither lose nor win; and so my name be but in print, and go about the world merrily from hand to hand, not a fig shall I care: they may say of me whatever they list."

"You remind me, Sancho," said Don Quixote, " of what happened to a famous poet of our own times, who wrote an abusive satire upon the ladies of the court; but, not having expressly named a certain female of rank, so that it was doubtful whether she was included in it or not, she took occasion to reproach him for the omission, and desired to know what he had seen in her that she was to be excluded, and commanded him, at his peril, to enlarge his satire, and introduce her in the supplement. The poet acquiesced, and did not spare her character; but the lady, in order to be famous, was well content to be infamous.

The same kind of ambition was that of the shepherd who set fire to the Temple of Diana, accounted one of the seven wonders of the world, only that his name might live in future ages; and though, in order to defeat his purpose, it was commanded by public edict that his name should never be mentioned either in speech or writing, yet it is known to have been Erostratus. A parallel instance is that which happened to the great emperor Charles the Fifth when he went to look over the famous church of the Rotunda, which by the ancients was called the Pantheon, or temple of all the gods, but now by a better name—the church of all saints. It is the only entire edifice remaining of heathen Rome, and one of the most considerable records of the greatness and magnificence of that city. It is circular in form, spacious, and very light within, though it has but one window, being a circular opening at the top, through which the emperor looked down to view the interior of the structure. He was attended by a Roman knight, who pointed out to him all the beauties of that noble edifice; and after they had descended from the skylight, the knight said to him, ' Sacred sir, a thousand times I felt inclined to clasp your majesty in my arms, and cast myself down with you from the top to the bottom of the church, that my name might be eternal.' ' I thank you,' answered the emperor, ' for not indulging your ambitious thoughts on this occasion, and shall take care in future that your loyalty be not exposed to so severe a trial, and therefore command you never to let me see you again.' He then dismissed him, but not without a princely token of his generosity. This love of fame, Sancho, is a very active principle within us. What, thinkest thou, cast Horatius down from the bridge, armed at all points, into the Tiber? What burnt the arm and hand of Mutius? What impelled Curtius to throw himself into the flaming gulf that opened itself in the midst of Rome? What made Cæsar pass the Rubicon in opposition to every presage? What made the valiant Spaniards, under the courteous and intrepid Cortes, destroy their ships on the shores of a new world? These and a multitude of other great exploits were the effects of that unquenchable thirst after distinction—that fame which mortals aspire to as the only meet recompense of great and glorious deeds; though we, who are Catholic Christian knights-errant, ought to fix our hopes on that higher reward placed in the celestial and eternal regions, which is happiness perfect and everlasting; unlike that shadow of glory which, being only of this world, must perish with it. Since, then, we seek a Christian reward, O my Sancho, let our works be conformable to the religion we profess! In slaying giants we must destroy pride and arrogance; we must vanquish envy by generosity; wrath, by a serene and humble spirit; gluttony and sloth, by temperance and vigilance; licentiousness, by chastity and inviolable fidelity to the sovereign mistresses of our hearts; indolence, by traversing the world in search of every honourable opportunity of obtaining renown as knights and Christians. Such, Sancho, are the means by which we must gain that applause which is the reward of exalted merit." " I understand very well what your worship has been saying," quoth

Sancho; "but, for all that, I wish you would be so kind as to dissolve me one doubt which has just come into my head." "*Resolve*, thou wouldst say, Sancho," said Don Quixote: "but declare it, in Heaven's name, and I will satisfy thee as far as I am able." "Pray tell me, sir," proceeded Sancho, "those Julys or Augusts, and all those mighty heroes you spoke of who are dead—where are they now?" "The Gentiles," answered Don Quixote, "are doubtless in hell; the Christians, if they were good Christians, are either in purgatory or in heaven." "Very

"We had better turn saints immediately, and we shall then soon get that fame we are seeking after."

well," quoth Sancho; "but pray, sir, tell me whether the sepulchres in which the bodies of those great lords lie interred have silver lamps burning before them, and whether the walls of their chapels are adorned with crutches, winding-sheets, old perukes, legs, waxen eyes, and the like; and if not with these, pray how are they adorned?" "The sepulchres of the heathens were for the most part sumptuous temples," answered Don Quixote; "but the ashes of Julius Cæsar were deposited in an urn, placed upon the top of a pyramid of stone of a prodigious magnitude, now called the obelisk of St. Peter. The sepulchre of the Emperor Adrian was a fortress in Rome, as large as a goodly-size

village, formerly called *Moles Adriani,* and now the castle of St. Angelo.
Queen Artemisia buried her husband Mausolus in a tomb which was
numbered among the seven wonders of the world; but neither these
nor any other of the numerous sepulchres of the Gentiles were decorated
with winding-sheets, or any other offerings or signs intended to denote
the holiness of the deceased." "That is what I am coming to," replied
Sancho; "and now pray tell me which is the most difficult, to raise a
dead man to life, or to slay a giant?" "The answer is very obvious,"
answered Don Quixote; "to raise a dead man." "There I have caught
you!" quoth Sancho. "Then his fame who raises the dead, gives sight
to the blind, makes the lame walk, and cures the sick; who has lamps
burning near his grave, and good Christians always in his chapels,
adoring his relics upon their knees—his fame, I say, shall be greater,
both in this world and the next, than that which all the heathen
emperors and knights-errant in the world ever had or ever shall have."
"I grant it," answered Don Quixote. "Then," replied Sancho, "the
bodies and relics of saints have this power and grace, and these privileges, or how do you call them? and with the license of our holy Mother
Church have their lamps, winding-sheets, crutches, pictures, perukes,
eyes, and legs, whereby they increase people's devotion and spread
abroad their own Christian fame. Kings themselves carry the bodies
or relics of saints upon their shoulders, kiss the fragments of their
bones, and adorn their chapels and most favourite altars with them."
"Certainly; but what wouldst thou infer from all this, Sancho?" quoth
Don Quixote. "What I mean," said Sancho, "is, that we had better
turn saints immediately, and we shall then soon get that fame we are
seeking after. And pray take notice, sir, that it was but yesterday—I
mean very lately—a couple of poor barefooted friars were canonised, and
people now reckon it a greater happiness to touch or kiss the iron chains
that bound them, and which are now held in greater veneration than
Orlando's sword in the armoury of our lord the king, Heaven save him!
So that it is better to be a poor friar of the meanest order than the
bravest knight-errant; because four dozen of good penitent lashes are
more esteemed in the sight of God than two thousand tilts with a lance,
though it be against giants, goblins, or dragons." "I confess," answered
Don Quixote, "all this is true; but we cannot all be friars, and many
and various are the ways by which God conducts His elect to heaven.
Chivalry is a kind of religious profession; and some knights are now
saints in glory." "True," quoth Sancho; "but I have heard say there
are more friars in heaven than knights-errant." "It may well be so,"
replied Don Quixote, "because their number is much greater than that
of knights-errant." "And yet," quoth Sancho, "there are abundance
of the errant sort." "Abundance, indeed," answered Don Quixote;
"but few who deserve the name of knights."

In this and the like conversation they passed that night and the
following day, without having encountered anything worth relating,
to the no little mortification of Don Quixote; but the next day they
came in view of the great city of Toboso, at the sight of which Don

Quixote's spirits were much elevated, and those of Sancho as much dejected, because he knew not the abode of Dulcinea, nor had he ever seen her in his life, any more than his master. Thus both were in a state of suffering, the one anxious to see her, and the other anxious because he had not seen her; for Sancho knew not what he should do in case his master should dispatch him to the city. Don Quixote having determined not to enter it until nightfall, he waited in the meantime under the shade of some oak trees, and then proceeded towards the city, where things befell them that were things indeed!

CHAPTER IX.

Which relates what will be found therein.

It was late at night when Don Quixote and Sancho left their retreat and entered Toboso. All the town was hushed in silence; for its inhabitants were sound asleep, stretched out at their ease. The night was clear, though Sancho wished it were otherwise, having occasion for its darkness to conceal his prevarications. No noise was heard in any part save the barking of dogs, which annoyed the ears of Don Quixote and disquieted Sancho's heart. Now and then, it is true, asses brayed, swine grunted, and cats mewed—sounds which seemed to be augmented by the absence of every other noise. All these circumstances the enamoured knight regarded as boding ill. Nevertheless, he said to his squire, " Son Sancho, lead on to Dulcinea's palace; for it is possible we may find her awake." " To what palace? Body of the sun!" answered Sancho, " that in which I saw her highness was but a little mean house." " It was, I suppose, some small apartment of her castle which she had retired to," said the knight, " to amuse herself with her damsels, as is usual with great ladies and princesses." " Since your worship," quoth Sancho, " will needs have my lady Dulcinea's house to be a castle, is this an hour to find the gates open? and is it fit that we should stand thundering at them till they open and let us in, putting the whole house in an uproar? " " First, however, let us find this castle," replied Don Quixote, " and then I will tell thee how it is proper to act. But look, Sancho—either my eyes deceive me, or that huge dark pile we see yonder must be Dulcinea's palace." " Then lead on yourself, sir," answered Sancho; " perhaps it may be so, though if I were to see it with my eyes and touch it with my hands, I will believe it just as much as that it is now day."

Don Quixote led the way, and having gone about two hundred paces, he came up to the edifice which cast the dark shade, and perceiving a large tower, he soon found that the building was no palace, but the principal church of the place; whereupon he said, " We are come to the church, Sancho." " I see we are," answered Sancho; " and pray

Heaven we be not come to our graves; for it is no very good sign to be rambling about churchyards at such hours, and especially since I have already told your worship, if I remember right, that this same lady's house stands in a blind alley." "God's curse light on thee, blockhead!" said the knight; "where hast thou ever found castles and royal palaces built in blind alleys?" "Sir," replied Sancho, "each country has its customs; so, perhaps, it is the fashion here in Toboso to build your palaces and great edifices in alleys; and therefore I beseech your worship to let me look about among these lanes or alleys just before me, and perhaps in one nook or other I may pop upon this same palace, which I wish I may see devoured by dogs for puzzling and bewildering us at this rate." "Speak with more respect, Sancho, of what regards my lady," said Don Quixote: "let us keep our holidays in peace, and not throw the rope after the bucket." "I will curb myself," answered Sancho; "but I cannot bear to think, that though I have seen our mistress's house but once, your worship will needs have me find it at midnight, when you cannot find it yourself, though you must have seen it thousands of times." "Thou wilt make me desperate, Sancho," quoth Don Quixote. "Come hither, heretic: have I not told thee a thousand times that I never saw the peerless Dulcinea in the whole course of my life, nor ever stepped over the threshold of her palace, and that I am enamoured by report alone, and the great fame of her wit and beauty?" "I hear it now," answered Sancho; "and to tell you the truth, I have seen her just as much as your worship." "How can that be?" cried Don Quixote; "didst thou not tell me that thou sawest her winnowing wheat?" "Take no heed of that, sir," replied the squire; "for the fact is, her message, and the sight of her too, were both by hearsay; and I can no more tell who the Lady Dulcinea is than I can buffet the moon." "Sancho, Sancho," answered Don Quixote, "there is a time to jest, and a time when jests are unseasonable. What! because I say that I never saw nor spoke to the mistress of my soul, must thou say so likewise, when thou knowest it to be untrue?"

Their conversation was here interrupted by the approach of a man with two mules; and by the sound of a ploughshare which they dragged along the ground, our travellers rightly guessed that he was a husbandman. As he came near, they heard him singing the ballad of the defeat of the French at Roncesvalles; upon which Don Quixote observed, "No good fortune to-night, Sancho: dost thou not hear what that peasant is singing?" "Yes, I do," answered Sancho; "but what is the defeat of Roncesvalles to us? If he had been singing the ballad of 'Calainos,' it would have had just as much to do with the good or bad ending of our business." The country fellow having now come up to them, Don Quixote said to him, "Good morrow, honest friend: canst thou direct me to the palace of the peerless princess, Donna Dulcinea del Toboso?" "Sir," answered the fellow, "I am a stranger here; for I have been but a few days in the service of a farmer of this town. But the parish priest or the sexton, who live in yonder house across the road, can either of them give your worship an account of that same lady princess; for they keep a register of all the inhabitants of Toboso — not that I think there is any princess living here, though there are several great ladies that may every one be a princess in her own house." "Among those, friend," said Don Quixote, "may be her for whom I am inquiring." "Not unlikely," answered the ploughman, "and so Heaven speed you, for it will soon be daybreak." Then pricking on his mules, he waited for no more questions.

Sancho seeing his master perplexed and dissatisfied, said to him, "Sir, the day comes on apace, and we shall soon have the sun upon us, which will not be very pleasant in the streets; so I think we had better get out of this place, and while your worship takes shelter in some wood hereabouts, I will return and leave not a corner in all the town unsearched for this house, castle, or palace of my lady; and it shall go hard with me but I find it: and as soon as I have done so, I will speak to her ladyship, and tell her where your worship is waiting for her orders and directions how you may see her without damage to her honour and reputation." "Sancho," quoth Don Quixote, "thou hast uttered a thousand sentences in the compass of a few words. Thy counsel I relish much, and shall most willingly follow it. Come on, son, and let us seek for some shelter: then shalt thou return and seek out my lady, from whose discretion and courtesy I expect more than miraculous favours." Sancho was impatient till he got his master out of the town, lest his lies should be detected. He therefore hastened on as fast as possible, and when they had got about the distance of two miles, the knight retired into a shady grove, while the squire returned in quest of the Lady Dulcinea, on which embassy things occurred well worthy of credit and renewed attention.

CHAPTER X.

Wherein is related the cunning used by Sancho in enchanting the Lady Dulcinea; with other events no less ludicrous than true.

EXPRESSING an apprehension that the contents of the present chapter would not be believed, the author of this grand history says he felt much inclined to suppress it, because the knight's frenzy appears herein to be carried to an excess beyond all conception. Notwithstanding this diffidence, he has, however, detailed the whole truth, without adding or diminishing, determined not to regard any doubts that might be entertained of his veracity; and he was in the right, for truth will ever rise above falsehood, like oil above water. He proceeds, therefore, as follows:

Don Quixote having retired into a grove near the city of Toboso, dispatched Sancho, with orders not to return into his presence till he had spoken to his lady, beseeching her that she would be pleased to grant her captive knight permission to wait upon her, and that she would deign to bestow on him her benediction, whereby he might secure complete success in all his encounters and arduous enterprises. Sancho promised to execute his commands, and to return with an answer no less favourable than that which he had formerly brought him. " Go, then, son," replied Don Quixote, " and be not in confusion when thou standest in the blaze of that sun of beauty. Happy art thou above all the squires in the world ! Deeply impress on thy memory the particulars of thy reception—whether she changes colour while thou art delivering thy embassy, and betrays agitation on hearing my name; whether her cushion cannot hold her, if perchance thou shouldst find her seated on the rich Estrado;* or, if standing, mark whether she is not obliged to sustain herself sometimes upon one foot and sometimes upon the other; whether she repeats her answer to thee three or four times; whether she changes it from soft to harsh, from harsh to soft again; whether she raises her hand to adjust her hair, though it be not disordered—in short, observe all her actions and motions; for by an accurate detail of them I shall be enabled to penetrate into the secret recesses of her heart touching the affair of my love; for let me tell thee, Sancho, if thou knowest it not already, that with lovers the external actions and gestures are couriers, which bear authentic tidings of what is passing in the interior of the soul. Go, friend, and may better fortune than mine conduct thee : be thou more successful than my anxious heart will bode during the painful period of thy absence ! " " I will go, and return quickly," quoth Sancho. " In the meantime, good sir, cheer up, and remember the saying, that ' a good heart breaks bad luck,' and ' if there is no hook there is no bacon,' and ' where we least expect it the hare starts;' this I say because, though we could not find the castle nor palace of my lady Dulcinea in the dark, now that it is daylight, I reckon I shall soon find it, and then—let me alone to deal with her." " Verily, Sancho," quoth Don Quixote, " thou dost apply thy proverbs most happily; yet Heaven grant me better luck in the attainment of my hopes ! "

Sancho now switched his Dapple, and set off, leaving Don Quixote on horseback, resting on his stirrups and leaning on his lance, full of melancholy and confused fancies, where we will leave him, and attend Sancho Panza, who departed no less perplexed and thoughtful; insomuch that, after he had got out of the grove and looked behind him to ascertain that his master was out of sight, he alighted, and sitting down at the foot of a tree, he began to hold a parley with himself. " Tell me now, brother Sancho," quoth he, " whither is your worship going? Are you going to seek some ass that is lost?" " No, verily." " Then what are you going to seek?" " Why I go to look for a thing of nothing— a princess, the sun of beauty, and all heaven together ! " " Well, Sancho, and where think you to find all this?" " Where? In the great city of Toboso." " Very well; and pray who sent you on this

---

* That part of the floor at the upper end of the room which is raised, and where the ladies sit upon cushions to receive visits,

errand?" "Why, the renowned knight Don Quixote de la Mancha, who redresses wrongs, and gives drink to the hungry and meat to the thirsty." "All this is mighty well; and do you know her house, Sancho?" "My master says it must be some royal palace or stately castle." "And have you ever seen her?" "Neither I nor my master have ever seen her." "And do you think it would be right or advisable that the people of Toboso should know you are coming to kidnip their princesses and lead their ladies astray? What if, for this offence, they should come and grind your ribs to powder with true dry basting, and not leave you a whole bone in your skin?" "Truly, they would be much in the right of it, unless they please to consider that I, being only a messenger, am not in fault." "Trust not to that, Sancho; for the Manchegans are very choleric, and their honour so ticklish that it will not bear touching." "God's my life! if we should be scented, woe be to us. But why do I go looking for a cat with three legs for another man's pleasure? Besides, to look for Dulcinea up and down Toboso is just as if one should look for Little Mary in Rabena, or a bachelor in Salamanca. The devil, and nobody else, has put me upon such a business!"

This was Sancho's soliloquy, the result of which was to return to it again. "Well," continued he, "there is a remedy for everything but death, who, in spite of our teeth, will have us in his clutches. This master of mine, I can plainly see, is mad enough for a straight waistcoat; and, in truth, I am not much better: nay, I am worse, in following and serving him, if there be any truth in the proverb, ' Show me who thou art with, and I will tell thee what thou art;' or in the other, ' Not with whom thou wert bred, but with whom thou art fed.' He, then, being in truth a madman, and so mad as frequently to mistake one thing for another, and not know black from white; as plainly appeared when he called the windmills giants, mules dromedaries, and the flock of sheep armies of fighting men, with many more things to the same tune; this being the case, I say, it will not be very difficult to make him believe that a country wench (the first I light upon) is the Lady Dulcinea; and should he not believe it, I will swear to it; and if he swears, I will outswear him; and if he persists, I will persist the more, so that mine shall still be uppermost, come what will of it. By this plan I may, perhaps, tire him of sending me on such errands; or he may take it into his head that some wicked enchanter has changed his lady's form, out of pure spite."

This project set Sancho's spirit at rest, and he reckoned his business as good as half done; so he stayed where he was till towards evening, that Don Quixote might suppose him travelling on his mission. Fortunately for him, just as he was going to mount his Dapple, he espied three country wenches coming from Toboso, each mounted on a young ass; but whether male or female the author declares not: probably they were females, as the countrywomen commonly rode upon she-asses; however, that being a matter of no great importance, it is unnecessary to be at the trouble of ascertaining the point. Sancho no sooner got sight of them than he rode back at a good pace to seek his master Don Quixote, whom he found breathing a thousand sighs and amorous lamentations. When Don Quixote saw him, he said, "Well, friend Sancho, am I to mark this day with a white or a black stone?" "Your worship," answered Sancho, "had better mark it with red ochre, as they do the inscriptions on the professors' chairs, to be the more easily read by the lookers-on." "Thou bringest me good news, then?" cried Don Quixote. "So good," answered Sancho, "that your worship has only to clap spurs to Rozinante, and get out upon the plain, to see the Lady Dulcinea del Toboso, who, with a couple of her damsels, is coming to pay your worship a visit." "Gracious Heaven!" exclaimed Don Quixote, "what dost thou say? Take care that thou beguilest not my real sorrow by a counterfeit joy." "What should I get," answered Sancho, "by deceiving your worship, only to be found out the next moment? Come, sir, put on, and you will see the princess our mistress all arrayed and adorned—in short, like herself. She and her damsels are one blaze of flaming gold; all strings of pearls, all diamonds, all rubies, all cloth of tissue above ten hands deep; their hair loose about their shoulders, like so many sunbeams blowing about in the wind; and what is more, they come mounted upon three pied belfreys, the finest you ever laid eyes on." "*Palfreys*, thou wouldst say, Sancho," quoth Don Quixote. "Well, well," answered Sancho, "belfreys and palfreys are much the same thing; but let them be mounted how they will, they are surely the finest creatures one would wish to see; especially my mistress the Princess Dulcinea, who dazzles one's senses." "Let us go, son Sancho," answered Don Quixote; "and as a reward for this welcome news, I bequeath to thee the choicest spoils I shall gain in my next adventure; and, if that will not satisfy thee, I bequeath thee the colts which my three mares will foal this year upon our village common." "I stick to the colts," answered Sancho, "for we cannot yet reckon up the worth of the spoils."

They were now got out of the wood, and saw the three wenches very near. Don Quixote looked eagerly along the road towards Toboso, and, seeing nobody but the three wenches, he asked Sancho, in much agitation, whether they were out of the city when he left them. "Out of the city!" answered Sancho; "are your worship's eyes in the nape of your neck, that you do not see them now before you, shining like the sun at noon-day?" "I see only three country girls," answered Don Quixote, "on three asses." "Now, Heaven keep me from the devil!" answered Sancho; "is it possible that three palfreys, or how do you call them? white as the driven snow, should look to you like asses? As the Lord liveth, you shall pluck off this beard of mine if it be so." "I tell thee, friend Sancho," answered Don Quixote, "that it is as certain they are asses as that I am Don Quixote and thou Sancho Panza—at least, so they seem to me." "Sir," quoth Sancho, "say not such a thing; but snuff those eyes of yours, and come and pay reverence to the mistress of your soul." So saying, he advanced forward to meet the peasant girls, and, alighting from Dapple, he laid hold of

one of their asses by the halter, and, bending both knees to the ground,
said to the girl, "Queen, princess, and duchess of beauty, let your
haughtiness and greatness be pleased to receive into grace and good-
liking your captive knight, who stands there turned into stone, all
disorder, and without any pulse, to find himself before your magnificent
presence. I am Sancho Panza, his squire, and he is that way-worn
knight Don Quixote de la Mancha, otherwise called the Knight of the
Sorrowful Figure."

Don Quixote had now placed himself on his knees by Sancho, and
with wild and staring eyes surveyed her whom Sancho called his queen;
and, seeing nothing but a peasant girl, with a broad face, flat nose,
coarse and homely, he was so confounded that he could not open his
lips. The wenches were also surprised to find themselves stopped by
two men so different in aspect, and both on their knees; but the lady
who was stopped, breaking silence, said in an angry tone, " Get out of
the road, plague on ye! and let us pass by, for we are in haste." " O

princess and universal lady of Toboso!" cried Sancho, "is not your magnificent heart melting to see, on his knees before your sublimated presence, the pillar and prop of knight-errantry?" "Heyday! what's here to do?" cried another of the girls; "look how your small gentry come to jeer us poor country girls, as if we could not give them as good as they bring: go! get off about your business, and let us mind ours; and so speed you well." "Rise, Sancho," said Don Quixote, on hearing this; "for I now perceive that fortune, not yet satisfied with persecuting me, has barred every avenue whereby relief might come to this wretched soul I bear about me in the flesh. And thou, O extreme of all that is valuable, summit of human perfection, thou sole balm to this disconsolate heart that adores thee, though now some wicked enchanter spreads clouds and cataracts over my eyes, changing, and to them only, thy peerless beauty into that of a poor rustic; if he has not converted mine also into that of some goblin, to render it horrible to thy view, bestow on me one kind and amorous look, and let this submissive posture, these bended knees, before thy disguised beauty, declare the humility with which my soul adores thee!" "Marry come up," quoth the wench, "with your idle gibberish! Get on with you, and let us go, and we shall take it kindly." Sancho now let go the halter, delighted that he had come off so well with his contrivance. The imaginary Dulcinea was no sooner set at liberty than, pricking her beast with a sharp-pointed stick which she held in her hand, she scoured along the field; but the ass, smarting more than usual under the goad, began to kick and wince in such a manner that down came the Lady Dulcinea to the ground. Don Quixote instantly ran to her assistance, and Sancho to replace the pannel that had got under the ass's belly. Don Quixote was then proceeding to raise his enchanted mistress, but the lady saved him that trouble; for, immediately upon getting up from the ground, she retired three or four steps back, took a little run, then, clapping both hands upon the ass's crupper, jumped into the saddle lighter than a falcon, and seated herself astride like a man. "By Saint Roque!" cried Sancho, "our lady mistress is lighter than a bird, and could teach the nimblest Cordovan or Mexican how to mount: she springs into the saddle at a jump, and without the help of spurs makes her palfrey run like a wild ass; and her damsels are not a whit short of her, for they all fly like the wind!" And this was the truth; for, Dulcinea being remounted, the other two made after her at full speed, without looking behind them for above half a league.

Don Quixote followed them with his eyes as far as he was able, and when they were out of sight, turning to Sancho, he said, "What dost thou think now, Sancho? See how I am persecuted by enchanters! Mark how far their malice extends, even to depriving me of the pleasure of seeing my mistress in her own proper form! Surely I was born to be an example of wretchedness, and the butt and mark at which all the arrows of ill fortune are aimed! And thou must have observed, too, Sancho, that these traitors were not contented with changing and transforming the countenance of my Dulcinea, but they must give her the base and uncouth figure of a country wench; at the same time robbing her of that which is peculiar to ladies of rank—the fragrant scent which they imbibe from being always among flowers and sweet perfumes: for, if thou wilt believe me, Sancho, when I approached to help Dulcinea upon her palfrey (as thou sayest, though it appeared to me but an ass) she gave me such a whiff of undigested garlic as almost poisoned my very soul." "Oh base rabble!" cried Sancho, "O barbarous and evil-minded enchanters! Oh that I might see you all strung and hung up by the gills like smoked herrings! Cunning ye are, much ye can, and much evil ye do. One would have thought it might have satisfied ye, rogues as ye are! to have changed the pearls of my lady's eyes into cork galls, and her hair of the purest gold into bristles of a red cow's tail, and all her features from beauty to ugliness, without meddling with her breath, by which we might have guessed at what was hid beneath her ugly crust—though, to say the truth, to me she did not appear in the least ugly, but rather all beauty, which was raised to the highest pitch by a mole she had on her right lip, like a whisker, with seven or eight red hairs on it, like threads of gold, and above a span long!" " As to the mole," said Don Quixote, " according to the correspondence subsisting between the moles of the face and those of the body, Dulcinea should have another on her person, on the same side as that on her face ; but, indeed, hairs of the length thou sayest are somewhat of the longest for moles." " Yet I can assure your worship," answered Sancho, "that there they were, and looked as if they had been born with her." " I believe it, friend," replied Don Quixote, " for Nature has placed nothing about Dulcinea but what is finished and perfect; and therefore, had she a hundred moles like those of which thou speakest, in her they would not be moles, but moons and resplendent stars. But tell me, Sancho, that which to me appeared to be a pannel, was it a side-saddle or a pillion?" "It was a side-saddle," answered Sancho, " with a field covering, worth half a kingdom for the richness of it." "And that I should not see all this!" exclaimed Don Quixote. "Again I say, and a thousand times will I repeat it, I am the most unfortunate of men!" The sly rogue Sancho had much difficulty to forbear laughing, to think how exquisitely his master was gulled. After more dialogue of the same kind, they mounted their beasts again, and followed the road to Saragossa, still intending to be present at a solemn festival annually held in that city; but before they reached it events befell them which, for their importance, variety, and novelty, well deserve to be recorded and read

CHAPTER XI.

*Of the strange adventure which befell the valorous Don Quixote, with the cart, or wain, of the Cortes of Death.**

DON QUIXOTE proceeded on his way at a slow pace, exceedingly pensive, musing on the base trick the enchanters had played him in transforming his lady Dulcinea into the homely figure of a peasant wench; nor could he devise any means of restoring her to her former state. In these meditations his mind was so absorbed that, without perceiving it, the bridle dropped on Rozinante's neck, who, taking advantage of the liberty thus given him, at every step turned aside to take a mouthful of the fresh grass with which those parts abounded. Sancho endeavoured to rouse him. "Sorrow," said he, "was made for man, not for beasts, sir; but if men give too much way to it, they become beasts. Take heart, sir; recollect yourself, and gather up Rozinante's reins: cheer up, awake, and show that you have courage befitting a knight-errant! What, in the devil's name, is the matter? Why are you so cast down? Are we here, or in France? Satan take all the Dulcineas in the world! The welfare of a single knight-errant is of more consequence than all the enchantments and transformations on earth." "Peace, Sancho!" cried Don Quixote, in no very faint voice; "peace, I say, and utter no blasphemies against that enchanted lady, of whose disgrace and misfortune I am the sole cause, since they proceed entirely from the envy that the wicked bear to me." "So say I," quoth Sancho; "for who saw her then and sees her now, his heart must melt with grief, I vow." "Well, indeed, mayest thou say so," replied Don Quixote; "thou who sawest her in the full lustre of her beauty, as the enchantment affected not thy sight, nor concealed her perfections from thee. Against me alone, and against my eyes, was the force of its poison directed. Nevertheless, Sancho, I suspect that thou didst not give me a true description of her beauty; for, if I remember right, thou saidst her eyes were of pearl; now, eyes that look like pearl are rather those of a fish than of a lady. I imagine the eyes of Dulcinea must be of verdant emeralds, arched over with two celestial bows, that serve for eyebrows. Thou must, therefore, take those pearls from her eyes, and apply them to her teeth; for doubtless, Sancho, thou hast mistaken teeth for eyes." "It may be," answered Sancho, "for her beauty confounded me as much as her ugliness did your worship. But let us recommend all to God, who alone knows what shall befall us

---

* These *Autos* are dramatic allegories, symbolical of religious mysteries; they were represented on the festival of the Corpus Christi, and the Octave, not only at the theatres, but before the councils of state, and even the tribune of the Holy Inquisition. These allegorical shows are now wisely prohibited.

in this vale of tears—this evil world of ours, in which there is scarcely anything to be found without some mixture of wickedness, imposture, and knavery. One thing, dear sir, troubles me more than all the rest; which is to think what must be done when your worship shall overcome some giant or knight-errant, and send him to present himself before the beauty of the Lady Dulcinea. Where shall this poor giant or miserable vanquished knight be able to find her? Methinks I see them sauntering up and down Toboso, and gaping about like fools for my lady Dulcinea; and though they should meet her in the middle of the street, they will know her no more than they would my father." "Perhaps, Sancho," answered Don Quixote, " the enchantment may not extend to the vision of vanquished knights or giants; however, we will make the experiment upon one or two of the first I overcome, and send them with orders to return and give me an account of their reception." "Your worship is quite in the right," replied Sancho, "for by this trial we shall surely come at the knowledge: and if she is hid from your worship alone, the misfortune will be more yours than hers: and so that the Lady Dulcinea have health and contentment, we, for our parts, ought to make shift and bear it as well as we can, seeking our adventures, and leaving it to Time to do his work, who is the best doctor for these and worse grievances."

Don Quixote would have answered Sancho, but was prevented by the passing of a cart across the road, full of the strangest-looking people imaginable. It was without any awning above or covering to the sides, and the carter who drove the mules had the appearance of a frightful demon. The first figure that caught Don Quixote's attention was that of Death, with a human visage; close to him sat an angel, with large painted wings; on the other side stood an emperor with a crown, seemingly of gold, on his head. At Death's feet sat the god Cupid, not blindfold, but with his bow, quiver, and arrows; a knight also appeared among them in complete armour, only instead of a morion or casque, he wore a hat with a large plume of feathers of divers colours; and there were several other persons of equal diversity in appearance. Such a sight coming thus abruptly upon them somewhat startled Don Quixote, and the heart of Sancho was struck with dismay. But with the knight surprise soon gave place to joy, for he anticipated some new and perilous adventure; and under this impression, with a resolution prepared for any danger, he planted himself just before the cart, and cried out in a loud menacing voice, " Carter, coachman, or devil, or whatever be thy denomination, tell me instantly what thou art, whither going, and who are the persons thou conveyest in that vehicle, which, by its freight, looks like Charon's ferry-boat?" To which the devil calmly replied, " Sir, we are travelling players belonging to Angulo el Malo's company. To-day, being the Octave of Corpus Christi, we have been performing a piece representing the ' Cortes of Death;' this evening we are to play it again in the village just before us; and, not having far to go, we travel in the dresses of our parts, to save trouble. This young man represents Death ; he an angel : that woman, who is our author's wife, plays a queen ; the other a soldier ; this one is an emperor; and I am the devil, one of the principal personages of the drama, for in this company I have all the chief parts. If your worship desires any further information I am ready to answer your questions ; for, being a devil, I know everything." " Upon the faith of a knight-errant," answered Don Quixote, " when I first espied this cart, I imagined some great adventure offered itself ; but appearances are not always to be trusted. Heaven be with you, good people ; go and perform your play, and if there be anything in which I may be of service to you, command me, for I will do it most readily, having been from my youth a great admirer of masques and theatrical representations."

While they were speaking, one of the motley crew came up capering towards them, in an antic dress, frisking about with his morris-bells, and three full-blown ox-bladders tied to the end of a stick. Approaching the knight, he flourished his bladders in the air, and bounced them against the ground close under the nose of Rozinante, who was so startled by the noise that Don Quixote lost all command over him, and having got the curb between his teeth, away he scampered over the plain, with more speed than might have been expected from such an assemblage of dry bones. Sancho, seeing his master's danger, leaped from Dapple and ran to his assistance ; but, before his squire could reach him, he was upon the ground, and close by him Rozinante, who fell with his master, the usual termination of Rozinante's frolics. Sancho had no sooner dismounted to assist Don Quixote than the bladder-dancing devil jumped upon Dapple, and thumping him with the bladders, fear at the noise, more than the smart, set him also flying over the field towards the village where they were going to act. Thus, Sancho, beholding at one and the same moment Dapple's flight and his master's fall, was at a loss to which of the two duties he should first attend ; but, like a good squire and faithful servant, the love he bore to his master prevailed over his affection for his ass ; though, as often as he saw the bladders hoisted in the air and fall upon the body of his Dapple, he felt the pangs and tortures of death, and he would rather those blows had fallen on the apple of his own eyes than on the least hair of his ass's tail.

In this tribulation he came up to Don Quixote, who was in a much worse plight than he could have wished ; and, as he helped him to get upon Rozinante, he said, " Sir, the devil has run away with Dapple." " What devil ? " demanded Don Quixote. " He with the bladders," answered Sancho. " I will recover him," replied Don Quixote, "though he should hide himself in the deepest and darkest dungeon of the earth. Follow me, Sancho ; for the cart moves but slowly, and the mules shall make compensation for the loss of Dapple." " Stay, sir," cried Sancho, " you may cool your anger, for I see the devil has left Dapple and gone his way." And so it was ; for Dapple and the devil having tumbled, as well as Rozinante and his master, the merry imp left him and made off on foot to the village, while Dapple turned back to his rightful owner. " Nevertheless," said Don Quixote, " it will not be amiss to chastise the

Sancho, beholding at one and the same moment Dapple's flight and his master's fall, was at a loss to which of the two duties he should first attend.

insolence of this devil on some of his company, even upon the emperor himself." "Good your worship," quoth Sancho, "do not think of such a thing, but take my advice, and never meddle with players, for they are a people mightily beloved. I have seen a player taken up for two murders, and get off scot-free. As they are merry folks and give pleasure, everybody favours them and is ready to stand their friend; particularly if they are of the king's or some nobleman's company, who look and dress like any princes." "That capering buffoon shall not escape with impunity, though he were favoured by the whole human race!" cried Don Quixote, as he rode off in pursuit of the cart, which was now very near the town, and he called aloud, "Halt a little, merry sirs; stay and let me teach you how to treat cattle belonging to the squires of knights-errant." Don Quixote's words were loud enough to be heard by the players, who, perceiving his adverse designs upon them, instantly jumped out of the cart, Death first, and after him the emperor, the carter-devil, and the angel; nor did the queen or the god Cupid stay behind; and, all armed with stones, waited in battle array, ready to receive Don Quixote at the points of their pebbles. Don Quixote, seeing the gallant squadron with arms uplifted, ready to discharge such a fearful volley, checked Rozinante with the bridle, and began to consider how he might most prudently attack them. While he paused, Sancho came up, and seeing him on the point of attacking that well-formed brigade, remonstrated with him. "It is mere madness, sir," said he, "to attempt such an enterprise. Pray consider there is no armour proof against stones and brick, unless you could thrust yourself into a bell of brass. Besides, it is not courage, but rashness, for one man singly to encounter an army where Death is present, and where emperors fight in person, assisted by good and bad angels. But if that be not reason enough, remember that, though these people all look like princes and emperors, there is not a real knight among them." "Now, indeed," said Don Quixote, "thou hast hit the point, Sancho, which can alone shake my resolution. I neither can nor ought to draw my sword, as I have often told thee, against those who are not dubbed knights. To thee it belongs, Sancho, to revenge the affront offered to thy Dapple; and from this spot I will encourage and assist thee by my voice and salutary instructions." "Good Christians should never avenge injuries," answered Sancho; "and I dare say that Dapple is as forgiving as myself, and ready to submit his case to my will and pleasure, which is to live peaceably with all the world, as long as Heaven is pleased to grant me life." "Since this is thy resolution, good Sancho, discreet Sancho, Christian Sancho, and honest Sancho," replied Don Quixote, "let us leave these phantoms, and seek better and more substantial adventures; for this country, I see, is likely to afford us many and very extraordinary ones." He then wheeled Rozinante about, Sancho took his Dapple, and Death, with his flying squadron, having returned to their cart, each pursued their way. Thus happily terminated the awful adventure of Death's caravan—thanks to the wholesome advice that Sancho Panza gave his master; who, the next day, encountering an enamoured knight-errant, met with an adventure not a whit less important than the one just related.

CHAPTER XII.

Of the strange adventure which befell the valorous Don Quixote with the brave Knight of the Mirrors.

DON QUIXOTE and his squire passed the night following their encounter with Death under some tall umbrageous trees; and, as they were re-freshing themselves, by Sancho's advice, from the store of provisions carried by Dapple, he said to his master, "What a fool, sir, should I have been had I chosen for my reward the spoils of your worship's first adventure, instead of the three ass-colts! It is a true saying, 'A sparrow in the hand is better than a vulture upon the wing.' " " However, Sancho," answered Don Quixote, " hadst thou suffered me to make the attack which I had premeditated, thy share of the booty would have been at least the emperor's crown of gold, and Cupid's painted wings; for I would have plucked them off perforce, and delivered them into thy hands." "The crowns and sceptres of your theatrical emperors," answered Sancho, " are never pure gold, but tinsel or copper." " That is true," replied Don Quixote; "nor would it be proper that the decorations of a play should be otherwise than counterfeit, like the drama itself, which I would have thee hold in due estimation, as well as the actors and authors, for they are all instruments of much benefit to the commonwealth, continually presenting a mirror before our eyes, in which we see lively representations of the actions of human life : nothing, indeed, more truly portrays to us what we are, and what we should be, than the drama. Tell me, hast thou never seen a play in which kings, emperors, popes, lords, and ladies are introduced, with divers other personages; one acting the ruffian, another the knave; one the merchant, another the soldier; one a designing fool, another a foolish lover; and observed that, when the play is done, and the actors undressed, they are all again upon a level ?" " Yes, marry have I," quoth Sancho. " The very same thing, then," said Don Quixote, " happens on the stage of this world, on which some play the part of emperors, others of popes— in short, every part that can be introduced in a comedy; but, at the conclusion of this drama of life, death strips us of the robes which make the difference between man and man, and leaves us all on one level in the grave." " A brave comparison !" quoth Sancho; "though not so new but that I have heard it many times, as well as that of the game at chess; which is that, while the game is going, every piece has its office, and, when it is ended, they are all huddled together and put into a bag; just as we are put together into the ground when we are dead." " Sancho," said Don Quixote, " thou art daily improving in sense." "And so I ought," answered Sancho; "for some of your worship's wisdom must needs stick to me; as dry and barren soil, by well dunging and digging, comes at last to bear good fruit. My meaning is, that your worship's conversation has been the dung laid upon the barren soil of my poor wit, and the tillage has been the time I have been in your service and company; by which I hope to produce fruit like any blessing, and such as will not disparage my teacher, nor let me stray from the paths of good breeding which your worship has made in my shallow understanding." Don Quixote smiled at Sancho's affected style; but he really did think him improved, and was frequently surprised by his observations, when he did not display his ignorance by soaring too high. His chief strength lay in proverbs, of which he had always abundance ready, though perhaps not always fitting the occasion, as may often have been remarked in the course of this history.

In this kind of conversation they spent a great part of the night, till Sancho felt disposed to let down the portcullises of his eyes, as he used to say when he was inclined to sleep. So, having unrigged his Dapple, he turned him loose into pasture; but he did not take off the saddle from Rozinante's back, it being the express command of his master that he should continue saddled whilst they kept the field, and were not sleeping under a roof, in conformity to an ancient established custom religiously observed among knights-errant, which was to take off the bridle, and hang it on the pommel of the saddle, but by no means to remove the saddle. Sancho observed this rule, and gave Rozinante the same liberty he had given to Dapple. And here it may be noticed that the friendship subsisting between this pair was so remarkable, that there is a tradition handed down from father to son, that the author of this faithful history compiled several chapters expressly upon that subject; but, to maintain the decorum due to an heroic work, he would not insert them. Nevertheless, he occasionally mentions these animals, and says, that when they came together they always fell to scratching one another with their teeth, and, when they were tired or satisfied, Rozinante would stretch his neck at least half a yard across that of Dapple, and both fixing their eyes attentively on the ground, would stand three days in that posture—at least as long as they were undisturbed, or till hunger compelled them to seek food. The author is said to have compared their friendship to that of Nisus and Euryalus, or that of Pylades and Orestes. How steady, then, must have been the friendship of these two peaceable animals — to the shame of men, who are so regardless of its laws! Hence the sayings, "A friend cannot find a friend;" "Reeds become darts;" and "From a friend to a friend, the bug," &c.* Nor let it be taken amiss that any comparison should be made between the mutual cordiality of animals and that of men; for much useful knowledge and many salutary precepts have been taught by the brute creation. We are indebted, for example, to the stork for the clyster, and for emetics to the dog; from which animal we may also learn gratitude, as well as vigilance from cranes, foresight from ants, modesty from elephants, and loyalty from horses.

At length Sancho fell asleep at the foot of a cork tree, while Don Quixote slumbered beneath a branching oak. But it was not long before he was disturbed by a noise near him: he started up, and looking in the direction whence the sounds proceeded, could discern two men on horseback, one of whom, dismounting, said to the other, "Alight, friend, and unbridle the horses; for this place will afford them pasture, and offers to me that silence and solitude which my serious thoughts require." As he spoke, he threw himself on the ground, and in this motion a rattling of armour was heard, which convinced Don Quixote that this was a knight-errant; and going to Sancho, who was fast asleep, he pulled him by the arm, and having with some difficulty aroused him, he said in a low voice, "Friend Sancho, we have got an adventure here." "Heaven send it be a good one," answered Sancho; "and pray, sir, where may this same adventure be?" "Where, sayest thou, Sancho?" replied

---

* "From a friend to a friend, a bug in the eye," is a proverb applied to the false professions of friendship.

Don Quixote: "turn thine eyes that way, and thou wilt see a knight-errant lying extended, who seems to me not over-happy in his mind; for I just now saw him dismount and throw himself upon the ground as if much oppressed with grief, and his armour rattled as he fell." "But how do you know," quoth Sancho, "that this is an adventure?" "Though I cannot yet positively call it an adventure, it has the usual signs of one. But listen: he is tuning an instrument, and seems to be preparing to sing." "By my troth, so he is," cried Sancho, "and he must be some knight or other in love." "As all knights-errant must be," quoth Don Quixote; "but hearken, and we shall discover his thoughts by his song, for out of the abundance of the heart the mouth speaketh." Sancho would have replied, but the Knight of the Wood, whose voice was only moderately good, began to sing, and they both attentively listened to the following words:

SONNET.

"Bright authoress of my good or ill,
  Prescribe the law I must observe:
My heart, obedient to thy will,
  Shall never from its duty swerve.

"If you refuse my griefs to know,
  The stifled anguish seals my fate;
But if your ears would drink my woe,
  Love shall himself the tale relate.

"Though contraries my heart compose,
  Hard as the diamond's solid frame,
And soft as yielding wax that flows,
  To thee, my fair, 't is still the same.

"Take it, for every stamp prepared:
  Imprint what characters you choose:
The faithful tablet, soft or hard,
  The dear impression ne'er shall lose."

With a deep sigh that seemed to be drawn from the very bottom of his heart, the Knight of the Wood ended his song; and after some pause, in a plaintive and dolorous voice he exclaimed, "O thou most beautiful and most ungrateful of womankind! O divine Casildea de Vandalia! wilt thou then suffer this thy captive knight to consume and pine away in continual peregrinations, and in severest toils? Is it not enough that I have caused thee to be acknowledged the most consummate beauty in the world, by all the knights of Navarre, of Leon, of Tartesia, of Castile, and, in fine, by all the knights of La Mancha?" "Not so," said Don Quixote; "for I am of La Mancha, and never have I made such an acknowledgment, nor ever will admit an assertion so prejudicial to the beauty of my mistress. Thou seest, Sancho, how this knight raves. But let us listen; perhaps he will make some further declaration." "Ay, marry will he," replied Sancho, "for he seems to be in a humour to complain for a month to come." But they were mistaken; for the knight, hearing voices near them, proceeded no further in his lamentations, but, rising up, said aloud in a courteous voice, " Who goes there? What are ye? of the number of the happy, or of the afflicted?" " Of the afflicted," answered Don Quixote. " Come to me, then," replied the Knight of the Wood, " and you will find sorrow and misery itself! " These expressions were uttered in so moving a tone that Don Quixote, followed by Sancho, went up to the mournful knight, who, taking his hand, said to him, " Sit down here, Sir Knight, for to be assured that you profess the order of chivalry, it is sufficient that I find you here, encompassed by solitude and the cold dews of night—the proper station for knights-errant." " A knight I am," replied Don Quixote, " and of the order you name; and, although my heart is the mansion of misery and woe, yet can I sympathise in the sorrows of others: from the strain I just now heard from you, I conclude that yours are of the amorous kind—arising, I mean, from a passion for some ungrateful fair."

Whilst thus discoursing, they were seated together on the ground, peaceably and sociably, not as if, at daybreak, they were to fall upon each other with mortal fury. " Perchance you, too, are in love, Sir Knight," said he of the wood to Don Quixote. " Such is my cruel destiny," answered Don Quixote; " though the sorrows that may arise from well-placed affections ought rather to be accounted blessings than calamities." " That is true," replied the Knight of the Wood, " provided our reason and understanding be not affected by disdain, which, when carried to excess, is more like vengeance." " I never was disdained by my mistress," answered Don Quixote. " No, verily," quoth Sancho, who stood close by, " for my lady is as gentle as a lamb, and as soft as butter." " Is this your squire?" demanded the Knight of the Wood. " He is," replied Don Quixote. " I never in my life saw a squire," said the Knight of the Wood, " who durst presume to speak where his lord was conversing: at least there stands mine, as tall as his father, and it cannot be proved that he ever opened his lips when I was speaking." " I' faith! " quoth Sancho, " I have talked, and can talk, before one as good as—and perhaps—but let that rest: perhaps the less said the better." The Knight of the Wood's squire now took Sancho by the arm, and said, " Let us two go where we may chat squire-like together, and leave these masters of ours to talk over their loves to each other; for I warrant they will not have done before to-morrow morning." " With all my heart," quoth Sancho; " and I will tell you who I am, that you may judge whether I am not fit to make one among the talking squires." The squires then withdrew, and a dialogue passed between them as lively as that of their masters was grave.

CHAPTER XIII.

Wherein is continued the adventure of the Knight of the Wood; with the wise and pleasant dialogue between the two squires.

SQUIRES and knights being thus separated, the latter were engaged on the subject of their loves, while the former gave an account to each other of their lives. The history first relates the conversation between the servants, and afterwards proceeds to that of the masters. Having retired a little apart, the Squire of the Wood said to Sancho, "This is a toilsome life we squires to knights-errant lead: in good truth, we eat our bread by the sweat of our brows, which is one of the curses laid upon our first parents." "You may say, too, that we eat it by the frost of our bodies," added Sancho; "for who has to bear more cold, as well as heat, than your miserable squires to knights-errant? It would not be quite so bad if we could always get something to eat, for good fare lessens care; but how often we must pass whole days without breaking our fast—unless it be upon air!" "All this may be endured," quoth he of the wood, "with the hopes of reward; for that knight-errant must be unlucky indeed who does not speedily recompense his squire with, at least, a handsome government, or some pretty earldom." "I," replied Sancho, "have already told my master that I should be satisfied with the government of an island; and he is so noble and so generous that he has promised it me a thousand times." "And I," said he of the wood, "should think myself amply rewarded for all my services with a canonry, and I have my master's word for it too." "Why, then," quoth Sancho, "belike your master is some knight of the Church, and so can bestow rewards of that kind on his squires: mine is only a layman. Some of his wise friends advised him once to be an archbishop, but he would be nothing but an emperor, and I trembled all the while, lest he should take a liking to the Church; because, you must know, I am not gifted that way—to say the truth, sir, though I look like a man, I am a very beast in such matters." "Let me tell you, friend," quoth he of the wood, "you are quite in the wrong; for these island governments are often more plague than profit. Some are crabbed, some beggarly, some—in short, the best of them are sure to bring more care than they are worth, and are mostly too heavy for the shoulders that have to bear them. I suspect it would be wiser in us to quit this thankless drudgery and stay at home, where we may find easier work and better pastime; for he must be a sorry squire who has not his nag, his brace of greyhounds, and an angling-rod to enjoy himself with at home." "I am not without these things," answered Sancho; "it is true I have no horse, but then I have an ass which is worth twice as much as my master's steed. Heaven send me a bad Easter, and may it be the first that comes, if I would swap with him, though he should offer me four bushels of barley to boot; no, faith, that would not I, though you may take for a joke the price I set upon my Dapple; for dapple, sir, is the colour of my ass. Greyhounds I cannot be in want of, as our town is overstocked with them : besides, the rarest sporting is that we find at other people's cost." "Really and truly, brother squire," answered he of the wood, "I have resolved with myself to quit the frolics of these knights-errant, and get home again and look after my children; for I have three like Indian pearls." "And I have two," quoth Sancho, "fit to be presented to the Pope himself in person; especially my girl that I am breeding up for a countess, if it please Heaven, in spite of her mother." "And pray, what may be the age of the young lady you are breeding up for a countess?" demanded he of the wood. "Fifteen years, or thereabouts," answered Sancho; "and she is as tall as a lance, as fresh as an April morning, and as strong as a porter." "These are qualifications," said he of the wood, "not only for a countess, but for a wood nymph ! Ah, the young slut ! how buxom must the jade be !" To this Sancho answered somewhat angrily, "She is no slut, nor was her mother one before her ; nor whilst I live shall either of them be so, God willing : so pray speak more civilly, for such language is unbecoming one brought up like you, among knights-errant, who are good breeding itself." "Why, brother squire, you don't understand what praising is !" quoth he of the wood. "What ! do you not know that when some knight at a bull feast gives the bull a home-thrust with his lance, or when a thing is well hit off, it is common to say, 'Ah, how cleverly the rascal did it '? which, though it seems to be a slander, is in fact a great commendation. I would have you renounce every son or daughter whose actions do not make them deserving of such compliments." "I do renounce them," answered Sancho; "and since you mean so well by it, you may call my wife and children all the sluts and jades you please, for all they do or say is excellent, and well worthy of such praises ; and that I may return and see them again, I beseech Heaven to deliver me from mortal sin— that is, from this dangerous profession of squireship, into which I have run a second time, drawn and tempted by a purse of a hundred ducats which I found one day among the mountains. In truth, the devil is continually setting before my eyes, here, there, and everywhere, a bag full of gold pistoles, so that methinks at every step I am laying my hand upon it, hugging it, and carrying it home, buying lands, settling rents, and living like a prince ; and while this runs in my head, I can bear all the toil which must be suffered with this foolish master of mine, who, to my knowledge, is more of the madman than the knight."

"Indeed, friend," said the Squire of the Wood, "you verify the proverb, which says that 'covetousness bursts the bag.' Truly, friend, now you talk of madmen, there is not a greater one in the world than my master. The old saying may be applied to him, 'Other folks' burdens break the ass's back ;' for he gives up his own wits to recover those of another, and in searching after that which, when found, may chance to hit him in the teeth." "By the way, he is in love, it seems," said Sancho. "Yes," quoth he of the wood, "with one Casildea de Vandalia, one of the most whimsical dames in the world; but that is not the foot he halts on at present: he has some other crotchets in his pate, which we shall hear more of anon." "There is no road so even but it has its stumbling-places," replied Sancho; "in other folks' houses they boil beans, but in mine, whole kettles full. Madness will have more followers than discretion, but if the common saying be true, that there is some comfort in having partners in grief, I may comfort myself with you, who serve as crack-brained a master as my own." "Crack-brained, but valiant," answered he of the wood, "and more knavish than either." "Mine," answered Sancho, "has nothing of the knave in him; so far from it, he has a soul as pure as a pitcher, and would not harm a fly: he bears no malice, and a child may persuade him it is night at noon-day: for which I love him as my life, and cannot find in my heart to leave him, in spite of all his pranks." "For all that, brother," quoth he of the wood, "if the blind lead the blind, both may fall into the ditch. We had better turn us fairly about, and go back to our homes; for they who seek adventures find them sometimes to their cost."

Here the Squire of the Wood, observing Sancho to spit very often, as if very thirsty, "Methinks," said he, "we have talked till our tongues cleave to the roofs of our mouths; but I have got, hanging at my saddle-bow, that which will loosen them." Then rising up, he quickly produced a large bottle of wine, and a pasty half a yard long, without any exaggeration; for it was made of so large a rabbit that Sancho thought verily it must contain a whole goat, or at least a kid; and after due examination, "How," said he, "do you carry such things about with you?" "Why, what did you think?" answered the other; "did you take me for some starveling squire? No, no, I have a better cupboard behind me on my horse than a general carries with him upon a march." Sancho fell to, without waiting for entreaties, and swallowed down huge mouthfuls in the dark. "Your worship," said he, "is indeed a squire, trusty and loyal, round and sound, magnificent and great withal, as this banquet proves (if it did not come by enchantment), and not a poor wretch like myself, with nothing in my wallet but a piece of cheese, and that so hard that you may knock out a giant's brains with it; and four dozens of carobes* to bear it company, with as many filberts—thanks to my master's stinginess, and to the fancy he has taken that knights-errant ought to feed, like cattle, upon roots and wild herbs." "Troth, brother," replied he of the wood, "I have no stomach for your wild pears, nor sweet thistles, nor your mountain roots: let our masters have them with their fancies and their laws of chivalry, and let them eat what they commend. I carry cold meats and this bottle at the pommel of my saddle, happen what will; and such

---

* A pod so called in La Mancha, with a flat pulse in it, which, green or ripe, is harsh, but sweet and pleasant after it is dried.

is my love and reverence for it, that I kiss and hug it every moment."
And as he spoke he put it into Sancho's hand, who grasped it, and,
applying it straightway to his mouth, continued gazing at the stars for a
quarter of an hour; then, having finished his draught, he let his head
fall on one side, and, fetching a deep sigh, said, " Oh, the rascal! how
catholic it is ! " " You see now," quoth he of the wood, " how properly
you commend this wine in calling it rascal." " I agree with you now,"
answered Sancho, " and own that it is no discredit to be called rascal
when it comes in the way of compliment. But tell me, by all you love
best, is not this wine of Ciudad Real?" " Thou art a rare taster,"
answered he of the wood; " it is indeed of no other growth, and has, besides, some years over its head." " Trust me for that," quoth Sancho:
" depend upon it I always hit right, and can guess to a hair. And this
is all natural in me : let me but smell them, and I will tell you the
country, the kind, the flavour, the age, strength, and all about it; for
you must know, I have had in my family, by the father's side, two of the
rarest tasters that were ever known in La Mancha ; and I will give you
a proof of their skill. A certain hogshead was given to each of them to
taste, and their opinion asked as to the condition, quality, goodness, or
badness of the wine. One tried it with the tip of his tongue ; the other
only put it to his nose. The first said the wine savoured of iron ; the
second said it had rather a twang of goat's leather. The owner protested that the vessel was clean and the wine neat, so that it could not
taste either of iron or leather. Notwistanding this, the two famous
tasters stood positively to what they had said. Time went on ; the
wine was sold off, and, on cleaning the cask, a small key, hanging to a
leathern thong, was found at the bottom. Judge then, sir, whether one
of that race may not be well entitled to give his opinion in these
matters." " That being the case," quoth he of the wood, " we should
leave off seeking adventures, and, since we have a good loaf, let us not
look for cheesecakes, but make haste and get home to our cots, for there
God will find us, if it be His will." " I will serve my master till he
reaches Saragossa," quoth Sancho; " then, mayhap, we shall turn over
a new leaf."

Thus the good squires went on talking, and eating, and drinking,
until it was full time that sleep should give their tongues a respite, and
allay their thirst, for to quench it seemed impossible ; and both of them,
still keeping hold of the almost empty bottle, fell fast asleep; in which
situation we will leave them at present.

CHAPTER XIV.

In which is continued the adventure of the Knight of the Wood.

PEACEABLY and amicably the two knights continued to converse; and among other things, the history informs us that he of the wood said to Don Quixote, "In fact, Sir Knight, I must confess that by destiny, or rather by choice, I became enamoured of the peerless Casildea de Vandalia:—peerless I call her, because she is without her peer, either in rank, beauty, or form. Casildea repaid my honourable and virtuous passion by employing me, as Hercules was employed by his step-mother, in many and various perils: promising, at the end of each of them, that the next should crown my hopes; but, alas! she still goes on, adding link after link to the chain of my labours, insomuch that they are now countless, nor can I tell when they are to cease, and my tenderness be returned. One time she commanded me to go and challenge Giralda,* the famous giantess of Seville, who is as stout and strong as if she were made of brass, and, though never stirring from one spot, is the most changeable and unsteady woman in the world. I came, I saw, I conquered—I made her stand still, and fixed her to a point; for, during a whole week, no wind blew but from the north. Another time she commanded me to weigh those ancient statues, the fierce bulls of Guisando,† an enterprise better suited to a porter than to a knight. Another time she commanded me to plunge headlong into Cabra's cave (direful mandate!) and bring her a particular detail of all the lies enclosed within its dark abyss. I stopped the motion of Giralda, I weighed the bulls of Guisando, I plunged headlong into the cavern of Cabra, and brought to light its hidden secrets; yet still my hopes are dead—Oh, how dead!—and her commands and disdains alive—Oh, how alive! In short, she has now commanded me to travel over all the provinces of Spain, and compel every knight whom I meet to confess that in beauty she excels all others now in existence, and that I am the most valiant and the most enamoured knight in the universe. In obedience to this command I have already traversed the greater part of Spain, and have vanquished divers knights who have had the presumption to contradict me. But what I value myself most upon is having vanquished, in single combat, that renowned knight, Don Quixote de la Mancha, and made him confess that my Casildea is more beautiful than his Dulcinea: and I reckon that, in this conquest alone, I have vanquished all the knights in the world; for this Don Quixote has con-

---

* A brass statue on a steeple at Seville, which serves for a weathercock.
† Two large statues in that town, supposed to have been placed there by Metellus, in the time of the Romans.

quered them all, and I having overcome him, his glory, his fame, and his honour are consequently transferred to me. All the innumerable exploits of the said Don Quixote I therefore consider as already mine, and placed to my account."

Don Quixote was amazed at the assertions of the Knight of the Wood, and had been every moment on the point of giving him the lie; but he restrained himself, that he might convict him of falsehood from his own mouth: and therefore he said, very calmly, "That you may have vanquished, Sir Knight, most of the knights-errant of Spain, or even of the whole world, I will not dispute; but that you have conquered Don Quixote de la Mancha I have much reason to doubt. Some one resembling him, I allow, it might have been, though, in truth, I believe there are not many like him." "How say you?" cried he of the wood: "by the canopy of heaven, I fought with Don Quixote, vanquished him, and made him surrender to me! He is a man of an erect figure, withered face, long and meagre limbs, grizzle-haired, hawk-nosed, with large black moustaches, and styles himself the Knight of the Sorrowful Figure. The name of his squire is Sancho Panza: he oppresses the back and governs the reins of a famous steed called Rozinante—in a word, the mistress of his thoughts is one Dulcinea del Toboso, formerly called Aldonza Lorenzo, as my Casildea, being of Andalusia, is now distinguished by the name of Casildea de Vandalia. And now, if I have not sufficiently proved what I have said, here is my sword, which shall make incredulity itself believe!" "Softly, Sir Knight," said Don Quixote, "and hear what I have to say. You must know that this Don Quixote you speak of is the dearest friend I have in the world, insomuch that he is, as it were, another self; and, notwithstanding the very accurate description you have given of him, I am convinced, by the evidence of my senses, that you have never subdued him. It is, indeed, possible that, as he is continually persecuted by enchanters, some one of these may have assumed his shape, and suffered himself to be vanquished, in order to defraud him of the fame which his exalted feats of chivalry have acquired him over the whole face of the earth. A proof of their malice occurred but a few days since, when they transformed the face and figure of the beautiful Dulcinea del Toboso into the form of a mean rustic wench. And now, if, after all, you doubt the truth of what I say, behold the true Don Quixote himself before you, ready to convince you of your error, by force of arms, on foot, or on horseback, or in whatever manner you please." He then rose up, and, grasping his sword, awaited the determination of the Knight of the Wood, who very calmly said in reply, "A good paymaster wants no pledge: he who could vanquish Signor Don Quixote under transformation may well hope to make him yield in his proper person. But as knights-errant should by no means perform their feats in the dark, like robbers and ruffians, let us wait for daylight, that the sun may witness our exploits; and let the condition of our combat be, that the conquered shall remain entirely at the mercy and disposal of the conqueror; provided that he require nothing of him but what a knight may with honour submit to." Don Quixote having expressed himself entirely satisfied with these conditions, they went to seek their squires, whom they found snoring, in the very same posture as that in which sleep had first surprised them. They were soon awakened by their masters, and ordered to prepare the steeds, so that they might be ready, at sunrise, for a bloody single combat. At this intelligence Sancho was thunderstruck, and ready to swoon away with fear for his master, from what he had been told by the Squire of the Wood of his knight's prowess. Both the squires, however, without saying a word, went to seek their cattle; and the three horses and Dapple, having smelt each other out, were found all very sociable together.

"You must understand, brother," said the Squire of the Wood to Sancho, "that it is not the custom in Andalusia for the seconds to stand idle, with their arms folded, while their godsons* are engaged in combat. So this is to give you notice, that while our masters are at it, we must fight too, and make splinters of one another." "This custom, Signor Squire," answered Sancho, "may pass among ruffians; but among the squires of knights-errant no such practice is thought of—at least, I have not heard my master talk of any such custom, and he knows by heart all the laws of knight-errantry. But supposing there is any such law, I shall not obey it. I would rather pay the penalty laid upon such peaceable squires, which, I dare say, cannot be above a couple of pounds of wax;† and that will cost me less money than plasters to cure a broken head. Besides, how can I fight, when I have got no sword, and never had one in my life?" "I know a remedy for that," said he of the wood: "here are a couple of linen bags of the same size; you shall take one, and I the other, and so, with equal weapons, we will have a bout at bag-blows." "With all my heart," answered Sancho; "for such a battle will only dust our jackets." "It must not be quite so, either," replied the other; "for, lest the wind should blow them aside, we must put in them half a dozen clean and smooth pebbles of equal weight; and thus we may brush one another, without much harm or damage." "Body of my father!" answered Sancho, "what sable fur, what bottoms of carded cotton, forsooth, you would put into the bags, that we may not break our bones to powder! But I tell you what, master, though they should be filled with balls of raw silk, I shall not fight. Let our masters fight, and take the consequences; but let us drink and live, for time takes care to rid us of our lives, without our seeking ways to go before our appointed term and season." "Nay," replied he of the wood, "do let us fight, if it be but for half an hour." "No, no," answered Sancho, "I shall not be so rude nor ungrateful as to have a quarrel with a gentleman after eating and drinking with him. Besides, who is there can set about dry fighting without being provoked to it?" "If that be all," quoth he of the wood, "I can easily manage

---

* In tilts and tournaments the seconds were a kind of godfathers to the principals, and certain ceremonies were performed on those occasions.

† Small offences, in Spain, are fined at a pound or two of white wax, for the tapers in churches, &c., and confessors frequently enjoin it as a penance.

it; for before we begin our fight, I will come up, and just give you three or four handsome cuffs, which will lay you flat at my feet, and awaken your choler, though it slept sounder than a dormouse." "Against that trick," answered Sancho, "I have another, not a whit behind it; which is, to take a good cudgel, and before you can come near enough to waken my choler, I will bastinado yours into so sound a sleep, that it shall never awake but in another world. Let me tell you, I am not a man to suffer my face to be handled, so let every one look to the arrow; though the safest way would be to let that same choler sleep on—for one man knows not what another can do, and some people go out for wool and come home shorn. In all times God blessed the peacemakers and cursed the peace-breakers. If a baited cat turns into a lion, Heaven knows what I, that am a man, may turn into; and therefore I warn you, Master Squire, that all the damage and mischief that may follow from our quarrel must be placed to your account." "Agreed," replied he of the wood. "God send us daylight, and we shall see what is to be done."

And now a thousand sorts of birds, glittering in their gay attire, began to chirp and warble in the trees, and, in a variety of joyous notes, seemed to hail the blushing Aurora, who now displayed her rising beauties from the bright arcades and balconies of the east, and gently shook from her locks a shower of liquid pearls, sprinkling that reviving treasure over all vegetation. The willows distilled their delicious manna, the fountains smiled, the brooks murmured, the woods and meads rejoiced at her approach. But scarcely had hill and dale received the welcome light of day, and objects become visible, when the first thing that presented itself to the eyes of Sancho Panza was the Squire of the Wood's nose, which was so large that it almost overshadowed his whole body. Its magnitude was indeed extraordinary; it was, moreover, a hawk-nose, full of warts and carbuncles, of the colour of a mulberry, and hanging two fingers' breadth below his mouth. The size, the colour, the carbuncles, and the crookedness, produced such a countenance of horror, that Sancho, at the sight thereof, began to tremble from head to foot, and he resolved within himself to take two hundred cuffs before he would be provoked to attack such a hobgoblin.

Don Quixote also surveyed his antagonist, but the beaver of his helmet being down, his face was concealed; it was evident, however, that he was a strong-made man, not very tall, and that over his armour he wore a kind of surtout, or loose coat, apparently of the finest gold cloth, besprinkled with little moons of polished glass, which made a very gay and shining appearance; a large plume of feathers, green, yellow, and white, waved above his helmet. His lance, which was leaning against a tree, was very large and thick, and headed with pointed steel above a span long. All these circumstances Don Quixote attentively marked, and inferred from appearances that he was a very potent knight, but he was not therefore daunted, like Sancho Panza: on the contrary, with a gallant spirit, he said to the Knight of the Mirrors, "Sir Knight, if your eagerness for combat has not exhausted your courtesy, I entreat

you to lift up your beaver a little, that I may see whether your countenance corresponds with your gallant demeanour." "Whether vanquished or victorious in this enterprise, Sir Knight," answered he of the
mirrors, "you will have time and leisure enough for seeing me; and if
I comply not now with your request, it is because I think it would be
an indignity to the beauteous Casildea de Vandalia to lose any time in

*The first thing that presented itself to the eyes of Sancho Panza was
the Squire of the Wood's nose.*

forcing you to make the confession required." "However, while we
are mounting our horses," said Don Quixote, "you can tell me whether
I resemble that Don Quixote whom you said you had vanquished."
"As like as one egg is to another," replied he of the mirrors; "though,
as you say you are persecuted by enchanters, I dare not affirm that you
are actually the same person." "I am satisfied that you acknowledge
you may be deceived," said Don Quixote; "however, to remove all
doubt, let us to horse, and in less time than you would have spent in

raising your beaver, if God, my mistress, and my arm avail me, I will see your face, and you shall be convinced I am not the vanquished Don Quixote."

They now mounted without more words, and Don Quixote wheeled Rozinante about to take sufficient ground for the encounter, while the other knight did the same; but before Don Quixote had gone twenty paces, he heard himself called by his opponent, who, meeting him half-way, said, " Remember, Sir Knight, our agreement; which is, that the conquered shall remain at the discretion of the conqueror." "I know it," answered Don Quixote, " provided that which is imposed shall not transgress the laws of chivalry." " Certainly," answered he of the mirrors. At this juncture the squire's strange nose presented itself to Don Quixote's sight, who was no less struck than Sancho, insomuch that he looked upon him as a monster, or some creature of a new species. Sancho seeing his master set forth to take his career, would not stay alone with Long-nose, lest, perchance, he should get a fillip from that dreadful snout, which would level him to the ground either by force or fright. So he ran after his master, holding by the stirrup-leather; and when he thought it was nearly time for him to face about, " I beseech your worship," he cried, " before you turn, to help me into yon cork tree, where I can see better and more to my liking the brave battle you are going to have with that knight." " I rather believe, Sancho," quoth Don Quixote, " that thou art for mounting a scaffold to see the bull-sports without danger." " To tell you the truth, sir," answered Sancho, " that squire's monstrous nose fills me with dread, and I dare not stand near him." " It is indeed a fearful sight," said Don Quixote, " to any other but myself; come, therefore, and I will help thee up."

While Don Quixote was engaged in helping Sancho up into the cork tree, the Knight of the Mirrors took as large a compass as he thought necessary, and believing that Don Quixote had done the same, without waiting for sound of trumpet, or any other signal, he turned about his horse, who was not a whit more active or more sightly than Rozinante, and at his best speed, though not exceeding a middling trot, he advanced to encounter the enemy; but, seeing him employed with Sancho, he reined in his steed, and stopped in the midst of his career; for which his horse was most thankful, being unable to stir any farther. Don Quixote, thinking his enemy was coming full speed against him, clapped spurs to Rozinante's lean flanks, and made him so bestir himself, that, as the history relates, this was the only time in his life that he approached to something like a gallop; and with this unprecedented fury he soon came up to where his adversary stood, striking his spurs rowel-deep into the sides of his charger, without being able to make him stir a finger's length from the place where he had been checked in his career. At this fortunate juncture Don Quixote met his adversary, embarrassed not only with his horse but his lance, which he either knew not how, or had not time, to fix in its rest; and therefore our knight, who saw not these per-plexities, assailed him with perfect security, and with such force that he soon brought him to the ground over his horse's crupper, leaving him

Don Quixote met his adversary, and assailed him with such force that he soon brought him to the ground.

motionless and without any signs of life.   Sancho, on seeing this, immediately slid down from the cork tree, and in all haste ran to his master, who alighted from Rozinante, and went up to the vanquished knight, when, unlacing his helmet, to see whether he was dead, or, if yet alive, to give him air, he beheld—but who can relate what he beheld without causing amazement, wonder, and terror in all that hear it?   He saw, says the history, the very face, the very figure, the very aspect, the very physiognomy, the very effigy and semblance of the bachelor Sampson Carrasco! "Come hither, Sancho," cried he aloud, "and see, but believe not; make haste, son, and mark what wizards and enchanters can do!" Sancho approached, and seeing the face of the bachelor Sampson Carrasco, he began to cross and bless himself a thousand times over. All this time the overthrown cavalier showed no signs of life. "My advice is," said Sancho, "that, at all events, your worship should thrust your sword down the throat of this man, who is so like the bachelor Sampson Carrasco, for in dispatching him, you may destroy one of those enchanters, your enemies." "Thou sayest not amiss," quoth Don Quixote, "for the fewer enemies the better." He then drew his sword to put Sancho's advice into execution, when the Squire of the Mirrors came running up, but without the frightful nose, and cried aloud, "Have a care, Signor Don Quixote, what you do; for it is the bachelor Sampson Carrasco, your friend, and I am his squire." Sancho, seeing his face now shorn of its deformity, exclaimed, "The nose! where is the nose?" "Here it is," said the other, taking from his right-hand pocket a pasteboard nose, formed and painted in the manner already described; and Sancho, now looking earnestly at him, made another exclamation. "Blessed Virgin defend me!" cried he, "is not this Tom Cecial, my neighbour?" "Indeed am I," answered the unnosed squire; "Tom Cecial I am, friend Sancho Panza, and I will tell you presently what tricks brought me hither; but now, good Sancho, entreat, in the meantime, your master not to injure the Knight of the Mirrors at his feet; for he is truly no other than the rash and ill-advised bachelor Sampson Carrasco, our townsman."

By this time the Knight of the Mirrors began to recover his senses, which Don Quixote perceiving, he clapped the point of his naked sword to his throat, and said, "You are a dead man, Sir Knight, if you confess not that the peerless Dulcinea del Toboso excels in beauty your Casildea de Vandalia; you must promise me also, on my sparing your life, to go to the city of Toboso, and present yourself before her from me, that she may dispose of you as she shall think fit; and if she leaves you at liberty, then shall you return to me without delay—the fame of my exploits being your guide—to relate to me the circumstances of your interview; these conditions being strictly conformable to the terms agreed upon before our encounter, and also to the rules of knight-errantry." "I confess," said the fallen knight, "that the Lady Dulcinea del Toboso's torn and dirty shoe is preferable to the ill-combed, though clean locks of Casildea; and I promise to go and return from her presence to yours, and give you the exact and particular account which you require of me."

"You must likewise confess and believe," added Don Quixote, "that the knight you vanquished was not Don Quixote de la Mancha, but some one resembling him; as I do confess and believe that, though resembling the bachelor Sampson Carrasco, you are not he, but some other whom my enemies have purposely transformed into his likeness, to restrain the impetuosity of my rage, and make me use with moderation the glory of my conquest." "I confess, judge, and believe everything precisely as you do yourself," answered the disjointed knight; "and now suffer me to rise, I beseech you, if my bruises do not prevent me." Don Quixote raised him, with the assistance of his squire, on whom Sancho still kept his eyes fixed; and though, from some conversation that passed between them, he had much reason to believe it was really his old friend Tom Cecial, he was so prepossessed by all that his master had said about enchanters, that he would not trust his own eyes. In short, both master and man persisted in their error; and the Knight of the Mirrors, with his squire, much out of humour, and in ill plight, went in search of some convenient place where he might searcloth himself and splinter his ribs. Don Quixote and Sancho continued their journey to Saragossa, where the history now leaves them, to give some account of the Knight of the Mirrors and his well-snouted squire.

CHAPTER XV.

Giving an account of the Knight of the Mirrors and his squire.

Don Quixote was exceedingly happy, elated, and vainglorious at his triumph over so valiant a knight as he imagined him of the mirrors to be, and from whose promise he hoped to learn whether his adored mistress still remained in a state of enchantment. But Don Quixote expected one thing, and he of the mirrors intended another—his only care at present being to get, as soon as possible, plasters for his bruises. The history then proceeds to tell us that, when the bachelor Sampson Carrasco advised Don Quixote to resume his functions of knight-errantry, he had previously consulted with the priest and the barber upon the best means of inducing Don Quixote to remain peaceably and quietly at home; and it was agreed by general vote, as well as by the particular advice of Carrasco, that they should let Don Quixote make another sally (since it seemed impossible to detain him), and that the bachelor should then also sally forth like a knight-errant, and take an opportunity of engaging him to fight; and after vanquishing him, which they held to be an easy matter, he should remain, according to a previous agreement, at the disposal of the conqueror, who should command him to return home, and not quit it for the space of two years, or till he had received further orders from him. They doubted not but that he would readily comply, rather than infringe the laws of chivalry; and they hoped that during this interval he might forget his follies, or that some means might be discovered of curing his malady. Carrasco engaged in the enterprise, and Tom Cecial, Sancho Panza's neighbour, a merry, shallow-brained fellow, proffered his service as squire. Sampson armed himself in the manner already described, and Tom Cecial fitted the counterfeit nose to his face for the purpose of disguising himself; and, following the same road that Don Quixote had taken, they were not far off when the adventure of Death's car took place; but it was in the wood they overtook him, which was the scene of the late action, and where, had it not been for Don Quixote's extraordinary conceit that the bachelor was not the bachelor, that gentleman, not meeting even so much as nests where he thought to find birds, would have been incapacitated for ever from taking the degree of licentiate.

Tom Cecial, after the unlucky issue of their expedition, said to the bachelor, "Most certainly, Signor Carrasco, we have been rightly served. It is easy to plan a thing, but very often difficult to get through with it. Don Quixote is mad, and we are in our senses; he gets off sound and laughing, and your worship remains sore and sorrowful: now, pray, which is the greater madman, he who is so because he cannot help it, or he who is so on purpose?" "The difference between these two sorts of madmen is," replied Sampson, "that he who cannot help it will remain so, and he who deliberately plays the fool may leave off when he thinks fit." "That being the case," said Tom Cecial, "I was mad when I desired to be your worship's squire, and now I desire to be so no longer, but shall hasten home again." "That you may do," answered Sampson; "but for myself, I cannot think of returning to mine till I have soundly banged this same Don Quixote. It is not now with the hope of curing him of his madness that I shall seek him, but a desire for revenge: the pain of my ribs will not allow me to entertain a more charitable purpose." In this humour they went on talking till they came to a village, where they luckily met with a bone-setter, who undertook to cure the unfortunate Sampson. Tom Cecial now returned home, leaving his master meditating schemes of revenge; and though the history will have occasion to mention him again hereafter, it must now attend the motions of our triumphant knight.

CHAPTER XVI.

Of what befell Don Quixote with a worthy gentleman of La Mancha.

DON QUIXOTE pursued his journey with pleasure, satisfaction, and self-complacency, as already described: imagining, because of his late victory, that he was the most valiant knight the world could then boast of. He cared neither for enchantments nor enchanters, and looked upon all the adventures which should henceforth befall him as already achieved and brought to a happy conclusion. He no longer remembered his innumerable sufferings during the progress of his chivalries—the stoning that demolished half his grinders, the ingratitude of the galley-slaves, nor the audacity of the Yanguesian carriers and their shower of packstaves: in short, he inwardly exclaimed that could he devise any means of disenchanting his lady Dulcinea, he should not envy the highest fortune that ever was or could be attained by the most prosperous knight-errant of past ages.

He was wholly absorbed in these reflections, when Sancho said to him, " Is it not strange, sir, that I have still before my eyes the monstrous nose of my neighbour, Tom Cecial?" " And dost thou really believe, Sancho," said Don Quixote, " that the Knight of the Mirrors was the bachelor Sampson Carrasco, and his squire thy friend Tom Cecial?" " I know not what to say about it," answered Sancho: " I only know that the marks he gave me of my house, wife, and children, could be given by nobody else; and his face, when the nose was off, was Tom Cecial's, just as I have often seen it, for he lives in the next house to my own; the tone of his voice, too, was the very same." " Come, come, Sancho," replied Don Quixote, " let us reason upon this matter. How can it be imagined that the bachelor Sampson Carrasco should come as a knight-errant, armed at all points, to fight with me? Was I ever his enemy? Have I ever given him occasion to bear me ill-will? Am I his rival? Or has he embraced the profession of arms, envying the fame I have acquired by them?" " But then, what are we to say, sir," answered Sancho, " to the likeness of that knight, whoever he may be, to the bachelor Sampson Carrasco, and his squire to my neighbour Tom Cecial? If it be enchantment, as your worship says, why were they to be made like those two, above all others in the world?" " Trust me, Sancho, the whole is an artifice," answered Don Quixote, " and a trick of the wicked magicians who persecute me. Knowing that I might be victorious, they cunningly contrived that my vanquished enemy should assume the appearance of the worthy bachelor, in order that the friendship which I bear him might interpose between the edge of my sword and the vigour of my arm, and by checking my just indignation, the wretch might escape with life, who by fraud and violence sought mine. Indeed, already thou knowest by experience, Sancho, how easy a thing it is for enchanters to change one face into another, making the fair foul, and the foul fair; since not two days ago thou sawest with thine own eyes the grace and beauty of the peerless Dulcinea in their highest perfection, while to me she appeared under the mean and disgusting exterior of a rude country wench, with cataracts on her eyes and a bad smell in her mouth. If, then, the wicked enchanter durst make so foul a transformation, no wonder at this deception of his, in order to snatch the glory of victory out of my hands! However, I am gratified in knowing that, whatever the form he pleased to assume, my triumph over him was complete." " Heaven knows the truth of all things," answered Sancho, who, well knowing the transformation of Dulcinea to have been a device of his own, was not quite satisfied with his master's elucidations; but he would make no reply, lest he should betray himself.

While thus discoursing, they were overtaken by a gentleman mounted on a very fine flea-bitten mare, and dressed in a green cloth riding-coat faced with murrey-coloured velvet, and a hunter's cap of the same. The mare's furniture corresponded in colour with his dress, and was adapted to field sports. A Moorish scimitar hung at his shoulder-belt, which was green and gold; his buskins were wrought like the belt, and his spurs were not gilt, but green, and polished so neatly, that, as they suited his clothes, they looked better than if they had been of pure gold. He saluted them courteously, and, spurring his mare, was passing on, when Don Quixote said to him, "If you are travelling our road, signor, and are not in haste, will you favour us with your company?" "Indeed, signor," replied he, "I should not have passed on, but I was afraid your horse might prove unruly in the company of my mare." "Sir," answered Sancho, "if that be all, you may safely trust your mare; for ours is the noblest and best-behaved horse in the world, and at such a time was never guilty of a roguish trick in his life but once, and then my master and I paid for it sevenfold. I say again, your worship need not fear; for if she were served up betwixt two dishes, I assure you he would not so much as look her in the face." The traveller checked his mare, his curiosity being excited by the appearance of Don Quixote, who rode without his helmet, which Sancho carried like a cloak-bag at the pommel of his ass's pannel; but if he stared at Don Quixote, he was himself surveyed with no less attention by the knight, who conceived him to be some person of consequence. His age seemed to be about fifty, though he had but few grey hairs: his face was of the aquiline form, of a countenance neither too gay nor too grave; and by his whole exterior it was evident that he was no ordinary person. It was not less manifest that the traveller, as he contemplated Don Quixote, thought he had never seen any one like him before. With wonder he gazed upon his tall person, his meagre, sallow visage, his lank horse, his armour, and stately deportment, altogether presenting a figure, like which nothing, for many centuries past, had been seen in that country.

Don Quixote perceived that he had attracted the attention of the traveller, and, being the pink of courtesy, and always desirous of pleasing, he anticipated his questions by saying, "You are probably surprised, signor, at my appearance, which is certainly uncommon in the present age; but this will be explained when I tell you that I am a knight in search of adventures. I left my country, mortgaged my estate, quitted ease and pleasures, and threw myself into the arms of fortune. I wished to revive chivalry, so long deceased: and for some time past, exposed to many vicissitudes, stumbling in one place, and rising again in another, I have prosecuted my design; succouring widows, protecting damsels, aiding wives and orphans—all the natural and proper duties of knights-errant. And thus, by many valorous and Christian exploits, I have acquired the deserved honour of being in print throughout all or most of the nations in the world. Thirty thousand copies are already published of my history, and, Heaven permitting, thirty thousand thousands more are likely to be printed. Finally, to sum up all in a single word, know that I am Don Quixote de la Mancha, otherwise called the Knight of the Sorrowful Figure! Though self-praise depreciates, I am compelled sometimes to pronounce my own commendations, but it is only when no friend is present to perform that office for me. And now, my worthy sir, that you know my profession and who I am, you will cease to wonder at my appearance."

After an interval of silence, the traveller in green said, in reply, "You are indeed right, signor, in conceiving me to be struck by your appearance ; but you have rather increased than lessened my wonder by the account you give of yourself. How ! is it possible that there are knights-errant now in the world, and that there are histories printed of real chivalries ? I had no idea there was anybody now upon earth who relieved widows, succoured damsels, aided wives, or protected orphans ; nor should yet have believed it, had I not been now convinced with my own eyes. Thank Heaven ! the history you mention of your exalted and true achievements must cast into oblivion all the fables of imaginary knights-errant which abound so much, to the detriment of good morals, and the prejudice and neglect of genuine history." "There is much to be said," answered Don Quixote, "upon the question of the truth or fiction of the histories of knights-errant." "Why, is there any one," answered he in green, "who doubts the falsehood of those histories ? " "I doubt it," replied Don Quixote ; "but no more of that at present ; for, if we travel together much farther, I hope to convince you, sir, that you have been wrong in suffering yourself to be carried in the stream with those who cavil at their truth." The traveller now first began to suspect the state of his companion's intellect, and watched for a further confirmation of his suspicion : but, before they entered into any other discourse, Don Quixote said that, since he had so fully described himself, he hoped he might be permitted to ask who he was. To which the traveller answered, "I, Sir Knight of the Sorrowful Figure, am a gentleman, and native of a village where, if it please Heaven, we shall dine to-day. My fortune is affluent, and my name is Don Diego de Miranda. I spend my time with my wife, my children, and my friends : my diversions are hunting and fishing ; but I keep neither hawks nor greyhounds, only some decoy partridges and a stout ferret. I have about six dozen of books, Spanish and Latin, some of history and some of devotion : those of chivalry have not come over my threshold. I am more inclined to the reading of profane than devout authors, provided they are well written, ingenious, and harmless in their tendency, though, in truth, there are very few books of this kind in Spain. Sometimes I eat with my neighbours and friends, and frequently I invite them : my table is neat and clean, and not parsimoniously furnished. I slander no one, nor do I listen to slander from others. I pry not into other men's lives, nor scrutinize their actions. I hear mass every day ; I share my substance with the poor, making no parade of my good works, lest hypocrisy and vainglory, those insidious enemies of the human breast, should find access to mine. It is always my endeavour to make peace between those who are at variance. I am devoted to our blessed Lady, and ever trust in the infinite mercy of God our Lord."

Sancho was very attentive to the account of this gentleman's life, which appeared to him to be good and holy ; and thinking that one of such a character must needs work miracles, he flung himself off his Dapple, and, running up to him, he laid hold of his right stirrup ; then, devoutly, and almost with tears, he kissed his feet more than once. " What mean you by this, brother ? " said the gentleman ; " why these embraces ? " " Pray let me kiss on," answered Sancho ; " for your worship is the first saint on horseback I ever saw in all my life." " I am not a saint," answered the gentleman, " but a great sinner : you, my friend, must indeed be good, as your simplicity proves." Sancho retired, and mounted his ass again ; having forced a smile from the profound gravity of his master, and caused fresh astonishment in Don Diego.

Don Quixote then asked him how many children he had, at the same time observing that the ancient philosophers, being without the true knowledge of God, held supreme happiness to consist in the gifts of nature and fortune, in having many friends and many good children. " I have one son," answered the gentleman, " and if I had him not, perhaps I should think myself happier : not that he is bad, but because he is not all that I would have him. He is eighteen years old, six of which he has spent at Salamanca, learning the Latin and Greek languages ; and when I wished him to proceed to other studies, I found him infatuated with poetry, and could not prevail upon him to look into the law, which it was my desire he should study ; nor into theology, the queen of all sciences. I was desirous that he should be an honour to his family, since we live in an age in which useful and virtuous literature is rewarded by the sovereign—I say virtuous, for letters without virtue are pearls upon a dunghill. He passes whole days in examining whether Homer expressed himself well in such a verse of the Iliad ; whether Martial, in such an epigram, be obscene or not ; whether such a line in Virgil should be understood this or that way ;—in a word, all his conversation is with these and other ancient poets, such as Horace, Persius, Juvenal, and Tibullus ; for the modern Spanish authors he holds in no esteem. At the same time, in spite of the contempt he seems to have for Spanish poetry, his thoughts are at this time entirely engrossed by a paraphrase on four verses sent him from Salamanca, and which, I believe, is intended for a scholastic prize."

" Children, my good sir," replied Don Quixote, " are the flesh and blood of their parents, and, whether good or bad, must be loved and cherished as part of themselves. It is the duty of parents to train them up, from their infancy, in the paths of virtue and good manners, and in Christian discipline, so that they may become the staff of their age and an honour to their posterity. As to forcing them to this or that pursuit, I do not hold it to be right, though I think there is a propriety in advising them ; and when the student is so fortunate as to have an inheritance, and therefore not compelled to study for his subsistance, I should be for indulging him in the pursuit of that science to which his genius is most inclined ; and, although that of poetry be less useful than delightful, it does not usually reflect disgrace on its votaries. Poetry I regard as a tender virgin, young and extremely beautiful, whom divers other virgins—namely, all the other sciences—are assiduous to enrich, to polish, and adorn. She is to be served by them, and they are to be ennobled through her. But this same virgin is not to be rudely handled, nor dragged through the streets, nor exposed in the market-place, nor posted on the corners of gates of palaces. She is of so exquisite a nature, that he who knows how to treat her will convert her into gold of the most inestimable value. He who possesses her should guard her with vigilance, neither suffering her to be polluted by obscene, nor degraded by dull and frivolous works. Although she must be in no wise venal, she is not, therefore, to despise the fair reward of honourable labours, either in heroic or dramatic composition. Buffoons must not come near her, neither must she be approached by the ignorant vulgar, who have no sense of her charms; and this term is equally applicable to all ranks, for whoever is ignorant is vulgar. He, therefore, who, with the qualifications I have named, devotes himself to poetry, will be honoured and esteemed by all nations distinguished for intellectual cultivation.

"With regard to your son's contempt for Spanish poetry, I think he is therein to blame. The great Homer, being a Greek, did not write in Latin, nor did Virgil, who was a Roman, write in Greek. In fact, all the ancient poets wrote in the language of their native country, and did not hunt after foreign tongues to express their own sublime conceptions. This custom, therefore, should prevail among all nations: the German poet should not be undervalued for writing in his own tongue; nor the Castilian—nor even the Biscayan—for writing the language of his province. But your son, I should imagine, does not dislike the Spanish poetry, but poets who are unacquainted with other languages, and deficient in that knowledge which might enrich, embellish, and invigorate their native powers: although, indeed, it is generally said that the gift of poesy is innate—that is, a poet is born a poet; and thus endowed by Heaven, apparently without study or art, composes things which verify the saying, *Est deus in nobis, &c.* Thus the poet of nature, who improves himself by art, rises far above him who is merely the creature of study: art may improve, but cannot surpass nature; and therefore it is the union of both which produces the perfect poet. Suffer, then, your son to proceed in the career which the star of his genius points out; for being so good a scholar, and having already happily mounted the first step of the sciences—that of the learned languages—he may, by their aid, attain the summit of literary eminence, which is no less an honour and an ornament to a gentleman, than a mitre to the ecclesiastic or the long robe to the lawyer. If your son write personal satires, chide him and tear his performances; but if he write like Horace, reprehending vice in general, commend him, for it is laudable in a poet to employ his pen in a virtuous cause. Let him direct the shafts of satire against vice, in all its various forms, but not level them at individuals, like some who, rather than not indulge their mischievous wit, will hazard a disgraceful banishment to the Isles of Pontus.* If the poet be correct in his

---

* Alluding to Ovid.

morals, his verse will partake of the same purity : the pen is the tongue of the mind, and what his conceptions are, such will be his productions. The wise and virtuous subject who is gifted with a poetic genius, is ever honoured and enriched by his sovereign, and crowned with the leaves of the tree which the thunderbolt hurts not, as a token that all should respect those brows which are so honourably adorned."

Here Don Quixote paused, having by his rational discourse made his companion waver in the opinion he had formed of his insanity. Sancho, in the meantime, not finding the conversation to his taste, had gone a short distance out of the road to beg a little milk of some shepherds whom he saw milking their ewes : and just as the traveller, highly satisfied with Don Quixote's ingenuity and good sense, was about to resume the conversation, Don Quixote perceived a cart with royal banners advancing on the same road, and believing it to be something that fell under his jurisdiction, he called aloud to Sancho to bring him his helmet. Sancho immediately left the shepherds, and pricking up Dapple, hastened to his master, who was about to be engaged in a most terrific and stupendous adventure.

CHAPTER XVII.

Wherein is set forth the extreme and highest point at which the unheard-of courage of Don Quixote ever did or ever could arrive; with the happy conclusion of the adventure of the lions.

LITTLE expecting a fresh adventure, Sancho, as the history carefully relates, was leisurely buying some curds of the shepherds; and, being summoned in such haste to his master, he knew not what to do with them, nor how to carry them ; so that, to prevent their being wasted, he poured them into the helmet ; and, satisfied with this excellent device, he hurried away to receive the commands of his lord. " Sancho," said the knight, " give me my helmet; for either I know little of adventures, or that which I descry yonder is one that will oblige me to have recourse to arms." He of the green riding-coat, hearing this, looked on all sides, and could see nothing but a cart coming towards them, with two or three small flags, by which he thought it probable that it was conveying some of the king's money. He mentioned his conjecture to Don Quixote; but he heeded him not—his imagination was too much possessed by adventures, and his only reply was, " Forewarned, forearmed : to be prepared is half the victory. I know, by experience, that I have enemies both visible and invisible, and I know not when, nor from what quarter, nor at what time, nor in what shape, they may attack me." He then took his helmet from Sancho's hand before he had discharged the curds, and, without observing its contents, clapped it hastily upon his head. The curds being squeezed and pressed, the whey began to run down the face and beard of the knight, to his great

"By the lady of my soul," he exclaimed, "these are curds which thou hast put here, thou base unmannerly squire!"

consternation. "What can this mean, Sancho?" said he; "methinks my skull is softening, or my brains melting, or I sweat from head to foot! If so, it is certainly not through fear, though I verily believe that this will prove a terrible adventure. Give me something to wipe myself, Sancho; for this copious sweat blinds me." Sancho said nothing, but gave him a cloth; at the same time thanking Heaven that his master had not found out the truth. Don Quixote wiped himself, and took off his helmet to see what it was so cool to his head; and, observing some white lumps in it, put them to his nose, and smelling them, "By the lady of my soul," he exclaimed, "these are curds which thou hast put here, thou base unmannerly squire!" Sancho replied with much coolness and cunning, " If they are curds, sir, give them to me, and I will eat them—No, now I think of it, the devil may eat them for me, for he only could have put them there. What! I offer to foul your worship's helmet! Egad! it seems as if I had my enchanters too, who persecute me as a creature and member of your worship, and have put that filthiness there to provoke your wrath against me. But, truly, this time they have missed their aim; for I trust to my master's good judgment, who will consider that I have neither curds, nor cream, nor anything like it; and that if I had, I should sooner have put them into my stomach than into your worship's helmet." " Well," said Don Quixote, " there may be something in that." The gentleman, who had been observing all that had passed, was astonished; and still more so at what followed; for Don Quixote, after having wiped his head, face, beard, and helmet, again put it on, and fixing himself firm in his stirrups, adjusting his sword, and grasping his lance, he exclaimed, " Now, come what may, I am prepared to encounter Satan himself!"

They were soon overtaken by the cart with flags, which was attended only by the driver, who rode upon one of the mules, and a man sitting upon the fore part of it. Don Quixote planted himself just before them, and said, " Whither go ye, brethren? What carriage is this? What does it contain, and what are those banners?" " The cart is mine," answered the carter, " and in it are two fierce lions, which the General of Oran is sending to court as a present to his majesty; the flags belong to our liege the king, to show that what is in the cart belongs to him." " And are the lions large?" demanded Don Quixote. " Larger never came from Africa to Spain," said the man on the front of the cart: " I am their keeper, and in my time have had charge of many lions, but never of any so large as these. They are a male and a female; the male is in the first cage, and the female is in that behind. Not having eaten to-day, they are now hungry; and therefore, sir, stand aside, for we must make haste to the place where they are to be fed." " What!" said Don Quixote, with a scornful smile, " Lion-whelps against me! Against me, your puny monsters! and at this time of day! By yon blessed sun! those who sent them hither shall see whether I am a man to be scared by lions. Alight, honest friend, and, since you are their keeper, open the cages and turn out your savages of the desert; for in the midst of this field will I make them know who Don Quixote de la Mancha is, in spite of the enchanters that sent them hither to me." " So, so," quoth the gentleman to himself, " our good knight has now given us a specimen of what he is; doubtless the curds have softened his skull, and made his brains mellow." Sancho now coming up to him, " For Heaven's sake, sir," cried he, " hinder my master from meddling with these lions; for if he does they will tear us all to pieces." " What, then, is your master so mad," answered the gentleman, " that you really fear he will attack such fierce animals?" " He is not mad," answered Sancho, " but daring." " I will make him desist," replied the gentleman; and, going up to Don Quixote, who was importuning the keeper to open the cages, " Sir," said he, " knights-errant should engage in adventures that, at least, afford some prospect of success, and not such as are altogether desperate; for the valour which borders on temerity has in it more of madness than courage. Besides, Sir Knight, these lions do not come to assail you : they are going to be presented to his majesty ; and it is, therefore, improper to detain them or retard their journey." " Sweet sir," answered Don Quixote, " go hence, and mind your decoy partridge and your stout ferret, and leave every one to his functions. This is mine, and I shall see whether these gentlemen lions will come against me or not." Then, turning to the keeper, he said, " I vow to Heaven, Don Rascal, if thou dost not instantly open the cages, with this lance I will pin thee to the cart." The carter seeing that the armed lunatic was resolute, " Good sir," said he, " for charity's sake be pleased to let me take off my mules and get with them out of danger before the lions are let loose; for should my cattle be killed, I am undone for ever, as I have no other means of living than by this cart and these mules." " Incredulous wretch !" cried Don Quixote, " unyoke and do as thou wilt; but thou shalt soon see that thy trouble might have been spared."

The carter alighted and unyoked in great haste. The keeper then said aloud, " Bear witness, all here present, that against my will, and by compulsion, I open the cages and let the lions loose. I protest against what this gentleman is doing, and declare all the mischief done by these beasts shall be placed to his account, with my salary and perquisites over and above. Pray, gentlemen, take care of yourselves before I open the door; for, as to myself, I am sure they will do me no hurt." Again the gentleman pressed Don Quixote to desit from so mad an action, declaring to him that he was thereby provoking God's wrath. Don Quixote replied that he knew what he was doing. The gentleman rejoined, and entreated him to consider well of it, for he was certainly deceived. " Nay, sir," replied Don Quixote, " if you will not be a spectator of what you think will prove a tragedy, spur your flea-bitten mare, and save yourself." Sancho too besought him, with tears in his eyes, to desist from an enterprise compared with which that of the windmills, the dreadful one of the fulling-mills, and in short, all the exploits he had performed in the whole course of his life, were mere tarts and cheesecakes. " Consider, sir," added Sancho, " here is no enchantment, nor anything like it; for I saw, through the grates and chinks of the cage, the paw of a true lion; and I guess, by the size of its claw, that it is bigger than a mountain." " Thy fears," answered Don Quixote, " would make it appear to thee larger than half the world. Retire, Sancho, and leave me; and if I perish here, thou knowest our old agreement : repair to Dulcinea—I say no more." To these he added other expressions, which showed the firmness of his purpose, and that all argument would be fruitless. The gentleman would fain have compelled him to desist, but thought himself unequally matched in weapons and armour, and that it would not be prudent to engage with a madman, whose violence and menaces against the keeper were now redoubled; the gentleman therefore spurred his mare, Sancho his Dapple, and the carter his mules, and all endeavoured to get as far off as possible from the cart before the lions were let loose. Sancho bewailed the death of his master, verily believing it would now overtake him between the paws of the lions : he cursed his hard fortune, and the unlucky hour when he again entered into his service. But, nothwithstanding his tears and lamentations, he kept urging on his Dapple to get far enough from the cart. The keeper, seeing that the fugitives were at a good distance, repeated his arguments and entreaties, but to no purpose : Don Quixote answered that he heard him, and desired he would trouble himself no more, but immediately obey his commands, and open the door.

Whilst the keeper was unbarring the first gate, Don Quixote deliberated within himself whether it would be best to engage on horseback or not; and finally determined it should be on foot, as Rozinante might be terrified at the sight of the lions. He therefore leaped from his horse, flung aside his lance, braced on his shield, and drew his sword ; then slowly advancing, with marvellous intrepidity and an undaunted heart, he planted himself before the lion's cage, devoutly commending himself first to God, and then to his mistress Dulcinea.

The keeper seeing Don Quixote fixed in his posture, and that he could not avoid letting loose the lion without incurring the resentment of the angry and daring knight, set wide open the door of the first cage, where the monster lay, which appeared to be of an extraordinary size, and of a hideous and frightful aspect. The first thing the creature did was to turn himself round in the cage, reach out a paw, and stretch himself at full length. Then he opened his mouth and yawned very leisurely ; after which he threw out some half-yard of tongue, wherewith he licked and washed his face. This done, he thrust his head out of the cage, and stared around on all sides with eyes like red-hot coals : a sight to have struck temerity itself with terror ! Don Quixote observed him with fixed attention, impatient for him to leap out of his den, that he might grapple with him and tear him to pieces—to such a height of extravagance was he transported by his unheard-of frenzy ! But the generous lion, more gentle than arrogant, taking no notice of his vapouring and bravadoes, after having stared about him, turned himself round, and, showing his posteriors to Don Quixote, calmly and quietly laid himself down again in the cage. Upon which Don Quixote ordered the keeper to give him some blows, and provoke him to come forth. "That I will not do," answered the keeper ; "for, should I provoke him, I shall be the first whom he will tear to pieces. Be satisfied, Signor Cavalier, with what is done, which is everything in point of courage, and do not tempt fortune a second time. The lion has the door open to him and the liberty to come forth ; and since he has not yet done so, he will not come out to-day. The greatness of your worship's courage is already sufficiently shown : no brave combatant, as I take it, is bound to do more than to challenge his foe, and await his coming in the field ; and if the antagonist does not meet him, the disgrace falls on him, while the challenger is entitled to the crown of victory." "That is true," answered Don Quixote : "shut the door, and give me a certificate, in the best form you can, of what you have here seen me perform. It should

Don Quixote observed him with fixed attention, impatient for him to leap out of his den, that
he might grapple with him and tear him to pieces.

be known that you opened the door to the lion; that I waited for him;
that he came not out; again I waited for him; again he came not out;
and again he laid himself down. I am bound to no more—enchantments, avaunt! So Heaven prosper right and justice, and true chivalry!
Shut the door, as I told thee, while I make a signal to the fugitive and
absent, that from your own mouth they may have an account of this
exploit."

The keeper closed the door, and Don Quixote, having fixed the linen
cloth with which he had wiped the curds from his face upon the point
of his lance, began to hail the troop in the distance, who, with the gentleman in green at their head, were still retiring, but looking round at
every step, when, suddenly, Sancho observed the signal of the white
cloth. "May I be hanged," cried he, "if my master has not vanquished the wild beasts, for he is calling to us!" They all stopped, and
saw that it was Don Quixote that made the sign; and, their fear in
some degree abating, they ventured to return slowly, till they could

distinctly hear the words of Don Quixote, who continued calling to them. When they had reached the cart again, Don Quixote said to the driver, "Now, friend, put on your mules again, and in Heaven's name proceed; and, Sancho, give two crowns to him and the keeper, to make them amends for this delay." "That I will, with all my heart," answered Sancho; "but what has become of the lions? are they dead or alive?" The keeper then very minutely, and with due pauses, gave an account of the conflict, enlarging, to the best of his skill, on the valour of Don Quixote, at sight of whom the daunted lion would not, or durst not, stir out of the cage, though he had held open the door a good while; and, upon his representing to the knight that it was tempting God to provoke the lion, and to force him out, he had at length, very reluctantly, permitted him to close it again. "What sayest thou to this, Sancho?" said Don Quixote; "can any enchantment prevail against true courage? Enchanters may, indeed, deprive me of good fortune, but of courage and resolution they never can." Sancho gave the gold crowns; the carter yoked his mules; the keeper thanked Don Quixote for his present, and promised to relate this valourous exploit to the king himself, when he arrived at court. "If, perchance, his majesty," said Don Quixote, "should inquire who performed it, tell him the Knight of the Lions; for henceforward I resolve that the title I have hitherto borne, of the Knight of the Sorrowful Figure, shall be thus changed, converted, and altered; and herein I follow the ancient practice of knights-errant, who changed their names at pleasure."

The cart now went forward, and Don Quixote, Sancho, and Don Diego di Miranda (which was the name of the traveller in green) pursued theirs. This gentleman had not spoken a word for some time, his attention having been totally engrossed by the singular conduct and language of Don Quixote, whom he accounted a sensible madman, or one whose madness was mingled with good sense. He had never seen the first part of our knight's history, or he would have felt less astonishment at what he had witnessed; but now he knew not what to think, seeing him in his conversation so intelligent and sensible, and in his actions so foolish, wild, and extravagant. "What," thought he, "could be more absurd than to put a helmet full of curds upon his head, and then believe that enchanters had softened his skull? Or what could equal his extravagance in seeking a contest with lions?"

Don Quixote interrupted these reflections by saying, "Doubtless, signor, you set me down as extravagant and mad; and no wonder if such should be your thoughts, for my actions indicate no less. Nevertheless, I would have you know that I am not quite so irrational as I possibly may appear to you. It is a gallant sight to see a cavalier in shining armour, prancing over the lists at some gay tournament, in sight of the ladies · it is a gallant sight when in the middle of a spacious square, a brave cavalier, before the eyes of his prince, transfixes with his lance a furious bull; and a gallant show do all those knights make who, in military or other exercises, entertain, enliven, and do honour to their prince's court; but far above all these is the knight-errant who, through deserts and solitudes, through cross-ways, through woods, and over mountains, goes in quest of perilous adventures, which he undertakes and accomplishes only to obtain a glorious and immortal fame. It is a nobler sight, I say, to behold a knight-errant in the act of succouring a widow in some desert, than a courtier knight complimenting a damsel in the city. All knights have their peculiar functions. Let the courtier serve the ladies, adorn his prince's court with rich liveries, entertain the poorer cavaliers at his splendid table, order his jousts, manage tournaments, and show himself great, liberal, and magnificent, above all, a good Christian, and thus will he fulfil his duties; but let the knight-errant search the remotest corners of the world; enter the most intricate labyrinths; assail, at every step, impossibilities; brave, in wild uncultivated deserts, the burning rays of the summer's sun and the keen inclemency of the winter's wind and frost; let not lions daunt him, nor spectres affright, nor dragons terrify him: for to seek, to attack, to conquer them all, is his particular duty. Therefore, sir, as it has fallen to my lot to be one of the number of knights-errant, I cannot decline undertaking whatever seems to me to come within my department; which was obviously the case in regard to the lions, although, at the same time, I knew it to be the excess of temerity. Well I know that fortitude is a virtue placed between the two extremes of cowardice and rashness; but it is better the valiant should rise to the extreme of temerity than sink to that of cowardice; for, as it is easier for the prodigal than the miser to become liberal, so it is much easier for the rash than the cowardly to become truly brave. In enterprises of every kind, believe me, Signor Don Diego, it is better to lose the game by a card too much than one too little; for it sounds better to be called rash and daring than timorous and cowardly."

"All that you have said and done, Signor Don Quixote," answered Don Diego, "is levelled by the line of right reason; and I think if the laws and ordinances of knight-errantry should be lost, they might be found in your worship's breast, as their proper depository and register. But, as it grows late, let us quicken our pace, and we shall reach my habitation, where you may repose yourself after your late toil, which, if not of the body, must have been a labour of the mind." "I accept your kind offer with thanks," said the knight; then, proceeding a little faster than before, they reached, about two o'clock in the afternoon, the mansion of Don Diego, whom Don Quixote called the Knight of the Green Riding-coat.

BOOK II.

CHAPTER XVIII.

Of what befell Don Quixote in the castle or house of the Knight of the Green Riding-coat; with other extraordinary matters.

Don Quixote, on approaching Don Diego's house, observed it to be a spacious mansion, having, after the country fashion, the arms of the family roughly carved in stone over the great gates, the buttery in the courtyard, the cellar under the porch, and likewise several earthen wine-jars placed around it, which, being of the ware of Toboso, recalled to his memory his enchanted and metamorphosed Dulcinea; whereupon, sighing deeply, he broke out into the following exclamation:

> "O pledges, once my comfort and relief,
> Though pleasing still, discovered now with grief!

O ye Tobosian jars, that bring back to my remembrance the sweet pledge of my most bitter sorrow!" This was overheard by the poetical scholar, Don Diego's son; he having, with his mother, come out to receive him; and both mother and son were not a little astonished at the appearance of their guest, who, alighting from Rozinante, very courteously desired leave to kiss the lady's hands. "Madam," said Don Diego, "this gentleman is Don Quixote de la Mancha, the wisest and most valiant knight-errant in the world; receive him, I pray, with your accustomed hospitality." The lady, whose name was Donna Christina, welcomed him with much kindness and courtesy, which Don Quixote returned in expressions of the utmost politeness. The same kind of compliments passed between him and the student, with whom Don Quixote was much pleased, judging him, by his conversation, to be a young man of wit and good sense.

Here the original author gives a particular account of Don Diego's house, describing all that is usually contained in the mansion of a wealthy country gentleman; but the translator of the history thought fit to pass over in silence these minute matters, as inconsistent with the general tenour of the work, which, while it carefully admits whatever is essential to truth, rejects all uninteresting and superfluous details.

Don Quixote was led into a hall, and Sancho having unarmed him, he remained in his wide Walloon breeches, and in a chamois doublet, stained all over with the rust of his armour; his band was of the college cut, unstarched, and without lace · his buskins were date-coloured, and his shoes waxed. He girt on his trusty sword, which was hung at a belt made of a sea-wolf's skin, on account of a weakness he was said to have been troubled with in his loins; and over the whole he wore a cloak of grey cloth. But, first of all, with five or six kettles of water (for there are doubts as to the exact number) he washed his head and face. The water still continued of a whey-colour—thanks to Sancho's gluttony, and his foul curds, that had so defiled his master's visage. Thus accoutred, with a graceful and gallant air Don Quixote walked into another hall, where the student was waiting to entertain him till the table was prepared; for the lady Donna Christina wished to show her noble guest that she knew how to regale such visitors.

While the knight was unarming, Don Lorenzo (for that was the name of Don Diego's son) had taken an opportunity to question his father concerning him. " Pray, sir," said he, " who is this gentleman? for my mother and I are completely puzzled both by his strange figure and the title you give him." " I scarcely know how to answer you, son," replied Don Diego; " and can only say that, from what I have witnessed, his tongue belies his actions; for he converses like a man of sense, and acts like an outrageous madman. Talk you to him, and feel the pulse of his understanding, and exercise all the discernment you possess to ascertain the real state of his intellects; for my own part, I suspect them to be in rather a distracted condition."

Don Lorenzo accordingly addressed himself to Don Quixote; and, among other things, in the course of their conversation Don Quixote said to Don Lorenzo, " Signor Don Diego de Miranda, your father, sir, has informed me of the rare talents you possess, and particularly that you are a great poet." " Certainly not a great poet," replied Lorenzo : " it is true I am fond of poetry, and honour the works of good poets; but have no claim to the title my father is pleased to confer upon me." " I do not dislike this modesty," answered Don Quixote; " for poets are usually very arrogant, each thinking himself the greatest in the world." " There is no rule without an exception," answered Don Lorenzo; " and surely there may be some who do not appear to be too conscious of their real merits." " Very few, I believe," said Don Quixote; " but I pray, sir, tell me what verses are those you have now in hand which your father says engross your thoughts; for if they be some gloss or paraphrase, I should be glad to see them, as I know something of that kind of writing. If they are intended for a poetical prize, I would advise you to endeavour to obtain the second. The first is always determined by favour or the high rank of the candidate; but the second is bestowed according to merit: so that the third becomes the second, and the first no more than the third, according to the usual practice in our universities. The first, however, I confess, makes a figure in the list of honours." " Hitherto," said Don Lorenzo to himself, " I have no reason to judge thee to be mad;—but let us proceed. I presume, sir," said he, " you have frequented the schools. What science, pray, has been your particular study?" " That of knight-errantry," answered Don Quixote, " which is equal to poetry, and even somewhat beyond it." " I am ignorant what science that is," replied Don Lorenzo, " never having heard of it before." " It is a science," replied Don Quixote, " which comprehends all, or most of the other sciences; for he who professes it must be learned in the law, and understand distributive and commutative justice, that he may know not only how to assign to each man what is truly his own, but what is proper for him to possess; he must be conversant in divinity, in order to be able to explain, clearly and distinctly, the Christian faith which he professes; he must be skilled in medicine, especially in botany, that he may know both how to cure the diseases with which he may be afflicted, and to collect the various remedies which Providence has scattered in the midst of the wilderness, nor be compelled on every emergency to be running in quest of a physician to heal him; he must be an astronomer, that he may, if necessary, ascertain by the stars the exact hour of the night, and what part or climate of the world he is in; he must understand mathematics, because he will have occasion for them; and, taking it for granted that he must be adorned with all the cardinal and theological virtues, I descend to other more minute particulars, and say that he must know how to swim as well as it is reported of Fish Nicholas;* he must know how to shoe a horse and repair his saddle and bridle: and to return to higher concerns, he must preserve his faith inviolable towards Heaven, and also to his mistress; he must be chaste in his thoughts, modest in his words, liberal in good works, valiant in exploits, patient in toils, charitable to the needy, and steadfastly adhering to the truth, even at the hazard of his life. Of all these great and small parts a good knight-errant is composed. Consider, then, Signor Don Lorenzo, whether the student of knight-errantry hath an easy task to accomplish, and whether such a science may not rank with the noblest that are taught in the schools." " If your description be just, I maintain that it is superior to all others," replied Don Lorenzo. " How! *if* it be just?" cried Don Quixote. " What I mean, sir," said Don Lorenzo, " is, that I question whether knights-errant do, or ever did, exist; and especially adorned with so many virtues." " How many are there in the world," exclaimed the knight, " who entertain such doubts! and I verily believe that, unless Heaven would vouchsafe, by some miracle, to convince them, every exertion of mine to that end would be fruitless. I shall not, therefore, waste time in useless endeavours, but will pray Heaven to enlighten you, and lead you to know how useful and necessary knight-errantry was in times past, and how beneficial it would be now were it restored—yes, now, in these sinful times, when sloth, idleness, gluttony, and luxury triumph." " Our guest has broke loose," quoth Don Lorenzo to himself; " still, it must be acknowledged he is a most extraordinary madman."

---

* A Sicilian, native of Catania, who lived in the latter part of the sixteenth century. He was commonly called Pesce-cola, or the Fish-Nicholas, and is said to have lived so much in the water, from his infancy, that he could cleave the waves in the midst of a storm like a marine animal.

Their conversation was now interrupted, as they were summoned to the dining-hall: but Don Diego took an opportunity of asking his son what opinion he had formed of his guest. " His madness, sir, is beyond the reach of all the doctors in the world," replied Don Lorenzo; " yet it is full of lucid intervals." They now sat down to the repast, which was such as Don Diego had said he usually gave to his visitors : neat, plentiful, and savoury. Don Quixote was, moreover, particularly pleased with the marvellous silence that prevailed throughout the whole house, as if it had been a convent of Carthusians.

The cloth being taken away, grace said, and their hands washed, Don Quixote earnestly entreated Don Lorenzo to repeat the verses which he intended for the prize. " I will do as you desire," replied he, " that I may not seem like those poets who, when entreated, refuse to produce their verses; but, if unasked, very often enforce them upon unwilling hearers : mine, however, were not written with any view to obtain a prize, but simply as an exercise." " It is the opinion of an ingenious friend of mine," said Don Quixote, " that these kinds of composition are not worth the trouble they require; because the paraphrase can never equal the text; they seldom exactly agree in sense, and often deviate widely. He says that the rules for this species of poetry are much too strict; suffering no interrogations, nor such expressions as ' said he,' ' I shall say,' and the like; nor changing verbs into nouns, nor altering the sense; with other restrictions, which, you well know, confine the writer." " Truly, Signor Don Quixote," said Don Lorenzo, " I would fain catch your worship tripping in some false Latin, but I cannot, for you slide through my fingers like an eel." " I do not comprehend your meaning," said Don Quixote. " I will explain myself at another time," replied Don Lorenzo, " and will now recite the text and its comment."

THE TEXT.

" Could I recall departed joy,
    Though barred the hopes of greater gain,
Or now the future hours employ
    That must succeed my present pain."

THE PARAPHRASE.

" All fortune's blessings disappear,
    She 's fickle as the wind ;
And now I find her as severe
    As once I thought her kind.
How soon the fleeting pleasures passed !
How long the lingering sorrows last !
    Unconstant goddess, in thy haste,
Do not thy prostrate slave destroy ;
    I 'd ne'er complain, but bless my fate,
Could I recall departed joy.

" Of all thy gifts I beg but this,
　　Glut all mankind with more,
Transport them with redoubled bliss,
　　But only mine restore.
With thought of pleasure once possessed,
I 'm now as curst as I was blessed:
　　Oh, would the charming hours return,
How pleased I 'd live, how free from pain !
　　I ne'er would pine, I ne'er would mourn,
Though barred the hopes of greater gain.

" But oh, the blessing I implore
　　Not fate itself can give ;
Since time elapsed exists no more,
　　No power can bid it live.
Our days soon vanish into nought,
And have no being but in thought.
　　Whate'er began must end at last ;
In vain we twice would youth enjoy,
　　In vain would we recall the past,
Or now the future hours employ.

" Deceived by hope and racked by fear,
　　No longer life can please ;
I 'll then no more its torments bear
　　Since death so soon can ease.
This hour I 'll die—but, let me pause—
A rising doubt my courage awes.
　　Assist, ye powers that rule my fate,
Alarm my thoughts, my rage restrain,
　　Convince my soul there 's yet a state
That must succeed my present pain."

As soon as Don Lorenzo had recited his verses, Don Quixote started up, and, grasping him by the hand, exclaimed in a loud voice, " By Heaven ! noble youth, there is not a better poet in the universe, and you deserve to wear the laurel, not of Cyprus, nor of Gaëta, as a certain poet said, whom Heaven forgive, but of the universities of Athens, did they now exist, and those of Paris, Bologna, and Salamanca ! If the judges deprive you of the first prize, may they be transfixed by the arrows of Apollo, and may the Muses never cross the threshold of their doors ! Be pleased, sir, to repeat some other of your more lofty verses, for I would fain have a further taste of your admirable genius."

How diverting that the young poet should be gratified by the praises of one whom he believed to be a madman ! O flattery, how potent is thy sway ! how wide are the bounds of thy pleasing jurisdiction ! This was verified in Don Lorenzo, who, yielding to the request of Don Quixote, repeated the following sonnet on the story of Pyramus and Thisbe :

SONNET.

" The nymph who Pyramus with love inspired
　Pierces the wall, with equal passion fired:
　Cupid from distant Cyprus thither flies,
　And views the secret breach with laughing eyes

*A day of sorrow to Sancho Panza, who was too sensible of the comforts that reigned in
Don Diego's house not to feel great unwillingness to return to the hunger of
the forests and wildernesses.*

> " Here silence, vocal, mutual vows conveys,
>   And, whisp'ring eloquent, their love betrays :
>   Though, chained by fear, their voices dare not pass,
>   Their souls, transmitted through the chink, embrace.
>
> " Ah, woful story of disastrous love !
>   Ill-fated haste, that did their ruin prove !
>   One death, one grave unite the faithful pair,
>   And in one common fame their mem'ries share."

"Now, Heaven be thanked," exclaimed Don Quixote, "that, among
the infinite number of rhymers now in being, I have at last met with
one who is truly a poet, which you, sir, have proved yourself by the
composition of that sonnet."

Four days was Don Quixote nobly regaled in Don Diego's house; at
the end of which he begged leave to depart, expressing his thanks for
the generous hospitality he had experienced; but as inactivity and

repose, he said, were unbecoming knights-errant, the duties of his function required him to proceed in quest of adventures, which he was told might be expected in abundance in those parts, and sufficient to occupy him until the time fixed for the tournament at Saragossa, where it was his intention to be present. Previously, however, he meant to visit the cave of Montesinos, concerning which so many extraordinary things were reported, and at the same time to discover, if possible, the true source of the seven lakes, commonly called the Lakes of Ruydera. Don Diego and his son applauded his honourable resolution, desiring him to furnish himself with whatever their house afforded for his accommodation, since his personal merit and noble profession justly claimed their services.

At length the day of his departure came — a day of joy to Don Quixote, but of sorrow to Sancho Panza, who was too sensible of the comforts and abundance that reigned in Don Diego's house not to feel great unwillingness to return to the hunger of forests and wildernesses, and to the misery of ill-provided wallets. However, these he filled and stuffed with what he thought most necessary; and Don Quixote, on taking leave of Don Lorenzo, said, " I know not whether I have mentioned it to you before, but if I have, I repeat it, that whenever you may feel disposed to shorten your way up the rugged steep that leads to the temple of fame, you have only to turn aside from the narrow path of poetry, and follow the still narrower one of knight-errantry, which may, nevertheless, raise you in a trice to imperial dignity." With these expressions Don Quixote completed, as it were, the evidence of his madness, especially when he added, " Heaven knows how willingly I would take Signor Don Lorenzo with me, to teach him how to spare the lowly and trample the oppressor under foot—virtues inseparable from my profession; but since your laudable exercises, as well as your youth, render that impossible, I shall content myself with admonishing you, in order to become eminent as a poet, to be guided by other men's opinions rather than your own; for no parents can see the deformity of their own children, and still stronger is the self-deception with respect to the offspring of the mind." The father and son again wondered at the medley of extravagance and good sense which they observed in Don Quixote, and the unfortunate obstinacy with which he persevered in the disastrous pursuit that seemed to occupy his whole soul. After repeating compliments and offers of service, and taking formal leave of the lady of the mansion, the knight and the squire—the one mounted upon Rozinante. the other upon Dapple—quitted their friends, and departed.

CHAPTER XIX.

Wherein is related the adventures of the enamoured shepherd; with other truly pleasing incidents.

DON QUIXOTE had not travelled far, when he overtook two persons like ecclesiastics or scholars, accompanied by two country fellows, all of whom were mounted upon asses. One of the scholars carried behind him a small bundle of linen and two pair of thread stockings, wrapped up in green buckram like a portmanteau; the other appeared to have nothing but a pair of new black fencing foils, with their points guarded. The countrymen carried other things, which showed that they had been making purchases in some large town, and were returning with them to their own village. But the scholars and the countrymen were astonished, as all others had been, on first seeing Don Quixote, and were curious to know what man this was, so different in appearance from all other men. Don Quixote saluted them, and hearing they were travelling the same road, he offered to bear them company, begging them to slacken their pace, as their asses went faster than his horse : and to oblige them he briefly told them who he was, and that his employment and profession was that of a knight-errant seeking adventures over the world. He told them his proper name was Don Quixote de la Mancha, and his appellative the Knight of the Lions.

All this to the countrymen was Greek or gibberish; but not so to the scholars, who soon discovered the soft part of Don Quixote's skull : they nevertheless viewed him with respectful attention, and one of them said, "If, Sir Knight, you are not fixed to one particular road, as those in search of adventures seldom are, come with us, and you will see one of the greatest and richest weddings that has ever been celebrated in La Mancha, or for many leagues round." "The nuptials of some prince, I presume?" said Don Quixote. "No," replied the scholar, "only that of a farmer and a country maid : he the wealthiest in this part of the country, and she the most beautiful that eyes ever beheld. The preparations are very uncommon; for the wedding is to be celebrated in a meadow near the village where the bride lives, who is called Quiteria the Fair, and the bridegroom Camacho the Rich : she is about the age of eighteen, and he twenty-two, both equally matched; though some nice folks, who have all the pedigrees of the world in their heads, pretend that the family of Quiteria the Fair has the advantage over that of Camacho; but that is now little regarded, for riches are able to solder up abundance of flaws. In short, this same Camacho is as liberal as a prince; and, intending to be at some cost in this wedding, has taken it into his head to convert a whole meadow into a kind of arbour, shading it so that the sun itself will find some difficulty to visit the green grass beneath. He will also have morris-dances, both with swords and bells; for there are people in the village who jingle and clatter them with great dexterity. As to the number of shoe-clappers* invited, it is impossible to count them; but what will give the greatest interest to this wedding is the effect it is expected to have on the slighted Basilius.

"This Basilius is a swain of the same village as Quiteria; his house is next to that of her parents, and separated only by a wall, whence Cupid took occasion to revive the ancient loves of Pyramus and Thisbe; for Basilius was in love with Quiteria from his childhood, and she returned his affection with a thousand modest favours, insomuch that the loves of the two children, Basilius and Quiteria, became the common talk of the village. When they were grown up, the father of Quiteria resolved to forbid Basilius the usual access to his family; and to relieve himself of all fears on his account, he determined to marry his daughter to the rich Camacho; not choosing to bestow her on Basilius, whose endowments are less the gifts of fortune than of nature: in truth, he is the most active youth we know: a great pitcher of the bar, an excellent wrestler, a great player at cricket, runs like a buck, leaps like a wild goat, and plays at ninepins as if by witchcraft; sings like a lark, and touches a guitar delightfully; and, above all, he handles a sword like the most skilful fencer." "For this accomplishment alone," said Don Quixote, "the youth deserves to marry not only the fair Quiteria, but Queen Guinevra herself, were she now alive, in spite of Sir Launcelot and all opposers." "To my wife with that," quoth Sancho, who had hitherto been silent and listening; "for she will have everybody marry their equal, according to the proverb, 'Every sheep to its like.' I shall take the part, too, of honest Basilius, and would have him marry the Lady Quiteria; and Heaven send them good luck; and a blessing"— meaning the contrary—"light upon all that would keep true lovers asunder." "If love only were to be considered," said Don Quixote, "parents would no longer have the privilege of judiciously matching their children. Were daughters left to choose for themselves, there are those who would prefer their father's serving-man, or throw themselves away on some fellow they might chance to see in the street: mistaking, perhaps, an impostor and swaggering poltroon for a gentleman, since passion too easily blinds the understanding, so indispensably necessary in deciding on that most important point, matrimony, which is peculiarly exposed to the danger of a mistake, and therefore needs all the caution that human prudence can supply, aided by the particular favour of Heaven. A person who proposes to take a long journey, if he is prudent, before he sets forward will look out for some safe and agreeable companion; and should not he who undertakes a journey for life use the same precaution, especially as his fellow-traveller is to be his companion at bed and board, and in all other situations? The wife is not a commodity which, when once bought, you can exchange or return; the mar-

---

* *Zapateadores.* Dancers that strike the soles of their shoes with the palms of their hands, in time and measure.

riage bargain, once struck, is irrevocable. It is a noose which, once thrown about the neck, turns to a Gordian knot, and cannot be unloosed till cut asunder by the scythe of death. I could say much more upon this subject, were I not prevented by my curiosity to hear something more from Signor Licentiate concerning the history of Basilius." To which the bachelor—or licentiate, as Don Quixote called him—answered, " I have nothing more to add, but that from the moment Basilius heard of the intended marriage of Quiteria to Camacho the rich, he has never been seen to smile nor speak coherently : he is always pensive and sad, and talking to himself—a certain and clear proof that he is distracted. He eats nothing but a little fruit ; and if he sleeps, it is in the fields, like cattle, upon the hard earth. Sometimes he casts his eyes up to heaven, and then fixes them on the ground, remaining motionless like a statue. In short, he gives such indications of a love-stricken heart, that we all expect that Quiteria's fatal ' Yes ' will be the sentence of his death."

" Heaven will order it better," said Sancho; "for God, who gives the wound, sends the cure. Nobody knows what is to come. A great many hours come in between this and to-morrow ; and in one hour, yea, in one minute, down falls the house. I have seen rain and sunshine at the same moment. A man may go to bed well at night, and not be able to stir next morning ; and tell me who can boast of having driven a nail in fortune's wheel ? Between the Yes and the No of a woman I would not undertake to thrust the point of a pin. Grant me only that Quiteria loves Basilius with all her heart, and I will promise him a bagful of good fortune : for Love, as I have heard say, wears spectacles, through which copper looks like gold, rags like rich apparel, and specks in the eye like pearls." "A curse on thee, Sancho !" said Don Quixote, " what wouldst thou be at ? When once thy stringing of proverbs begins, Judas alone—I wish he had thee !—can have patience to the end. Tell me, animal ! what knowest thou of nails and wheels, or of anything else ? " " Oh, if I am not understood," replied Sancho, " no wonder that what I say passes for nonsense. But no matter for that, I understand myself ; neither have I said many foolish things, only your worship is such a cricket." " *Critic*—not cricket, fool !—thou corrupter of good language !" said the knight. " Pray, sir, do not be so sharp upon me," answered Sancho ; " for I was not bred at court, nor studied in Salamanca, to know whether my words have a letter short or one too many. As Heaven shall save me, it is unreasonable to expect that beggarly Sayagues* should talk like Toledans—nay, even some of *them* are not over-nicely spoken." " You are in the right, friend," quoth the licentiate, " for how should they who live among the tan-yards, or stroll about the market of Zocodover, speak so well as those who are all day walking up and down the cloisters of the great church ? Yet they are all Toledans. Purity, propriety, and elegance of style will always be found among polite, well-bred, and sensible men, though born in Majalahonda : —sensible, I say, because though habit and example do much, good

---

* The people about Zamora, the poorest in Spain

sense is the foundation of good language. I, gentlemen, for my sins, have studied the canon law in Salamanca, and pique myself a little upon expressing myself in clear, plain, and significant terms." "If you had not piqued yourself still more upon managing those foils," said the other scholar, "you might by this time have been at the head of your class, whereas now you are at its tail."

"Look you, bachelor," answered the licentiate, "if you fancy dexterity in the use of the sword of no moment, you are grossly mistaken." "I do not only fancy so," replied Corchuelo, "but what is more, I am convinced of it, and, if you please, will convince you also by experience: try your foils against my nerves and bodily strength, and you will soon confess that I am in the right. Alight, and make use of your measured steps, your circles, and angles, and science, yet I hope to make you see the stars at noon-day with my artless and vulgar dexterity; for I trust, under Heaven, that the man is yet unborn who shall make me turn my back, or be able to stand his ground against me." "As to turning your back or not, I say nothing," replied the adept; "though it may happen that in the first spot you fix your foot on, your grave may be opened, were it only for your contempt of skill." "We shall see that presently," answered Corchuelo; and, hastily alighting, he snatched one of the foils which the licentiate carried upon his ass. "Hold, gentlemen!" cried Don Quixote at this moment, "my interposition may be necessary here; let me be judge of the field, and see that this long-controverted question is decided fairly."

Then, dismounting from Rozinante, and grasping his lance, he planted himself in the midst of the road, just as the licentiate had placed himself in a graceful position to receive his antagonist, who flew at him like a fury—cut and thrust, back-strokes and fore-strokes, single and double: laying it on thicker than hail, with all the rage of a provoked lion. But the licentiate not only warded off the tempest, but checked its fury, by making his adversary kiss the button of his foil, though not with quite so much devotion as if it had been a relic. In short, the licentiate, by dint of clean thrust, counted him all the buttons of a little cassock he had on, and tore the skirts so that they hung in rags, like the tails of the polypus. Twice he struck off his hat, and so worried and wearied him that, through spite, choler, and rage, he flung away the foil into the air with such force, that one of the country fellows present, who happened to be a notary, and went himself to fetch it, made oath that it was thrown near three-quarters of a league; which testimony has served, and still serves, to demonstrate that strength is overcome by art. Corchuelo sat down quite spent, and Sancho, going up to him, said, "Take my advice, Master Bachelor, and henceforward let your challenges be only to wrestle or pitch the bar; but as to fencing, meddle no more with it, for I have heard it said of your fencers that they can thrust you the point of a sword through the eye of a needle." "I am satisfied," answered Corchuelo, "and have learned by experience a truth I could not otherwise have believed." He then got up, embraced the licentiate, and they were better friends than ever.

Being unwilling to wait for the scrivener who was gone to fetch the foil, they determined to press forward, that they might reach betimes the village of Quiteria, whither they were all bound. On their way, the licentiate explained to them the merits of the fencing art, which he so well defended by reason and by mathematical demonstration, that all were convinced of the usefulness of the science, and Corchuelo was completely cured of his incredulity.

It now began to grow dark, and as they approached the village there appeared before them a new heaven, blazing with innumerable stars. At the same time they heard the sweet and mingled sounds of various instruments—such as flutes, tambourines, psalters, cymbals, drums, and bells; and, drawing still nearer, they perceived a spacious arbour, formed near the entrance into the town, hung round with lights that shone undisturbed by the breeze; for it was so calm that not a leaf was seen to move. The musicians, who are the life and joy of such festivals, paraded in bands up and down this delightful place, some dancing, others singing, and others playing upon different instruments: in short, nothing was there to be seen but mirth and pleasure. Several were employed in raising scaffolds, from which they might commodiously behold the shows and entertainments of the following day, that were to be dedicated to the nuptial ceremony of the rich Camacho and the obsequies of poor Basilius. Don Quixote refused to enter the town, though pressed by the countrymen and the bachelor; pleading what appeared to him a sufficient excuse—the practice of knights-errant to sleep in fields and forests, rather than in towns, though under gilded roofs: he therefore turned a little out of the road, much against Sancho's will, who had not yet forgotten the good lodging he had met with in the hospitable mansion of Don Diego.

CHAPTER XX.

Giving an account of the marriage of Camacho the Rich, and also the adventure of Basilius the Poor.

SCARCELY had the beautiful Aurora appeared, and given bright Phœbus time, by the warmth of his early rays, to exhale the liquid pearls that hung glittering on his golden hair, when Don Quixote, shaking off sloth from his drowsy members, rose up, and proceeded to call his squire Sancho Panza; but, finding him still snoring, he paused, and said, " O happy thou, above all that live on the face of the earth, who, neither envying nor envied, canst take thy needful rest with tranquillity of soul, neither persecuted by enchanters nor affrighted by their machinations! Sleep on—a hundred times I say, sleep on! No jealousies on thy lady's account keep thee in perpetual watchings, nor do anxious thoughts of debts unpaid awake thee; nor care how on the morrow thou and thy little straitened family shall be provided for. Ambition disquiets thee not, nor does the vain pomp of the world disturb thee; for thy chief concern is the care of thy ass, since to me is committed the comfort and protection of thine own person : a burden imposed on the master by nature and custom. The servant sleeps, the master lies awake, considering how he is to maintain, assist, and do him kindness. The pain of seeing the heavens obdurate in withholding the moisture necessary to refresh the earth, touches only the master, who is bound to provide in times of sterility and famine for those who served him in the season of fertility and abundance."

To all this Sancho answered not a word, for he was asleep ; nor would he have soon awaked, had not Don Quixote jogged him with the butt-end of his lance. At last he awoke, drowsy and yawning; and, after turning his face on all sides, he said, " From yonder bower, if I mistake not, there comes a steam and smell that savours more of broiled rashers than of herbs and rushes :—by my faith, a wedding that smells so well in the beginning must needs be a dainty one !" " Peace, glutton !" quoth Don Quixote, " and let us go and see this marriage, and what becomes of the disdained Basilius." " Hang him," quoth Sancho, " it matters not what becomes of him : if he is poor, he cannot think to wed Quiteria. A pleasant fancy, forsooth, for a fellow who has not a groat in his pocket to look for a yoke-mate above the clouds. Faith, sir, in my opinion a poor man should be contented with what he finds, and not be seeking for truffles at the bottom of the sea. I dare wager an arm that Camacho can cover Basilius with reals from head to foot; and if so, Quiteria would be a pretty jade, truly, to leave the fine clothes and jewels that Camacho can give her, for the bar-pitching and fencing of Basilius ! The bravest pitch of the bar or cleverest push of the foil will not fetch me a pint of wine from the vintner's : such talents and graces are not marketable wares—let Count Dirlos have them for me; but should they light on a man that has wherewithal—may my life show as well as they do when so coupled ! Upon a good foundation a good building may be raised; and the best bottom and foundation in the world is money." " For the love of Heaven, Sancho," quoth Don Quixote, "put an end to thy harangue. I verily believe, wert thou suffered to go on, thy prating would leave thee no time either to eat or sleep." " Be pleased to remember, sir," said Sancho, " the articles of our agreement before we sallied from home this last time; one of which was that you were to let me talk as much as I pleased, so it were not anything against my neighbour, nor against your worship's authority; and to my think-ing, I have made no breach yet in the bargain." " I do not remember any such article, Sancho," answered Don Quixote; " and though it were so, it is my pleasure that thou shouldst now hold thy peace, and come along; for already the musical instruments which we heard last night begin again to cheer the valleys, and doubtless the espousals will be celebrated in the cool of the morning."

Sancho obeyed his master's commands; and saddling and pannelling their steeds, they both mounted, and at a slow pace entered the artificial shade. The first thing that presented itself to Sancho's sight was a whole bullock spitted upon a large elm. The fire by which it was roasted was composed of a mountain of wood, and round it were placed six huge pots—not cast in common moulds, but each large enough to contain a whole shamble of flesh. Entire sheep were swallowed up in them, and floated like so many pigeons. The hares ready flayed, and

The first thing that presented itself to Sancho's sight was a whole bullock spitted upon a large elm.

the fowls plucked, that hung about the branches, in order to be buried in these cauldrons, were without number. Infinite was the wild-fowl and venison hanging about the trees to receive the cool air. Sancho counted about threescore skins, each holding above twenty-four quarts, and all, as appeared afterwards, full of generous wines. Hillocks, too, he saw, of the whitest bread, arranged like heaps of wheat on the thresh-ing-floor, and cheeses, piled up in the manner of bricks, formed a kind of wall. Two cauldrons of oil, larger than dyers' vats, stood ready for frying all sorts of batter-ware: and, with a couple of stout peels, they shovelled them up when fried, and forthwith immersed them in a kettle of prepared honey that stood near. The men and women cooks were about fifty in number, all clean, all active, and all in good humour. In the bullock's distended belly were sewed up a dozen sucking pigs, to make it savoury and tender. The spices of various kinds, which seemed to have been bought, not by the pound, but by the hundredweight, were deposited in a great chest, and open to every hand. In short, the preparation for the wedding was all rustic, but in sufficient abundance to have feasted an army.

Sancho beheld all with wonder and delight. The first that captivated and subdued his inclinations were the flesh-pots, out of which he would have been glad to have filled a moderate pipkin; next the wine-skins drew his affections; and lastly the products of the frying-pans—if such capacious vessels might be so called; and, being unable any longer to abstain, he ventured to approach one of the busy cooks, and in persuasive and hungry terms begged leave to sop a luncheon of bread in one of the pots. To which the cook answered, " This, friend, is not a day for hunger to be abroad—thanks to rich Camacho. Alight, and look about you for a ladle to skim out a fowl or two, and much good may they do you." " I see no ladle," answered Sancho. " Stay," said the cook· " Heaven save me, what a helpless varlet!" So saying, he laid hold of a kettle, and sousing it into one of the half-jars, he fished out three pullets and a couple of geese, and said to Sancho, " Eat, friend, and make a breakfast of this scum, to stay your stomach till dinner-time." " I have nothing to put it in," answered Sancho. " Then take ladle and all," quoth the cook ; " for Camacho's riches and joy supply everything."

While Sancho was thus employed, Don Quixote stood observing the entrance of a dozen peasants at one side of the spacious arbour, each mounted on a beautiful mare, in rich and gay caparisons, hung round with little bells. They were clad in holiday apparel, and in a regular troop made sundry careers about the meadow, with a joyful Moorish cry of " Long live Camacho and Quiteria! he as rich as she is fair, and she the fairest of the world!" Don Quixote hearing this, said to himself, " These people, it is plain, have never seen my Dulcinea del Toboso, otherwise they would have been less extravagant in the praise of their Quiteria." Soon after there entered, on different sides of the arbour, various sets of dancers, among which was one consisting of four and twenty sword-dancers; handsome, sprightly swains, all arrayed in fine white linen, and handkerchiefs wrought with several colours of fine silk. One of those mounted on horseback inquired of a young man who led the sword-dance, whether any of his comrades were hurt. " No," replied the youth, " thank Heaven, as yet we are all well :" and instantly he twined himself in among his companions with so many turns, and so dexterously, that although Don Quixote had often seen such dances before, none had ever pleased him so well. Another dance also delighted him much, performed by twelve damsels, young and beautiful, all clad in green stuff of Cuenza, having their hair partly plaited and partly flowing, all of golden hue, rivalling the sun itself, and covered with garlands of jessamine, roses, and woodbine. They were led up by a venerable old man and an ancient matron, to whom the occasion had given more agility than might have been expected from their years. A Zamora bagpipe regulated their motions, which, being no less sprightly and graceful than their looks were modest and maidenly, more lovely dancers were never seen in the world.

A pantomimic dance now succeeded, by eight nymphs, divided into two ranks—"Cupid" leading the one, and "Interest" the other; the former equipped with wings, bow, quiver, and arrows; the latter gorgeously apparelled with rich and variously-coloured silks, embroidered with gold. The nymphs in Cupid's band displayed their names, written in large letters, on their backs. "Poetry" was the first; then succeeded "Discretion," "Good Lineage," and "Valour." The followers of "Interest" were "Liberality," "Bounty," "Wealth," and "Security." This band was preceded by a wooden castle drawn by savages, clad so naturally in ivy and green cloth, coarse and shaggy, that Sancho was startled. On the front and sides of the edifice was written, "The Castle of Reserve." Four skilful musicians played on the tabor and pipe; Cupid began the dance, and after two movements he raised his eyes, and, bending his bow, pointed an arrow towards a damsel that stood on the battlements of the castle; at the same time addressing to her the following verses:

> "I am the god whose power extends
> Through the wide ocean, earth, and sky;
> To my soft sway all nature bends,
> Compelled by beauty to comply.

> "Fearless I rule in calm and storm;
> Indulge my pleasure to the full;
> Things deemed impossible perform;
> Bestow, resume, ordain, annul."

Cupid, having finished his address, shot an arrow over the castle, and retired to his station; upon which Interest stepped forth, and after two similar movements, the music ceasing, he said—

> "My power exceeds the might of love,
> For Cupid bows to me alone;
> Of all things framed by Heaven above,
> The most respected, sought, and known.

> "My name is Interest; mine aid
> But few obtain, though all desire:
> Yet shall thy virtue, beauteous maid,
> My constant services acquire."

Interest then withdrew, and Poetry advanced; and fixing her eyes on the damsel of the castle, she said—

" Let Poetry, whose strain divine
      The wondrous power of song displays,
  His heart to thee, fair nymph, consign,
      Transported in melodious lays.

" If haply thou wilt not refuse
      To grant my supplicated boon,
  Thy fame shall, wafted by the Muse,
      Surmount the circle of the moon."

Poetry having retired from the side of Interest, Liberality advanced;
and after making her movements, said—

" My name is Liberality,
      Alike beneficent and wise,
  To shun wild prodigality,
      And sordid avarice despise.

" Yet, for thy favour lavish grown,
      A prodigal I mean to prove—
  An honourable vice, I own—
      But giving is the test of love."

In this manner each personage of the two parties advanced and
retreated, performing a movement and reciting verses, some elegant and
some ridiculous; of which Don Quixote, though he had a very good
memory, only treasured up the foregoing.   Afterwards the groups mingled together in a lively and graceful dance; and when Cupid passed
before the castle, he shot his arrows aloft, but Interest flung gilded
balls against it.   After having danced for some time, Interest drew out
a large purse of Roman cat-skin which seemed to be full of money, and
throwing it at the castle, it separated and fell to pieces, leaving the
damsel exposed and without defence.   Whereupon Interest with his
followers, casting a large golden chain about her neck, seemed to take
her prisoner and lead her away captive, while Love and his party endeavoured to rescue her : all their motions during this contest being
regulated by the musical accompaniments.   The contending parties were
at length separated by the savages, who with great dexterity repaired
the shattered castle, wherein the damsel was again enclosed as before ;
and thus the piece ended, to the great satisfaction of the spectators.

Don Quixote asked one of the nymphs, Who had composed and
arranged the show?   She told him that it was a clergyman of that
village, who had a notable head-piece for such kind of inventions.   " I
would venture a wager," said Don Quixote, " that this bachelor, or clergyman, is more a friend to Camacho than to Basilius, and understands
satire better than vespers; for in his dance he has ingeniously opposed
the talents of Basilius to the riches of Camacho."   " I hold with Camacho," quoth Sancho, who stood listening : " the king is my cock."   " It
is plain," said Don Quixote, " that thou art an arrant bumpkin, and one
of those who always cry, ' Long live the conqueror !' "   " I know not who
I am one of," answered Sancho ; " but this I know, I shall never get

such elegant scum from Basilius's pots as I have done from Camacho's." And showing his kettleful of geese and hens, he laid hold of one, and began to eat with notable good-will and appetite. " A fig for the talents of Basilius !" said he, " for so much thou art worth as thou hast, and so much hast as thou art worth. There are but two lineages in the world, as my grandmother used to say : ' the Haves and the Have-nots,' and she stuck to the Haves. Now-a-days, Master Don Quixote, people are more inclined to feel the pulse of Have than of Know. An ass with golden furniture makes a better figure than a horse with a pack-saddle : so that I tell you again, I hold with Camacho, for the plentiful scum of his kettles are geese and hens, hares and conies; while that of Basilius, if he has any, must be mere dish-water."

" Is thy speech finished, Sancho ?" quoth Don Quixote. " I must have done," replied Sancho, " because I see your worship is about to be angry at what I am saying; were it not for that, I have work cut out for three days." " Heaven grant that I may see thee dumb before I die !" said Don Quixote. " At the rate we go on," quoth Sancho, " before you die I shall be mumbling clay; in which case I may not speak a word till the end of the world, or at least till doomsday." " Though it be so ordered," said Don Quixote, " thy silence, O Sancho, will never balance thy past, present, and future prating. Besides, according to the course of nature, I must die before thee, and therefore it will never be my fate to see thy tongue at rest, not even when drinking or sleeping." " Faith, sir," quoth Sancho, " there is no trust-ing to goodman Death, who devours lambs as well as sheep; and I have heard our vicar say, ' he tramples just the same upon the high towers of kings, and the low cottages of the poor.' That same ghastly gentleman is more powerful than dainty : far from being squeamish, he eats of everything, and snatches at all; stuffing his wallets with people of all ages and degrees. He is not a reaper that sleeps away the mid-day heat, for he cuts down and mows at all hours, the dry grass as well as the green. Nor does he stand to chew, but devours and swal-lows down all that comes in his way; having a wolfish appetite that is never satisfied; and, though he has no belly, he seems to have a perpetual dropsy, and a raging thirst for the lives of all that live, whom he gulps down just as one would drink a jug of cold water." " Hold, Sancho," said Don Quixote, " while thou art well, and do not spoil thy work by over-doing ; for, in truth, what thou hast said of death, in thy rustic phrase, might become the mouth of a good preacher. If thou hadst but discretion, Sancho, equal to thy natural abilities, thou mightest take to the pulpit, and go preaching about the world." " A good liver is the best preacher," replied Sancho, " and that is all the divinity I know." " Or need know," said Don Quixote; " but I can in nowise comprehend how, since the fear of Heaven is the beginning of wisdom, thou, who art more afraid of a lizard than of Him, shouldst know so much as thou dost." " Good your worship, judge of your own chival-ries, I beseech you," answered Sancho, " and meddle not with other men's fears or valours ; for I am as pretty a fearer of God as any of my neighbours; so pray let me whip off this scum, for all besides is idle talk, which one day or other we must give an account of in the next world." Whereupon he began a fresh assault upon his kettle, with so long-winded an appetite as to awaken that of Don Quixote, who doubtless would have assisted him had he not been prevented by that which must forthwith be related.

CHAPTER XXI.

In which is continued the history of Camacho's wedding; with other delightful incidents.

As Don Quixote and Sancho were engaged in the conversation mentioned in the preceding chapter, they suddenly heard a great outcry and noise raised by those mounted on the mares, shouting as they gallopped to meet the bride and bridegroom, who were entering the bower, saluted by a thousand musical instruments of all kinds and inventions, accompanied by the parish priest and kindred on both sides, and by a number of the better class of people from the neighbouring towns, all in their holiday apparel. When Sancho espied the bride, he said, " In good faith, she is not clad like a country girl, but like any court lady ! By the mass ! her breast-piece seems to me at this distance to be of rich coral, and her gown, instead of green stuff of Cuenza, is no less than a thirty-piled velvet ! Besides, the trimming, I vow, is of satin ! Do but observe her hands—instead of rings of jet, let me never thrive but they are of gold, aye, and of real gold, with pearls as white as a curd, every one of them worth an eye of one's head. Ah, jade ! and what fine hair she has ! If it be not false, I never saw longer nor fairer in all my life. Then her sprightliness and mien, why, she is a very moving palm tree, laden with branches of dates, for just so look the trinklets hanging at her hair and about her neck. By my soul, the girl is so covered with plate that she might pass the banks of the Flanders."*

Don Quixote smiled at Sancho's homely praises; at the same time he thought that, excepting the mistress of his soul, he had never seen a more beautiful woman. The fair Quiteria looked a little pale, occasioned, perhaps, by a want of rest the preceding night, which brides usually employ in preparing their wedding finery.

The bridal pair proceeded towards a theatre on one side of the arbour, decorated with tapestry and garlands, where the nuptial ceremony was to be performed, and whence they were to view the dances and shows prepared for the occasion. Immediately on their arrival

---

* To pass the bank of Flanders is a phrase commonly used to express the attempt or execution of an arduous enterprise. They are dangerous sand-banks formed by the waves of the sea.

at that place, a loud noise was heard at a distance, amidst which a voice was distinguished calling aloud, "Hold a little, rash and thoughtless people!" On turning their heads they saw that these words were uttered by a man who was advancing towards them, clad in a black doublet, welted with flaming crimson. He was crowned with a garland of mournful cypress, and held in his hand a large truncheon; and, as he drew near, all recognized the gallant Basilius, and waited in fearful expectation of some disastrous result from this unseasonable visit. At length he came up, tired and out of breath, and placed himself just before the betrothed couple; then, pressing his staff, which was pointed with steel, into the ground, he fixed his eyes on Quiteria, and, in a broken and tremulous voice, thus addressed her: "Ah, false and forgetful Quiteria, well thou knowest that, by the laws of our holy religion, thou canst not marry another man whilst I am living; neither art thou ignorant that, while waiting till time and mine own industry should improve my fortune, I have never failed in the respect due to thy honour. But thou hast cast aside every obligation due to my lawful love, and art going to make another man master of what is mine: a man who is not only enriched, but rendered eminently happy in his wealth; and, in obedience to the will of Heaven, the only impediment to his supreme felicity I will remove, by withdrawing this wretched being. Long live the rich Camacho with the ungrateful Quiteria! Long and happily may they live, and let poor Basilius die, who would have risen to good fortune had not poverty clipped his wings and laid him in an early grave!"

But so saying, he plucked his staff from the ground, and, drawing out a short tuck, to which it had served as a scabbard, he fixed what might be called the hilt into the ground, and, with a nimble spring and resolute air, he threw himself on the point, which instantly appearing at his back, the poor wretch lay stretched on the ground, pierced through and through, and weltering in his blood.

His friends, struck with horror and grief, rushed forward to help him, and Don Quixote, dismounting, hastened also to lend his aid, and taking the dying man in his arms, found that he was still alive. They would have drawn out the tuck, but the priest who was present thought that it should not be done till he had made his confession; as, the moment it was taken out of his body, he would certainly expire. But Basilius, not having quite lost the power of utterance, in a faint and doleful voice said, "If, cruel Quiteria, in this my last and fatal agony, thou wouldst give me thy hand as my spouse, I should hope my rashness might find pardon in heaven, since it procured me the blessing of being thine." Upon which the priest advised him to attend rather to the salvation of his soul than to his bodily appetites, and seriously implore pardon of God for his sins, especially for this last desperate action. Basilius replied that he could not make any confession till Quiteria had given him her hand in marriage, as that would be a solace to his mind, and enable him to confess his sins.

Don Quixote, hearing the wounded man's request, said, in a loud voice, that Basilius had made a very just and reasonable request, and, moreover, a very practicable one; and that it would be equally honourable for Signor Camacho to take Quiteria a widow of the brave Basilius, as if he received her at her father's hand; nothing being required but the simple word "Yes," which could be of no consequence, since, in these espousals, the nuptial bed must be the grave. Camacho heard all this, and was perplexed and undecided what to do or say; but so much was he importuned by the friends of Basilius to permit Quiteria to give him her hand, and thereby save his soul from perdition, that they at length moved, nay forced him to say that, if it pleased Quiteria to give it to him, he should not object, since it was only delaying for a moment the accomplishment of his wishes. They all immediately applied to Quiteria, and, with entreaties, tears, and persuasive arguments, pressed and importuned her to give her hand to Basilius; but she, harder than marble, and more immoveable than a statue, returned no answer, until the priest told her that she must decide promptly, as the soul of Basilius was already between his teeth, and there was no time for hesitation.

Then the beautiful Quiteria, in silence, and to all appearance troubled and sad, approached Basilius, whose eyes were already turned in his head, and he breathed short and quick, muttering the name of Quiteria, and giving tokens of dying more like a heathen than a Christian. At last, Quiteria, kneeling down by him, made signs to him for his hand. Basilius unclosed his eyes, and fixing them steadfastly upon her, said, "O Quiteria, thou relentest at a time when thy pity is a sword to put a final period to this wretched life; for now I have not strength to bear the glory thou conferrest upon me in making me thine, nor will it suspend the pain which shortly will veil my eyes with the dreadful shadow of death. What I beg of thee, O fatal star of mine! is that thou give not thy hand out of compliment, or again to deceive me, but to declare that thou bestowest it upon me as thy lawful husband, without any compulsion on thy will; for it would be cruel in this extremity to deal falsely or impose on him who has been so true to thee." Here he fainted, and the bystanders thought his soul was just departing. Quiteria, all modesty and bashfulness, taking Basilius's right hand in hers, said, "No force would be sufficient to bias my will; and therefore, with all the freedom I have, I give thee my hand to be thy lawful wife, and receive thine, if it be as freely given, and if the anguish caused by thy rash act doth not trouble and prevent thee." "Yes, I give it thee," answered Basilius, "neither discomposed nor confused, but with the clearest understanding that Heaven was ever pleased to bestow on me; and so I give and engage myself to be thy husband." "And I to be thy wife," answered Quiteria, "whether thou livest many years, or art carried from my arms to the grave." "For one so much wounded," observed Sancho, "this young man talks a great deal. Advise him to leave off his courtship, and mind the business of his soul; though to my thinking he has it more on his tongue than between his teeth."

Basilius and Quiteria being thus, with hands joined, the tender-hearted priest, with tears in his eyes, pronounced the benediction upon them, and prayed to Heaven for the repose of the bridegroom's soul; who, as soon as he had received the benediction, suddenly started up, and nimbly drew out the tuck which was sheathed in his body. All the spectators were astonished, and some, more simple than the rest, cried out, "A miracle! a miracle!" But Basilius replied, "No miracle, no miracle, but a stratagem!" The priest, astonished and confounded, ran to feel, with both his hands, the wound, and found that the sword had passed, not through Basilius's flesh and ribs, but through a hollow iron pipe, cunningly fitted to the place, and filled with blood, so prepared as not to congeal. In short, the priest, Camacho, and the rest of the spectators found they were imposed upon and completely duped. The bride showed no signs of regret at the artifice: on the contrary, hearing it said that the marriage, as being fraudulent, was not valid, she said that she confirmed it anew; it was, therefore, generally supposed that the matter had been concerted with the privity and concurrence of both parties; which so enraged Camacho and his friends, that they immediately had recourse to vengeance, and, unsheathing abundance of swords, they fell upon Basilius, in whose behalf as many more were instantly drawn, and Don Quixote, leading the van on horseback, his lance couched, and well covered with his shield, made them all give way. Sancho, who took no pleasure in such kind of frays, retired to the jars out of which he had gotten his charming skimmings; regarding that place as a sanctuary which none would dare to violate.

Don Quixote then cried aloud, "Hold, sirs, hold! It is not right to avenge the injuries committed against us by love. Remember that the arts of warfare and courtship are in some points alike. In war, stratagems are lawful; so likewise are they in the conflicts and rivalships of love, if the means employed be not dishonourable. Quiteria and Basilius were destined for each other by the just and favouring will of Heaven. Camacho is rich, and may purchase his pleasure when, where, and how he pleases: Basilius has but this one ewe-lamb, and no one, however powerful, has a right to take it from him; for those whom God hath joined, let no man sunder; and whoever shall attempt it must first pass the point of this lance." Then he brandished it with such vigour and dexterity that he struck terror into all those who did not know him.

Quiteria's disdain made such an impression upon Camacho, that he initantly banished her from his heart. The persuasions, therefore, of the priest, who was a prudent, well-meaning man, had their effect: Camacho and his party sheathed their weapons, and remained satisfied, blaming rather the fickleness of Quiteria than the cunning of Basilius. With much reason Camacho thought within himself that, if Quiteria loved Basilius when a virgin, she would love him also when married; and that he had more cause to thank Heaven for so fortunate an escape than to repine at the loss he had sustained. The disappointed bridegroom and his followers, being thus consoled and appeased, those of Basilius were so likewise; and the rich Camacho, to show that his mind was free from resentment, would have the diversions and entertainments go on as if they had been really married. The happy pair, however, not choosing to share in them, retired to their own dwelling, accompanied by their joyful adherents : for if the rich man can draw after him attendants and flatterers, the poor man who is virtuous and deserving is followed by friends who honour and support him. Don Quixote joined the party of Basilius, having been invited by them as a person of worth and bravery; while Sancho, finding it impossible to remain and share the relishing delights of Camacho's festival, which continued till night, with a heavy heart accompanied his master, leaving behind the flesh-pots of Egypt, the skimmings of which, though now almost consumed, still reminded him of the glorious abundance he had lost. Pensive and sorrowful, therefore, though not hungry, without alighting from Dapple, he followed the tract of Rozinante.

CHAPTER XXII.

Wherein is related the grand adventure of the Cave of Montesinos, situated in the heart of La Mancha, which the valorous Don Quixote happily accomplished.

Looking upon themselves as greatly obliged for the valour he had shown in defending their cause, the newly-married couple made much of Don Quixote ; and judging of his wisdom by his valour, they accounted him a Cid in arms and a Cicero in eloquence; and during three days honest Sancho solaced himself at their expense. The bridegroom explained to them his stratagem of the feigned wound, and told them it was a device of his own, and had been concerted with the fair Quiteria. He confessed, too, that he had let some of his friends into the secret, that they might support his deception. " That ought not to be called deception which aims at a virtuous end," said Don Quixote; " and no end is more excellent than the marriage of true lovers; though love," added he, " has its enemies, and none greater than hunger and poverty; for love is all gaiety, joy, and content."

This he intended as a hint to Basilius, whom he wished to draw from the pursuit of his favourite exercises; for, though they procured him fame, they were unprofitable; and it was now his duty to exert himself for the improvement of his circumstances, by lawful and praiseworthy means, which are never wanting to the prudent and active. " The poor, yet honourable man," said he, " admitting that honour and poverty can be united, in a beautiful wife possesses a precious jewel, and whoever deprives him of her, despoils him of his honour. The chaste and beautiful wife of an indigent man deserves the palm and laurel crowns of victory and triumph. Beauty of itself attracts admiration and love, and the royal eagles and other towering birds stoop to the tempting lure ; but if it be found unprotected and exposed to poverty, kites and vultures are continually hovering round it, and watching it as their natural prey. Well, therefore, may she be called the crown of her husband who main-tains her ground in so perilous a situation. It was the opinion of a certain sage, O discreet Basilius, that the world contained only one good woman, and he advised every man to persuade himself that she was fallen to his lot, and he would then live contented. Although unmarried myself, I would venture to offer counsel to one who should require it in the choice of a wife. In the first place, I would advise him to consider the purity of her fame more than her fortune: a virtuous woman seeks a fair reputation not only by being good, but by appearing to be so; for a woman suffers more in the world's opinion by public indecorum than secret wantonness. If the woman you bring to your house be virtuous, it is an easy matter to keep her so, and even to improve her good qualities; but if she be otherwise, you will have much trouble to correct her; for it is not easy to pass from one extreme to the other: it may not be impossible, but certainly it is very difficult."

To all this Sancho listened, and said to himself, "This master of mine tells me, when I speak of things of marrow and substance, that I might take a pulpit in my hand, and go about the world preaching; and well may I say to him, that whenever he begins to string sentences and give out his advice, he may not only take a pulpit in his hand, but two upon each finger, and stroll about your market-places, crying out, 'Mouth, what will you have?' The devil take thee for a knight-errant that knows everything! I verily thought that he only knew what belonged to his chivalries, but he pecks at everything, and thrusts his spoon into every dish." Sancho muttered this so very loud that he was overheard by his master, who said, "Sancho, what art thou muttering?" "Nothing at all," answered Sancho; "I was only saying to myself that I wished I had heard your worship preach in this way before I was married; then perhaps I should have been able to say now, 'The ox that is loose is best licked.'" "Is thy Teresa, then, so bad, Sancho?" quoth Don Quixote. "She is not very bad," answered Sancho; "neither is she very good, at least not quite so good as I would have her." "Thou art in the wrong, Sancho," said Don Quixote, "to speak ill of thy wife, who is the mother of thy children." "We owe each other nothing upon that score," answered Sancho, "for she speaks as ill of me, whenever the fancy takes her, especially when she is jealous; and then Satan himself cannot bear with her."

Three days they remained with the new-married couple, where they were served and treated like kings; at the end of which time, Don Quixote requested the student who was so dexterous a fencer, to procure him a guide to the Cave of Montesinos; for he had a great desire to descend into it, in order to see with his own eyes if the wonders reported of it were really true. The student told him he would introduce him to a young relation of his, a good scholar, and much given to reading books of chivalry, who would very gladly accompany him to the very mouth of the cave, and also show him the Lakes of Ruydera, so famous in La Mancha, and even all over Spain; adding that he would find him a very entertaining companion, as he knew how to write books and dedicate them to princes. In short, the cousin appeared, mounted on an ass with foal, whose pack-saddle was covered with a doubled piece of an old carpet or sacking. Sancho saddled Rozinante, pannelled Dapple, and replenished his wallets: those of the scholar being also well provided; and thus, after taking leave of their friends and commending themselves to Heaven, they set out, bending their course directly towards the famous Cave of Montesinos.

Upon the road, Don Quixote asked the scholar what were his exercises, his profession, and his studies. He replied that his studies and profession were literary, and his employment composing books for the press, on useful and entertaining subjects. Among others, he said he had published one that was entitled, " A Treatise on Liveries," wherein he had described seven hundred and three liveries; with their colours, mottoes, and cyphers; forming a collection from which gentlemen, without the trouble of inventing, might select according to their fancy; for, being adapted to all occasions, the jealous, the disdained, the forsaken, and the absent might all there be united. " I have likewise," said he, " just produced another book, which I intend to call ' The Metamorphoses, or Spanish Ovid.' The idea is perfectly novel; for, in a burlesque imitation of Ovid, I have given the origin and history of the Giralda of Seville, the Angel of La Magdalena,* the Conduit of Vecinguerra at Cordova, the bulls of Guisando, the Sierra Morena, the fountains of Leganitos, and the Lavapies in Madrid, not forgetting the Piojo, the golden pipe, and the Priory; and all these with their several transformations, allegories, and metaphors, in such a manner as at once to surprise, instruct, and entertain. Another book of mine I call ' A Supplement to Virgil Polydore,'† which treats of the invention of things: a work of vast erudition and study; because I have there supplied many important matters omitted by Polydore, and explained them in a superior style. Virgil, for instance, forgot to tell us who was the first in the world that caught a cold, and who was first anointed for the French disease. These points I settle with the utmost precision, on the testimony of above five and twenty authors, whom I have cited; so that your worship may judge whether I have not laboured well, and whether the whole world is not likely to profit by such a performance."

Sancho, who had been attentive to the student's discourse, said, " Tell me, sir—so may Heaven send you good luck with your books—can you resolve me—but I know you can, since you know everything—who was the first man that scratched his head? I, for my part, am of opinion it must have been our father Adam." " Certainly," answered the scholar; " for there is no doubt but Adam had a head and hair; and,

---

* The Angel of La Magdalena is a shapeless figure placed for a weathercock on the steeple of the church of St. Magdalen at Salamanca. The conduit of Vecinguerra carries the rain-water from the streets of Cordova to the Guadalquiver. The fountains of Leganitos, &c., are all situated in the promenades and public places of Madrid.

† He should have said Polydore Virgil. He was a learned Italian, who published, in 1499, the treatise *De rerum Inventoribus.*

this being granted, he, being the first man in the world, must needs have been the first who scratched his head." "That is what I think," said Sancho; "but tell me now, who was the first tumbler in the world?" "Truly, brother," answered the scholar, "I cannot determine that point till I have given it some consideration, which I will surely do when I return to my books, and will satisfy you when we see each other again, for I hope this will not be the last time." "Look ye, sir," replied Sancho, "be at no trouble about the matter, for I have already hit upon the answer to my question. Know, then, that the first tumbler was Lucifer, when he was cast or thrown headlong from heaven, and came tumbling down to the lowest abyss." "You are in the right, friend," quoth the scholar. "That question and answer are not thine, Sancho," said Don Quixote; "thou hast heard them before." "Say no more, sir," replied Sancho, "for, in good faith, if we fall to questioning and answering, we shall not have done before to-morrow morning; besides, for foolish questions and foolish answers I need not be obliged to any of my neighbours." "Sancho," quoth Don Quixote, "thou hast said more than thou art aware of; for some there are who bestow much labour in examining and explaining things which, when known, are not worth recollecting."

In such conversation they pleasantly passed that day, and at night took up their lodging in a small village, which the scholar told Don Quixote was distant but two leagues from the Cave of Montesinos, and that if he persevered in his resolution to enter into it, it was necessary to be provided with a rope, by which he might let himself down. Don Quixote declared that if it reached to the abyss he would see the bottom. They procured, therefore, near a hundred fathom of cord; and about two in the afternoon of the following day arrived at the mouth of the cave, which they found to be wide and spacious, but so much overgrown with briers, thorns, and wild fig trees, as to be almost concealed. On perceiving the cave they alighted, and the scholar and Sancho proceeded to bind the cord fast round Don Quixote, and, while they were thus employed, Sancho said, "Have a care, sir, dear sir, what you are about: do not bury yourself alive, nor hang yourself dangling like a flask of wine let down to cool in a well; for it is no business of your worship to pry into that hole, which must needs be worse than any dungeon." "Tie on," replied Don Quixote, "and hold thy peace; for such an enterprise as this, friend Sancho, was reserved for me alone." The guide then said, "I beseech your worship, Signor Don Quixote, to be observant, and with a hundred eyes see, explore, and examine what is below; perhaps many things may there be discovered worthy of being inserted in my book of Metamorphoses." "The drum," quoth Sancho, "is in a hand that knows full well how to rattle it."

The knight being well bound, not over his armour, but his doublet, he said, "We have been careless in neglecting to provide a bell, to be tied to me with this rope, by the tinkling of which you might have heard me still descending, and thereby have known that I was alive; but since that is now impossible, be Heaven my guide!" Kneeling down, he first supplicated Heaven for protection and success in an adventure so new, and seemingly so perilous; then raising his voice, he said, " O mistress of every act and movement of my life, most illustrious and peerless Dulcinea del Toboso! if the prayers and requests of this thy adventurous lover reach thy ears, by the power of thy unparalleled beauty I conjure thee to listen to them, and grant me thy favour and protection in this moment of fearful necessity, when I am on the point of plunging, engulfing, and precipitating myself into the profound abyss before me, solely to prove to the world that, if thou favourest me, there is no impossibility I will not attempt and overcome."

So saying, he drew near to the cavity, and observing that the entrance was so choked with vegetation as to be almost impenetrable, he drew his sword, and began to cut and hew down the brambles and bushes with which it was covered; whereupon, disturbed at the noise and rustling which he made, presently out rushed such a flight of huge daws and ravens, as well as bats and other night-birds, that he was thrown down; and had he been as superstitious as he was Catholic, he would have taken it for an ill omen, and relinquished the enterprise. Rising again upon his legs, and seeing no more creatures fly out, the scholar and Sancho let him down into the fearful cavern; and, as he entered, Sancho gave him his blessing, and, making a thousand crosses over him, said, " God, and the Rock of France, together with the Trinity of Gaëta,* speed thee, thou flower and cream and skimming of knights-errant! There thou goest, Hector of the world, heart of steel, and arm of brass! Once more, Heaven guide thee, and send thee back safe and sound to the light of this world, which thou art now forsaking for that horrible den of darkness." The scholar also added his prayers to those of Sancho for the knight's success and happy return.

Don Quixote went down, still calling as he descended for more rope, which they gave him by little and little; and when the voice, owing to the windings of the cave, could be heard no longer, and the hundred fathom of cordage was all let down, they thought that they should pull him up again, since they could give him no more rope. However, after the lapse of about half an hour, they began to gather up the rope, which they did so easily that it appeared to have no weight attached to it, whence they conjectured that Don Quixote remained in the cave: Sancho, in this belief, wept bitterly, and pulled up the rope in great haste, to know the truth; but having drawn it to a little above eight fathoms, they had the satisfaction again to feel the weight. In short, after raising it up to about the tenth fathom, they could see the knight very distinctly; upon which Sancho immediately called to him, saying, " Welcome back again to us, dear sir, for we began to fear you meant to stay below!" But Don Quixote answered not a word; and being now drawn entirely out, they perceived

---

* The Rock of France is a lofty mountain in the district of Alberca. The Trinity of Gaëta is a chapel and convent, founded by King Ferdinand V. of Arragon, on the summit of a promontory before the port of Gaëta, and dedicated to the Holy Trinity.

Having drawn it to a little above eight fathoms, they had the satisfaction again to feel the weight.

that his eyes were shut, as if he were asleep. They then laid him along the ground and unbound him; but as he still did not awake, they turned, pulled, and shook him so much, that at last he came to himself, stretching and yawning, just as if he had awaked out of a deep and heavy sleep; and looking wildly about him, he said, "Heaven forgive ye, my friends, for having brought me away from the most delicious and charming state that ever mortal enjoyed! In truth, I am now thoroughly satisfied that all the pleasures of this life pass away like a shadow or dream, or fade like a flower of the field. O unhappy Montesinos! O desperately wounded Durandarte! O unhappy Belerma! O weeping Guadiana! And ye, unfortunate daughters of Ruydera, whose waters show what floods of tears have streamed from your fair eyes!"

The scholar and Sancho listened to Don Quixote's words, which he uttered as if drawn with excessive pain from his entrails. They entreated him to explain, and to tell them what he had seen in that bottomless pit. "Pit, do you call it?" said Don Quixote; "call it so no more, for it deserves not that name, as you shall presently hear." He then told them that he wanted food extremely, and desired they would give him something to eat. The scholar's carpet was accordingly spread upon the grass, and they immediately applied to the pantry of his wallets, and being all three seated in loving and social fellowship, they made their dinner and supper at one meal. When all were satisfied, and the carpet removed, Don Quixote de la Mancha said, " Remain where you are, my sons, and listen to me with attention."

CHAPTER XXIII.

Of the wonderful things which the accomplished Don Quixote de la Mancha declared he had seen in the Cave of Montesinos, from the extraordinary nature of which, this adventure is held to be apocryphal.

It was about four o'clock in the afternoon, when the sun, being covered by clouds, its temperate rays gave Don Quixote an opportunity, without heat or fatigue, of relating to his two illustrious hearers what he had seen in the Cave of Montesinos ; and he began in the following manner :

"About twelve or fourteen fathoms deep in this dungeon, there is on the right hand a hollow space, wide enough to contain a large waggon, together with its mules, and faintly lighted by some distant apertures above. This cavity I happened to see, as I journeyed on through the dark without knowing whither I was going; and as I was just then beginning to be weary of hanging by the rope, I determined to enter, in order to rest a little. I called out to you aloud, and desired you not to let down more rope till I bid you; but it seems you heard me not. I then collected the cord you had let down, and coiling it up into a heap or bundle, I sat down upon it, full of thought, meditating how I might descend to the bottom, having nothing to support my weight. In this situation, pensive and embarrassed, a deep sleep suddenly came over me, from which, I know not how, I as suddenly awoke, and found that I had been transported into a verdant lawn, the most delightful that Nature could create, or the liveliest fancy imagine. I rubbed my eyes, wiped them, and perceived that I was not asleep, but really awake. Nevertheless, I felt my head and breast, to be assured that it was I myself, and not some empty and counterfeit illusion; but sensation, feeling, and the coherent discourse I held with myself, convinced me that I was the identical person which I am at this moment. I soon discovered a royal and splendid palace or castle, whereof the walls and battlements seemed to be composed of bright and transparent crystal; and as I gazed upon it, the great gates of the portal opened, and a venerable old man issued forth and advanced towards me. He was clad in a long mourning cloak of purple baize, which trailed upon the ground ; over his shoulders and breast he wore a kind of collegiate tippet of green satin; he had a black Milan cap on his head, and his hoary beard reached below his girdle. He carried no weapons, but held a rosary of beads in his hand as large as walnuts, and every tenth bead the size of an ordinary ostrich egg. His mien, his gait, his gravity, and his goodly presence, each singly and conjointly filled me with surprise and admiration. On coming up, he embraced me, and said, 'The day is at length arrived, most renowned and valiant Don Quixote de la Mancha, that we, who are enclosed in this enchanted solitude, have long hoped would bring thee hither, that thou mayest proclaim to the world the things prodigious and incredible that lie concealed in this subterranean place, commonly called the Cave of Montesinos—an exploit reserved for your invincible heart and stupendous courage. Come with me, illustrious sir, that I may show you the wonders contained in this transparent castle, of which I am warder and perpetual guard; for I am Montesinos himself, from whom this cave derives its name.' He had no sooner told me that he was Montesinos than I asked him whether it was true what was reported in the world above, that with a little dagger he had taken out the heart of his great friend Durandarte, and conveyed it to the Lady Belerma, agreeable to his dying request. He replied that the whole was true, excepting as to the dagger; for it was not a small dagger, but a bright poniard, sharper than an awl."

"That poniard," interrupted Sancho, "must have been made by Raymond de Hozes, of Seville." "I know not who was the maker," said Don Quixote, "but on reflection, it could not have been Raymond de Hozes, who lived but the other day, whereas the battle of Roncesvalles, where this misfortune happened, was fought some ages ago. But that question is of no importance, and does not affect the truth and connection of the story." "True," answered the scholar; "pray go on, Signor Don Quixote, for I listen to your account with the greatest pleasure imaginable." "And I relate it with no less," answered Don Quixote: "and so to proceed—the venerable Montesinos conducted me to the crystalline palace, where, in a lower hall, formed of alabaster, and extremely cool, there stood a marble tomb of exquisite workmanship, whereon I saw extended a knight, not of brass, or marble, or jasper, as is usual with other monuments, but of pure flesh and bones. His right hand, which seemed to me somewhat hairy and nervous (a token of great strength), was laid on the region of his heart; and before I could ask any question, Montesinos, perceiving my attention fixed on the sepulchre, said, 'This is my friend Durandarte, the flower and model of all the enamoured and valiant knights-errant of his time. He is kept here enchanted, as well as myself and many others of both sexes, by that French enchanter, Merlin, said to be the devil's son, which, however, I do not credit, though indeed I believe he knows one point more than the devil himself. How or why we are thus enchanted, no one can tell; but time will explain it, and that, too, I imagine, at no distant period. What astonishes me is, that I am as certain as that it is now day, that Durandarte expired in my arms, and that, after he was dead, with these hands I pulled out his heart, which could not have weighed less than two pounds: confirming the opinion of naturalists that a man's valour is in proportion to the size of his heart. Yet, certain as it is that this cavalier is really dead, how comes it to pass that ever and anon he sighs and moans as if he were alive?' Scarcely were these words uttered, than the wretched Durandarte, crying out aloud, said, 'O my cousin Montesinos! at the moment my soul was departing, my last request of you was, that, after ripping my heart out of my breast, with either a poniard or a dagger, you should carry it to Belerma.' The venerable Montesinos hearing this, threw himself on his knees before the complaining knight, and, with tears in his eyes, said to him, 'Long, long since, O Durandarte, dearest cousin, long since did I fulfil what you enjoined on that sad day when you expired. I took out your heart with all imaginable care, not leaving the smallest particle of it within your breast; I then wiped it with a lace handkerchief, and set off at full speed with it for France, having first laid your dear remains in the earth, shedding as many tears as sufficed to wash my hands and clean away the blood with which they were smeared by raking into your entrails; and furthermore, dear cousin of my soul, at the first place I stopped after leaving Roncesvalles, I sprinkled a little salt over your heart, and thereby kept it, if not fresh, at least from emitting any unpleasant odour, until it was presented to the Lady Belerma; who, together with you and myself, and your squire Guadiana, and the duenna Ruydera, with her seven daughters and two nieces, as well as several others of your friends and acquaintance, have been long confined here, enchanted by the sage Merlin; and, though it is now above five hundred years since, we are still alive. It is true, Ruydera and her daughters and nieces have left us, having so far moved the compassion of Merlin by their incessant weeping, that he turned them into as many lakes, which at this time, in the world of the living and the province of La Mancha, are called the Lakes of Ruydera. The seven sisters belong to the kings of Spain, and the two nieces to the most holy Order of Saint John. Guadiana also, your squire, bewailing your misfortune, was in like manner changed into a river, still retaining his name; but when he reached the surface of the earth, and saw the sun of another sky, he was so grieved at the thought of forsaking you, that he plunged again into the bowels of the earth: nevertheless, he was compelled by the laws of nature to rise again, and occasionally show himself to the eyes of men and the light of heaven. The lakes which I have mentioned supply him with their waters, and with them, joined by several others, he makes his majestic entrance into the kingdom of Portugal. Yet, wherever he flows, his grief and melancholy still continue, breeding only coarse and unsavoury fish, very different from those of the golden Tagus. All this, O my dearest cousin, I have often told you before; and since you make me no answer, I fancy you either do not believe, or do not hear me, which, Heaven knows, afflicts me very much. But now I have other tidings to communicate, which, if they do not alleviate, will in no wise increase, your sorrow. Open your eyes, and behold here in your presence, that great knight, of whom the sage Merlin has foretold so

"The female who closed the procession was the Lady Belerma herself."

many wonders—that same Don Quixote de la Mancha, I say, who has revived with new splendour the long-neglected order of knight-errantry, and by whose prowess and favour it may, perhaps, be our good fortune to be released from the spells by which we are here held in confinement; for great exploits are reserved for great men.' 'And though it should not be so,' answered the wretched Durandarte, in a faint and low voice, 'though it should prove otherwise, O cousin, I can only say—patience, and shuffle the cards.' Then turning himself on one side, he relapsed into his accustomed silence.

"At that moment, hearing loud cries and lamentations, with other sounds of distress, I turned my head, and saw, through the crystal walls of the palace, a procession of beautiful damsels in two lines, all attired in mourning, and with white turbans, in the Turkish fashion. These were followed by a lady—for so she seemed by the gravity of her air— clad also in black, with a white veil, so long that it reached to the ground. Her turban was twice the size of the largest of the others; she was beetled-browed, her nose somewhat flattish, her mouth wide, but her lips red; her teeth, which she sometimes displayed, were thin-set and uneven, though as white as blanched almonds. She carried in her hand a fine linen handkerchief, in which I could discern a human heart, withered and dry like that of a mummy. Montesinos told me that the damsels whom I saw were the attendants of Durandarte and Belerma —all enchanted like their master and mistress—and that the female who closed the procession was the Lady Belerma herself, who four days in the week walked in that manner with her damsels, singing, or rather weeping, dirges over the body and piteous heart of his cousin; and that if she appeared to me less beautiful than fame reported, it was occasioned by the bad nights and worse days she passed in that state of enchantment; as might be seen by her sallow complexion and the deep furrows in her face. 'Nor is the hollowness of her eyes and pallid skin to be attributed to any disorders incident to women, since with these she has not for months and years been visited, but merely to that deep affliction which incessantly preys on her heart for the untimely death of her lover, still renewed and kept alive by what she continually carries in her hands; indeed, had it not been for this, the great Dulcinea del Toboso herself, so much celebrated here and over the whole world, would scarcely have equalled her in beauty of person or sweetness of manner.' 'Softly,' said I, 'good Signor Montesinos: comparisons, you know, are odious, and therefore let them be spared, I beseech you. The peerless Dulcinea is what she is, and the Lady Donna Belerma is what she is and what she has been; and there let it rest.' 'Pardon me, Signor Don Quixote,' said Montesinos, 'I might have guessed that your worship was the Lady Dulcinea's knight, and ought to have bit my tongue off rather than it should have compared her to anything less than heaven itself.' This satisfaction being given me by the great Montesinos, my heart recovered from the shock it had sustained on hearing my mistress compared with Belerma."

"I wonder," quoth Sancho, "that your worship did not give the old fellow a hearty kicking, and pluck his beard for him till you had not left a single hair on his chin." "No, friend Sancho," answered Don Quixote, "it did not become me to do so; for we are all bound to respect the aged, although not of the order of knighthood; still more those who are so, and who besides are enchanted; but, trust me, Sancho, in other discourse which we held together, I fairly matched him."

Here the scholar said, "I cannot imagine, Signor Don Quixote, how it was possible, having been so short a space of time below, that your worship should have seen so many things, and have heard and said so much." "How long, then, may it be since I descended?" quoth Don Quixote. "A little above an hour," answered Sancho. "That cannot be," replied Don Quixote, "for night came on, and was followed by morning three times successively; so that I must have sojourned three days in those remote and hidden parts." "My master," said Sancho, "must needs be in the right; for, as everything has happened to him in the way of enchantment, what seems to us but an hour may there seem full three days and three nights." "Doubtless it must be so," answered Don Quixote. "I hope," said the scholar, "your worship was not without food all this time?" "Not one mouthful did I taste," said the knight, "nor was I sensible of hunger." "What, then, do not the enchanted eat?" said the scholar. "No," answered Don Quixote; "although some think that their nails and beards still continue to grow." "And pray, sir," said Sancho, "do they never sleep?" "Certainly never," said Don Quixote: "at least, during the three days that I have been amongst them, not one of them has closed an eye, nor have I slept myself." "Here," said Sancho, "the proverb is right—'tell me thy company, and I will tell thee what thou art.' If your worship keeps company with those who fast and watch, no wonder that you neither eat nor sleep yourself. But pardon me, good master of mine, if I tell your worship that, of all you have been saying, Heaven—I was going to say the devil—take me if I believe one word." "How!" said the scholar, "do you think that Signor Don Quixote would lie? But, were he so disposed, he has not had time to invent and fabricate such a tale." "I do not think my master lies," answered Sancho. "What, then, dost thou think?" said Don Quixote. "I think," answered Sancho, "that the necromancers, or that same Merlin who enchanted all those whom your worship says you saw and talked with there below, have crammed into your head all the stuff you have told us, and all that you have yet to say."

"All that is possible," said Don Quixote, "only that it happens not to be so; for what I have related I saw with my own eyes and touched with my own hands. But what wilt thou say, when I tell thee that, among an infinite number of wonderful and surprising things shown to me by Montesinos, whereof I will give an account hereafter (for this is not the time or place to speak of them), he pointed out to me three country wenches, dancing and capering like kids about those charming fields, and no sooner did I behold them, than I recognized in one of the three the peerless Dulcinea herself, and in the other two the very same wenches that attended her, and with whom we held some parley on the road from Toboso? Upon my asking Montesinos whether he knew them, he said they were strangers to him, though he believed them to be some ladies of quality lately enchanted, having made their appearance there but a few days before. Nor should that excite my wonder, he said, for many distinguished ladies, both of the past and present times, were enchanted there under different forms; among whom he had discovered Queen Guinevra, and her duenna, Quintoniana, cupbearer to Launcelot when he came from Britain."

When Sancho heard his master say all this, he was ready to run distracted, or to die with laughter; for, knowing that he was himself Dulcinea's enchanter, he now made no doubt that his master had lost his senses, and was raving mad. "In an evil hour and a woful day, dear master of mine," said he, "did you go down to the other world; and in a luckless moment did you meet with Signor Montesinos, who has sent you back to us in this plight. Your worship left us in your right senses, such as Heaven had given you, speaking sentences and giving advice at every turn; but now—Lord bless us, how you talk!" "As I know thee, Sancho," answered Don Quixote, "I heed not thy words." "Nor I your worship's," replied Sancho: "you may kill or strike me, if you please, for all those I have said or shall say, without you correct and mend your own. But tell me, sir, now we are at peace, how or by what token did you know the lady your mistress? and, if you spoke to her, what said you, and what did she answer?" "I knew her," answered Don Quixote, "because her apparel was the same that she wore when you showed her to me. I spoke to her, but she answered me not a word; on the contrary, she turned her back upon me, and fled with the speed of an arrow. I would have followed her, but Montesinos dissuaded me from the attempt, as I should certainly lose my labour; and besides, the hour approached when I must quit the cave and return to the upper world; he assured me, however, that in due time I should be informed of the means of disenchanting himself, Belerma, Durandarte, and all the rest who were there. While we were thus talking, a circumstance occurred that gave me much concern. Suddenly one of the companions of the unfortunate Dulcinea came up to my side, all in tears, and in a low and troubled voice said to me, 'My lady Dulcinea del Toboso kisses your worship's hand, and desires to know how you do: and being at this time a little straitened for money, she earnestly entreats your worship would be pleased to lend her, upon this new cotton petticoat that I have brought here, six reals, or what you can spare, which she promises to return very shortly.' This message astonished me, and, turning to Montesinos, I said to him, 'Is it possible, Signor Montesinos, that persons of quality under enchantment are exposed to necessity?' To which he answered, 'Believe, Signor Don Quixote de la Mancha, that what is called necessity prevails everywhere, and extends to all, not sparing even those who are enchanted: and since the Lady Dulcinea sends to request a loan of six reals, and the pledge seems to be unexceptionable, give them to her, for without doubt she is in great need.' 'I will take no pawn,' answered I; 'nor can I send her what she desires, for I have but four reals in my pocket. I therefore send her those four reals,' being the same thou gavest me the other day, Sancho, to bestow in alms on the poor we should meet with upon the road: and I said to the damsel, 'Tell your lady, friend, that I am grieved to the soul at her distresses, and wish I was as rich as a Fucar,* to remedy them. But pray let her be told that I neither can nor will have health while deprived of her amiable presence and discreet conversation; and that I earnestly beseech that she will vouchsafe to let herself be seen and conversed with by this her captive and wayworn knight; tell her, also, that, when she least expects it, she will hear that I have made a vow like that made by the Marquis of Mantua, when he found his nephew Valdovinos ready to expire on the mountain: which was, not to eat bread upon a tablecloth, and other matters of the same kind,

---

* A rich German family of the name of Fugger, ennobled by Charles V.

till he had revenged his death. In like manner will I take no rest, but traverse the seven parts of the universe with more diligence than did the Infant Don Pedro of Portugal, until her disenchantment be accomplished.' 'All this, and more, your worship owes my lady,' answered the damsel; and, taking the four reals, instead of making me a courtesy, she cut a caper full two yards high in the air, and fled."

"Now, Heaven defend us!" cried Sancho: "is it possible that there should be anything like this in the world, and that enchanters and enchantments should so bewitch and change my master's good understanding? O sir! sir! for Heaven's sake look to yourself, take care of your good name, and give no credit to these vanities, which have robbed you of your senses." "Thou lovest me, Sancho, I know," said Don Quixote, "and therefore I am induced to pardon thy prattle. To thy inexperienced mind whatever is uncommon appears impossible; but, as I have said before, a time may come when I will tell thee of some things which I have seen below, whereof the truth cannot be doubted, and that will make thee give credit to what I have already related."

CHAPTER XXIV.

In which are recounted a thousand trifling matters, equally pertinent and necessary to the right understanding of this grand history.

THE translator of this great work from the original of its first author, Cid Hamet Benengeli, says, when he came to the chapter that records the adventure of the Cave of Montesinos, he found on the margin these words in Hamet's own handwriting:

"I cannot persuade myself that the whole of what is related in this chapter, as having happened to Don Quixote in the Cave of Montesinos, is really true; because the adventures in which he has hitherto been engaged are all natural and probable, whereas this of the cave is neither one nor the other, but exceeds all reasonable bounds, and therefore cannot be credited. On the other hand, if we recollect the honour and scrupulous veracity of the noble Don Quixote, it seems utterly impossible that he could be capable of telling a lie: sooner, indeed, would he submit to be transfixed with arrows than be guilty of a deviation from truth. Besides, if we consider the minute and circumstantial details that he entered into, it seems a still greater impossibility that he could in so short a time have invented such a mass of extravagance. Should this adventure, however, be considered as apocryphal, let it be remembered that the fault is not mine. I write it without affirming either its truth or falsehood; therefore, discerning and judicious reader, judge for thyself, as I neither can nor ought to do more—unless it be just to apprise thee that Don Quixote, on his death-bed, is said to have acknowledged that this adventure was all a fiction, invented only because it accorded and squared with the tales he had been accustomed to read in his favourite books." But to proceed with our history.

The scholar was astonished no less at the boldness of Sancho Panza than at the patience of his master, but attributed his present mildness to the satisfaction he had just received in beholding his mistress Dulcinea del Toboso, though enchanted; for, had it not been so, he conceived that Sancho's freedom of speech would have had what it richly deserved—a manual chastisement. In truth, he thought him much too presuming with the knight, to whom now addressing himself, he said, " For my own part, Signor Don Quixote, I account myself most fortunate in having undertaken this journey, as I have thereby made four important acquisitions. The first is the honour of your worship's acquaintance, which I esteem a great happiness; the second is a knowledge of the secrets enclosed in this wonderful cave, the metamorphoses of Guadiana and the Lakes of Ruydera, which will be of notable use in my Spanish Ovid now in hand; my third advantage is the discovery of the antiquity of cards, which, it now appears, were in use at least in the days of the Emperor Charlemagne, as may be gathered from the words that fell from Durandarte, when, after that long speech of Montesinos, he awaked, and said, ' Patience, and shuffle the cards.' Now, as he could not have learnt this phrase during his enchantment, he must have learnt it in France in the days of Charlemagne; and this discovery also comes in opportunely for my ' Supplement to Polydore Virgil on Antiquities;' for I believe that in his treatise he has wholly neglected the subject of cards—a defect that will now be supplied by me, which will be of great importance, especially as I shall be able to quote an authority so grave and authentic as that of Signor Durandarte. And finally, it has, in the fourth place, been my good fortune thus to come at the knowledge of the true source of the river Guadiana which has hitherto remained unknown."

" There is much reason in what you say," quoth the knight; " but if, by Heaven's will, you should obtain a license for printing your books, which I much doubt, to whom would you inscribe them?" " O sir," said the scholar, " we have lords and grandees in abundance, and are therefore in no want of patrons." " Not so many as you may imagine," said Don Quixote; " for all those who are worthy of such a token of respect are not equally disposed to make that generous return which seems due to the labour, as well as the politeness, of the author. It is my happiness to know of one exalted personage* who makes ample amends for what is wanting in the rest, and with so liberal a measure that, if I might presume to make it known, I should infallibly stir up envy in many a noble breast. But let this rest till a more convenient season; for it is now time to consider where we shall lodge to-night." " Not far hence," said the scholar, " is a hermitage, the dwelling of a recluse, who, they say, was once a soldier, and is now accounted a

---

* The Count de Lemos, Don Pedro Fernandes de Castro.

"Hold, honest friend," said Don Quixote to him, "methinks you go faster than is convenient for that mule."

pious Christian, wise and charitable. Near his hermitage he has built at his own cost a small house, which, however, is large enough to accommodate the strangers who visit him." "Does that same hermit keep poultry?" said Sancho. "Few hermits are without them," answered Don Quixote; "for such holy men now are not like the hermits of old in the deserts of Egypt, who were clad with leaves of the palm tree, and fed on roots of the earth. By commending these, however, I do not mean to reflect upon the hermits of our times; I would only infer that the penances of these days do not equal the austerities and strictness of former times; but this is no reason why they may not be good; at least I account them so: and, at the worst, he who only wears the garb of piety does less harm than the audacious and open sinner."

While they were thus discoursing they perceived a man coming towards them, walking very fast, and switching on a mule laden with lances and halberds. When he came up to them he saluted them, and passed on. "Hold, honest friend," said Don Quixote to him, "methinks you go faster than is convenient for that mule." "I cannot stay," answered the man, "as the weapons which I am carrying are to be made use of to-morrow. I have no time to lose, and so adieu. But, if you would know for what use they are intended, I shall lodge to-night at the inn beyond the hermitage, and should you be travelling on the same road, you will find me there, where I will tell you wonders; and, once more, Heaven be with you." He then pricked on his mule at such a rate that Don Quixote had no time to inquire after the wonders which he had to tell; but, as he was not a little curious and eager for anything new, he determined immediately to hasten forwards to the inn, and pass the night there, without touching at the hermitage. They accordingly mounted, and took the direct road to the inn, at which they arrived a little before nightfall. The scholar proposed calling at the hermitage just to allay their thirst; upon which Sancho Panza instantly steered Dapple in that direction, and Don Quixote and the scholar followed his example; but, as Sancho's ill-luck would have it, the hospitable sage was not at home, as they were told by the under-hermit, of whom they requested some wine. He told them that his master had no wine, but, if they would like water, he would give them some with great pleasure. "If I had wanted water," quoth Sancho, "there are wells in abundance on the road. Oh, the wedding of Camacho, and the plenty of Don Diego's house! When shall I meet with your like again?"

Quitting the hermitage, they spurred on towards the inn, and soon overtook a lad who was walking leisurely before them. He carried a sword upon his shoulder, and upon it a roll or bundle that seemed to contain his apparel, such as breeches, a cloak, and a shirt or two; for he had on an old velvet jerkin, with some tatters of a satin lining, below which his shirt hung out at large; his stockings were silk, and his shoes square-toed, after the court fashion. He seemed to be about eighteen or nineteen years of age; his countenance was lively and his body active. He went on gaily singing, to cheer him on his way; and just as they overtook him, they heard the following lines, which the scholar failed not to commit to memory:

> "For want of the pence to the wars I must go:
> Ah! had I but money, it would not be so."

"You travel very airily, sir," said Don Quixote to him; "pray, may I ask whither you are bound?" "Heat and poverty," replied the youth, "make me travel in this way; and my intention, sir, is to join the army." "From heat it may well be; but why poverty?" said Don Quixote. "Sir," replied the youth, "I carry in this bundle a pair of velvet trousers, fellows to my jacket; if I wear them out upon the road, they will do me no credit in the city, and I have no money to buy others; for this reason, sir, as well as for coolness, I go thus till I overtake some companies of infantry, which are not twelve leagues hence, where I mean to enlist myself, and then shall be sure to meet with some baggage-waggon to convey me to the place of embarkation, which, they say, is Carthagena: for I had rather serve the king in his wars abroad than be the lacquey of any beggarly courtier at home." "And pray, sir, have you no appointment?" said the scholar. "Had I served some grandee or other person of distinction," answered the youth, "possibly I might have been so rewarded; for in the service of such masters it is no uncommon thing to rise into ensigns or captains, from the servants' hall; but it was always my scurvy fate to be dangling upon foreigners or fellows without a home, who allow so pitiful a salary that half of it goes in starching a ruff; and it would be a miracle indeed for a poor page to meet with preferments in such situations." "But tell me, friend," quoth Don Quixote, "is it possible that, during all the time you have been in service, you could not procure yourself a livery?" "I have had two," answered the page; "but as he who quits a monastery before he confesses is stripped of his habit, and his old clothes are returned him, just so did my masters treat me; for when the business for which they came to court was done, they hurried back into the country, taking away the liveries which they had only given to make a flourish in the town."

"A notable *espilorcheria*,* as the Italians say," quoth Don Quixote: "however, consider yourself as fortunate in having quitted your former life, with so laudable an intention; for there is nothing more honourable, next to the service you owe to God, than to serve your king and natural lord, especially in the profession of arms, which, if less profitable than learning, far exceeds it in glory. More great families, it is true, have been established by learning, yet there is in the martial character a certain splendour, which seems to exalt it far above all other pursuits. But allow me, sir, to offer you a piece of advice, which, believe me, you will find worth your attention. Never suffer your mind to dwell on the adverse events of your life; for the worst that can befall you is death, and when attended with honour there is no event so glorious. Julius Cæsar, that valorous Roman, being asked which was the kind of death to be preferred, 'That,' said he, 'which is sudden and unforeseen.' Though he answered like a heathen who knew not the true God, yet, considering human infirmity, it was well said. For, supposing you should be cut off in the very first encounter, either by cannon-shot or the springing of a mine, what does it signify? it is but dying, which is inevitable, and, being over, there it ends. Terence observes that the corpse of the man who is slain in battle looks better than the living soldier who has saved himself by flight; and the good soldier rises in estimation according to the measure of his obedience to those who command him. Observe, moreover, my son, that a soldier had better smell of gunpowder than of musk; and if old age overtakes you in this noble profession, though lamed and maimed, and covered with wounds, it will find you also covered with honour, and of such honour as poverty itself cannot deprive you. From poverty, indeed, you are secure; for care is now taken that veteran and disabled soldiers shall not be exposed to want, nor be treated as many do their negro slaves, when old and past service, turning them out of their houses, and, under pretence of giving them freedom, leave them slaves to hunger, from which they can

---

* A mean and sordid action.

have no relief but in death. I will not say more to you at present; but get up behind me and go with us to the inn, where you shall sup with me, and to-morrow morning pursue your journey; and may Heaven prosper and reward your good intentions." The page declined Don Quixote's offer of riding behind him, but readily accepted his invitation to supper. Sancho now muttered to himself, " The Lord bless thee for a master!" said he: " who would believe that one who can say so many good things, should tell us such nonsense and riddles about that cave? Well, we shall see what will come of it."

They reached the inn just at the close of day, and Sancho was pleased that his master did not, as usual, mistake it for a castle. Don Quixote immediately inquired for the man with the lances and halberds, and was told by the landlord that he was in the stable attending his mule. There also the scholar and Sancho disposed of their beasts, failing not to honour Rozinante with the best manger and best stall in the stable.

CHAPTER XXV.

Wherein is begun the braying adventure, and the diverting one of the puppet-show, with the memorable divinations of the wonderful ape.

DON QUIXOTE being all impatience to hear the wonders which had been promised him by the arms-carrier, immediately went in search of him, and having found him in the stable, he begged him to relate without delay what he had promised on the road. " My wonders," said the man, " must be told at leasure, and not on the wing. Wait, good sir, till I have done with my mule, and then I will tell you things that will amaze you." " It shall not be delayed on that account," answered Don Quixote, " for I will help you." And so in truth he did, winnowing the barley and cleaning the manger; which condescension induced the man the more willingly to tell his tale. Seating himself, therefore, on a stone bench at the outside of the door, and having Don Quixote (who sat next to him), and the scholar, the page, Sancho Panza, and the innkeeper, for his senate and auditors, he began in the following manner:

" You must know, gentlemen, that in a town four leagues and a half from this place, a certain alderman happened to lose his ass, all through the artful contrivance (too long to be told) of a wench, his maid-servant; and though he tried every means to recover his beast, it was to no purpose. Fifteen days passed, as public fame reports, after the ass was missing, and while the unlucky alderman was standing in the market-place, another alderman of the same town came up to him, and said, ' Pay me for my good news, gossip, for your ass has made its appearance.' ' Most willingly, neighbour,' answered the other; ' but tell me—where has he been seen?' ' On the mountain,' answered the other; ' I saw him there this morning, with no pannel or furniture upon him of any kind, and so lank that it was grievious to behold him. I would have driven him before me and brought him to you, but he is already become so shy that when I went near him he took to his heels and fled to a distance from me. Now, if you like it, we will both go seek him; but first let me put up this of mine at home, and I will return instantly.' 'You will do me a great favour,' said the owner of the lost ass, 'and I shall be happy at any time to do as much for you.'

"With all these particulars and in these very words is the story told by all who are thoroughly acquainted with the truth of the affair. In short, the two aldermen, hand in hand and side by side, trudged together up the hill; and on coming to the place where they expected to find the ass, they found him not, nor was he anywhere to be seen, though they made diligent search. Being thus disappointed, the alderman who had seen him said to the other, 'Hark you, friend, I have thought of a stratagem by which we shall certainly discover this animal, even though he had crept into the bowels of the earth, instead of the mountain; and it is this: I can bray marvellously well, and if you can do a little in that way the business is done.' 'A little, say you, neighbour?' quoth the other; 'before Heaven, in braying I yield to none— no, not to asses themselves.' 'We shall soon see that,' answered the second alderman; 'go you on one side of the mountain, while I take the other, and let us walk round it, and every now and then you shall bray, and I will bray; and the ass will certainly hear and answer us, if he still remains in these parts.' 'Verily, neighbour, your device is excellent, and worthy your good parts,' said the owner of the ass. They then separated, according to agreement, and both began braying at the same instant, with such marvellous truth of imitation that, mutually deceived, each ran towards the other, not doubting that the ass was found; and, on meeting, the loser said, 'Is it possible, friend, that it was not my ass that brayed?' 'No, it was I,' answered the other. 'I declare, then,' said the owner, 'that as far as regards braying, there is not the least difference between you and an ass; for in my life I never heard anything more natural.' 'These praises and compliments,' answered the author of the stratagem, 'belong rather to you than to me, friend; for by Him that made me, you could give the odds of two brays to the greatest and most skilful brayer in the world; for your tones are rich, your time correct, your notes well sustainnd, and cadences abrupt and beautiful; in short, I own myself vanquished, and yield to you the palm in this rare talent.' 'Truly,' answered the ass-owner, 'I shall value and esteem myself the more henceforth, since I am not without some endowment. It is true, I fancy that I brayed indifferently well, yet never flattered myself that I excelled so much as you are pleased to say.' 'I tell you,' answered the second, 'there are rare abilities often lost to the world, and they are ill bestowed on those who know not how to employ them to advantage.' 'Right, brother,' quoth the owner, 'though, except in cases like the present, ours may not turn to much account: and even in this business, Heaven grant it may prove of service

" This said, they separated again, to resume their braying; and each time were deceived as before, and met again, till they at length agreed, as a signal, to distinguish their own voices from that of the ass, that they should bray twice together, one immediately after the other. Thus, doubling their brayings, they made the tour of the whole mountain, without having any answer from the stray ass, not even by signs. How, indeed, could the poor creature answer, whom at last they found in a thicket, half devoured by wolves? On seeing the body, the owner said, 'Truly, I wondered at his silence; for, had he not been dead, he certainly would have answered us, or he were no true ass; nevertheless, neighbour, though I have found him dead, my trouble in the search has been well repaid in listening to your exquisite braying.' 'It is in good hands, friend,' answered the other; 'for, if the abbot sings well, the novice comes not far behind him.'

" Hereupon they returned home hoarse and disconsolate, and told their friends and neighbours all that had happened to them in their search after the ass, each of them extolling the other for his excellence in braying. The story spread all over the adjacent villages, and the devil, who sleeps not, as he loves to sow discord wherever he can, raising a bustle in the wind, and mischief out of nothing, so ordered it that all the neighbouring villagers, at the sight of any of our townspeople, would immediately begin to bray, hitting us, as it were, in the teeth with the notable talent of our aldermen. The boys fell to it, which was the same as falling into the hands and mouths of a legion of devils; and thus braying far and wide, insomuch that the natives of the town of Bray are as well known and distinguished as the negroes are from white men. And this unhappy jest has been carried so far that our people have often sallied out in arms against their scoffers, and given them battle, neither king nor rook, nor fear nor shame, being able to restrain them. To-morrow, I believe, or next day, those of our town will take the field against the people of another village about two leagues from us, being one of those which persecute us most: and I have brought the lances and halberds which you saw, that we may be well prepared for them. Now these are the wonders I promised you; and if you do not think them such, I have no better for you." And here the honest man ended his story.

At this juncture a man entered the inn, clad from head to foot in chamois-skin, hose, doublet, and breeches, and called with a loud voice, "Master Host, have you any lodging? for here comes the divining ape and the puppet-show of 'Melisendra's Deliverance.'" "What, Master Peter!" quoth the innkeeper, "body of me! then we shall have a rare night of it." This same Master Peter, it should be observed, had his left eye, and almost half his cheek, covered with a patch of green taffeta, a sign that something was wrong on that side of his face. "Welcome, Master Peter," continued the landlord: "where is the ape and the puppet-show? I do not see them." "They are hard by," answered the man in leather; "I came before, to see if we could find lodging here." "I would turn out the Duke of Alva himself to make room for Master Peter," answered the innkeeper: "let the ape and the puppets come; for there are guests this evening in the inn who will be good customers to you, I warrant." "Be it so, in God's name," answered he of the patch; "and I will lower the price, and reckon myself well paid with only bearing my charges. I shall now go back and bring on the cart with my ape and puppets." For which purpose he immediately hastened away.

Don Quixote now inquired of the landlord concerning this Master Peter. "He is," said the landlord, "a famous puppet-player, who has been some time past travelling about these parts with a show of the deliverance of Melisendra by the famous Don Gayferos; one of the best stories and the best performance that has been seen for many a day. He has also an ape, whose talents go beyond all other apes, and even those of men; for if a question be put to him, he listens attentively, then leaps upon his master's shoulders, and, putting his mouth to his ear, whispers the answer to the question he has been asked, which Master Peter repeats aloud. He can tell both what is to come and what is past; and though in foretelling things to come he does not always hit the mark exactly, yet for the most part he is not so much out; so that we are inclined to believe the devil must be in him. His fee is two reals for every question the ape answers, or his master answers for him, which is all the same; so that Master Peter is thought to be rich. He is a rare fellow, too, and lives the merriest life in the world; talks more than six, and drinks more than a dozen, and all by the help of his tongue, his ape, and his puppets."

By this time Master Peter had returned with his cart, in which he carried his puppets, and also his ape, which was large and without a tail, with posteriors as bare as felt, and a countenance most ugly. Don Quixote immediately began to question him, saying, "Signor Diviner, pray tell me what fish do we catch, and what will be our fortune? See, here are my two reals," bidding Sancho to give them to Master Peter, who, answering for the ape, said, "My ape, signor, gives no reply nor information regarding the future : he knows something of the past and a little of the present." "Bodikins!" quoth Sancho, "I would not give a brass farthing to be told what has happened to me; for who can tell that better than myself? and I am not such a fool as to pay for hearing what I already know. But since he knows what is now passing, here are my two reals—and now, good Master Ape, tell me what my wife Teresa is doing at this moment—I say, what is she busied about?" Master Peter would not take the money, saying, "I will not be paid beforehand, nor take your reward before the service is performed." Then giving with his right hand two or three claps upon his left shoulder, at one spring the ape jumped upon it, and laying its mouth to his ear, chattered and grated his teeth. Having made these grimaces for the space of a *Credo*, at another skip down it jumped on the ground, and straightway Master Peter ran and threw himself on his knees before Don Quixote, and embracing his legs, said, "These legs I embrace, just as I would embrace the two pillars of Hercules, O illustrious reviver of the long-forgotten order of chivalry! O never-sufficiently-extolled knight, Don Quixote de la Mancha! thou reviver of drooping hearts, the prop and stay of the falling, the raiser of the fallen, the staff and comfort to all who are unfortunate!"

Don Quixote was thunderstruck, Sancho confounded, the scholar surprised,—in short, the page, the braying-man, the innkeeper, and every one present were astonished at this harangue of the puppet-player, who proceeded, saying, "And thou, O good Sancho Panza, the best squire to the best knight in the world, rejoice, for thy good wife Teresa is well, and at this instant is dressing a pound of flax. Moreover, by her left side stands a broken-mouthed pitcher, which holds a very pretty scantling of wine, with which, ever and anon, she cheers her spirits at her work." "Egad, I verily believe it," answered Sancho, "for she is a blessed one; and were she not a little jealous, I would not swap her for the giantess Andandona, who, in my master's opinion, was a brave lady, and a special housewife; though my Teresa, I warrant, is one of those who take care of themselves, though others whistle for it."

"Well," quoth Don Quixote, "he who reads and travels much, sees and learns much. What testimony but that of my own eyes could have persuaded me that there apes in the world which have the power of divination? Yes, I am indeed Don Quixote de la Mancha, as this good animal has declared, though he has rather exaggerated in regard to my merits; but, whatever I may be, I thank Heaven for endowing me with a tender and compassionate heart, inclined to do good to all, and harm to none." "If I had money," said the page, "I would ask Master Ape what is to befall me in my intended expedition." To which Master Peter, who had now risen from Don Quixote's feet, answered, "I have already told you that this little beast gives no answers concerning things to come; otherwise, your being without money should have been no hindrance; for to serve Signor Don Quixote here present, I would willingly give up all views of profit. And now, as in duty bound, to give pleasure, I intend to put my puppet-show in order, and entertain all the company in the inn *gratis.*" The innkeeper rejoiced at hearing this, and pointed out a convenient place for setting up the show, which was done in an instant.

Don Quixote was not entirely satisfied with the ape's divinations, thinking it very improbable that such a creature should, of itself, know anything either of future or past: therefore, whilst Master Peter was preparing his show, he drew Sancho aside to a corner of the stable, where, in a low voice, he said to him, "I have been considering, Sancho, the strange power of this ape, and am convinced that Master Peter, his owner, must have a tacit or express pact with the devil." "Nay," quoth Sancho, "if the pack be express from the devil, it must needs be a very sooty pack; but what advantage would it be to this same Master Peter to have such a pack?" "Thou dost not comprehend me, Sancho," said Don Quixote; "I only mean that he must certainly have made some agreement with the devil to infuse this power into the ape, whereby he gains much worldly wealth, and, in return for the favour, he gives up his soul, which is the chief aim of that great enemy of mankind. What induces me to this belief is finding that the ape answers only questions relative to things past or present, which is exactly what is known by the devil, who knows nothing of the future, except by conjecture, wherein he must be often mistaken; for it is the prerogative of God alone truly to comprehend all things : to Him nothing is past or future, everything is present. This being the fact, it is plain the ape is inspired by the devil : and I marvel much he has not been questioned by our Holy Inquisition, and examined by torture till he acknowledges the authority under which he acts. It is certain that this ape is no astrologer: neither he nor his master know how to raise one of those figures called judical, although now so much in fashion that there is scarcely a maid-servant, page, or labouring mechanic who does not pretend to raise a figure and draw conclusions from the stars, as if it were no more than a trick at cards; thus degrading, by ignorance and imposture, a science no less wonderful than true. I know a lady who asked one of these pretenders whether her little lap-dog would breed, and, if so, what would be the number and colour of its offspring. To which Master Astrologer, after raising his figure, answered that the bitch would certainly have three whelps, one green, one carnation, and the other mottled. It happened that the bitch died some two days after of a surfeit; yet was Master Figure-raiser still accounted, like the rest of his brethren, an infallible astrologer."

"But for all that," quoth Sancho, "I should like your worship to desire Master Peter to ask his ape whether all that was true which you told about the Cave of Montesinos; because, for my own part, begging your worship's pardon, I take it to be all fibs and nonsense, or at least only a dream." "Thou mayest think what thou wilt," answered Don Quixote; "however, I will do as thou advisest, although I feel some scruples on the subject."

Here they were interrupted by Master Peter, who came to inform Don Quixote that the show was ready, and to request he would come to see it, assuring him that he would find it worthy of his attention. The knight told him that he had a question to put to the ape first, as he desired to be informed by it whether the things which happened to him in the Cave of Montesinos were realities, or only sleeping fancies; though he had a suspicion himself that they were a mixture of both. Master Peter immediately brought his ape, and placing him before Don Quixote and Sancho, said, "Look you, Master Ape, this worthy knight would know whether certain things which befell him in the Cave of Montesinos were real or visionary." Then making the usual signal, the ape leaped upon his left shoulder, and, after seeming to whisper in his ear, Master Peter said, "The ape tells me that some of the things your worship saw, or which befell you in the said cave, are not true, and some probable; which is all he now knows concerning this matter, for his virtue has just left him; but if your worship desires to hear more, on Friday next, when his faculty will return, he will answer to your heart's content." "There now," quoth Sancho, "did I not say you would never make me believe all you told us about that same cave?—no, nor half of it." "That will hereafter appear," answered Don Quixote; "for time brings all things to light, though hidden within the bowels of the earth : and now we will drop the subject for the present, and see the puppet-play, for I am of opinion there must be some novelty in it." "Some?" exclaimed Master Peter; "sixty thousand novelties shall you see in this play of mine! I assure you, Signor Don Quixote, it is one of the rarest sights that the world affords this day. *Operibus credite et non verbis;* so let us to work, for it grows late, and we have a great deal to do, to say, and to show."

Don Quixote and Sancho complied with his request, and repaired to the place where the show was set out, filled in every part with small wax candles, so that it made a gay and brilliant appearance. Master Peter, who was to manage the figures, placed himself behind the show, and in front of the scene stood his boy, whose office it was to relate the story and expound the mystery of the piece; holding a wand in his hand to point to the several figures as they entered.

All the people of the inn being fixed, some standing opposite to the show, and Don Quixote, Sancho, the page, and the scholar seated in the best places, the young interpreter began to say what will be heard or seen by those who may choose to read or listen to what is recorded in the following chapter.

CHAPTER XXVI.

Wherein is continued the pleasant adventure of the puppet-player; with sundry other matters, all, in truth, sufficiently good.

TYRIANS and Trojans were all silent — that is, all the spectators of the show hung upon the lips of the expounder of its wonders, when from behind the scene their ears were saluted with the sound of drums and trumpets, and discharges of artillery. These flourishes being over, the boy raised his voice and said, "Gentlemen, we here present you with a true story, taken out of the French chronicles and Spanish ballads, which are in everybody's mouth, and sung by the boys about the streets. It tells you how Don Gayferos delivers his spouse Melisendra, who was imprisoned by the Moors in the city of Sansuenna, now called Saragossa; and there you may see how Don Gayferos is playing at tables, according to the ballad —

> " ' Gayferos now at tables plays,
> Forgetful of his lady dear.'

That personage whom you see with a crown on his head and a sceptre in his hands is the Emperor Charlemagne, the fair Melisendra's reputed father, who, vexed at the idleness and negligence of his son-in-law,

All the spectators of the show hung upon the lips of the expounder of its wonders.

comes forth to chide him: and pray mark with what passion and vehemence he rates him—one would think he had a mind to give him half a dozen raps over the pate with his sceptre; indeed, there are some authors who say he actually gave them, and sound ones too; and after having laid it on roundly about the injury his honour sustained in not delivering his spouse, it is reported that he made use of these very words —'I have said enough—look to it.' Pray observe, gentlemen, how the emperor turns his back, and leaves Don Gayferos in a fret

"See him now in a rage, tossing the table-board one way and pieces another! Now calling hastily for his armour, and now asking Don Orlando, his cousin, to lend him his sword, Durindana, which Don Orlando refuses, though he offers to bear him company in his perilous undertaking; but the furious knight will not accept of his help, saying that he is able alone to deliver his spouse, though she were thrust down to the centre of the earth. Hereupon he goes out to arm himself, in order to set forward immediately. Now, gentlemen, turn your eyes towards that tower which appears yonder, which you are to suppose to be one of the Moorish towers of Saragossa, now called the Aljaferia; and that lady in a Moorish habit, who appears in the balcony, is the peerless Melisendra, who from that window has cast many a wistful look towards the road that leads to France, and soothed her captivity by thinking of the city of Paris and her dear husband. Now behold a strange incident, the like perhaps you never heard of before. Do you not see that Moor stealing along softly, and how, step by step, with his finger on his mouth, he comes behind Melisendra? Hear what a smack he gives on her sweet lips, and see how she spits and wipes her mouth with her white smock-sleeves, and how she frets, and tears her beauteous hair from pure vexation!—as if that was to blame for the indignity. Observe, also, the grave Moor who stands in that open gallery—he is Marsilius, King of Sansuenna, who, seeing the insolence of the Moor, though he is a kinsman and a great favourite, orders him to be seized immediately, and two hundred stripes given him, and to be led through the principal streets of the city, with criers before to proclaim his crime, followed by the public whippers with their rods; and see now, how all this is put in execution almost as soon as the fault is committed; for among the Moors there are no citations, nor indictments, nor delays of the law, as among us."

"Boy, boy!" said Don Quixote, "on with your story in a straight line, and leave your curves and transversals. I can tell you there is often much need of formal process and deliberate trial to come at the truth."

Master Peter also, from behind, said, "None of your flourishes, boy, but do as the gentleman bids you, and then you cannot be wrong: sing your song plainly, and meddle not with counterpoints, for they will only put you out." "Very well," quoth the boy; and proceeded, saying.

"The figure you see there on horseback, muffled up in a Gascoigne cloak, is Don Gayferos himself, whom his lady (after being revenged on the impertinence of the Moor) sees from the battlements of the tower, and, taking him for a stranger, holds that discourse with him which is recorded in the ballad:

> " ' If towards France your course you bend,
> Let me entreat you, gentle friend,
> Make diligent inquiry there
> For Gayferos, my husband dear.'

The rest I omit, because length begets loathing. It is sufficient that Don Gayferos makes himself known to her, as you may perceive by the signs of joy she discovers, and especially now that you see how nimbly she lets herself down from the balcony, to get on horseback behind her loving spouse. But alas, poor lady! the border of her under-petticoat has caught one of the iron rails of the balcony, and there she hangs dangling in the air without being able to reach the ground. But see how Heaven is merciful, and sends relief in the greatest distress! For

"Hold, base-born rabble!—follow him not, or expect to feel the fury of my resentment!"

now comes Don Gayferos, and, without caring for the richness of her petticoat, see how he lays hold of her, and, tearing her from the hooks, brings her at once to the ground, and then, at a spring, sets her behind him on the crupper, astride, like a man, bidding her hold very fast, and clasp her arms about him till they cross and meet over his breast, that she may not fall; because the Lady Melisendra was not accustomed to that way of riding.

"Now, gentlemen, observe; hear how the horse neighs and shows how proud he is of the burden of his valiant master and his fair mistress. See how they now wheel about, and, turning their backs upon the city, scamper away merrily and joyfully to Paris. Peace be with ye, O ye matchless pair of faithful lovers! Safe and sound may you reach your desired country, without impediment, accident, or ill-luck on your journey! May you live as long as Nestor, among friends and relations rejoicing in your happiness, and——"

"Stay, stay, boy," said Master Peter, "none of your flights, I beseech you; for affectation is the devil." The boy, making no reply, went on with his story.

"Now, sirs," said he, "quickly as this was done, idle and evil eyes, that pry into everything, are not wanting to mark the descent and mounting of the fair Melisendra, and to give notice to King Marsilius, who immediately ordered an alarm to be sounded; and now observe the hurry and tumult which follow! See how the whole city shakes with the ringing of bells in the steeples of the mosques——"

"Not so," quoth Don Quixote, "Master Peter is very much out as to the ringing of bells, which were not used by the Moors, but kettle-drums and a kind of dulcimer, like our waits; and, therefore, to introduce the ringing of bells in Sansuenna is a gross absurdity."

Upon which Master Peter left off ringing, and said: "Signor Don Quixote, if you stand upon these trifles we shall never please you; do not be so severe a critic. Have we not thousands of comedies full of such mistakes and blunders, and yet are they not everywhere listened to, not only with applause, but admiration?—Go on, boy, and let these folks talk; for, so that my bags are filled, I care not if there are as many absurdities as there are motes in the sun." "You are in the right," quoth Don Quixote; and the boy proceeded.

"See, gentlemen, the squadrons of glittering cavalry that now rush out of the city, in pursuit of the two Catholic lovers! How many trumpets sound, how many dulcimers play, and how many drums and kettle-drums rattle! Alack, I fear the fugitives will be overtaken and brought back tied to their own horse's tail, which would be a lamentable spectacle."

Don Quixote, roused at the din, and seeing such a number of Moors, thought it incumbent on him to succour the flying pair; and, rising up, said in a loud voice, "It shall never be said while I live that I suffered such a wrong to be committed against so famous a knight and so daring a lover as Don Gayferos. Hold, base-born rabble!—follow him not, or expect to feel the fury of my resentment!"

'T was no sooner said than done: he unsheathed his sword, and at one spring he planted himself close to the show, and, with the utmost fury, began to rain hacks and slashes on the Moorish puppets, overthrowing some, and beheading others, laming this, and demolishing that; and among other mighty strokes, one fell with mortal force in such a direction that, had not Master Peter dexterously slipped aside, he would have taken off his head as clean as if it had been made of sugar-paste.

"Hold, Signor Don Quixote!" cried out the showman, "hold for pity's sake!—these are not real Moors that you are cutting and destroying, but puppets of pasteboard. Think of what you are doing: sinner that I am! you will ruin me for ever." These remonstrances were lost upon the exasperated knight, who still laid about him, showering down and redoubling his blows, fore-stroke and back-stroke, with such fury, that in less than the saying of two *Credos* he demolished the whole machine, hacking to pieces all the tackling and figures. King Marsilius was in a grievous condition, and the Emperor Charlemagne's head, as well as crown, cleft in twain! The whole audience was in a consternation; the ape flew to the top of the house, the scholar and the page were panic-struck, and Sancho trembled exceedingly; for, as he afterwards declared, when the storm was over, he had never seen his master in such a rage before.

After this chastisement of the Moors, and the general destruction which accompanied it, Don Quixote's fury began to abate, and he calmly said, "I wish all those were at this moment present who obstinately refuse to be convinced of the infinite benefit that knights-errant are to the world; for, had I not been fortunately at hand, what would have become of the good Don Gayferos and the fair Melisendra? No doubt these infidel dogs would have overtaken them by this time, and treated them with their wonted cruelty. Long live knight-errantry, above all things in the world!" "In Heaven's name let it live, and let me die!" replied Master Peter, in a dolorous tone, "for such is my wretched fate that I can say with King Loderigo, 'Yesterday I was a sovereign of Spain, and to-day I have not a foot of land to call my own.' It is not half an hour ago, nor scarcely half a minute, since I was master of kings and emperors, my stalls full of horses, and my trunks and sacks full of fine things; now I am destitute and wretched, poor, and a beggar; and to aggravate my grief, I have lost my ape, who, in truth, will make me sweat for it before I catch him again; and all this through the rash fury of this doughty knight, who is said to protect orphans, redress wrongs, and do other charitable deeds: but, Heaven be praised, he has failed in all these good offices towards my wretched self. Well may he be called the Knight of the Sorrowful Figure, for, alas! I am undone for ever by the sorrowful disfigurement I see before me."

Sancho Panza was moved to compassion by Master Peter's lamentations, and said to him, "Come, do not weep, Master Peter; for it breaks my heart to see you grieve and take on so. I can assure you my master Don Quixote is too Catholic and scrupulous a Christian to let any poor man come to loss by him: when he finds out that he has done you wrong he will certainly make you amends, with interest." "Truly," said Master Peter, "if his worship would but make good part of the damage he has done me I should be satisfied, and he would acquit his conscience; for he that takes from his neighbour, and does not make restitution, can never be saved, that's certain." "I allow it," said Don Quixote; "but as yet I am not aware that I have anything of yours, Master Peter." "How!" answered Peter; "see the relics that lie on the hard and barren ground! How were they scattered and annihilated but by the invincible force of your powerful arm? To whom did their bodies belong but to me? How did I maintain myself but by them?" "Here," said Don Quixote, "is a fresh confirmation of what I have often thought, and can now no longer doubt, that those enchanters who persecute me are continually leading me into error by first allowing me to see things as they really are, and then transforming them to my eyes into whatever shape they please. I protest to you, gentlemen, that the spectacle we have just beheld seemed to me a real occurrence, and I doubted not the identity of Melisendra, Don Gayferos, Marsilius, and Charlemagne. I was, therefore, moved with indignation at what I conceived to be injustice, and, in compliance with the duty of my profession as a knight-errant, I wished to assist and succour the fugitives : and with this good intention I did what you have witnessed. If I have been deceived, and things have fallen out unhappily, it is not I who am to blame, but my wicked persecutors. Nevertheless, though this error of mine proceeded not from malice, yet I will condemn myself in costs— consider, Master Peter, your demand for the damaged figures, and I will pay it you down in current and lawful money of Castile."

Master Peter made him a low bow, saying, "I expected no less from the unexampled Christianity of the valorous Don Quixote de la Mancha, the true protector of all needy and distressed wanderers; and let Master Innkeeper and the great Sancho be umpires and appraisers between your worship and me, of what the demolished figures are, or might be, worth."

The innkeeper and Sancho consented; whereupon Master Peter, taking up Marsilius, King of Saragossa, without a head, "You see," said he, "how impossible it is to restore this king to his former state, and therefore I think, with submission to better judgment, that you must award me for his death and destruction four reals and a half." "Proceed," quoth Don Quixote. "Then for this gash from top to bottom," continued Master Peter, taking up the Emperor Charlemagne, "I think five reals and a quartillo would not be too much." "Nor too little," quoth Sancho. "Nor yet too much," added the innkeeper; "but split the difference, and set him down five reals." "Give him the whole of his demand," quoth Don Quixote; "for a quartillo more or less is immaterial on this disastrous occasion: but be quick, Master Peter, for supper-time approaches, and I feel symptoms of hunger." "For this figure," quoth Master Peter, "wanting a nose and an eye, which is the fair Melisendra, I must have, and can abate nothing of, two reals and twelve maravedis." "Nay," said Don Quixote, "the devil is in it if Melisendra, with her husband, be not by this time, at least, upon the borders of France; for the horse they rode seemed to me to fly rather than gallop; and therefore do not pretend to sell me a cat for a coney, showing me here Melisendra without a nose, whereas, at this very instant, the happy pair are probably solacing themselves at their ease, far out of the reach of their enemies. Heaven help every one to what is their just due: proceed, Master Peter, but let us have plain dealing." Master Peter finding that Don Quixote began to waver, and was returning to his old theme, and not choosing that he should escape, he changed his ground, and said, "No, now I recollect, this cannot be Melisendra, but one of her waiting-maids, and so with sixty maravedis I shall be content and well enough paid."

Thus he went on, setting his price upon the dead and wounded, which the arbitrators moderated to the satisfaction of both parties; and the whole amounted to forty reals and three quartillos, which Sancho having paid down, Master Peter demanded two reals more for the trouble he should have in catching his ape. "Give him the two reals, Sancho," said Don Quixote; "and now I would give two hundred more to be assured that the Lady Melisendra and Signor Don Gayferos are at this time in France and among their friends." "Nobody can tell us that better than my ape," said Master Peter; "but the devil himself cannot catch him now; though perhaps either his love for me, or hunger, will force him to return at night. However, to-morrow is a new day, and we shall then see each other again."

The bustle of the puppet-show being quite over, they all supped together in peace and good fellowship, at the expense of Don Quixote, whose liberality was boundless. The man who carried the lances and halberts left the inn before daybreak, and after the sun had risen, the scholar and the page came to take leave of Don Quixote; the former to return home, and the latter to pursue his intended journey; Don Quixote having given him a dozen reals to assist in defraying his expenses. Master Peter had no mind for any further intercourse with Don Quixote, whom he knew perfectly well, and therefore he also arose before the sun, and, collecting the fragments of his show, he set off with his ape in quest of adventures of his own; while the innkeeper, who was not so well acquainted with Don Quixote, was equally surprised at his madness and liberality. In short, Sancho, by order of his master, paid him well; and about eight in the morning, having taken leave of him, they left the inn and proceeded on their journey, where we will leave them, to relate other things necessary to the elucidation of this famous history.

CHAPTER XXVII.

Wherein is related who Master Peter and his ape were; with Don Quixote's ill success in the braying adventure, which terminated neither as wished nor intended.

CID HAMET, the author of this great work, begins the present chapter with these words, "I swear as a Catholic Christian." On which his translator observes that Cid Hamet's swearing as a Catholic Christian, although he was a Moor, meant only that as a Catholic Christian, when he swears, utters nothing but the truth, so he, with equal veracity, will set down nothing in writing of Don Quixote but what is strictly true; especially in the account that is now to be given of the person hitherto called Master Peter, and of the divining ape, whose answers created such amazement throughout all that part of the country. He says, then, that whoever has read the former part of this history must well remember Gines de Passamonte, who among other galley-slaves was liberated by Don Quixote in the Sierra Morena: a benefit for which he was but ill requited by that mischievous and disorderly crew.

This Gines de Passamonte, whom Don Quixote called Ginesillo de Parapilla, was the person who stole Sancho Panza's Dapple; and the time and manner of that theft not having been inserted in the former part of this history, through the neglect of the printers, many have ascribed the omission to want of memory in the author. But in fact Gines stole the animal while Sancho Panza was asleep upon his back, by the same artifice which Brunello practised when he carried off Sacripante's horse from between his legs, at the siege of Albraca; although Sancho afterwards recovered his Dapple, as hath already been related.

This Gines then (whose rogueries and crimes were so numerous and flagrant as to fill a large volume, which he compiled himself), being afraid of falling into the hands of justice, passed over into the kingdom of Arragon, and there, after covering his left eye, he set up the trade of showman, in which, as well as the art of legerdemain, he was a skilful practitioner. From a party of Christians just redeemed from slavery, whom he chanced to meet with, he purchased his ape, which he forthwith instructed to leap upon his shoulder and mutter in his ear, as before described. Thus prepared, he commenced his avocations; and his practice was, before he entered any town, to make inquiries in the neighbourhood concerning its inhabitants and passing events, and, bearing them carefully in his memory, he first exhibited his show, which represented sometimes one story and sometimes another, but all pleasant, gay, and popular. After this he propounded to his auditors the rare talents of his ape, assuring them of his knowledge of the past and present, at the same time confessing his ignorance of the future. Though his regular fee was two reals, he was always disposed to accommodate his customers; and if he found people unwilling to pay the expense of his oracle, he sometimes poured forth his knowledge gratuitously, which gained him unspeakable credit and numerous followers. Even when perfectly ignorant of the queries proposed to him, he contrived so to adapt his answers, that as people were seldom troublesome in their scruples, he was able to deceive all, and fill his pockets.

No sooner had Master Peter Passamonte entered the inn than he recognized the knight and squire, and therefore had no difficulty in exciting their astonishment; but the adventure would have cost him dear had he not been so lucky as to elude the sword of Don Quixote, when he sliced off the head of King Marsilius and demolished his cavalry, as related in the foregoing chapter. This may suffice concerning Master Peter and his ape.

Let us now return to our illustrious knight of La Mancha, who, after quitting the inn, determined to visit the banks of the river Ebro and the neighbouring country: finding that he would have time sufficient for that purpose before the tournaments at Saragossa began. With this intention he pursued his journey, and travelled two days without encountering anything worth recording, till, on the third day, as he was ascending a hill, he heard a distant sound of drums, trumpets, and other martial instruments, which at first he imagined to proceed from a body of military on the march; and spurring Rozinante, he ascended a rising ground, whence he perceived, as he thought, in the valley beneath, above two hundred men, armed with various weapons, as spears, cross-bows, partisans, halberds, and spikes, with some firearms. He then descended, and advanced so near the troop that he could distinguish their banners, with the devices they bore; especially one upon a banner or pennant of white satin, on which an ass was painted to the life, of the small Sardinian breed, with its head raised, its mouth open in the very posture of braying, and over it was written in large characters,

> " The bailiffs twain
> Brayed not in vain."

From this motto Don Quixote concluded that these were the inhabitants of the braying town, which opinion he communicated to Sancho, and told him also what was written on the banner. He likewise said that the person who had given them an account of this affair was mistaken in calling the two brayers aldermen, since, according to the motto, it appeared they were not aldermen, but bailiffs. "That breaks no squares, sir," answered Sancho Panza; "for it might happen that the aldermen who brayed have in process of time become bailiffs of their town, and therefore may properly be called by both titles; though it signifies nothing to the truth of the history whether they were bailiffs or aldermen; for one is as likely to bray as the other."

They soon ascertained that it was the derided town sallying forth to attack another, which had ridiculed them more than was reasonable or becoming in good neighbours. Don Quixote advanced towards them, to the no small concern of Sancho, who never had any liking to meddle in such matters, and he was presently surrounded by the motley band, who supposed him to be some friend to their cause. Don Quixote then raising his vizor, with an easy and graceful deportment, approached the ass-banner, and all the chiefs of the army collected around him, being struck with the same astonishment which the first sight of him usually excited. Don Quixote, seeing them gaze so earnestly at him, without being spoken to by any of the party, took advantage of this silence, and addressed them in the following manner :

" It is my intention, most worthy gentlemen, to address you, and I earnestly entreat you not to interrupt my discourse, unless you find it offensive or tiresome : for in that case, upon the least sign from you, I will put a seal on my lips and a bridle on my tongue." They all desired him to say what he pleased, and promised to hear him with attention. With this license, Don Quixote proceeded. "Gentlemen," said he, " I am a knight-errant : arms are my exercise, and my profession is that of relieving the distressed and giving aid to the weak. I am no stranger to the cause of your agitation, nor to the events which have provoked your resentment and impelled you to arms. I have, therefore, often reflected on your case, and find that, according to the laws of duel, you are mistaken in thinking yourselves insulted; for no one person can insult a whole city, unless, when treason has been committed within it, not know-ing the guilty person, he should accuse the whole body. Of this we have an example in Don Diego Ordonnez de Lara, who challenged the whole people of Zamora, because he did not know that Vellido Dolfos alone had murdered his king: and therefore, every individual being charged with that crime, it belonged to the whole to answer and to revenge the imputation. It is true that Signor Don Diego went somewhat too far, and exceeded the just limits of challenge; for certainly it was not necessary to include in it the dead and the unborn, the waters, the bread, and several other particulars therein mentioned. But let that pass, for when choler overflows the tongue is under no government. Since, then, it is impossible that an individual should affront a whole kingdom, province, or city, it is clear that there is no reason for your marching out to take revenge upon what cannot be considered as an offence worthy of your resentment. It would be a fine business, truly, if all those towns which, by the vulgar, are nicknamed from their trades, and called the cheesemongers, the costermongers, the fishmongers, the soapboilers, and other appellations,* should be so absurd as to think themselves insulted, and to seek vengeance with their swords upon this and every slight provocation! No, no; such doings Heaven neither wills or permits. In well-ordered states, men are required to unsheathe their swords and hazard their lives and property upon four different accounts: first, to defend the holy Catholic faith; secondly, in selfdefence, which is agreeable to natural and divine law; thirdly, in defence of personal honour, family, reputation, and worldly wealth; fourthly, in obedience to the commands of their sovereign, in a just war; to these may be added a fifth (which, indeed, will properly rank with the second), and that is, the defence of our country. These are the principal occasions upon which an appeal to the sword is justifiable; but to have recourse to it for trifles, and things rather to excite mirth than anger, is equally wicked and senseless. Besides, to take unjust revenge (and no revenge can be just) is acting in direct opposition to our holy religion, by which we are enjoined to forgive our enemies, and do good to those who hate us—a precept which, though it seems difficult to obey, yet it is only so to the worldly-minded, who have more of the flesh than the spirit: for the Redeemer of mankind, whose words could never deceive, said that His yoke was easy and His burden light; and therefore He would not require from us what was impossible to be performed. So that, gentlemen, by every law, human and divine, you are bound to sheathe your swords, and let your resentment sleep."

"The devil fetch me," quoth Sancho to himself, "if this master of mine be not a perfect priest; or, if not, he is as like one as one egg is like another." Don Quixote took breath a little, and perceiving his auditors were still attentive, he would have continued his harangue, had he not been prevented by the zeal of his squire, who seized the opportunity offered him by a pause to make a speech in his turn.

"Gentlemen," said he, "my master Don Quixote de la Mancha,

---

* The cities so called are Valladolid, Toledo, Madrid, and probably Getafe.

*Feeling a shower of stones come thick upon him, he turned Rozinante about,
and got out from among them.*

once called the Knight of the Sorrowful Figure, and now the Knight
of the Lions, is a choice scholar, and understands Latin, and talks
the vulgar tongue like any bachelor of arts; and in all he meddles or
advises, proceeds like an old soldier, having all the laws and statutes
of what is called duelling at his fingers' ends; and so you have nothing
to do but to follow his advice, and while you abide by that, let the
blame be mine if ever you make a false step. And, indeed, as you
have already been told, it is mighty foolish in you to be offended at
hearing any one bray. When I was a boy I well remember nobody ever
hindered me from braying as often as I pleased; and I could do it so
rarely that all the asses in the town answered me; yet for all that was
I still the son of my parents, who were very honest people: and though
I must say a few of the proudest of my neighbours envied me the
gift, yet I cared not a rush; and, to convince you that I speak the
truth, do but listen to me; for this art, like that of swimming, once
learned, is never forgotten."

Then putting his hands to his nostrils, he began to bray so strenu-
ously that the adjacent valleys resounded again; whereupon a man who
stood near him, supposing that he was mocking them, raised his pole,
and gave him such a blow that it brought the unlucky squire to the

ground. Don Quixote, seeing him so ill-treated, made at the striker with his lance, but was instantly opposed by so many of his comrades, that he saw that it was impossible for him to be so revenged : on the contrary, feeling a shower of stones come thick upon him, and seeing a thousand cross-bows presented, and as many guns levelled at him, he turned Rozinante about, and, as fast as he could gallop, got out from among them, heartily recommending himself to Heaven, and praying, as he fled, to be delivered from so imminent a danger ; at the same time expecting at every step to be pierced through and through with bullets, he went on drawing his breath at every moment, to try whether or not it failed him. The rustic battalion, however, seeing him fly, were contented to save their ammunition. As for Sancho, they set him again upon his ass, though scarcely recovered from the blow, and suffered him to follow his master—not that he had power to guide him, but Dapple, unwilling to be separated from Rozinante, naturally followed his steps. Don Quixote having got to a considerable distance, at length ventured to look back, and, seeing only Sancho slowly following, he stopped, and waited till he came up. The army kept the field till nightfall, when, no enemy coming forth to battle, they joyfully returned home : and had they known the practice of the ancient Greeks, they would have erected a trophy in that place.

CHAPTER XXVIII.

*Concerning things which, Benengeli says, he who reads of them will know,
if he reads with attention*

WHEN the valiant man flies he must have discovered foul play ; and it is then the part of the wise to reserve themselves for a better occasion. This truth was verified in Don Quixote, who, not choosing to expose himself to the fury of an incensed and evil-disposed multitude, prudently retired out of their reach, without once recollecting his faithful squire, or the perilous situation in which he left him ; nor did he stop till he got as far off as he deemed sufficient for his safety. Sancho followed the track of his master, hanging, as before described, athwart his ass, and having recovered his senses, at length came up to him ; when, unable to support himself, he dropped from his pack-saddle at Rozinante's feet, overcome with the pain of the bruises and blows he had received.

Don Quixote dismounted to examine the state of Sancho's body : but finding no bones broken, and the skin whole from head to foot, he said, angrily, " In an evil hour, Sancho, must thou needs show thy skill in braying : where didst thou learn that it was proper to name a halter in the house of a man that was hanged ? To thy braying music what counterpoise couldst thou expect but that of a cudgel ? Return thanks to Heaven, Sancho, that instead of crossing thy back with a cudgel, they did not make the sign of the cross on thee with a scimitar." "I am not now in a condition to answer," replied Sancho, "for methinks I speak through my shoulders. Let us mount, and be gone from this place. As for braying, I will have done with it for ever; but not with telling that knights-errant can fly, and leave their faithful squires to be beaten to powder in the midst of their enemies." "To retire is not to fly," answered Don Quixote; "for thou must know, Sancho, that the valour which has not prudence for its basis is termed rashness, and the successful exploits of the rash are rather to be ascribed to good fortune than to courage. I confess I did retire, but not fly: and herein I imitated sundry valiant persons who have reserved themselves for better purposes, whereof history furnishes abundance of examples; but being of no profit to thee, or pleasure to myself, I shall not now mention them."

By this time Sancho had mounted again, with the assistance of his master, who likewise got upon Rozinante, and they proceeded slowly towards a grove of poplars which they discovered about a quarter of a league off, Sancho every now and then heaving most profound sighs, accompanied by dolorous groans: and, when asked the cause of his distress, he said that, from the nape of his neck to the lowest point of his back-bone, he was so bruised and sore that the pain made him mad. "Doubtless," said Don Quixote, "this pain must have been caused by the pole with which they struck thee, and which, being long, extended over the whole of thy back, including all the parts which now grieve thee so much; and, had the weapon been still larger, thy pain would have been increased." "Before Heaven," quoth Sancho, "your worship hath relieved me from a mighty doubt, and explained it, forsooth, in notable terms! Body o' me! was the cause of my pain so hidden that it was necessary to tell me that I felt pain in all those parts which the pole reached? If my ankles had ached, then might you have tried to unriddle the cause; but to find out that I am pained because I was beaten is, truly, no great matter. In faith, master of mine, other men's harms are easily borne. I descry land more and more every day, and see plainly how little I am to expect from following your worship; for if this time you could suffer me to be basted, I may reckon upon returning, again and again, to our old blanketing and other pranks. My back bears the mischief now, but next it may fall on my eyes. It would be much better for me, only that I am a beast, and shall never in my life do anything that is right—better, I say, would it be for me to return home to my wife and children, and strive to maintain and bring them up with the little Heaven shall be pleased to give me, and not be following your worship through roads without a road, and pathless paths, drinking ill and eating worse. And as for sleeping—good squire, measure out seven feet of earth, and if that be not sufficient, prithee take as many more and welcome, and stretch out to your heart's content! I should like to see the first who set knight-errantry on foot burnt to ashes; or, at least, the first that would needs be squire to such idiots as all the knights-errant of former times must have been—of the present I say nothing, for, your worship being one of them, I am bound to pay them respect, and because I know that, in regard to talking and understanding, your worship knows a point beyond the devil himself."

"I would lay a good wager with thee, Sancho," quoth Don Quixote, "that now thou art talking, and without interruption, thou feelest no pain in thy body. Go on, my son, and say all that comes into thy head, or to thy tongue; for, so thou art relieved from pain, I shall take pleasure even in the vexation thy impertinence occasions me; nay, more, if thou hast really so great a desire to return home to thy wife and children, God forbid that I should hinder thee. Thou hast money of mine in thy hands: see how long it is since we made this third sally from our town, and how much thou couldst have earned monthly, and pay thyself." "When I served Thomas Carrasco," replied Sancho, "father of the bachelor Sampson Carrasco, whom your worship knows full well, I got two ducats a month, besides my victuals: with your worship I cannot tell what I may get; but I am sure it is greater drudgery to be squire to a knight-errant than servant to a farmer; for, if we work for husbandmen, though we labour hard in the day, at night we are sure of supper from the pot, and a bed to sleep on, which is more than I have found since I have been in your worship's service—the scum of Camacho's pots excepted, and the short time we were at the houses of Don Diego and Basilius: all the rest of the time I have had no other bed than the hard ground, and no other covering than the sky, whether foul or fair; living upon scraps of bad bread and worse cheese, and drinking such water as chance put in our way."

"I confess, Sancho," said Don Quixote, "that all thou sayest is true: how much dost thou think I ought to pay thee more than what thou hadst from Thomas Carrasco?" "I think," quoth Sancho, "if your worship adds two reals a month, I should reckon myself well paid. This is for the wages due for my labour; but as to the promise your worship made of the government of an island, it would be fair that you add six reals more, making thirty in all." "Very well," replied Don Quixote; "it is five and twenty days since we sallied forth from our village, and, according to the wages thou hast allotted thyself, calculate the proportion and see what I owe thee, and pay thyself, as I said before, with thine own hand." "Body o' me!" quoth Sancho, "your worship is clean out of the reckoning; for as to the promised land, we must reckon from the day you promised me to the present hour." "How long then is it since I promised it to thee?" said Don Quixote. "If I remember right," answered Sancho, "it is about twenty years and three days, more or less."

Here Don Quixote, clapping his forehead with the palm of his hand, began to laugh heartily, and said, "Why, all my sallies, including the time I sojourned in the Sierra Morena, have scarcely taken up more than two months, and dost thou say, Sancho, it is twenty years since I promised thee an island? I perceive that thou art determined to lay claim to all the money thou hast of mine : if such be thy wish, take it, and much good may it do thee; for to rid myself of so worthless a squire I will gladly be left poor and penniless. But tell me, thou perverter of the squirely ordinances of knight-errantry! where hast thou seen or read that any squire to knight-errant ever presumed to bargain with his master, and say, So much per month you must give me to serve you? Launch, launch out, thou base reptile! thou hobgoblin!—for such thou art—launch out, I say, into the *mare magnum* of their histories, and if thou canst find that any squire has ever said, or thought, as thou hast done, I will give thee leave to nail it on my forehead, and write fool upon my face in capitals. Turn about the bridle, or halter, of Dapple, and get home! for not one single step farther shalt thou go with me. O bread ill-bestowed! O promises ill-placed! O man, that hast more of the beast than of the human creature! Now, when I thought of establishing thee, and in such a way that, in spite of thy wife, thou shouldst have been styled ‘your lordship,’ now dost thou leave me? now, when I had just taken a firm and effectual resolution to make thee lord of the best island in the world? But, as thou thyself hast often said, ‘honey is not for the mouth of an ass.’ An ass thou art, an ass thou wilt continue to be, and an ass thou wilt die; for I verily believe thou wilt never acquire even sense enough to know that thou art a beast!”

Sancho looked at his master with a sad and sorrowful countenance, all the time he thus reproached and rated him; and when the storm was passed, with tears in his eyes and in a faint and doleful voice he said, “I confess, dear sir, that to be a complete ass I want nothing but a tail, and if your worship will be pleased to put one on me, I shall deem it well placed, and will then serve you as your faithful ass all the days I have yet to live. Pardon me, sir, I entreat you; have pity on my ignorance, and consider that, if my tongue runs too fast, it is more from folly than evil meaning: ‘ he who errs and mends, himself to Heaven commends.’ ” “ I should have wondered much, Sancho,” quoth Don Quixote, “ if thy proverbs had been wanting upon such an occasion. Well, I forgive thee, on the promise of thy amendment, and in the hope that henceforth thou mayest prove less craving and selfish. I would hope also to see thy mind prepared to wait with becoming patience the due accomplishment of my promises, which, though deferred, are not on that account the less certain.” Sancho promised compliance, though to do it he should have to draw strength out of weakness.

They now entered the poplar-grove, and Don Quixote seated himself at the foot of an elm, and Sancho under a beech—for it is admitted that such trees are always provided with feet, but never with hands. In that situation they passed the night : Sancho suffering from the pain of his bruises, and his master indulging his wonted meditations; nevertheless they both slept, and in the morning pursued their way towards the banks of the famous Ebro, where that befell them which shall be related in the ensuing chapter.

CHAPTER XXIX.

Of the famous adventure of the enchanted bark.

AFTER travelling leisurely for two days, Don Quixote and his squire reached the banks of the river Ebro, and the knight experienced much pleasure while he contemplated the verdure of its margin, the smoothness of its current, and the abundance of its crystal waters. Cheered and delighted with the scene, a thousand tender recollections rushed upon his mind, and particularly what he had witnessed in the Cave of Montesinos; for although Master Peter's ape had pronounced a part only of those wonders to be true, he rather inclined to believe the whole than allow any part to be doubtful : quite the reverse of Sancho, who held them all to be false.

Thus musing and sauntering along, they observed a small vessel, without oars or any kind of tackle, fastened by a rope to the shore. Don Quixote looked round him on all sides, and, seeing nobody, he alighted, and ordered Sancho to do the same, and make fast both their beasts to the trunk of a poplar or willow that grew by the side of the river. On Sancho's requesting to know why he was to do so, " Thou must know," said Don Quixote, "that this vessel is placed here expressly for my reception, and in order that I might proceed therein to the succour of some knight or other person of high degree, who is in extreme distress; for such is the practice of enchanters, as we learn in the books of chivalry, when some knight happens to be involved in a situation of extraordinary peril, from which he can only be delivered by the hand of another knight. Then, although distant from each other two or three thousand leagues, and even more, they either snatch him up in a cloud, or, as thus, provide him with a boat, and in less than the twinkling of an eye convey him through the air, or over the surface of the ocean, whereever they list, or where his aid is required. This bark, therefore, O Sancho, must be placed here for that sole purpose, as certainly as it is now day : haste, then, before it is spent; tie Dapple and Rozinante together, and the hand of Providence be our guide ! for embark I will, although holy friars themselves should entreat me to desist." " Since it must be so," said Sancho, " and that your worship is determined to be always running into these vagaries, there is nothing left for me but to obey; following the proverb, ' do your master's bidding, and sit down with him at his table.' But for all that, to discharge my conscience, I am bound to tell your worship that, to my mind, this same boat belongs to no enchanter, but to some fisherman on this part of the river; for here, it is said, they catch the best shads in the world."

This caution Sancho ventured to give, while, with much grief of soul, he was tying the cattle where they were to be left under the protection of enchanters. Don Quixote told him to be under no concern about forsaking those animals; for he by whom they were themselves to be transported to far distant longitudes, would take care that they should not want food. "I do not understand your logitudes," said Sancho, "nor have I ever heard of such a word in all my life." "Longitude," replied Don Quixote, "means length;—but no wonder thou dost not understand it, for thou art not bound to know Latin; though there are some who pretend to know it, and are as ignorant as thyself." "Now they are tied," quoth Sancho, "what is next to be done?" "What?" answered Don Quixote; "why, cross ourselves and weigh anchor—I mean embark—and cut the rope with which the vessel is now tied." Then, leaping into it, followed by Sancho, he cut the cord, and the boat floated gently from the shore; and when Sancho saw himself a few yards from the bank, he began to quake with fear; but on hearing his friend Dapple bray, and seeing Rozinante struggle to get loose, he was quite overcome. "The poor ass," said he, "brays for pure grief at being deserted, and Rozinante is endeavouring to get loose, that he may plunge into the river and follow us. O dearest friends, abide where you are in peace, and may the mad freak, which is the cause of our doleful parting, be quickly followed by a repentance that will bring us back again to your sweet company."

Here he began to weep so bitterly that Don Quixote lost all patience. "Of what art thou afraid, cowardly wretch?" cried he: "heart of butter! why weepest thou? Who pursues, who annoys thee — soul of a house rat? Or what dost thou want, poor wretch, in the very bowels of abundance? Peradventure thou art trudging barefoot over the Riphean mountains? No, seated like an archduke, thou art gently gliding down the stream of this charming river, whence in a short space we shall issue out into the boundless ocean, which doubtless we have already entered, and must have gone at least seven or eight hundred leagues. If I had but an astrolabe here, to take the elevation of the pole, I would tell thee what distance we have gone; though, if I am not much mistaken, we are already past, or shall presently pass, the equinoctial line, which divides and cuts the world in equal halves." "And when we come to that line your worship speaks of," quoth Sancho, "how far shall we have travelled?" "A mighty distance," replied Don Quixote, "for of the three hundred and sixty degrees into which the terraqueous globe is divided, according to the system and computation of Ptolemy, the greatest of all geographers, we shall at least have travelled one-half when we come to that line." "By the Lord!" quoth Sancho, "your worship has brought a pretty fellow to witness, that same Tolmy—how d' ye call him? with his amputation, to vouch for the truth of what you say."

Don Quixote smiled at Sancho's blunders, and said, "Thou must know, Sancho, that one of the signs by which the Spaniards, and those who travel by sea to the East Indies, discover they have passed the line of which I told thee, is that all the vermin upon every man in the ship die; nor, after passing it, is one to be found in the vessel, though they would give its weight in gold for it; and, therefore, Sancho, pass thy hand over thy body, and if thou findest any live thing, we shall have no doubts upon that score, and if not, we shall then know that we have certainly passed the line." "Not a word of that do I believe," quoth Sancho; "however, I will do as your worship bids me, though I know not what occasion there is for making this experiment, since I see with mine own eyes that we have not got five yards from the bank, for yonder stand Rozinante and Dapple in the very place where we left them; and, from points which I now mark, I vow to Heaven we do not move an ant's pace." "Sancho," said Don Quixote, "make the trial I bid thee, and take no further care: thou knowest not what colours are, nor the lines, parallels, zodiacs, ecliptics, poles, solstices, equinoctials, planets, signs, and other points and measures of which the celestial and terrestrial globes are composed; for if thou knewest all these things, or but a part of them, thou wouldst plainly perceive what parallels we have cut, what signs we have seen, and what constellations we have left behind us, and are just now leaving. Once more, then, I bid thee feel thyself all over, and fish; for my part, I am of opinion that thou art as clean as a sheet of smooth white paper." Accordingly Sancho passed his hand lightly over his left ham, then lifting up his head, and looking significantly at his master, he said, "Either the experiment is false, or we have have not yet arrived where your worship says—no, not by many leagues." "Why," said Don Quixote, "hast thou met with something, then?" "Aye, sir, several somethings," replied Sancho, and, shaking his fingers, he washed his whole hand in the river, on the surface of which the boat was gently gliding—not moved by the secret influence of enchantment, but by the current, which was then gentle, and the whole surface smooth and calm.

At this time several corn mills appeared before them in the midst of the stream, which Don Quixote no sooner espied than he exclaimed in a loud voice, "Behold, O Sancho! seest thou yon city, castle, or fortress? —there lies some knight under oppression, or some queen, infanta, or princess, confined in evil plight, to whose relief I am brought hither." "What the devil of a city, fortress, or castle do you talk of, sir?" quoth Sancho; "do you not see that they are mills, standing in the river for the grinding of corn?" "Peace, Sancho," quoth Don Quixote; "for though they seem to be mills, they are not so. How often must I tell thee that enchanters have the power to transform whatever they please? I do not say that things are totally changed by them, but to our eyes they are made to appear so; whereof we have had a woful proof in the transformation of Dulcinea, the sole refuge of my hopes."

The boat having now got into the current of the river, was carried on with more celerity than before; and, as it approached the mill, the labourers within, seeing it drifting towards them, and just entering the mill-stream, several of them ran out in haste with long poles to stop it; and, their faces and clothes being all covered with meal-dust, they had a ghostly appearance. "Devils of men!" said they, bawling aloud,

Standing up in the boat, he began to threaten the millers aloud. "Ill-advised scoundrels!" said he, "set at liberty the person ye keep under oppression in that castle of yours."

"what do you there? Are you mad, or do you intend to drown your-selves, or be torn to pieces by the wheels?"

"Did I not tell thee, Sancho," said Don Quixote, "that we should certainly arrive where it would be necessary for me to display the valour of my arm? Look, what assassins and hobgoblins come out to oppose us! See their horrid visages with which they think to scare us! Now, rascals, have at you!" Then standing up in the boat, he began to threaten the millers aloud. "Ill-advised scoundrels!" said he, "set at liberty the person ye keep under oppression in that castle or fortress of yours, whether he be of high or low degree; for I am Don Quixote de la Mancha, otherwise called the Knight of the Lions, for whom, by Heaven's high destiny, the happy accomplishment of this adventure is reserved." So saying, he drew his sword, and began to flourish with it in the air, as if he would smite the millers, who, not understanding his menaces, endeavoured to stop the boat, now on the point of entering into the swift current that rushed under the wheels. Sancho fell upon his knees and prayed devoutly to Heaven for his deliverance, which was accomplished by the agility and adroitness of the millers with their poles; but not without oversetting the boat, whereby the knight and squire were plunged into the water. Although Don Quixote could swim like a goose, the weight of his armour now carried him twice to the bottom; and, had it not been for the millers, who leaped into the river and hauled them both out, they must inevitably have perished.

After having been dragged on shore, much more wet than thirsty, Sancho again fell on his knees, and long and devoutly prayed that Heaven would thenceforward protect him from the dangers to which he was likely to be exposed through the rash enterprises of his master. Now came the fishermen, owners of the boat, which had been entirely destroyed by the mill-wheels, and loudly demanded reparation for the loss they had sustained, and for that purpose began to strip Sancho, when Don Quixote, with as much unconcern as if nothing had happened, gravely told the millers and fishermen that he would willingly pay for the boat on condition of their delivering up, free and without ransom, the person or persons whom they unjustly detained in their castle. "What persons, or what castles, madman! do you mean?" said one of the millers; "would you carry off those who come to have their corn ground at our mills?" "There let it rest," thought Don Quixote to himself: "it is only preaching to the desert to endeavour, either by argument or entreaty, to incite these dregs of human kind to a generous action! In this adventure it is manifest that two powerful enchanters must have engaged, the one frustrating what the other attempts; the one providing me a bark, and the other oversetting it. Heaven help me! in this world there is nothing but plots and counterplots, mines and countermines!—I can do no more." Then casting a look of melancholy towards the mills, "Friends," he said, "whoever ye are that live immured in that prison, pardon me, I beseech you, for not having delivered you from affliction; by your ill fate and mine it is ordained that this adventure should be reserved for some more fortunate knight!" He then compounded with the fishermen, and agreed to give them fifty reals for the boat, which sum Sancho with much reluctance paid down, saying, "A couple more of such embarkations as this will sink our whole capital." The fishermen and millers stood gazing with astonishment at two figures so far out of the fashion and semblance of other men, and were quite at a loss to find out the meaning of Don Quixote's speeches; but, conceiving their intellects to be disordered, they left them, the millers retiring to their mills, and the fishermen to their cabins; whereupon, Don Quixote and Sancho, like a pair of senseless animals themselves, returned to the animals they had left; and thus ended the adventure of the enchanted bark.

CHAPTER XXX.

Of what befell Don Quixote with a fair huntress.

Low-spirited, wet, and out of humour, the knight and squire reached their cattle; Sancho more especially was grieved to the very soul to have encroached so much upon their stock of money, all that was taken thence seeming to him as so much taken from the apples of his eyes. In short, they mounted, without exchanging a word, and silently quitted the banks of that famous river: Don Quixote buried in amorous meditations, and Sancho in those of his preferment, which seemed at that moment to be very dim and remote; for, dull as he was, he saw clearly enough that his master's actions were for the most part little better than crazy, and he only waited for an opportunity, without coming to accounts and reckonings, to steal off and march home. But fortune was kinder to him than he expected.

It happened on the following day, near sunset, as they were issuing from a forest, that Don Quixote espied sundry persons at a distance, who, it appeared, as he drew nearer to them, were taking the diversion of hawking; and among them he remarked a gay lady mounted on a palfry, or milk-white pad, with green furniture and a side-saddle of cloth of silver. Her own attire was also green, and so rich and beautiful that she was elegance itself. On her left hand she carried a hawk; whence Don Quixote conjectured that she must be a lady of high rank, and mistress of the hunting-party (as in truth she was), and therefore he said to his squire, " Hasten, Sancho, and make known to the lady of the palfry and the hawk, that I, the Knight of the Lions, humbly salute her highness, and, with her gracious leave, would be proud to kiss her fair hands, and serve her to the utmost of my power and her highness's commands ; but take especial care, Sancho, how thou deliverest my message, and be mindful not to interlard thy embassy with any of thy proverbs." " So, then," quoth Sancho, " you must quit the interlarder !—but why this to me ? as if this, forsooth, were the first time I had carried messages to high and mighty ladies !" " Excepting that to the Lady Dulcinea," replied Don Quixote, " I know of none thou hast carried—at least, none from me." " That is true," answered Sancho; " but a good paymaster needs no surety ; and where there is plenty, dinner is soon dressed : I mean, there is no need of schooling me ; for I am prepared for all, and know something of everything." " I believe it, Sancho," quoth Don Quixote ; " go, then, and Heaven direct thee."

Sancho set off at a good rate, forcing Dapple out of his usual pace, and went up to the fair huntress ; then alighting, and kneeling before her, he said, " Beauteous lady, that knight yonder, called the Knight of the Lions, is my master, and I am his squire, Sancho Panza by name.

That same Knight of the Lions, lately called the Knight of the Sorrowful Figure, sends me to beg your grandeur would be pleased to give leave that, with your liking and good-will, he may approach and accomplish his wishes, which, as he says and I believe, are no other than to serve your exalted beauty, which if your ladyship grant, you will do a thing that will redound to the great benefit of your highness; and to him it will be a mighty favour and satisfaction."

"Truly, good squire," answered the lady, "you have delivered your message with all the circumstances which such embassies require. Rise up, I pray; for it is not fit the squire of so renowned a knight as he of the Sorrowful Figure, of whom we have already heard much in these parts, should remain upon his knees. Rise, friend, and desire your master, by all means, to honour us with his company, that my lord duke and I may pay him our respects at a rural mansion we have here, hard by." Sancho rose up, no less amazed at the lady's beauty than at her affability and courteous deportment, and yet more that her ladyship should have any knowledge of his master, the Knight of the Sorrowful Figure! And if she did not give him his true title, he concluded it was because he had assumed it so lately. "Pray," said the duchess (whose title is yet unknown), "is not your master the person of whom there is a history in print, called 'The ingenious gentleman Don Quixote de la Mancha,' and who has for the mistress of his affections a certain lady named Dulcinea del Toboso?" "The very same," answered Sancho; "and that squire of his, called Sancho Panza, who is, or ought to be, spoken of in the same history, am I, unless I was changed in the cradle—I mean in the printing." "I am much delighted by what you tell me," quoth the duchess; "go to your master, good Panza, and give him my invitation and hearty welcome to my house; and tell him that nothing could happen to me which would afford me greater pleasure."

Sancho, overjoyed at this gracious answer, hastened back to his master, and repeated to him all that the great lady had said to him; extolling to the skies, in his rustic phrase, her extraordinary beauty and courteous behaviour. Don Quixote seated himself handsomely in his saddle, adjusted his vizor, enlivened Rozinante's mettle, and assuming a polite and stately deportment, advanced to kiss the hand of the duchess. Her grace in the meantime having called the duke her husband, had already given him an account of the embassy she had just received; and, as they had read the first part of this history, and were, therefore, aware of the extravagant humour of Don Quixote, they waited for him with infinite pleasure and the most eager desire to be acquainted with him, determined to indulge his humour to the utmost, and, while he remained with them, to treat him as a knight-errant, with all the ceremonies described in books of chivalry, which they took pleasure in reading.

Don Quixote now arrived, with his beaver up; and signifying his intention to alight, Sancho was hastening to hold his stirrup, but unfornately, in dismounting from Dapple, his foot caught in one of the rope-stirrups in such a manner that it was impossible for him to disentangle himself, and he hung by it, with his face and breast on the ground. Don Quixote, who was not accustomed to alight without having his stirrup held, thinking that Sancho was already there to do his office, threw his body off with a swing of his right leg, that brought down Rozinante's saddle; and the girth giving way, both he and the saddle, to his great shame and mortification, came to the ground, where he lay, muttering between his teeth many a heavy execration against the unfortunate Sancho, who was still hanging by the leg. The duke having commanded some of his attendants to relieve the knight and squire, they raised Don Quixote, who, though much discomposed by his fall, and limping, made an effort to approach and kneel before the lord and lady. The duke, however, would by no means suffer it; on the contrary, alighting from his horse, he immediately went up and embraced him, saying, " I am very sorry, Sir Knight, that such a mischance should happen to you on your first arrival on my domains; but the negligence of squires is often the occasion of even greater disasters." " The moment cannot be unfortunate that introduces me to your highness," replied Don Quixote, " and had my fall been to the centre of the deep abyss, the glory of seeing your highness would have raised me thence. My squire, whom Heaven confound! is better at letting loose his tongue to utter impertinence then at securing a saddle : but whether down or up, on horseback or on foot, I shall always be at the service of your highness, and that of my lady duchess your worthy consort—the sovereign lady of beauty, and universal princess of all courtesy." " Softly, dear Signor Don Quixote de la Mancha," quoth the duke; " for, while the peerless Dulcinea del Toboso exists, no other beauty can be named."

Sancho Panza had now got freed from the noose, and being near, before his master could answer, he said, " It cannot be denied—nay, it must be declared, that my lady Dulcinea del Toboso is a rare beauty; but, ' where we are least aware, there starts the hare.' I have heard say that what they call Nature is like a potter who makes earthen vessels, and he who makes one handsome vessel may also make two, and three, and a hundred. This I say, because, by my faith, her highness there comes not a whit behind my mistress, the Lady Dulcinea del Toboso." Don Quixote here turned to the duchess, and said, " I assure your grace, never any knight-errant in the world had a more conceited and troublesome prater for his squire than I have : of this he will give ample proof, if it please your highness to accept of my service for some days." " I am glad to hear that my friend Sancho is conceited," replied the duchess; " it is a sign he has good sense; for wit and gay conceits, as you well know, Signor Don Quixote, proceed not from dull heads; and, since you acknowledge that Sancho has wit and pleasantry, I shall henceforth pronounce him to be wise—" " And a prater," added Don Quixote. " So much the better," said the duke; " for many good things cannot be expressed in a few words ; and, that we may not throw away all our time upon them, come on, Sir Knight of the Sorrowful

Figure." "Of the Lions, your highness should say," quoth Sancho; "the Sorrowful Figure is no more." "Of the Lions, then, let it be," continued the duke. "I say, come on, Sir Knight of the Lions, to a castle of mine hard by, where you shall be received in a manner suitable to a person of your distinction, and as the duchess and I are accustomed to receive all knights-errant who honour us with their society."

By this time, Sancho having adjusted and well-girthed Rozinante's saddle, Don Quixote remounted, and thus he and the duke, who rode a stately courser, with the duchess between them, proceeded towards the castle. The duchess requested Sancho to be near her, being mightily pleased with his arch observations; nor did Sancho require much entreaty, but, joining the other three, made a fourth in the conversation, to the great satisfaction of the duke and duchess, who looked upon themselves as highly fortunate in having to introduce such guests to their castle, and the prospect of enjoying the company of such a knight-errant and such an errant squire.

CHAPTER XXXI.

Which treats of many and great things.

Sancho's joy was excessive on seeing himself, as he thought, a favourite with the duchess, not doubting but that he should find in her castle the same abundance that prevailed in the mansion of Don Diego and Basilius; for good cheer was the delight of his heart, and therefore he always took care to seize by the forelock every opportunity to indulge that passion. Now the history relates that, before they came to the rural mansion or castle of the duke, his highness rode on before, and gave directions to his servants in what manner they were to behave to Don Quixote; therefore, when he arrived with the duchess at the castle-gate, there immediately issued out two lacqueys or grooms, clad in a kind of robe or gown of fine crimson satin reaching to their feet; and, taking Don Quixote in their arms, they privately said to him, "Go, great sir, and assist our lady the duchess to alight."

The knight accordingly hastened to offer his services, which, after much ceremony and many compliments, her grace positively declined, saying that she would not alight from her palfry, but into the duke's arms, as she did not think herself worthy to charge so great a knight with so unprofitable a burden. At length the duke came out and lifted her from her horse; and on their entering into a large inner court of the castle, two beautiful damsels advanced and threw over Don Quixote's shoulders a large mantle of the finest scarlet, and in an instant all the galleries of the courtyard were crowded with men and women, the domestic household of his grace, crying aloud, "Welcome the flower and cream of knights-errant!" Then they sprinkled whole bottles of sweet-scented

Six damsels attended to take off his armour and serve as pages.

waters upon the knight, and also upon the duke and duchess; all which Don Quixote observed with surprise and pleasure; being now, for the first time, thoroughly convinced that he was a true knight, and no imaginary one, since he was treated just like the knights-errant of former times.

Sancho, abandoning Dapple, attached himself closely to the duchess, and entered with her into the castle; but his conscience soon reproached him with having left his ass alone and unprovided for. He therefore approached a reverend duenna, who amongst others came out to receive the duchess, and said to her in a low voice, "Mistress Gonzalez, or pray, madam, what may your name be?" "Donna Rodriguez de Grijalva," answered the duenna: "what would you have with me, friend?" "I wish, Madam Donna Rodriguez," replied Sancho, "you would be so good as to step to the castle-gate, where you will find a dapple ass of mine; and be so kind as to order him to be put into the stable, or put him there yourself; for the poor thing is a little timorous, and cannot abide to be alone." "If the master be of the same web as the man," an-

swered the duenna, " we are finely thriven! Go, brother—it was an evil
hour for you and him that brought you hither—and look after your
beast yourself, for the duennas of this house are not accustomed to do
such offices." " How now!" answered Sancho; "I have heard my
master say—and he is a notable hand at history—that when Lancelot
came from Britain ladies took care of his person, and duennas of his
horse: and as for my ass, whatever you may think, faith! I would not
swap him for Signor Launcelot's steed." " Hark ye, friend : if you are
a dealer in jests, take your wares to another market—here they will
not pass—a fig, say I, for your whole budget!" " I thank you for
that," quoth Sancho, " for I am sure it will be a ripe one : if sixty 's
the game, you will not lose it for want of a trick."

" You beast!" cried the duenna, foaming with rage; " whether I am
old or not, to Heaven I account, and not to thee—rascal, garlic-eating
stinkard!" This she uttered so loud that the duchess turned towards
them, and, seeing the duenna in such agitation, and her face and eyes
in a flame, asked her with whom she was so angry. " With this man
here," answered the duenna, " who has desired me, in good earnest, to
go and put into the stable an ass of his that stands at the castle-gate;
raking up, as an example, the tale of one Launcelot, whose steed was
attended by ladies; and, to complete his impertinence, he coolly tells me
that I am old!" " That, indeed," said the duchess, " is an affront
which cannot be endured." Then, turning to Sancho, " Be assured,
friend Sancho," said she, " you are mistaken on that point : the veil
which Donna Rodriguez wears is more for authority and fashion than
on account of her years." " May I never again know a prosperous
one," quoth Sancho, " if I meant her any offence. I only spoke because
of the great love I bear to my ass, and I thought that I could not do
better than recommend him to the charitable care of the good Signora
Donna Rodriguez." Don Quixote, hearing this altercation, now in-
terfered. " Sancho," said he, " is this a fit place for such discourse ?"
" Sir," answered Sancho, " every one must speak of his wants, let him
be where he will. Here I bethought me of Dapple, and here I spoke
of him; and if I had thought of him in the stable I should have
spoken of him there." To which the duke said, " Sancho is very
much in the right, and deserves no censure. Dapple shall have provender to his heart's content; and let Sancho take no further care, for
he shall be treated like his own person."

With this conversation — pleasing to all but Don Quixote — they
ascended the great stairs, and conducted the knight into a spacious
hall, sumptuously hung with cloth of gold and rich brocade. Six
damsels attended to take off his armour and serve as pages, all tutored
by the duke and duchess in their behaviour towards him, in order to
confirm his delusion. Don Quixote, being now unarmed, remained in
his straight breeches and chamois doubtlet, lean, tall, and stiff, with his
cheeks shrunk into his head; making such a figure that the damsels
who waited on him had much difficulty to restrain their mirth, and
observe in his presence that decorum which had been strictly enjoined

by their lord and lady. They begged that he would suffer himself to be undressed, for the purpose of changing his linen; but he would by no means consent, saying that modesty was as becoming a knight-errant as courage. However, he bade them give the shirt to Sancho; and, retiring with him to an apartment where there was a rich bed, he pulled off his clothes, and there put it on.

Being thus alone with Sancho, he said to him, "Tell me, buffoon and blockhead! dost thou imagine it a becoming thing to abuse and insult a duenna so venerable and so worthy of respect? Was that a time to think of Dapple? Or is it probable that these noble persons would suffer our beasts to fare poorly, when they treat their owners so honourably? For the love of Heaven, Sancho, restrain thyself, and discover not the grain, lest it should be seen how coarse the web is of which thou art spun. Remember, sinner, the master is esteemed in proportion as his servants are respectable and well-behaved; and one of the greatest advantages which the great enjoy over other men is that they are served by domestics of a superior mould. Dost thou not consider — plague to thyself, and torment to me!—that if it is perceived that thou art a rude clown or a conceited fool, they will be apt to think that I am an impostor, or some knight of the sharping order? Avoid, friend Sancho, pray avoid, these impertinences; for whoever sets up for a talker and a wit sinks at the first trip into a contemptible buffoon. Bridle thy tongue: consider and deliberate upon thy words before they quit thy lips; and recollect that we are now in a place whence, by the help of Heaven and the valour of my arm, we may depart bettered by three, or perhaps five-fold, in fortune and reputation." Sancho promised him faithfully to sew up his mouth or bite his tongue before he spoke a word that was not duly considered and to the purpose, and assured him that he need be under no fear of his saying anything that would tend to his worship's discredit.

Don Quixote then dressed himself, girt on his sword, threw the scarlet mantle over his shoulders, put on a green satin cap which the damsels had given him, and thus equipped, marched out into the great saloon, where he found the damsels drawn up on each side in two equal ranks, and all of them provided with an equipage for washing his hands, which they administered with many reverences and much ceremony. Then came twelve pages, with the major-domo, to conduct him to dinner, the lord and lady being now waiting for him; and, having placed him in the midst of them with great pomp and ceremony, they proceeded to another hall, where a rich table was spread out with four covers only. The duke and duchess came to the door to receive him, accompanied by a grave ecclesiastic—one of those who govern great men's houses; one of those who, not being nobly born themselves, are unable to direct the conduct of those who are so; who would have the liberality of the great measured by the narrowness of their own souls: making those whom they govern penurious, under the pretence of teaching them to be prudent. One of this species was the grave ecclesiastic who came out with the duke to receive Don Quixote. After a thousand courtly compliments mutually interchanged, Don Quixote advanced towards the table, between the duke and duchess, and, on preparing to seat themselves, they offered the upper end to Don Quixote, who would have declined it but for the pressing importunities of the duke. The ecclesiastic seated himself opposite to the knight, and the duke and duchess on each side.

Sancho was present all the while, in amazement to see the honour paid by those great people to his master; and whilst the numerous entreaties and ceremonies were passing between the duke and Don Quixote, before he would sit down at the head of the table, he said, "With your honour's leave I will tell you a story of what happened in our town about seats." Don Quixote immediately began to tremble, not doubting that he was going to say something absurd. Sancho observed him, and, understanding his looks, he said, "Be not afraid, sir, of my breaking loose, or saying anything that is not pat to the purpose. I have not forgotten the advice your worship gave me awhile ago, about talking much or little, well or ill." "I remember nothing, Sancho," answered Don Quixote; "say what thou wilt, so thou sayest it quickly." "What I would say," quoth Sancho, "is very true, for my master Don Quixote, who is present, will not suffer me to lie." "Lie as much as thou wilt for me, Sancho," replied Don Quixote; "I shall not hinder thee; but take heed what thou art going to say." "I have heeded it over and over again, so that it is as safe as if I had the game in my hand, as you shall presently see" "Your graces will do well," said Don Quixote, "to order this blockhead to retire, that you may get rid of his troublesome folly." "By the life of the duke," quoth the duchess, "Sancho shall not stir a jot from me: I have a great regard for him, and am assured of his discretion." "Many happy years may your holiness live," quoth Sancho, "for the good opinion you have of me, little as I deserve it. But the tale I would tell is this :

"A certain gentleman of our town, very rich, and of a good family —for he was descended from the Alamos of Medina del Campo, and married Donna Mencia de Quinnones, who was daughter to Don Alonzo de Maranon, knight of the Order of St. James, the same that was drowned in the Herradura, about whom that quarrel happened in our town, in which it was said my master Don Quixote had a hand, and Tommy the mad-cap, son of Balvastro the blacksmith, was hurt—pray, good master of mine, is not all this true? Speak, I beseech you, that their worships may not take me for some lying prater." "As yet," said the ecclesiastic, "I take you rather for a prater than for a liar; but I know not what I shall next take you for." "Thou hast produced so many witnesses and so many proofs," said Don Quixote, "that I cannot say but thou mayest probably be speaking truth; but for Heaven's sake shorten thy story, or it will last these two days." "He shall shorten nothing," quoth the duchess; "and, to please me, he shall tell it his own way, although he were not to finish these six days; and, should it last so long, they would be to me days of delight."

"I must tell you, then," proceeded Sancho, "that this same gentleman—whom I know as well as I do my right hand from my left, for it is not a bow-shot from my house to his—invited a husbandman to dine with him—a poor man, but mainly honest." "On, friend," said the chaplain, " for, at the rate you proceed, your tale will not reach its end till you reach the other world." " I shall stop," replied Sancho, " before I get half-way thither, if it please Heaven. This same farmer, coming to the house of the gentleman his inviter—God rest his soul, for he is dead and gone; and, moreover, died like an angel, as it is said, for I was not by myself, being at that time gone a reaping to Tembleque." " Prithee, son," said the ecclesiastic, " come back quickly from Tembleque, and stay not to bury the gentleman, unless you are determined upon more burials;—pray make an end of your tale." " The business, then," quoth Sancho, " was this: they being ready to sit down to table— methinks I see them plainer than ever." The duke and duchess were highly diverted at the impatience of the good ecclesiastic, and at the length and pauses of Sancho's tale; but Don Quixote was almost suffocated with rage and vexation. " I say, then," quoth Sancho, " that as they were both standing before the dinner-table, just ready to sit down, the farmer insisted that the gentleman should take the upper end of the table, and the gentleman as positively pressed the farmer to take it, saying he ought to be master in his own house. But the countryman, piquing himself upon his good breeding, still refused to comply, till the gentleman, losing all patience, laid both his hands upon the farmer's shoulders, and made him sit down by main force, saying, ' Sit thee down, clodpole! for in whatever place I am seated, that is the upper end to thee.' This is my tale, and truly I think it comes in here pretty much to the purpose."

The natural brown of Don Quixote's face was flushed with anger and shame at Sancho's insinuations, so that the duke and duchess, seeing his distress, endeavoured to restrain their laughter; and, to prevent further impertinence from Sancho, the duchess asked Don Quixote what news he had last received of the Lady Dulcinea, and whether he had lately sent her any presents of giants or caitiffs, since he must certainly have vanquished many. " Alas, madam!" answered he, " my misfortunes have had a beginning, but they will never have an end. Giants I have conquered, and robbers, and wicked caitiffs, and many have I sent to the mistress of my soul; but where should they find her, transformed as she now is into the homeliest rustic wench that the imagination ever conceived?" " I know not, sir, how that can be," quoth Sancho, " for to me she appeared the most beautiful creature in the world: at least for nimbleness, or in a kind of a spring she has with her, I am sure no stage tumbler can go beyond her. In good faith, my lady duchess, she springs from the ground upon an ass as if she were a cat." " Have you seen her enchanted, Sancho?" quoth the duke. " Seen her!" answered Sancho; " who the devil was it but I that first hit upon the business of her enchantment? Yes, she is as much enchanted as my father."

The ecclesiastic, when he heard talk of giants, caitiffs, and enchantments, began to suspect that this must be the Don Quixote de la Mancha whose history the duke was often reading; and he had as frequently reproved him for so doing; telling him it was idle to read such fooleries. Being assured of the truth of his suspicion, with much indignation he said to the duke, " Your excellency will be accountable to Heaven for the actions of this poor man : this Don Quixote, or Don Coxcomb, or whatever you are pleased to call him, cannot be quite so mad as your excellency would make him by thus encouraging his extravagant fancies." Then turning to Don Quixote, he said, " And you, Signor Addle-pate, who has thrust it into your brain that you are a knight-errant, and that you vanquish giants and robbers? Go, get you home in a good hour, and in such are you now admonished ; return to your family, and look to your children, if you have any : mind your affairs, and cease to be a vagabond about the world, sucking the wind, and drawing on yourself the derision of all that know you or know you not. Where, with a murrain, have you ever found that there are, or even were, in the world such creatures as knights-errant? Where are there giants in Spain, or caitiffs in La Mancha, or enchanted Dulcineas, or all the rabble rout of follies that are told of you ? " Don Quixote was very attentive to the words of the reverend gentleman, and, finding that he was now silent, regardless of the respect due to the duke and duchess, up he started with indignation and fury in his looks, and said—but his answer deserves a chapter to itself.

CHAPTER XXXII.

Of the answer Don Quixote gave to his reprover ; with other grave and pleasing events.

SPRINGING to his feet, Don Quixote, trembling like quicksilver from head to foot, in an agitated voice said, " The place where I am, and the presence of the noble personages before whom I stand, as well as the respect which I have ever entertained for your profession, restrain my just indignation ; for these reasons, and because I know, as all the world knows, that the weapons of gownsmen, like those of women, are their tongues, with the same weapon, in equal combat, I will engage your reverence, from whom good counsel might have been expected, rather than scurrility. Charitable and wholesome reproof requires a different language ; at least it must be owned that reproach so public, as well as rude, exceeds the bounds of decent reprehension. Mildness, sir, would have been better than asperity ; but was it either just or decent, at once, and without knowledge of the fault, plainly to proclaim the offender madman and idiot? Tell me, I beseech your reverence, for which of the follies you have observed in me do you thus condemn and revile me, desiring me to go home and take care of my house, and of my wife and children, without knowing whether I have either ? What ! is there nothing more to do, then, but boldly enter into other men's houses, and govern the masters, for a poor pedagogue who never saw more of the world than twenty or thirty leagues around him, rashly to presume to give laws to chivalry, and pass judgments upon knights-errant? Is it, forsooth, idleness, or time misspent, to range the world, not seeking its pleasures, but its hardships, through which good men aspire to the seat of immortality? If men, high born and of liberal minds, were to proclaim me a madman, I should regard it as an irreparable affront; but to be esteemed a fool by pedants who never trod the path of chivalry, I value it not a rush. A knight I am, and a knight I will die, if it be Heaven's good will. Some choose the spacious field of proud ambition; others the mean path of servile and base flattery; some seek the way of deceitful hypocrisy, and others that of true religion: but I, directed by the star that rules my fate, take the narrow path of knight-errantry; despising wealth, but thirsting for honour. I have redressed grievances, righted wrongs, chastised insolence, vanquished giants, and trampled upon hobgoblins: I am enamoured—for knights-errant must be so; but I am conscious of no licentious passion—my love is of the chaste Platonic kind. My intentions are always directed to virtuous ends—to do good to all, and injury to none. Whether he who thus means, thus acts, and thus lives, deserves to be called fool, let your highnesses judge, most excellent duke and duchess."

"Well said, i' faith!" quoth Sancho. "Say no more for yourself, good lord and master, for there is nothing more in the world to be said, thought, or done. And besides, this gentleman denying, as he has denied, that there neither are, nor ever were, knights-errant, no wonder if he knows nothing of what he has been talking about." "So, then," said the ecclesiastic, "you, I suppose, are the same Sancho Panza they talk of, to whom it is said your master has promised an island?" "I am that Sancho," replied the squire, "and deserve it too, as well as any other he whatever. Of such as me it is said, 'Keep company with the good, and thou wilt be one of them;' and, 'Not with whom thou wert bred, but with whom thou hast fed;' and, 'He that leaneth against a good tree, a good shelter findeth he.' I have leaned and stuck close to a good master these many months, and shall be such another as he, if it be God's good pleasure; and if he lives, and I live, neither shall he want kingdoms to rule, nor I islands to govern."

"That you shall not, friend Sancho," said the duke, "for in the name of Signor Don Quixote, I promise you the government of one of mine now vacant, and of no inconsiderable value."

"Kneel, Sancho," said Don Quixote, "and kiss his excellency's feet, for the favour he has done thee." Sancho did so; upon which the ecclesiastic got up from the table in great wrath, saying, "By the habit I wear, I could find in my heart to say that your excellency is as simple as these sinners; no wonder they are mad, since wise men authorize their follies! Your excellency may stay with them, if you please; but while they are in this house I will remain in my own, and save myself the trouble of reproving where I cannot amend." Then, without saying another word, and leaving his meal unfinished, away he went, in spite of the entreaties of the duke and duchess : though, indeed, the duke could not say much, through laughter at his foolish petulance.

As soon as his laughter would allow him, the duke said to Don Quixote, " Sir Knight of the Lions, you have answered so well for yourself and your profession, that you can require no further satisfaction of the angry clergyman ; especially if you consider that, whatever he might say, it was impossible for him, as you well know, to affront a person of your character." " It is true, my lord," answered Don Quixote; " whoever cannot receive an affront cannot give one. Women, children, and churchman, as they cannot defend themselves if attacked, so they cannot be affronted, because, as your excellency better knows, there is this difference between an injury and an affront : an affront must come from a person who not only gives it, but who can maintain it when it is given ; an injury may come from any hand. A man, for example, walking in the street, is unexpectedly set upon by ten armed men, who beat him : he draws his sword to avenge the injury, but, the assailants overpowering him by numbers, he is compelled to forego the satisfaction he desired : this person is injured, but not affronted. Again, let us suppose one man to come secretly behind another and strike him with a cudgel, then run away : the man pursues him, but the offender escapes : he who received the blow is injured, it is true, but has received no affront, because the violence offered is not maintained. If he who gave the blow, though it was done basely, stands his ground to answer for the deed, then he who was struck is both injured and affronted : injured because he was struck in a secret and cowardly manner, and affronted because he who gave the blow stood his ground to maintain what he had done. According to the laws of duel, therefore, I may be injured, but not affronted ; for, as women and children can neither resent nor maintain opposition, so it is with the clergy, who carry no weapons, either offensive or defensive ; and, though they have a right to ward off all violence offered to themselves, they can offer no affront that demands honourable satisfaction. Upon consideration, therefore, although I before said I was injured, I now affirm that it could not be ; for he who can receive no affront can give none ; and, consequently, I neither ought, nor do, feel any resentment for what that good man said to me — only I could have wished he had stayed a little longer, that I might have convinced him of his error in supposing that knights-errant never existed in the world. Indeed, had Amadis, or any of his numerous descendants, heard so strange an assertion, I am persuaded it would have gone hard with his reverence." " That I will swear," quoth Sancho : " at one slash they would have cleft him from top to bottom like a pomegranate ; they were not folks to be so jested with. Ods life ! had Reynaldos de Montalvan heard the little gentleman talk at that rate, he would have given him such a gag as would have stopped his mouth for three years at least. Aye, aye, let him fall into their clutches, and see how he will get out again !" The duchess was overcome with laughter at Sancho's zeal, and thought him more diverting and mad than his master ; indeed many others at that time were of the same opinion.

*The damsel who held the basin now respectfully approached the knight
and placed it under his beard.*

At length, Don Quixote being pacified and calm, and the dinner
ended, the cloth was removed; whereupon four damsels entered, one with
a silver ewer, another with a basin, also of silver, a third with two fine
clean towels over her shoulder, and the fourth with her sleeves tucked
up to her elbows, and in her white hands (for doubtless they were white)
a wash-ball of Naples soap. The damsel who held the basin now respectfully approached the knight, and placed it under his beard; while he,
wondering at the ceremony, yet believing it to be the custom of that
country to wash beards instead of hands, obediently thrust out his chin
as far as he could; whereupon the ewer began to rain upon his face,
while the damsel of the wash-ball lathered his beard with great dexterity,
covering with a snow-white froth, not only the beard, but the whole face
of the submissive knight, even over his eyes, which he was compelled to
close. The duke and duchess, who were not in the secret, were eager to

know the issue of this extraordinary ablution. The barber damsel having raised a lather a span high, pretended that the water was all used, and ordered the girl with the ewer to fetch more, telling her that Signor Don Quixote would stay till she came back. Thus he was left, the strangest and most ridiculous figure imaginable, to the gaze of all that were present; and, seeing him with his neck half an ell long, more than moderately swarthy, his eyes half-shut, and his whole visage under a covering of white foam, it was marvellous, and a sign of great discretion, that they were able to preserve their gravity.

The damsels concerned in the jest gazed steadfastly on the ground, not daring to look at their lord or lady, who were divided between anger and mirth, not knowing whether to chastise the girls for their boldness, or reward them for the amusement their device had afforded. The water nymph returned, and the beard-washing was finished, when she who was charged with the towels performed the office of wiping and drying with much deliberation; and thus the ceremony being concluded, the four damsels at once, making him a profound reverence, were retiring, when the duke, to prevent Don Quixote from suspecting the jest, called the damsel with the basin, and said, " Come and do your duty, and take care that you have water enough." The girl, who was shrewd and active, went up, and applied the basin to the duke's chin in the same manner she had done to that of Don Quixote; and with equal adroitness, but more celerity, repeated the ceremony of lathering, washing, and wiping; and the whole being done, they made their courtesies, and retired. The duke, however, had declared, as it afterwards appeared, that he would have chastised them for their pertness, if they had refused to serve him in the same manner.

Sancho was very attentive to this washing ceremony. " Heaven guide me ! " said he, muttering to himself; " is it the custom, I wonder, of this place to wash the beards of squires, as well as of knights? On my conscience and soul, I need it much; and if they would give me a stroke of a razor, I should take it for a still greater favour." " What are you saying to yourself, Sancho ?" quoth the duchess. " I say, madam," answered Sancho, " that in other houses of the great, I have always heard that, when the cloth is taken away, the custom is to bring water to wash hands, but not suds to scour beards; and therefore one must live long to see much. It is also said, he who lives long must suffer much; though, if I am not mistaken, to be so scoured must be rather a pleasure than a pain." " Be under no concern, friend Sancho," quoth the duchess; " for I will order my damsels to see to your washing, and to lay you a bucking too, if needful." " For the present, if my beard get a scouring I shall be content," said Sancho; " for the rest, Heaven will provide hereafter." " Here, steward," said the duchess, " attend to the wishes of good Sancho, and do precisely as he would have you." He answered that Signor Sancho should in all things be punctually obeyed; and he then went to dinner, and took Sancho along with him.

Meantime, Don Quixote remained with the duke and duchess, discoursing on divers matters relating to arms and knight-errantry. The duchess entreated Don Quixote, since he seemed to have so happy a memory, that he would delineate and describe the beauty and accomplishments of the Lady Dulcinea del Toboso; for, if fame spoke the truth, she must needs be the fairest creature in the world, and, consequently, in La Mancha. "Madam," said Don Quixote, heaving a deep sigh, "if I could pluck out my heart and place it before you on this table, your highness would there behold her painted to the life, and I might save my tongue the fruitless labour of describing that which can scarcely be conceived; for how am I to delineate or describe the perfections of that paragon of excellence? My shoulders are unequal to so mighty a burden : it is a task worthy of the pencils of Parrhasius, Timantes, and Apelles, and the chisel of Lysippus, to produce, in speaking pictures, or statues of bronze or marble, a copy of her beauties, and Ciceronian and Demosthenian eloquence to describe them."

"Pray, Signor Don Quixote," said the duchess, "what do you mean by Demosthenian?—a word I do not recollect ever hearing." "Demosthenian eloquence," answered Don Quixote, "means the eloquence of Demosthenes, as Ciceronian is that of Cicero, who were the two greatest orators and rhetoricians in the world." "That is true," said the duke, "and you betrayed your ignorance in asking such a question; nevertheless, Signor Don Quixote would give us great pleasure by endeavouring to paint her to us; for though it be only a rough sketch, doubtless she will appear such as the most beautiful may envy." "Ah! my lord, so she certainly would," answered Don Quixote, "had not the misfortune which lately befell her blurred and defaced the lovely idea, and razed it from my memory : such a misfortune, that I ought rather to bewail what she suffers than describe what she is; for your excellencies must know that, going, not many days since, to kiss her hands and receive her benediction, with her commands and license for this third sally, I found her quite another person than her I sought for. I found her enchanted and transformed from a princess into a country wench, from beautiful to ugly, from an angel to a fiend, from fragrant to pestiferous, from courtly to rustic, from light to darkness, from a dignified lady to a jumping Joan—in fine, from Dulcinea del Toboso to an unsightly bumpkin of Sayago." "Heaven defend me!" exclaimed the duke, elevating his voice, "what villain can have done the world so much injury? who has deprived it of the beauty that delighted it, the grace that charmed, and the modesty that did it honour?" "Who?" answered Don Quixote, "who could it be but some malicious enchanter, of the many that persecute me : that wicked brood that was sent into the world only to obscure and annihilate the exploits of the good, and to blazon forth and magnify the actions of the wicked? Enchanters have hitherto persecuted me; enchanters now persecute me; and so they will continue to do until they have overwhelmed me and my lofty chivalries into the profound abyss of oblivion. Yes, even in the most sensible part they injure and wound me : well knowing that to deprive a knight-errant of his mistress is to deprive him of the eyes he sees with, the sun that enlightens him, and the food that sustains him; for, as I have often said, and now repeat it, a knight-errant without a mistress is like a tree without leaves, an edifice without cement, and a shadow without the material substance by which it should be cast."

" All this," said the duchess, " is not to be denied ; yet if the published history of Don Quixote, so much applauded by all nations, be worthy of credit, we are bound by that authority, if I am not mistaken, to think that there is no such lady in the world, she being only an imaginary lady, begotten and born of your own brain, and dressed out with all the graces and perfections of your fancy !" " There is much to be said upon this point," answered Don Quixote. " Heavens knows whether there be a Dulcinea in the world or not, and whether she be imaginary or not imaginary : these are things not to be too nicely inquired into. I neither begot nor brought forth my mistress, though I contemplate her as a lady endowed with all those qualifications which may spread the glory of her name over the whole world—such as possessing beauty without blemish, dignity without pride, love with modesty, politeness springing from courtesy, and courtesy from good-breeding, and, finally, of illustrious descent ; for the beauty that is of a noble race shines with more splendour than that which is meanly born." " That cannot be doubted," quoth the duke ; " but Signor Don Quixote must here give me leave to speak on the authority of the history of his exploits ; for there, although it be allowed that, either in or out of Toboso, there is actually a Dulcinea, and that she is no less beautiful and accomplished than your worship has described her, it does not appear that, in respect to high descent, she is upon a level with the Orianas, the Alastrajareas, Madasimas, and many others, whose names, as you well know, are celebrated in history."

" The Lady Dulcinea," replied Don Quixote, " is the daughter of her own works ; and your grace will acknowledge that virtue ennobles blood, and that a virtuous person of humble birth is more estimable than a vicious person of rank. Besides, that incomparable lady has endowments which may raise her to a crown and sceptre ; for still greater miracles are within the power of a beautiful and virtuous woman. And though she may not, in form, possess the advantage you question, the want is more than compensated by that mine of intrinsic worth which is her true inheritance." " Certainly, Signor Don Quixote," cried the duchess, " you tread with great caution, and, as the saying is, with the plummet in hand ; nevertheless, I am determined to believe, and make all my family, and even my lord duke, if necessary, believe, that there is a Dulcinea del Toboso, and that she is at this moment living, beautiful, highly born, and well deserving that such a knight as Signor Don Quixote should be her servant, which is the highest commendation I can bestow upon her. But there yet remains a small matter on my mind, concerning which I cannot entirely excuse my friend Sancho ; and it is this : in the history of your deeds we are told that, when Sancho Panza took your worship's letter to the Lady Dulcinea, he found her winnowing a sack of wheat, and that, too, of the coarsest kind—a circumstance that seems incompatible with her high birth."

To this Don Quixote replied, " Your grace must know that, whether directed by the inscrutable will of fate, or contrived by the malice of envious enchanters, it is certain that all, or the greater part, of what has befallen me, is of a more extraordinary nature than what usually happens to other knights-errant; and it is well known that the most famous of that order had their privileges : one was exempt from the power of enchantment; the flesh of another was impenetrable to wounds, as was the case with the renowned Orlando, one of the twelve peers of France, who, it is said, was invulnerable except in the heel of the left foot, and that, too, accessible to no weapon but the point of a large pin ; so that Bernardo del Carpio (who killed him at Roncesvalles), perceiving that he could not wound him with steel, snatched him from the ground, and squeezed him to death betwixt his arms; recollecting, probably, that the giant Antæus was so destroyed by Hercules. It may fairly be presumed, therefore, that I have some of those privileges—not that of being invulnerable, for experience has often shown me that I am made of tender flesh, and by no means impenetrable; nor that of being exempt from the power of enchantment, for I have already been confined in a cage, into which, but for that power, the whole world could never have forced me. However, since I freed myself thence, I am inclined to believe no other can reach me; and therefore these enchanters, seeing they cannot practise their wicked artifices upon my person, wreak their vengeance upon the object of my affections; hoping, by their evil treatment of her in whom I exist, to take that life which would, otherwise, be proof against their incantations. I am convinced, therefore, that, when Sancho delivered my message to the Lady Dulcinea, they presented her to him in the form of a country wench engaged in the mean employment of winnowing wheat. But, as I have said before, what she seemed to winnow was not red, neither was it wheat, but grains of oriental pearl : and, in confirmation of this, I must tell your excellencies that, passing lately through Toboso, I could nowhere find the palace of Dulcinea ; nay more, not many days ago she was seen by my squire in her proper figure, the most beautiful that can be imagined, while at the same moment she appeared to me as a coarse, ugly country wench, and her language, instead of being discretion itself, was no less offensive. Thus, then, it appears that, since I am not, and probably cannot be, enchanted, she is made to suffer : she is the enchanted, the injured, the metamorphosed, and transformed ; in her my enemies have revenged themselves on me, and for her I shall live in perpetual tears till I see her restored to her pristine state.

" All this I say, that nothing injurious to my lady may be inferred from what Sancho has related of her sifting and winnowing ; for, if she appeared so changed to me at one time, no wonder that she should seem transformed to him at another. Assuredly, the peerless Dulcinea is highly born, and allied in blood to the best and most ancient families of Toboso, which town will, from her name, be no less famous in after ages than Troy is for its Helen, and Spain for its Cava ; though on a more honourable account. And in regard to my squire Sancho Panza,

I beg your highnesses will do him the justice to believe that never was knight-errant served by a squire of more pleasantry. His shrewdness and simplicity appear at times so curiously mingled, that it is amusing to consider which of the two prevails: he has cunning enough to be suspected of knavery, and absurdity enough to be thought a fool. He doubts everything, yet he believes everything; and, when I imagine him about to sink into a downright idiot, out comes some observation so pithy and sagacious that I know not where to stop in my admiration. In short, I would not exchange him for any other squire, though a city were offered me in addition; and therefore I am in doubt whether I shall do well to send him to the government your highness has conferred on him, though I perceive in him a capacity so well suited to such an office, that, with but a moderate addition of polish to his understanding, he will be a perfect master in the art of governing. Besides, we know by sundry proofs, that neither great talents nor much learning are necessary to such appointments; for there are hundreds of governors who, though they can scarcely read, yet in their duty are as sharp as hawks. The chief requisite is a good intention: those who have no other desire than to act uprightly will always find able and virtuous counsellors to instruct them. Governors, being soldiers, and therefore probably unlearned, have often need of an assistant to be ready with advice. My counsel to Sancho would be, ' All bribes to refuse, but insist on his dues;' with some other little matters which lie in my breast, and which shall come forth in proper time for Sancho's benefit and the welfare of the island he is to govern."

In this manner were the duke, the duchess, and Don Quixote conversing, when suddenly a great noise of many voices was heard in another part of the palace, and presently Sancho rushed into the saloon, with a terrified countenance, and a dish-clout under his chin, followed by a number of kitchen helpers and other inferior servants; one of whom carried a trough full of something that seemed to be dish-water, with which he followed close upon Sancho, and made many efforts to place it under his chin, while another scullion seemed equally eager to wash his beard with it.

"What is the matter, fellows?" quoth the duchess; "what would you do with this good man? do you not know that he is a governor-elect?" "This gentleman," said the roguish beard-washer, "will not suffer himself to be washed, according to custom, and as our lord the duke and his master have been." "Yes, I will," answered Sancho, in great wrath, "but I would have cleaner towels and clearer suds, and not such filthy hands; for there is no such difference between me and my master that he should be washed with angel water and I with devil's ley. The customs of countries or of great men's houses are good as far as they are agreeable; but this of beard scouring, here, is worse than the friar's scourge. My beard is clean, and I have no need of such refreshings; and he who offers to scour me, or touch a hair of my head—my beard, I should say—with due reverence be it spoken, shall feel the full weight of my fist upon his skull; for such ceremonies

The duchess was convulsed with laughter at Sancho's remonstrances and rage.

and soapings to my thinking look more like jokes and jibes than a civil welcome."

The duchess was convulsed with laughter at Sancho's remonstrances and rage, but Don Quixote could not endure to behold his squire so accoutred with a filthy towel, and baited by a kitchen rabble. Making, therefore, a low bow to the duke and duchess, as if requesting their permission to speak, he said to the greasy tribe, in a solemn voice, "Hark ye, good people, be pleased to let the young man alone, and return whence ye came, or whither ye list; for my squire is as clean as another man, and these troughs are as odious to him as a narrow-necked jug. Take my advice, and leave him; for neither he nor I understand this kind of jesting." "No, no," quoth Sancho, interrupting his master,

" let them go on with their sport, and see whether I will bear it or no.
Let them bring hither a comb, or what else they please, and curry this
beard, and if they find anything there that should not be there, I will
give them leave to shear me cross-wise."

" Sancho Panza is perfectly right," said the duchess, " and will be
so in whatever he shall say : he is clean, and, as he truly says, needs
no washing ; and, if he be not pleased with our custom, he is master of
his own will.   Besides, unmannerly scourers, you who are so forward
to purify others, are yourselves shamefully idle—in truth, I should say
impudent—to bring your troughs and greasy dish-clouts to such a personage and such a beard, instead of ewers and basins of pure gold,
and towels of Dutch diaper.   Out of my sight, barbarians ! low-born
wretches ! who cannot help showing the spite and envy you bear to the
squires of knights-errant ! "

The roguish crew, and even the major-domo, who accompanied them,
thought the duchess was in earnest, and, hastily removing the foul cloth
from Sancho's neck, they slunk away in confusion.   The squire, on being
thus delivered from what he thought imminent danger, threw himself on
his knees before the duchess.   " Heaven bless your highness," quoth he ;
" great persons are able to do great kindnessess.   For my part, I know
not how to repay your ladyship for that you have just done me, and can
only wish myself dubbed a knight-errant, that I may employ all the days
of my life in the service of so high a lady.   A peasant I am, Sancho
Panza my name ; I am married, I have children, and I serve as a squire :
if with any one of these I can be serviceable to your grandeur, I shall be
nimbler in obeying than your ladyship in commanding."

" It plainly appears, Sancho," answered the duchess, " that you have
learned to be courteous in the school of courtesy itself—I mean, it is
evident that you have been bred under the wing of Signor Don Quixote,
who is the very cream of complaisance, and the flower of ceremony.
Well may it fare with such a master and such a man !—the one the polar
star of knight-errantry, and the other the bright luminary of squire-like
fidelity !   Rise up, friend Sancho, and be assured I will reward your
courtesy by prevailing with my lord duke to hasten the performance of
the promise he has made you of a government."

Here the conversation ceased, and Don Quixote went to repose during
the heat of the day ; and the duchess desired Sancho, if he had no inclination to sleep, to pass the afternoon with her and her damsels in a very
cool apartment.   Sancho said, in reply, that, though he was wont to
sleep four or five hours a day during the afternoon heats of the summer,
yet, to wait upon her highness, he would endeavour, with all his might,
not to sleep at all that day, and would be at her service.   He accordingly retired with the duchess ; while the duke made further arrangements concerning the treatment of Don Quixote, being desirous that it
should in all things be strictly conformable to the style in which it is
recorded the knights of former times were treated.

BOOK III.

CHAPTER XXXIII.

Of the relishing conversation which passed between the duchess, her damsels, and Sancho Panza—worthy to be read and noted.

THE history then relates that Sancho Panza did not take his afternoon sleep, but, in compliance with his promise, went immediately after his dinner to see the duchess, who, being delighted to hear him talk, desired him to sit down by her on a stool, although Sancho, out of pure good manners, would have declined it ; but the duchess told him that he must be seated as a governor and talk as a squire, since in both those capacities he deserved the very seat of the famous champion Cid Ruy Diaz. Sancho therefore submitted, and placed himself close by the duchess, while all her damsels and duennas drew near and stood in silent attention to hear the conversation. "Now that we are alone," said the duchess, " where nobody can overhear us, I wish Signor Governor would satisfy me as to certain doubts that have arisen from the printed history of the great Don Quixote : one of which is that, as honest Sancho never saw Dulcinea—I mean the Lady Dulcinea del Toboso—nor delivered to her the letter of Don Quixote, which was left in the pocket-book in the Sierra Morena, I would be glad to know how he could presume to feign an answer to that letter, or assert that he found her winnowing wheat, which he must have known to be altogether false, and much to the prejudice of the peerless Dulcinea's character, as well as inconsistent with the duty and fidelity of a trusty squire."

At these words, without making any reply, Sancho got up from his stool, and with his body bent, and the tip of his forefinger on his lips, he stepped softly round the room, lifting up the hangings ; and this done, he sat himself down again, and said, "Now, madam, that I am sure that nobody but the company present can hear us, I will answer, without fear, to all you ask of me : and the first thing I tell you is that I take my master Don Quixote for a downright madman ; and though sometimes he will talk in a way which, to my thinking, and in the opinion of all who hear him, is so much to the purpose that Satan himself could not speak better, yet, for all that, I believe him to be really and truly mad. Now, this being so, as in my mind it is, nothing is more easy than to make him believe anything, though it has neither head nor tail ; like that affair of the answer to the letter, and another matter of some six or eight days' standing, which is not yet in print—I mean the enchantment of my mistress Donna Dulcinea; for you must know I made him believe she was enchanted, though it was no more true than that the moon is a horn lantern."

The duchess desired him to tell her the particulars of that enchantment or jest; and Sancho recounted the whole exactly as it had passed, very much to the entertainment of his hearers. "From what honest Sancho has told me," said the duchess, "a certain scruple troubles me, and something whispers in my ear, saying, 'Since Don Quixote de la Mancha is such a lunatic and simpleton, surely Sancho Panza, his squire, who knows it, and yet follows and serves him, relying on his vain promises, must be more mad than his master! Now this being the case, it will surely turn to bad account, lady duchess, if to such a Sancho Panza thou givest an island to govern; for how should he who rules himself so ill be able to govern others?'"

"Faith, madam," quoth Sancho, "that same scruple is an honest scruple, and need not speak in a whisper, but plain out, or as it lists; for I know it says true, and had I been wise, I should long since have left my master; but such is my lot, or such my evil-errantry, I cannot help it—follow him I must: we are both of the same town, I have eaten his bread, I love him, and he returns my love; he gave me his ass-colts; above all, I am faithful, so that nothing in the world can part us but the sexton's spade and shovel; and if your highness does not choose to give me the government you promised, God made me without it, and perhaps it may be all the better for my conscience if I do not get it; for fool as I am, I understand the proverb, 'The pismire had wings to her sorrow;' and perhaps it may be easier for Sancho the squire to get to heaven than for Sancho the governor. They make as good bread here as in France; and by night all cats are grey; unhappy is he who has not breakfasted at three; and no stomach is a span bigger than another, and may be filled, as they say, with straw or with hay. Of the little birds in the air, God himself takes the care; and four yards of coarse cloth of Cuenza are warmer than as many of fine Segovia serge; and in travelling from this world to the next, the road is no wider for the prince than the peasant. The Pope's body takes up no more room than that of the sexton, though a loftier person; for in the grave we must pack close together, whether we like it or not; so good night to all. And let me tell you again that, if your highness will not give me the island because I am a fool, I will be wise enough not to care a fig for it. I have heard say the devil lurks behind the cross: all is not gold that glitters. From the plough-tail Bamba was raised to the throne of Spain, and from his riches and revels was Roderigo cast down to be devoured by serpents, if ancient ballads tell the truth."

"And how should they lie?" said the duenna Rodriguez, who was among the attendants. "I remember one that relates to a king named Roderigo, who was shut up all alive in a tomb full of toads snakes, and lizards; and how, after two days' imprisonment, his voice was heard from the tomb, crying in a dolorous tone, 'Now they gnaw me, now they gnaw me in the part by which I sinned the most!' And according to this, the gentleman has much reason to say he would rather be a poor labourer than a king, to be devoured by such vermin."

The duchess was highly amused with Sancho's proverbs and philosophy, as well as the simplicity of her duenna. "My good Sancho knows full well," said she, "that the promise of a knight is held so sacred by him that he will perform it even at the expense of life. The duke, my lord and husband, though he is not of the errant order, is nevertheless a knight, and therefore will infallibly keep his word as to the promised government. Let Sancho, then, be of good cheer; for, in spite of the envy and malice of the world, before he is aware of it he may find himself seated in the state chair of his island and territory, in full possession of a government for which he would refuse one of brocade three storeys high. What I charge him is, to take heed how he governs his vassals, and forget not that they are well born and of approved loyalty." "As to the matter of governing," answered Sancho, "let me alone for that. I am naturally charitable and good to the poor, and 'None shall dare the loaf to steal from him that sifts and kneads the meal.' By my beads! they shall put no false dice upon me. An old dog is not to be coaxed with a crust, and I know how to snuff my eyes and keep the cobwebs from them; for I can tell where the shoe pinches. All this I say to assure your highness that the good shall have me hand and heart, while the bad shall find neither the one nor t' other. And, as to governing well, the main point, in my mind, is to make a good beginning; and, that being done, who knows but that by the time I have been fifteen days a governor, my fingers may get so nimble in the office that they will tickle it off better than the drudgery I was bred to in the field?"

"You are in the right, Sancho," quoth the duchess, "for everything wants time: men are not scholars at their birth, and bishops are made of men, not of stones. But, to return to the subject we were just now upon, concerning the transformation of the Lady Dulcinea. I have reason to think that Sancho's artifice to deceive his master, and make him believe the peasant girl to be Dulcinea enchanted, was, in fact, all a contrivance of some one of the magicians who persecute Don Quixote; for, really and in truth, I know from very good authority that the country wench who so lightly sprang upon her ass was verily Dulcinea del Toboso herself; and that my good Sancho, in thinking he had deceived his master, was himself much more deceived; and there is no more doubt of this than of any other things that we never saw. For Signor Sancho Panza must know that here also we have our enchanters, who favour us and tell us faithfully all that passes in the world; and believe me, Sancho, the jumping wench was really Dulcinea, and is as certainly charmed as the mother that bore her; and, when we least expect it, we shall see her again in her own true shape: then will Sancho discover that it was he who has been imposed upon, and not his master."

"All that might well be," quoth Sancho; "and now I begin to believe what my master told of Montesinos' cave, where he saw my lady Dulcinea del Toboso in exactly the same figure and dress as when it came into my head to enchant her, with my own will, as I fancied, though, as your ladyship says, it must have been quite otherwise. Lord bless us! How can it be supposed that my poor head-piece could, in an instant, have contrived so cunning a device, or who could think my master such a goose as to believe so unlikely a matter, upon no better voucher than myself? But, madam, your goodness will know better than to think the worse of me for all that. Lack-a-day! it cannot be expected that an ignorant lout, as I am, should be able to smell out the tricks and wiles of wicked magicians. I contrived the thing with no intention to offend my master, but only to escape his chiding; and if it has happened otherwise, God is in heaven, and He is the judge of hearts." "That is honestly spoken," quoth the duchess; "but, Sancho, did you not mention something of Montesinos' cave? I should be glad to know what you meant." Sancho then gave her highness an account of that adventure, with its circumstances; and when he had done, "See now," quoth the duchess, "if this does not confirm what I have just said! for, since the great Don Quixote affirms that he saw the very same country wench whom Sancho met coming from Toboso, she certainly must be Dulcinea, and it shows that the enchanters hereabouts are very busy and excessively officious."

"Well," quoth Sancho Panza, "if my lady be enchanted, so much the worse for her. I do not think myself bound to quarrel with my master's enemies, for they must needs be many, and very wicked ones too. Still I must say, and it cannot be denied, that she I saw was a country wench: a country wench at least I took her to be, and such I thought her; and if that same lass really happened to be Dulcinea, I am not to be called to account for it, nor ought it to be laid at my door. Sancho, truly, would have enough to do if he must answer for all, and at every turn to be told that Sancho said it, Sancho did it, Sancho came back, Sancho returned; as if Sancho were anybody they pleased, and not that very Sancho Panza handed about in print all the world over, as Sampson Carrasco told me, who, at least, has been bachelorized at Salamanca; and such persons cannot lie, unless when they have a mind to do so, or when it may turn to good account: so that there is no reason to meddle or make with me, since I have a good name, and, as I have heard my master say, a good name is better than bags of gold. Case me but in that same government, and you shall see wonders; for a good squire will make a good governor."

"Sancho speaks like an oracle," quoth the duchess; "all that he has now said are so many sentences of Cato, or at least extracted from the very marrow of Michael Verino himself—'*florentibus occidit annis:*' in short, to speak in his own way, a bad cloak often covers a good drinker."

"Truly, madam," answered Sancho, "I never in my life drank for any bad purpose; for thirst, perhaps, I have, as I am no hypocrite. I drink when I want it, and if it is offered to me, rather than be thought ill-mannered; for when a friend drinks one's health, who can be so hard-hearted as not to pledge him? But though I put on the shoes, they are no dirtier for me. And truly there is no fear of that, for water is your common drink of squires-errant, who are always wandering about woods, forests, meadows, mountains, and craggy rocks, where no one merciful drop of wine is to be got, though they would give an eye for it." "In truth, I believe it," said the duchess: " but, as it grows late, go, Sancho, and repose yourself, and we will talk of these matters again hereafter, and orders shall speedily be given about casing you, as you call it, in the government."

Sancho again kissed the duchess's hand, and begged of her, as a favour, that good care might be taken of his Dapple, for he was the light of his eyes. " What mean you by Dapple?" quoth the duchess. "I mean my ass, please your highness," replied Sancho; "for not to give him that name, I commonly call him Dapple; and I desired this good mistress here, when I first came into the castle, to take care of him, which made her as angry as if I had called her old and ugly; yet in my mind, it would be more proper and natural for duennas to take charge of asses than strut about like ladies in rooms of state. Heaven save me! what a deadly grudge a certain gentleman in our town had for these madams." " Some filthy clown, I make no question," quoth Donna Rodriguez; "for had he been a gentleman, and known what good breeding was, he would have placed them under the horns of the moon."

"Enough," quoth the duchess, "let us have no more of this: peace, Donna Rodriguez; and you, Signor Panza, be quiet, and leave the care of making much of Dapple to me; for being a jewel of Sancho's, I will lay him upon the apple of my eye." "Let him lie in the stable, my good lady," answered Sancho, "for upon the apple of your grandeur's eye neither he nor I are worthy to lie one single moment, — 'slife! they should stick me like a sheep sooner than I would consent to such a thing; for though my master says that, in respect to good manners, we should rather lose the game by a card too much than too little, yet, when the business in hand is about asses and eyes, we should step warily, with compass in hand." " Carry him, Sancho," quoth the duchess, "to your government, and there you may regale him as you please, and set him free from further labour." "Think not, my lady duchess," quoth Sancho, " that you have said much; for I have seen more asses than one go to governments, and therefore, if I should carry mine, it would be nothing new." The relish of Sancho's conversation was not lost upon the duchess, who, after dismissing him to his repose, went to give the duke an account of all that had passed between them. They afterwards consulted together how they should practise some jest upon Don Quixote, to humour his knight-errantry; and indeed they devised many of that kind, so ingenious and appropriate as to be accounted among the prime adventures that occur in this great history.

CHAPTER XXXIV.

Giving an account of the method prescribed for disenchanting the peerless Dulcinea del Tobosc; which is one of the most famous adventures in this book.

THE duke and duchess were extremely diverted with the humours of their two guests; and resolving to improve their sport by practising some pleasantries that should have the appearance of a romantic adventure, they contrived to dress up a very choice entertainment from Don Quixote's account of the cave of Montesinos : taking that subject because the duchess had observed, with astonishment, that Sancho now believed his lady Dulcinea was really enchanted, although he himself had been her sole enchanter ! Accordingly, after the servants had been well instructed as to their deportment towards Don Quixote, a boar-hunt was proposed, and it was determined to set out in five or six days with a princely train of huntsmen. The knight was presented with a hunting suit proper for the occasion, which, however, he declined, saying that he must soon return to the severe duties of his profession, when, having no sumpters or wardrobes, such things would be superfluous. But Sancho readily accepted a suit of fine green cloth which was offered to him, intending to sell it on the first opportunity.

The appointed day being come, Don Quixote armed himself, and Sancho in his new suit mounted Dapple (which he preferred to a horse that was offered him), and joined the troop of hunters. The duchess issued forth magnificently attired, and Don Quixote, out of pure politeness, would hold the reins of the palfrey, though the duke was unwilling to allow it. Having arrived at the proposed scene of their diversion, which was in a wood between two lofty mountains, they posted themselves in places where the toils were to be pitched; and all the party having taken their different stations, the sport began with prodigious noise and clamour, insomuch that, between the shouts of the huntsmen, the cry of the hounds, and the sound of the horns, they could not hear each other. The duchess alighted, and, with a boar-spear in her hand, took her stand in a place where she expected the boars would pass. The duke and Don Quixote dismounted also, and placed themselves by her side; while Sancho took his station behind them all, with his Dapple, whom he would not quit, lest some mischance should befall him. Scarcely had they ranged themselves in order, when a hideous boar of monstrous size rushed out of cover, pursued by the dogs and hunters, and made directly towards them, gnashing his teeth, and tossing foam with his mouth. Don Quixote, on seeing him approach, braced his shield, and, drawing his sword, stepped before the rest to meet him. The duke joined him with his boar-spear, and the duchess would have

Sancho was no sooner released than he began to examine the rent in his hunting suit.

been the foremost, had not the duke prevented her. Sancho alone
stood aghast, and, at the sight of the fierce animal, leaving even his
Dapple, ran in terror towards a lofty oak, in which he hoped to be
secure; but his hopes were in vain, for, as he was struggling to reach
the top, and had got half-way up, unfortunately a branch to which he
clung gave way, and, falling with it, he was caught by the stump of
another, and here left suspended in the air, so that he could neither get
up nor down. Finding himself in this situation, with his new green
coat tearing, and almost in reach of the terrible creature, should it
chance to come that way, he began to bawl so loud, and to call for help
so vehemently, that all who heard him and did not see him thought
verily he was between the teeth of some wild beast. The tusked boar,
however, was soon laid at length by the numerous spears that were
levelled at him from all sides; at which time Sancho's cries and lamentations reached the ears of Don Quixote, who, turning round, beheld
him hanging from the oak with his head downwards, and close by him

stood Dapple, who never forsook him in adversity; indeed, it was remarked by Cid Hamet, that he seldom saw Sancho Panza without his Dapple, or Dapple without Sancho Panza: such was the amity and cordial love that subsisted between them! Don Quixote hastened to the assistance of his squire, who was no sooner released than he began to examine the rent in his hunting suit, which grieved him to the soul; for he looked upon that suit as a rich inheritance.

The huge animal they had slain was laid across a sumpter-mule, and after covering it with branches of rosemary and myrtle, they carried it, as the spoils of victory, to a large field tent, erected in the midst of the wood, where a sumptuous entertainment was prepared, worthy of the magnificence of the donor. Sancho, showing the wounds of the torn garments to the duchess, said, "Had hares or birds been our game, I should not have had this misfortune. For my own part, I cannot think what pleasure there can be in beating about for a monster that, if it reaches you with a tusk, may be the death of you. There is an old ballad which says—

> " ' May fate of Fabila be thine,
> And make thee food for bears or swine.' "

"That Fabila," said Don Quixote, "was a king of the Goths, who, going to the chase, was devoured by a bear." "What I mean," quoth Sancho, "is, that I would not have kings and other great folks run into such dangers merely for pleasure; and, indeed, methinks it ought to be none to kill poor beasts that never meant any harm." "You are mistaken, Sancho," said the duke; "hunting wild beasts is the most proper exercise for knights and princes. The chase is an image of war: there you have stratagems, artifices, and ambuscades to be employed, in order to overcome your enemy with safety to yourself; there, too, you are often exposed to the extremes of cold and heat; idleness and ease are despised; the body acquires health and vigorous activity: in short, it is an exercise which may be beneficial to many, and injurious to none. Besides, it is not a vulgar amusement, but, like hawking, is the peculiar sport of the great. Therefore, Sancho, change your opinion before you become a governor; for then you will find your account in these diversions." "Not so, i' faith," replied Sancho; "the good governor and the broken leg should keep at home. It would be fine indeed for people to come after him about business, and find him gadding about in the mountains for his pleasure. At that rate what would become of his government? In good truth, sir, hunting, and such-like pastimes, are rather for your idle companions than for governors. The way I mean to divert myself shall be with brag at Easter, and bowls on Sundays and holidays; as for your hunting, it befits neither my condition nor conscience." "Heaven grant you prove as good as you promise," said the duke; "but saying and doing are often wide apart." "Be that as it will," replied Sancho; "the good paymaster wants no pawn; and God's help is better than early rising; and the belly carries the legs, and not the legs the belly:—I mean that, with the help of Heaven and a good intention, I warrant I shall govern better than a goss-hawk. Ay, ay, let them put their fingers in my mouth, and try whether or not I can bite." "A curse upon thy proverbs!" said Don Quixote; "when will the day come that I shall hear thee utter one coherent sentence without that base intermixture? Let this blockhead alone, I beseech your excellencies; he will grind your souls to death, not between two, but two thousand proverbs—all timed as well, and as much to the purpose, as I wish God may grant him health, or me, if I desire to hear them." "Sancho Panza's proverbs," said the duchess, "though more numerous than those of the Greek commentator, are equally admirable for their sententious brevity. For my own part, I must confess they give me more pleasure than many others, more aptly suited and better timed."

After this and such-like pleasant conversation, they left the tent, and retired into the wood to examine their nets and snares. The day passed, and night came on, not clear and calm, like the usual evening in summer, but in a kind of murky twilight, extremely favourable to the projects of the duke and duchess. Soon after the close of day, the wood suddenly seemed to be in flames on all sides, and from every quarter was heard the sound of numerous trumpets and other martial instruments, as if great bodies of cavalry were passing through the wood. All present seemed petrified with astonishment at what they heard and saw. To these noises others succeeded, like the Moorish yells at the onset of battle. Trumpets, clarions, drums, and fifes were heard all at once, so loud and incessant, that he must have been without sense who did not lose it in the midst of so discordant and horrible a din. The duke and duchess were alarmed, Don Quixote in amazement, and Sancho Panza trembled: in short, even those who were in the secret were terrified, and consternation held them all in silence. A post-boy, habited like a fiend, now made his appearance, blowing, as he passed onward, a monstrous horn, which produced a hoarse and frightful sound.

"Ho, courier!" cried the duke, "who are you? Whither go you? And what soldiers are those who seem to be crossing this wood?" To which the courier answered in a terrific voice, "I am the devil, and am going in quest of Don Quixote de la Mancha. Those you inquire about are six troops of enchanters, conducting the peerless Dulcinea del Toboso, accompanied by the gallant Frenchman Montesinos, who comes to inform her knight by what means she is to be released from the power of enchantment." "If you were the devil, as you say, and, indeed, appear to be," quoth the knight, "you would have known that I who now stand before you am that same Don Quixote de la Mancha." "Before Heaven, and on my conscience," replied the devil, "in my hurry and distraction I did not see him." This devil," quoth Sancho, "must needs be an honest fellow and a good Christian, else he would not have sworn by Heaven and his conscience; for my part, I verily believe there are some good people, even in hell." The devil now, without alighting, directed his eyes to Don Quixote, and said, "To thee, Knight of the Lions—and may I see thee between their paws!—I am sent by the valiant but unfortunate Montesinos, by whom I am directed to command thee to wait his arrival on the very spot wherever I should find thee. With him comes the Lady Dulcinea del Toboso, in order to inform thee by what means thou mayest deliver her from the thraldom of enchantment. Thou hast heard my message; I now return. Devils like myself have thee in their keeping! and good angels that noble pair!" All were in perplexity, but especially the knight and squire : Sancho to see how Dulcinea must be enchanted in spite of plain truth, and Don Quixote from certain qualms respecting the truth of his adventures in the cave of Montesinos. While he stood musing on this subject, the duke said to him, "Do you mean to wait, Signor Don Quixote?" "Why not?" answered he; "here will I wait, intrepid and firm, though all hell should come to assault me." "By my faith!" quoth Sancho, "if I should see another devil, and hear another such horn, I will no more stay here than in Flanders."

The night now grew darker, and numerous lights were seen glancing through the wood, like those exhalations which in the air appear like shooting stars. A dreadful noise was likewise heard, like that caused by the ponderous wheels of an ox-waggon, from whose harsh and continued creaking, it is said, wolves and bears fly away in terror. The turmoil, however, still increased, for at the four quarters of the wood hostile armies seemed to be engaged : here was heard the dreadful thunder of artillery; there volleys of innumerable musketeers; the clashing of arms, and shouts of nearer combatants, joined with the Moorish war-whoop at a distance; in short, the horns, clarions, trumpets, drums, cannon, muskets, and, above all, the frightful creaking of the waggons, formed altogether so tremendous a din, that Don Quixote had need of all his courage to stand firm and wait the issue. But Sancho's heart quite failed him, and he fell down in a swoon at the duchess's feet. Cold water being brought at her grace's command, it was sprinkled upon his face, and his senses returned just in time to witness the arrival of one of the creaking waggons. It was drawn by four heavy oxen, all covered with black palls, having also a large flaming torch fastened to each horn. On the floor of the waggon was placed a seat, much elevated, on which sat a venerable old man, with a beard whiter than snow, that reached below his girdle. His vestment was a long gown of black buckram (for the carriage was so illuminated that everything might be easily distinguished), and the drivers were two demons, clothed also in black, and of such hideous aspect that Sancho, having once seen them, shut his eyes, and would not venture upon a second look.

When the waggon had arrived opposite the party, the venerable person within it arose from his seat, and, standing erect, with a solemn voice he said, "I am the sage Lirgandeo." He then sat down, and the waggon went forward. After that another waggon passed in the same manner, with another old man enthroned, who, when the carriage stopped, arose, and, in a voice no less solemn, said, "I am the sage Alquife, the great friend of Urganda the Unknown." He passed on, and a third waggon advanced at the same pace, but the person seated on the throne was not an old man like the two former, but a man of a robust form and ill-favoured countenance, who, when he came near, stood up as the others had done, and said, in a voice hoarse and diabolical, "I am Arcalaus the enchanter, mortal enemy of Amadis de Gaul and all his race," and immediately proceeded onward. The three waggons halting at a little distance, the painful noise of their wheels ceased, and it was followed by the sweet and harmonious sounds of music, very delightful to Sancho's ears, who, taking it for a favourable omen, said to the duchess (from whose side he had not stirred an inch), "Where there is music, madam, there can be no mischief." "No, nor where there is light and splendour," answered the duchess. "Flame may give light," replied Sancho, "and bonfires may illuminate; yet we may easily be burnt by them; but music is always a sign of feasting and merriment." "That will be seen presently," quoth Don Quixote, who was listening; and he said right, for it will be found in the next chapter.

CHAPTER XXXV.

Wherein is continued the account of the method prescribed to Don Quixote for disenchanting Dulcinea; with other wonderful events.

As THE agreeable music approached, they observed that it attended a stately triumphal car, drawn by six grey mules, covered with white linen; and upon each of them rode a penitent of light,* clothed also in white, and holding a lighted torch in his hand. The car was more than double the size of the others which had passed, and twelve penitents were ranged in order within it, all carrying lighted torches; a sight which at once caused surprise and terror. Upon an elevated throne sat a nymph, covered with a thousand veils of silver tissue bespangled with innumerable flowers of gold, so that her dress, if not rich, was gay and glittering. Over her head was thrown a transparent gauze, so thin that through its folds might be seen a most beautiful face; and from the multitude of lights, it was easy to discern that she was young as well as beautiful; for she was evidently under twenty years of age, though not less than seventeen. Close by her sat a figure, clad in a magnificent robe, reaching to the feet, having his head covered with a black veil. The moment this vast machine arrived opposite to where the duke and duchess and Don Quixote stood, the attending music ceased, as well as the harps and lutes within the car. The figure in the gown then stood up, and throwing open the robe and uncovering his face, displayed the

* In England also, to be clothed in a white sheet, and bear a candle or torch in the hand, is a penance; and in the same manner the *amende honourable* is performed in France.

ghastly countenance of Death, looking so terrific that Don Quixote started, Sancho was struck with terror, and even the duke and duchess seemed to betray some symptoms of fear. This living Death, standing erect, in a dull and drowsy tone, and with a sleepy articulation, spoke as follows :

> " Merlin I am, miscalled the devil's son
> In lying annals, authorised by time :
> Monarch supreme, and great depositary
> Of magic art and Zoroastic skill ;
> Rival of envious ages, that would hide
> The glorious deeds of errant cavaliers,
> Favoured by me and my peculiar charge ;
> Though vile enchanters, still on mischief bent,
> To plague mankind their baleful art employ,
> Merlin's soft nature, ever prone to good,
> His power inclines to bless the human race.
>
> " In Hade's chambers, where my busied ghost
> Was forming spells and mystic characters,
> Dulcinea's voice, peerless Tobosan maid,
> With mournful accents reached my pitying ears :
> I knew her woe, her metamorphosed form
> From high-born beauty in a palace graced,
> To the loathed features of a cottage wench.
> With sympathizing grief I straight revolved
> The numerous tomes of my detested art,
> And in the hollow of this skeleton
> My soul inclosing, hither am I come,
> To tell the cure of such uncommon ills.
>
> " O glory thou of all that case their limbs
> In polished steel and fenceful adamant !
> Light, beacon, polar star, and glorious guide
> Of all who, starting from the lazy down,
> Banish ignoble sleep for the rude toil
> And hardy exercise of errant arms !
> Spain's boasted pride, La Mancha's matchless knight,
> Whose valiant deeds outstrip pursuing fame !
> Wouldst thou to beauty's pristine state restore
> Th' enchanted dame, Sancho, thy faithful squire,
> Must to his brawny shoulders, bare exposed,
> Three thousand and three hundred stripes apply,
> Such as may sting and give him smarting pain :
> The authors of her change have thus decreed,
> And this is Merlin's errand from the shades."

" What ! " quoth Sancho, " three thousand lashes ! Odd's-flesh ! I will as soon give myself three stabs as three single lashes—much less three thousand ! The devil take this way of disenchanting ! I cannot see what my shoulders have to do with enchantment. Before Heaven ! if Signor Merlin can find out no other way to disenchant the Lady Dulcinea del Toboso, enchanted she may go to her grave for me ! " " Not lash thyself, thou garlic-eating wretch ! " quoth Don Quixote ; " I shall take thee to a tree, and tie thee naked as thou wert born, and there, not three thousand and three hundred, but six thousand six hundred lashes will I give thee, and those so well laid on that three thousand three hundred hard tugs shall not tug them off. So answer me not a word, scoundrel! or I will tear thy very soul out!" "It must not be so," said Merlin; "the lashes that honest Sancho is to receive must not be applied by force, but with his good-will, and at whatever time he pleases, for no term is fixed: and furthermore, he is allowed, if he please, to save himself half the trouble of applying so many lashes, by having half the number laid on by another hand, provided that hand be somewhat heavier than his own." "Neither another hand nor my own," quoth Sancho; "no hand, either heavy or light, shall touch my flesh. Was the Lady Dulcinea brought forth by me, that my shoulders must pay for the transgressions of her eyes? My master, indeed, who is part of her, since at every step he is calling her his life, his soul, his support, and stay—he it is who ought to lash himself for her, and do all that is needful for her delivery; but for me to whip myself—no, I pronounce it!"

No sooner had Sancho thus declared himself, than the spangled nymph who sat by the side of Merlin arose, and throwing aside her veil, discovered a face of extraordinary beauty; and with a masculine air, and no very amiable voice, addressed herself to Sancho: "O wretched squire —with no more soul than a pitcher! thou heart of cork and bowels of flint!—hadst thou been required, nose-slitting thief! to throw thyself from some high tower: hadst thou been desired, enemy of human kind! to eat a dozen of toads, two dozen of lizards, and three dozen of snakes; hadst thou been requested to kill thy wife and children with some bloody and sharp scimitar—no wonder if thou hadst betrayed some squeamishness; but to hesitate about three thousand three hundred lashes, which there is not a wretched schoolboy but receives every month, it amazes, stupefies, and affrights the tender feelings of all who hear it, and even of all who shall hereafter be told it. Cast, thou marble-hearted wretch!— cast, I say, those huge goggle eyes upon these lovely balls of mine, that shine like glittering stars, and thou wilt see them weep, drop by drop, and stream after stream, making furrows, tracks, and paths down these beautiful cheeks! Relent, malicious and evil-minded monster! Be moved by my blooming youth, which, though yet in its teens, is pining and withering beneath the vile bark of a peasant wench; and if at this moment I appear otherwise, it is by the special favour of Signor Merlin, here present, hoping that these charms may soften that iron heart; for the tears of afflicted beauty turn rocks into cotton, and tigers into lambs. Lash, untamed beast! lash away on that brawny flesh of thine, and rouse from that base sloth which only inclines thee to eat and eat again; and restore to me the delicacy of my skin, the sweetness of my temper, and all the charms of beauty. And if for my sake thou wilt not be mollified into reasonable compliance, let the anguish of that miserable knight stir thee to compassion—thy master I mean, whose soul I see sticking crosswise in his throat, not ten inches from his lips, waiting only thy cruel or kind answer either to fly out of his mouth or return joyfully into his bosom."

Don Quixote here putting his finger to his throat, "Before Heaven!"

said he, " Dulcinea is right, for I here feel my soul sticking in my throat,
like the stopper of a crossbow ! "　" What say you to that, Sancho ? "
quoth the duchess.　" I say, madam," answered Sancho, " what I have
already said, that as to the lashes, I pronounce them."　" *Renounce*, you
should say, Sancho," quoth the duke, " and not pronounce."　" Please
your grandeur to let me alone," replied Sancho, " for I cannot stand
now to a letter more or less : these lashes so torment me that I know
not what I say or do.　But I would fain know one thing from the Lady
Dulcinea del Toboso, and that is, where she learnt her manner of asking
a favour?　She comes to desire me to tear my flesh with stripes, and at
the same time lays upon me such a bead-roll of ill names that the devil
may bear them for me.　What ! does she think my flesh is made of
brass ? or that I care a rush whether she is enchanted or not ?　Where
are the presents she has brought to soften me ?　Instead of a basket
of fine linen shirts, nightcaps, and socks (though I wear none), here is
nothing but abuse.　Every one knows that ' the golden load is a burden
light ; ' that ' gifts will make their way through stone walls : ' ' pray
devoutly and hammer on stoutly ; ' and ' one take is worth two I 'll
give thee 's.'　There 's his worship my master, too, instead of wheedling
and coaxing me to make myself wool and carded cotton, threatens to
tie me naked to a tree and double the dose of stripes.　These tender-
hearted gentlefolks ought to remember, too, that they not only desire to
have a squire whipped, but a governor, making no more of it than saying,
' Drink with your cherries.'　Let them learn — plague take them ! — let
them learn how to ask and entreat, and mind their breeding.　All times
are not alike, nor are men always in a humour for all things.　At this
moment my heart is ready to burst with grief to see this rent in my
jacket, and people come to desire that I would also tear my flesh, and
that, too, of my own good-will : I have just as much mind to the thing
as to turn Turk."

" In truth, friend Sancho," said the duke, " if you do not relent and
become softer than a ripe fig, you finger no government of mine.　It
would be a fine thing, indeed, were I to send my good islanders a cruel,
flinty-hearted tyrant, whom neither the tears of afflicted damsels nor the
admonitions of wise, reverend, and ancient enchanters can move to compassion !　Really, Sancho, I am compelled to say—no stripes, no government."　" May I not be allowed two days, my lord," quoth Sancho, " to
consider what is best for me to do ? "　In nowise can that be," cried
Merlin : " on this spot and at this instant you must determine ; for
Dulcinea must either return to Montesinos' cave and to her rustic shape,
or in her present form be carried to the Elysian fields, there to wait until
the penance be completed."　" Come, friend Sancho," said the duchess,
" be of good cheer, and show yourself grateful to your master, whose
bread you have eaten, and to whose generous nature and noble feats of
chivalry we are all so much beholden.　Come, my son, give your consent,
and let the devil go to the devil ; leave fear to the cowardly ; a good
heart breaks bad fortune, as you well know."

" Hark you, Signor Merlin," quoth Sancho, addressing himself to the

Don Quixote clung about Sancho's neck, giving him a thousand kisses.

sage; "pray, will you tell me one thing—how comes it about that the devil courier just now brought a message to my master from Signor Montesinos, saying that he would be here anon, to give directions about this disenchantment, and yet we have seen nothing of him all this while?" "Pshaw!" replied Merlin, "the devil is an ass and a lying rascal: he was sent from me, and not from Montesinos, who is still in his cave contriving, or rather awaiting, the end of his enchantment, for the back is yet unflayed. If he owes you money, or you have any other business with him, he shall be forthcoming in a trice, when and where you think fit; and therefore come to a decision, and consent to this small penance, from which both your soul and body will receive marvellous benefit; your soul by an act of charity, and your body by a wholesome and timely blood-letting." " How the world swarms with doctors!" quoth Sancho; "the very enchanters seem to be of the trade! Well, since everybody tells me so, though the thing is out of all reason, I promise to give myself the three thousand three hundred lashes, upon condition that I may lay them on whenever I please, without being tied to days or times; and I will endeavour to get out of debt as soon as I possibly can, that the beauty of my lady Dulcinea del Toboso may shine forth to all the world; as it seems she is really beautiful, which I much doubted. Another condition is, that I will not be bound to draw blood, and if some lashes happen only to fly-flap, they shall all go into the account. Moreover, if I should mistake in the reckoning, Signor Merlin here, who knows everything, shall give me notice how many I want, or have exceeded."

" As for the exceedings, there is no need of keeping account of them," answered Merlin; " for when the number is completed, that instant will the Lady Dulcinea del Toboso be disenchanted, and come full of gratitude in search of good Sancho, to thank and even reward him for the generous deed. So that no scruples are necessary about surplus and deficiency; and Heaven forbid that I should allow anybody to be cheated of a single hair of their head." " Go to, then, in God's name," quoth Sancho; " I must submit to my ill fortune: I say I consent to the penance upon the conditions I have mentioned."

No sooner had Sancho pronounced his consent than the innumerable instruments poured forth their music, the volleys of musketry were discharged, while Don Quixote clung about Sancho's neck, giving him, on his forehead and brawny cheeks, a thousand kisses; the duke and duchess, and all who were present, likewise testified their satisfaction. The car now moved on, and in departing the fair Dulcinea bowed her head to the duke and duchess, and made a low courtesy to Sancho.

By this time the cheerful and joyous dawn began to appear, the flowerets of the field expanded their fragrant beauties to the light, and brooks and streams, in gentle murmurs, ran to pay expecting rivers their crystal tribute. The earth rejoiced, the sky was clear, and the air serene and calm; all, combined and separately, giving manifest tokens that the day, which followed fast upon Aurora's heels, would be bright and fair. The duke and duchess, having happily executed their ingenious project, returned highly gratified to their castle, and determined on the continuation of fictions which afforded more pleasures than realities.

CHAPTER XXXVI.

Wherein is recorded the strange and inconceivable adventure of the ill-used duenna, or the Countess of Trifaldi; and likewise Sancho Panza's letter to his wife Teresa Panza.

THE whole contrivance of the former adventure was the work of the duke's steward, a man of a humorous and facetious turn of mind. He it was who composed the verses, instructed a page to perform the part of Dulcinea, and personated himself the shade of Merlin. Assisted by the duke and duchess, he now prepared another scene still more entertaining than the former.

The next day the duchess inquired of Sancho if he had begun his penance for the relief of his unhappy lady. "By my faith, I have," said he, "for last night I gave myself five lashes." The duchess desired to know how he had given them. "With the palm of my hand," said he. "That," replied the duchess, "is rather clapping than whipping, and I am of opinion Signor Merlin will not be so easily satisfied. My good Sancho must get a rod of briers or of whipcord, that the strokes may be followed by sufficient smarting; for letters written in blood cannot be disputed, and the deliverance of a great lady like Dulcinea is not to be purchased with a song." "Give me, then, madam, some rod or bough," quoth Sancho, "and I will use it, if it does not smart too much; for I would have your ladyship know that, though I am a clown, my flesh has more of the cotton than of the rush, and there is no reason why I should flay myself for other folks' gain." "Fear not," answered the duchess, "it shall be my care to provide you with a whip that shall suit you exactly, and agree with the tenderness of your flesh as if it were its own brother." "But now, my dear lady," quoth Sancho, "you must know that I have written a letter to my wife Teresa Panza, giving her an account of all that has befallen me since I parted from her:—here it is in my bosom, and it wants nothing but the name on the outside. I wish your discretion would read it, for methinks it is written like a governor—I mean in the manner that governors ought to write." "And who indited it?" demanded the duchess. "Who should indite it but I myself, sinner as I am?" replied Sancho. "And did you write it too?" said the duchess. "No, indeed," answered Sancho, "for I can neither read nor write, though I can set my mark." "Let us see it," said the duchess, "for I dare say it shows the quality and extent of your genius." Sancho took the letter out of his bosom, unsealed it, and the duchess having taken it, read as follows:

SANCHO PANZA'S LETTER TO HIS WIFE TERESA PANZA.

"If I have been finely lashed, I have been finely mounted up; if I have got a good government, it has cost me many good lashes. This, my dear Teresa, thou canst not understand at present; another time thou wilt. Thou must know, Teresa, that I am determined that thou shalt ride in thy coach, which is somewhat to the purpose; for all other ways of going are no better than creeping upon all fours, like a cat. Thou shalt be a governor's wife: see then whether anybody will dare to tread on thy heels. I here send thee a green hunting suit, which my lady duchess gave me: fit it up so that it may serve our daughter for a jacket and petticoat. They say in this country that my master Don Quixote is a sensible madman and a pleasant fool, and that I am not a whit behind him. We have been in Montesinos' cave, and the sage Merlin, the wizard, has pitched upon me to disenchant the Lady Dulcinea del Toboso, who among you is called Aldonza Lorenzo. When I have given myself three thousand and three hundred lashes, lacking five, she will be as free from enchantment as the mother that bore her. Say nothing of this to anybody; for, bring your affairs into council, and one will cry it is white, another it is black. A few days hence I shall go to the government, whither I go with a huge desire to get money; and I am told it is the same with all new governors. I will first see how matters stand, and send thee word whether or not thou shalt come to me. Dapple is well, and sends thee his hearty service; part with him I will not, though I were to be made the great Turk. The duchess, my mistress, kisses thy hands a thousand times over; return her two thousand; for, as my master says, nothing is cheaper than civil words. God has not been pleased to throw in my way another portmanteau, and another hundred crowns, as once before; but take no heed, my dear Teresa, for he that has the game in his hand need not mind the loss of a trick—the government will make up for all. One thing only troubles me: I am told if I once try it I shall eat my very fingers after it; and if so, it will not be much of a bargain: though, indeed, the crippled and maimed enjoy a petty-canonry in the alms they receive; so that, one way or another, thou art sure to be rich and happy. God send it may be so—as He easily can, and keep me for thy sake.

"Thy husband, the governor,
"SANCHO PANZA.

"From this Castle, the 20th of July, 1614."

The duchess, having read the letter, said to Sancho, "In two things the good governor is a little out of the way: the one in saying, or insinuating, that this government is conferred on him on account of the lashes he is to give himself; whereas he cannot deny, for he knows it well, that, when my lord duke promised it to him, nobody dreamt of lashes; the other is, that he appears to be covetous, and I hope no harm may come of it; for avarice bursts the bag, and the covetous governor doeth ungoverned justice." "Truly, madam, that is not my meaning," replied Sancho; "and, if your highness does not like this letter, it is but tearing it, and writing a new one, which, mayhap, may prove worse, if left to thy mending." "No, no," replied the duchess, "this is a very good one, and the duke shall see it."

They then repaired to a garden, where they were to dine that day; and there Sancho's letter was shown to the duke, who read it with great pleasure. After dinner, as Sancho was entertaining the company with some of his relishing conversation, they suddenly heard the dismal sound of an unbraced drum, accompanied by a fife. All were surprised at this martial and doleful harmony, especially Don Quixote, who was so agitated that he could scarcely keep his seat. As for Sancho, it is enough to say that fear carried him to his usual refuge, which was

As for Sancho, it is enough to say that fear carried him to his usual refuge, which was the duchess's side, or the skirts of her petticoat.

the duchess's side, or the skirts of her petticoat; for the sounds which they heard were truly dismal and melancholy. While they were thus held in suspense, two young men, clad in mourning robes trailing upon the ground, entered the garden, each of them beating a great drum, covered also with black; and with these a third, playing on the fife, in mourning like the rest. These were followed by a person of gigantic stature, not dressed, but rather enveloped, in a robe of the blackest dye, the train whereof was of immoderate length, and over it he wore a broad black belt, in which was slung a mighty scimitar, enclosed within a sable scabbard. His face was covered by a thin black veil, through which might be discovered a long beard, white as snow. He marched forward, regulating his steps to the sound of the drums, with much gravity and stateliness. In short, his dark robe, his enormous bulk, his solemn deportment, and the funereal gloom of his figure, together with his attendants, might well produce the surprise that appeared on every countenance.

With all imaginable respect and formality he approached and knelt down before the duke, who received him standing, and would in nowise suffer him to speak till he rose up. The monstrous apparition, then rising, lifted up his veil, and exposed to view his fearful length of beard—the longest, whitest, and most luxuriant that ever human eyes beheld; then, fixing his eyes on the duke, in a voice grave and sonorous he said, " Most high and potent lord, my name is Trifaldin of the White Beard, and I am squire to the Countess Trifaldi, otherwise called the Afflicted Duenna, from whom I bear a message to your highness, requesting that you will be pleased to give her ladyship permission to approach, and relate to your magnificence the unhappy and wonderful circumstances of her misfortune. But, first, she desires to know whether the valorous and invincible knight, Don Quixote de la Mancha, resides at this time in your castle ; for in quest of him she has travelled on foot, and fasting, from the kingdom of Candaya to this your territory ; an exertion miraculous and incredible, were it not wrought by enchantment. She is now at the outward gate of this castle, and only waits your highness's invitation to enter."

Having said this, he hemmed, stroked his beard from top to bottom, and with much gravity and composure stood expecting the duke's answer, which was to this effect : " Worthy Trifaldin of the White Beard, long since have we been apprised of the afflictions of my lady the Countess Trifaldi, who, through the malice of enchanters, is too truly called the Dolorous Duenna : tell her, therefore, stupendous squire, that she may enter, and that the valiant knight Don Quixote de la Mancha is here present, from whose generous assistance she may safely promise herself all the redress she requires. Tell her also that, if my aid be necessary, she may command my services, since, as a knight, I am bound to protect all women, more especially injured and afflicted matrons like her ladyship." Trifaldin, on receiving the duke's answer, bent one knee to the ground ; then giving a signal to his musical attendants, he retired with the same solemnity as he had entered, leaving all in astonishment at the majesty of his figure and deportment.

The duke, then turning to Don Quixote, said, " It is evident, Sir Knight, that neither the clouds of malice nor of ignorance can obscure the light of your valour and virtue : six days have scarcely elapsed since you have honoured this castle with your presence, and, behold, the afflicted and oppressed flock hither in quest of you from far distant countries ; not in coaches, or upon dromedaries, but on foot, and fasting !—such is their confidence in the strength of that arm, the fame whereof spreads over the whole face of the earth." " I wish, my lord duke," answered Don Quixote, " that holy person, who but a few days since expressed himself with so much acrimony against knights-errant, were now here, that he might have ascertained, with his own eyes, whether or not such knights were necessary in the world ; at least he would be forced to acknowledge that the afflicted and disconsolate, in extraordinary cases and in overwhelming calamities, fly not for relief to the houses of scholars, nor to village priests, nor to the country gentleman who never travels out of sight of his own domain, nor to the lazy courtier, who rather inquires after news to tell again than endeavours to perform deeds worthy of being related by others. No : remedy for the injured, support for the distressed, protection for damsels, and consolation for widows, are nowhere so readily to be found as among knights-errant ; and I give infinite thanks to Heaven that I am one, and shall not repine at any hardships or evils that I may endure in so honourable a vocation. Let the afflicted lady come forward and make known her request, and, be it whatever it may, she may rely on the strength of this arm, and the resolute courage of my soul."

CHAPTER XXXVII.

In which is continued the famous adventure of the Afflicted Duenna.

THE duke and duchess were extremely delighted to find Don Quixote wrought up into a mood so favourable to their design; but Sancho was not so well satisfied. "I should be sorry," said he, "that this Madam Duenna should lay any stumbling-block in the way of my promised government; for I have heard an apothecary of Toledo, who talked like any goldfinch, say that no good ever comes of meddling with duennas. Odds my life! what an enemy to them was that apothecary! If, then, duennas of every quality and condition are troublesome and impertinent, what must those be who come in the doldrums? which seems to be the case with this same Countess Three-skirts, or Three-tails—for skirts and tails, in my country, are all one." "Hold thy peace, Sancho," said Don Quixote; "for as this lady duenna comes in quest of me from so remote a country, she cannot be one of those who fall under that apothecary's displeasure. Besides, thou must have noticed that this lady is a countess; and when countesses serve as duennas, it must be as attendants upon queens and empresses; having houses of their own, where they command, and are served by other duennas." "Yes, in sooth, so it is," said Donna Rodriguez (who was present); "and my lady duchess has duennas in her service who might have been countesses themselves had it pleased fortune; but 'laws go on kings' errands;' and let no one speak ill of duennas, especially of ancient maiden ones; for, though I am not of that number, yet I can easily conceive the advantage a maiden duenna has over one that is a widow. But let them take heed, for he who attempts to clip us will be left with the shears in his hand."

"For all that," replied Sancho, "there is still so much to be sheared about your duennas, as my barber tells me, that it is better not to stir the rice though it burn to the pot." "These squires," quoth Donna Rodriguez, "are our sworn enemies; and being, as it were, evil spirits that prowl about antechambers, continually watching us the hours they are not at their beads—which are not a few—they can find no other pastime than reviling us, and will dig our bones only to give another death-blow to our reputations. But let me tell these jesters that, in spite of their flouts, we shall live in the world—ay, and in the best families too, though we starve for it, and cover our delicate or not delicate bodies with black weeds, as dunghills are sometimes covered with tapestry on a procession day. Foul slanderers!—by my faith, if I were allowed, and the occasion required it, I would prove to all here present, and to the whole world besides, that there is no virtue that is not contained in a duenna." " I am of opinion," quoth the duchess, "that my good Donna Rodriguez is very much in the right; but she must wait for a more proper opportunity to finish the debate, and confute and confound the calumnies of that wicked apothecary, and also to root out the ill opinion which the great Sancho Panza fosters in his breast." "I care not to dispute with her," quoth Sancho, "for, ever since the fumes of government have got into my head, I have given up all my squireship notions, and care not a fig for all the duennas in the world."

This dialogue about duennas would have continued, had not the sound of the drum and fife announced the approach of the afflicted lady. The duchess asked the duke whether it would not be proper for him to go and meet her, since she was a countess, and a person of quality. "Look you," quoth Sancho, before the duke could answer, "in regard to her being a countess, it is fitting your highness should go to receive her; but, inasmuch as she is a duenna, I am of opinion you should not stir a step." "Who desires thee to intermeddle in this matter, Sancho?" said Don Quixote. "Who, sir," answered Sancho, "but I myself? have I not a right to intermeddle, being a squire who has learned the rules of good manners in the school of your worship? Have I not had the flower of courtesy for my master, who has often told me that one may as well lose the game by a card too much as a card too little; and a word is enough to the wise." "Sancho is right," quoth the duke; "but let us see what kind of a countess this is, and then we shall judge what courtesy is due to her." The drums and fife now advanced as before—but here the author ended this short chapter, and began another with the continuation of the same adventure, which is one of the most remarkable in the history.

CHAPTER XXXVIII.

Which contains the account given by the Afflicted Duenna of her misfortunes.

THE doleful musicians were followed by twelve duennas, in two ranks, clad in large mourning robes, seemingly of milled serge, and covered with white veils of thin muslin that almost reached to their feet. Then came the Countess Trifaldi herself, led by her squire Trifaldin of the White Beard. She was clad in a robe of the finest serge, which, had it been napped, each grain would have been of the size of a good ronceval pea. The train, or tail (call it by either name), was divided into three separate portions, and supported by three pages, and spread out, making a regular mathematical figure with three angles; whence it was conjectured she obtained the name of Trifaldi, or Three-skirts. Indeed, Benengeli says that was the fact; her real name being Countess of Lobuna, or Wolf-land, from the multitude of wolves produced in that earldom; and, had they been foxes instead of wolves, she would have been styled Countess Zorruna, according to the custom of those nations for the great to take their titles from the things with which the country most abounded. This great countess, however, was induced, from the singular form of her garments, to exchange her original title of Lobuna for that of Trifaldi. The twelve duennas, with the lady, advanced slowly in procession, having their faces covered with black veils—not transparent, like that of the squire Trifaldin, but so thick that nothing could be seen through them.

On the approach of this battalion of duennas, the duke, duchess, Don Quixote, and all the other spectators, rose from their seats; and now the attendant duennas halted, and separating, opened a passage through which their afflicted lady, still led by the squire Trifaldin, advanced towards the noble party, who stepped some dozen paces forward to receive her. She then cast herself on her knees, and, with a voice rather harsh and coarse than clear and delicate, said, " I entreat your graces will not condescend to so much courtesy to this your valet—I mean your handmaid; for my mind, already bewildered with affliction, will only be still more confounded. Alas! my unparalleled misfortune has seized and carried off my understanding, I know not whither; but surely it must be to a great distance, for the more I seek it the farther it seems from me." " He must be wholly destitute of understanding, lady countess," quoth the duke, " who could not discern your merit by your person, which alone claims all the cream of courtesy and all the flower of well-bred ceremony." Then raising her by the hand, he led her to a chair close by the duchess, who also received her with much politeness.

During the ceremony Don Quixote was silent, and Sancho dying with impatience to see the face of the Trifaldi, or of some one of her many duennas; but it was impossible till they chose to unveil themselves. All was expectation, and not a whisper was heard, till at length the afflicted lady began in these words : " Confident I am, most potent lord, most beautiful lady, and most discreet spectators, that my most unfortunate miserableness will find, in your generous and compassionate natures, a most merciful sanctuary; for so doleful and dolorous is my wretched state that it is sufficient to mollify marble, to soften adamant, and melt down the steel of the hardest hearts. But, before the rehearsal of my misfortunes is commenced on the public stage of your hearing faculties, I earnestly desire to be informed whether this noble circle be adorned by that renownedissimo knight, Don Quixote de la Manchissima, and his squirissimo Panza." " That same Panza," said Sancho, before any other could answer, " stands here before you, and also Don Quixotissimo; and therefore, most dolorous duennissima, say what you willissima; for we are all ready to be your most humble servantissimos."

Upon this Don Quixote stood up, and, addressing himself to the doleful countess, he said, " If your misfortunes, afflicted lady, can admit of remedy from the valour or fortitude of a knight-errant, the little all that I possess shall be employed in your service. I am Don Quixote de la Mancha, whose function it is to relieve every species of distress; you need not, therefore, madam, implore benevolence, nor have recourse to preambles, but plainly, and without circumlocution, declare your grievances, for you have auditors who will bestow commiseration if not redress." On hearing this, the afflicted duenna attempted to throw herself at Don Quixote's feet—in truth she did so, and struggling to kiss them, said, " I prostrate myself, O invincible knight, before these feet and legs, which are the bases and pillars of knight-errantry, and will kiss these feet, whose steps lead to the end and termination of my misfortunes ! O valorous knight-errant, whose true exploits surpass and obscure the fabulous feats of the Amadises, Esplandians, and Belianises of old !"

Then, leaving Don Quixote, she turned to Sancho Panza, and taking him by the hand, said, " O thou, the most trusty squire that ever served knight-errant in present or in past ages, whose goodness is of greater extent than that beard of my usher Trifaldin; well mayest thou boast that, in serving Don Quixote, thou dost serve, in epitome, all the knights-errant that ever shone in the annals of chivalry ! I conjure thee, by thy natural benevolence and inviolable fidelity, to intercede with thy lord in my behalf, that the light of his favour may forthwith shine upon the humblest and unhappiest of countesses." To which Sancho answered, " Whether my goodness, Madam Countess, be or be not as long and as broad as your squire's beard, is no concern of mine : so that my soul be well bearded and whiskered when it departs this life, I care little or nothing for beards here below : but without all this coaxing and beseeching, I will put in a word for you to my master, who I know has a kindness for me ; besides, just now he stands in need of me about a certain business ; so, take my word for it, he shall do what he can for you. Now pray unload your griefs, madam ; let us hear all you have to say, and leave us to manage the matter."

The duke and duchess could scarcely preserve their gravity on seeing this adventure take so pleasant a turn, and were highly pleased with the ingenuity and good management of the Countess Trifaldi, who, returning to her seat, thus began her tale of sorrow : " The famous kingdom of Candaya, which lies between the great Taprobana and the South Sea, two leagues beyond Cape Camorin, had for its queen the Lady Donna Maguncia, widow of King Archipiela, who died, leaving the Infanta Antonomasia, their only child, heiress to the crown. This princess was brought up and educated under my care and instruction, I being the eldest and chief of the duennas in the household of her royal mother. Now, in process of time the young Antonomasia arrived at the age of fourteen, with such perfection of beauty that nature could not raise it a pitch higher ; and, what is more, discretion itself was but a child to her ; for she was as discreet as fair, and she was the fairest creature living ; and so she still remains, if the envious fates and hard-hearted

destinies have not cut short her thread of life. But sure they have not
done it; for Heaven would never permit that so much injury should be
done to the earth as to lop off prematurely the loveliest branch that ever
adorned the garden of the world. Her wondrous beauty, which my
feeble tongue can never sufficiently extol, attracted innumerable adorers;
and princes of her own, and every other nation, became her slaves.
Among the rest, a private cavalier of the court had the audacity to
aspire to that earthly heaven; confiding in his youth, his gallantry, his
sprightly and happy wit, with numerous other graces and qualifications.
Indeed, I must confess to your highnesses—though with reverence be it
spoken — he could touch the guitar to a miracle. He was, besides, a
poet and a fine dancer, and had so rare a talent for making bird-cages
that he might have gained his living by it in case of need. So many
parts and elegant endowments were sufficient to have moved a mountain, much more the tender heart of a virgin. But all his graces and
accomplishments would have proved ineffectual against the virtue of
my beautiful charge, had not the robber and ruffian first artfully contrived to make a conquest of me. The assassin and barbarous vagabond
began with endeavouring to obtain my good-will and suborn my inclination, that I might betray my trust, and deliver up to him the keys of the
fortress I guarded. In short, he so plied me with toys and trinkets,
and so insinuated himself into my soul, that I was bewitched. But that
which chiefly brought me down, and levelled me with the ground, was a
copy of verses which I heard him sing one night under my window;
and if I remember right, the words were these:

> "'The tyrant fair whose beauty sent
>   The throbbing mischief to my heart,
> The more my anguish to augment,
>   Forbids me to reveal the smart.'

"The words of this song were to me so many pearls, and his voice was
sweeter than honey; and many a time since have I thought, reflecting
on the evils I incurred, that poets — at least, your amorous poets —
should be banished from all good and well-regulated commonwealths;
for, instead of composing pathetic verses like those of the Marquis of
Mantua, which make women and children weep, they exercise their skill
in soft strokes and tender touches, which pierce the soul, and, entering
the body like lightning, consume all within, while the garment is left
unsinged. Another time he sang:

> "'Come, death, with gently-stealing pace,
>   And take me unperceived away,
> Nor let me see thy wished-for face,
>   Lest joy my fleeting life should stay."

"Thus was I assailed with these and such-like couplets, that astonish,
and when chanted, are bewitching. But when our poets deign to compose a kind of verses much in fashion with us, called roundelays—good
Heaven! they are no sooner heard than the whole frame is in a state of

emotion; the soul is seized with a kind of quaking, a titillation of the fancy, a pleasing delirium of all the senses! I therefore say again, most noble auditors, that such versifiers deserve to be banished to the Isle of Lizards; though, in truth, the blame lies chiefly with the simpletons who commend, and the idiots who suffer themselves to be deluded by such things; and had I been a wise and discreet duenna, the nightly chanting of his verses would not have moved me, nor should I have lent an ear to such expressions as ' Dying I live; in ice I burn; I shiver in flames; in despair I hope; I fly, yet stay;' with other flim-flams of the like stamp, of which such kind of writings are full. Then again, when they promise to bestow on us the phœnix of Arabia, the crown of Ariadne, the ringlets of Apollo, the pearls of the South Sea, the gold of Tiber, and the balsam of Pencaya, how beautiful are their pens! how liberal in promises which they cannot perform! But, woe is me, unhappy wretch! Whither do I stray? What madness impels me to dwell on the faults of others, who have so many of mine own to answer for? Woe is me again, miserable creature! No, it was not his verses that vanquished me, but my own weakness: music did not subdue me; no, it was my own levity, my ignorance and lack of caution that melted me down, that opened the way and smoothed the passage for Don Clavijo;—for that is the name of the treacherous cavalier. Thus being made the go-between, the wicked man was often in the chamber of the—not by him, but by me—betrayed Antonomasia, as her lawful spouse; for, sinner as I am, never would I have consented unless he had been her true husband that he should have come within the shadow of her shoe-string! No, no; marriage must be the forerunner of any business of this kind undertaken by me. The only mischief in the affair was that they were ill-sorted, Don Clavijo being but a private gentleman, and the Infanta Antonomasia, as I have already said, heiress of the kingdom.

" For some time this intercourse, enveloped in the sagacity of my circumspection, was concealed from every eye. At length circumstances occurred which I feared might lead to a discovery; we laid our three heads together, and determined that, before their indiscretion should come to light, Don Clavijo should demand Antonomasia in marriage before the vicar, in virtue of a contract signed and given him by the infanta herself to be his wife, and so worded by wit, that the force of Samson could not have broken through it. Our plan was immediately carried into execution; the vicar examined the contract, took the lady's confession, and she was placed in the custody of an honest alguazil." " Bless me!" said Sancho, " alguazils too, and poets, and songs, and roundelays, in Candaya! I swear the world is the same everywhere! But pray get on, good Madam Trifaldi, for it grows late, and I am on thorns till I know the end of this long story." " I shall be brief." answered the countess.

CHAPTER XXXIX.

Wherein the duenna Trifaldi continues her stupendous and memorable history.

EVERY word uttered by Sancho was the cause of much delight to the duchess, and disgust to Don Quixote, who having commanded him to hold his peace, the afflicted lady went on. "After many questions and answers," said she, "the infanta stood firm to her engagement, without varying a tittle from her first declaration; the vicar, therefore, confirmed their union as lawful man and wife, which so affected the Queen Donna Maguncia, mother to the Infanta Antonomasia, that three days after we buried her." "She died, then, I suppose?" quoth Sancho. "Assuredly," replied the squire Trifaldin; "in Candaya we do not bury the living, but the dead." "Nevertheless, Master Squire," said Sancho, "it has happened before now that people only in a swoon have been buried for dead; and methinks Queen Maguncia ought rather to have swooned than died in good earnest; for while there is life there is hope; and the young lady's offence was not so much out of the way that her mother should have taken it so to heart. Had she married one of her pages, or some serving-man of the family, as I have been told many have done, it would have been a bad business and past cure; but as she made choice of a well-bred young cavalier of such good parts, faith and troth, though mayhap it was foolish, it was no such mighty matter: for, as my master says, who is here present and will not let me lie, bishops are made out of learned men, and why may not kings and emperors be made out of cavaliers—especially if they be errant?" "Thou art in the right, Sancho," said Don Quixote; "for a knight-errant with but two grains of good luck is next in the order of promotion to the greatest lord in the world. But let the afflicted lady proceed; for I fancy the bitter part of this hitherto sweet story is still behind." "Bitter!" answered the countess — "ay, and so bitter that, in comparison, wormwood is sweet and rue savoury!

"The queen being really dead, and not in a swoon, we buried her; and scarcely had we covered her with earth and pronounced the last farewell, when, '*Quis talia fando temperet a lacrymis?*'—lo, upon the queen's sepulchre who should appear, mounted on a wooden horse, but her cousin-german, the giant Malambruno! Yes, that cruel necromancer came expressly to avenge the death of his cousin, and to chastise the presumptuous Don Clavijo and the foolish Antonomasia, both of whom, by his cursed art, he instantly transformed—she into a monkey of brass, and him into a frightful crocodile of some strange metal; fixing upon them at the same time a plate of metal, engraven with Syriac characters; which being first rendered into the Candayan, and now into the Castilian language, have this meaning: 'These two presumptuous lovers shall not regain their pristine form till the valorous Manchegan engages with me in single combat; since for his mighty arm alone have the destinies reserved the achievement of that stupendous adventure.' No sooner was the wicked deed performed, than out he drew from its scabbard a dreadful scimitar, and taking me by the hair of my head, he seemed preparing to cut my throat, or whip off my head at a blow !

"*Scarcely had we covered her with earth and pronounced the last farewell, when, lo, who should appear, mounted on a wooden horse, but her cousin-german the giant Malambruno !*"

Though struck with horror, and almost speechless, trembling and weeping, I begged for mercy in such moving tones and melting words that I at last prevailed on him to stop the cruel execution which he meditated. In short, he ordered into his presence all the duennas of the palace, being those you see here present—and, after having expatiated on our fault, inveighed against duennas, their wicked plots and worse intrigues, and reviled all for the crime of which I alone was guilty, he said, though he would vouchsafe to spare our lives, he would inflict on us a punishment that should be a lasting shame. At the same instant, we all felt the pores of our faces open, and a sharp pain all over them, like the pricking of needle-points; upon which we clapped our hands to our faces, and found them in the condition you shall now behold."

Hereupon the afflicted lady and the rest of the duennas lifted up the veils which had hitherto concealed them, and discovered their faces planted with beards of all colours, black, brown, white, and piebald! The duke and duchess viewed the spectacle with surprise, and Don Quixote, Sancho, and the rest were all lost in amazement.

"Thus," continued Trifaldi, "hath that wicked and evil-minded felon Malambruno punished us!—covering our soft and delicate faces with these rugged bristles. Would to Heaven he had struck off our heads with his huge scimitar, rather than have obscured the light of our countenances with such an odious cloud! Whither, noble lords and lady,—Oh that I could utter what I have now to say with rivers of tears! but alas, the torrent is spent, and excess of grief has left our eyes without moisture, and as dry as beards of corn!—whither, I say, can a duenna go, whose chin is covered with a beard? What relation will own her? What charitable person will show her compassion or afford her relief? Even at the best, when the grain of her skin is the smoothest, and her face tortured and set off with a thousand different washes and ointments —with all this, how seldom does she meet with good-will from either man or woman! What then will become of her when her face is become a forest? O duennas! my dear partners in misfortune and companions in grief! in an evil hour were we brought into the world! Oh!"—here, being overcome with the strong sense of her calamity, she fell into a swoon.

CHAPTER XL.

Which treats of matters relating and appertaining to this adventure, and to this memorable history.

VERY grateful ought all who delight in histories of this kind to be to the original author of the present work, Cid Hamet, for his punctilious regard for truth, in allowing no circumstance to escape his pen, and the curious exactness with which he notes and sets down everything just as it happened, nothing, however minute, being omitted! He lays open the inmost thoughts, speaks for the silent, clears up doubts, resolves arguments; in fine, satisfies, to the smallest particle, the most acute and inquisitive minds. O most incomparable author! O happy Don Quixote! O famous Dulcinea! O facetious Sancho Panza! Jointly and severally may ye live through endless ages, for the delight and recreation of mankind!

The history then proceeds to relate that when Sancho saw the afflicted lady faint away, he said, " Upon the word of an honest man, and by the blood of all my ancestors, the Panzas, I swear I never heard or saw, nor has my master ever told me, nor did such an adventure as this ever enter into his thoughts ! A thousand devils take thee—not to say curse thee, Malambruno, for an enchanter and giant ! Couldst thou, beast ! hit upon no other punishment for these poor sinners, than clapping beards upon them ? Had it not been better (for them I am sure it would) to have whipt off half their noses, though they had snuffled for it, than to have covered their faces with scrubbing-brushes ? And what is worse, I 'll wager a trifle that they have not wherewithal to pay for shaving." " That is true, indeed, sir," answered one of the twelve : " we have not wherewithal to satisfy the barber, and therefore, as a shaving shift, some of us lay on plasters of pitch, which being pulled off with a jerk, take up roots and all, and thereby free us of this stubble for a while. As for the women who, in Candaya, go about from house to house to take off the superfluous hairs of the body, and trim the eyebrows, and do other private jobs for ladies, we, the duennas of her ladyship, would never have anything to do with them ; for they are, most of them, no better than they should be ; and therefore, if we are not relieved by Signor Don Quixote, with beards we shall live, and with beards be carried to our graves." " I would pluck off my own in the land of the Moors," said Don Quixote, " if I failed to deliver you from yours."

" Ah, valorous knight ! " cried the Trifaldi, at that moment recovering from her fainting fit, " the sweet tinkling of that promise reached my hearing faculty, and restored me to life. Once again, then, illustrious knight-errant and invincible hero ! let me beseech that your gracious promises may be converted into deeds." " The business shall not sleep with me," answered Don Quixote ; " therefore say, madam, what I am to do, and you shall soon be convinced of my readiness to serve you." " Be it known, then, to you, sir," replied the afflicted dame, " that from this place to the kingdom of Candaya, by land, is computed to be about five thousand leagues, one or two more or less ; but, through the air in a direct line, it is three thousand two hundred and twenty-seven. You are likewise to understand that Malambruno told me that, whenever fortune should direct me to the knight who was to be our deliverer, he would send him a steed—not like the vicious jades let out for hire, for it should be that very wooden horse upon which Peter of Provence carried off the fair Magalona. This horse is governed by a peg in his forehead, which serves instead of a bridle, and he flies as swiftly through the air as if the devil himself was switching him. This famous steed, tradition reports to have been formed by the cunning hand of Merlin the enchanter, who sometimes allowed him to be used by his particular friends, or those who paid him handsomely ; and he it was who lent him to his friend, the valiant Peter, when, as I said before, he stole the fair Magalona ; whisking her through the air behind him on the crupper, and leaving all that beheld him from the earth gaping with astonishment. Since the time of Peter to the present moment, we know of none that have mounted him ; but this we know, that Malambruno, by his art, has now got possession of him, and by this means posts about to every part of the world. To-day he is here, to-morrow in France, and the next day in Potosi; and the best of it is, that this same horse neither eats nor sleeps, nor wants shoeing; and, without wings, he ambles so smoothly that in his most rapid flight the rider may carry in his hand a cup full of water without spilling a drop! No wonder, then, that the fair Magalona took such delight in riding him."

"As for easy going," quoth Sancho, "commend me to my Dapple, though he is no highflyer; but by land I will match him against all the amblers in the world." The gravity of the company was disturbed for a moment by Sancho's observation; but the unhappy lady proceeded: "Now, this horse," said she, "if it be Malambruno's intention that our misfortunes should have an end, will be here this very evening; for he told me that the sign by which I should be assured of my having arrived in the presence of my deliverer, would be his sending me the horse thither with all convenient dispatch." "Pray," quoth Sancho, "how many will that same horse carry?" "Two persons," answered the lady, "one in the saddle, and the other on the crupper; and generally these two persons are the knight and his squire, when there is no stolen damsel in the case." "I would fain know," quoth Sancho, "by what name he is called." "His name," answered the Trifaldi, "is not the same as the horse of Bellerophon, which was the Pegasus; nor is he called Bucephalus, like that of Alexander the Great; nor Brilladore, like that of Orlando Furioso; nor is it Bayarte, which belonged to Reynaldos of Montalvan; nor Frontino, which was the steed of Rogero; nor is it Boötes, nor Pyrois—names given, it is said, to the horses of the sun; neither is he called Orelia, like the horse which the unfortunate Roderigo, the last king of the Goths in Spain, mounted in that battle wherein he lost his kingdom and his life."

"I will venture a wager," quoth Sancho, "since they have given him none of these famous and well-known names, neither have they given him that of my master's horse Rozinante, which in fitness goes beyond all the names you have mentioned." "It is very true," answered the bearded lady; "yet the name he bears is correct and significant, for he is called Clavileno el Aligero; * whereby his miraculous peg, his wooden frame, and extraordinary speed, are all curiously expressed: so that, in respect of his name, he may vie with the renowned Rozinante." "I dislike not his name," replied Sancho; "but with what bridle or what halter is he guided?" "I have already told you," answered the Trifaldi, "that he is guided by a peg, which the rider turning this way and that, makes him go either aloft in the air, or else sweeping, and, as it were, brushing the earth; or in the middle region: a course which the discreet and wise generally endeavour to keep." "I have a mighty desire to see him," quoth Sancho; "but to think I will get upon him, either in the saddle or behind upon the crupper, is to look for pears upon an elm-tree. It were a jest, indeed, for me, who can

---

* Wooden-peg the Winged; compounded of *clave*, a nail, and *leno*, wood.

hardly sit upon my own Dapple, though upon a pannel softer than silk, to think of bestriding a wooden crupper, without either pillow or cushion! In faith, I do not intend to flay myself to unbeard the best lady in the land. Let every one shave or shear as he likes best; I have no mind for so long a journey: my master may travel by himself. Besides, I have nothing to do with it—I am not wanted for the taking off these beards, as well as the business of my lady Dulcinea." "Indeed, my friend, you are," said the Trifaldi; "and so much need is there of your kind help, that without it nothing can be done." "In the name of all the saints in heaven!" quoth Sancho, "what have squires to do with their masters' adventures? Are we always to share the trouble, and they to reap all the glory? Body o' me! it might be something if the writers who recount their adventures would but set down in their books, ' such a knight achieved such an adventure, with the help of such a one, his squire, without whom the devil a bit could he have done it.' I say it would be something if we had our due; but, instead of this, they coolly tell us that 'Don Paralipomenon of the Three Stars finished the notable adventure of the six goblins,' and the like, without once mentioning his squire any more than if he had been a thousand miles off; though mayhap he, poor devil, was in the thick of it all the while! In truth, my good lord and lady, I say again, my master may manage this adventure by himself; and much good may it do him. I will stay with my lady duchess here, and perhaps when he comes back he may find Madam Dulcinea's business pretty forward; for I intend at my leisure whiles to lay it on to some purpose, so that I shall not have a hair to shelter me."

"Nevertheless, honest Sancho," quoth the duchess, "if your company be really necessary, you will not refuse to go; indeed, all good people will make it their business to entreat you; for piteous, truly, would it be that, through your groundless fears, these poor ladies should remain in this unseemly plight." "Odds my life!" exclaimed Sancho, "were this piece of charity undertaken for modest maidens, or poor charity-girls, a man might engage to undergo something; but to take all this trouble to rid duennas of their beards!—plague take them!—I had rather see the whole finical and squeamish tribe bearded, from the highest to the lowest of them!" "You seem to be upon bad terms with duennas, friend Sancho," said the duchess, "and are of the same mind as the Toledan apothecary; but in truth you are in the wrong; for I have duennas in my family who might serve as models to all duennas; and here is my Donna Rodriguez, who will not allow me to say otherwise." "Your excellency may say what you please," said Rodriguez; "but Heaven knows the truth of everything; and, good or bad, bearded or smooth, such as we are, our mothers brought us forth like other women; and, since God has cast us into the world, He knows why and wherefore; and upon His mercy I rely, and not upon anybody's beard whatever."

"Enough, Signora Rodriguez," quoth Don Quoixote; "as for you, Lady Trifaldi, and your persecuted friends, I trust that Heaven will speedily look with a pitying eye upon your sorrows, and that Sancho will do his duty, in obedience to my wishes. Would that Clavileno were here, and on his back Malambruno himself! for I am confident no razor would more easily shave your ladyship's beards than my sword shall shave off Malambruno's head from his shoulders. If Heaven in its wisdom permits the wicked to prosper, it is but for a time." "Ah, valorous knight!" exclaimed the afflicted lady, "may all the stars of the celestial regions regard your excellency with eyes of benignity, and impart strength to your arm and courage to your heart, to be the shield and refuge of the reviled and oppressed duennian order, abominated by apothecaries, calumniated by squires, and scoffed at by pages! Scorn betake the wretch who, in the flower of her age, doth not rather profess herself a nun than a duenna! Forlorn and despised as we are, although our descent were to be traced in a direct line from Hector of Troy himself, our ladies would not cease to 'thee' and 'thou' us, were they to be made queens for their condescension. O giant Malambruno! who, though an enchanter, art punctual in thy promises, send us the incomparable Clavileno, that our misfortunes may cease; for if the heats come on, and these beards of ours remain, woe be to us!" The Trifaldi uttered this with so much pathos that she drew tears from the eyes of all present; and so much was the heart of Sancho moved, that he secretly resolved to accompany his master to the farthest part of the world, if that would contribute to remove the bristles which deformed those venerable faces.

CHAPTER XLI.

Of the arrival of Clavileno, with the conclusion of this prolix adventure.

EVENING now came on, which was the time when the famous horse Clavileno was expected to arrive, whose delay troubled Don Quixote much, being apprehensive that, by its not arriving, either he was not the knight for whom this adventure was reserved, or that Malambruno had not the courage to meet him in single combat. But lo, on a sudden, four savages entered the garden, all clad in green ivy, and bearing on their shoulders a large wooden horse! They set him upon his legs on the ground, and one of the savages said, "Let the knight mount who has the courage to bestride this wondrous machine." "Not I," quoth Sancho; "for neither have I courage, nor am I a knight." "And let the squire, if he has one," continued the savage, "mount the crupper, and trust to valorous Malambruno; for no other shall do him harm. Turn but the pin on his forehead, and he will rush through the air to the spot where Malambruno waits; and to shun the danger of a lofty flight, let the eyes of the riders be covered till the neighing of the horse shall give the signal of his completed journey. Having thus spoken, he left Clavileno, and with courteous demeanour departed with his companions.

The afflicted lady no sooner perceived the horse than, almost with tears, addressing herself to Don Quixote, " Valorous knight," said she, " Malambruno has kept his word ; here is the horse ; our beards are increasing, and every one of us, with every hair of them, entreat and conjure you to shave and shear us. Mount, therefore, with your squire behind you, and give a happy beginning to your journey." " Madam," said Don Quixote, " I will do it with all my heart, without waiting for either cushion or spurs, so great is my desire to see your ladyship and these your unfortunate friends shaven and clean." " That will not I," quoth Sancho, " either with a bad or good will, or anywise ; and if this shaving cannot be done without my mounting that crupper, let my master seek some other squire, or these madams some other barber ; for, being no wizard, I have no stomach for these journeys. What will my islanders say when they hear that their governor goes riding upon the wind ? Besides, it is three thousand leagues from here to Candaya, —what if the horse should tire upon the road, or the giant be fickle and change his mind ? Seven years, at least, it would take us to travel home, and by that time I should have neither island or islanders that would own me ! No, no, I know better things ; I know, too, that delay breeds danger ; and when they bring you a heifer, be ready with the rope. These gentlewomen's beards must excuse me ;—faith ! St. Peter is well at Rome ; and so am I too, in this house, where I am made much of, and, through the noble master thereof, hope to see myself a governor."

" Friend Sancho," said the duke, " your island neither floats nor stirs, and therefore it will keep till your return ; indeed, so fast is it rooted in the earth, that three good pulls would not tear it from its place ; and, as you know that all offices of any value are obtained by some service or other consideration, what I expect in return for this government I have confered upon you, is only that you attend your master on this memorable occasion ; and, whether you return upon Clavileno with the expedition his speed promises, or be it your fortune to return on foot, like a pilgrim, from house to house and from inn to inn,—however it may be, you will find your island where you left it, and your islanders with the same desire to receive you for their governor. My good-will is equally unchangeable ; and to doubt that truth, Signor Sancho, would be a notorious injury to the inclination I have to serve you." " Good your worship, say no more," quoth Sancho ; " I am a poor squire, and my shoulders cannot bear the weight of so much kindness. Let my master mount, let my eyes be covered, and good luck go with us. But tell me, when we are aloft, may I not say my prayers and entreat all the saints and angels to help me ?" " Yes, surely," answered the Trifaldi, " you may invoke whomsoever you please ; for Malambruno is a Christian, and performs his enchantments with great discretion and much precaution." " Well, let us away," quoth Sancho, " and Heaven prosper us !" " Since the memorable business of the fulling-mill," said Don Quixote, "I have never seen thee, Sancho, in such trepidation; and were I superstitious, as some people, this extraordinary fear of thine would a little discourage me. But come hither, friend; for, with the leave of these nobles, I would speak a word or two with thee in private."

Don Quixote then drew Sancho aside among some trees out of hearing, and, taking hold of both his hands, said to him, "Thou seest, my good Sancho, the long journey we are about to undertake; the period of our return is uncertain, and Heaven alone knows what leisure or convenience our affairs may admit during our absence; I earnestly beg, therefore, now that opportunity serves, thou wilt retire to thy chamber, as if to fetch something necessary for the journey, and there in a trice give thyself, if it be but five hundred lashes, in part of the three thousand and three hundred for which thou art pledged; for work well begun is half ended." "By my soul," quoth Sancho, "your worship is stark mad! I am just going to gallop a thousand leagues upon a bare board, and you would have me first flay my body!—verily, verily, your worship is out of all reason. Let us go and shave these duennas, and on my return I promise to make such dispatch in getting out of debt, that your worship shall be contented,—can I say more?" "With that promise," said Don Quixote, "I feel somewhat comforted, and believe thou wilt perform it; for, though thou art not over-wise, thou art true blue in thine integrity." "I am not blue, but brown," quoth Sancho; "but though I were a mixture of both, I would make good my promise."

The knight and squire now returned to the company; and as they were preparing to mount Clavileno, Don Quixote said, "Hoodwink thyself, Sancho, and get up: he that sends for us from countries so remote cannot surely intend to betray us, for he would gain little glory by deceiving those who confide in him. And supposing the success of the adventure should not be equal to our hopes, yet of the glory of so brave an attempt no malice can deprive us." "Let us be gone, sir," quoth Sancho, "for the beards and tears of these ladies have pierced my heart, and I shall not eat to do me good till I see them smooth again. Mount, sir, and hoodwink first, for if I am to have the crupper, your worship, who sits in the saddle, must get up first." "That is true," replied Don Quixote; and, pulling a handkerchief out of his pocket, he requested the afflicted lady to place the bandage over his eyes; but it was no sooner done than he uncovered them again, saying, "I remember to have read in the 'Æneid' of Virgil, that the fatal wooden horse dedicated by the Greeks to their tutelary goddess Minerva, was filled with armed knights, who by that stratagem got admittance into Troy, and wrought its downfall. Will it not, therefore, be prudent, before I trust myself upon Clavileno, to examine what may be in his body?" "There is no need of that," said the Trifaldi; "for I am confident Malambruno has nothing in him of the traitor: your worship may mount him without fear, and should any harm ensue, let the blame fall on me alone."

Don Quixote, now considering that to betray any further doubts would be a reflection on his courage, vaulted at once into his saddle. He then tried the pin, which he found would turn very easily; stirrups he had none, so that, with his legs dangling, he looked like a figure in some Roman triumph woven in Flemish tapestry.

Very slowly, and much against his will, Sancho then got up behind, fixing himself as well as he could upon the crupper; and finding it very deficient in softness, he humbly begged the duke to accommodate him, if possible, with some pillow or cushion, even though it were from the duchess's state sofa, or from one of the page's beds, as the horse's crupper seemed rather to be of marble than of wood; but the Trifaldi, interfering, assured him that Clavileno would not endure any more furniture upon him; but that, by sitting sideways, as women ride, he would find himself greatly relieved. Sancho followed her advice; and, after taking leave of the company, he suffered his eyes to be covered. But soon after he raised the bandage, and looking sorrowfully at his friends, begged them, with a countenance of woe, to assist him at that perilous crisis with a few *Paternosters* and *Ave Marias*, as they hoped for the same charity from others when in the like extremity. "What, then!" said Don Quixote, "art thou a thief in the hands of the executioner, and at the point of death, that thou hast recourse to such prayers? Dastardly wretch without a soul! dost thou not know that the fair Magalona sat in the same place, and, if there be truth in history, alighted from it, not into the grave, but into the throne of France? And do not I sit by thee—I that may vie with the valorous Peter, who pressed this very seat that I now press? Cover, cover thine eyes, heartless animal, and publish not thy shame—at least in my presence." "Hoodwink me, then," answered Sancho; "but, since I must neither pray myself, nor beg others to do it for me, no wonder if I am afraid that we may be followed by a legion of devils, who may watch their opportunity to fly away with us."

They were now blindfolded, and Don Quixote feeling himself firmly seated, put his hand to the peg, upon which all the duennas, and the whole company, raised their voices at once, calling out, "Speed you well, valorous knight! Heaven guide thee, undaunted squire! now you fly aloft!—see how they cut the air more swiftly than an arrow! how they mount and soar, and astonish the world below! Steady, steady, valorous Sancho! you seem to reel and totter in your seat—beware of falling; for, should you drop from that tremendous height, your fall would be more terrible than that of Phaeton!" Sancho, hearing all this, pressed closer to his master, and, grasping him fast, said, "How can they say, sir, that we are got so high, when we hear them as plain as if they were close by us?" "Take no heed of that, Sancho," said Don Quixote, "for in these extraordinary flights, to see or hear a thousand leagues is nothing. But squeeze me not quite so hard, good Sancho, or thou wilt unhorse me. In truth, I see not why thou shouldst be so alarmed, for I can safely swear, an easier-paced steed I never rode in all my life: faith, it goes as glibly as if it did not move at all! Banish fear, my friend; the business goes on swimmingly, with a gale fresh

He instantly blew up with a prodigious report, and threw his riders to the ground.

and fair behind us." "Gad, I think so too!" quoth Sancho, "for I feel the wind here, as if a thousand pairs of bellows were puffing at my back." And, indeed, this was the fact, as sundry large bellows were just then pouring upon them an artificial storm; in truth, so well was this adventure managed and contrived, that nothing was wanting to make it complete. Don Quixote now feeling the wind, "Without doubt," said he, "we have now reached the second region of the air, where the hail and snow are formed: thunder and lightning are engendered in the third region; and, if we go on mounting at this rate, we shall soon be in the region of fire; and how to manage this peg I know not, so as to avoid mounting to where we shall be burnt alive."

Just at that time some flax, set on fire at the end of a long cane, was held near their faces; the warmth of which being felt, "May I be hanged," said Sancho, " if we are not already there, or very near it, for half my beard is singed off—I have a huge mind, sir, to peep out and see whereabouts we are." " Heaven forbid such rashness ! " said Don Quixote : "remember the true story of the licentiate Toralvo, who was carried by devils, hoodwinked, riding on a cane, with his eyes shut, and in twelve hours reached Rome, where, lighting on the Tower of Nona, he saw the tumult, witnessed the assault and death of the Constable of Bourbon, and the next morning returned to Madrid, where he gave an account of all that he had seen. During his passage through the air, he said that a devil told him to open his eyes, which he did, and found himself, as he thought, so near the body of the moon that he could have laid hold of it with his hand ; but that he durst not look downwards to the earth, lest his brain should turn. Therefore, Sancho, let us not run the risk of uncovering in such a place, but rather trust to him who has taken charge of us, as he will be responsible : perhaps we are just now soaring aloft to a certain height, in order to come souse down upon the kingdom of Candaya, like a hawk upon a heron ; and, though it seems not more than half an hour since we left the garden, doubtless we have travelled through an amazing space." " As to that I can say nothing," quoth Sancho Panza ; " I can only say that if Madam Magalona was content to ride upon this crupper without a cushion, her flesh could not have been the tenderest in the world."

This conversation between the two heroes was overheard by the duke and duchess, and all who were in the garden, to their great diversion ; and, being now disposed to finish the adventure, they applied some lighted flax to Clavileno's tail; upon which, his body being full of combustibles, he instantly blew up with a prodigious report, and threw his riders to the ground. The Trifaldi, with the whole bearded squadron of duennas, vanished, and all that remained in the garden were laid stretched on the ground as if in a trance. Don Quixote and Sancho got upon their legs in but an indifferent plight, and looking round, were amazed to find themselves in the same garden with such a number of people strewed about them on all sides ; but their wonder was increased when, on a huge lance sticking in the earth, they beheld a sheet of white parchment attached to it by silken strings, whereon was written in letters of gold, the following words :

" The renowned knight, Don Quixote de la Mancha, has achieved the stupendous adventure of Trifaldi the Afflicted and her companions in grief only by attempting it. Malambruno is satisfied, his wrath is appeased, the beards of the unhappy have vanished, and Don Clavijo and Antonomasia have recovered their pristine state. When the squirely penance shall be completed, then shall the white dove, delivered from the cruel talons of the pursuing hawks, be enfolded in the arms of her beloved turtle : such is the will of Merlin, prince of enchanters."

Don Quixote having read the prophetic decree, and perceiving at once that it referred to the disenchantment of Dulcinea, he expressed his gratitude to Heaven for having, with so much ease, performed so great an exploit, whereby many venerable females had been happily rescued from disgrace. He then went to the spot where the duke and duchess lay on the ground, and, taking the duke by the arm, he said, " Courage, courage, my good lord; the adventure is over without damage to the bars, as you will find by that record." The duke gradually, as if awaking from a sound sleep, seemed to recover his senses, as did the duchess and the rest of the party; expressing, at the same time, so much wonder and affright that what they feigned so well seemed almost reality to themselves.

Though scarcely awake, the duke eagerly looked at the scroll, and, having read it, with open arms embraced Don Quixote, declaring him to be the bravest of knights. Sancho looked all about for the afflicted dame, to see what kind of face she had when beardless, and whether she was now as goodly to the sight as her stately presence seemed to promise; but he was told that, when Clavileno came tumbling down in the flames through the air, the Trifaldi, with her whole train, vanished, with not a beard to be seen among them—every hair was gone, root and branch !

The duchess inquired of Sancho how he had fared during that long voyage. " Why, truly, madam," answered he, " I have seen wonders; for as we were passing through the region of fire, as my master called it, I had, you must know, a mighty mind to take a peep; and though my master would not consent to it, I, who have an itch to know everything, and a hankering after what is forbidden, could not help, softly and unperceived, shoving the cloth a little aside, when through a crevice I looked down, and there I saw (Heaven bless us !) the earth so far off that it looked to me no bigger than a grain of mustard-seed, and the men that walked upon it little bigger than hazel-nuts !—only think, then, what a height we must have been!" "Take care what you say, friend," said the duchess; " had it been so, you could not have seen the earth nor the people upon it : a hazel-nut, good man, would have covered the whole earth." " Like enough," said Sancho, " but for all that, I had a side view of it, and saw it all." " Take heed, Sancho," said the duchess, "for one cannot see the whole of anything by a side view." " I know nothing about views," replied Sancho; " I only know that your ladyship should remember that, since we flew by enchantment, by enchantment I might see the whole earth, and all the men upon it, in whatever way I looked; and, if your ladyship will not credit that, neither will you believe me when I tell you that, thrusting up the kerchief close to my eyebrows, I found myself so near to heaven that it was not above a span and a half from me (bless us all ! what a place it is for bigness !) and it so fell out that we passed close by the place where the seven little she-goats* are kept; and, by my faith, having been a goatherd in my youth, I no sooner saw them than I longed to play with them awhile; and had I not done it, I verily believe I should have died;

---

* The Pleiades are vulgarly called, in Spain, " the seven little she-goats."

so what did I, but, without saying a word, softly slide down from Clavileno, and play with the sweet little creatures, which are like so many violets, for almost three-quarters of an hour; and all the while Clavileno seemed not to move from the place, nor stir a jot."

"And while honest Sancho was diverting himself with the goats," quoth the duke, "how did Signor Don Quixote amuse himself?" To which the knight answered, "As these and such-like concerns are out of the order of nature, I do not wonder at Sancho's assertions; for my own part, I can truly say I neither looked up nor down, and saw neither heaven nor earth, nor sea nor sands. It is nevertheless certain that I was sensible of our passing through the region of air, and even touched upon that of fire; but that we passed beyond it I cannot believe; for, the fiery region lying between the sphere of the moon and the uppermost region of the air, we could not reach that heaven where the seven goats are which Sancho speaks of, without being burnt; and since we were not burnt, either Sancho lies or Sancho dreams." "I neither lie nor dream," answered Sancho; "only ask me the marks of these same goats, and by them you may guess whether I speak the truth or not." "Tell us what they were, Sancho," quoth the duchess. "Two of them," replied Sancho, "are green, two carnation, two blue, and one motley-coloured." "A new kind of goats are those," said the duke; "in our region of the earth we have none of such colours." "The reason is plain," quoth Sancho; "your highness will allow that there must be some difference between the goats of heaven and those of earth." "Prithee, Sancho," said the duke, "was there a he-goat among them?" "Not one, sir," answered Sancho; "and I was told that none are suffered to pass beyond the horns of the moon."

They did not choose to question Sancho any more concerning his journey, perceiving him to be in the humour to ramble all over the heavens, and tell them of all that was passing there, without having stirred a foot from the place where he mounted.

Thus concluded the adventure of the Afflicted Duenna, which furnished the duke and duchess with a subject of mirth, not only at the time, but for the rest of their lives, and Sancho something to relate had he lived for ages. "Sancho," said Don Quixote (whispering him in the ear). "if thou wouldst have us credit all thou hast told us of heaven, I expect thee to believe what I saw in Montesinos' cave—I say no more."

CHAPTER XLII.

Containing the instructions which Don Quixote gave to Sancho Panza before he went to his government ; and with other well-considered matters.

THE duke and duchess being so well pleased with the Afflicted Duenna, were encouraged to proceed with other projects, seeing that there was nothing too extravagant for the credulity of the knight and squire. The necessary orders were accordingly issued to their servants and vassals with regard to their behaviour towards Sancho in his government of the promised island. The day after the flight of Clavileno, the duke bid Sancho prepare and get himself in readiness to assume his office, for his islanders were already wishing for him as for rain in May. Sancho made a low bow, and said, " Ever since my journey to heaven, when I looked down and saw the earth so very small, my desire to be a governor has partly cooled ; for what mighty matter is it to command on a spot no bigger than a grain of mustard-seed ? Where is the majesty and pomp of governing half a dozen creatures no bigger than hazel-nuts ? If your lordship will be pleased to offer me some small portion of heaven, though it be but half a league, I would jump at it sooner than for the largest island in the world."

" Look you, friend Sancho," answered the duke, " I can give away no part of heaven, not even a nail's breadth ; for God has reserved to Himself the disposal of such favours ; but what it is in my power to give, I give you with all my heart ; and the island I now present to you is ready made, round and sound, well proportioned, and above measure fruitful, and where, by good management, you may yourself, with the riches of the earth, purchase an inheritance in heaven." "Well, then," answered Sancho, " let this island be forthcoming, and it shall go hard with me but I will be such a governor that, in spite of rogues, heaven will take me in. Nor is it out of covetousness that I forsake my humble cottage and aspire to greater things, but the desire I have to taste what it is to be a governor." " If once you taste it, Sancho," quoth the duke, " you will lick your fingers after it ; so sweet it is to command and be obeyed. And certain I am, when your master becomes an emperor, of which there is no doubt, as matters proceed so well, it would be impossible to wrest his power from him, and his only regret will be that he had it not sooner." " Faith, sir, you are in the right," quoth Sancho ; " it is pleasant to govern, though it be but a flock of sheep." " Let me be buried with you, Sancho," replied the duke, " if you know not something of everything, and I doubt not you will prove a pearl of a governor. But enough of this for the present ; to-morrow you surely depart for your island, and this evening you shall be fitted with suitable apparel and with all things necessary for your appointment." "Clothe me as you will," said Sancho, "I shall still be Sancho Panza." "That is true," said the duke; "but the garb should always be suitable to the office and rank of the wearer. For a lawyer to be habited like a soldier, or a soldier like a priest, would be preposterous; and you, Sancho, must be clad partly like a scholar, and partly like a soldier, as, in the office you will hold, arms and learning are united." "As for learning," replied Sancho, "I have not much of that, for I hardly know my A B C; but to be a good governor it will be enough that I am able to make my Christ-cross; and as to arms, I shall handle such as are given me till I fall, and so God help me." "With so good an intention," quoth the duke, "Sancho cannot do wrong." At this time Don Quixote came up to them, and hearing how soon Sancho was to depart to his government, he took him by the hand, and, with the duke's leave, led him to his chamber, in order to give him some advice respecting his conduct in office; and, having entered, he shut the door, and, almost by force, made Sancho sit down by him, and with much solemnity addressed him in these words:

"I am thankful to Heaven, friend Sancho, that even before fortune has crowned my hopes, prosperity has gone forth to meet thee. I, who had trusted in my own success for the reward of thy services, am still but on the road to advancement, whilst thou, prematurely, and before all reasonable expectation, art come into full possession of thy wishes. Some must bribe, importune, solicit, attend early, pray, persist, and yet do not obtain what they desire; whilst another comes, and, without knowing how, jumps at once into the preferment for which so many had sued in vain. It is truly said that 'merit does much, but fortune more.' Thou, who in respect to me art but a very simpleton, without either early rising or late watching, without labour of body or mind, by the air alone of knight-errantry breathing on thee, findest thyself the governor of an island, as if it were a trifle, a thing of no account!

"All this I say, friend Sancho, that thou mayest not ascribe the favour done thee to thine own merit, but give thanks, first to Heaven, which disposeth things so kindly; and, in the next place, acknowledge with gratitude the inherent grandeur of the profession of knight-errantry. Thy heart being disposed to believe what I have now said to thee, be attentive, my son, to me, thy Cato, who will be thy counsellor, thy north star, and thy guide, to conduct and steer thee safe into port, out of that tempestuous sea upon which thou art going to embark, and where thou wilt be in danger of being swallowed up in the gulf of confusion.

"First, my son, fear God; for to fear Him is wisdom; and being wise, thou canst not err.

"Secondly, consider what thou art, and endeavour to know thyself, which is the most difficult study of all others. The knowledge of thyself will preserve thee from vanity, and the fate of the frog that foolishly vied with the ox will serve thee as a caution; the recollection, too, of having been formerly a swineherd in thine own country will be to thee, in the loftiness of thy pride, like the ugly feet of the peacock." "It is true," said Sancho, " that I once kept swine; but I was only a boy then : when I grew towards man I looked after geese, and not hogs. But this, methinks, is nothing to the purpose; for all governors are not descended from kings." " That I grant," replied Don Quixote ; " and therefore those who have not the advantage of noble descent should fail not to grace the dignity of the office they bear with gentleness and modesty, which, when accompanied with discretion, will silence those murmurs which few situations in life can escape.

" Conceal not the meanness of thy family, nor think it disgraceful to be descended from peasants; for, when it is seen that thou art not thy-self ashamed, none will endeavour to make thee so; and deem it more meritorious to be a virtuous humble man than a lofty sinner. Infinite is the number of those who, born of low extraction, have risen to the highest dignities, both in church and state; and of this truth I could tire thee with examples.

" Remember, Sancho, if thou takest virtue for the rule of life, and valuest thyself upon acting in all things conformably thereto, thou wilt have no cause to envy lords and princes ; for blood is inherited, but virtue is a common property, and may be acquired by all; it has, more-over, an intrinsic worth which blood has not. This being so, if perad-venture any one of thy kindred visit thee in thy government, do not slight or affront him ; but receive, cherish, and make much of him; for in so doing thou wilt please God, who allows none of His creatures to be despised ; and thou wilt also manifest therein a well-disposed nature.

" If thou takest thy wife with thee (and it is not well for those who are appointed to governments to be long separated from their families), teach, instruct, and polish her from her natural rudeness; for it often happens that all the consideration a wise governor can acquire is lost by an ill-bred and foolish woman.

" If thou shouldst become a widower (an event which is possible), and thy station entitles thee to a better match, seek not one to serve thee for a hook and angling-rod, or a friar's hood to receive alms in ;* for, be-lieve me, whatever the judge's wife receives, the husband must account for at the general judgment, and shall be made to pay fourfold for all that of which he has rendered no account during his life.

" Be not under the dominion of thine own will : it is the vice of the ignorant, who vainly presume on their own understanding.

" Let the tears of the poor find more compassion, but not more justice, from thee than the applications of the wealthy.

" Be equally solicitous to sift out the truth amidst the presents and promises of the rich, and the sighs and entreaties of the poor.

" Whenever equity may justly temper the rigour of the law, let not the whole force of it bear upon the delinquent ; for it is better that a judge should lean on the side of compassion than severity.

---

* An allusion to the proverb, *" No quiero, mas echadmelo en mi capilla ;"* that is, " I will not, but throw it into my hood." It is applied to the begging friars, who refuse to take money, but suffer it to be thrown into their hoods.

" If perchance the scales of justice be not correctly balanced, let the error be imputable to pity, not to gold.

" If perchance the cause of thine enemy come before thee, forget thy injuries, and think only on the merits of the case.

" Let not private affection blind thee in another man's cause; for the errors thou shalt thereby commit are often without remedy, and at the expense both of thy reputation and fortune.

" When a beautiful woman comes before thee to demand justice, consider maturely the nature of her claim, without regarding either her tears or her sighs, unless thou wouldst expose thy judgment to the danger of being lost in the one, and thy integrity in the other.

" Revile not with words him whom thou hast to correct with deeds : the punishment which the unhappy wretch is doomed to suffer is sufficient, without the addition of abusive language.

" When the criminal stands before thee, recollect the frail and depraved nature of man, and, as much as thou canst, without injustice to the suffering party, show pity and clemency ; for though the attributes of God are all equally adorable, yet His mercy is more shining and attractive in our eyes than His justice.

" If, Sancho, thou observest these precepts, thy days will be long and thy fame eternal, thy recompense full, and thy felicity unspeakable. Thou shalt marry thy children to thy heart's content, and they and thy grandchildren shall want neither honours nor titles. Beloved by all men, thy days shall pass in peace and tranquillity ; and when the inevitable period comes, death shall steal on thee in a good and venerable old age, and thy grandchildren's children, with their tender and pious hands, shall close thine eyes.

" The advice I have just given thee, Sancho, regards the good and ornament of thy mind ; now listen to the directions I have to give concerning thy person and deportment."

CHAPTER XLIII.

Of the second series of instructions Don Quixote gave to Sancho Panza.

Who that has duly considered Don Quixote's instructions to his squire would not have taken him for a person of singular intelligence and discretion ? But, in truth, as it has often been said in the progress of this great history, he raved only on the subject of chivalry ; on all others he manifested a sound and discriminating understanding ; wherefore his judgment and his actions appeared continually at variance. But, in these second instructions given to Sancho, which showed much ingenuity, his wisdom and frenzy are both singularly conspicuous.

During the whole of this private conference, Sancho listened to his master with great attention, and endeavoured so to register his counsel in his mind, that he might thereby be enabled to bear the burden of government, and acquit himself honourably.   Don Quixote now proceeded :

" As to the regulation of thine own person and domestic concerns," said he, " in the first place, Sancho, I enjoin thee to be cleanly in all things.   Keep the nails of thy fingers constantly and neatly pared, nor suffer them to grow as some do, who ignorantly imagine that long nails beautify the hand, and account the excess of that excrement simply a finger-nail, whereas it is rather the talon of the lizard-hunting kestrel— a foul and unsightly object.

" Go not loose and unbuttoned, Sancho ; for a slovenly dress betokens a careless mind ; or, as in the case of Julius Cæsar, it may be attributed to cunning.

" Examine prudently the income of thy office, and if it will afford thee to give liveries to thy servants, give them such as are decent and lasting, rather than gaudy and modish ; and what thou shalt thus save in thy servants bestow on the poor; so shalt thou have attendants both in heaven and earth, — a provision which our vainglorious great never think of.

" Eat neither garlic nor onions, lest the smell betray thy rusticity. Walk with gravity, and speak deliberately, but not so as to seem to be listening to thyself; for affectation is odious.

" Eat little at dinner and less at supper ; for the health of the whole body is tempered in the laboratory of the stomach.

" Drink with moderation ; for inebriety never keeps a secret nor performs a promise.

" Take heed, Sancho, not to chew on both sides of thy mouth at once, and by no means to eruct before company."   " I know not what you mean by *eruct,*" quoth Sancho.   " To eruct," said Don Quixote, " means to belch — a filthy, though very significant word ; and therefore the polite, instead of saying ' belch,' make use of the word ' eruct,' which is borrowed from the Latin ; and from belchings they say ' eructations ;' and though it is true that some do not yet understand these terms, it matters not much, for in time, by use and custom, their meaning will be known to all; and it is by such innovations that languages are enriched."   " By my faith, sir," quoth Sancho, " I shall bear in mind this counsel about not belching, for in truth, I am hugely given to it."   " *Eructing,* Sancho, not belching," said Don Quixote.   " Eructing it shall be henceforward," quoth Sancho, " and, egad ! I shall never forget it."

" In the next place, Sancho, do not intermix in thy discourse such a multitude of proverbs as thou wert wont to do ; for though proverbs are concise and pithy sentences, thou dost so often drag them in by the head and shoulders, that they seem rather the maxims of folly than of wisdom."   " Heaven alone can remedy that," quoth Sancho ; " for I know more than a handful of proverbs, and when I talk, they crowd so thick into my mouth, that they quarrel which shall get out first; so out they come haphazard, and no wonder if they should sometimes not be very pat to the purpose.   But I will take heed in future to utter only such as become the gravity of my place; for ' in a plentiful house supper is soon dressed;' ' he that cuts does not deal;' and, ' with the repique in hand the game is sure;' ' he is no fool who can both spend and spare.' ''

" So, so! there, out with them, Sancho," quoth Don Quixote; " spare them not;—my mother whips me and I still tear on. While I am warning thee from the prodigal use of proverbs, thou pourest upon me a whole litany of them, as fitting to the present purpose as if thou hadst sung, ' Hey down derry!' Attend to me, Sancho. I do not say a proverb is amiss when aptly and seasonably applied; but to be for ever discharging them, right or wrong, hit or miss, renders conversation insipid and vulgar.

" When thou art on horseback, do not throw thy body backward over the crupper, nor stretch thy legs out stiff and straddling from the horse's belly; neither let them hang dangling, as if thou wert still upon Dapple; for by their deportment and air on horseback gentlemen are distinguished from grooms.

" Let thy sleep be moderate; for he who rises not with the sun enjoys not the day; and remember, Sancho, that diligence is the mother of good fortune, and that sloth, her adversary, never arrived at the attainment of a good wish.

" At this time I have but one more admonition to give thee, which, though it concerns not thy person, it is well worthy of thy careful remembrance. It is this,—never undertake to decide contests concerning lineage, or the pre-eminence of families; since, in the comparison, one must of necessity have the advantage, and he whom thou hast humbled will hate thee, and he who is preferred will not reward thee.

" As for thy dress, wear breeches and hose, a long coat, and a cloak somewhat longer; but for trousers or trunk-hose, think not of them: they are not becoming either gentlemen or governors.

" This is all the advice, friend Sancho, that occurs to me at present; hereafter, as occasions offer, my instructions will be ready, provided thou art mindful to inform me of the state of thy affairs." " Sir," answered Sancho, " I see very well that all your worship has told me is wholesome and profitable; but what shall I be the better for it if I cannot keep it in my head? It is true I shall not easily forget what you said about paring my nails, and marrying again if the opportunity offered; but as for your other quirks and quillets, I protest they have already gone out of my head as clean as last year's clouds; and therefore let me have them in writing; for, though I cannot read them myself, I will give them to my confessor, that he may repeat and drive them into me in time of need."

" Heaven defend me!" said Don Quixote, " how scurvy doth it look in a governor to be unable to read or write! Indeed, Sancho, I must needs tell thee that when a man has not been taught to read, or is left-handed, it argues that his parentage was very low, or that in early life he was so indocile and perverse that his teachers could beat nothing good into him. Truly, this is a great defect in thee, and therefore I would have thee learn to write, if it were only thy name." " That I

can do already," quoth Sancho; " for when I was steward of the Brotherhood in our village, I learned to make certain marks like those
upon wool-packs, which, they told me, stood for my name. But at the
worst, I can feign a lameness in my right hand, and get another to sign
for me : there is a remedy for everything but death ; and having the
staff in my hand, I can do what I please. Besides, as your worship
knows, he whose father is mayor* — and I, being governor, am, I trow,
something more than mayor. Ay, ay, let them come that list, and play
at bo-peep, — ay, fleer and backbite me ; but they may come for wool,
and go back shorn : ' his home is savoury whom God loves ;'— besides,
' the rich man's blunders pass current for wise maxims ;' so that I
being a governor, and therefore wealthy, and bountiful to boot — as I

" Heaven defend me !" said Don Quixote, " how scurvy doth it look in a governor
to be unable to read or write!"

intend to be—nobody will see any blemish in me. No, no, ' let the clown
daub himself with honey, and he will never want flies.' ' As much as
you have, just so much you are worth,' said my grandam ; ' revenge
yourself upon the rich who can.' " " Heaven confound thee !" exclaimed
Don Quixote; " sixty thousand devils take thee and thy proverbs !
This hour or more thou hast been stringing thy musty wares, poisoning
and torturing me without mercy. Take my word for it, these proverbs
will one day bring thee to the gallows ; — they will surely provoke thy
people to rebellion ! Where dost thou find them ? How shouldst thou
apply them, idiot ? for I toil and sweat as if I were delving the ground
to utter but one, and apply it properly."

---

* The entire proverb is, " He whose father is mayor goes safe to his trial."

" Before Heaven, master of mine," replied Sancho, "your worship complains of very trifles. Why, in the devil's name, are you angry that I make use of my own goods? for other stock I have none, nor any stock but proverbs upon proverbs; and just now I have four ready to pop out, all pat and fitting as pears in a pannier — but I am dumb; Silence is my name." *   " Then art thou vilely miscalled," quoth Don Quixote "being an eternal blabber. Nevertheless, I would fain know these four proverbs that come so pat to the purpose; for I have been rummaging my own memory, which is no bad one, but for the soul of me can find none." " Can there be better," quoth Sancho, "than— ' Never venture your fingers between two eye-teeth;' and with ' Get out of my house — what would you have with my wife?' there is no arguing; and, ' Whether the pitcher hits the stone, or the stone hits the pitcher, it goes ill with the pitcher.' All these, your worship must see, fit to a hair. Let no one meddle with the governor or his deputy, or he will come off the worst, like him who claps his finger between two eye-teeth, and though they were not eye-teeth, 't is enough if they be but teeth. To what a governor says there is no replying, any more than to ' Get out of my house—what business have you with my wife?' Then as to the stone and the pitcher—a blind man may see that. So he who points to the mote in another man's eye should first look to the beam in his own, that it may not be said of him, ' The dead woman was afraid of her that was flayed.' Besides, your worship knows well that the fool knows more in his own house than the wise in that of another."

" Not so, Sancho," answered Don Quixote; "the fool knows nothing, either in his own or any other house; for knowledge is not to be erected upon so bad a foundation as folly. But here let it rest, Sancho, for if thou governest ill, though the fault will be thine, the shame will be mine. However, I am comforted in having given thee the best counsel in my power; and therein having done my duty, I am acquitted both of my obligation and promise: so God speed thee, Sancho, and govern thee in thy government, and deliver me from the fears I entertain that thou wilt turn the whole island topsy-turvy!—which, indeed, I might prevent, by letting the duke know what thou art, and telling him that all that paunch-gut and little carcase of thine is nothing but a sack full of proverbs and impertinence."

" Look you, sir," replied Sancho, " if your worship thinks I am not fit for this government, I renounce it from this time; for I have more regard for a single nail's-breadth of my soul than for my whole body; and plain Sancho can live as well upon bread and onions as governor Sancho upon capon and partridge. Besides, sleep makes us all alike, great and small, rich and poor. Call to mind, too, who first put this whim of governor into my head — who was it but yourself? for, alack! I know no more about governing islands than a bustard; and if you fancy that, in case I should be a governor, the devil will have me — in God's name, let me rather go to heaven plain Sancho than a governor

---

* The proverb is, "To keep silence well is called *Santo.*"

to the other place." "Before Heaven, Sancho," quoth Don Quixote, "for those last words of thine I think that thou deservest to be governor of a thousand islands. Thou hast a good disposition, without which knowledge is of no value. Pray to God, and endeavour not to err in thy intention; I mean, let it ever be thy unshaken purpose and design to do right in whatever business occurs; for Heaven constantly favours a good intention. And now let us go to dinner, for I believe their highnesses wait for us."

CHAPTER XLIV.

How Sancho Panza was conducted to his government, and of the strange adventure which befell Don Quixote in the castle.

WE have been told that there is a manifest difference between the translation and the original in the beginning of this chapter; the translator having entirely omitted what the historian, Cid Hamet, here took occasion to say of himself, where he laments his ever having engaged in a work like the present, of so dry and limited a subject, wherein he was confined to a dull narrative of the transactions of the crazy knight and his squire; not daring to launch out into episodes and digressions, that would have yielded both pleasure and profit in abundance. To have his invention, his hand, and his pen thus tied down to a single subject, and confined to so scanty a list of characters, he thought an insupportable hardship, as it gave him endless trouble, and promised him nothing for his pains. In the First Part he had endeavoured, he said, to make amends for the defect here complained of, by introducing such tales as "The Curious Impertinent," and "The Captive;" and though these, it is true, did not, strictly, make a part of the history, the same objection could not apply to other stories which are there brought in, and appear so naturally connected with Don Quixote's affair that they could not well be omitted. But finding, he said, the attention of his readers so engrossed by the exploits of his mad hero, that they have none to bestow on his novels, and that, being run over in haste, their reception is not proportioned to their merit, which would have been sufficiently obvious if they had been published separately, and unmixed with the extravagances of Don Quixote and the simplicities of his squire; finding this to be the case, he has in the Second Part admitted no unconnected tales, and only such episodes as arose out of the events that actually occurred, and even these with all possible brevity. But although he has thus consented to restrain his genius, and to keep within the narrow limits of a simple narrative — thereby suppressing knowledge and talents sufficient to treat of the whole universe, he hopes his book will not do him any discredit, but that he may be applauded for what he has written, and yet more for what he has omitted in obedience to the restrictions imposed on him. He then goes on with his history, where the translator has taken it up, as follows :

Don Quixote, in the evening of the day in which Sancho had received his admonitions, gave him a copy of them in writing, that he might get them read to him occasionally; but they were no sooner delivered to Sancho than he dropped them, and they fell into the duke's hands, who communicated them to the duchess, and both were again surprised at the good sense and madness of Don Quixote. That very evening, in prosecution of their merry project, they dispatched Sancho, with a large retinue, to the place which to him was to be an island. The person who had the management of the business was steward to the duke; a man of much humour, and who had, besides, a good understanding— indeed, without that there can be no true pleasantry. He it was who had already personated the Countess Trifaldi in the manner before related; and being so well qualified, and likewise so well tutored by his lord and lady as to his behaviour towards Sancho, no wonder he performed his part to admiration. Now, it so happened that the moment Sancho cast his eyes upon this same steward, he fancied he saw the very face of the Trifaldi; and, on turning to his master, "The devil fetch me for an honest man and a true believer," said he, "if your worship will not own that the face of this steward is the very same as that of the afflicted lady."

Don Quixote looked at the steward very earnestly, and, after having viewed him from head to foot, he said, "There is no need, Sancho, of giving thyself to the devil either for thy honesty or faith ; for, though I know not thy meaning, I plainly see the steward's face is similar to that of the afflicted lady : yet is the steward not the afflicted lady, for that would imply a palpable contradiction, which, were we now to examine and inquire into, would only involve us in doubts and difficulties that might be still more inexplicable. Believe me, friend, it is our duty earnestly to pray that we may be protected from the wicked wizards and enchanters that infest us." "Egad, sir, it is no jesting matter," quoth Sancho, "for I heard him speak just now, and methought the very voice of Madam Trifaldi sounded in my ears. But I say nothing—only I shall keep my eye upon him, and time will show whether I am right or wrong." "Do so, Sancho," quoth Don Quixote ; "and fail not to give me advice of all thou mayest discover in this affair, and of all that happens to thee in thy government."

At length Sancho set out with a numerous train. He was dressed like one of the long robe, wearing a loose gown of sad-coloured camlet, and a cap of the same. He was mounted upon a mule, which he rode gineta fashion, and behind him, by the duke's order, was led his Dapple adorned with shining trappings of silk, which so delighted Sancho that every now and then he turned his head to look upon him, and thought himself so happy that he would not have changed conditions with the Emperor of Germany. On taking leave of the duke and duchess, he kissed their hands ; at the same time he received his master's blessing, not without tears on both sides.

Now, loving reader, let honest Sancho depart in peace, and in a happy hour: the accounts hereafter given of his conduct in office may, perchance, excite thy mirth; but at the same time let us attend to what befell his master on the same night; at which if thou dost not laugh outright, at least thou wilt show thy teeth, and grin like a monkey; for it is the property of all the noble knight's adventures to produce either surprise or merriment.

It is related, then, that, immediately after Sancho's departure, Don Quixote began to feel the solitary state in which he was now left, and had it been possible for him to have revoked the commission, and deprived Sancho of his government, he would certainly have done it. The duchess, perceiving this change, inquired the cause of his sadness; adding that, if it was on account of Sancho's absence, her home contained abundance of squires, duennas, and damsels, all ready to serve him to his heart's desire. " It is true, madam," answered Don Quixote, " that Sancho's absence somewhat weighs upon my heart, but that is not the principal cause of my apparent sadness; and of all your excellency's kind offers I accept only of the good-will with which they are tendered; saving that I humbly entreat that your excellency will be pleased to permit me to wait upon myself in my own apartment." " By my faith, Signor Don Quixote," quoth the duchess, " that must not be: you shall be served by four of my damsels, all beautiful as roses." " To me," answered Don Quixote, " they will not be roses, but even as thorns pricking me to the soul;—they must in nowise enter my chamber. If your grace would continue your favours to me, unmerited as they are, suffer me to be alone, and leave me without attendants in my chamber, that I may still keep a wall betwixt my passions and my modesty: a practice I would not forego for all your highness's liberality towards me; in truth, I would rather sleep in my garments than consent that others should undress me."

" Enough, enough, Signor Don Quixote," replied the duchess: " I will surely give orders that not so much as a fly shall enter your chamber, much less a damsel. I would by no means be accessory to the violation of Signor Don Quixote's delicacy; for, by what I can perceive, the most conspicuous of his virtues is modesty. You shall undress and dress by yourself, your own way, when and how you please; for no intruders shall invade the privacy of your chamber, in which you will find all the accommodation proper for those who sleep with their doors closed, that there may be no necessity for opening them. May the great Dulcinea del Toboso live a thousand ages, and may her name be extended over the whole circumference of the earth, for meriting the love of so valiant and so chaste a knight! And may indulgent Heaven infuse into the heart of Sancho Panza, our governor, a disposition to finish his penance speedily, that the world may again enjoy the beauty of so exalted a lady." " Madam," returned Don Quixote, " your highness has spoken like yourself. From the mouth of so excellent a lady nothing but what is good and generous can proceed; and Dulcinea will be more happy and more renowned by the praises your grace bestows upon her than by all the applause lavished by the most eloquent orators upon earth." " Sir Knight," said the duchess, " I must now remind you that the hour of refreshment draws near : let us to supper, for the duke, perhaps, is waiting for us, and we will retire early, for you must needs be weary after your long journey yesterday to Candaya." " Not in the least, madam," answered Don Quixote. " I can assure your grace that in all my life I never bestrode a horse of an easier or better pace than Clavileno ; and I cannot imagine what should induce Malambruno to deprive himself of so swift and so gentle a steed, and without scruple thus rashly to destroy him." " It is not impossible," said the duchess, " that repenting of the mischief he had done to the Countess Trifaldi and her attendants, as well as to many other persons, and of the iniquities he had committed as a wizard and an enchanter, he was determined to destroy all the implements of his art, and accordingly he burnt Clavileno as the principal, being the engine which enabled him to rove all over the world ; and thus by his memorable destruction, and the record which he had caused to be set up, has eternized the memory of the great Don Quixote de la Mancha."

Don Quixote repeated his thanks to the duchess ; and after supper he retired to his chamber, where, conformably to his determination, he remained alone, suffering no attendants to approach him, lest he should be moved to transgress those bounds of virtuous decorum which he had ever observed towards his lady Dulcinea, and always bearing in mind the chastity of Amadis, that flower and mirror of knights-errant. He closed his door after him, and undressed himself by the light of two wax candles ; but on pulling off his stockings—Oh, direful mishap, unworthy of such a personage ! — forth bursts, not sighs, nor anything else unbecoming the purity of his manners, but some dozen stitches in one of his stockings, giving it the resemblance of a lattice window ! The good knight was extremely afflicted, and would have given an ounce of silver to have had just then a drachm of green silk—I say green, because his stockings were of that colour.

Here Benengeli exclaims, " O poverty, poverty ! I cannot imagine what could have induced the great Cordovan poet to call thee ' a holy, thankless gift !' I, though a Moor, have learnt by the intercourse I have had with the Christians, that holiness consists in charity, humility, faith, obedience, and poverty. Yet I maintain that a man must be much indebted to God's grace who can be contented in poverty ; unless, indeed, it be of that kind to which one of their greatest saints alludes, saying, ' Possess all things as not possessing them,' — which is no other than poverty in spirit. But thou I mean, O second poverty ! accursed indigence ! it is of thee I would now speak — why dost thou intrude upon gentlemen, and delight in persecuting the well born in preference to all others ? Why dost thou force them to cobble their own shoes, and on the same threadbare garments wear buttons of every kind and colour ? Why must their ruffs be, for the most part, ill-plaited and worse starched ?" (By the way, this shows the antiquity both of starch and ruffs.) " Wretched is the poor gentleman who, while he pampers his honour, starves his body; dining scurvily or fasting unseen with his door locked; then out in the street he marches, making a hypocrite of his toothpick, and picking where, alas! there is nothing to pick! Wretched he, I say, whose honour is in a state of continual alarm; who thinks that, at the distance of a league, every one discovers the patch upon his shoe, the greasiness of his hat, the threadbareness of his cloak, and even the cravings of his stomach."

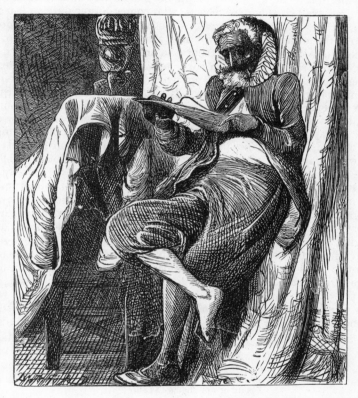

Melancholy reflections must have passed through Don Quixote's mind as he surveyed the fracture in his stocking.

All these melancholy reflections must have passed through Don Quixote's mind as he surveyed the fracture in his stocking; nevertheless, he was much comforted on finding that Sancho had left him a pair of travelling boots, in which he immediately resolved to make his appearance the next day. He now laid himself down, pensive and heavy-hearted, not more for lack of Sancho than for the misfortune of his stocking, which he would gladly have darned, even with silk of another colour — that most expressive token of gentlemanly poverty! His lights were now extinguished, but the weather was sultry, and he could not compose himself to sleep; he therefore got out of bed, and opened a casement which looked into the garden, which he had no sooner done than he heard the voices of some persons walking on the terrace below. He listened, and could distinctly hear these words: "Press me not to sing, dear Emerencia, for you know, ever since this stranger entered our castle and my eyes beheld him, I cannot sing, I can only weep. Besides, my lady does not sleep sound, and I would not for the world she should find us here. But though she should not awake, what would my singing avail, if this new Æneas, who comes hither only to leave me forlorn, awakes not to hear it?" "Do not fancy so, dear Altisidora," answered the other, "for I doubt not that the duchess is asleep, and everybody else in the house except the master of your heart and disturber of your repose; he, I am sure, is awake, for even now I heard his casement open. Sing, my unhappy friend, in a low and sweet voice to the sound of your lute, and if my lady should hear us, we will plead in excuse the excessive heat of the weather." "My fears are not on that account, my Emerencia," answered Altisidora, "but I fear lest my song should betray my heart, and that, by those who know not the mighty force of love, I might be taken for a light and wanton damsel; but come what may, I will venture: better a blush in the face than a blot in the heart." And presently she began to touch a lute so sweetly that Don Quixote was delighted and surprised; at the same time an infinite number of similar adventures rushed into his mind, of casements, grates, and gardens, serenades, courtships, and swoonings, with which his memory was well stored; and he forthwith imagined that some damsel belonging to the duchess had become enamoured of him. Though somewhat fearful of the beautiful foe, he resolved to fortify his heart, and on no account to yield; so, commending himself with fervent devotion to his mistress Dulcinea del Toboso, he determined to listen to the music; and, to let the damsel know he was there, he gave a feigned sneeze, at which they were not a little pleased, as they desired above all things that he should hear them. The lute being now tuned, Altisidora began the following

SONG.

"Wake, Sir Knight, now love's invading;
 Sleep in Holland sheets no more;
When a nymph is serenading,
 'T is an errant shame to snore.

"Hear a damsel, tall and slender,
 Moaning in most rueful guise,
With heart almost burned to cinder,
 By the sunbeams of thine eyes.

"To free damsels from disaster
 Is, they say, your daily care:
Can you then deny a plaster
 To a wounded virgin here?

"Tell me, doughty youth, who cursed thee
 With such humours and ill luck?
Was't some sullen bear dry-nursed thee,
 Or she-dragon gave thee suck?

" Dulcinea, that virago,
 Well may brag of such a Cid,
Now her fame is up, and may go
 From Toledo to Madrid.

" Would she but her prize surrender,
 (Judge how on thy face I doat!)
In exchange I'd gladly send her
 My best gown and petticoat.

" Happy I, would fortune doom me
 But to have me near thy bed,
Stroke thee, pat thee, currycomb thee,
 And hunt o'er thy knightly head.

" But I ask too much, sincerely,
 And I doubt I ne'er must do't,
I'd but kiss your toe, and fairly
 Get the length thus of your foot.

" How I'd rig thee, and what riches
 Should be heaped upon thy bones!
Caps and socks, and cloaks and breeches,
 Matchless pearls and precious stones.

" Do not from above, like Nero,
 See me burn and slight my woe,
But to quench my fires, my hero,
 Cast a pitying eye below.

" I'm a virgin pullet, truly;
 One more tender ne'er was seen:
A mere chicken fledged but newly:—
 Hang me if I'm yet fifteen.

" Wind and limb, all's tight about me;
 My hair dangles to my feet;
I am straight too:—if you doubt me,
 Trust your eyes, come down and see't

" I've a bob nose has no fellow,
 And a sparrow's mouth as rare,
Teeth like bright topazes, yellow;
 Yet I'm deemed a beauty here.

" You know what a rare musician
 (If you hearken) courts your choice;
I dare say my disposition
 Is as taking as my voice."

Here ended the song of the beauteous Altisidora, and began the alarm of the courted Don Quixote; who, fetching a deep sigh, said within himself, " Why am I so unhappy a knight-errant that no damsel can see but she must presently fall in love with me? Why is the peerless Dulcinea so unlucky that she must not be suffered singly to enjoy this my incomparable constancy? Queens, what would ye have with her? Empresses, why do ye persecute her? Damsels from fourteen to fifteen, why do ye plague her? Leave, leave the poor creature; let her triumph and glory in the lot which Love bestowed upon her in the conquest of my heart and the surrender of my soul. Take notice, ye enamoured multitude, that to Dulcinea alone I am paste and sugar, and to all others flint. To her I am honey, and to the rest of ye aloes. To me, Dulcinea alone is beautiful, discreet, lively, modest, and well born ; all the rest of her sex foul, foolish, fickle, and base born. To be hers, and hers alone, nature sent me into the world. Let Altisidora weep or sing, let the lady despair on whose account I was buffeted in the castle of the enchanted Moor. Boiled or roasted, Dulcinea's I must be, clean, well bred, and chaste, in spite of all the necromantic powers on earth."

Having so said, he clapped-to the casement, and, in despite and sorrow, as if some great misfortune had befallen him, threw himself upon his bed, where we will leave him for the present, to attend the great Sancho Panza, who is desirous of beginning his famous government.

CHAPTER XLV.

How the great Sancho Panza took possession of his island, and of the manner of his beginning to govern it.

O THOU ceaseless discoverer of the antipodes, torch of the world, eye of heaven, and sweet cause of earthen wine-coolers ;* here Thymbrius, there Phœbus ; here archer, there physician, father of poesy, inventor of music ; thou who always risest, and, though thou seemest to do so, never settest : to thee I speak, O sun ! thee I invoke to favour and enlighten the obscurity of my genius, that I may be able punctually to describe the government of the great Sancho Panza : without thee I find myself indolent, dispirited, and confused !

Sancho, then, with all his attendants, arrived at a town containing about a thousand inhabitants, which was one of the largest and best the duke had. They gave him to understand that it was called the island of Barataria, either because Barataria was really the name of the place, or because he obtained the government of it at so cheap a rate. On his arrival near the gates of the town, which was walled about, the municipal officers came out to receive him. The bells rung, and, with all the demonstrations of a general joy, and a great deal of pomp, the people conducted him to the great church to give thanks to God. Presently after, with certain ridiculous ceremonies, they presented him the keys of the town, and constituted him perpetual governor of the island of Barataria. The garb, the beard, the thickness and shortness of the new governor, surprised all who were not in the secret, and, indeed, those

---

* In Spain they call *cantimploras* small glass decanters or very small earthen pitchers, which, to cool the water in the summer, are hung in a current of air. Hence the odd epithet Cervantes applies to the sun.

who were, who were not a few. In fine, as soon as they had brought him out of the church, they carried him to the tribunal of justice, and placed him in the chair. The duke's steward then said to him, " It is an ancient custom here, my lord governor, that he who comes to take possession of this famous island is obliged to answer a question put to him, which is to be somewhat intricate and difficult. By his answer the people are enabled to feel the pulse of their new governor's understanding, and, accordingly, are either glad or sorry for his coming."

While the steward was saying this, Sancho was staring at some capital letters written on the wall opposite to his chair, and, being unable to read, he asked what that writing was on the wall. He was answered, " Sir, it is there written on what day your honour took possession of this island. The inscription runs thus: 'This day, such a day of the month and year, Signor Don Sancho Panza took possession of this island. Long may he enjoy it.'" " Pray who is it they call Don Sancho Panza?" demanded Sancho. " Your lordship," answered the steward ; " for no other Panza, besides him now in the chair, ever came into this island." " Take notice, then, brother," returned Sancho, " that the *Don* does not belong to me, nor ever did to any of my family. I am called plain Sancho Panza : my father was a Sancho, and my grandfather was a Sancho, and they were all Panzas, without any addition of *Dons,* or any other title whatever. I fancy there are more *Dons* than stones in this island. But enough : God knows my meaning; and, perhaps, if my government lasts four days, I may weed out these *Dons* that overrun the country, and, by their numbers, are as troublesome as mosquitoes and cousins.* On with your question, Master Steward, and I will answer the best I can, let the people be sorry or rejoice."

About this time two men came into the court, the one clad like a country fellow, and the other like a tailor, with a pair of shears in his hand; and the tailor said, " My lord governor, I and this countryman come before your worship by reason this honest man came yesterday to my shop (saving your presence, I am a tailor, and have passed my examination, God be thanked), and putting a piece of cloth into my hands, asked me, 'Sir, is there enough of this to make me a cap?' I, measuring the piece, answered Yes. Now he, thinking that doubtless I had a mind to cabbage some of the cloth, grounding his conceit upon his own knavery, and upon the common ill opinion of tailors, bade me view it again, and see if there was not enough for two. I guessed his drift, and told him there was. Persisting in his knavish intentions, my customer went on increasing the number of caps, and I still saying Yes, till we came to five caps. A little time ago he came to claim them. I offered them to him, but he refuses to pay me for the making, and insists I shall either return him his cloth or pay him for it." " Is all this so, brother?" demanded Sancho. " Yes," answered the man ; " but pray, my lord, make him produce the five caps he has made me." " With all my heart," an-

---

* Many plebeians in Cervantes' time already arrogated to themselves the title of *Don* which was, until then, reserved exclusively for the nobility.

swered the tailor; and pulling his hand from under his cloak, he showed the five caps on the ends of his fingers and thumb, saying, "Here are the five caps this honest man would have me make, and on my soul and conscience, not a shred of the cloth is left, and I submit the work to be viewed by any inspectors of the trade." All present laughed at the number of the caps and the novelty of the suit. Sancho reflected a moment, and then said, "I am of opinion there needs no great delay in this suit, and it may be decided very equitably off-hand. Therefore I pronounce that the tailor lose the making, and the countryman the stuff, and that the caps be confiscated to the use of the poor; and there is an end of that."

If the sentence Sancho afterwards passed on the purse of the herdsman caused the admiration of all the bystanders, this excited their laughter. However, what the governor commanded was executed, and two old men next presented themselves before him. One of them carried a cane in his hand for a staff; and the other, who had no staff, said to Sancho, "My lord, some time ago I lent this man ten crowns of gold to oblige and serve him, upon condition that he should return them on demand. I let some time pass without asking for them, being loth to put him to a greater strait to pay me than he was in when I lent them. But at length, thinking it full time to be repaid, I asked him for my money more than once, but to no purpose: he not only refuses payment, but denies the debt, and says I never lent him any such sum, or, if I did, that he had already paid me. I have no witnesses to the loan, nor has he of the payment which he pretends to have made, but which I deny; yet if he will swear before your worship that he has returned the money, I from this minute acquit him before God and the world." "What say you to this, old gentleman?" quoth Sancho. "I confess, my lord," replied the old fellow, "that he did lend me the money; and if your worship pleases to hold down your wand of justice, since he leaves it to my oath, I will swear I have really and truly returned it to him." The governor accordingly held down his wand, and the old fellow, seeming encumbered with his staff, gave it to his creditor to hold while he was swearing; and then taking hold of the cross of the wand, he said it was true indeed the other had lent him ten crowns, but that he had restored them to him into his own hand; but having, he supposed, forgotten it, he was continually dunning him for them. Upon which his lordship the governor demanded of the creditor what he had to say in reply to the solemn declaration he had heard. He said that he submitted, and could not doubt that his debtor had sworn to the truth; for he believed him to be an honest man and a good Christian; and that, as the fault must have been in his own memory, he would thenceforward ask him no more for his money. The debtor now took his staff again, and, bowing to the governor, went out of court.

Sancho having observed the defendant take his staff and walk away, and noticing also the resignation of the plaintiff, he began to meditate, and laying the forefinger of his right hand upon his forehead, he continued a short time apparently full of thought; and then, raising his

"Justice, my lord governor, justice! Woe is me! he has robbed me of what I have kept above these three and twenty years."

head, he ordered the old man with the staff to be called back; and when he had returned, "Honest friend," said the governor, "give me that staff, for I have occasion for it." "With all my heart," answered the old fellow, and delivered it into his hand. Sancho took it, and immediately giving it to the other old man, he said, "There, take that, and go about your business, in God's name, for you are now paid." "I paid, my lord!" answered the old man; "what! is this cane worth ten golden crowns?" "Yes," quoth the governor, "or I am the greatest dunce in the world: and it shall now appear whether or not I have a head to govern a whole kingdom." He then ordered the cane to be broken in court; which being done, ten crowns of gold were found within it. All the spectators were struck with admiration, and began to look upon their new governor as a second Solomon. They asked him how he had discovered that the ten crowns were in the cane. He told them that, having observed the defendant give it to the plaintiff to hold, while he took his oath that he had truly restored the money into his own hands, and that being done, he took his staff again, it came into his head that the money in dispute must be inclosed within it. From this, he added, they might see that it sometimes pleased God to direct the judgments of those who govern, though otherwise little better than blockheads. Besides, he had heard the curate of his parish tell of such another business, which was still in his mind; indeed, he had so special a memory, that were it not that he was so unlucky as to forget all that he chiefly wanted to remember, there would not have been a better in the whole island. The cause being ended, the two old men went away, the one abashed, and the other satisfied; and the secretary, who minuted down the words, actions, and behaviour of Sancho Panza, could not yet determine in his own mind whether he should set him down for wise or simple.

This cause was no sooner ended than there came into court a woman, keeping fast hold of a man clad like a rich herdsman. She came, crying aloud, "Justice, my lord governor, justice! If I cannot find it on earth, I will seek it in heaven! Lord governor of my soul, this wicked man surprised me in the middle of a field, and used me as if I had been a dish-clout! Woe is me! he has robbed me of what I have kept above these three and twenty years. Have I been as hard as a cork tree, and preserved myself as entire as a salamander in the fire, or as wool among briers, that this honest man should come with his clean hands to harm me!" "That remains to be inquired into," said Sancho; "let us now proceed to see whether this gallant's hands are clean or not;" and, turning to the man, he asked him what he had to say in answer to this woman's complaint. The man, all in confusion, replied: "Sir, I am a poor herdsman, and deal in swine; and this morning I went out of this town, after having sold, under correction be it spoken, four hogs, and what between dues and exactions, the officers took from me little less than they were worth. As I was returning home, by the way I lighted upon this good dame, and the author of all mischief, brought us together. I gave her money, but she, not contented, laid hold of me, and has never let me go till she has dragged me to this place. She says I wronged her; but, by the oath I have taken, or am to take, she lies. This is the whole truth."

Then the governor asked him if he had any silver money about him. The man answered that he had about twenty ducats in a leathern purse in his bosom. Sancho ordered him to produce it, and deliver it just as it was to the plaintiff. He did so, trembling. The woman took the purse, and making a thousand courtesies, and praying to God for the life and health of the lord governor, who took such care of poor orphans and maidens, out of the court she went, holding the purse with both hands, taking care first to see that the money that was in it was silver.

She had no sooner left the room than Sancho said to the herdsman, who was in tears, and whose eyes and heart were gone after his purse:

" Honest man, follow that woman, and take away the purse from her, whether she will or not, and come back hither with it." This was not said to one deaf or stupid, for the man instantly flew after her like lightning, and went about doing what he was bidden.

All present were in great suspense, expecting the issue of this suit. In a few minutes came in the man and the woman, clinging together closer than the first time, she with her petticoat tucked up, and the purse lapped up in it, and the man struggling to take it from her, but in vain, she defended it so stoutly. " Justice from God and the world ! " cried she, at the top of her lungs : " see, my lord governor, the impudence and want of fear of this varlet, who, in the midst of the town and of the street, would take from me the purse your worship commanded to be given to me." " And has he got it ? " demanded the governor. " Got it ! " answered the woman ; " I would sooner let him take away my life than my purse. A pretty baby I should be, indeed ! Other-guise cats must claw my beard, and not such pitiful, sneaking fools as this. Pincers and hammers, crows and chisels, shall not get it out of my clutches, nor even the paws of a lion. My soul and body shall sooner part." " She is in the right," added the man : " I yield myself worsted and spent, and confess I have not strength enough to take it from her." That said, he left her.

Then said the governor to the woman, " Give me that purse, chaste and valiant heroine." She presently delivered it, and the governor returned it to the man, and said to the violent damsel, " Sister of mine, had you shown the same, or but half as much, courage and resolution in defending yourself as you have done in defending your purse, the strength of Hercules could not have harmed you. Begone, in God's name, and in an ill hour, and be not found in all this island, nor in six leagues round about it, upon pain of two hundred stripes. Begone instantly, I say, thou prating, shameless, cheating hussey ! " The woman was confounded, and went away hanging down her head and not very well pleased. " Now, friend," said the governor to the man, " in Heaven's name get you home with your money, and henceforward, if you would avoid worse luck, yoke not with such cattle." The countryman thanked him in the best manner he could, and went his way, leaving all the court in admiration at the acuteness and wisdom of their new governor : all of whose sentences and decrees, being noted down by the appointed historiographer, were immediately transmitted to the duke, who waited for these accounts with the utmost impatience. Here let us leave honest Sancho, and return to his master, who earnestly requires our attendance, Altisidora's serenade having strangely discomposed his mind.

CHAPTER XLVI.

Of the dreadful bell-ringing, and the catish consternation into which Don Quixote was thrown in the course of the enamoured Altisidora's amour.

WE left the great Don Quixote in bed, harassed with reflections on the conduct of the love-stricken Altisidora; not to mention others which arose from the disaster of his stocking. He carried them with him to his couch, and had they been fleas, they could not more effectually have disturbed his rest. But time is ever moving; nothing can impede his course, and on he came prancing, leading up at a brisk pace the welcome morn; which was no sooner perceived by Don Quixote, than, forsaking his pillow, he hastily put on his chamois doublet, and also his travelling boots, to conceal the misfortune of his stocking. He then threw over his shoulders his scarlet mantle, and put on his head a green velvet cap trimmed with silver lace; his sharp and trusty blade he next slung over his shoulder by its belt, and now, taking up a large rosary, which he always carried about him, he marched with great state and solemnity towards the antechamber, where the duke and duchess expected him; and, as he passed through the gallery, he encountered Altisidora and her damsel friend, who had placed themselves in his way.

The moment Altisidora caught sight of him, she pretended to fall into a swoon, and dropped into the arms of her companion, who in haste began to unclasp her bosom. Don Quixote, observing this, approached them, and turning to the damsel, "I well know the meaning of this," said he, "and whence these faintings proceed." "It is more than I do," replied her friend, "for this I am sure of, that no damsel in all this family had better health than Altisidora; I have never heard so much as a sigh from her since I have known her: ill betide all the knights-errant in the world, say I, if they are all so ungrateful. Pray, my lord Don Quixote, for pity's sake leave this place; for this poor young creature will not come to herself while you are near." "Madam," said the knight, "be pleased to order a lute to be left in my chamber to-night, and I will comfort this poor damsel as far as I am able; for love in the beginning is most easily cured."

He then retreated, to avoid observation; and Altisidora, immediately recovering from her swoon, said to her companion, "By all means let him have the lute, for doubtless he intends to give us some music, which, being his, cannot but be precious." When they gave the duchess an account of their jest, and of Don Quixote's desire to have a lute in his apartment, she was exceedingly diverted, and seized the occasion, in concert with the duke and her women, to plot new schemes of harmless merriment. With great glee, therefore, they waited for night, which, notwithstanding their impatience, did not seem tardy in its approach, since the day was spent in relishing conversation with Don Quixote.

On the same day the duchess had also dispatched a page of hers (one who had personated Dulcinea in the wood) to Teresa Panza, with her husband's letter and the bundle he had left to be sent; charging him to bring back an exact account of all that should pass.

At the hour of eleven Don Quixote retired to his chamber, where he found a lute, as he had desired. After touching the instrument lightly, he opened his casement, and, on listening, heard footsteps in the garden; whereupon he again ran over the strings of the instrument, and, after tuning it as nicely as he could, he hemmed, cleared his throat, and then, with a hoarse though not unmusical voice, sang the following song, which he had himself composed that day :

> " Love, with idleness its friend,
> O'er a maiden gains its end ;
> But let business and employment
> Fill up every careful moment ;
> These an antidote will prove
> 'Gainst the poisonous arts of love.
> Maidens that aspire to marry
> In their looks reserve should carry
> Modesty their price should raise,
> And be the herald of their praise.
> Knights, whom toils of arms employ,
> With the free may laugh and toy ;
> But the modest only choose
> When they tie the nuptial noose.
> Love that rises with the sun,
> With his setting beams is gone :
> Love that guest-like visits hearts,
> When the banquet 's o'er departs ;
> And the love that comes to-day,
> And to-morrow wings its way,
> Leaves no traces on the soul,
> Its affections to control.
> Where a sovereign beauty reigns,
> Fruitless are a rival's pains—
> O'er a finished picture who
> E'er a second picture drew ?
> Fair Dulcinea, queen of beauty,
> Rules my heart and claims its duty ;
> Nothing there can take her place,
> Nought her image can erase.
> Whether fortune smile or frown,
> Constancy 's the lover's crown ;
> And, its force divine to prove,
> Miracles performs in love."

Thus far had Don Quixote proceeded in his song, which was heard by the duke and duchess, Altisidora, and almost all the inmates of the castle, when suddenly, from an open gallery directly over Don Quixote's window, a rope was let down, to which above a hundred little tinkling bells were fastened ; and immediately after, a huge sackful of cats, each furnished with similar bells tied to their tails, was also let down to the window. The noise made by these cats and bells was so great and strange, that the duke and duchess, though the inventors of the jest, were alarmed, and Don Quixote himself was panic-struck. Two or three of the cats made their way into his room, where, scouring about from side to side, it seemed as if a legion of devils had broken loose, and were flying about the room. They soon extinguished the lights in the chamber, and endeavoured to make their escape. In the meantime the rope to which the bells were fastened was playing its part, and added to the discord, insomuch that those who were not in the secret of the plot were amazed and confounded.

Don Quixot seized his sword, and made thrusts at the casement, crying out aloud, " Avaunt, ye malicious enchanters ! avaunt, ye wizard tribe ! for I am Don Quixote de la Mancha, against whom your wicked arts avail not." Then, assailing the cats in the room, they fled to the window, where they all escaped except one, which, being hard pressed by the knight, sprang at his face, and, fixing his claws in his nose, made him roar so loud, that the duke and duchess hearing, and guessing the cause, ran up in haste to his chamber, which they opened with a master-key, and there they found the poor gentleman endeavouring to disengage the creature from his face. On observing the unequal combat, the duke hastened to relieve Don Quixote; but he cried out, " Let no one take him off! leave me to battle with this demon, this wizard, this enchanter ! I will teach him what it is to deal with Don Quixote de la Mancha !" The cat, however, not regarding these menaces, kept her hold till the duke happily disengaged the furious animal, and put him out of the window.

Don Quixote's face was hideously scratched all over, not excepting his nose, which had fared but ill ; nevertheless, he was much dissatisfied by the interference which had prevented him from chastising that villanous enchanter. Oil of Aparicio was brought for him, and Altisidora herself with her lily-white hands bound up his wounds ; and while she was so employed, she said to him in a low voice, " All these misadventures befall thee, hard-hearted knight, as a punishment for your stubborn disdain ; and Heaven grant that Sancho, your squire, may forget to whip himself, that your darling Dulcinea may never be released from her enchantment, nor you ever be blest with her embraces—at least, so long as I, your unhappy adorer, shall live." To all this Don Quixote answered only with a profound sigh, and then stretched himself at full length upon his bed, thanking the duke and duchess, not for their assistance against that catish, bell-ringing crew of rascally enchanters, which he despised, but for their kind intention in coming to his succour. His noble friends then left him to repose, not a little concerned at the event of their jest, on which they had not calculated ; for it was far from their intention that it should prove so severe to the worthy knight as to cost him five days' confinement to his chamber. During that period, however, an adventure befell him more relishing than the former, but which cannot in this place be recorded, as the historian must now turn to Sancho Panza, who had hitherto proceeded very smoothly in his government.

Sancho Panza was conducted from the court of justice to a sumptuous palace, where in a great hall he found a magnificent entertainment prepared.

CHAPTER XLVII.

Giving a further account of Sancho's behaviour in his government.

THE history relates that Sancho Panza was conducted from the court of justice to a sumptuous palace, where in a great hall he found a magnificent entertainment prepared. He had no sooner entered than his ears were saluted by the sound of many instruments, and four pages served him with water to wash his hands, which the governor received with becoming gravity. The music having ceased, Sancho now sat down to dinner in a chair of state placed at the upper end of the table; for there was but one seat, and only one plate and napkin. A personage who, as it afterwards appeared, was a physician, took his stand at one side of his chair with a whalebone rod in his hand. They then removed the beau-

tiful white cloth, which covered a variety of fruits and other eatables.
Grace was said by one in a student's dress, and a laced bib was placed
by a page under Sancho's chin. Another, who performed the office of
sewer, now set a plate of fruit before him; but he had scarcely tasted it,
when, on being touched by the wand-bearer, it was snatched away, and
another, containing meat, instantly supplied its place. Yet, before
Sancho could make a beginning, it vanished, like the former, on a signal
of the wand.

The governor was surprised at this proceeding, and, looking around
him, asked if this dinner was only to show off their sleight of hand.
" My lord," said the wand-bearer, " your lordship's food must here be
watched with the same care as is customary with the governors of other
islands. I am a doctor of physic, sir, and my duty, for which I receive
a salary, is to watch over the governor's health, whereof I am more
careful than of my own. I study his constitution night and day, that I
may know how to restore him when sick ; and therefore think it incumbent on me to pay especial regard to his meals, at which I constantly
preside, to see that he eats what is good and salutary, and prevent his
touching whatever I may imagine may be prejudicial to his health or
offensive to his stomach. It was for that reason, my lord," continued
he, " I ordered the dish of fruit to be taken away, as being too watery,
and that other dish as being too hot, and over-seasoned with spices,
which are apt to provoke thirst ; and he that drinks much destroys and
consumes the radical moisture which is the fuel of life."

" Well, then," quoth Sancho, " that plate of roasted partridges, which
seem to me to be very well seasoned, I suppose will do me no manner
of harm ? " " Hold," said the doctor ; " my lord governor shall not
eat them while I live to prevent it." " Pray, why not ? " quoth Sancho.
" Because," answered the doctor, " our great master Hippocrates, the
north star and luminary of medicine, says in one of his aphorisms,
' *Omnis saturatio mala, perdicis autem pessima ;*' which means, ' All re-
pletion is bad, but that from partridges the worst.' " " If it be so," quoth
Sancho, " pray cast your eye, Signor Doctor, over all these dishes here
on the table, and see which will do me the most good or the least harm,
and let me eat of it, without whisking it away with your conjuring-
stick ; for by my soul, and as Heaven shall give me life to enjoy this
government, I am dying with hunger ; and to deny me food—let Signor
Doctor say what he will—is not the way to lengthen my life, but to cut
it short."

" Your worship is in the right, my lord governor," answered the physician, " and therefore I am of opinion you should not eat of these stewed
rabbits, as being a food that is tough and acute ; of that veal, indeed,
you might have taken a little, had it been neither roasted nor stewed ;
but as it is, not a morsel." " What think you, then," said Sancho, " of
that huge dish there, smoking hot, which I take to be an olla-podrida ?
—for, among the many things contained in it, I may surely light upon
something both wholesome and toothsome." " *Absit !* " quoth the
doctor ; " far be such a thought from us. Olla-podrida ! there is no

worse dish in the world ;—leave them to prebends and rectors of colleges, or lusty feeders at country weddings ; but let them not be seen on the tables of governors, where nothing contrary to health and delicacy should be tolerated. Simple medicines are always more estimable and safe, for in them there can be no mistake ; whereas, in such as are compounded, all is hazard and uncertainty. Therefore, what I would at present advise my lord governor to eat, in order to corroborate and preserve his health, is about a hundred small rolled-up wafers, with some thin slices of marmalade, that may sit upon the stomach and help digestion."

Sancho, hearing this, threw himself backward in his chair, and, looking at the doctor from head to foot very seriously, asked him his name, and where he had studied. To which he answered, " My lord governor, my name is Doctor Pedro Rezio de Aguero ; I am a native of a place called Tirteafuera, lying between Caraquel and Almoddobar del Campo, on the right hand, and I have taken my doctor's degrees in the university of Ossuna." " Then, hark you," said Sancho, in a rage, " Signor Doctor Pedro Rezio de Aguero, native of Tirteafuera, lying on the right hand as we go from Caraquel to Almoddobar del Campo, graduate in Ossuna, get out of my sight this instant ! or, by the light of heaven, I will take a cudgel, and, beginning with your carcase, will so belabour all the physic-mongers in the island, that not one of the tribe shall be left ! —I mean of those like yourself, who are ignorant quacks; for those who are learned and wise I shall make much of, and honour as so many angels. I say again, Signor Pedro Rezio, begone ! or I shall take the chair I sit on, and comb your head to some tune ; and, if I am called to an account for it when I give up my office, I shall prove that I have done a good service, in ridding the world of a bad physician, who is a public executioner. Body of me ! give me something to eat, or let them take back their government ; for an office that will not find a man in victuals is not worth two beans."

On seeing the governor in such a fury, the doctor would have fled out in the hall, had not the sound of a courier's horn at that instant been heard in the street. " A courier from my lord duke," said the sewer (who had looked out of the window), " and he must certainly have brought despatches of importance." The courier entered hastily, foaming with sweat and in great agitation, and, pulling a packet out of his bosom, he delivered it into the governor's hands, and by him it was given to the steward, telling him to read the superscription, which was this : " To Don Sancho Panza, Governor of the Island of Barataria. To be delivered only to himself or to his secretary." " Who is my secretary ?" said Sancho. " It is I, my lord," answered one who was present, " for I can read and write, and am, besides, a Biscayan." " With that addition," quoth Sancho, " you may very well be secretary to the emperor himself. Open the packet and see what it holds." The new secretary did so, and, having run his eye over the contents, he said it was a business which required privacy. Accordingly Sancho commanded all to retire excepting the steward and sewer ; and when the hall was cleared, the secretary read the following letter :

"It has just come to my knowledge, Signor Don Sancho Panza, that certain enemies of mine intend very soon to make a desperate attack, by night, upon the island under your command; it is necessary, therefore, to be vigilant and alert, that you may not be taken by surprise. I have also received intelligence from trusty spies, that four persons in disguise are now in your town, sent thither by the enemy, who, fearful of your great talents, have a design upon your life. Keep a strict watch; be careful who are admitted to you, and eat nothing sent you as a present. I will not fail to send you assistance if you are in want of it. Whatever may be attempted, I have full reliance on your activity and judgment.

　　　　　　　　　　　　　　　　　　　　　　" Your friend, the DUKE.

"From this place, the 16th of August, at four in the morning."

Sancho was astonished at this information, and the others appeared to be no less so. At length, turning to the steward, " I will tell you," said he, " the first thing to be done, which is, to clap Doctor Rezio into a dungeon; for if anybody has a design to kill me, it is he, and that by the most lingering and the worst of all deaths—starvation." " Be that as it may," said the steward, " it is my opinion your honour would do well to eat none of the meat here upon the table, for it was presented by some nuns, and it is a saying, 'The devil lurks behind the cross.'" " You are in the right," quoth Sancho, " and for the present give me only a piece of bread and some four pounds of grapes—there can be no poison in them; for, in truth, I cannot live without food, and if we must keep in readiness for these battles that threaten us, it is fit that we should be well fed; for the stomach upholds the heart, and the heart the man. Do you, Mr. Secretary, answer the letter of my lord duke, and tell him his commands shall be obeyed throughout most faithfully; and present my dutiful respects to my lady duchess, and beg her not to forget to send a special messenger with my letter and bundle to my wife Teresa Panza, which I shall take as a particular favour, and will be her humble servant to the utmost of my power. And, by the way, you may put in my hearty service to my master, Don Quixote de la Mancha, that he may see that I am neither forgetful nor ungrateful; and as to the rest, I leave it to you, as a good secretary and a true Biscayan, to add whatever you please, or that may turn to the best account. Now away with this cloth, and bring me something that may be eaten, and then let these spies, murderers, and enchanters, see how they meddle with me or my island."

A page now entered, saying, " Here is a countryman who would speak with your lordship on business, as he says, of great importance." " It is very strange," quoth Sancho, " that these men of business should be so silly as not to see that this is not a time for such matters. What! we who govern and are judges, belike, are not made of flesh and bone like other men? We are made of marble-stone, forsooth, and have no need of rest or refreshment? Before Heaven, and upon my conscience, if my government lasts, as I have a glimmering it will not, I shall hamper more than one of these men of business! Well, for this once, tell the fellow to come in; but first see that he is no spy, nor one of my murderers." " He looks, my lord," answered the page, " like a simple fellow; and I am much mistaken if he be not as harmless as a crust of bread." "Your worship need not fear," quoth the steward, "since we are with you." "But now that Doctor Pedro Rezio is gone," quoth Sancho, "may I not have something to eat of substance and weight, though it were but a luncheon of bread and an onion?" "At night your honour shall have no cause to complain," quoth the sewer; "supper shall make up for the want of dinner." "Heaven grant it may," replied Sancho.

The countryman, who was of a goodly presence, then came in, and it might be seen a thousand leagues off that he was an honest, good soul. "Which among you is the lord governor?" said he. "Who should it be," answered the secretary, "but he who is seated in the chair?" "I humble myself in his presence," quoth the countryman; and, kneeling down, he begged for his hand to kiss. Sancho refused it, and commanded him to rise and tell his business. The countryman did so, and said, "My lord, I am a husbandman, a native of Miguel Terra, two leagues from Ciudad Real." "What! another Tirteafuera?" quoth Sancho: "say on, brother; for let me tell you, I know Miguel Terra very well: it is not very far from my own village." "The business is this, sir," continued the peasant: "by the mercy of Heaven I was married in peace and in the face of the holy Roman Catholic Church. I have two sons, bred scholars: the younger studies for bachelor, and the elder for licentiate. I am a widower—for my wife died, or rather a wicked physician killed her by improper medicines, when she was pregnant; and if it had been God's will that the child had been born, and had proved a son, I would have put him to study for doctor, that he might not envy his two brothers the bachelor and the licentiate." "So that, if your wife," quoth Sancho, "had not died, or had not been killed, you would not now be a widower?" "No, certainly, my lord," answered the peasant. "We are much the nearer," replied Sancho; "go on, friend; for this is an hour rather for bed than business."

"I say, then," quoth the countryman, "that my son who is to be the bachelor fell in love with a damsel in the same village, called Clara Perlerino, daughter of Andres Perlerino, a very rich farmer; which name of Perlerino came to them not by lineal or any other descent, but because all of that race are paralytic; and to mend the name they call them Perlerinos. Indeed, to say the truth, the damsel is like any oriental pearl, and looked at on the right side, seems a very flower of the field; but on the left not quite so fair, for on that side she wants an eye, which she lost by the small-pox; and though the pits in her face are many and deep, her admirers say they are not pits, but graves in which the hearts of her lovers are buried. So clean and delicate, too, is she, that, to prevent defiling her face, she carries her nose so hooked up that it seemes to fly from her mouth: yet for all that she looks charmingly; for she has a large mouth; and did she not lack half a score or a dozen front teeth, she might pass and make a figure among the fairest. I say nothing of her lips, for they are so thin, that were it the fashion to reel lips, one might make a skein of them; but, being of a different colour from what is usual in lips, they have a marvellous appearance; for they are streaked with blue, green, and orange-tawny. Pardon me, good my lord governor, if I paint so minutely the parts of her who is about to become my daughter ; for in truth I love and admire her more than I can tell." "Paint what you will," quoth Sancho, "for I am mightily taken with the picture ; and had I but dined, I would have desired no better dessert." "It shall be always at your service," replied the peasant, "and the time may come when we may be acquainted, though we are not so now ; and I can assure you, my lord, if I could but paint her genteel air, and the tallness of her person, you would be amazed ; but that cannot be, because she is doubled and folded up together in such wise that her knees touch her mouth ; yet you may see plainly that, could she but stand upright, her head for certain would touch the ceiling. In fine, long ere now would she have given her hand to my bachelor in marriage, but that she cannot stretch it out, it is so shrunk ; nevertheless, her long guttered nails show the goodness of its make."

" So far, so good," quoth Sancho ; "and now, brother, that you have painted her from head to foot, what is it you would be at ? come to the point, without so many windings and turnings." "What I desire, my lord," answered the countryman, "is, that your lordship would do me the favour to give me a letter of recommendation to her father, begging his consent to the match, since we are pretty equal in the gifts of fortune and of nature ; for, to say the truth, my lord governor, my son is possessed, and scarcely a day passes in which the evil spirits do not torment him three or four times ; and having thereby once fallen into the fire, his face is as shrivelled as a piece of scorched parchment, and his eyes are somewhat bleared and running ; but, bless him ! he has the temper of an angel ; and did he not buffet and belabour himself, he would be a very saint for gentleness."

" Would you have anything else, honest friend ? " said Sancho. " One thing more I would ask," quoth the peasant, " but that I dare not ;— yet out it shall :—come what may, it shall not rot in my breast. I say, then, my lord, I could wish your worship to give me three or six hundred ducats towards mending the fortune of my bachelor—I mean, to assist in furnishing his house ; for it is agreed they shall live by themselves, without being subject to the impertinences of their fathers-in-law." " Well," quoth Sancho, " see if there is anything else you would have, and be not squeamish in asking." " No, nothing more," answered the peasant. The governor then rising, and seizing the chair on which he had been seated, exclaimed, " I vow to Heaven, Don Lubberly, saucy bumpkin, if you do not instantly get out of my sight, I will break your head with this chair ! Son of a rascal, and the devil's own painter ! At this time of day to come and ask me for six hundred ducats ! Where should I have them, villain ! And if I had them, idiot ! why should I give them to thee ? What care I for Miguel Terra, or for the whole race of the Perlerinos ? Begone, I say ! or by the life of my lord duke, I will be as good as my word. Thou art no native of Miguel Terra, but some scoffer sent from the devil to tempt me. Impudent scoundrel! I have not yet had the government a day and a half, and you expect I should have six hundred ducats!" The sewer made signs to the countryman to go out of the hall, which he did, hanging down his head, and seemingly much afraid lest the governor should put his threat into execution; for the knave knew very well how to play his part.

But let us leave Sancho in his passion—peace be with him! and turn to Don Quixote, whom we left with his face bound up, and under cure of his catish wounds, which were eight days in healing. In the course of that time, circumstances occurred to him which Cid Hamet promises to relate with the same truth and precision which he has observed in everything, however minute, appertaining to this history.

CHAPTER XLVIII.

Of what befell Don Quixote with Donna Rodriguez, the duchess's deunna; together with other incidents worthy to be written and held in eternal remembrance.

THE sore-wounded Don Quixote was exceedingly discontented and melancholy, with his face bound up, and marked, not by the hand of God, but by the claws of a cat: such are the misfortunes incident to knight-errantry! During six days he appeared not in public. One night, in the course of that time, lying stretched on his bed, awake and meditating on his misfortunes, and the persecution he had suffered from Altisidora, he heard a key applied to his chamber-door, and immediately concluded that the enamoured damsel herself was coming, with a determination to overcome by temptation the fidelity he owed to his lady Dulcinea del Toboso. "No," said he, not doubting the truth of what he fancied, and speaking so loud as to be overheard, "no, not the greatest beauty upon earth shall prevail upon me to cease adoring her whose image is engraven and stamped in the bottom of my soul and in the inmost recesses of my heart! Whether, my dearest lady! thou be now transformed into a garlic-eating wench, or into one of the nymphs of the golden Tagus, who weave in silk and gold their glittering webs; or whether thou art detained by Merlin or Montesinos —wherever thou art, mine thou shalt be, and wherever I am, thine I have been and thine I will remain!"

As he concluded these words, the door opened, and he rose up in the bed, wrapped from top to toe in a quilt of yellow satin, a woollen cap on his head, and his face and moustachios bound up—his face on account of its scratches, and his moustachios to keep them from flagging; in which guise a more extraordinary phantom imagination never conceived. He riveted his eyes on the door, and when he expected to see the captivated and sorrowful Altisidora enter, he perceived something that resembled a most reverend duenna gliding in, covered with a long white veil that reached from head to foot. Between the forefinger and thumb of her left hand she carried half a lighted candle, and held her right over it to keep the glare from her eyes, which were hidden behind a huge pair of spectacles. She advanced very slowly and with cautious tread, and as Don Quixote gazed at her form and face from his watch-tower, he was convinced that some witch or sorceress was come in that disguise to do him secret mischief, and therefore began to cross himself with much diligence.

The apparition kept moving forward, and having reached the middle of the room, it paused and raised its eyes, as if remarking how devoutly the knight was crossing himself: and if he was alarmed at seeing such a figure, she was no less dismayed at the sight of him—so lank, so yellow, enveloped in the quilt, and disfigured with bandages! "Jesu! what do I see?" she exclaimed—and in her fright the candle fell out of her hand. Finding herself in the dark, she endeavoured to regain the door, but her feet becoming entangled in the skirts of her garment, she stumbled and fell. Don Quixote was in the utmost consternation. "Phantom!" he cried, "or whatever thou art, say, I conjure thee, what art thou and what requirest thou of me? If thou art a soul in torment, tell me, and I will do all I can to help thee, for I am a Catholic Christian, and love to do good to all mankind. It was for that purpose I took upon me the profession of knight-errantry, which engages me to relieve even the souls in purgatory."

The fallen duenna hearing herself thus exorcised, guessed at Don Quixote's fear by her own, and in a low and doleful voice answered, "Signor Don Quixote (if peradventure your worship be Don Quixote), I am no phantom, nor apparition, nor soul in purgatory, as your worship seems to think, but Donna Rodriguez, duenna of honour to my lady duchess, and am come to your worship with one of those cases of distress which your worship is wont to remedy." "Tell me then, Signora Donna Rodriguez," quoth Don Quixote, "if it happens that your ladyship comes in quality of love-messenger? because, if so, I would have you understand that your labour will be fruitless—thanks to the peerless beauty of my mistress, Dulcinea del Toboso. To be plain, Signora Donna Rodriguez, on condition you waive all tender messages, you may go and light your candle and return hither, and we will discourse on whatever you please to command—with that exception." "I bring messages, good sir!" answered the duenna; "your worship mistakes me much: it is not so late in life with me yet as to be compelled to take such base employment; for, Heaven be praised! my soul is still in my body, and all my teeth in my head, except a few snatched from me by this cold province of Arragon. But wait, sir, till I have lighted my candle, when I will return and communicate my griefs to your worship, who are the redresser of all the grievances in the world." Thereupon she quitted the room without waiting for a reply from the knight, whom she left in a state of great suspense.

A thousand thoughts now crowded into his mind touching this new adventure, and he was of opinion that he had judged and acted improperly to expose himself to the hazard of breaking his plighted troth to his lady; and he said to himself, "Who knows but the devil, that father of mischief, means to deceive me now with a duenna, though he could not effect it with empresses, queens, duchesses, and ladies of high degree? For I have often heard wise men say, ' the devil finds a better bait in a flat-nosed than a hawk-nosed woman;' and who can tell but this soli-tude, this opportunity, and this silence, may awaken my desires, and make me now, at these years, fall where I never yet stumbled? In such cases, better it were to fly than hazard a battle. But why do I talk so idly? Surely I have lost my senses to imagine that an antiquated, white-veiled, lank, and spectacled duenna should awaken a single un-chaste thought in the most abandoned libertine in the world. Is there a duenna upon earth who can boast of wholesome flesh and blood? Is there a duenna upon the globe who is not impertinent, affected, and loathsome? Avaunt, then, ye rabble of duennas! useless, disgusting, and unprofitable! Wisely did that good lady act who placed near her sofa a couple of painted images, accoutred like those ancient waiting-women, as if at their work : finding the state and decorum of her rank quite as well supported by these dumb imitations."

So saying, he jumped off the bed, intending to lock the door so as to prevent the duenna's return; but before he could effect his purpose, Signora Rodriguez entered with a lighted taper of white wax; and coming at once upon Don Quixote, wrapped up in his quilt, with bandages and nightcap, she was again alarmed, and, retreating two or three steps, she said, "Sir Knight, am I safe? for I take it to be no sign of modesty that your worship has got out of bed." "I should rather ask you that question, madam," answered Don Quixote, "and therefore tell me if I am safe and secure from any assault." "Of whom, or from whom, Sir Knight, do you demand that security?" answered the duenna. "From you, madam," replied Don Quixote; "for I am not made of marble, nor you, I suppose, of brass; nor is it noonday, but midnight, and even later, if I am not mistaken; and, moreover, we are in a room retired, and more secret than the cave in which the bold and traitorous Æneas wooed the beautiful and tender-hearted Dido. But, madam, give me your hand; for I desire no greater security than my own continence and reserve, and what that most reverend veil inspires." So saying, he kissed his right hand, and took hold of hers, which she gave him with the same ceremony.

Here Cid Hamet makes a parenthesis, and swears by Mahomet he would have given the better of his two vests to have seen the knight and matron walking from the chamber-door to the bedside. He then proceeds to inform us that Don Quixote resumed his situation in bed, and Donna Rodriguez sat down in a chair at some little distance from it, without taking off her spectacles or setting down her candle. Don Quixote covered himself up close, all but his face; and after a short pause, the first who broke silence was the knight. "Now, Signora Donna Rodriguez," said he, "you may unbosom all that is in your oppressed and afflicted heart; for you shall be listened to by me with chaste ears, and assisted with compassionate deeds." "That I verily believe," said the duenna; "and no other than so Christian an answer could be expected from a person of your worship's courtly and seemly presence. The case, then, is this, noble signor, that though you see me sitting in this chair, and in the midst of the kingdom of Arragon, and in the garb of a poor persecuted duenna, I was born in the Asturias of Oviedo, and of a family allied to some of the best of that province. But my hard fate and the neglect of my parents, who fell, I know not how, into a state of poverty, carried me to Madrid, where, from prudence and the fear of what might be worse, they placed me in the service of a court lady, and I can assure your worship that, in making needle-cases and plain work, I was never in my life outdone. My parents left me in service, and returned to their own country, where, in a few years after, they died, and, I doubt not, went to heaven; for they were very good and Catholic Christians. Then was I left an orphan, and reduced to the sorrowful condition of such court servants—wretched wages, and slender allowance. About the same time—Heaven knows, without my giving him the least cause for it!—the gentleman usher of the family fell in love with me. He was somewhat stricken in years, with a fine beard, a comely person, and, what is more, as good a gentleman as the king himself, for he was a mountaineer. We did not carry our love so secretly but that it came to the notice of my lady, who without more ado, and to prevent slander, had us duly married in the face of our holy mother the Roman Catholic Church; from which marriage sprang a daughter, to complete my good fortune, if fortune had been mine: not that I died in childbed, for in due time I was safely delivered; but alas! my husband died soon after of fright; and had I but time to tell you how it was, your worship, I am sure, would be all astonishment."

Here Donna Rodriguez shed many tears of tender recollection. " Pardon me, good Signor Don Quixote," said she, "for I cannot command myself: as often as I call to mind my poor ill-fated spouse, these tears will flow. Heaven be my aid! With what stateliness was he wont to carry my lady behind him on a princely mule as black as jet itself; for in those times coaches and side-saddles were not in fashion, as it is said they now are—ladies rode behind their squires. Pardon me, for I cannot help telling you at least this one circumstance, because it proves the good breeding and punctilio of my worthy husband. It happened that, on entering the street of Santiago, which is very narrow, a judge of one of the courts, with two of his officers before him, appeared, and as soon as my good squire saw him, he turned his mule about, as if he would follow him. My lady, who was behind him, said to him in a low voice, 'What are you doing, blockhead? am not I here?' The judge civilly stopped his horse, and said, 'Proceed on your way, sir, for it is rather my duty to attend my lady Donna Casilda—my mistress's name; but my husband persisted, cap in hand, in his intention to follow the judge. On which my lady, full of rage and indignation, pulled out a great pin, or rather, I believe, a bodkin, and stuck it into his back; whereupon my husband bawled out, and, writhing with the smart, down he came with his lady to the ground. Two of her footmen ran to assist her, as well as the judge and his officers, and the gate of Guadalajara—I mean the idle people that stood there—were all in an uproar. My mistress was forced to walk home on foot, and my husband repaired to a barber-surgeon's, declaring he was quite run through and through. The courtesy and good breeding of my spouse was soon in everybody's mouth, so that the very boys in the street gathered about him and teased him with their gibes when he walked abroad. On this account, and

Donna Rodriguez sat down in a chair at some little distance, without taking off her spectacles. Don Quixote covered himself up close, all but his face.

because he was a little short-sighted, my lady dismissed him from her service; which he took so to heart, poor man! that I verily believe it brought him to the grave. Thus, sir, I was left a poor helpless widow, and with a daughter to keep, fair as a flower, and who went on increasing in beauty like the foam of the sea. At length, as I had the reputation of being an excellent workwoman at my needle, my lady duchess, who was then newly married to my lord duke, took me to live with her here in Arragon, and also my daughter, who grew up with a world of accomplishments. She sings like any lark, dances like a fairy, capers like any wild thing, reads and writes like a schoolmaster, and casts accounts as exact as a miser. I say nothing of her cleanliness, for surely the running brook is not more pure; and she is now, if I remember right, just sixteen years of age, five months and three days, one more or less. To make short, sir, the son of a very rich farmer, who lives here on my lord duke's land, was smitten with my daughter; and how he managed matters I cannot tell, but the truth is simply this, that under promise of being her husband, he has fooled my daughter, and now refuses to make good his word. The duke is no stranger to this business, for I have complained to him again and again, and begged he would be so gracious as to command this young man to wed my daughter; but he turns a deaf ear to my complaints, and will hardly vouchsafe to listen to me; and the reason is, that the cozening knave's father is rich, and lends his grace money, and is bound for him on all occasions; therefore he would not in any way disoblige him. Now, good sir, my humble desire is that your worship would kindly take upon you to redress this wrong, either by entreaty or by force of arms; since all the world says your worship was born to redress grievances, to right the injured, and succour the wretched. Be pleased, sir, I entreat you, to take pity on a fatherless daughter, and let her youth, her beauty, and all her other good parts move you to compassion; for, on my conscience, among all my lady's damsels there is not one that comes up to the sole of her shoe—no, not she who is cried up as the liveliest and finest of them all, whom they call Altisidora—she is not to be named with my daughter; for, let me tell you, dear sir, that all is not gold that glitters, and that that same little Altisidora, after all, has more self-conceit than beauty; besides, she is none of the soundest, for her breath is so foul that nobody can stand near her for a moment. Nay, indeed, as for that, even my lady duchess—but, mum! for they say walls have ears."

"What of my lady duchess?" quoth Don Quixote; "tell me, Madam Rodriguez, I conjure you." "Your entreaties," said the duenna, "cannot be resisted; and I must tell you the truth. Has not your worship observed the beauty of my lady duchess?—that softness, that clearness of complexion, smooth and shining like any polished sword; those cheeks of milk and crimson, with the sun in the one, and the moon in the other; and that stateliness with which she treads, as if she disdained the very ground she walks on, that one would think her the goddess of health dispensing the blessing wherever she goes? Let me tell you, sir, she may thank God for it in the first place, and in the next, two issues, one in each leg, that carry off all the bad humours in which, the physicians say, her ladyship abounds." "Holy Virgin!" quoth Don Quixote, "is it possible that my lady duchess should have such drains? I should never have credited such a thing, though barefooted friars themselves had sworn it; but, since Madam Donna Rodriguez says it, so it must needs be. Yet assuredly from such perfection no ill humours can flow, but rather liquid amber. Well, I am now convinced that such conduits may be of importance to health."

Scarcely had Don Quixote said this, when the chamber-door suddenly burst open, which so startled Donna Rodriguez that the candle fell out of her hand, leaving the room as dark as a wolf's mouth; when instantly the poor duenna felt her throat griped by two hands, and so hard that she had not power to cry out, while other two hands so unmercifully be-slapped with a slipper, as it seemed, her scantily-protected and shrinking form, that she was presently in a woful plight. Yet, notwithstanding the compassion which Don Quixote felt for her, he remained quietly in bed, being at a great loss what to think of the matter, and doubtful whether the same calamity might not fall on himself. Nor were his apprehensions groundless; for, after having well curried the duenna, who durst not cry out, the silent executioners then came to Don Quixote, and, turning up the bed-clothes, they so pinched and tweaked him all over, that he could not forbear laying about him with his fists, in his own defence; till at last, after a scuffle of almost half an hour, the silent and invisible phantoms vanished. Donna Rodriguez then adjusted her disordered garments, and, bewailing her misfortune, hastened out of the chamber without speaking a word to the knight; who, vexed with the pinching he had received, remained in deep thought, utterly at a loss to conceive who the malicious enchanter could be that had treated him so rudely. This will be explained in its proper place; at present the order of the history requires that our attention should be turned to Sancho Panza.

CHAPTER XLIX.

Of what befell Sancho Panza in going the round of his island.

NEVER was the great governor more out of humour than when we left him, from the provocation he had received from the knave of a peasant, who was one of the steward's instruments for executing the duke's pro-jects upon Sancho. Nevertheless, simple, rough, and round as he was, he held out toughly against them all; and, addressing himself to those about him, among others the doctor Pedro Rezio (who had returned after the private despatch had been read), " I now plainly perceive," said he, " that judges and governors must or ought to be made of brass, to endure the importunities of your men of business, who, intent upon their own affairs alone, will take no denial, but must needs be heard at all hours and at all times; and if his poor lordship does not think fit to attend to them, either because he cannot, or because it is not a time for business, then, forsooth, they murmur and peck at him, rake up the ashes of his grandfather, and gnaw the very flesh from their bones. Men of business—out upon them! meddling, troublesome fools!—take the proper times and seasons for your affairs, and come not when men should eat and sleep; for judges are made of flesh and blood, and must give to their nature what nature requires; except, indeed, miserable I, who am forbidden to do so by mine — thanks to Signor Pedro Rezio

Tirteafuera, here present, who would have me die of hunger, and swear that this kind of dying is the only way to live. God grant the same life to him, and all those of his tribe!—I mean quacks and impostors; for good physicians deserve palms and laurels." All who knew Sancho Panza were in admiration at his improved oratory, which they could not account for, unless it be that offices and weighty employments quicken and polish some men's minds, as they perplex and stupefy others.

At length the bowels of Doctor Pedro Rezio de Tirteafuera relented, and he promised the governor he should sup that night, although it were in direct opposition to all the aphorisms of Hippocrates. With this promise his excellency was satisfied, and looked forward with great impatience to the hour of supper; and though time, as he thought, stood stock-still, yet the wished-for moment came at last, when messes of cow-beef, hashed with onions, and boiled calves' feet, somewhat of the stalest, were set before him. Nevertheless, he laid about him with more relish than if they had given him Milan godwits, Roman pheasants, veal of Sorrento, partridges of Moron, or geese of Lavajos; and, in the midst of supper, turning to the doctor, " Look you, Master Doctor," said he, " never trouble yourself again to provide me your delicacies or your tit-bits; for they will only unhinge my stomach, which is accustomed to goats'-flesh, cow-beef, and bacon, with turnips and onions; and if you ply me with court kickshaws, it will only make my stomach queasy and loathing. However, if Master Sewer will now and then set before me one of those — how do you call them? — olla podridas,* which are a jumble of all sorts of good things, and to my thinking the stronger they are the better they smack—but stuff them as you will, so it be but an eatable—I shall take it kindly, and will one day make you amends. So let nobody p'ay their jests upon me; for either we are or we are not; and let us all live and eat together in peace and good friendship; for when God sends daylight it is morning to all. I will govern this island without either waiving right or pocketing bribe. So let every one keep a good look-out, and each mind his own business; for I would have them to know the devil is in the wind, and if they put me upon it, they shall see wonders. Ay, ay; make yourselves honey, and the wasps will devour you."

" Indeed, my lord governor," quoth the sewer, " your lordship is much in the right in all you have said; and I dare engage, in the name of all the inhabitants of this island, that they will serve your worship with all punctuality, love, and good-will; for your gentle way of governing, from the very first, leaves us no room to do or think anything to the disadvantage of your worship." " I believe as much," replied Sancho, " and they would be little better than fools if they did or thought otherwise; therefore I tell you, once again, it is my pleasure that you look well to me and my Dapple in the article of food; for that is the main point: and when the hour comes, we will go the round, as my

---

* A dish composed of beef, mutton, pork, with sometimes poultry or game, vegetables and a variety of other ingredients.

intention is to clear this island of all manner of filth and rubbish, especially vagabonds, idlers, and sharpers; for I would have you know, friends, that your idle and lazy people in a commonwealth are like drones in a bee-hive, which devour the honey that the labouring bees gather. My design is to protect the peasants, maintain the gentry in their privileges, reward virtue, and above all to have a special regard to religion and the reverence due to holy men. What think you of this, my good friends? Do I say something, or do I crack my brains to no purpose?" "My lord governor speaks so well," replied the steward, "that I am all admiration to hear one devoid of learning, like your worship, utter so many notable things, so far beyond the expectation of your subjects, or those who appointed you. But every day produces something new in the world; jests turn into earnest, and the biters are bit."

The governor having supped by license of Signor Doctor Rezio, they prepared for going the round, and he set out with the secretary, the steward, the sewer, and the historiographer, who had the charge of recording his actions, together with serjeants and notaries: altogether forming a little battalion. Sancho, with his rod of office, marched in the midst of them, making a goodly show. After traversing a few streets, they heard the clashing of swords, and hastening to the place, they found two men fighting. On seeing the officers coming they desisted, and one of them said, "Help, in the name of Heaven and the king! Are people to be attacked here, and robbed in the open streets?" "Hold, honest man," quoth Sancho, "and tell me what is the occasion of this fray, for I am the governor."

His antagonist, interposing, said, "My lord governor, I will briefly relate the matter. Your honour must know that this gentleman is just come from the gaming-house over the way, where he has been winning above a thousand reals, and Heaven knows how, except that I, happening to be present, was induced, even against my conscience, to give judgment in his favour in many a doubtful point; and when I expected he would have given me something, though it were but the small matter of a crown, by way of present, as it is usual with gentlemen of character like myself, who stand by ready to back unreasonable demands and to prevent quarrels, up he got, with his pockets filled, and marched out of the house. Surprised and vexed at such conduct, I followed him, civilly reminded him that he could not refuse me the small sum of eight reals, as he knew me to be a man of honour without either office or pension, my parents having brought me up to nothing; yet this knave, who is as great a thief as Cacus and as arrant a sharper as Andradilla, would give me but four reals! Think, my lord governor, what a shameless and unconscionable fellow he is! But, as I live, had it not been for your worship coming, I would have made him disgorge his winnings, and taught him how to balance accounts."

"What say you to this, friend?" quoth Sancho to the other. He acknowledged that what his adversary had said was true: he meant to give him no more than four reals, for he was continually giving him something; and they who expect snacks should be modest, and take cheerfully whatever is given them, and not haggle with the winners, unless they know them to be sharpers, and their gains unfairly gotten; and that he was no such person was evident from his resisting an un-reasonable demand; for cheats are always at the mercy of the accomplices. "That is very true," quoth the steward: "be pleased, my lord governor, to say what shall be done with these men."

"What shall be done," replied Sancho, "is this: you, Master Winner, whether by fair play or foul, instantly give your hackster here a hundred reals, and lay down thirty more for the poor prisoners; and you, sir, who have neither office nor pension, nor honest employment, take the hundred reals, and, some time to-morrow, be sure you get out of this island, nor set foot in it again these ten years, unless you would finish your banishment in the next life; for if I find you here, I will make you swing on a gibbet—at least the hangman shall do it for me; so let no man reply, or he shall repent it." The decree was immediately executed: the one disbursed, the other received; the one quitted the island, the other went home; and the governer said, "Either my power is small, or I will demolish these gaming-houses; for I strongly suspect that much harm comes of them." "The house here before us," said one of the officers, "I fear your honour cannot put down; being kept by a person of quality, whose losses far exceed his gains. Your worship may exert your authority against petty gaming-houses, which do more harm and shelter more abuses than those of the gentry, where notorious cheats dare not show their faces; and since the vice of play is become so common, it is better that it should be permitted in the houses of the great than in those of low condition, where night after night un-fortunate gulls are taken in, and stripped of their very skins." "Well, Master Notary," quoth Sancho, "I know there is much to be said on the subject."

Just at that moment a serjeant came up to him holding fast a young man. "My lord governor," said he, "this youth was coming towards us, but as soon as he perceived us to be officers of justice, he turned about and ran off like a deer—a sure sign he is after some mischief. I pursued him; and had he not stumbled and fallen, I should never have overtaken him." "Why did you fly from the officer, young man?" quoth Sancho. "My lord," said the youth, "it was to avoid the many questions that officers of justice usually ask." "What is your trade?" asked Sancho. "A weaver," answered the youth. "And what do you weave?" quoth Sancho. "Iron heads for spears, an it please your worship." "So, then," returned Sancho, "you are pleased to be jocose with me, and set up for a wit! 'tis mighty well. And pray, may I ask whither you were going?" "To take the air, sir," replied the lad. "And pray, where do people take the air in this island?" said Sancho. "Where it blows," answered the youth. "Good," quoth Sancho; "you answer to the purpose: a notable youth, truly! But hark you, sir: I am the air which you seek, and will blow in your poop, and drive you into safe custody. Here, secure him, and carry him straight to prison. I will make him sleep there to-night, without air." "Not so, by my

Two or three lanterns were held up to her face, by the light of which they perceived it to be that of a female about sixteen years of age.

faith," said the youth; "your worship shall as soon make the king, as make me sleep there." "I not make you sleep in prison!" exclaimed Sancho: "have I not power to confine or release you as I please?" "Whatever your worship's power may be, you shall not force me to sleep in prison."

"We shall see that," replied Sancho: "away with him immediately, and let him be convinced to his cost; and should the gaoler be found to practise in his favour, and allow him to sleep out of his custody, I will sconce him in the penalty of two thousand ducats." "All this is very pleasant," answered the youth; "but no man living shall make me sleep to-night in prison: in that I am fixed." "Tell me, devil incarnate!" quoth Sancho, "hast thou some angel at thy beck, to come and break the fetters with which I mean to tether thee?" "Good my lord," said the youngster, with a smile, "let us not trifle, but come to the point. Your worship, I own, may clap me in a dungeon, and load me with chains and fetters, and lay what commands you please upon the gaoler; yet if I choose not to sleep, can your worship, with all your power, force me to sleep?" "No, certainly," said the secretary, "and the young man has made out his meaning." "Well, then," quoth Sancho, "if you keep awake, it is from your own liking, and not to cross my will?" "Certainly not, my lord," said the youth. "Then go, get thee home and sleep," quoth Sancho, "and Heaven send thee a good night's rest, for I will not be thy hindrance. But have a care another time how you sport with justice; for you may chance to meet with some man in office who will not relish your jokes, but crack your noddle in return." The youth went his way, and the governor continued his round.

Soon after two serjeants came up, saying, "We have brought you, my lord governor, one in disguise who seems to be a man, but is, in fact, a woman, and no ugly one either." Two or three lanterns were immediately held up to her face, by the light of which they indeed perceived it to be that of a female seemingly about sixteen years of age. She was beautiful as a thousand pearls, with her hair inclosed under a net of gold and green silk. They viewed her from head to foot, and observed that her stockings were flesh-coloured, her garters of white taffeta, with tassels of gold and seed pearl; her breeches were of green and gold tissue, her cloak of the same, under which she wore a very fine waistcoat of white and gold stuff, and her shoes were white, like those worn by men. She had no sword, but a very rich dagger; and on her fingers were many valuable rings. All were struck with admiration of the maiden, but nobody knew her, not even the inhabitants of the town. Indeed, those who were in the secret of these jests were as much interested as the rest, for this circumstance was not of their contriving, and being, therefore, unexpected, their surprise and curiosity were more strongly excited.

The governor admired the young lady's beauty, and asked her who she was, whither she was going, and what had induced her to dress herself in that habit. With downcast eyes, she modestly answered, "I hope, sir, you will excuse my answering so publicly what I wish so much to be kept a secret. Of one thing be assured, gentlemen, I am no thief, nor a criminal, but an unhappy maiden, who, from a jealous and rigorous confinement, have been tempted to transgress the rules of decorum." The steward, on hearing this, said, "Be pleased, my lord governor, to order your attendants to retire, that this lady may speak more freely."

The governor did so, and they all removed to a distance, excepting the steward, the sewer, and the secretary; upon which the damsel proceeded thus: " I am the daughter, gentlemen, of Pedro Perez Mazorca, who farms the wool of this town, and often comes to my father's house."

" This will not pass, madam," said the steward; " for I know Pedro Perez very well, and I am sure he has neither sons nor daughters; besides, after telling us he is your father, you immediately say that he comes often to your father's house." " I took notice of that," quoth Sancho. " Indeed, gentlemen," said she, " I am in such confusion that I know not what I say; but the truth is, I am daughter to Diego de la Llana, whom you all must know." " That may be true," answered the steward, " for I know Don Diego de la Llana: he is a gentleman of birth and fortune, and has a son and a daughter; and, since he has been a widower, nobody in this town can say they have seen the face of his daughter, for he keeps her so confined that he hardly suffers the sun to look upon her; the common report, too, is, that she is extremely handsome."

" What you say is true, sir," said the damsel, " and whether fame lies or not as to my beauty, you, gentlemen, who have seen me, may judge." She then began to weep most bitterly; upon which the secretary whispered the sewer, " Something of importance, surely, must have caused a person of so much consequence as this young lady to leave her own house in such a dress, and at this unseasonable hour." " No doubt of that," replied the sewer: " besides, this suspicion is confirmed by her tears." Sancho comforted her as well as he could, and desired her to tell the whole matter without fear, for they would be her friends, and serve her in the best manner they were able.

" The truth is, gentlemen," replied she, " that since my mother died, which is now ten years ago, my father has kept me close confined (we have a chapel in the house, where we hear mass); and in all that time I have seen nothing but the sun in the heavens by day, and the moon and stars by night; nor do I know what streets, squares, or churches are; nor even men, excepting my father and brother, and Pedro Perez the wool farmer, whose constant visits to our house led me to say he was my father, to conceal the truth. This close confinement, and being forbidden to set my foot out of doors, though it were but to church, has for many days and months past disquieted me very much, and gave me a constant longing to see the world, or at least the town where I was born; and I persuaded myself that this desire was neither unlawful nor unbecoming. When I heard talk of bull-fights, running at the ring, and theatrical shows, I asked my brother, who is a year younger than myself, to tell me what those things were, and several others that I have never seen. He described them all as well as he could, but it only inflamed my curiosity to see them myself. In a word, to shorten the story of my ruin, I prayed and entreated my brother—Oh that I had never so prayed nor entreated!"—and here a flood of tears interrupted her narrative. " Pray, madam," said the steward, " be comforted, and proceed, for your words and tears keep us all in anxious suspense." "I have but few more words," answered the damsel, "though many tears to shed; for misplaced desires like mine can be atoned for in no other way."

The beauty of the damsel had made an impressson on the soul of the sewer, and again he held up his lantern to have another view of her, when he verily thought her tears were orient pearls and dew-drops of the morning, and he heartily wished her misfortune might not be so great as her tears and sighs seemed to indicate. But the governor was out of all patience at the length of her story, and therefore bid her make an end, and keep them no longer, as it grew late, and they had much ground yet to pass over. As well as the frequent interruption of sobs and sighs would let her, she continued, saying, "My misfortune and misery is no other than this, that I desired my brother to let me put on his clothes, and take me out some night when my father was asleep, to see the town. Yielding to my frequent entreaties, he at length gave me this habit, and dressed himself in a suit of mine, which fits him exactly, and he looks like a beautiful girl, for he has yet no beard; and this night, about an hour ago, we contrived to get out of the house, and with no other guide than a footboy and our own unruly fancies, we have walked through the whole town; and as we were returning home, we saw a great company of people before us, which my brother said was the round, and that we must run, or rather fly, for if we should be discovered it would be worse for us. Upon which he set off at full speed, leaving me to follow him; but I had not got many paces before I stumbled and fell, and that instant a man seized me and brought me hither, where my indiscreet longing has covered me with shame." "Has nothing, then," quoth Sancho, "befallen you but this?—you mentioned at first something of jealousy, I think, which had brought you from home." "Nothing," said she, "has befallen me but what I have said, nor has anything brought me out but a desire to see the world, which went no farther than seeing the streets of this town."

The truth of the damsel's story was now confirmed by the arrival of two other serjeants, who had overtaken and seized the brother as he fled from the sister. The female dress of the youth was only a rich petticoat and a blue damask mantle bordered with gold; on his head he had no other ornament or cover than his own hair, which appeared like so many waves of gold. The governor, the steward, and the sewer examined him apart, and, out of the hearing of his sister, asked him why he had disguised himself in that manner. With no less bashfulness and distress, he repeated the same story they had heard from his sister, to the great satisfaction of the enamoured sewer. "Really, young gentlefolks," said the governor, "this seems only a piece of childish folly, and all these sobs and tears might well have been spared in giving an account of your frolic. Had you but told us your names, and said you had got out of your father's house only to satisfy your curiosity, there would have been an end of the story." "That is true," answered the damsel; "but my confusion was so great, that I knew not what I said, or how to behave myself." "Well, madam," said Sancho, "there is no harm done : we will see you safe to your father's house, who, perhaps, has not missed you; and henceforward be not so childish nor so eager to get abroad; for 'the modest maiden and the broken leg should keep at home;' 'the woman and the hen are lost by gadding;' and 'she who wishes to see, wishes no less to be seen.' I say no more."

The young man thanked the governor for the favour he intended them in seeing them safe home, whither they all went; and, having reached the house, the youth threw a pebble up at a grated window, which immediately brought down one of the domestics, who opened the door, and they went in, leaving every one in admiration of their beauty and graceful demeanour, and much entertained by their desire of seeing the world by night. The sewer, finding that his heart was pierced through and through, secretly resolved to demand the young lady in marriage of her father the next day, and he flattered himself that, being a servant of the duke, he should not be refused. Sancho, too, had some thoughts of matching the young man with his daughter Sanchica, and determined to bring it about the first opportunity; feeling assured that no man's son would think himself too good for a governor's daughter. Thus ended the night's round of the great Sancho : two days after also ended his government, which put an end to his great designs and expectations, as shall hereafter be shown.

CHAPTER L.

Which declares who were the enchanters and executioners that whipped the duenna and pinched and scratched Don Quixote; and also the success of the page who carried Sancho's letter to his wife, Teresa Panza.

CID HAMET, the most laborious and careful investigator into the minutest particles of this true history, says that, when Donna Rodriguez went out of her chamber to go to that of Don Quixote, another duenna, who had slept with her, observed her; and as all duennas are addicted to listening, prying into, and smelling out everything, she followed her, and with so light a foot that the good Rodriguez did not hear it; and no sooner had she entered Don Quixote's chamber, than the other, that she might not be deficient in the laudable practice of tale-bearing, in which duennas usually excel, hastened to acquaint the duchess that Donna Rodriguez was then actually in Don Quixote's chamber. The duchess immediately told the duke; and having gained his permission to go with Altisidora to satisfy her curiosity respecting this night visit of her duenna, they silently posted themselves at the door of the knight's apartment, where they stood listening to all that was said within; but when the duchess heard her secret imperfection exposed, neither she nor

Altisidora could bear it, and so, brimful of rage and eager for revenge, they bounced into the chamber, and, seizing the offenders, inflicted the whipping and pinching before mentioned, and in the manner already related; for nothing awakens the wrath of women and inflames them with a desire of vengeance more effectually than affronts levelled at their beauty, or other objects of their vanity.

The duke was much diverted with his lady's account of this night adventure; and the duchess, being still merrily disposed, now dispatched a messenger extraordinary to Teresa Panza with her husband's letter (for Sancho, having his head so full of the great concerns of his government, had quite forgotten it), and with another from herself, to which she added as a present a large string of rich coral beads.

Now, the story tells us that the messenger employed on this occasion was a shrewd fellow, and the same page who personated Dulcinea in the wood, and being desirous to please his lord and lady, he set off with much glee to Sancho's village. Having arrived near it, he inquired of some women whom he saw washing in a brook if there lived not in that town one Teresa Panza, wife of one Sancho Panza, squire to a knight called Don Quixote de la Mancha. "That Teresa Panza is my mother," said a young lass who was washing among the rest, "and that Sancho my own father, and that knight our master." "Are they so?" quoth the page: "come, then, my good girl, and lead me to your mother; for I have a letter and a token for her from that same father of yours." "That I will, with all my heart, sir," answered the girl (who seemed to be about fourteen years of age), and, leaving the linen she was washing to one of her companions, without stopping to cover either her head or feet, away she ran, skipping along before the page's horse bare-legged, and her hair dishevelled.

"Come along, sir, an't please you," quoth she, "for our house stands hard by, and you will find my mother in trouble enough for being so long without tidings of my father." "Well," said the page, "I now bring her news that will cheer her heart, I warrant her." So on he went, with his guide running, skipping, and capering before him, till they reached the village; and, before she got up to the house, she called out aloud, "Mother, mother, come out! here's a gentleman who brings letters and other things from my good father."

At these words out came her mother Teresa Panza with a distaff in her hand, for she was spinning flax. She was clad in a russet petticoat, so short that it looked as if it had been docked at the placket, with a jacket of the same, and the sleeves of her under-garment hanging about it. She appeared about forty years of age, and was strong, hale, sinewy, and hard as a hazel-nut.

"What is the matter, girl?" quoth she, seeing her daughter with the page; "what gentleman is that?" "It is an humble servant of my Lady Donna Teresa Panza," answered the page; and, throwing himself from his horse, with great respect he went and kneeled before the Lady Teresa, saying, "Be pleased, Signora Donna Teresa, to give me your lady-ship's hand to kiss, as the lawful wife of Signor Don Sancho Panza, sole governor of the island of Barataria." "Alack-a-day, good sir, how you talk!" she replied: "I am no court dame, but a poor countrywoman, daughter of a ploughman, and wife indeed of a squire-errant, but no governor." "Your ladyship," answered the page, "is the most worthy wife of a thrice-worthy governor; and to confirm the truth of what I say, be pleased, madam, to receive what I here bring you." He then drew the letter from his pocket, and a string of corals, each bead set in gold, and, putting it about her neck, he said, "This letter is from my lord governor, and another that I have here, and those corals, are from my lady duchess, who sends me to your ladyship."

Teresa and her daughter were all astonishment. "May I die," said the girl, "if our master Don Quixote be not at the bottom of this—

The page, throwing himself from his horse, with great respect went and kneeled before the Lady Teresa.

as sure as day he has given my father the government or earldom he has so often promised him." "It is even so," answered the page; "and for Signor Don Quixote's sake, my Lord Sancho is now governor of the island of Barataria, as the letter will inform you." "Pray, young gentleman," quoth Teresa, "be pleased to read it; for though I can spin, I cannot read a jot." "Nor I neither, i' faith," cried Sanchica; "but stay a little, and I will fetch one who can, either the bachelor Sampson Carrasco or the priest himself, who will come with all their hearts to hear news of my father." "You need not take that trouble," said the page; "for I can read, though I cannot spin, and will read it to you." Which he accordingly did; but as its contents have already been given, it is not here repeated. He then produced the letter from the duchess, and read as follows:

"Friend Teresa,—

"Finding your husband Sancho worthy of my esteem for his honesty and good understanding, I prevailed upon the duke my spouse, to make him governor of one of the many islands in his possession. I am informed he governs like any hawk; at which I and my lord duke are mightily pleased, and give many thanks to Heaven that I have not been deceived in my choice, for Madam Teresa may be assured that it is no easy matter to find a good governor—and God make me as good as Sancho governs well. I have sent you, my dear friend, a string of corals set in gold—I wish they were oriental pearls; but, whoever gives thee a bone has no mind to see thee dead: the time will come when we shall be better acquainted, and converse with each other, and then Heaven knows what may happen. Commend me to your daughter Sanchica, and tell her from me to get herself ready; for I mean to have her highly married when she least expects it. I am told the acorns near your town are very large—pray send me some two dozen of them; for I shall value them the more as coming from your hand. Write to me immediately, to inform me of your health and welfare; and, if you want anything, you need but open your mouth, and it shall be measured. So God keep you.

"From this place.   "Your loving friend, the DUCHESS."

"Ah!" quoth Teresa, at hearing the letter, "how good, how plain, how humble a lady! Let me be buried with such ladies as this, I say, and not with such proud madams as this town affords, who think, because they are gentlefolks, the wind must not blow upon them, and go flaunting to church as if they were queens! They seem to think it a disgrace to look upon a peasant woman: and yet you see how this good lady, though she be a duchess, calls me friend, and treats me as if I were her equal!—and equal may I see her to the highest steeple in La Mancha! As to the acorns, sir, I will send her ladyship a peck of them, and such as, for their size, people shall come from far and near to see and admire. But for the present, Sanchica, let us make much of this gentleman. Do you take care of his horse, child, and bring some new-laid eggs out of the stable, and slice some rashers of bacon, and let us entertain him like any prince; for his good news and his own good looks deserve no less. Meanwhile I will step and carry my neighbours the joyful tidings, especially our good priest and Master Nicholas the barber, who are and have always been such friends to your father." "Yes, I will," answered Sanchica; "but hark you, mother: half that string of corals comes to me; for sure the great lady knows better than to send them all to you." "It is all for thee, daughter," answered Teresa, "but let me wear it a few days about my neck, for truly methinks it cheers my very heart." "You will be no less cheered," quoth the page, "when you see the bundle I have in this portmanteau: it is a habit of superfine cloth, which the governor wore only one day at a hunting match, and he has sent it all to Signorina Sanchica." "May he live a thousand years!" answered Sanchica; "and the bearer neither more nor less—ay, and two thousand, if need be!"

Teresa now went out of the house with the letters, and the beads about her neck, and playing as she went along with her finger upon the letter, as if they had been a timbrel, when accidentally meeting the priest and Sampson Carrasco, she began dancing and capering before them." "Faith and troth," cried she, "we have no poor relations now: —we have got a government! Ay, ay, let the proudest she amongst them all meddle with me, I will make her know her distance." "What is the matter, Teresa Panza? What madness is this?" quoth the priest; "and what papers have you got there?" "No other madness," quoth she, "but that these are letters from duchesses and governors, and these about my neck are true coral; and the *Ave Marias* and the *Paternosters* are of beaten gold; and I am a governor's lady—that's all!" "Heaven be our aid!" they exclaimed; "we know not what you mean, Teresa." "Here," said she, giving them the letters, "take these, read, and believe your own eyes." The priest having read them so that Sampson Carrasco heard the contents, they both stared at each other in astonishment. The bachelor asked who had brought those letters. Teresa said if they would come home with her they should see the messenger, who was a youth like any golden pine tree, and that he had brought her another present worth twice as much. The priest took the string of corals from her neck, and examined them again and again; and being satisfied that they were genuine, his wonder increased, and he said, "By the habit I wear, I know not what to say nor what to think of these letters and these presents! On the one hand, I see and feel the fineness of these corals, and on the other I read that a duchess sends to desire a dozen or two of acorns!" "Make these things tally if you can," quoth Carrasco: "let us go and see the messenger, who may explain the difficulties which puzzle us."

They then returned with Teresa, and found the page sifting a little barley for his horse, and Sanchica cutting a rasher to fry with eggs for the page's dinner, whose appearance and behaviour they both liked; and, after the usual compliments, Sampson requested him to give them some intelligence of Don Quixote and Sancho Panza; for though they had read a letter from Sancho to his wife, and another from a duchess, still they were confounded, and could not divine what Sancho's government could mean, and especially of an island; well knowing that all or most of those in the Mediterranean belonged to his majesty. "Gentlemen," answered the page, "that Signor Sancho Panza is a governor is beyond all doubt; but whether it be an island or not that he governs I cannot say; I only know that it is a place containing above a thousand inhabitants. And as to my lady duchess sending to beg a few acorns, if you knew how humble and affable she is, it would give you no surprise: she will even send and borrow a comb of one of her neighbours. The ladies of Arragon, gentlemen, I would have you to know, though as high in rank, are not so proud and ceremonious as the ladies of Castile—they are much more condescending."

Sanchica now came in with her lap full of eggs. "Pray, sir," said she to the page, "does my father, now he is a governor, wear trunk-hose?"* "I never observed," answered the page; "but doubtless he does." "God's my life!" replied Sanchica, "what a sight to see my father in long breeches! Is it not strange that ever since I was born I

---

* Trunk-hose were prohibited by royal decree shortly after the publication of "Don Quixote."

have longed to see my father with breeches of that fashion laced to his girdle?" "I warrant you will have that pleasure if you live," answered the page; "before Heaven, if his government lasts but two months, he is likely to travel with a cape to his cap."* The priest and the bachelor clearly saw that the page spoke jestingly; but the fineness of the corals, and also the hunting-suit sent by Sancho, which Teresa had already shown them, again perplexed them exceedingly. They could not forbear smiling at Sanchica's longing, and still more when they heard Teresa say, "Master Priest, do look about and see if anybody be going to Madrid or Toledo, who may buy me a farthingale, right and tight, and fashionable, and one of the best that is to be had; for, truly, I am resolved not to shame my husband's government; and if they vex me I will get to that same court myself, and ride in my coach as well as the best of them there; for she who has a governor for her husband may very well have a coach, and afford it too, i' faith!" "Ay, marry," quoth Sanchica, "and would to Heaven it were to-day, rather than to-morrow; though folks that saw me coached with my lady mother should say, 'Do but see the bumpkin there, daughter of such an one, stuffed with garlic!—how she flaunts it about, and lolls in her coach like any she-Pope!' But let them jeer, so they trudge in the dirt, and I ride in my coach, with my feet above the ground. A bad year and a worse month to all the murmurers in the world! While I go warm, let 'em laugh that like it: say I well, mother?" "Ay, mighty well, daughter," answered Teresa; "and, indeed, my good man, Sancho, foretold me all this, and still greater luck; and thou shalt see, daughter, it will never stop till it has made me a countess; for luck only wants a beginning; and, as I have often heard your father say—who, as he is yours, so is he the father of proverbs—'When they give you a heifer, make haste with the halter; when they offer thee a governorship, lay hold of it; when an earldom is put before thee, lay your claws on it; and when they whistle to thee with a good gift, snap at it; if not, sleep on, and give no answer to the good luck that raps at your door.'" "Ay, indeed," quoth Sanchica, "what care I though they be spiteful, and say, when they see me step it stately and bridle it—'Look, look there at the dog in a doublet! the higher it mounts, the more it shows.'"

"Surely," said the priest, "the whole race of Panzas were born with their bellies stuffed with proverbs, for I never knew one of them that did not throw them out at every turn." "I believe so too," quoth the page; "even his honour the governor Sancho utters them very thick; and though often not much to the purpose, they are mightily relished, and my lady duchess and the duke commend them highly." "You persist, then, in affirming, sir," said the bachelor, "that Sancho is really a governor, and that these presents and letters are in truth sent by a duchess? As for us, though we touch the presents and have read the letters, we have no faith, and are inclined to think it one of the adven-

---

* It was customary for men of quality to wear a veil or mask depending from the covering worn on the head, in order to shield the face from the sun.

tures of our countryman Don Quixote, and take it all for enchantment; indeed, friend, I would fain touch you, to be certain you are a messenger of flesh and blood, and not an illusion." "All I know of myself, gentlemen," answered the page, "is, that I am really a messenger, and that Signor Sancho Panza is actually a governor; and that my lord duke and his duchess can give and have given him that government; in which I have heard that he behaves himself in a notable manner. Now, whether there be enchantment in this or not I leave to you to determine; for, by the life of my parents,* who are living, and whom I dearly love, I know nothing more of the matter." "It may be so," replied the bachelor; "but *dubitat Augustinus!*" "Doubt who will," answered the page: "the truth is what I tell you, and truth will always rise uppermost, as the oil does above water; but if you will not believe me, *Operibus credite, et non verbis;*—come one of you gentlemen along with me, and be satisfied with your eyes of what your ears will not convince you." "That jaunt is for me," quoth Sanchica: "take me behind you, sir, upon your nag, for I have a huge mind to see his worship my father." "The daughters of governors," said the page, "must not travel unattended, but in coaches and litters, and with a handsome train of servants." "By the mass!" quoth Sanchica, "I can go a journey as well on an ass's colt as in a coach; I am none of your tender squeamish things—not I." "Peace, wench!" quoth Teresa; "thou knowest not what thou sayest: the gentleman is in the right, for, 'according to reason, each thing in its season.' When it was Sancho, it was Sancha; and when governor, 'my lady.' Say I not right, sir?" "My lady Teresa says more than she imagines," quoth the page; "but pray give me something to eat, and dispatch me quickly, for I intend to return home this night." "Be pleased, then, sir," said the priest, "to take a humble meal with me, for Madam Teresa has more good-will than good cheer to welcome so worthy a guest." The page refused at first, but at length thought it best to comply, and the priest very willingly took him home with him, that he might have an opportunity to inform himself more at large concerning Don Quixote and his exploits. The bachelor offered Teresa to write answers to her letters; but, as she looked upon him to be somewhat of a wag, she would not let him meddle in her concerns; so she gave a couple of eggs and a modicum of bread to a noviciate friar who was a penman, and he wrote two letters for her, one to her husband, and the other to the duchess, both of her own inditing; and they are none of the worst things recorded in this great history, as will be seen hereafter.

---

* To swear by the life of one's parents was a common mode of adjuration in the time of Cervantes.

CHAPTER LI.

Of the progress of Sancho Panza's government; with other entertaining matters.

Now THE morning dawned that succeeded the night of the governor's round; the remainder of which the sewer passed, not in sleep, but in pleasing thoughts of the lovely face and charming air of the disguised damsel; and the steward in writing an account to his lord and lady of the words and actions of the new governor, who appeared to him a marvellous mixture of ignorance and sagacity. His lordship being risen, they gave him, by order of Doctor Pedro Rezio, a little conserve and four draughts of clear spring water, which, however, he would gladly have exchanged for a luncheon of bread and a few grapes. But, seeing it was rather a matter of compulsion than choice, he submitted, although with much grief of heart and mortification of appetite; being assured by his doctor that spare and delicate food sharpened that acute judgment which was so necessary for persons in authority and high employment, where a brawny strength of body is much less needful than a vigorous understanding. By this sophistry Sancho was induced to struggle with hunger, while inwardly he cursed the government, and even him that gave it.

Nevertheless, on this fasting fare did the worthy magistrate attend to the administration of justice; and the first business that occurred on that day was an appeal to his judgment in a case which was thus stated by a stranger—the appellant: "My lord," said he, "there is a river which passes through the domains of a certain lord, dividing it into two parts—I beseech your honour to give me your attention, for it is a case of great importance and some difficulty. I say, then, that upon this river there was a bridge, and at one end of it a gallows, and a kind of court-house, where four judges sit to try and pass sentence upon those who are found to transgress a certain law enacted by the proprietor, which runs thus: 'Whoever would pass over this bridge, must first declare upon oath whence he comes, and upon what business he is going; and if he swears the truth, he shall pass over; but if he swears to a falsehood, he shall certainly die upon the gibbet there provided.' After this law was made known many persons ventured over it, and the truth of what they swore being admitted, they were allowed freely to pass. But a man now comes, demanding a passage over the bridge; and, on taking the required oath, he swears that he is going to be executed upon the gibbet before him, and that he has no other business. The judges deliberated, but would not decide. 'If we let this man pass freely,' said they, 'he will have sworn falsely, and by the law he ought to die; and, if we hang him, he will verify his oath, and he, having sworn the truth, ought to have passed unmolested, as the law ordains.'

The case, my lord, is yet suspended, for the judges know not how to act; and therefore, having heard of your lordship's great wisdom and acuteness, they have sent me humbly to beseech your lordship on their behalf, to give your opinion in so intricate and perplexing a case." "To deal plainly with you," said Sancho, "these gentlemen judges who sent you to me might have saved themselves and you the labour; for I have more of the blunt than the acute in me. However, let me hear your question once more, that I may understand it the better, and mayhap I may chance to hit the right nail on the head." The man accordingly told his tale once or twice more, and when he had done, the governor thus delivered his opinion: "To my thinking," said he, "this matter may soon be settled; and I will tell you how. The man, you say, swears he is going to die upon the gallows, and if he is hanged, it would be against the law, because he swore the truth; and if they do not hang him, why then he swore a lie, and ought to have suffered." "It is just as you say, my lord governor," said the messenger, "and nothing more is wanting to a right understanding of the case." "I say, then," continued Sancho, "that they must let that part of the man pass that swore the truth, and hang that part that swore the lie, and thereby the law will be obeyed." "If so, my lord," replied the stranger, "the man must be divided into two parts; and thereby he will certainly die, and thus the law, which we are bound to observe, is in no respect complied with." "Harkee, honest man," said Sancho: "either I have no brains, or there is as much reason to put this passenger to death as to let him live and pass the bridge; for if the truth saves him, the lie also condemns him; and, this being so, you may tell those gentlemen who sent you to me, that since the reasons for condemning and acquitting him are equal, they should let the man pass freely; for it is always more commendable to do good than to do harm; and this advice I would give you under my hand, if I could write. Nor do I speak thus of my own head, but on the authority of my master, Don Quixote, who, on the night before the day I came to govern this island, told me, among many other good things, that when justice was doubtful, I should lean to the side of mercy; and God has been pleased to bring it to my mind in the present case, in which it comes pat to the purpose." "It does so," answered the steward; "and, for my part, I think Lycurgus himself, who gave laws to the Lacedæmonians, could not have decided more wisely than the great Panza has done. And now let the business of the court cease for this morning, and I will give orders that my lord governor shall dine to-day much to his satisfaction." "That," quoth Sancho, "is what I desire: give us fair play, feed us well, and then let cases and questions rain upon me ever so thick, I will dispatch them in a trice."

The steward was as good as his word, for it would have gone much against his conscience to starve so excellent a governor; besides, he intended to come to a conclusion with him that very night, and to play off the last trick he had in commission.

Now Sancho, having dined to his heart's content, though against all the rules and aphorisms of Doctor Tirteafuera, when the cloth was removed, a courier arrived with a letter from Don Quixote to the governor. Sancho desired the secretary to read it first to himself, and then, if it contained nothing that required secresy, to read it aloud. The secretary having done as he was commanded, "My lord," said he, "well may it be read aloud, for what Signor Don Quixote writes to your lordship deserves to be engraven in letters of gold. Pray listen to me.

"DON QUIXOTE DE LA MANCHA TO SANCHO PANZA, GOVERNOR OF THE ISLAND OF BARATARIA.

"When I expected, friend Sancho, to have heard only of thy carelessness and blunders, I have had accounts of thy vigilance and discretion; for which I return particular thanks to Heaven, that can raise up the lowest from their poverty, and convert the fool into a wise man. I am told that as a governor thou art a man; yet as a man thou art scarcely above the brute creature—such is the humility of thy demeanour. But I would observe to thee, Sancho, that it is often expedient and necessary, for the due support of authority, to act in contradiction to the humility of the heart. The personal adornments of one that is raised to a high situation must correspond with his present greatness, and not with his former lowliness: let thy apparel, therefore, be good and becoming; for the hedgestake, when decorated, no longer appears what it really is. I do not mean that thou shouldst wear jewels or finery; nor, being a judge, would I have thee dress like a soldier; but adorn thyself in a manner suitable to thy employment. To gain the good-will of thy people, two things, among others, thou must not fail to observe: one is to be courteous to all—that, indeed, I have already told thee; the other is to take especial care that the people be exposed to no scarcity of food; for with the poor, hunger is, of all afflictions, the most insupportable. Publish few edicts, but let those be good; and, above all, see they are well observed; for edicts that are not kept are the same as not made, and serve only to show that the prince, though he had wisdom and authority to make them, had not the courage to insist upon their execution. Laws that threaten, and are not enforced, become like King Log, whose croaking subjects first feared, then despised him. Be a father to virtue, and a stepfather to vice. Be not always severe, nor always mild; but choose the happy mean between them, which is the true point of discretion. Visit the prisons, the shambles, and the markets; for there the presence of the governor is highly necessary: such attention is a comfort to the prisoner hoping for release; it is a terror to the butchers, who then dare not make use of false weights; and the same effect is produced on all other dealers. Shouldst thou unhappily be secretly inclined to avarice, to gluttony, or women, which I hope thou art not, avoid showing thyself guilty of these vices; for, when those who are concerned with thee discover thy ruling passion, they will assault thee on that quarter, nor leave thee till they have effected thy destruction. View and review, consider and reconsider the counsels and documents I gave thee in writing before thy departure hence to thy government; and in them thou wilt find a choice supply to sustain thee through the toils and difficulties which governors must continually encounter. Write to thy patrons, the duke and duchess, and show thyself grateful; for ingratitude is the daughter of pride, and one of the greatest sins; whereas, he who is grateful to those that have done him service, thereby testifies that he will be grateful also to God, his constant benefactor.

"My lady duchess has dispatched a messenger to thy wife Teresa, with thy hunting-suit, and also a present from herself. We expect an answer every moment. I have been a little out of order with a certain cat-clawing which befell me, not much to the advantage of my nose; but it was nothing, for if there are enchanters who persecute me, there are others who defend me. Let me know if the steward who is with thee had any hand in the actions of the Trifaldi, as thou hast suspected; and give me advice from time to time of all that happens to thee, since the distance between us is so short. I think of quitting this idle life very soon, for I was not born for luxury and ease. A circumstance has occurred which may, I believe, tend to deprive me of the favour of the duke and duchess; but, though it afflicts me much. it affects not my determination, for I must comply with

He took his secretary with him into his private chamber, being desirous to send an immediate answer to his master, and ordered him to write what he should dictate to him.

the duties of my profession in preference to any other claim ; as it is often said, *Amicus Plato, sed magis amica veritas.* I write this in Latin, being persuaded that thou hast learned that language since thy promotion. Farewell, and God have thee in His keeping: so mayest thou escape the pity of the world.

"Thy friend, DON QUIXOTE DE LA MANCHA.

Sancho listened with great attention to the letter, which was praised for its wisdom by all who heard it ; and, rising from table, he took his secretary with him into his private chamber, being desirous to send an immediate answer to his master ; and he ordered him to write, without adding or diminishing a tittle, what he should dictate to him.   He was obeyed, and the answer was as follows :

"SANCHO PANZA TO DON QUIXOTE DE LA MANCHA.

"I am so taken up with business, that I have scarcely time either to scratch my head or even to pare my nails, and therefore, Heaven help me ! I wear them very long. I tell your worship this that you may not wonder why I have given you no account before of my well or ill being in this government, where I suffer more hunger than when we both wandered about through woods and deserts.

"My lord duke wrote to me the other day, to tell me of certain spies that were come into this island to take away my life; but, as yet, I have been able to find none, except a certain doctor, hired by the islanders to kill their governors. He calls himself Doctor Pedro Rezio, and is a native of Tirteafuera; so your worship may see by his name that one is in danger of dying under his hands. The same doctor owns that he does not cure distempers, but prevents them, for which he prescribes nothing but fasting and fasting, till he reduces his patient to bare bones; as if a consumption was not worse than a fever. In short, by this man's help, I am in a fair way to perish by hunger and vexation; and, instead of coming hither, as I expected, to eat hot and drink cool, and lay my body at night between Holland sheets, upon soft beds of down, I am come to do penance, like a hermit; and this goes so much against me, that I do believe the devil will have me at last.

"Hitherto I have neither touched fee nor bribe, and how I am to fare hereafter I know not; but I have been told that it was the custom with the governors of this island, on taking possession, to receive a good round sum by way of gift or loan from the towns-people, and furthermore, that it is the same in all other governments.

"One night, as I was going the round, I met a very comely damsel in man's clothes, and a brother of hers in those of a woman. My sewer fell in love with the girl, and has thoughts of making her his wife, and I have pitched upon the youth for my son-in-law. To-day we both intend to disclose our minds to their father, who is one Diego de la Llana, a gentleman, and as good a Christian as one can desire.

"I visit the markets, as your worship advised me, and yesterday I found a huckster-woman pretending to sell new hazel-nuts, and, finding that she had mixed them with such as were old and rotten, I condemned them all to the use of the hospital boys, who well know how to pick the good from the bad, and forbade her to appear in the market again for fifteen days. The people say I did well in this matter, for it is a common opinion in this town that there is not a worse sort of people than your market women; for they are all shameless, hard-hearted, and impudent; and I verily believe it is so, by those I have seen in other places.

"I am mightily pleased that my lady duchess has written to my wife, Teresa Panza, and sent her the present your worship mentions; I hope one time or other to requite her goodness: pray kiss her honour's hands in my name, and tell her she has not thrown her favours into a rent sack, as she will find.

"I should be grieved to hear that you had any cross reckonings with my lord and lady; for if your worship quarrels with them, 't is I must come to the ground; and, since you warn me, of all things, not to be ungrateful, it would ill become your worship to be so towards those who have done you so many kindnesses, and entertained you so nobly in their castle.

"The cat business I don't understand—one of the tricks, mayhap, of your worship's old enemies the enchanters; but I shall know more about it when we meet.

"I would fain send your worship a token, but I cannot tell what, unless it be some little clyster-pipes which they make here very curiously; but, if I continue in office, I shall get fees and other pickings worth sending you. If my wife, Teresa Panza, writes to me, be so kind as to pay the postage and send me the letter; for I have a mighty desire to know how it fares with her, and my house and children. So Heaven protect your worship from evil-minded enchanters, and bring me safe and sound out of this government; which I very much doubt, seeing how I am treated by Doctor Pedro Rezio.

"Your worship's servant,

"Sancho Panza, the Governor."

The secretary sealed the letter, and it was forthwith dispatched by the courier; and, as it was now judged expedient to release the governor from the troubles of office, measures were concerted by those who had the management of these jests. Sancho passed that afternoon in making divers regulations for the benefit of his people. Among others, he strictly prohibited the monopoly and forestalling of provisions; wines he allowed to be imported from all parts, requiring only the merchant to declare of what growth it was, that a just price might be set upon it; and whoever adulterated it, or gave it a false name, should be punished with death. He moderated the prices of all sorts of hose and shoes, especially the latter, the current price of which he thought exorbitant. He limited the wages of servants, which were mounting fast to an extravagant height. He laid several penalties upon all those who should sing lewd and immoral songs either by day or by night; and prohibited the vagrant blind from going about singing their miracles in rhyme, unless they could produce unquestionable evidence of their truth; being persuaded that such counterfeit tales brought discredit upon those which were genuine. He appointed an overseer of the poor—not to persecute them, but to examine their true claims; for under the disguise of pretended lameness and counterfeit sores, are often found sturdy thieves and hale drunkards. In short, he made many good and wholesome ordinances, which are still observed in that town; and, bearing his name, are called, "The Regulations of the great Governor Sancho Panza."

CHAPTER LII.

In which is recorded the adventure of the second afflicted matron, otherwise called Donna Rodriguez.

CID HAMET relates that Don Quixote, being now properly healed of his wounds, began to think the life he led in that castle was against all he rules of his profession, and therefore he determined to request his notble host and hostess to grant him their permission to depart for Saragossa, as the approaching tournament drew near, wherein he proposed to win the suit of armour which was the prize at that festival.

But as he was dining one day with their highnesses, and preparing to unfold his purpose, lo! two women, clad in deep mourning, entered the great hall; and one of them, advancing towards the table, threw herself at Don Quixote's feet, which she embraced, at the same time pouring forth so many groans that all present were astonished, and the duke and duchess suspected it to be some jest of their domestics; yet the groans and sobs of the female appeared so much like real distress that they were in doubt, until the compassionate Don Quixote raised her from the ground, and prevailed with her to remove the veil from her weeping visage, when, to their surprise, they beheld the duenna Donna Rodriguez, accompanied by her unfortunate daughter, who had been deluded by the rich farmer's son. The discovery was a fresh cause of amazement, especially to the duke and duchess; for, though they knew the good woman's simplicity and folly, they had not thought her quite so absurd. At length Donna Rodriguez, turning to her lord and lady, "May it please your excellencies," said she, to permit me to speak with this gentleman, by whom I hope to be relieved from a perplexity in which we are involved by a cruel impudent villain?" The duke told her that she had his permission to say whatever she pleased to Don Quixote. Whereupon, addressing herself to the knight, she said, " It is not long, valorous knight, since I gave you an account how basely and treacherously a wicked peasant had used my poor dear child, this unfortunate girl here present, and you promised me to stand up in her defence and see her righted; and now I understand that you are about to leave this castle in search of good adventures—which Heaven send you: my desire is that, before you go forth to the wide world, you would challenge that graceless villain, and force him to wed my daughter, as he promised before he overcame her simple nature; for to expect justice in this affair from my lord duke would, for the reasons I mentioned to you, be to look for pears on an elm tree; so Heaven preserve your worship, and still be our defence."

" Worthy madam," replied Don Quixote, with much gravity and stateliness, "moderate your tears—or rather dry them up, and spare your sighs; for I take upon me the charge of seeing your daughter's wrongs redressed: though it had been better if she had not been so ready to believe the promises of lovers, who for the most part are forward to make promises, and very slow to perform them. However, I will, with my lord duke's leave, depart immediately in search of this ungracious youth, and will challenge and slay him if he refuse to perform his contract; for the chief end and purpose of my profession is, to spare the humble, and chastise the proud; I mean, to succour the wretched, and destroy the oppressor." " Sir Knight," said the duke, " you need not trouble yourself to seek the rustic of whom this good duenna complains; nor need you ask my permission to challenge him: regard him as already challenged, and leave it to me to oblige him to answer it, and meet you in person here in this castle, within the lists, where all the usual ceremonies shall be observed, and impartial justice distributed, conformable to the practice of all princes who grant the lists to combatants within the bounds of their territories." " Upon that assurance," said Don Quixote, " with your grace's leave, I waive on this occasion the punctilios of my gentility, and degrade myself to the level of the offender, that he may be qualified to meet me in equal combat. Thus, then, though absent, I challenge and defy him, upon account of the injury he has done in deceiving this poor girl, who through his fault is in great distress; and he shall either perform his promise of becoming her lawful husband, or die in the contest." Thereupon, pulling off his glove, he cast it into the middle of the hall, and the duke immediately took it up, declaring, as he had done before, that he accepted the challenge in the name of his vassal, and that the combat should take place six days after, in the inner court of his castle: the arms to be those customary among knights—namely, a lance, shield, and laced suit of armour, and all the other pieces, without deceit, fraud, or any superstition whatever, to be first viewed and examined by the judges of the field.

"But first it will be necessary," he further said, "that this good duenna here, and this simple damsel, should commit the justice of their cause to the hand of their champion Don Quixote ; for otherwise the challenge would become void, and nothing be done." "I dó commit it," answered the duenna. "And I too," added the daughter, all in tears, ashamed and confused.

The day being fixed, and the duke determined within himself what should be done, the mourning supplicants retired ; at the same time the duchess gave orders that they should not be regarded as domestics, but as ladies-errant, who came to seek justice in her castle. A separate apartment was therefore allotted to them, and they were served as strangers —to the amusement of the rest of the household, who could not imagine what was to be the end of the folly and presumption on the part of the duenna and her forsaken daughter.

A choice dessert to their entertainment now succeeded, and to give it a happy completion, in came the page who had carried the letters and presents to Governor Sancho's wife Teresa. The duke and duchess were much pleased at his return, and eager to learn the particulars of his journey. He said, in reply to their inquiries, that he could not give his report so publicly, nor in a few words, and therefore entreated their graces would be pleased to hear it in private, and in the meantime accept of what amusement the letters he had brought might afford. He thereupon delivered his packet, when one of the letters was found to be addressed "To my lady duchess of I know not where," and the other, "To my husband, Sancho Panza, Governor of the island of Barataria, whom God prosper more years than me." The duchess's cake was dough, as it is said, till she had perused her letter, which she eagerly opened, and, after hastily running her eye over it, finding nothing that required secresy, she read it aloud to the duke and the rest of the company, and the following were its contents :

TERESA PANZA'S LETTER TO THE DUCHESS.

"My lady,—The letter your greatness sent to me made me right glad, and, in faith, I longed for it mightily. The string of corals is very good, and my husband's hunting-suit comes not short of it. All the people in our town talk of your ladyship's goodness in making my husband a governor, though nobody believes it ; especially the priest and Master Nicholas the barber, and the bachelor Sampson Carrasco. But what care I ? for so long as the thing is so as it is, they may say what they list ; though, to own the truth, I should not have believed it myself but for the corals and the habit ; for in this village everybody takes my husband for a dolt, and cannot think what government he can be good for, but over a herd of goats. Heaven be his guide, and speed him in what is best for his children. As for me, dear honey-sweet madam, I am bent upon making hay while the sun shines, and hie me to court, to loll in my coach, though it makes a thousand that I could name stare their eyes out to see me. So pray bid my husband to send me a little money—and let it be enough ; for I reckon it is dear living at court, where bread sells for sixpence, and meat for thirty maravedis the pound, which is a judgment ; and if he is not for my going, let him send me word in time, for my feet tingle to be on the tramp ; and, besides, my neighbours all tell me that if I and my daughter go stately and fine at court, my husband will be better known by me than I by him ; and to be sure, many will ask, What ladies are those in that coach ? and will be told by a footman of ours that 't is the wife and daughter of Sancho Panza, Governor of the island of Barataria ;

and so shall my husband be known, and I much looked upon—to Rome for everything!

"I am as sorry as sorry can be, that hereabouts there has been no gathering of acorns this year of any account; but, for all that, I send your highness about half a peck, which I went to the hills for, and with my own hands picked them one by one, and could find no better—I wish they had been as big as ostrich eggs.

"Pray let not your mightiness forget to write to me, and I will take care to answer, and send you tidings of my health, and all the news of the village where I now remain, praying our Lord to preserve your greatness, and not to forget me. My daughter Sanchica and my son kiss your ladyship's hands.

"She who is more minded to see than to write to your ladyship,
"Your servant, TERESA PANZA.'

Teresa's letter gave great pleasure to all who heard it, especially the duke and duchess, insomuch that her grace asked Don Quixote if he thought her letter to the governor might with propriety be opened, as it must needs be admirable; to which he replied that, to satisfy her highness' curiosity, he would open it. Accordingly he did so, and found it to contain what follows:

TERESA PANZA'S LETTER TO HER HUSBAND SANCHO PANZA.

"I received thy letter, dear husband of my soul, and I vow and swear to thee, as I am a Catholic Christian, that I was within two fingers' breath of running mad with joy. Yes, indeed, when I came to hear that thou wast a governor, methought I should have dropped down dead for mere gladness; for 't is said, thou know'st, that sudden joy kills as soon as great sorrow. And as for our daughter Sanchica, verily, she could not contain herself, for pure pleasure. There I had before my eyes thy suit, and the corals sent by my lady duchess about my neck, and the letters in my hands, and the young man that brought them standing by; yet, for all that, I thought it could be nothing but a dream; for who could think that a goatherd should ever come to be a governor of islands? My mother used to say that 'he who would see much must live long.' I say this because, if I live longer, I hope to see more;—no, faith, I shall not rest till I see thee a tax-farmer, or a collector of the customs; for though they be offices that send many to the devil, there is much money to be touched and turned. My lady duchess will tell thee how I have a huge longing to go to court: think of it, and let me know thy mind; for I would fain do thee credit there by riding in a coach.

"Neither the priest, the barber, the bachelor, nor even the sexton can yet believe thou art a governor, and will have it that it is all a cheat, or a matter of enchantment, like the rest of thy master Don Quixote's affairs; and Sampson says he will find thee out, and drive this government out of thy pate, and scour thy master's brains. But I only laugh at them, and look upon my string of corals, and think how to make thy suit of green into a habit for our daughter. I sent my lady duchess a parcel of acorns :—I wish they had been of gold. Prithee send me some strings of pearl, if they are in fashion in that same island. The news of our town is that Berrueca has married her daughter to a sorry painter, who came here and undertook any sort of work. The corporation employed him to paint the king's arms over the gate of the town-house. He asked them two ducats for the job, which they paid beforehand; so he fell to it, and worked eight days, at the end of which he had made nothing of it, and said he could not bring his hand to paint such trumpery, and returned the money; yet, for all that, he married in the name of a good workman. The truth is, he has left his brushes and taken up the spade, and goes to the field like a gentleman. Pedro de Lobo's son has taken orders, and shaven his crown, meaning to be a priest. Minguilla, Mingo Silvato's niece, hearing of it, is suing him upon a promise of marriage. We have had no olives this year, nor is there a drop of vinegar to be had in all the town. A company of foot soldiers passed through here, and carried off with them three girls—I will not say who they are; mayhap they will return, and somebody or other may marry them, with all their faults. Sanchica makes bone-lace, and gets eight maravedis a day, which she drops into a saving-box, to help her towards household stuff; but now that she is a governor's daughter she has no need to work, for thou wilt give her a portion without it. The fountain in our market-place is dried up. A thunder-bolt fell upon the pillory, and there may they all light! I expect an answer to this, and about my going to court. And so God grant thee more years than myself, or as many, for I would not willingly leave thee behind me.

"Thy wife, TERESA PANZA."

This letter caused much merriment, applause, and admiration; and to complete all, the courier now arrived who brought the letter sent by Sancho to his master, which was also read aloud, and occasioned the governor's folly to be much questioned. The duchess retired to hear from the page the particulars of his journey to Sancho's village, all of which he related very minutely, without omitting a single circumstance. He delivered the acorns, also a cheese, which Teresa presented as an excellent one, and better than those of Tronchon. These the duchess received with great satisfaction. And here we will leave them, to record how the government of the great Sancho Panza, the flower and mirror of all island governors, ended.

———◆———

BOOK IV.

CHAPTER LIII.

Of the toilsome end and conclusion of Sancho Panza's government.

IT is in vain to expect uniformity in the affairs of this life; the whole seems rather to be in a course of perpetual change. The seasons from year to year run in their appointed circle—spring is succeeded by sum-mer, summer by autumn, and autumn by winter, which is again followed by the season of renovation; and thus they perform their everlasting round. But man's mortal career has no such renewal: from infancy to age it hastens onward to its end, and to the beginning of that state which has neither change nor termination. Such are the reflections of Cid Hamet, the Mahometan philosopher; for many, by a natural sense, with-out the light of faith, have discovered the changeful uncertainty of our present condition, and the eternal duration of that which is to come. In this place, however, our author alludes only to the instability of Sancho's fortune, and the brief duration of his government, which so suddenly expired, dissolved, and vanished like a dream.

The governor being in bed on the seventh night of his administration, not sated with bread nor wine, but with sitting in judgment, deciding causes, and making statutes and proclamations; and just at the moment when sleep, in despite of hunger, was closing his eyelids, he heard such a noise of bells and voices that he verily thought the whole island had been sinking. He started up in his bed, and listened with great attention, to find out, if possible, the cause of so alarming an uproar; but far from discovering it, his confusion and terror were only augmented by the din of an infinite number of trumpets and drums being added to the former noises. Quitting his bed, he put on his slippers, on account of the damp floor; but, without nightgown or other apparel, he opened his chamber-door, and saw more than twenty persons coming along a gallery with lighted torches in their hands, and their swords drawn, all crying aloud, "Arm, arm, my lord governor, arm!—a world of enemies have got into the island, and we are undone for ever, if your conduct and valour do not save us." Thus advancing, with noise and disorder, they came up to where Sancho stood, astonished and stupefied with what he heard and saw. "Arm yourself quickly, my lord," said one of them, "unless you would be ruined, and the whole island with you." "What have I to do with arming," replied Sancho, "who know nothing of arms or fighting? It were better to leave these matters to my master Don Quixote, who will dispatch them and secure us in a trice; for, as I am a sinner to Heaven, I understand nothing at all of these hurly-burlys." "How, Signor Governor!" said another; "what faint-heartedness is this? Here we bring you arms and weapons—harness yourself, my lord, and come forth to the market-place, and be our leader and our captain, which, as governor, you ought to be." "Why, then, arm me, in God's name," replied Sancho: and instantly they brought two large old targets, which they had provided for the occasion, and, without allowing him to put on other garments, clapped them over his shirt, the one before and the other behind. They thrust his arms through holes they had made in them, and bound them so fast together with cords, that the poor commander remained cased and boarded up as stiff and straight as a spindle, without power to bend his knees or stir a single step. They then put a lance into his hand, upon which he leaned to keep himself up; and thus accoutred, they desired him to lead on and animate his people; for he being their north-pole, their lantern, and their morning star, their affairs could not fail to have a prosperous issue. "How should I march—wretch that I am!" said the governor, "when I cannot stir a joint between these boards, that press into my flesh? Your only way is to carry me in your arms, and lay me athwart, or set me upright, at some gate, which I will maintain either with my lance or my body." "Fie, Signor Governor!" said another, "it is more fear than the targets that hinders your marching. Hasten and exert yourself, for time advances, the enemy pours in upon us, and every moment increases our danger."

The unfortunate governor, thus urged and upbraided, made efforts to move, and down he fell, with such violence that he thought every bone had been broken ; and there he lay, like a tortoise in his shell, or like a flitch of bacon packed between two boards, or like a boat on the sands keel upwards. Though they saw his disaster, those jesting rogues had no compassion ; on the contrary, putting out their torches, they renewed the alarm, and, with terrible noise and precipitation, trampled over his body, and bestowed numerous blows upon the targets, insomuch that, if he had not contrived to shelter his head between the bucklers, it had gone hard with the poor governor, who, pent up within his narrow lodging, and sweating with fear, prayed from the bottom of his heart for deliverance from that horrible situation. Some kicked him, others stumbled and fell over him, and one among them jumped upon his body, and there stood as on a watch-tower, issuing his orders to the troops. "There, boys, there ! that way the enemy charges thickest ! defend that breach ! secure yon gate ! down with those scaling ladders ! this way with your kettles of melted pitch, resin, and flaming oil ; quick ! fly !—get woolpacks, and barricade the streets ! " In short, he called for all the instruments of death, and everything employed in the defence of a city besieged and stormed. All this while Sancho, pressed and battered, lay and heard what was passing, and often said to himself, " Oh that it would please the Lord that this island were but taken, and I could see myself either dead or delivered out of this devil's den !" Heaven at last heard his prayers, and, when least expecting it, he was cheered with shouts of triumph. " Victory ! victory !" they cried : " the enemy is routed. Rise, Signor Governor, enjoy the conquest, and divide the spoils taken from the foe by the valour of that invincible arm !" " Raise me up," quoth Sancho, in a woful tone ; and when they had placed him upon his legs, he said, " All the enemies I have routed may be nailed to my forehead. I will divide no spoils ; but I beg and entreat some friend, if I have any, to give me a draught of wine to keep me from choking with thirst, and help me to dry up this sweat, for I am almost turned into water." They untied the targets, wiped him, and brought him wine ; and, when seated upon his bed, such had been his fatigue, agony, and terror, that he fainted away. Those concerned in the joke were now sorry they had laid it on so heavily, but were consoled on seeing him recover. He asked them what time it was, and they told him it was daybreak. He said no more, but proceeded in silence to put on his clothes, while the rest looked on, curious to know what were his intentions.

At length, having put on his clothes, which he did slowly and with much difficulty, from his bruises, he bent his way to the stable, followed by all present, and going straight to Dapple, he embraced him, and gave him a kiss of peace on his forehead. " Come hither," said he, with tears in his eyes, " my friend, and the partner of my fatigues and miseries. When I consorted with thee, and had no other care but mending thy furniture, and feeding that little carcase of thine, happy were my hours, my days, and my years ; but since I forsook thee, and mounted the towers of ambition and pride, a thousand toils, a thousand torments, and ten thousand tribulations, have seized and worried my soul." While he thus spoke, he fixed the pannel upon his ass without interruption from anybody, and when he had done, with great difficulty and pain he got upon him, and said to the steward, the secretary, and the doctor, Pedro Rezio, and many others who were present, "Make way, gentlemen, make way, and let me return to my ancient liberty ; let me seek the life I have left, that I may rise again from this grave. I was not born to be a governor, nor to defend islands nor cities from enemies that break in upon them. I understand better how to plough and dig, to plant and prune vines, than to make laws and to take care of provinces and kingdoms. Saint Peter is well at Rome — I mean to say, that nothing becomes a man so well as the employment he was born for. In my hand a sickle is better than a sceptre. I had rather have my bellyful of my own poor porridge, than to be mocked with dainties by an officious doctor who would kill me with hunger ; I had rather lay under the shade of an oak in summer, and wrap myself in a jerkin of double sheep's-skin in winter, at my liberty, than lay me down, under the slavery of a government, between Holland sheets, and be robed in fine sables. Heaven be with you, gentlefolks : tell my lord duke that naked was I born, and naked I am ; I neither win nor lose ; for without a penny came I to this government, and without a penny do I leave it— all governors cannot say the like. Make way, gentlemen, I beseech you, that I may go and plaster myself, for I verily believe all my ribs are broken—thanks to the enemies who have been trampling over me all night long."

" It must not be so, Signor Governor," said the doctor, " I will give your lordship a balsamic draught, good against all kinds of bruises, that shall presently restore you to your former health and vigour ; and as to your food, my lord, I promise to amend that, and let you eat abundantly of whatever you desire." " Your promises come too late, Mr. Doctor," quoth Sancho ; " I will as soon turn Turk as remain here. These tricks are not to be played twice. 'Fore Heaven, I will no more hold this nor any other government, though it were served up to me in a covered dish, than I will fly to heaven without wings. I am of the race of the Panzas, who are made of stubborn stuff ; and if they once cry, Odd ! odds it shall be, come of it what will. Here will I leave the flimsy wings that raised me aloft to be pecked at by martlets and other small birds ; and be content to walk upon plain ground, with a plain foot ; for though it be not adorned with pink Cordovan shoes, it will not wait for hempen sandals. Every sheep with its like ; stretch not your feet beyond your sheet : so let me be gone, for it grows late." " Signor Governor," said the steward, " we would not presume to hinder your departure, although we are grieved to lose you, because of your wise and Christian conduct ; but your lordship knows that every governor before he lays down his authority is bound to render an account of his administration. Be pleased, my lord, to do so for the time which you have been among us ; then peace be with you." " Nobody can require that of me," replied Sancho, " but my lord duke : to him I go, and to him I shall give a fair and square account ; though, in going away naked as I do, there needs nothing more to show that I have governed like an angel." " Before Heaven," said Doctor Pedro Rezio, " the great Sancho is in the right, and I am of opinion we should let him go ; for without doubt his highness will be glad to see him." They all agreed, therefore, that he should be allowed to depart, and also offered to attend him and provide him with whatever was necessary or convenient for his journey. Sancho told them he wanted only a little barley for Dapple, and half a cheese and half a loaf for himself ; that having so short a distance to travel, nothing more would be needful. Hereupon they all embraced him, which kindness he returned with tears in his eyes, and he left them in admiration both of his good sense and unalterable firmness.

CHAPTER LIV.

Which treats of matters relating to this particular history, and to no other.

THE duke and duchess resolved that Don Quixote's challenge of their vassal should not be neglected; and though the young man had fled into Flanders to avoid having Donna Rodriguez for his mother-in-law, they made choice of a Gascon lacquey, named Tosilos, to supply his place, and for that purpose gave him instructions how to perform his part ; and the duke informed Don Quixote that his opponent would in four days present himself in the lists, armed as a knight, and prepared to maintain that the damsel lied by half his beard, and even by the whole beard, in saying that he had given her a promise of marriage. The information was highly delightful to Don Quixote, who flattered himself that the occasion would offer him an opportunity of performing wonders, and thought himself singularly fortunate that he should be able in the presence of such noble spectators to give proofs of the valour of his heart and the strength of his arm ; and so with infinite content he waited the four days, which his eager impatience made him think were so many ages.

Now, letting them pass, as we have done many other matters, we will turn to our friend Sancho, who, partly glad and partly sorrowful, was hastening as fast as his Dapple would carry him to his master, whose society he loved better than being governor of all the islands in the world. He had not, however, proceeded far from this island, city, or town (for which of these it was, he had never given himself the trouble to determine), when he saw on the high road six pilgrims with their staves, being foreigners of that class who were wont to sing their supplications for alms. As they drew near, they placed themselves in order, and began their song in the language of their country ; but Sancho understood nothing except the word signifying alms, whence he concluded that alms was the object of their chanting ; and being, as Cid Hamet says, extremely charitable, he took the half loaf and half cheese out of his wallet, and gave it them, making signs at the same time that he had nothing else to give.

They received his donation eagerly, saying, "*Guelte, guelte.*" * "I do not understand you," answered Sancho ; "what is it you would have, good people ?" One of them then drew out of his bosom a purse, and showing it to Sancho, intimated that it was money they wanted ; upon which Sancho, placing his thumb to his throat, and extending his hand upward, gave them to understand he had not a penny in the world. Then clapping heels to Dapple, he made way through them ; but as he passed by, one of them, looking at him with particular attention, caught hold of him, and throwing his arms about his waist, "God be my aid !" said he, in good Castilian : "what is it I see ? Is it possible I hold in my arms my dear friend and good neighbour, Sancho Panza ? Yes, truly, it must be so, for I am neither drunk nor sleeping." Sancho, much surprised to hear himself called by his name, and to be embraced by the stranger pilgrim, stared at him for some time without speaking a word ; but though he viewed him earnestly, he could not recollect him. "How !" said the pilgrim, observing his amazement, "have you forgotten your neighbour Ricote, the Morisco shopkeeper of your town ?" Sancho at length, after a fresh examination, recognized the face of an old acquaint-ance, and, without alighting from his beast, he embraced him, and said, "Who in the name of fortune, Ricote, would know you in this covering ? Tell me how you came to be thus Frenchified, and how you dare venture to come again into Spain, where, if you are found out, egad ! that coat of yours will not save you ?" "If you do not discover me, Sancho," answered the pilgrim, "I am safe enough, for in this habit nobody can know me. But go with us to yonder poplar grove, where my comrades mean to dine and rest themselves, and you shall eat with us. They are honest souls, I can assure you. There I shall have an opportunity to tell you what has befallen me since I was obliged to leave the town by the king's edict, which, as you know, caused so much misery to our people."

Sancho consented, and after Ricote had conferred with his comrades, they all retired together to the poplar grove, which was far enough out of the high road. There they flung down their staves, and putting off their pilgrim's attire, every man appeared in his doublet, excepting Ricote, who was somewhat advanced in years. They were all good-looking young fellows ; each had his wallet, which, as it soon appeared, was well stored, at least with relishing incentives to thirst, and such as provoke it at two leagues' distance. They laid themselves along on the ground, and, making the grass their table-cloth, there was presently a comfortable display of bread, salt, nuts, and cheese, with some bacon bones, which, though they would not bear picking, were to be sucked with advantage. Caviére too was produced—a kind of black eatable, made of the roes of fish : a notable awakener of thirst. Even olives were not wanting, and though somewhat dry, they were savoury and in

---

* A Dutch word, signifying "money."

The finishing of the wine was the beginning of a sound sleep, which seized them all,
upon their very board and table-cloth.

good keeping. But the glory of the feast was six bottles of wine: each
wallet being charged with one, even that of honest Ricote, who from a
Moor had become a German or Hollander, and like the rest drew forth
his bottle, which in size might vie with the other five. They now began
their feast, dwelling upon each morsel with great relish and satisfaction,
and as if they were determined to make the most of them; then pausing,
they all together raised their arms and bottles aloft into the air, mouth
to mouth, and with eyes fixed upwards, as if taking aim at the heavens ;
and in this posture, waving their heads from side to side in token of the
pleasure they received, they continued a long time, transfusing the precious fluid into their stomachs. Sancho beheld all this, and, nothing
grieved thereat, but rather in compliance with a proverb he well knew,
" When in Rome, do as Rome does," he asked Ricote for his bottle,
and took his aim as the others had done, and with equal delight. Four
times the bottles were tilted with effect, but the fifth was to no purpose,
for, alas ! they were now all empty and as dry as a rush, which struck a
damp on the spirits of the party. Nevertheless, one or other of them

would ever and anon take Sancho by the hand, saying, " Spaniard and Dutchman, all one, goot companion." " Well said, i'faith!" replied Sancho, " goot companion I vow to gad!"—then burst into a fit of laughing which held him an hour, losing at the time all recollection of the events of his government; for care has no control over the time that is spent in eating and drinking. In short, the finishing of the wine was the beginning of a sound sleep, which seized them all, upon their very board and table-cloth—Ricote and Sancho excepted: they having drunk less and eaten more, remained awake, and leaving their companions in a deep sleep, went a little aside and sat down under the shade of a beech tree, where Ricote, in pure Castilian, without once stumbling into his Morisco jargon, spoke as follows :

" You well know, friend Sancho, the dread and terror which his majesty's proclamation everywhere produced among our people ; * at least it had that effect upon me, and to such a degree that I almost imagined its dreadful penalty had already fallen upon my own family before the time limited for our departure from Spain. I endeavoured, however, to provide for our safety, as the prudent man does, who, expecting to be deprived of his habitation, looks out for another before he is turned out of doors. I quitted the town alone, in search of some place where I might conveniently remove my family, without that hurry and confusion which generally prevailed ; for the wisest among us clearly saw that the proclamations of his majesty were no empty threats, but would certainly be carried into effect at the time which had been fixed. In this belief I was the more confirmed from knowing the dangerous designs of our people, so that I could not but think that the king was inspired by Heaven to adopt so wise a measure. Not that we were all culpable; some of us were steady and true Christians, but their number was so small as to bear no proportion to those who were otherwise. In short, the country could no longer shelter the serpent in its bosom, and our expul-

---

* When the Moors were in possession of Spain, they allowed the Christians to remain in the country, with the free exercise of their holy religion, but subject to certain imposts. On the restoration of the Christian power, the Moors were likewise suffered to reside in separate quarters, paying tribute, as well as the Jews, to our king and nobles. In the year 1525, Charles V. ordered, on pain of death, all the Moors in Spain either to embrace the Christian faith or leave the country. Numbers were thus banished, but many remained and received baptism, though not all with equal sincerity. Their language, their national dances, songs, fêtes, and nuptial ceremonies, were all prohibited. These descendants of the conquerors of Spain were called Moriscos, or the New Proselytes, to distinguish them from the old Christians.

These Moriscos were detected in a conspiracy with the Grand Signor and some of the chiefs of Barbary. On the discovery of this plot, various councils of prelates and ministers were held, in which opinions were divided as to the question of expulsion; a measure which, as the only security for religion and the country, was, in the end, wisely adopted. Edicts were issued for general banishment, with the exception only of children of eight years of age; ordering likewise that the property they were allowed to carry away with them, consisting of their goods and chattels, or the money they might derive from the sale of them, should be all registered at the ports. On pain of death, no treasures were to be concealed, no Morisco harboured, nor suffered to return to Spain; which orders were, nevertheless, occasionally transgressed.

sion was just and necessary; a punishment which, though some might treat lightly, to us is the most terrible that can be inflicted. In whatever part of the world we are driven, our affections are centred here; this alone is our country; here alone we find the compassion which our misery and misfortunes demand; for in Barbary, and other parts of Africa, where we expected to be received and cherished, it is there we are most neglected and maltreated. We knew not our happiness till we lost it; and so great is the desire that we feel to return to Spain, that the most of those who, like myself, can speak the language—and they are not a few—forsake even their wives and children to revisit the country they love so much. Now it is we feel the truth of the saying, 'Sweet is our native land!'

"After quitting our village, I made the best of my way to France; but there, though I was well received, my stay was short, as I wished to examine other countries. From France, therefore, I went to Italy, and thence to Germany, where I thought we might live without restraint: the inhabitants being not over-scrupulous, and almost in every part of the country enjoy liberty of conscience. There I engaged a house situated in a village near Augsburgh, and soon after joined these adventurers in an excursion to Spain, whither great numbers come every year to visit the usual resorts of devotees: regarding it as their Indies, to which they are certain of making a profitable voyage. They traverse the whole kingdom, and there is not a village where they are not certain to get meat and drink, and at least a real in money: generally managing matters so well as to amass above a hundred crowns clear gain, which they change into gold, and hide either in the hollow of their staves, the patches of their garments, or some other private way; and thus, in spite of the numerous searchers and other officers, convey it safely into their own country.

"My object, however, in coming hither, is not to collect alms, but, if possible, to carry off the treasure I left behind when I went away, which, being buried in a place without the town, I can do with little danger. That being done, I intend to write or go to my wife and daughter, who, I know, are in Algiers, and contrive means for their reaching some port of France, and thence carry them into Germany, where we will wait, and see how Providence will dispose of us. Francisca, my wife, I know is a good Catholic Christian, and also my daughter Ricota; and, though I am not entirely so, yet I am more of the Christian than the Mahometan, and make it my constant prayer to the Almighty to open the eyes of my understanding, and make me know how best to serve Him. But what surprises me much is that my wife and daughter should have preferred going to Barbary rather than to France, where they might have lived as Christians."

"Mayhap, neighbour," said Sancho, "that was not their choice; for John Tiopeyo, your wife's brother, who carried them away, being a rank Moor, would certainly go where he liked best to stay; and I can tell you another thing, which is, that it may be lost labour now to seek for your hidden treasure, for the report was that a power of jewels and money had been taken from your wife and brother-in-law, which they were carrying off without being registered." "That may be," replied Ricote; "but I am sure, Sancho, they did not touch my hoard; for being afraid of some mischance, I never told them where I had hidden it; and therefore if you will go with me, and help me to carry it off, and conceal it, I will give you two hundred crowns, with which you may relieve your wants; for I know, friend, that they are not a few." "I would do it," answered Sancho, "but that I am not at all covetous. Had it been so with me, it was but this morning I quitted an employment out of which I could have covered the walls of my house with beaten gold, and, in six months, have eaten my victuals out of silver plates. And so, for that reason, and because, to my thinking, it would be treason against the king to favour his enemies, I will not go with you, though, instead of two hundred crowns, you should lay me down twice as much." "And pray, what employment is it you have quitted, Sancho?" demanded Ricote. "I have been governor of an island," answered Sancho, "and such a one, in faith, as you would not easily match." "Where might this island be?" said Ricote. "Where?" replied Sancho, "why, about two leagues off, and it is called Barataria." "Prithee, not so fast, friend Sancho," quoth Ricote: "islands are in the sea: there can be no islands here on land." "No, say you?" quoth Sancho; "I tell you, neighbour, it was but this very morning that I left it; yesterday I was there, governing at my pleasure, like any dragon: yet for all that, I turned my back upon it, for that same office of governor, as I take it, is a ticklish and dangerous thing." "And what have you got by your governorship?" demanded Ricote. "I have got," replied Sancho, "experience enough to know that I am fit to govern nothing but a herd of cattle, and that the riches to be gained in such governments must be paid for in hard labour, toil, and watching, ay, and hunger too; for your island governors eat next to nothing, especially if they have physicians to look after their health." "The meaning of all this," said Ricote, "I cannot comprehend; but it seems to me you talk wildly; for who should give you islands to govern? Are wise men now so scarce that they must needs make you a governor? Say no more, man, but come along with me, as I said before, and help me dig up my treasure—for, in truth, I may give it that name—and you shall have wherewithal to banish care." "Hark you, friend," said Sancho, 'I have already told you my mind upon the point; be satisfied that I will not betray you, and so in God's name go your way, and let me go mine; for I have heard that ' Well-got wealth may meet disaster, but ill-got wealth destroys its master.' "

"Well, Sancho," said Ricote, "I will not press you further; but tell me, were you in the village when my wife and daughter and my brother-in-law went away?" "Truly, I was," replied Sancho; "and I can tell you too that your daughter looked so comely that all the town went out to see her, and everybody said that there was none to be compared with her. Poor damsel! she wept bitterly on leaving us, and embraced all her friends and acquaintances, and all that came to see her, and desired them to recommend her to God and to our Lady His mother; and so piteously that even I could not help shedding tears, though not much of a weeper; in faith, many thought of stopping her on the road, and carrying her off, but the king's proclamation kept them in awe. Don Pedro Gregorio, the rich heir, was more moved than all, for they say he was mightily in love with her; and, since she went away, he has never been seen in our town, so that we all thought he followed to steal her away; but as yet we have heard nothing more of the matter." "I long had a suspicion," quoth Ricote, "that this gentleman was smitten with my daughter, but, trusting to her virtue, it gave me no uneasiness; for you must have heard, Sancho, that the Moorish women seldom or never hold amorous intercourse with old Christians; and my daughter, who, as I believe, minded religion more than love, thought but little of his courtship." "Heaven grant it," replied Sancho, "for otherwise it would go ill with them both. And now let me begone, friend, for to-night I intend to join my master Don Quixote." "God be with you, brother Sancho," said Ricote; "my comrades are stirring, and it is time for us also to be on our way." They then embraced each other; Sancho mounted his Dapple, and Ricote leaned on his pilgrim's staff, and so they parted.

CHAPTER LV.

Of what befell Sancho on his way; and other matters, which will be known when read.

It was so late before Sancho parted with his friend Ricote, that he could not reach the duke's castle that day, although he was within half a league of it, when night, somewhat darker than usual, overtook him: but as it was summer-time, this gave him little concern, and therefore he turned out of the road, intending to proceed no farther till the morning. But in seeking a convenient shelter for the night, his ill-luck so ordered it that he and Dapple fell together into a cavity, among the ruins of an old building. The hole was deep, and Sancho, in the course of his descent, devoutly recommended himself to Heaven, not expecting to stop till he came to the utmost depth of the abyss; but therein he was mistaken, for he had not much exceeded three fathoms before Dapple felt the ground, with Sancho still upon his back, without having received the smallest damage. He forthwith examined the condition of his body, held his breath, and felt all about him, and, finding himself whole and in catholic health, he thought he could never be sufficiently grateful to Heaven for his wonderful preservation; for he verily believed he had been dashed into a thousand pieces. He then groped about the pit, in the hope of discovering some means of getting out, but found that the sides were perpendicular, smooth, and without either hold or footing, which grieved him much, especially when he heard Dapple groan most piteously; nor did he lament without good cause, for in truth he was in a bad plight. "Woe is me!" exclaimed Sancho: "what sudden and unlooked-for mischances perpetually befall us poor wretches who live in this miserable world! Who could have thought that he who but yesterday saw himself on a throne, a governor of an island, with officers and servants at his call, should, to-day, find himself buried in a pit, alone, helpless, and cut off from all relief? Here must I and my ass perish with hunger, unless we die first, he with bruises, and I with grief; for I cannot reckon upon my master's luck in the Cave of Montesinos, where, it seems, he met with better entertainment than in his own house, and where he found the cloth ready laid, and the bed ready made. There he saw beautiful and pleasant visions; and here, if I see anything, it will be toads and snakes. Unfortunate that I am! what are my follies and my f. n∴es come to? Whenever it shall please Heaven that I shall be found, here will my bones be taken up, clean, white, and bare, and those of my trusty Dapple with them: by which, peradventure, it will be guessed who we are—at least by those who know that Sancho Panza never left his ass, nor did his ass ever leave Sancho Panza. Wretches that we are! not to have the comfort of dying among our friends, where at least there would be some to grieve for us, and, at our last gasp, to close our eyes. O my dear companion and friend! how ill have I requited thy faithful services! Forgive me, and pray to fortune, in the best manner thou canst, to bring us out of this miserable pickle; and I here promise thee, besides doubling thy allowance of provender, to set a crown of laurel upon thy head, that thou mayest look like any poet-laureate."

Thus did Sancho Panza bewail his misfortune; and though his ass listened to all he said, yet not a word did he answer: such was the poor beast's anguish and distress! At length, after having passed all that night in sad complaints and bitter wailings, daylight began to appear, whereby Sancho was soon confirmed in what he so much feared—that it was utterly impossible to escape from that dungeon without help. He therefore had recourse to his voice, and set up a vigorous outcry, in the hope of making somebody hear him; but, alas! it was all in vain, for not a human creature was within hearing, and after many trials he gave himself up as dead and buried. Seeing that his dear Dapple was yet lying upon his back, with his mouth upwards, he endeavoured to get him upon his legs, which, with much ado, he accomplished, though the poor animal could scarcely stand; he then took a luncheon of bread out of his wallet (which had shared in the disaster), and gave it to his beast, saying to him, "Bread is relief for all kind of grief:" all of which the ass appeared to take very kindly. At last, however, Sancho perceived a crevice on one side of the pit large enough to admit the body of a man. He immediately thrust himself into the hole, and creeping upon all-fours, he found it to enlarge as he proceeded, and that it led into another cavity, which, by a ray of light that glanced through some cranny above, he saw was large and spacious. He saw also that it led into another vault equally capacious; and having made this discovery, he returned for his ass, and by removing the earth about the hole, he soon made it large it enough for Dapple to pass. Then laying hold of his halter, he led him along through the several cavities, to try if he could not find a way out on the other side. Thus he went on, sometimes in the dusk, sometimes in the dark, but always in fear and trembling. "Heavens defend me!" said he, "what a chicken-hearted fellow am I! This now, which to me is a sad mishap, to my master Don Quixote would have been a choice adventure. These caves and dungeons, belike, he would have taken for beautiful gardens and stately palaces of Galiana, and would have reckoned upon their ending in some pleasant flowery meadow; while I, poor, helpless, heartless wretch that I am, expect some other pit still deeper to open suddenly under my feet and swallow me up. Oh, welcome the ill luck that comes alone!" Thus he went on, lamenting and despairing; and when he had gone, as he supposed, somewhat more than half a league, he perceived a kind of glimmering light, like that of day, breaking through some aperture above that seemed to him an entrance to the other world; in which situation Cid Hamet leaves him for awhile, and returns to Don Quixote, who with great pleasure looked forward to the day appointed for the combat, by which he hoped to venge the injury done to the honour of Donna Rodriguez' daughter.

One morning, as the knight was riding out to exercise and prepare himself for the approaching conflict, now urging, now checking the mettle of his steed, it happened that Rozinante, in one of his curvetings, pitched his feet so near the brink of a deep cave, that had not Don Quixote used his reins with all his skill, he must inevitably have fallen into it. But, having escaped that danger, he was curious to examine the chasm, and as he was earnestly surveying it, still sitting on his horse, he thought he heard a noise issuing from below, like a human voice; and listening more attentively, he distinctly heard these words: "Ho! above there! is there any Christian that hears me, or any charitable gentleman to take pity on a sinner buried alive—a poor governor without a government?" Don Quixote thought it was the voice of Sancho Panza; at which he was greatly amazed, and, raising his voice as high he could, he cried, "Who are you below there? Who is it that complains?" "Who should be here, and who complains," answered the voice, "but the most wretched soul alive, Sancho Panza, governor, for his sins and evil-errantry, of the island of Barataria, and late squire to the famous knight Don Quixote de la Mancha."

On hearing this, Don Quixote's wonder and alarm increased; for he conceived that Sancho Panza was dead, and that his soul was there doing penance; and in this persuasion, he said, "I conjure thee, as far as a Catholic Christian may, to tell me who thou art; and if thou art a soul in purgatory, let me know what I can do for thee; for since my profession obliges me to aid and succour all that are afflicted in this world, I shall also be ready to aid and assist the distressed in the world below, where they cannot help themselves." "Surely," answered the voice from below, "it is my master, Don Quixote de la Mancha, who speaks to me—by the sound of the voice it can be no other!" "Don Quixote I am," replied the knight, "he whose profession and duty it is to relieve and succour the living and the dead in their necessities. Tell me, then, who thou art, for I am amazed at what I hear. If thou art really my squire Sancho Panza, and art dead, since the devils have not got thee, and through God's mercy thou art still in purgatory, our holy mother the Roman Catholic Church has power by her supplications to deliver thee from the pains which afflict thee; and I will myself solicit her in thy behalf, as far as my estate and purse will go: speak, therefore, and tell me quickly who thou art?" "Why, then, I vow to Heaven," said the voice, "and will swear by whatever your worship pleases, Signor Don Quixote de la Mancha, that I am your squire Sancho Panza, and that I never died in the whole course of my life; but that, having left my government for reasons and causes that require more leisure to be told, I fell last night into this cavern, where I now am, and Dapple with me, who will not let me lie; and, as a further proof, here the good creature stands by me."

Now it would seem the ass understood what Sancho said, and willing to add his testimony, at that instant began to bray so lustily that the whole cave resounded. "A credible witness!" quoth Don Quixote: "that bray I know as well as if I myself had brought it forth; and thy voice, too, I know, my dear Sancho—wait a little, and I will go to the duke's castle and bring some people to get thee out of this pit, into which thou hast certainly been cast for thy sins." "Pray go, for the Lord's sake," quoth Sancho, "and return speedily; for I cannot bear any longer to be buried alive, and am dying with fear." Don Quixote left him, and hastened to the castle to tell the duke and duchess what had happened to Sancho Panza; at which they were not a little surprised, though they readily accounted for his being there, and conceived that he might easily have fallen down the pit, which was well known, and had been there time out of mind; but they could not imagine how he should have left his government without their having been apprised of it. Ropes and pullies were, however, immediately sent; and, with much labour and many hands, Dapple and his master were drawn out of that gloomy den, to the welcome light of the sun.

A certain scholar, who was present at Sancho's deliverance, said, "Thus should all bad governors quit their governments; even as this sinner comes out of the depth of this abyss; pale, hungry, and penniless!" "Harkye, brother," said Sancho, who had overheard him, "it is now eight or ten days since I began to govern the island that was given to me, and in all that time I never had my bellyful but once. Doctors persecuted me, enemies trampled over me and bruised my bones, but no leisure had I either to touch a bribe or receive my dues; and this being the fact, methinks I deserve not to come out of it in this fashion. But, man proposes and God disposes; and He knows what is best and fittest for everybody; and, as is the reason, such is the season; and, let nobody say, I will not drink of this cup; for where one expected to find a flitch, there may not be even a pin to hang it on! Heaven

knows my mind, and that is enough. I could say much, but I say
nothing."   "Be not angry, Sancho, nor concerned at what may be
said," quoth Don Quixote, "otherwise thou wilt never be at peace.
Keep but a safe conscience, and let people say what they will ; for as
well mayest thou think to barricade the plain, as to tie up the tongue of
slander. If a governor comes rich from his government, they say he has
plundered it ; and if he leaves it poor, that he has been a fool."   "I

*With much labour and many hands, Dapple and his master were drawn out of that gloomy
den, to the welcome light of the sun.*

warrant," answered Sancho, "that for this bout. they will rather take
me for a fool than a thief."
     In such discourse, amidst a rabblement of boys and other followers,
they arrived at the castle, where the duke and duchess were already in
a gallery waiting for them. Sancho would not go up to see the duke
till he had first taken the necessary care of Dapple in the stable, because
the poor creature, he said, had had but an indifferent night's lodging ;
and, that done, he went up to the duke and duchess, and kneeling
before them, he said, "My lord and lady, you made me governor of

your island of Barataria; and not from any desert of mine, but because your grandeurs would have it so. Naked I entered it, and naked have I left it : I neither win nor lose. Whether I have governed well or ill, there are witnesses, who may say what they please. I have cleared up doubts, and pronounced sentences, and all the while famished with hunger : so far it was ordered by Pedro Rezio, native of Tirteafuera, doctor in ordinary to the island and its governor. Enemies attacked us by night ; and, though they put us in great danger, I heard many say that the island was delivered ; and according as they speak the truth, so help them Heaven. In short, I have by this time been able to reckon up the cares and burdens the trade of governing brings with it, and find them, by my own account, too heavy for my shoulders or ribs to bear— they are not arrows for my quiver ; and so before the government left me, I even resolved to leave the government ; and yesterday morning, turning my back on the island, I left it just as I found it, with the same streets, the same houses, with the selfsame roofs to them as they had when I first entered it. I have neither borrowed nor hoarded ; and though I intended to make some wholesome laws, I made none, fearing they would not be observed, which is the same as if they were not made. I came away, as I said, from the island without any company but my Dapple. In the dark, I fell headlong into a pit, and crept along under-ground, till this morning by the light of the sun I discovered a way out, though not so easy a one but that if Heaven had not sent my master Don Quixote, there I might have stayed till the end of the world. So that, my lord duke and my lady duchess, behold here your governor Sancho Panza, who in the ten days that he held his office, found out by experience that he would not give a single farthing to be governor, not of an island only, but even of the whole world. This, then, being the case, kissing your honours' feet, and imitating the boys at play, who cry, ' Leap and away,' I give a leap out of the government, and pass over to the service of my master Don Quixote ; for, after all, though with him I eat my bread in bodily fear, at least I have my bellyful ; and, for my part, so I have but that well stuffed, it is all one to me whether it be with carrots or partridges."

Here Sancho ended his long speech, Don Quixote dreading all the while a thousand absurdities, and when he had ended with so few, he gave thanks to Heaven in his heart. The duke embraced Sancho, and said that it grieved him to the soul he had left the government so soon ; but that he would take care he should have some other employment in his territories, of less trouble and more profit. The duchess was no less kind, and ordered that he should be taken good care of ; for he seemed to be much bruised and in wretched plight.

CHAPTER LVI.

Of the prodigious and unparalleled battle between Don Quixote de la Mancha, and the lacquey Tosilos, in defence of the duenna Donna Rodriguez' daughter.

THE duke and duchess repented not of the jest they had practised upon Sancho Panza, when the steward, on his return, gave them a minute relation of almost every word and action of the governor during that time; and he failed not to enlarge upon the assault of the island, with his terror and final abdication, which gave them not a little entertainment. The history then tells that the appointed day of combat arrived; nor had the duke neglected to give his lacquey Tosilos all the necessary instructions how to vanquish his antagonist, and yet neither kill nor wound him; for which purpose he gave orders that the iron heads of their lances should be taken off, because, as he told Don Quixote, that Christianity upon which he valued himself forbade that in this battle their lives should be exposed to danger; and though contrary to the decree of the holy council, which prohibits such encounters, he should allow them free field-room in his own territories; but he did not wish the affair pushed to the utmost extremity. Don Quixote begged his excellency would arrange all things as he deemed best, and assured him that he would acquiesce in every particular.

On the dreadful day, the duke having commanded a spacious scaffold to be erected before the court of the castle for the judges of the field, and the two duennas, mother and daughter, appellants, an infinite number of people, from all the neighbouring towns and villages, flocked to see the novel spectacle; for, in latter times, nothing like it had ever been seen or heard of in that country, either by the living or the dead.

The first who entered the lists was the master of the ceremonies, who walked over the ground, and examined it in every part, to guard against foul play, and see that there was nothing on the surface to occasion stumbling or falling. The duennas now entered, and took seats, covered with veils, even to their breasts, and betraying much emotion. Don Quixote next presented himself in the lists, and soon after the sound of trumpets announced the entrance of the great Tosilos, mounted on a stately steed, making the earth shake beneath him; with vizor down, and stiffly cased within a suit of strong and shining armour. The horse seemed to be a Frieslander, broad-built and flea-bitten, with abundance of hair upon each fetlock. The courageous Tosilos came well instructed by the duke his lord how to behave towards the valorous Don Quixote de la Mancha, and cautioned in nowise to hurt him, and also to be careful to elude his adversary at the first onset, lest he should himself be slain, which would be inevitable if he met him in full career. He traversed the enclosure, and, advancing toward the duennas, surveyed the lady who demanded him for her husband. The marshal of the field, attended by Don Quixote and Tosilos, now formally demanded of the duennas whether they consented that Don Quixote de la Mancha should maintain their right. They answered that they did, and that whatever he should do in their behalf they would confirm, and hold to be right, firm, and valid.

The duke and duchess now took their seats in a balcony over the barriers, which were crowded by an infinite number of people, all in full expectation of beholding this terrible and extraordinary conflict. It was stipulated between Don Quixote and Tosilos, that if the former should conquer his adversary, the latter should be obliged to marry Donna Rodriguez' daughter; and if he should be overcome, his adversary should be released from his engagement with the lady, and every other claim on her account. And now the master of the ceremonies divided the sun equally between them, and fixed each at his post. The drums beat; the sound of trumpets filled the air, earth shook beneath the steeds of the combatants; the hearts of the gazing multitude palpitated, some with fear, some with hope, for the issue of this affair: finally Don Quixote, recommending himself to Heaven and to his lady Dulcinea del Toboso, stood waiting the signal for the onset. But our lacquey's thoughts were differently employed; for it so happened that, while he stood looking at his female enemy, she appeared to him the most beautiful woman he had ever seen in his life, and the little blind boy called Cupid seized the opportunity of adding a lacquey's heart to the list of his trophies. Softly and unperceived, therefore, he approached his victim, and, taking aim at the left side of the devoted youth, with an arrow two yards long he pierced his heart through and through; and this the amorous archer could do with perfect safety, for he is invisible, and goes and comes when and where he pleases, and to none is he accountable. So that when the signal was given for the onset, our lacquey stood transported, contemplating the beauty of her who was now the mistress of his liberty, and therefore attended not to the trumpet's sound. It was not so with Don Quixote, who, instantly spurring forward, advanced towards his enemy at Rozinante's best speed; while his trusty squire Sancho cried aloud, " God guide you, cream and flower of knights-errant! Heaven give you victory, for the right is on your side! "

Though Tosilos saw Don Quixote making towards him, he stirred not a step from the place where he stood, but loudly calling the marshal of the field to him, he said, " Is not this combat, sir, to decide whether I shall marry or not marry that young lady? " " It is," answered the marshal. " Then," quoth the lacquey, " my conscience will not let me proceed any further; and I declare that I yield myself vanquished, and am ready to marry that gentlewoman this moment." The marshal was surprised at what Tosilos said, and, being privy to the contrivance, he was at a loss how to answer him. Don Quixote, perceiving that his adversary was not advancing, stopped short in the midst of his career. The duke could not conceive why the combat was retarded; and, when the marshal explained the cause, he was angry at the disappointment.

In the meantime, however, Tosilos approached Donna Rodriguez, and said aloud, "I am willing, good madam, to marry your daughter, and would not seek by strife and bloodshed what I may have peaceably and without danger." "Since that is the case," said the valorous Don Quixote, "I am absolved from my promise: let them be married, in God's name, and, as God has given her, Saint Peter bless her."

The duke now came down into the court of the castle, and, going up to Tosilos, he said, "Is it true, knight, that you yield yourself vanquished, and that, instigated by your timorous conscience, you intend to marry this damsel?" "Yes, an't please your grace," replied Tosilos. "And, faith, 't is the wisest course," quoth Sancho Panza. "What you would give to the mouse give to the cat, and you will save trouble." Tosilos was, in the meantime, unlacing his helmet, to do which he begged for prompt assistance, as his spirits and breath were just failing him, unable to remain any longer pent up in so strait a lodging. They presently unarmed him, and, the face of the lacquey being exposed to view, Donna Rodriguez and her daughter cried aloud, "A cheat! a cheat! Tosilos, my lord duke's lacquey, is put upon us instead of our true spouse! Justice from Heaven and the king against so much deceit, not to say villany!" "Afflict not yourselves, ladies," quoth Don Quixote, "for this is neither deceit nor villany; or, if it be so, the duke is not to blame, but the wicked enchanters, my persecutors, who, envying me the glory I should have acquired by this conquest, have transformed the countenance of your husband into that of another, who, you say, is a lacquey belonging to my lord duke. Take my advice, and, in spite of the malice of my enemies, marry him; for, without doubt, he is the very man you desire for your husband."

The duke, hearing this, angry as he was, could not forbear laughing. "Truly," said he, "so many extraordinary things happen every day to the great Don Quixote, that I am inclined to believe this is not my lacquey; but, for our better satisfaction, and to detect the artifice, let us, if you please, defer the marriage for fifteen days; and in the meantime keep this doubtful youth in safe custody; by that time, perhaps, he may return to his own proper form: for doubtless the malice of those wicked magicians against the noble Don Quixote cannot last so long; especially when they find these tricks and transformations avail them so little." "Oh, sir," quoth Sancho, "the wicked wretches are for ever at this work, changing from one shape to another whatever my master has to do with. It was but lately they turned a famous knight he had beaten, called the Knight of the Mirrors, into the very shape of the bachelor Sampson Carrasco, a fellow townsman and special friend of ours; and more than that, they changed my lady Dulcinea del Toboso from a princess into a downright country bumpkin; so that I verily believe this lacquey here will live and die a lacquey all the days of his life." "Let him be who he will," said the duenna's daughter, "as he demands me to wife, I take it kindly of him; for I had rather be lawful wife to a lacquey than the cast mistress of a gentleman, though, indeed, he who deluded me is not one."

All these events, in short, ended with the imprisonment of Tosilos, where it was determined he should remain until it was seen in what his transformation would end; and although the victory was adjudged to Don Quixote by general acclamation, the greater part of the spectators were disappointed and out of humour that the long-expected combatants had not hacked each other to pieces ; as the rabble are wont to repine when the criminal is pardoned whom they expected to see hanged. The crowd now dispersed ; the duke and Don Quixote returned to the castle, after ordering the lacquey into close keeping. Donña Rodriguez and her daughter were extremely well pleased to see that, one way or other, this business was likely to end in matrimony; and Tosilos was consoled with the like expectation.

CHAPTER LVII.

Which ralates how Don Quixote took his leave of the duke, and oj what befell him' with the witty and wanton Altisidora, one of the duchess's damsels.

EVEN Don Quixote now thought it full time to quit so inactive a life as that which he had led in the castle, deeming himself culpable in living thus in indolence, amidst the luxuries prepared for him, as a knight-errant, by the duke and duchess; and he believed he should have to account to Heaven for this neglect of the duties of his profession. He therefore requested permission of their graces to depart, which they granted him, but with every expression of regret. The duchess gave Sancho Panza his wife's letters, which he wept over, saying, " Who could have thought that all the mighty hopes which my wife puffed herself up with on the news of my government should come at last to this, and that it should again be my lot to follow my master Don Quixote, in search of hungry and toilsome adventures ! I am thankful, however, that my Teresa has behaved like herself in sending the acorns to her highness, which if she had not done, and proved herself ungrateful, I should never have forgiven her ; and my comfort is that the present could not be called a bribe, for they were not sent till I was a governor ; and, indeed, it is fitting that all who receive a benefit should show themselves grateful, though it be only a trifle. Naked I went into the government, and naked came I out of it ; so I can say with a clear conscience, which is no small matter, naked I came into the world, and naked I am; I neither win nor lose."

In this manner Sancho communed with himself while preparing for his departure. That same evening Don Quixote took leave of the duke and duchess, and early the next morning he sallied forth, completely armed, into the great court, the surrounding galleries of which were

crowded with the inmates of the castle, all eager to behold the knight
nor were the duke and duchess absent on that occasion. Sancho was
mounted upon Dapple, his wallets well furnished, and himself much
pleased; for the duke's steward, who had played the part of the Trifaldi,
had given him, unknown to Don Quixote, a little purse with two hundred crowns in gold, to supply the occasions of the journey. And now,
whilst all were gazing at Don Quixote, the arch and witty Altisidora,
who was with the duennas and damsels of the duchess, came forward,
and, in a doleful tone, addressed herself to him in the following rhymes:

> " Stay, cruel knight,
> Take not thy flight,
> Nor spur thy battered jade
> Thy haste restrain,
> Draw in the rein,
> And hear a love-sick maid.
> Why dost thou fly ?
> No snake am I,
> That poison those I love.
> Gentle I am
> As any lamb,
> And harmless as a dove.
> Thy cruel scorn
> Has left forlorn
> A nymph whose charms may vie
> With theirs who sport
> In Cynthia's court,
> Though Venus' self were by.
> Since, fugitive knight, to no purpose I woo thee,
> Barabbas's fate still pursue and undo thee !
>
> " Like ravenous kite,
> That takes its flight
> Soon as 't has stolen a chicken,
> Thou bear'st away
> My heart thy prey,
> And leav'st me here to sicken.
> Three nightcaps, too,
> And garters blue,
> That did to legs belong
> Smooth to the sight,
> As marble white,
> And, faith, almost as strong.
> Two thousand groans,
> As many moans,
> And sighs enough to fire
> Old Priam's town,
> And burn it down,
> Did it again aspire.
> Since, fugitive knight, to no purpose I woo thee,
> Barabbas's fate still pursue and undo thee !
>
> " May Sancho ne'er
> His back so bare
> Fly-flap as is his duty;

And thou still want
To disenchant
Dulcinea's injured beauty.
May still transformed,
And still deformed,
Toboso's nymph remain,
In recompense
Of thy offence,
Thy scorn and cold disdain.
When thou dost wield
Thy sword in field,
In combat or in quarrel,
Ill luck and harms
Attend thy arms,
Instead of fame and laurel.
Since, fugitive knight, to no purpose I woo thee,
Barabbas's fate still pursue and undo thee!

" May thy disgrace
Fill ev'ry place,
Thy falsehood ne'er be hid,
But round the world
Be tossed and hurled,
From Seville to Madrid.
If, brisk and gay,
Thou sitt'st to play
At ombre or at chess,
May ne'er spadill
Attend thy will,
Nor luck thy movements bless.
Though thou with care
Thy corns dost pare,
May blood the pen-knife follow ;
May thy gums rage,
And nought assuage
The pain of tooth that 's hollow.
Since, fugitive knight, to no purpose I woo thee,
Barabbas's fate still pursue and undo thee!"

Whilst Altisidora thus poured forth her tuneful complaints, Don Quixote stood looking at her attentively ; and when she had done, without making her any answer, he turned to Sancho and said, " By the memory of thy forefathers, dear Sancho, I conjure thee to answer me truly—hast thou the nightcaps and garters which this love-sick damsel speaks of ? " " I confess to the three nightcaps, sir," quoth Sancho ; " but as to the garters, I know nothing about them."

The duchess was astonished at Altisidora's levity, for though she knew her to be gay, easy, and free, yet she did not think she would venture so far, ; and not being in the secret of this jest, her surprise was the greater. " I think, Sir Knight," said the duke (meaning to carry on the joke), " that it does not well beseem your worship, after the hospitable entertainment you have received in this castle, to carry off three nightcaps, at least, if not my damsel's garters : these are indications of a disposition that ill becomes your character. Return her the garters ; if not, I defy you to mortal combat, and fear not that your knavish en-

chanters should change my face as they have done that of my lacquey."
"Heaven forbid," answered Don Quixote, "that I should unsheathe my
sword against your illustrious person, from whom I have received so many
favours. The nightcaps shall be restored; for Sancho says that he has
them; but as for the garters, it is impossible, for neither he nor I ever
had them; if your damsel look well to her hiding-corners, I make no
question but she will find them. I, my lord duke, was never a pilferer,
nor, if Heaven forsake me not, shall I ever become one. This damsel
talks (as she owns) like one in love, which is no fault of mine; and,
therefore, I have no reason to ask pardon either of her or of your excellency, whom I entreat to think better of me, and again desire your permission to depart."

"Farewell, Signor Don Quixote," said the duchess, "and Heaven
send you so prosperous a journey that we may always hear happy tidings
of your exploits. Go, and Heaven be with you; for the longer you stay
the more you stir up the flames that scorch the hearts of these tender
damsels while they gaze on you. As for this wanton, take my word, I
will so deal with her that she shall not again offend, either in word or
deed." "Hear me but one word more, O valorous Don Quixote!"
quoth Altisidora; "pardon me for having charged you with stealing my
garters, for, on my soul and conscience, they are on my legs! and I
have blundered like the man who looked about for the ass he was riding."
"Did I not tell you," quoth Sancho, "that I am a rare hider of stolen
goods? Had I been that way given, my government would have offered
many a fair opportunity." Don Quixote made his obeisance to the duke
and duchess, and to all the spectators; then, turning Rozinante's head,
he sallied out at the castle-gate, and, followed by Sancho upon Dapple,
took the road leading to Saragossa.

CHAPTER LVIII.

Showing how adventures crowded so fast upon Don Quixote that they trod
upon each other's heels.

On finding himself in the open country, unrestrained and free from
the troublesome fondness of Altisidora, Don Quixote felt all his chivalric
ardour revive within him, and turning to his squire, he said, "Liberty,
friend Sancho, is one of the choicest gifts that Heaven hath bestowed
upon man, and exceeds in value all the treasures which the earth contains within its bosom, or the sea covers. Liberty, as well as honour,
man ought to preserve at the hazard of his life; for without it life is
insupportable. Thou knowest, Sancho, the luxury and abundance we
enjoyed in the hospitable mansion we have just left; yet, amidst those
seasoned banquets, those cool and delicious liquors, I felt as if I had

suffered the extremity of hunger and thirst, because I did not enjoy them with the same freedom as if they had been my own. The mind is oppressed and enthralled by favours and benefits to which it can make no return. Happy the man to whom Heaven hath given a morsel of bread without laying him under an obligation to any but Heaven itself!" "For all that," quoth Sancho, "we ought to feel ourselves much bound to the duke's steward for the two hundred crowns in gold which he gave me in a purse I carry here, next my heart, as a cordial and comfort in case of need; for we are not likely to find many castles where we shall be made so much of, but more likely inns, where we shall be rib-roasted."

Thus discoursing, the knight and squire-errant proceeded on their way, when having travelled a little more than half a league, they observed a dozen men, who looked like peasants, seated on a little patch of green near the road, with their cloaks spread under them, eating their dinner on the grass. Close to where they sat were spread sundry pieces of white cloth, like sheets, separate from each other, and which seemed to be covers to something on the ground beneath them. Don Quixote approached the eating party, and, after courteously saluting them, asked what they had under those sheets? "They are figures carved in wood, sir," said one of them, "intended for an altar-piece we are erecting in our village, and we carry them covered that they may not be soiled or broken." "With your permission," said Don Quixote, "I should be glad to see them; for things of that kind, carried with so much care, must doubtless be good." "Ay, indeed are they, sir," answered one of the men, "as their price will testify; for, in truth, there is not one of them but stands us in above fifty ducats; and of the truth of what I say your worship shall presently be satisfied." Then rising up and leaving his repast, he took off the covering from the first figure, which was gilt, and appeared to be St. George on horseback, piercing with his lance a serpent coiled at the feet of his horse, and represented with its usual fierceness. "That figure," said Don Quixote, "represents one of the greatest knights-errant that ever served the holy cause. He was, besides, the champion of the fair, and was called Don St. George. Now let us see what is beneath that other cloth."

On being uncovered, it appeared to be St. Martin, mounted on horse-back also, and in the act of dividing his cloak with the beggar. "St. Martin!" exclaimed Don Quixote, "he also was one of the Christian adventurers: a knight, I believe, more liberal than valiant, as thou mayest perceive, Sancho, by his giving half his cloak to that wretch; and doubtless it was then winter, otherwise he would have given the whole: so great was his charity." "That was not the reason," quoth Sancho; "but he had a mind to follow the proverb, that says, 'What to give, and what to keep, requires a head-piece wide and deep.'" Don Quixote smiled, and desired to see another of their figures. The patron of Spain was now presented to him, mounted on a fierce charger; he appeared grasping a bloody sword, and trampling upon the bodies of slaughtered Moors. "There," said Don Quixote, "was a knight indeed! one of Christ's own squadron. He was called Don St. Diego, the Moor-killer, one of the most valiant saints and knights of which the world ever boasted, or that heaven now containeth."

Another cloth being removed, the figure of St. Paul was produced, as at the moment of his conversion, when thrown from his horse, and with other attending circumstances. Seeing that event represented with so much animation that St. Paul appeared to be actually answering the voice from heaven, Don Quixote said, "This holy personage was at one time the greatest enemy to the church of God, and afterwards the greatest defender it will ever have; a knight-errant in his life, and an unshaken martyr at his death; an unwearied labourer in Christ's vineyard; an instructor of the Gentiles: heaven was his school, and his great teacher and master our Lord Himself!" Don Quixote now desired the figures might be again covered, having seen all. "I regard the sight of these things," said he, "as a favourable omen; for these saints and knights professed what I profess, with this only difference, that, being saints, they fought after a heavenly manner, whereas I, a sinner, fight in the way of this world. By the exercise of arms they gained heaven—for heaven must be won by exertion; and I cannot yet tell what will be the event of my labours; but could my Dulcinea del Toboso be relieved from her suffering, my condition being in that case improved, and my understanding wisely directed, I might perhaps, take a better course than I now do." "Heaven hear him," quoth Sancho, "and let sin be deaf!" The men wondered no less at the figure than at the words of Don Quixote, without understanding half what he meant by them. They finished their repast, packed up their images, and, taking their leave of Don Quixote, pursued their journey. Sancho was more than ever astonished at his master's knowledge, and fully convinced that there was no history nor event in the world which he had not at his fingers' ends and nailed on his memory.

"Truly, master of mine," quoth Sancho, "if what has happened to us to-day may be called an adventure, it has been one of the sweetest and most pleasant that has ever befallen us in the whole course of our rambles; faith, we are clear of it without either blows or bodily fear! We have neither laid our hands to our weapons, nor beaten the earth with our bodies; neither are we famished for want of food! Heaven be praised that I have seen all this with my own eyes!" "Thou sayest well, Sancho," quoth Don Quixote, "but I must tell thee that times are wont to vary and change their course; and what are commonly accounted omens by the vulgar, though not within the scope of reason, the wise will, nevertheless, regard as incidents of lucky aspect. Your watcher of omens rises betimes, and going abroad, meets a Franciscan friar, whereupon he hurries back again as if a furious dragon had crossed his way. Another happens to spill the salt upon the table, and straightway his soul is overcast with the dread of coming evil: as if nature had willed that such trivial accidents should give notice of ensuing mischances! The wise man and good Christian will not, however, pry too curiously into the counsels of Heaven. Scipio, on arriving in Africa, stumbled as he leaped on shore; his soldiers took it for an ill omen, but he, embracing the ground, said, 'Africa, thou canst not escape me—I have thee fast.' For my own part, Sancho, I cannot but consider as a favourable prognostic our meeting those holy sculptures." "I verily believe it," answered Sancho; "and I should be glad if your worship would tell me why the Spaniards, when they rush into battle, call upon that Saint Diego, the Moor-killer, and cry, 'Saint Iago, and close Spain!' Is Spain, then, so open as to want closing? what do you make of that ceremony?" "Sancho, thou art very shallow in these matters," said Don Quixote: "thou must know that Heaven gave the mighty champion of the red cross to Spain, to be its patron and protector, especially in its desperate conflicts with the Moors: and therefore it is they invoke him in all their battles; and oft, at such times, has he been seen overthrowing, trampling down, destroying, and slaughtering the infidel squadrons: of which I could recount to thee many examples recorded in the true histories of our country."

"1 am amazed, sir," said Sancho, suddenly changing the subject, "at the impudence of Altisidora, the duchess's waiting woman. I warrant you that same mischief-maker they call Love must have mauled and mangled her full sorely. They say he is a boy, short-sighted, or rather, blind; yet set a heart before him, and, as sure as death, he'll whip an arrow through it. I have heard say, too, that the weapons he makes use of, though sharp, are blunted and turned aside by the armour of modesty and maidenly coyness; but with that same Altisidora, methinks they are rather whetted than blunted." "Look you, Sancho," quoth Don Quixote, "Love has no respect of persons, and laughs at the admonitions of reason; like Death, he pursues his game both in the stately palaces of kings and the humble huts of shepherds. When he has got a soul fairly into his clutches, his first business is to deprive it of all shame and fear; as you have remarked in Altisidora, who, being without either, made an open declaration of her desires, which produced in my breast embarrassment instead of compassion."

"Shocking cruelty! monstrous ingratitude!" cried Sancho. "I can say, for myself, that the least kind word from her would have subdued me, and made me her slave. O wretch! what a heart of marble, what bowels of brass, and what a soul of plaster! But I wonder much what the damsel saw in your worship that so took her fancy. Where was the finery, the gallantry, the gaiety, and the sweet face, which, one by one or altogether, made her fall in love with you? for in plain truth, if I look at your worship from the tip of your toe to the top of your head, I see more to be frightened at than to love. Beauty, they say, is the chief thing in love matters; but, your worship having none, I cannot guess what the poor thing was so taken with." "Hearken to me, Sancho," said Don Quixote: "there are two kinds of beauty, the one of the mind, the other of the body. That of the mind shines forth in good sense and good conduct; in modesty, liberality, and courtesy; and all these qualities may be found in one who has no personal attractions; and when that species of beauty captivates, it produces a vehement and

Just as he was about to break through the frail enclosure, two lovely shepherdesses, issuing from the covert, suddenly presented themselves before him.

superior passion. I well know, Sancho, that I am not handsome; but I know also that I am not deformed; and a man of worth, if he be not hideous, may inspire love, provided he has those qualities of the mind which I have mentioned."

While the knight and squire were conversing in this manner, they entered a wood that was near the road side, but had not penetrated far when Don Quixote found himself entangled among some nets of green thread which were extended from tree to tree; and, surprised at the incident, he said, "These nets, Sancho, surely promise some new and extraordinary adventure—may I die this moment if it be not some new device of the enchanters, my enemies, to stop my way, out of revenge for having slighted the wanton Altisidora! But I would have them know that, if these nets were chains of adamant, or stronger than that in which the jealous god of blacksmiths entangled Mars and Venus, to me they would be nets of rushes and yarn!" Just as he was about to break through the frail enclosure, two lovely shepherdesses, issuing from the covert, suddenly presented themselves before him; at least their dress resembled that of shepherdesses, excepting that it was of fine brocade and rich gold tabby. Their hair, bright as sunbeams, flowed over their shoulders; and chaplets composed of laurel and interwoven with the purple amaranth adorned their heads; and they appeared to be from fifteen to eighteen years of age.

Sancho was dazzled, and Don Quixote amazed, at so unexpected a vision, which the sun himself must have stopped in his course to admire. "Hold! Signor Cavalier," said one of them; "pray do not break the nets we have placed here, not to offend you, but to divert ourselves; and as you may wish to know why we spread them, and who we are, I will, in a few words, tell you. About two leagues off, sir, there is a village where many persons of quality and wealth reside, several of whom lately made up a company, of friends, neighbours, and relations, to come and take their diversion at this place, which is accounted the most delightful in these parts. Here we have formed among ourselves a new Arcadia: the young men have put on the dress of shepherds, and the maidens that of shepherdesses. We have learned by heart two eclogues, one by our admired Garcilaso, and the other by the excellent Camoëns, in his own Portuguese tongue; which, however, we have not yet recited, as it was only yesterday that we came hither. Our tents are pitched among the trees, near the side of a beautiful stream. Last night we spread these nets to catch such simple birds as our calls could allure into the snare; and now, sir, if you please to be our guest, you shall be entertained liberally and courteously, for we allow neither care nor sorrow to be of our party."

"Truly, fair lady," answered Don Quixote, "Actæon was not more lost in admiration and surprise when unawares he saw Diana bathing, than I am in beholding your beauty. I approve and admire your project, and return thanks for your kind invitation, and, if I can do you any service, lay your commands upon me, in full assurance of being obeyed; for by my profession I am enjoined to be grateful and useful to all, but especially to persons of your condition; and were these nets, which probably cover but a small space, extended over the whole surface of the earth, I would seek new worlds, by which I might pass, rather than injure them. And, that you may afford some credit to a declaration which may seem extravagant, know, ladies, that he who makes it is no other than Don Quixote de la Mancha — if, perchance, that name has ever reached your ears."

"Bless me!" exclaimed the other shepherdess, addressing her companion, "what good fortune, my dear friend, has befallen us! See you this gentleman here before us? Believe me, he is the most valiant, the most enamoured, and the most courteous knight in the whole world, if the history of his exploits, which is in print, does not deceive us. I have read it, my dear, through and through; and I will lay a wager that the good man who attends him is that very Sancho Panza, his squire, whose pleasantries none can equal." "I' faith, madam, it is very true," quoth Sancho; "I am, indeed, that same jocular person and squire, and this gentleman is my master, the very Don Quixote de la Mancha you have read of in print." "Pray, my dear," said the other, "let us entreat him to stay, for our fathers and brothers will be infinitely pleased to have him here. I also have heard what you say of his valour and great merit, and, above all, that he is the most true and constant of lovers, and that his mistress, who is called Dulcinea del Toboso, bears away the palm from all the beauties in Spain." "And with great justice," quoth Don Quixote, "unless your wondrous charms should make it questionable. But do not, I beseech you, ladies, endeavour to detain me; for the indispensable duties of my profession allow me no intermission of labour."

At this moment a brother of one of the fair damsels came up to them, dressed as a shepherd, and with the same richness and gaiety. They instantly told him that the persons he saw were the valorous Don Quixote de la Mancha, and his squire Sancho Panza, whom he also knew by their history. The gay shepherd saluted the knight, and so urgently importuned him to honour their party with his presence, that, unable to refuse, he at length accepted their invitation. Just at that time the nets were drawn, and a great number of small birds, deceived by their artifices, were taken. The gallant party assembled on that occasion, being not less than thirty in number, all in pastoral habits, received Don Quixote and his squire in a manner very much to their satisfaction; for none were strangers to the knight's history. They all now repaired together to the tents, where they found the tables spread with elegance and plenty. The place of honour was given to Don Quixote, and all gazed on him with admiration.

When the cloth was removed, the knight with much gravity, and in an audible voice, thus addressed the company: "Of all the sins that men commit, though some say pride, in my opinion ingratitude is the worst: it is truly said that hell is full of the ungrateful. From that foul crime I have endeavoured to abstain ever since I enjoyed the use of reason; and if I cannot return the good offices done me by equal benefits, I substitute my desire to repay them; and if this be not enough, I publish them; for he who proclaims the favours he has received, would return them if he could; and generally the power of the receiver is unequal to that of the giver: like the bounty of Heaven, to which no man can make an equal return. But, though utterly unable to repay the unspeakable benificence of God, gratitude affords a humble compensation suited to our limited powers. This, I fear, is my present situation; and my ability not reaching the measure of your kindness, I can only show my gratitude by doing that little which is in my power. I therefore engage to maintain, for two whole days, in the middle of the king's highway leading to Saragossa, that these lady-shepherdesses in disguise are the most beautiful and the most courteous damsels in the world; excepting only the peerless Dulcinea del Toboso, the sole mistress of my thoughts — without offence to any present be it spoken."

Here Sancho, who had been listening to him with great attention, could no longer bridle his tongue. "Is it possible," cried he, "that any one should have the boldness to say and swear that this master of mine is a madman? Tell me, gentlemen shepherds, is there a village priest living, though ever so wise, or ever so good a scholar, who could speak as he has spoken? Or is there a knight-errant, though ever so renowned for valour, who could make such an offer as he has done?" Don Quixote turned to Sancho, and, with a wrathful countenance, said, "Is it possible, O Sancho, that there should be a single person on the globe who would not say that all over thou art an idiot, lined with the same, and bordered with I know not what of mischief and knavery? Who gave thee authority to meddle with what belongs to me, or to busy thyself with my folly or my discretion? Be silent, brute! make no reply; but go and saddle Rozinante, if he be unsaddled, and let us depart, that I may perform what I have engaged; for, relying on the justice of my cause, I consider all those who shall presume to dispute the point with me as already vanquished." Then in great haste, and with marks of furious indignation in his countenance, he arose from his seat, and rushed forth, leaving the company in amazement, and doubtful whether to regard him as a lunatic or a man of sense.

They nevertheless endeavoured to dissuade him from his challenge, telling him that they were sufficiently assured of his grateful nature, as well as his valour, by the true history of his exploits. Resolute, however, in his purpose, the knight was not to be moved; and, being now mounted upon Rozinante, bracing his shield and grasping his lance, he planted himself in the middle of the highway, not far from the Arcadian tents. Sancho followed upon his Dapple, with all the pastoral company, who were curious to see the event of so arrogant and extraordinary a defiance.

Don Quixote, being thus posted, made the air resound with such words as these: " O ye passengers, whoever ye are, knights, squires, travellers on foot and on horseback, who now pass this way, or shall pass in the course of these two successive days! know that Don Quixote de la Mancha, knight-errant, is posted here, ready to maintain that the nymphs who inhabit these meadows and groves excel in beauty and courtesy all the rest of the world, excepting only the mistress of my soul, Dulcinea del Toboso! Let him, therefore, who dares to uphold the contrary, forthwith show himself, for here I stand ready to receive him."

Twice he repeated the same words, and twice they were repeated in vain. But better fortune soon followed, for it so happened that a number of horsemen appeared, several of them armed with lances, hastily advancing in a body. Those who had accompanied Don Quixote no sooner saw them than they retired to a distance, thinking it might be dangerous to remain. Don Quixote alone, with an intrepid heart, stood firm, and Sancho Panza sheltered himself close under Rozinante's crupper. When the troop of horsemen came up, one of the foremost called aloud to Don Quixote, "Get out of the way, fool of a man! or these bulls will trample you to dust." " Caitiffs!" replied Don Quixote, " I fear not your bulls, though they were the fiercest that ever bellowed on the banks of Xarama. Confess, ye scoundrels! unsight, unseen, that what I here proclaimed is true; if not, I challenge ye to battle."

The herdsmen had no time to answer, nor Don Quixote to get out of the way, had he been willing; for now a herd of fierce bulls, together with some tame kine, hurried past, with a multitude of herdsmen and others driving them to a neighbouring town, where they were to be baited. Don Quixote, Sancho, Rozinante, and Dapple were in a moment overturned, and, after being trampled upon without mercy, were left sprawling on the ground. After the whole had passed, here lay Sancho mauled, and Don Quixote stunned, Dapple bruised, and Rozinante in no enviable plight! Nevertheless, they all contrived to recover the use of their legs; and the knight, in great haste, stumbling and reeling, began to pursue the herd, crying aloud, "Hold! stop! scoundrels! a single knight defies ye all, who scorns the coward maxim, 'Make a bridge of silver for a flying enemy.'" But the drovers had no time to attend to him, and made no more account of his threats than of last year's clouds. Fatigue obliged Don Quixote to desist from the pursuit; and, more enraged than revenged, he sat down in the road, to wait for Sancho, Rozinante, and Dapple. On their coming up, the knight and squire mounted again, and, with more shame than satisfaction, pursued their journey, without taking leave of the shepherds of New Arcadia.

CHAPTER LIX.

Wherein is related an extraordinary accident which befell Don Quixote, and which may pass for an adventure.

Don Quixote and Sancho removed, by immersion in the waters of a clear fountain, which they found in a cool and shady grove, the fatigue, the dust, and other effects caused by the rude encounter of the bulls. Here the way-worn pair seated themselves; and after giving liberty to Rozinante and Dapple, Sancho had recourse to the store of his wallet, and speedily drew out what he was wont to call his sauce. He rinsed his mouth, and Don Quixote washed his face, by which they were in some degree refreshed; but the knight, from pure chagrin, refused to eat, and Sancho abstained from pure good manners, though waiting and wishing for his master to begin. At length, seeing his master so wrapped in thought as to forget to convey a morsel to his mouth, he opened his own, and, banishing all kind of ceremony, made a fierce attack upon the bread and cheese before him.

"Eat, friend Sancho," said Don Quixote, "and support life, which to thee is of more importance than to me, and leave me to expire under my reflections and the severity of my misfortunes. I, Sancho, was born to live dying, and thou to die eating; and thou wilt allow that I speak truth when thou considerest that I, who am recorded in history, renowned in arms, courteous in deeds, respected by princes, and courted by damsels, should, after all, instead of psalms, triumphs, and crowns, earned and merited by my valorous exploits, have this morning seen myself trod upon, kicked, and bruised under the feet of filthy and impure beasts !—the thought thereof dulls the edge of my teeth, unhinges my jaws, sickens my appetite, and benumbs my hands, so that I am now awaiting death in its cruellest form—hunger."

" If so," quoth Sancho (still eating as he spoke), " your worship does not approve the proverb, which says, ' Let Martha die, so that she die well fed.' For my part, I have no mind to kill myself; but rather, like the shoemaker, who with teeth stretches his leather to make it fit for his purpose, I will by eating try all I can to stretch out my life, till it reaches as far as it may please Heaven ; and let me tell you, sir, that there is no greater folly than to give way to despair. Believe what I say, and when you have eaten, try to sleep a little upon this green mattress, and I warrant on waking you will find yourself another man."

Don Quixote followed Sancho's advice, thinking he reasoned more like a philosopher than a fool ; at the same time, he said, " Ah, Sancho, if thou wouldst do for me what I am going to propose, my sorrow would be diminished, and my relief more certain ; it is only this : whilst I endeavour by thy advice to compose myself to sleep, do thou step aside a little, and after making due preparations, give thyself, with the reins of Rozinante's bridle, some three or four hundred smart lashes, in part of the three thousand and odd which thou art bound to give thyself for the disenchantment of Dulcinea ; for, in truth, it is a great pity the poor lady should continue under enchantment through thy carelessness and neglect."

" There is a great deal to be said as to that," quoth Sancho ; " but for the present let us both sleep, and afterwards Heaven knows what may happen. Besides, I would have you remember, sir, that this lashing one's self in cold blood is no easy matter ; especially when the strokes light upon a body so tender without, and so ill-stored within, as mine is. Let my lady Dulcinea have a little patience, and mayhap, when she least thinks of it, she shall see my body a perfect sieve by dint of lashing. Until death all is life : I am still alive, and with a full intention to make good my promise." Don Quixote thanked him, ate a little, and Sancho much ; and both of them laid themselves down to sleep, leaving Rozinante and Dapple, those inseparable companions and friends, at their own discretion, either to repose or feed upon the tender grass, of which they here had abundance.

They awoke somewhat late in the day, mounted again, and pursued their journey, hastening to reach what seemed to be an inn, about a league before them. An inn it is here called, because Don Quixote himself gave it that name ; not happening, as usual, to mistake it for a castle. Having arrived there, they inquired of the host if he could provide them with lodging, and he promised as good accommodation and entertainment as could be found in Saragossa. On alighting, Sancho's first care was to deposit his travelling larder in a chamber, of which the landlord gave him the key. He then led Rozinante and Dapple to the stable, and, after seeing them well provided for, he went to receive the

*Both of them laid themselves down to sleep, leaving Rozinante and Dapple, those inseparable
companions and friends, at their own discretion.*

further commands of his master, whom he found seated on a stone
bench; the squire blessing himself that the knight had not taken the
inn for a castle.

Supper-time approaching, Don Quixote retired to his apartment, and
Sancho inquired of the host what they could have to eat. The landlord
told him his palate should be suited — for whatever the air, earth, and
sea produced, of birds, beast, or fish, that inn was abundantly provided
with. "There is no need of all that," quoth Sancho; "roast us but a
couple of chickens, and we shall be satisfied; for my master hath a
delicate stomach, and I am no glutton." "As for chickens," said the
innkeeper, "truly, we have none, for the kites have devoured them."
"Then let a pullet be roasted," said Sancho; "only see that it be tender."
"A pullet? my father!" answered the host; "faith and troth, I sent
above fifty yesterday to the city to be sold; but, excepting pullets, ask
for whatever you will." "Why, then," quoth Sancho, "e'en give us a
good joint of veal or kid, for they cannot be wanting." "Veal or kid?"
replied the host, "ah, now I remember we have none in the house at
present, for it is all eaten; but next week there will be enough and to
spare." "We are much the better for that," answered Sancho; "but
I dare say all these deficiencies will be made up with plenty of eggs and

bacon." "'Fore Heaven," answered the host, "my customer is a choice guesser! I told him I had neither pullets nor hens, and he expects me to have eggs! Talk of other delicacies, but ask no more for hens."

"Body of me!" quoth Sancho, "let us come to something—tell me, in short, what you have, Master Host, and let us have done with your flourishes." "Then," quoth the innkeeper, "what I really and truly have is a pair of cow-heels, that may be taken for calves' feet; or a pair of calves' feet that are like cow-heels. They are stewed with peas, onions, and bacon, and at this very moment are crying out, 'Come eat me! come eat me!'" "From this moment I mark them as my own," quoth Sancho; "let nobody lay a finger on them. I will pay you well, for there is nothing like them — give me but cow-heel, and I care not a fig for calves' feet." "They are yours," said the host: "nobody shall touch them; for my other guests, merely for gentility sake, bring their cook, their sewer, and provisions along with them." "As to the matter of gentility," quoth Sancho, "nobody is more a gentleman than my master; but his calling allows of no cooking nor butlering as we travel. No, faith; we clap us down in the midst of a green field, and fill our bellies with acorns or medlars." Such was the conversation Sancho held with the innkeeper, and he now chose to break it off, without answering the inquiries which the host made respecting his master's calling.

Supper being prepared, and Don Quixote in his chamber, the host carried in his dish of cow-heel, and, without ceremony, sat himself down to supper. The adjoining room being separated from that occupied by Don Quixote only by a thin partition, he could distinctly hear the voices of persons within. "Don Jeronimo," said one of them, "I entreat you, till supper is brought in, to let us have another chapter of 'Don Quixote de la Mancha.'" The knight hearing himself named, got up, and listening attentively, he heard another person answer, "Why, Signor Don John, would you have us read such absurdities? Whoever has read the First Part of the 'History of Don Quixote de la Mancha' cannot be pleased with the Second." "But for all that," said Don John, "let us read it; for there is no book so bad as not to have something good in it. What displeases me most in this Second Part is, that the author describes Don Quixote as no longer enamoured of Dulcinea del Toboso."

On hearing this, Don Quixote, full of wrath and indignation, raised his voice, and said, "Whoever shall say that Don Quixote de la Mancha has forgotten, or ever can forget, Dulcinea del Toboso, I will make him know, with equal arms, that he asserts what is not true; for neither can the peerless Dulcinea be forgotten, nor Don Quixote ever cease to remember her. His motto is constancy, and to maintain it his pleasure and his duty." "Who is it that speaks to us?" replied one in the other room. "Who should it be," quoth Sancho, "but Don Quixote de la Mancha himself? — who will make good all he says and all he shall say, for a good paymaster is in no want of a pawn."

At these words two gentlemen rushed into the room, and one of them, throwing his arms about Don Quixote's neck, said, "Your person belies not your name, nor can your name do otherwise than give credit to your person. I cannot doubt, signor, of your being the true Don Quixote de la Mancha, the north and morning star of knight-errantry, in despite of him who would usurp your name, and annihilate your exploits, as the author of this book has vainly attempted." Don Quixote, without making any reply, took up the book; and, after turning over some of the leaves, he laid it down again, saying, "In the little I have seen of this volume, three things I have noticed, for which the author deserves reprehension. The first is some expressions in the preface; the next that his language is Arragonian, for he sometimes omits the articles; and the third is a much more serious objection, inasmuch as he shows his ignorance and disregard of truth in a material point of the history; for he says that the wife of my squire, Sancho Panza, is called Mary Gutierrez, whereas her name is Teresa Panza; and he who errs in a circumstance of such importance may well be suspected of inaccuracy in the rest of the history."

Here Sancho put in his word. "Pretty work, indeed, of that same history-maker! Sure he knows much of our concerns, to call my wife, Teresa Panza, Mary Gutierrez! Pray, your worship, look into it again, and see whether I am there, and if my name be changed too." "By what you say, friend," quoth Don Jeronimo; "I presume you are Sancho Panza, squire to Signor Don Quixote?" "That I am," replied Sancho, "and value myself upon it." "In faith, then," said the gentleman, "this last author treats you but scurvily, and not as you seem to deserve. He describes you as a dull fool and a glutton, without pleasantry—in short, quite a different Sancho from him represented in the First Part of your master's history." "Heaven forgive him!" quoth Sancho; "he might as well have left me alone; for 'He who knows the instrument should play on it;' and 'Saint Peter is well at Rome.'" The two gentlemen entreated Don Quixote to go to their chamber and sup with them, as they well knew the inn had nothing fit for his entertainment. Don Quixote, who was always courteous, consented to their request, and Sancho remained with the flesh-pot, *cum mero mixto imperio :** placing himself at the head of the table, with the innkeeper for his messmate, whose love for cow-heel was equal to that of the squire.

While they were at supper, Don John asked Don Quixote when he had heard from the Lady Dulcinea del Toboso; whether she was married; whether she was yet a mother, or likely to be so; or whether, if still a virgin, she retained, with modest reserve and maidenly decorum, a grateful sense of the love and constancy of Signor Don Quixote. "Dulcinea," said the knight, "is still a maiden, and my devotion to her more fixed than ever; our correspondence as heretofore; but, alas! her own beautiful person is transformed into that of a coarse country

---

* That is, with a deputed or subordinate power.

wench." He then related every particular concerning the enchantment of the Lady Dulcinea. He also gave them an account of his descent into the Cave of Montesinos, and informed them of the instructions given by the sage Merlin for the deliverance of his mistress. Great was the satisfaction the two gentlemen received at hearing Don Quixote relate his strange adventures; and they were equally surprised at his extravagances and the elegance of his narrative. One moment they thought him a man of extraordinary judgment, and the next that he was totally bereaved of his senses; nor could they decide what degree to assign him between wisdom and folly.

Sancho, having finishd his supper, left the innkeeper fully dosed with liquor, and joined his master's party in the next chamber. Immediately on entering, he said, "May I die, gentlemen, if the writer of that book which you have got has any mind that he and I should eat a friendly meal together; he calls me a glutton, you say—egad! I wish he may not set me down a drunkard too." "In faith, he does," quoth Don Jeronimo; "though I do not remember his words; only this I know, that they are scandalous, and false into the bargain, as I see plainly by the countenance of honest Sancho here before me." "Take my word for it, gentlemen," quoth the squire, "the Sancho and Don Quixote of that history are in nowise like the men that are so called in the book made by Cid Hamet Benengeli; for they are truly we two: — my master, valiant, discreet, and a true lover; and I, a plain, merry-conceited fellow, but neither a glutton nor a drunkard." "I believe it," quoth Don John; "and were such a thing possible, I would have it ordered that none should dare to record the deeds of the great Don Quixote but Cid Hamet himself, his first historian; as Alexander commanded that none but Apelles should presume to draw his portrait, being a subject too lofty to be treated by one of inferior talent." "Treat me who will," said Don Quixote, "so that they do not maltreat me; for patience itself will not submit to be overladen with injuries." "No injury," quoth Don John, "can be offered to Signor Don Quixote that he is not able to avenge, should he fail to ward it off with the buckler of his patience, which seems to me both ample and strong."

In such conversation they passed the greater part of the night; and though Don John would fain have had Don Quixote read more of the book, he declined it, saying he deemed it read; and, by the sample he had seen, he pronounced it foolish throughout. He was unwilling, also, to indulge the scribbler's vanity so far as to let him think he had read his book, should he happen to learn that it had been put into his hands. "And besides, it is proper," he added, "that the eyes as well as the thoughts should be turned from everything filthy and obscene."

They then asked him which way he was travelling, and he told them that he should go to Saragossa, to be present at the jousts of that city, for the annual prize of a suit of armour. Don John told him that, in the new history, Don Quixote is said to have been there, running at the ring, of which the author gives a wretched account; dull in the contrivance, mean in style, miserably poor in devices, and rich only in absurdity. " For that very reason," answered Don Quixote, " I will not set foot in Saragossa; and thus I shall expose the falsity of this new historian, and all the world will be convinced that I am not the Don Quixote of whom he speaks." " In that you will do wisely," said Don Jeronimo; "and at Barcelona there are other jousts, where Signor Don Quixote may have a full opportunity to display his valour." " To Barcelona I will go, gentlemen," replied the knight; " and now permit me to take my leave, for it is time to retire to rest, and be pleased to rank me among the number of your best friends and faithful servants." "And me too," quoth Sancho; "for, mavhap, you may find me good for something."

Don Quixote and Sancho then retired to their chamber, leaving the two strangers surprised at the medley of sense and madness they had witnessed, and with a full conviction that these were the genuine Don Quixote and Sancho, and those of the Arragonese author certainly spurious. Don Quixote arose early, and, tapping at the partition of the other room, he again bid his new friends adieu. Sancho paid the innkeeper most magnificently, and at the same time advised him either to boast less of the provision of his inn, or to supply it better.

CHAPTER LX.

Of what befell Don Quixote on his way to Barcelona.

In the morning, which was cool, and promised a temperate day, Don Quixote left the inn, having first informed himself which was the most direct road to Barcelona, avoiding Saragossa; for he was determined to prove the falsehood of the new history, which he understood had so grossly misrepresented him. Six days he pursued his course without meeting with any adventure worth recording; at the end of which time, leaving the high road, night overtook them among some shady trees, but whether of cork or oak it does not appear—Cid Hamet, in this instance, not observing his wonted minuteness of description. Master and man having alighted, they laid themselves down at the foot of these trees. Sancho had already taken his afternoon's collation, and therefore he rushed at once into the arms of sleep; but Don Quixote, not from hunger, but his restless imagination, could not close his eyes. Agitated by a thousand fancies, now he thought himself in the Cave of Montesinos; now he saw his Dulcinea, in her odious disguise, spring upon her ass; the next moment he heard the words of the sage Merlin, declaring the means of her deliverance; then again he was in despair when he recollected the unfeeling negligence of his squire, who, he believed, had given himself only five lashes! a number so small compared with those yet remaining, that, overwhelmed with grief and indignation, he thus argued with himself:—" If Alexander the Great cut the Gordian knot, saying, ' To cut is the same as to untie,' and became thereby the universal lord of all Asia, exactly the same may happen now in the disenchantment of Dulcinea, if the lashes be applied by force; for if the virtue of this remedy consist in Sancho's receiving three thousand lashes, what is it to me whether they are applied by himself or another, since the efficacy lies in his receiving them, from whatever hand they may come ? "

Under this conviction, Don Quixote approached his sleeping squire, having first taken Rozinante's reins and adjusted them so that he might use them with effect. He then began to untruss his points—though it is generally thought that he had only that one in the front which kept up his breeches. Sancho was soon roused, and cried out, " What is the matter? Who is untrussing me ? " " It is I," answered Don Quixote, " who am come to atone for thy neglect, and to remedy my own troubles. I am come to whip thee, Sancho, and to discharge, at least in part, the debt for which thou art bound. Dulcinea is perishing; thou livest unconcerned; I am dying with desire; and therefore untruss of thine own accord; for it is my intention to give thee, in this convenient solitude, at least two thousand lashes." " No, indeed," quoth Sancho; " body o' me ! keep off, or the dead shall hear of it ! The strokes I am bound to give myself must be with my own will and when I please. At present I am not in the humour. Let your worship be content that I promise to flog and flay myself as soon as ever I am so inclined." " There is no trusting to thy courtesy, Sancho," said Don Quixote; " for thou art hard-hearted, and, though a peasant, of very tender flesh." He then struggled with Sancho, and endeavoured by force to uncover him. Upon which Sancho jumped up, then closing with his master, he threw his arms about him, tripped up his heels, and laid him flat on his back; whereupon, setting his right knee upon his breast, he held his hands down so fast that he could not stir, and scarcely could breathe. " How, traitor ! " exclaimed the knight, " dost thou rebel against thy master and natural lord? Dost thou raise thy hand against him who feeds thee ? " " I neither raise up nor pull down," answered Sancho; " I only defend myself, who am my own lord. If your worship will promise me to let me alone, and not talk about whipping at present, I will set you at liberty; if not, ' Here thou diest, traitor, enemy to Donna Sancha.' "* Don Quixote gave him the promise he desired, and swore, by the life of his best thoughts, he would not touch a hair of his garment, but leave the whipping entirely to his own discretion.

Sancho now removed to another place, and, as he was going to lay himself under another tree, he thought something touched his head; and, reaching up his hands, he felt a couple of dangling feet, with hose and shoes. Trembling with fear, he moved on a little farther, but was incommoded by other legs; upon which he called to his master for help. Don Quixote went up to him, and asked him what was the matter;

---

* Sancho here quotes the last line of an old ballad.

*Sancho jumped up, then closing with his master, he threw his arms about him,
tripped up his heels, and laid him flat on his back.*

when Sancho told him that all the trees were full of men's feet and legs.
Don Quixote felt them, and immediately guessing the cause, he said,
" Be not afraid, Sancho ; doubtless these are the legs of robbers and
banditti, who have been punished for their crimes ; for here the officers
of justice hang them by scores at a time, when they can lay hold of
them ; and from this circumstance I conclude we are not far from Barcelona." In truth, Don Quixote was right in his conjecture, for when day
began to dawn, they plainly saw that the legs they had felt in the dark
belonged to the bodies of thieves.

But if they were alarmed at these dead banditti, how much more were
they disturbed at being suddenly surrounded by more than forty of their
living comrades, who commanded them to stand, and not to move till
their captain came up. Don Quixote was on foot, his horse unbridled,
his lance leaning against a tree at some distance ; in short, being de-
fenceless, he thought it best to cross his hands, hang down his head,
and reserve himself for better occasions. The robbers, however, were

not idle, but immediately fell to work upon Dapple, and in a trice emptied both wallet and cloak-bag. Fortunately for Sancho, he had secured the crowns given him by the duke, with his other money, in a belt which he wore about his waist; nevertheless, they would not have escaped the searching eyes of these good people, who spare not even what is hid between the flesh and the skin, had they not been checked by the arrival of their captain. His age seemed to be about four and thirty, his body was robust, his stature tall, his visage austere, and his complexion swarthy: he was mounted upon a powerful steed, clad in a coat of steel, and his belt was stuck round with pistols. Observing that his squires (for so they call men of their vocation) were about to rifle Sancho, he commanded them to forbear, and was instantly obeyed, and thus the girdle escaped. He wondered to see a lance standing against a tree, a target on the ground, and Don Quixote in armour, and pensive, with the most sad and melancholy countenance that sadness itself could frame.

Going up to the knight, he said, "Be not so dejected, good sir, for you are not fallen into the hands of a cruel Osiris, but into those of Roque Guinart, who has more of compassion in his nature than cruelty." "My dejection," answered Don Quixote, "is not on account of having fallen into your hands, O valorous Roque, whose fame extends over the whole earth, but for my negligence in having suffered myself to be surprised by your soldiers, contrary to the bounden duty of a knight-errant, which requires that I should be continually on the alert, and, at all hours, my own sentinel: for, let me tell you, illustrious Roque, had they met me on horseback, with my lance and my target, they would have found it no very easy task to make me yield. Know, sir, I am Don Quixote de la Mancha, he with whose exploits the whole globe resounds."

Roque Guinart presently perceived Don Quixote's infirmity, and that it had in it more of madness than valour; and though he had sometimes heard his name mentioned, he always thought that what had been said of him was a fiction, conceiving that such a character could not exist; he was therefore delighted with this meeting, as he might now know, from his own observations, what degree of credit was really due to the reports in circulation. "Be not concerned," said Roque, addressing himself to Don Quixote, "nor tax Fortune with unkindness: by thus stumbling, you may chance to stand more firmly than ever; for Heaven, by strange and circuitous ways, incomprehensible to men, is wont to raise the fallen and enrich the needy."

Don Quixote was about to return his thanks for this courteous reception, when suddenly a noise was heard near them, like the trampling of many horses; but it was caused by one only, upon which came at full speed, a youth, seemingly about twenty years of age, clad in green damask, edged with gold lace, trousers, and a loose coat; his hat cocked in the Walloon fashion, with straight waxed leather boots, spurs, dagger, a gold-hilted sword; a carbine in his hand, and a brace of pistols by his side. Roque, hearing the noise of a horse, turned his head, and observed this handsome youth advancing towards him : " Valiant Roque," said the cavalier, "you are the person I have been seeking; for with you I hope to find some comfort, though not a remedy, in my afflictions. Not to keep you in suspense, because I perceive that you do not know me, I will tell you who I am. I am Claudia Jeronima, daughter of Simon Forte, your intimate friend, and the particular enemy of Claquel Torellas, who is also yours, being of the faction which is averse to you. You know, too, that Torellas has a son, called Don Vincente de Torellas, —at least, so he was called not two hours ago. That son of his—to shorten the story of my misfortune—ah, what sorrow he has brought upon me !—that son, I say, saw me, and courted me; I listened to him, and loved him, unknown to my father; for there is no woman, however retired or secluded, but finds opportunity to gratify her unruly desires. In short, he promised to be my spouse, and I pledged myself to become his, without proceeding any further. Yesterday I was informed that forgetting his engagement to me, he was going to be married to another, and that this morning the ceremony was to be performed. The news confounded me, and I lost all patience. My father being out of town, I took the opportunity of equipping myself as you now see me; and by the speed of this horse I overtook Don Vincente about a league hence, and, without stopping to reproach him or hear his excuses, I fired at him, not only with this piece, but with both my pistols, and lodged, I believe, not a few balls in his body; thus washing away with blood the stains of my honour. I left him with the servants, who either dared not or could not prevent the execution of my purpose, and am come to seek your assistance to get to France, where I have relations with whom I may live; and to entreat you, likewise, to protect my father from any cruel revenge on the part of Don Vincente's numerous kindred."

Roque was struck with the gallantry, bravery, figure, and also the adventure of the beautiful Claudia; and said to her, " Come, madam, and let us first be assured of your enemy's death, and then we will consider what is proper to be done for you." Don Quixote, who had listened attentively to Claudia's narration and the reply of Roque Guinart, now interposed, saying, " Let no one trouble himself with the defence of this lady, for I take it upon myself. Give me my horse and my arms, and wait for me here, while I go in quest of the perjured knight, and, whether living or dead, make him fulfil his promise to so much beauty." "Ay, ay, let nobody doubt that," quoth Sancho : "my master is a special hand at match-making. 'Twas but the other day he made a young rogue consent to marry a damsel he would fain have left in the lurch, after he had given her his word; and had not the enchanters who always torment his worship changed the bridegroom into a lacquey, that same maid by this time would have been a matron."

Roque, who was more intent upon Claudia's business than the discourse of master and man, heard them not; and, after commanding his squires to restore to Sancho all they had taken from Dapple, and likewise to retire to the place where they had lodged the night before, he went off immediately with Claudia, at full speed, in quest of the wounded or dead Don Vincente. They presently arrived at the place where Claudia had overtaken him, and found nothing there except the blood which had been newly spilt; but, looking round, at a considerable distance they saw some persons ascending a hill, and concluded (as indeed it proved) that it was Don Vincente being conveyed by his servants either to a doctor or his grave. They instantly pushed forward to overtake them, which they soon effected, and found Don Vincente in the arms of his servants, entreating them, in a low and feeble voice, to let him die in that place, for he could no longer endure the pain of his wounds.

Claudia and Roque, throwing themselves from their horses, drew near; the servants were startled at the appearance of Roque, and Claudia was troubled at the sight of Don Vincente; when, divided between tenderness and resentment, she approached him, and, taking hold of his hand, said, " Had you but given me this hand, according to our contract, you would not have been reduced to this extremity." The wounded cavalier opened his almost closed eyes, and, recognizing Claudia, he said, " I perceive, fair and mistaken lady, that it is to your hand I owe my death; a punishment unmerited by me, for neither in thought nor deed could I offend you." " It is not true, then," said Claudia, "that, this very morning, you were going to be married to Leonora, daughter of the rich Balvastro?" " No, certainly," answered Don Vincente; "my evil fortune must have borne you that news, to excite your jealousy to bereave me of life; but since I leave it in your arms, I esteem myself happy; and, to assure you of this truth, take my hand, and, if you are willing, receive me for your husband; for I can now give you no other satisfaction for the injury which you imagine you have received."

Claudia pressed his hand, and such was the anguish of her heart, that she swooned away upon the bloody bosom of Don Vincente, and at the same moment he was seized with a mortal paroxysm. Roque was confounded, and knew not what to do; the servants ran for water, with which they sprinkled their faces; Claudia recovered, but Don Vincente was left in the sleep of death. When Claudia was convinced that her beloved husband no longer breathed, she rent the air with her groans and pierced the sky with her lamentations. She tore her hair, scattered it in the wind, and with her own merciless hands wounded and disfigured her face, with every other demonstration of grief, distraction, and despair. " O rash and cruel woman!" she exclaimed, " with what facility wert thou moved to this evil deed! O maddening sting of jealousy! how deadly thy effects! O my dear husband! whose love for me hath given thee, for thy bridal bed, a cold grave!"

So piteous, indeed, were the lamentations of Claudia, that they forced tears even from the eyes of Roque, where they were seldom or never seen before. The servants wept and lamented; Claudia was recovered from one fainting-fit only to fall into another; and all around was a scene of sorrow. At length Roque Guinart ordered the attendants to take up the body of Don Vincente, and convey it to the town where his father dwelt, which was not far distant, that it might be there interred. Claudia told Roque that it was her determination to retire to a nunnery, of which her aunt was abbess, there to spend what remained of her wretched life, looking to heavenly nuptials and an eternal spouse. Roque applauded her good design, offering to conduct her wherever it was her desire to go, and to defend her father against the relatives of Don Vincente, or any one who should offer violence to him. Claudia expressed her thanks in the best manner she could, but declined his company, and, overwhelmed with affliction, took her leave of him. At the same time Don Vincente's servants carried off his dead body, and Roque returned to his companions. Thus ended the amour of Claudia Jeronima; and no wonder that it was so calamitous, since it was brought about by the cruel and irresistible power of jealousy.

Roque Guinart found his band of desperadoes in the place he had appointed to meet them, and Don Quixote in the midst of them, endeavouring in a formal speech to persuade them to quit that kind of life, so prejudicial both to soul and body. But his auditors were chiefly Gascons, a wild and ungovernable race, and therefore his harangue made but little impression upon them. Roque having asked Sancho Panza whether they had restored to him all the property which had been taken from Dapple, he said they had returned all but three nightcaps, which were worth three cities. "What does the fellow say?" quoth one of the party; "I have got them, and they are not worth three reals." "That is true," quoth Don Quixote; "but my squire justly values the gift for the sake of the giver." Roque Guinart insisted upon their being immediately restored; then, after commanding his men to draw up in a line before him, he caused all the clothes, jewels, and money, and, in short, all they had plundered since the last division, to be brought out and spread before them; which being done, he made a short appraisement, reducing into money what could not be divided, and shared the whole among his company with the utmost exactness and impartiality.

After sharing the booty in this manner, by which all were satisfied, Roque said to Don Quixote, "If I were not thus exact in dealing with these fellows, there would be no living with them." "Well," quoth Sancho, "justice must needs be a good thing, for it is necessary, I see, even among thieves." On hearing this, one of the squires raised the butt-end of his piece, and would surely have split poor Sancho's head, if Roque had not called out to him to forbear. Terrified at his narrow escape, Sancho resolved to seal up his lips while he remained in such company.

Just at this time intelligence was brought by the scouts that, not far distant, on the Barcelona road, a large body of people were seen coming that way. "Can you discover," said Roque, "whether they are such as we look for, or such as look for us?" "Such as we look for, sir." "Away, then," said Roque, "and bring them hither straight—and see that none escape." The command was instantly obeyed: the band sallied forth, while Don Quixote and Sancho remained with the chief, anxious to see what would follow. In the meantime Roque conversed with the knight on his own way of living. "This life of ours must appear strange to you, Signor Don Quixote; new accidents, new adventures in constant succession, and all full of danger and disquiet: it is a state, I confess, in which there is no repose, either for body or mind. Injuries I could not brook, and a thirst for revenge, first led me into it, contrary to my nature; for the savage asperity of my present behaviour is a disguise to my heart, which is gentle and humane. Yet, unnatural as it is, having plunged into it, I persevere; and, as one sin is followed by another, and mischief is added to mischief, my own resentments are now so linked with those of others, and I am so involved in wrongs, and factions, and engagements, that nothing but the hand of Providence can snatch me out of this entangled maze. Nevertheless, I despair not of coming, at last, into a safe and quiet harbour.'

Don Quixote was surprised at these sober reflections, so different from what he should have expected from a banditti chief, whose occupation was robbery and murder. "Signor Roque," said he, "the beginning of a cure consists in the knowledge of the distemper, and in the patient's willingness to take the medicines prescribed to him by his physician. You are sick; you know your malady, and God, our Physician, is ready with medicines that, in time, will certainly effect a cure. Besides, sinners of good understanding are nearer to amendment than those who are devoid of it; and, as your superior sense is manifest, be of good cheer, and hope for your entire recovery. If in this desirable work you would take the shortest way, and at once enter that of your salvation, come with me, and I will teach you to be a knight-errant—a profession it is true, full of labours and disasters, but which, being placed to the account of penance, will not fail to lead you to honour and felicity." Roque smiled at Don Quixote's counsel, but, changing the discourse, he related to him the tragical adventure of Claudia Jeronima, which grieved Sancho to the heart, for he had been much captivated by the beauty, grace, and sprightliness of the young lady.

The party which had been dispatched by Roque now returned with their captives, who consisted of two gentlemen on horseback, two pilgrims on foot, and a coach full of women, attended by six servants, some on foot and some on horseback, and also two muleteers belonging to the gentlemen. They were surrounded by the victors, who, as well as the vanquished, waited in profound silence till the great Roque should declare his will. He first asked the gentlemen who they were, whither they were going, and what money they had. "We are captains of infantry, sir," said one of them, "and are going to join our companies, which are at Naples, and, for that purpose, intend to embark at Barcelona, where, it is said, four galleys are about to sail for Sicily. Two or three hundred crowns is somewhere about the amount of our cash, and with that sum we accounted ourselves rich, considering that we are soldiers, whose purses are seldom overladen." The pilgrims being questioned in the same manner, said their intention was to embark for Rome, and that they had about them some threescore reals. The coach now came under examination, and Roque was informed by one of the attendants that the persons within were the Lady Donna Guiomar de Quinones, wife of the Regent of the Vicarship of Naples, her younger daughter, a waiting-maid, and a duenna; that six servants accompanied them, and their money amounted to six hundred crowns. " It appears, then," said Roque Guinart, " that we have here nine hundred crowns and sixty reals : my soldiers are sixty in number; see how much falls to the share of each ; for I am myself but an indifferent accountant."

His armed ruffians, on hearing this, cried out, " Long live Roque Guinart, in spite of the dogs that seek his ruin !" But the officers looked chapfallen, the lady regent much dejected, and the pilgrims nothing pleased at witnessing this confiscation of their effects. Roque held them awhile in suspense, but would not long protract their sufferings, which was visible a bow-shot off, and therefore, turning to the captains, he said, " Pray, gentlemen, do me the favour to lend me sixty crowns ; and you, lady regent, fourscore, as a slight perquisite which these honest gentlemen of mine expect; for ' the abbot must eat that sings for his meat ;' and you may then depart, and prosecute your journey without molestation; being secured by a pass which I will give you, in case of your meeting with any other of my people, who are dispersed about this part of the country ; for it is not a practice with me to molest soldiers, and I should be loath, madam, to be found wanting in respect to the fair sex—especially to ladies of your quality."

The captains were liberal in their acknowledgments to Roque for his courtesy and moderation, in having generously left them a part of their money ; and Donna Guiomar de Quinones would have thrown herself out of the coach to kiss the feet and hands of the great Roque, but he would not suffer it, and entreated her pardon for the injury he was forced to do them, in compliance with the duties of an office which his evil fortune had imposed upon him. The lady then ordered the fourscore crowns to be immediately paid to him, as her share of the assessment; the captains had already disbursed their quota, and the pilgrims were proceeding to offer their little all, when Roque told them to wait; then, turning to his men, he said, " Of these crowns, two fall to each man's share, and twenty remain : let ten be given to these pilgrims, and the other ten to this honest squire, that, in relating his travels, he may have cause to speak well of us." Then, producing his writing implements, with which he was always provided, he gave them a pass, directed to the chiefs of his several parties ; and, taking his leave, he dismissed them, all admiring his generosity, his gallantry, and extraordinary conduct, and looking upon him rather as an Alexander the Great than a notorious robber.*

On the departure of the travellers, one of Roque's men seemed dis-

---

* Pellicer proves that this robber, Guinart, properly named Pedro Rocha Guinarda, was a person actually existing in the time of Cervantes, and the captain of a band of freebooters. About the same period there were likewise other Andalusian robbers in Sierra Cabrilla, who were no less equitable, and even more scrupulous, than the great Roque himself. Their garb was that of good reformed people, and they took from travellers but half their property.

posed to murmur, saying, in his Catalonian dialect, "This captain of ours is wondrous charitable, and would do better among friars than with those of our trade; but if he must be giving, let it be with his own." The wretch spoke not so low but that Roque overheard him, and, drawing his sword, he almost cleft his head in two, saying, "Thus I chastise the mutinous." The rest were silent and overawed; such was their obedience to his authority. Roque then withdrew a little, and wrote a letter to a friend at Barcelona, to inform him that he had with him the famous Don Quixote de la Mancha, of whom so much had been reported, and that, being on his way to Barcelona, he might be sure to see him there on the approaching festival of St. John the Baptist, parading the strand, armed at all points, mounted on his steed Rozinante, and attended by his squire Sancho Panza upon an ass; adding that he had found him wonderfully sagacious and entertaining. He also desired him to give notice of this to his friends the Niarra, that they might be diverted with the knight, and enjoy a pleasure which he thought too good for his enemies, the Cadells, though he feared it was impossible to prevent their coming in for a share of what all the world must know and be delighted with. He dispatched this epistle by one of his troop, who, changing the habit of his vocation for that of a peasant, entered the city, and delivered it as directed.

CHAPTER LXI.

Of what befell Don Quixote at his entrance into Barcelona; with other events more true than ingenious.

THREE days and three nights Don Quixote sojourned with the great Roque; and had he remained with him three hundred years, in such a mode of life he might still have found new matter for observation and wonder. Here they sleep, there they eat, sometimes flying from they know not what, at others lying in wait for they know not whom; often forced to steal their nap standing, and every moment liable to be roused. Now they appear on this side of the country, now on that; always on the watch, sending out spies, posting sentinels, blowing the matches of their muskets—though they had but few, being chiefly armed with pistols. Roque passed the nights apart from his followers, making no man privy to his lodgings; for the numerous proclamations which the Viceroy of Barcelona had published against him, setting a price upon his head, kept him in continual apprehension of surprise, and even of the treachery of his own followers; making his life irksome and wretched beyond measure.

Roque, Don Quixote, and Sancho, attended by six squires, set out for Barcelona, and, taking the most secret and unfrequented ways, at night reached the strand on the eve of St. John. Roque now embraced the knight and squire, giving to Sancho the promised ten crowns; and thus they parted, with many friendly expressions, and a thousand offers of service on both sides.

Roque returned back, and Don Quixote remained there on horseback, waiting for daybreak : and it was not long before the beautiful Aurora appeared in the golden balconies of the east, cheering the flowery fields, while at the same time the ears were regaled with the sound of numerous kettle-drums and jingling morrice-bells, mixed with the noise of horsemen coming out of the city. Aurora now retired, and the glorious sun gradually rising, at length appeared, broad as an ample shield, on the verge of the horizon. Don Quixote and Sancho now beheld the sea, which to them was a wondrous novelty, and seemed so boundless and so vast, that the Lakes of Ruydera, which they had seen in La Mancha, could not be compared to it. They saw the galleys, too, lying at anchor near the shore, which, on removing their awnings, appeared covered with flags and pennants all flickering in the wind, and kissing the surface of the water. Within them was heard the sound of trumpets, hautboys, and other martial instruments, that filled the air with sweet and cheering harmony. Presently the vessels were put in motion, and on the calm sea began a counterfeit engagement; at the same time a numerous body of cavaliers, in gorgeous liveries and nobly mounted, issued from the city, and performed corresponding movements on shore. Cannon were discharged on board the galleys, which were answered by those on the ramparts; and thus the air was rent by mimic thunder. The cheerful sea, the serene sky, only now and then obscured by the smoke of the artillery, seemed to exhilarate and gladden every heart.

Sancho wondered that the bulky monsters which he saw moving on the water should have so many legs; and while his master stood in silent astonishment at the marvellous scene before him, the body of gay cavaliers came gallopping up towards him, shouting in the Moorish manner; and one of them—the person to whom Roque had written—came forward, and said, "Welcome to our city, thou mirror, and beacon, and polar star of knight-errantry! Welcome, I a gainsay, O valorous Don Quixote de la Mancha, not the spurious, the fictitious, the apocryphal one, lately sent amongst us in lying histories, but the true, the legitimate, the genuine Quixote of Cid Hamet Benengeli, the flower of historians!" Don Quixote answered not a word, nor did the cavaliers wait for any answer, but, wheeling round with all their followers, they began to curvet in a circle about Don Quixote, who, turning to Sancho, said, "These people seem to know us well, Sancho; I dare engage they have read our history, and even that of the Arragonese, lately printed."

The gentleman who spoke to Don Quixote again addressed him, saying, "Be pleased, Signor Don Quixote, to accompany us, for we are all the intimate and devoted friends of Roque Guinart." To which Don Quixote replied, "If courtesy beget courtesy, yours, good sir, springs from that of the great Roque. Conduct me whither you please, for I am wholly at your disposal." The gentleman answered in expressions no less polite, and enclosing him in the midst of them, they all proceeded, to the sound of martial music, towards the city; at the entrance of which the father of mischief so ordered it that, among the boys, all of whom are his willing instruments, two, more audacious than the rest, contrived to insinuate themselves within the crowd of horsemen, and one lifting Dapple's tail, and the other that of Rozinante, they lodged under each a handful of briers, the stings whereof being soon felt by the poor animals, they clapped their tails only the closer, which so augmented their suffering that, plunging and kicking from excess of pain, they quickly brought their riders to the ground. Don Quixote, abashed and indignant at the affront, hastened to relieve his tormented steed, while Sancho performed the same kind office for Dapple. Their cavalier escort would have chastised the offenders, but the young rogues presently found shelter in the rabble that followed. The knight and the squire then mounted again, and, accompanied by the same music and acclamations, proceeded until they reached the conductor's house, which was large and handsome, declaring the owner to be a man of wealth and consideration; and there we will leave them — for such is the will and pleasure of the author of this history, Cid Hamet Benengeli.

CHAPTER LXII.

Which treats of the adventure of the enchanted head; with other trifling matters that must not be omitted.

LEARNED, rich, sensible, and good-humoured, was Don Antonio Moreno, the present host of Don Quixote; and, being cheerfully disposed, with such an inmate, he soon began to consider how he might extract amusement from his whimsical infirmity; but without offence to his guest—for the jest that gives pain is no jest, nor is that lawful pastime which inflicts an injury. Having prevailed upon the knight to take off his armour, he led him to a balcony at the front of his house, and there, in his straight chamois doublet (which has already been mentioned), exposed him to the populace, who stood gazing at him as if he had been some strange baboon. The gay cavaliers again appeared, and paraded before him as in compliment to him alone, and not in honour of that days's festival. Sancho was highly delighted to find unexpectedly what he fancied to be another Camacho's wedding, another house like that of Don Diego de Miranda, and another duke's castle.

On that day several of Don Antonio's friends dined with him, all paying homage and respect to Don Quixote as a knight-errant; with which his vanity was so flattered that he could scarcely conceal the delight which it gave him. And such was the power of Sancho's wit, that every servant of the house, and indeed all who heard him, hung, as it were, upon his lips. While sitting at table, Don Antonio said to

him, " We are told here, honest Sancho, that you are so great a lover
of capons and sausages, that, when you have crammed your belly, you
stuff your pockets with the fragments for another day." " 'T is not true,
an't please your worship : I am not so filthy, nor am I glutton, as my
master Don Quixote here present can bear witness ; for he knows we
have often lived day after day, ay, a whole week together, upon a handful
of acorns or hazel-nuts.   It is true, I own, that if they give a heifer, I
make haste with a halter ;—my way is to take things as I find them,
and eat what comes to hand ; and whoever has said that I am given to
greediness, take my word for it, he is very much out ; and I would tell
my mind in another manner, but for the respect due to the honourable
beards here at table."

" In truth, gentlemen," said Don Quixote, " the frugality of my
squire and his cleanliness in eating deserve to be recorded on plates of
brass, to remain an eternal memorial for ages to come. I confess that,
when in great want of food, he may appear somewhat ravenous, eating
fast and chewing on both sides of his mouth ; but, as for cleanliness,
he is therein most punctilious ; and when he was a governor, such was
his nicety in eating, that he would take up grapes, and even the grains
of a pomegranate, with the point of a fork."   " How ! " quoth Don
Antonio, " has Sancho been a governor ? "   " Yes, i' faith, I have,"
replied Sancho, " and of an island called Barataria.   Ten days I
governed it at my own will and pleasure ; but I paid for it in sleepless
nights, and learned to hate with all my heart the trade of governing, and
made such haste to leave it that I fell into a pit, which I thought would
be my grave, but I escaped alive out of it by a miracle."   Hereupon
Don Quixote related minutely all the circumstances of Sancho's government, to the great entertainment of the hearers.

The dinner being ended, Don Quixote was led by his host into a
distant apartment, in which there was no other furniture than a small
table, apparently of jasper, supported by a pillar of the same, and upon
it was placed a bust, seemingly of bronze, the effigy of some high personage.   After taking a turn or two in the room, Don Antonio said,
" Signor Don Quixote, now that we are alone, I will make known to you
one of the most extraordinary circumstances, or rather, I should say,
one of the greatest wonders, imaginable, upon condition that what I
shall communicate be deposited in the inmost recesses of secresy."
" It shall be there buried," answered Don Quixote ; " and, to be more
secure, I will cover it with a tombstone ; besides, I would have you
know, Signor Don Antonio " (for by this time he had learned his
name), " that you are addressing one who, though he has ears to hear,
has no tongue to betray : so that if it please you to deposit it in my
breast, be assured it is plunged into the abyss of silence."   " I am
satisfied," said Don Antonio, " and, confiding in your promise, I will
at once raise your astonishment, and disburden my own breast of a
secret which I have long borne with pain, from the want of some person
worthy to be made a confidant in matters which are not to be revealed
to everybody."

Thus having, by his long preamble, strongly excited Don Quixote's curiosity, Don Antonio made him examine carefully the brazen head, the table, and the jasper pedestal upon which it stood; he then said, "Know, Signor Don Quixote, that this extraordinary bust is the production of one of the greatest enchanters or wizards that ever existed. He was, I believe, a Polander, and a disciple of the famous Escotillo,* of whom so many wonders are related. He was here in my house, and, for the reward of a thousand crowns, fabricated this head for me, which has the virtue and property of answering to every question that is put to it. After much study and labour, drawing figures, erecting schemes, and frequent observation of the stars, he completed his work. To-day being Friday, it is mute, but to-morrow, signor, you shall surely witness its marvellous powers. In the meantime you may prepare your questions, for you may rely on hearing the truth."

Don Quixote was much astonished at what he heard, and could scarcely credit Don Antonio's relation; but, considering how soon he should be satisfied, he was content to suspend his opinion, and express his acknowledgments to Don Antonio for so great a proof of his favour. Then leaving the chamber, and carefully locking the door, they both returned to the saloon, where the rest of the company were diverting themselves with Sancho's account of his master's adventures.

The same evening they carried Don Quixote abroad, to take the air, mounted on a large easy-paced mule, with handsome furniture, himself unarmed, and with a long wrapping-coat of tawny-coloured cloth, so warm that it would have put even frost into a sweat. They had given private orders to the servants to find amusement for Sancho, so as to prevent his leaving the house, as they had secretly fixed on the back of Don Quixote's coat a parchment, on which was written in capital letters— "This is Don Quixote de la Mancha."

They had no sooner set out, than the parchment attracted the eyes of the passengers, and the inscription being read aloud, Don Quixote heard his name so frequently repeated that, turning to Don Antonio with much complacency, he said, "How great the prerogative of knight-errantry, since its professors are known and renowned over the whole earth! Observe, Signor Don Antonio, even the very boys of this city know me, although they never could have seen me before!" "It is very true, Signor Don Quixote," answered Don Antonio; "for, as fire is discovered by its own light, so is virtue by its own excellence: and no renown equals in splendour that which is acquired by the profession of arms."

As Don Quixote thus rode along amidst the applause of the people, a Castilian who had read the label on his back exclaimed, "What! Don Quixote de la Mancha! Now the devil take thee! How hast thou got here alive after the many drubbings and bastings thou hast received? Mad indeed thou art! Had thy folly been confined to thyself, the mischief had been less; but thou hast the property of converting into

---

* Michael Scotus.

They had secretly fixed on the back of Don Quixote's coat a parchment, on which was written in capital letters—" This is Don Quixote de la Mancha."

fools and madmen all that keep thee company—witness these gentlemen here, thy present associates. Get home, blockhead! to thy wife and children; look after thy house, and leave these fooleries, that eat into thy brain and skim off the cream of thy understanding!"

" Go, friend," said Don Antonio, "look after your own business, and give your advice where it is required; Signor Don Quixote is wise, and we, his friends, know what we are doing. Virtue demands our homage wherever it is found; begone, therefore, in an evil hour, nor meddle where you are not called." " Truly," answered the Castilian, "your worship is in the right; for to give that lunatic advice, is to kick against the pricks. Yet am I grieved that the good sense which he is said to have should run to waste and be lost in the mire of knight-errantry. And may the evil hour, as your worship said, overtake me and all my generation, if ever you catch me giving advice again to anybody, asked or not asked, though I were to live to the age of Methusalem." So saying, the adviser went his way; but the rabble still pressing upon them to read the inscription, Don Antonio contrived to have it removed, that they might proceed without interruption.

On the approach of night the cavalcade returned home, where preparations were made for a ball by the wife of Don Antonio, an accomplished and beautiful lady, who had invited other friends, both to do honour to her guest, and to entertain them with his singular humour. The ball, which was preceded by a splendid repast, began about ten o'clock at night. Among the ladies, there were two of an arch and jocose disposition, who, though they were modest, behaved with more freedom than usual; and, to divert themselves and the rest, so plied Don Quixote with dancing that they worried both his soul and body. A sight it was indeed to behold his figure, long, lank, lean, and swarthy, straitened in his clothes, so awkward, and with so little agility.

These roguish ladies took occasion privately to pay their court to him, and he as often repelled them; till, at last, finding himself so pressed by their loving attention — " *Fugite, partes adversæ !* " cried he aloud : " avaunt, ladies ! your desires are poison to my soul ! Leave me to repose, ye unwelcome thoughts, for the peerless Dulcinea del Toboso is the sole queen of my heart ! " He then threw himself on the floor, where he lay quite shattered by the violence of his exertions. Don Antonio ordered that the wearied knight should be taken up and carried to bed. Sancho was among the first to lend a helping hand; and as he raised him up, " What, in Heaven's name, sir," said he, " put you upon this business ? Think you that all who are valiant must be caperers, or all knights-errant dancing-masters ? If so, you are much mistaken, I can tell you. Body of me ! some that I know would rather cut a giant's weasand than a caper. Had you been for the shoe-jig,* I could have done your business for you, for I can frisk it away like any jer-falcon; but as for your fine dancing, I cannot work a stitch at it." The company were much diverted by Sancho's remarks, who now led his master to bed, where he left him well covered up, to sweat away the ill effects of his dancing.

The next day, Don Antonio determined to make experiment of the enchanted head; and for that purpose the knight and squire, the two mischievous ladies (who had been invited by Don Antonio's lady to sleep there that night), and two other friends, were conducted to the chamber in which the head was placed. After locking the door, Don Antonio proceeded to explain to them the properties of the miraculous bust, of which, he said, he should now for the first time make trial, but laid them all under an injunction of secresy. The artifice was known only to the two gentlemen, who, had they not been apprised of it, would have been no less astonished than the rest at so ingenious a contrivance. The first who approached the head was Don Antonio himself, who whispered in its ear, not so low but he was overheard by all, " Tell me," said he, " thou wondrous head, by the virtue inherent in thee, what are my present thoughts ? " In a clear and distinct voice, without any perceptible motion of its lips, the head replied, " I have no knowledge of thoughts."

All were astonished to hear articulate sounds proceed from the head,

---

* *Zapatera.* When the dancers slap the sole of their shoe with the palm of their hand, in time and measure.

being convinced that no human creature present had uttered them. "Then tell me," said Don Antonio, "how many persons are here assembled?" "Thou and thy wife, with two of thy friends, and two of hers; and also a famous knight, called Don Quixote de la Mancha, with his squire, Sancho Panza."

At these words, the hair on every head stood erect with amazement and fear. "Miraculous head!" exclaimed Don Antonio (retiring a little from the bust), "I am now convinced he was no impostor from whose hands I received thee, O wise, oracular, and eloquent head! Let the experiment be now repeated by some other."

As women are commonly impatient and inquisitive, one of the two ladies next approached the oracle. "Tell me, head," said she, "what means shall I take to improve my beauty?" "Be modest," replied the head. "I have done," said the lady.

Her companion then went up and said, "I would be glad to know, wondrous head, whether I am beloved by my husband." "That thou mayest discover by his conduct towards thee," said the oracle. "That is true," said the married lady, "and the question was needless; for surely by a man's actions may be seen the true disposition of his mind."

One of the gentlemen now approached the bust, and said, "Who am I?" "Thou knowest," was the answer. "That is not an answer to my question—tell me, head, knowest thou who I am?" "Don Pedro Noriz," replied the head. "'Tis enough: amazing bust!" exclaimed the gentlemen, "thou knowest everything."

The other gentleman then put his question. "Tell me, head, I beseech thee," said he, "what are the chief wishes of my son and heir?" "Thou hast already heard that I speak not of thoughts," answered the head, "yet be assured thy son wishes to see thee entombed." "Truly, I believe it," said the gentleman; "it is but too plain. I have done."

Then came the lady of Don Antonio, and said, "I know not what to ask thee, yet I would fain know if I shall enjoy my dear husband many years." Then listening, she heard these words: "Yes, surely, from temperance and a sound body thou mayest expect no less."

Now came the flower of chivalry. "Tell me, thou oracle of truth," said the knight, "was it a reality or only an illusion that I beheld in the Cave of Montesinos? Will the penance imposed on my squire, Sancho Panza, ever be performed? and will Dulcinea ever be disenchanted?" "What thou sawest in the cave," replied the bust, "partakes both of truth and falsehood: Sancho's penance will be slow in performance; and in due time the disenchantment of Dulcinea will be accomplished." "I am satisfied," said Don Quixote; "when I shall see the lady of my soul released from her present thraldom, fortune will have nothing more to give me."

The last querist was Sancho. "Shall I," quoth he, "have another government? Shall I quit this hungry life of squireship? Shall I see again my wife and children?" "If thou returnest home," said the oracle, "there shalt thou be a governor, and see again thy wife and

children; and shouldst thou quit service, thou wilt cease to be a squire."
"Odds my life!" quoth Sancho Panza, "I could have told as much
myself, and the prophet Perogrullo * could have told me no more."
"Beast!" quoth Don Quixote, "what answer wouldst thou have? Is
it not enough that the answers given thee should correspond with the
questions?" "Yes, truly, sir, quite enough; only I wish it had not
been so sparing of its knowledge."

Thus ended the examination of the enchanted head, which left the
whole company in amazement, excepting Don Antonio's two friends.
Cid Hamet Benengeli, however, was determined to divulge the secret
of this mysterious head, that the world might not ascribe its extraordinary properties to witchcraft or necromancy. He declares, therefore,
that Don Antonio caused it to be made in imitation of one which he had
seen at Madrid, intending it for his own amusement, and to surprise the
ignorant; and he thus describes the machine: The table, including its
legs and four eagle-claws, was made of wood, and coloured in imitation
of jasper. The head, being a resemblance of one of the Cæsars, and
painted like bronze, was hollow, with an opening below corresponding
with another in the middle of the table, which passed through the leg,
and was continued, by means of a metal tube, through the floor of the
chamber into another beneath, where a person stood ready to receive
the questions, and return answers to the same: the voice ascending and
descending as clear and articulate as through a speaking-trumpet; and,
as no marks of the passage of communication were visible, it was impossible to detect the cheat. A shrewd, sensible youth, nephew to Don
Antonio, was on this occasion the respondent, having been previously
instructed by his uncle in what concerned the several persons with whom
he was to communicate. The first question he readily answered, and to
the rest he replied as his judgment directed.

Cid Hamet further observes that this oracular machine continued to
afford amusement to its owner during eight days; when it got abroad
that Don Antonio was in possession of an enchanted head that could
speak and give answers to all questions; and, apprehensive that it might
come to the ears of the watchful sentinels of our faith, he thought it
prudent to acquaint the officers of the Inquisition with the particulars;
upon which they commanded him to destroy the bust, in order to avert
the rage of the ignorant populace, who might think the possession of it
scandalous and profane. Nevertheless, in the opinion of Don Quixote
and Sancho it remained still an enchanted head,† and a true solver of

---

* The Spanish saying, "The prophecies of Perogrullo" is of similar satirical meaning
as the "Vérités de M. de la Palaisse," of the French.

† By the importance given to the enchanted head, it would seem that in the time of
Cervantes it was a novelty in Spain, where the people, being accustomed to hear much of
miracles wrought by the aid of good or bad agents, were likely to view it with extraordinary interest, and perhaps give full credit to its oracular powers; for which reason, no
doubt, the grave historian Cid Hamet has here thought it necessary to set the world
right, and show that it was all a trick, having really nothing in it either magical or supernatural.

questions; more, indeed, to the satisfaction of the knight than of his squire. The gentlemen of the city, out of complaisance to Don Antonio, and for the entertainment of Don Quixote—or, rather, for their own amusement—appointed a public running at the ring, which should take place in six days: but they were disappointed by an accident that will be hereafter told.

Don Quixote, being now desirous to view the city, thought he should be able to do it on foot with less molestation from the boys than if he rode; he therefore set out with Sancho to perambulate the streets, attended by two servants assigned him by Don Antonio. Now, it happened that, as they passed through a certain street, Don Quixote saw, in large letters, written over a door—" Here books are printed;" at which he was much pleased, for, never having seen the operation of printing, he was curious to know how it was performed. He entered it, with his followers, and saw workmen drawing off the sheets in one place, correcting in another, composing in this, revising in that—in short, all that was to be seen in a great printing-house.

The knight inquired successively of several workmen what they were employed upon, and was gratified by their ready information. Making the same inquiry of one man, he answered, " I am composing for the press, sir, a work which that gentleman there "—pointing to a person of grave appearance—" has translated from the Italian into our Castilian." " What title does it bear ? " said Don Quixote. " The book in Italian, sir," replied the author, "is called ' Le Bagatelle.' " " And what answers to *Bagatelle* in our language ? " said Don Quixote. " ' Le Bagatelle,' " said the author, " signifies trifles; but though its title promises little, it contains much good and substanial matter." " I know a little," quoth Don Quixote, " of the Tuscan language, and pique myself upon my recitation of some of Ariosto's stanzas; but, good sir, tell me, I beseech you (and I ask not to ascertain your skill, but merely out of curiosity), have you ever, in the course of your studies, met with the word *pignata ?* " " Yes, frequently," replied the author. " And how do you translate it into Castilian ? " quoth Don Quixote. " How should I translate it," replied the author, " but by the word *olla ?* "

" Body of me ! " said Don Quixote, " what a progress you have made, signor, in the Tuscan language ! I would venture a good wager that where the Tuscan says *piace*, you say, in Castilian, *plaze*; and where he says *piu*, you say, *mas*; and *su* you translate by the word *arriba;* and *giu* by *abaxo*." " I do so, most certainly," quoth the author, " for such are the corresponding words." " And yet I dare say, sir," quoth Don Quixote, " that you are scarcely known in the world :—but it is the fate of all ingenious men. What abilities are lost, what genius obscured, and what talents despised ! Nevertheless, I cannot but think that translation from one language into another, unless it be from the noblest of all languages, Greek and Latin, is like presenting the back of a piece of tapestry, where, though the figures are seen, they are obscured by innumerable knots and ends of thread, very different from the smooth and agreeable texture of the proper face of the work : and to translate easy

languages of a similar construction requires no more talent than tran-
scribing one paper from another. But I would not hence infer that
translating is not a laudable exercise, for a man may be worse and more
unprofitably employed. Nor can my observation apply to the two celebrated translators, Doctor Christopher de Figueroa, in his 'Pastor Fido,'
and Don John de Xaurigui, in his 'Aminta;' who, with singular felicity,
have made it difficult to decide which is the translation and which the
original. But tell me, signor, is this book printed at your charge, or
have you sold the copyright to some bookseller?"

"I print it, sir, on my own account," answered the author, "and
expect a thousand ducats by this first impression of two thousand copies:
at six reals each copy they will go off in a trice." "'T is mighty well,"
quoth Don Quixote; "though I fear you know but little of the tricks of
booksellers, and the juggling there is amongst them. Take my word
for it, you will find a burden of two thousand volumes upon your back
no trifling matter—especially if the book be deficient in sprightliness."
"What, sir!" cried the author, "would you have me give my labour
to a bookseller, who, if he paid me three maravedis for it, would think it
abundant, and say I was favoured? No, sir, fame is not my object; of
that I am already secure: profit is what I now seek, without which fame
is nothing."

"Well, Heaven prosper you, sir!" said the knight, who, passing on,
observed a man correcting a sheet of a book entitled, "The Light of the
Soul." On seeing the title he said, "Books of this kind, numerous as
they already are, ought still to be encouraged; for numerous are the be-
nighted sinners that require to be enlightened." He went forward, and
saw another book under the corrector's hand, and, on inquiring the title,
they told him it was the Second Part of the ingenious gentleman Don
Quixote de la Mancha, written by such a one, of Tordesillas. "I know
something of that book," quoth Don Quixote, "and, on my conscience,
I thought it had been burnt long before now for its stupidity; but its
Martinmas * will come, as it does to every hog. Works of invention are
only so far good as they come near to truth and probability, as general
history is valuable in proportion as it is authentic."

So saying, he went out of the printing-house, apparently in disgust.
On the same day Don Antonio proposed to show him the galleys at
that time lying in the road; which delighted Sancho, as the sight was
new to him. Don Antonio gave notice to the commodore of the four
galleys of his intention to visit him that afternoon, with his guest, the
renowned Don Quixote de la Mancha, whose name by this time was well
known in the city: and what befell him there shall be told in the following chapter.

---

* The feast of St. Martin was the time for killing hogs for bacon.

CHAPTER LXIII.

Of Sancho Panza's misfortune on board the galleys; and the extraordinary adventure of the beautiful Moor.

DON QUIXOTE made many profound reflections on the answers of the enchanted head, none giving him the slightest hint of any imposition practised upon him, and all centering in the promise, on which he relied, of the disenchantment of Dulcinea; and he exulted at the prospect of its speedy accomplishment. As for Sancho, though he abhorred being a governor, he still felt some desire to command again and be obeyed :— such, unfortunately, is the effect of power once enjoyed, though it were only the shadow of it!

In the afternoon, Don Antonio Moreno and his two friends, with Don Quixote and Sancho, sallied forth, with an intention to go on board the galleys; and the commodore, who was already apprised of their coming, no sooner perceived them approach the shore than he ordered all the galleys to strike their awnings, and the musicians to play; at the same time he sent out the pinnace, spread with rich carpets and crimson velvet cushions, to convey them on board. The moment Don Quixote entered the boat, he was saluted by a discharge of artillery from the forecastle guns of the captain galley, which was repeated by the rest; and as he ascended the side of the vessel, the crew gave him three cheers, agreeable to the custom of receiving persons of rank and distinction. When on deck, the commander, who was a nobleman of Valencia,* gave him his hand, and embracing him, said, " This day, Sir Knight, will I mark with white, as one of the most fortunate of my life, in having been introduced to Signor Don Quixote de la Mancha, in whom is combined and centered all that is valuable in knight-errantry."

Don Quixote replied to him in terms no less courteous, exceedingly elated to find himself so honoured. The visitors were then conducted to the quarter-deck, which was richly adorned, and there seated themselves. Presently the signal was given for the rowers to strip, when instantly a vast range of naked bodies were exposed to view, that filled Sancho with terror; and when, in a moment after, the whole deck was covered with its awning, he thought all the devils were let loose. But this prelude was sugar-cake and honey compared with what followed.

Sancho had seated himself on the right side of the deck, and close to the sternmost rower, who, being instructed what he was to do, seized upon the squire, and, lifting him up, tossed him to the next man, and he to a third, and so on, passing from bank to bank through the whole range of slaves, with such astonishing celerity that he lost his sight

---

* Don Pedro Coloma, Count d'Elda, commanded the squadron of Barcelona in 1014, when the Moors were expelled from Spain.

with the motion, and fancied that the devils themselves were carrying him away; nor did he stop till he had made the circuit of the vessel and was again replaced on the quarter-deck, where they left the poor man, bruised, breathless, and in a cold sweat. scarcely knowing what had befallen him.

Don Quixote, who beheld Sancho's flight without wings, asked the general if that was a ceremony commonly practised upon persons first coming aboard the galleys; for if so, added he, he must claim an exemption, having no inclination to perform the like exercise; then, rising up and grasping his sword, he vowed to God that if any one presumed to lay hold of him to toss him in that manner, he would hew their souls out.

At that instant they struck the awning, and, with a great noise, lowered the main-yard from the top of the mast to the bottom. Sancho thought the sky was falling off its hinges and tumbling upon his head; and stooping down, he clapped it in terror between his legs. Nor was Don Quixote without alarm, as plainly appeared by his countenance and manner. With the same swiftness and noise, the yard was again hoisted, and during all these operations not a word was heard. The boatswain now made the signal for weighing anchor, and, at the same time, with his whip, laid about him upon the shoulders of the slaves, while the vessel gradually moved from the shore. Sancho seeing so many red feet (for such the oars appeared to him) in motion all at once, said to himself, " Ay, these indeed are real enchantments ! and not the things we have seen before !—I wonder what these unhappy wretches have done to be flogged at this rate. And how does that whistling fellow dare to whip so many ? Surely this must be purgatory at least."

Don Quixote seeing with what attention Sancho observed all that passed, " Ah, friend Sancho," said he, " if thou wouldst now but strip to the waist, and place thyself among these gentlemen, how easily and expeditiously mightest thou put an end to the enchantment of Dulcinea ! For, having so many companions in pain, thou wouldst feel but little of thine own : besides, the sage Merlin would perhaps reckon every lash coming from so good a hand, for ten of those which, sooner or later, thou must give thyself."

The commander would have asked what lashes he spoke of, and what he meant by the disenchantment of Dulcinea, but was prevented by information that a signal was perceived on the fort of Montjuich, of a vessel with oars being in sight to the westward. On hearing this, he leaped upon the middle gangway and cheered the rowers, saying, " Pull away, my lads ! let her not escape us : she must be some Moorish thief." The other galley now coming up to the commodore for orders, two were commanded to push out to sea immediately, while he attacked them on the land side, and thus they would be more certain of their prey. The crew of the different galleys plied their oars with such diligence that they seemed to fly. A vessel was soon descried about two miles off, which they judged to be one of fourteen or fifteen banks of oars; but on discovering the galleys in chase, she immediately made off, in the hope of

"I have sworn to hang every man I took prisoner, especially that beardless rogue there, master of the brigantine;" pointing to one who had his hands tied, and a rope about his neck.

escaping by her swiftness. Unfortunately, however, for her, the captain galley was a remarkably fast sailer, and gained upon her so quickly that the corsairs, seeing they could not escape a superior force, dropped their oars, in order to yield themselves prisoners, and not exasperate the commander of the galley by their obstinacy. But fortune ordained otherwise; for, just as the captain galley had nearly closed with her, and she was summoned to surrender, two drunken Turks, who with twelve others were on board, discharged their muskets, with which they killed two soldiers who were on the prow; whereupon the commander swore he would not leave a man of them alive; and, coming up with all fury to board her, she slipped away under the oars of the galley. The galley ran ahead some distance: in the meantime the corsairs, as their case was desperate, endeavoured to make off; but their presumption only aggravated their misfortune, for the captain galley presently overtook them again, when, clapping her oars on the vessel, she was instantly taken possession of, without more bloodshed.

By this time the two other galleys had come up, and all three returned, with the captured vessel, to their former station near the shore, where a multitude of people had assembled to see what had been taken. On coming to anchor, the commander sent the pinnace on shore for the viceroy, whom he saw waiting to be conveyed on board, and at the same time ordered the main-yard to be lowered, intending, without delay, to hang the master of the vessel and the rest of the Turks he had taken in her, about six and thirty in number, all stout fellows, and most of them musketeers. The commander inquired which was their master, when one of the captives (who was afterwards discovered to be a Spanish renegado), answering him in Castilian, "That young man, sir, is our captain," said he, pointing to a youth of singular grace and beauty, seemingly under twenty years of age. "Tell me, ill-advised dog," said the commodore, "what moved you to kill my soldiers, when you saw it was impossible to escape? Is this the respect due to captain galleys? Know you not that temerity is not valour, and that doubtful hopes should make men bold, but not rash?"

The youth would have replied, but the commodore left him to receive the viceroy, who was at the moment entering the galley, with a numerous train of servants and others. "You have had a fine chase, commodore," said the viceroy. "So fine," answered the other, "that the sport is not yet over, as your excellency shall see." "How so?" replied the viceroy. "Because," replied the commodore, "these dogs, against all law and reason, and the custom of war, having killed two of my best soldiers, I have sworn to hang every man I took prisoner, especially that beardless rogue there, master of the brigantine;" pointing to one who had his hands tied and a rope about his neck, standing in expectation of immediate death.

The viceroy was much struck with his youth, his handsome person, and resigned behaviour, and felt a great desire to save him. "Tell me, corsair," said he, "what art thou? a Turk, Moor, or renegado?" "I am neither Turk, Moor, nor renegado," replied the youth, in the Castilian tongue. "What, then, art thou?" demanded the viceroy. "A Christian woman, sir," answered the youth. "A woman and a Christian in this garb, and in such a post!" said the viceroy: "this is indeed more wonderful than credible."

"Gentlemen," said the youth, "allow me to tell you the brief story of my life; it will not long delay your revenge." The request was urged so piteously, that it was impossible to deny it, and the commodore told him to proceed, but not to expect pardon for his offence. The youth then spoke as follows:

"I am of that unhappy nation whose miseries are fresh in your memories. My parents being of the Moorish race, I was hurried into Barbary by the current of their misfortunes, but more especially by the obstinacy of two of my uncles, with whom I in vain pleaded that I was a Christian. True as my declaration was, it had no influence either on them or the officers charged with our expulsion, who believed it to be only a pretext for remaining in the country where I was born. My father, a prudent man, was a true Christian, and my mother also, from whom, with a mother's early nourishment, I imbibed the Catholic faith.

" I was virtuously reared and educated, and neither in language nor behaviour gave indication of my Moorish descent. With these endowments, as I grew up what little beauty I have began to appear, and in spite of my reserve and seclusion, I was seen by a youth called Don Gaspar Gregorio, eldest son of a gentleman whose estate was close to the town in which we lived. How we met and conversed together, how he was distracted for me, and how I was little less so for him, would be tedious to relate, especially at a time when I am under apprehensions that the cruel cord which threatens me may cut short my narrative. I will therefore only say that Don Gregorio resolved to bear me company in our banishment; and accordingly he joined the Moorish exiles, whose language he understood, and getting acquainted with my two uncles, who had the charge of me, we all went together to Barbary, and took up our residence at Algiers, or, I should rather say, purgatory itself. My father, on the first notice of our banishment, had prudently retired to a place of refuge in some other Christian country, leaving much valuable property in pearls and jewels secreted in a certain place, which he discovered to me alone, with strict orders not to touch it until his return.

" On arriving at Algiers, the king, understanding that I was beautiful and rich—a report which afterwards turned to my advantage—sent for me, and asked me many questions concerning my country and the wealth I had brought with me. I told him where we had resided, and also what money and jewels had been left concealed, and said that if I might be permitted to return, the treasures could be easily brought away. This I told him in the hope that his avarice would protect me from his violence.

" While the king was making these inquiries, information was brought to him that a youth of extraordinary beauty had accompanied me from Spain. I knew that they could mean no other than Don Gaspar Gregorio, for he indeed is most beautiful, and I was alarmed to think of the danger to which he was exposed among barbarians, where, as I was told, a handsome youth is more valued than the most beautiful woman. The king ordered him to be brought into his presence, asking me, at the same time, if what had been said of him was true. Inspired, as I believe, by some good angel, I told him that the person they so commended was not a young man, but one of my own sex, and begged his permission to have her dressed in her proper attire, whereby her full beauty would be seen, and she would be spared the confusion of appearing before his majesty in that unbecoming habit. He consented, and said that the next day he would speak with me about my returning to Spain for the treasure that had been left behind. I then repaired to Don Gaspar, and having informed him of his danger, dressed him like a Moorish lady, and the same day introduced him as a female to the king. His majesty was struck with admiration, and determined to reserve the supposed lady as a present to the Grand Signor; and in the meantime, to avoid the temptation of so great a beauty among his own women, he gave him in charge to a Moorish lady of distinction, to whose house he was immediately conveyed.

"The grief which this separation caused—for I will not deny that I love him—can only be imagined by those who have felt the pangs of parting love. By the king's order, I presently embarked in this vessel, accompanied by the two Turks—the same that killed your soldiers—and this man also, who spoke to you first, and whom, though a renegado, I know to be a Christian in his heart, and more inclined to stay in Spain than to return to Barbary. The rest are Moors and Turks employed as rowers: their orders were to set me and the renegado on shore, in the habits of Christians, on the nearest coast of Spain; but these insolent Turks, regardless of their duty, must needs cruise along the coast, in the hope of taking some prize before they had landed us; fearing, if we had been first set on shore, we might be induced to give information that such a vessel was at sea, and thereby expose her to be taken. Last night we made this shore, not suspecting that any galleys were so near us; but, being discovered, we are now in your hands. Don Gregorio remains among the Moors as a woman, and in danger of his life; and here am I, with my hands bound, expecting, or rather fearing, to lose that life which, indeed, is now scarcely worth preserving. This, sir, is my lamentable story, equally true and wretched. All I entreat of you is to let me die like a Christian, since, as I have told you, I have no share in the guilt of my nation."

Here she ceased, and the tears that filled her lovely eyes drew many from those of her auditors. The viceroy himself was much affected, being a humane and compassionate man, and he went up to her to untie the cord with which her beautiful hands were fastened.

While the Christian Moor was relating her story, an old pilgrim, who came aboard the galley with the viceroy's attendants, fixed his eyes on her, and scarcely had she finished, when, rushing towards her, he cried, " O Anna Felix! my dear and unfortunate daughter! I am thy father Ricote, and was returning to seek thee, being unable to live without thee, who art my very soul."

At these words Sancho raised his head, which he had hitherto held down, ruminating on what he had lately suffered, and, staring at the pilgrim, recognized the same Ricote which he had met with on the day he had quitted his government. He was also satisfied that the damsel was indeed his daughter, who now, being unbound, was embracing her father, mingling her tears with his. "This, gentlemen," said he, " is my daughter, happy in her name alone. Anna Felix she is called, with the surname of Ricote, as famous for her own beauty as for her father's riches. I left my native country to seek in foreign kingdoms a safe retreat; and having found one in Germany, I returned in this pilgrim's habit to seek my daughter and take away the property I had left. My daughter was gone, but the treasure I have in my possession; and now, by a strange turn of fortune, I have found her, who is my greatest treasure. If our innocence and our united tears, through the uprightness of your justice, can open the gates of mercy, let it be extended to us, who never in thought offended you, nor in anywise conspired with those of our nation who have been justly banished."

Sancho now putting in his word, said, "I know Ricote well, and answer for the truth of what he says of Anna Felix being his daughter; but, as for the story of going and coming, and of his good or bad intentions, I meddle not with them."

An accident so remarkable could not fail to make a strong impression upon all who were present; so that the commodore, sharing in the common feeling, said to the fair captive : " My oath, madam, is washed away with your tears : live, fair Anna Felix, all the years Heaven has allotted you, and let punishment fall on the slaves who alone are guilty." Upon which he gave orders that the two Turks who had killed his soldiers should be hanged at the yard-arm. But the viceroy earnestly pleaded for their pardon, as the crime they had committed was rather the effect of frenzy than design; and the commander, whose rage had now subsided, yielded, not unwillingly, to his request.

They now consulted on the means of Don Gregorio's deliverance. Ricote offered jewels, then in his possession, to the amount of more than two thousand ducats, towards effecting it; but the expedient most approved of was the proposal of the renegado, who offered to return to Algiers in a small bark of six banks, manned with Christians, for he knew when and where he might land, and was, moreover, acquainted with the house in which Don Gregorio was kept. Some doubts were expressed whether the Christian sailors could be safely trusted with the renegado; but they were removed by the confidence in him expressed by Anna Felix, and the promise of her father to ransom them in case they should be taken.

The viceroy then returned on shore, charging Don Antonio Moreno with the care of Ricote and his daughter; desiring him at the same time to command anything that, in his own house, might conduce to their entertainment : such was the kindness and good-will inspired by beauty and misfortune.

CHAPTER LXIV.

Treating of the adventure which gave Don Quixote more vexation than any which had hitherto befallen him.

IT is related in this history that the wife of Don Antonio Moreno received Anna Felix with extreme pleasure, and was equally delighted with her beauty and good sense, for the young lady excelled in both; and from all parts of the city people came in crowds to see her, as if they had been brought together by the sound of bell. Don Quixote took occasion to inform Don Antonio that he could by no means approve of the expedient they had adopted for the redemption of Don Gregorio, as being more dangerous than promising: a much surer way, he added, would be to land him, with his horse and arms, in Barbary, and they would see that he would fetch the young gentleman off in spite of the whole Moorish race—as Don Gayferos had done by his spouse Melisendra.

"Remember, sir," quoth Sancho, "that when Signor Don Gayferos rescued his wife, and carried her into France, it was all done on dry land; but here, if we chance to rescue Don Gregorio, our road lies directly over the sea." "For all things except death there is a remedy," replied Don Quixote: "let a vessel be ready on shore to receive us, and the whole world shall not prevent our embarkation." "O master of mine, you are a rare contriver," said Sancho; "but saying is one thing, and doing another. For my part, I stick to the renegado, who seems an honest, good sort of man." "If the renegado should fail," said Don Antonio, "it will then be time for us to accept the offer of the great Don Quixote." Two days after, the renegado sailed in a small bark of twelve oars, with a crew of stout and resolute fellows, and in two days after that, the galleys departed for the Levant, the viceroy having promised the commodore an account of the fortunes of Don Gregorio and Anna Felix.

One morning, Don Quixote having sallied forth to take the air on the strand, armed at all points—his favourite costume, for arms, he said, were his ornament, and fighting his recreation—he observed a knight advancing towards him, armed also like himself, and bearing a shield, on which was portrayed a resplendent moon; and when near enough to be heard, in an elevated voice he addressed himself to Don Quixote, saying, "Illustrious knight, and never-enough-renowned Don Quixote de la Mancha, I am the Knight of the White Moon, of whose incredible achievements, peradventure, you have heard. I come to engage in combat with you, and to try the strength of your arm, in order to make you confess that my mistress, whoever she may be, is beyond comparison more beautiful than your Dulcinea del Toboso:—a truth, which if you fairly confess, you will spare your own life, and me the trouble of taking it. The terms of the combat I require are that if the victory be mine, you relinquish arms and the search of adventures for the space of one year, and that, returning forthwith to your own dwelling, you there live during that period in a state of profound quiet, which will tend both to your temporal and spiritual welfare; but if, on the contrary, my head shall lie at your mercy, then shall the spoils of my horse and arms be yours, and the fame of my exploits transferred to you. Consider which is best for you, and determine quickly, for this very day must decide our fate."

Don Quixote was no less surprised at the arrogance of the Knight of the White Moon, than the reason he gave for challenging him; and, with much gravity and composure, he answered, "Knight of the White

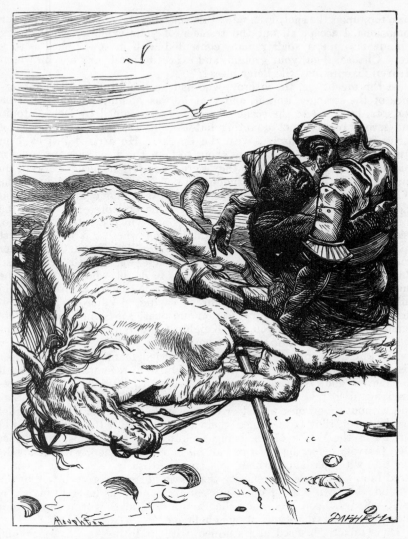

They now raised Don Quixote from the ground, and, uncovering his face, found him pale and bedewed with cold sweat, and Rozinante in such a plight that he was unable to stir.

Moon, whose achievements have not as yet reached my ears, I dare swear you have never seen the illustrious Dulcinea; for, if so, I am confident you would have taken care not to engage in this trial, since the sight of her must have convinced you that there never was, nor ever can be, beauty comparable to hers; and, therefore, without giving you the lie, I only affirm that you are mistaken, and accept your challenge, and that, too, upon the spot, even now, this very day, as you desire. Of your conditions, I accept all but the transfer of your exploits, which being unknown to me, I shall remain contented with my own, such as they are. Choose, then, your ground, and expect to meet me; and he whom Heaven favours may St. Peter bless!"

In the meantime, the viceroy, who had been informed of the appearance of the stranger knight, and that he was holding parley with Don Quixote, hastened to the scene of action, accompanied by Don Antonio and several others; not doubting but that it was some new device of theirs to amuse themselves with the knight. He arrived just as Don Quixote had wheeled Rozinante about to take the necessary ground for his career, and perceiving that they were ready for the onset, he went up and inquired the cause of so sudden an encounter. The Knight of the White Moon told him it was a question of pre-eminence in beauty, and then briefly repeated what he had said to Don Quixote, mentioning the conditions of the combat. The viceroy, in a whisper to Don Antonio, asked him if he knew the stranger knight, and whether it was some jest upon Don Quixote. Don Antonio assured him in reply that he neither knew who he was, nor whether this challenge was in jest or earnest. Puzzled with this answer, the viceroy was in doubt whether or not he should interpose, and prevent the encounter; but being assured it could only be some pleasantry, he withdrew, saying, " Valorous knights, if there be no choice between confession and death; if Signor Don Quixote persists in denying, and you, Sir Knight of the White Moon, in affirming—to it, gentlemen, in Heaven's name!"

The knights hereupon made their acknowledgments to the viceroy for his gracious permission; and now Don Quixote, recommending himself to Heaven, and (as usual on such occasions) to his lady Dulcinea, retired again to take a larger compass, seeing his adversary do the like: and without sound of trumpet or other warlike instrument to give signal for the onset, they both turned their horses about at the same instant; but he of the White Moon, being mounted on the fleetest steed, met Don Quixote before he had run half his career, and then, without touching him with his lance, which he seemed purposely to raise, he encountered him with such impetuosity that both horse and rider came to the ground; he then sprang upon him, and clapping his lance to his vizor, said, " Knight, you are vanquished and a dead man, if you confess not according to the conditions of our challenge."

Don Quixote, bruised and stunned, without lifting up his vizor, and as if speaking from a tomb, said in a feeble and low voice, " Dulcinea del Toboso is the most beautiful woman in the world, and I am the most unfortunate knight on earth, nor is it just that my weakness should discredit this truth : knight, push on your lance, and take away my life, since you have despoiled me of my honour."

" Not so, by my life!" quoth he of the White Moon; " long may the beauty and fame of the Lady Dulcinea del Toboso flourish! All I demand of the great Don Quixote is, that he submit to one year's domestic repose and respite from the exercise of arms."

The viceroy, Don Antonio, with many others, were witnesses to all that passed, and now heard Don Quixote promise that, since he required nothing of him to the prejudice of his lady Dulcinea, he should fulfil the terms of their engagement with the punctuality of a true knight.

This declaration being made, he of the White Moon turned about his horse, and, bowing to the viceroy, at a half-gallop entered the city, whither the viceroy ordered Don Antonio to follow him, and by all means to learn who he was. They now raised Don Quixote from the ground, and, uncovering his face, found him pale and bedewed with cold sweat, and Rozinante in such a plight that he was unable to stir.

Sancho, quite sorrowful and cast down, knew not what to do or say: sometimes he fancied he was dreaming; at others that the whole was an affair of witchcraft and enchantment. He saw his master discomfited, and bound by his oath to lay aside arms during a whole year! His glory, therefore, he thought, was for ever extinguished, and his hopes of greatness scattered like smoke to the wind. Indeed, he was afraid that both horse and rider were crippled, and hoped that it would prove no worse.

Finally, the vanquished knight was conveyed to the city in a chair, which had been ordered by the viceroy, who returned thither himself, impatient for some information concerning the knight who had left Don Quixote in such evil plight.

CHAPTER LXV.

In which an account is given who the Knight of the White Moon was, and of the deliverance of Don Gregorio; with other events.

DON ANTONIO MORENO rode into the city after the Knight of the White Moon, who was also pursued to his inn by a swarm of boys; and he had no sooner entered the chamber where his squire waited to disarm him, than he was greeted by the inquisitive Don Antonio. Conjecturing the object of his visit, he said, "I doubt not, signor, but that your design is to learn who I am; and as there is no cause for concealment, while my servant is unarming me, I will inform you without reserve. My name, signor, is the bachelor Sampson Carrasco, and I am of the same town with Don Quixote de la Mancha, whose madness and folly have excited the pity of all who knew him. I have felt, for my own part, particularly concerned, and, believing his recovery to depend upon his remaining quietly at home, my projects have been solely directed to that end. About three months ago I sallied forth on the highway like a knight-errant, styling myself the Knight of the Mirrors, intending to fight and conquer my friend without doing him harm, and making his submission to my will the condition of our combat. Never doubting of success, I expected to send him home for twelve months, and hoped that, during that time, he might be restored to his senses. But fortune ordained it otherwise, for he was the victor: he tumbled me from my horse, and thereby defeated my design. He pursued his journey, and I returned home, vanquished, abashed, and hurt by my fall. However, I did not relinquish my project, as you have seen this day; and, as he is so exact and punctual in observing the laws of knight-errantry, he will doubtless observe my injunctions. And now, sir, I have only to beg that you will not discover me to Don Quixote, that my good intentions may take effect, and his understanding be restored to him, which, when freed from the follies of chivalry, is excellent."

"O sir!" exclaimed Don Antonio, "what have you to answer for in robbing the world of so diverting a madman? Is it not plain, sir, that no benefit to be derived from his recovery can be set against the pleasure which his extravagances afford? But I fancy, sir, his case is beyond the reach of your art; and, Heaven forgive me! I cannot forbear wishing you may fail in your endeavours; for by his cure we should lose, not only the pleasantries of the knight, but those of his squire, which are enough to transform Melancholy herself into mirth. Nevertheless, I will be silent, and wait in the full expectation that Signor Carrasco will lose his labour." "Yet, all things considered," said the bachelor, "the business is in a promising way—I have no doubt of success."

Don Antonio then politely took his leave; and that same day the bachelor, after having his armour tied upon the back of a mule, mounted his charger and quitted the city, directing his course homewards, where he arrived without meeting with any adventure on the road worthy of a place in this faithful history. Don Antonio reported his conversation with the bachelor Carrasco to the viceroy, who regretted that such conditions should have been imposed upon Don Quixote, as they might put an end to that diversion which he had so liberally supplied to all who were acquainted with his whimsical turn of mind.

During six days Don Quixote kept his bed, melancholy, thoughtful, and out of humour, still dwelling upon his unfortunate overthrow. Sancho strove hard to comfort him. "Cheer up, my dear master," said he: "pluck up a good heart, sir, and be thankful you have come off without a broken rib. Remember, sir, 'they that give must take;' and 'every hook has not its flitch.'. Come, come, sir—a fig for the doctor! you have no need of him. Let us pack up, and be jogging homeward, and leave this rambling up and down to seek adventures the Lord knows where. Odds bodikins! after all I am the greatest loser, though mayhap your worship suffers the most; for though, after a taste of governing, I now loathe it, I have never lost my longing for an earldom or countship, which I may whistle for if your worship refuses to be a king, by giving up knight-errantry." "Peace, friend Sancho," quoth Don Quixote, "and remember that my retirement is not to exceed a year, and then I will resume my honourable profession, and shall not want a kingdom for myself, nor an earldom for thee." "Heaven grant it, and sin be

deaf!" quoth Sancho; "for I have always been told that good expectation is better than bad possession."

Here their conversation was interrupted by Don Antonio, who entered
the chamber with signs of great joy. "Reward me, Signor Don
Quixote," said he, "for my good news—Don Gregorio and the renegado are safe in the harbour—in the harbour, said I?—by this time they
are at the viceroy's palace, and will be here presently." Don Quixote
seemed to revive by this intelligence. "Truly," said he, "I am almost
sorry at what you tell me, for had it happened otherwise, I should have
gone over to Barbary, where, by the force of my arm, I should have
given liberty not only to Don Gregorio, but to all the Christian captives
in that land of slavery. But what do I say? wretch that I am! Am I
not vanquished? Am I not overthrown? Am I not forbidden to unsheathe my sword for twelve whole months? Why, then, do I promise
and vaunt? A distaff better becomes my hand than a sword!"

"No more, sir," quoth Sancho: "let the hen live, though she have
the pip: to-day for you, and to-morrow for me; and, as for these
matters of encounters and bangs, never trouble your head about them:
he that falls to-day may rise to-morrow; unless he chooses to lie in bed
and groan, instead of getting into heart and spirits, ready for fresh encounters. Rise, dear sir, and welcome Don Gregorio; for, by the bustle
in the house, I reckon he is come."

And this was the fact. Don Gregorio, after giving the viceroy an
account of the expedition, impatient to see his Anna Felix, hastened,
with his deliverer, the renegado, to Don Antonio's house. The female
dress, in which he had escaped, he had exchanged for that of a captive
who had come off with them; yet even in that disguise his handsome
exterior commanded respect and admiration. He was young, too, for he
seemed to be not more than seventeen or eighteen years of age. Ricote
and his daughter went out to meet him—the father with tears, and the
daughter with modest joy. The young couple did not embrace, for true
and ardent love shrinks from public freedom of behaviour. Their beauty
was universally admired, and though they spoke not to each other, their
eyes modestly revealed their joyful and pure emotions. The renegado
gave a short account of his voyage, and the means he had employed to
accomplish the purpose of the expedition; and Don Gregorio told the
story of his difficulties and embarrassments during his confinement, with
good sense and discretion above his years. Ricote fully satisfied the
boatmen, as well as the renegado, who was forthwith restored to the
bosom of the Church, and from a rotten member became, through penance and true repentance, clean and sound.

A few days after, the viceroy and Don Antonio consulted together
how permission might be obtained for Anna Felix and her father to
reside in Spain; being convinced there was nothing improper in such an
indulgence to so Christian a daughter and so well-disposed a father.
Don Antonio offered to negotiate the affair himself at court, having
occasion to go thither upon other business; and intimated that much
might be done there by favour or gold. "No," said Ricote, who was

present; " there is nothing to be expected from such means; neither prayers, promises, nor gold avail with the great Bernardino de Velasco, Count of Salazar, who was charged by the king with our expulsion; and, though disposed to temper justice with mercy, yet, seeing the whole body of our nation corrupt, instead of emollients he has applied caustics as the only remedy; thus, by his prudence, sagacity, and vigilance, as well as by his threats, he has successfully accomplished the great work, in spite of the numerous artifices of our people to evade his commands, or elude his Argus eyes, which are ever on the watch lest any noxious roots should still lurk in the soil, to shoot up again, and poison the wholesome vegetation of the country: a heroic determination of the great Philip III., and only to be equalled by his wisdom in placing the mighty task in such hands."

" Nevertheless," said Don Antonio, " when I arrive at court, I will make every exertion possible, and leave the rest to Providence. Don Gregorio shall go with me, to console his parents for the affliction they must have suffered in his absence; Anna Felix shall stay at my house with my wife, or in a monastery; and I know my lord the viceroy will be pleased to entertain honest Ricote until the success of my negotiation be seen." The viceroy consented to all that was proposed; but Don Gregorio, on being informed of what had passed, expressed great unwillingness to leave his fair mistress. At length, however, considering that he might return to her after he had seen his parents, he acquiesced; so Anna Felix remained with Don Antonio's lady, and Ricote in the mansion of the viceroy.

The time fixed for Don Antonio's departure now arrived, and many sighs, tears, and other expressions of passionate sorrow attended the separation of the lovers. Ricote offered Don Gregorio a thousand crowns, but he declined them, and accepted only the loan of five from Don Antonio. Two days afterwards, Don Quixote, who had hitherto been unable to travel on account of his bruises, set forward on his journey home, Sancho trudging after him on foot—because Dapple was now employed in bearing his master's armour.

CHAPTER LXVI.

Treating of matters which he who reads will see, and he who listens to them, when read, will hear.

As Don Quixote was leaving the city of Barcelona, he cast his eyes to the spot whereon he had been defeated; and pausing, he cried, " There stood Troy! there my evil destiny, not cowardice, despoiled me of my glory; there I experienced the fickleness of fortune; there the lustre of my exploits was obscured; and, lastly, there fell my happiness, never more to rise!" Upon which Sancho said to him, " Great hearts, dear sir, should be patient under misfortunes, as well as joyful when all goes well; and in that I judge by myself, for when I was made a governor, I was blithe and merry, and now that I am a poor squire on foot, I am not sad. I have heard say, that she they call Fortune is a drunken, freakish dame, and withal so blind that she does not see what she is about; neither whom she raises, nor whom she pulls down."

" Thou art much of a philosopher, Sancho," said Don Quixote, " and hast spoken very judiciously. Where thou hast learned it I know not; but one thing I must tell thee, which is, that there is no such thing in the world as fortune, nor do the events which fall out, whether good or evil, proceed from chance, but by the particular appointment of Heaven; and hence comes the saying that every man is the maker of his own fortune. I have been so of mine; but, not acting with all the prudence necessary, my presumption has undone me. I ought to have recollected that the feeble Rozinante was not a match for the powerful steed of the Knight of the White Moon. However, I ventured; I did my best: I was overthrown: and, though I lost my glory, I still retain my integrity, and therefore shall not fail in my promise. When I was a knight, daring and valiant, my arms gave credit to my exploits; and now that I am only a dismounted squire, my word at least shall be respected. March on, then, friend Sancho, and let us pass at home the year of our noviciate; by which retreat we shall acquire fresh vigour to return to the never-by-me-to-be-forgotten exercise of arms."

" Sir," replied Sancho, as he trotted by his side, " this way of marching is not so pleasant that I must needs be in such haste: let us hang this armour upon some tree, like the thieves we see there dangling, and when I am mounted again upon Dapple, with my feet from the ground, we will travel at any pace your worship pleases; but to think that I can foot it all the way at this rate is to expect what cannot be." " I approve thy advice, Sancho," answered Don Quixote: " my armour shall be suspended as a trophy; and beneath or round it we will carve on the tree that which was written on the trophy of Orlando's arms:

> " Let none presume these arms to move
> Who Roldan's fury dare not prove."

" That is just as I would have it," quoth Sancho; " and, were it not for the want of Rozinante on the road, it would not be amiss to leave him dangling too." " Now I think of it," said Don Quixote, " neither him nor the armour will I suffer to be hanged, that it may not be said, ' For good service, bad recompense.' " " Faith, that is well too," said Sancho, " for 't is a saying among the wise, that the fault of the ass should not be laid on the pack-saddle; and, since your worship is alone to blame in this business, punish yourself, and let not your rage fall upon the poor armour, battered and bruised in your service; nor upon your meek and gentle beast that carries you, nor yet upon my tender feet, making them suffer more than feet can bear."

In such-like discourse they passed all that day, and even four more, without meeting anything to impede their journey; but on the fifth, it being a holiday, as they entered a village, they observed a great number of people regaling themselves at the door of an inn. When Don Quixote and Sancho drew near to them, a peasant said aloud to the rest, "One of these two gentlemen who are coming this way, and who know not the parties, shall decide our wager." "That I will do with all my heart," answered Don Quixote, "and most impartially, when I am made acquainted with it." "Why, the business, good sir, is this," quoth the peasant: "an inhabitant of our village, who is so corpulent that he weighs eleven arrobas, has challenged a neighbour, who weighs not above five, to run with him a hundred yards, upon condition of carrying equal weight. Now he that gave the challenge, being asked how the weight should be made equal, says that the other, who weighs but five arrobas, should carry a weight of six more, and then both lean and fat will be equal." "Not so," quoth Sancho, before Don Quixote could return an answer; "and it is my business, who was so lately a governor and judge, as all the world knows, to set this matter right, and give my opinion in all disputes." "In Heaven's name, do so," said Don Quixote; "for I am unfit to throw crumbs to a cat, my brain is so troubled and out of order."

With this license, Sancho addressed the country fellows who crowded about him: "Brothers," said he, "I must tell you the fat man is wrong; there is no manner of reason in what he asks; for, if the custom is fair for him that is challenged to choose his weapons, it must be unjust for the other to make him take such as will be sure to hinder him from gaining the victory; and therefore my sentence is that the fat man who gave the challenge should cut, pare, slice, and shave away the flesh from such parts of his body as can best spare it, and when he has brought it down to the weight of five arrobas, then will he be a fair match for the other, and they may race it upon even terms." "I vow," quoth one of the peasants, "this gentleman has spoken like a saint, and given sentence like a canon; but I warrant the fat fellow loves his flesh too well to part with a sliver of it, much less with the weight of six arrobas." "Then the best way," quoth another of the countrymen, "will be not to run at all; for then neither lean will break his back with the weight, nor fat lose flesh; but let us spend half the wager in wine, and take these gentlemen to share it with us in the tavern that has the best; so 'Give me the cloak when it rains.'" "I return you thanks, gentlemen, for your kind proposal," answered Don Quixote, "but I cannot accept it; for melancholy thoughts and disastrous events oblige me to travel in haste, and to appear thus uncivil."

Whereupon, clapping spurs to Rozinante, he departed, leaving them in surprise both at the strangeness of his figure, and the acuteness of him whom they took to be his servant. "If the man be so wise," said one of them, "heaven bless us! what must his master be? If they go to study at Salamanca, my life for it, they will become judges at a court in a trice. Nothing more easy—it wants only hard study, good luck, and favour, and when a man least thinks of it, he finds himself with a white rod in his hand, or a mitre on his head."

That night the master and man took up their lodging in the middle of a field, under the spangled roof of heaven; and the next day, while pursuing their journey, they saw a man coming towards them on foot, with a wallet about his neck, and a javelin, or half-pike, in his hand—the proper equipment of a foot-post; who, when he had got near them, quickened his pace, and, running up to Don Quixote, embraced his right thigh—for he could reach no higher,—and, testifying great joy, he said, "Oh! Signor Don Quixote de la Mancha! how rejoiced will my lord duke be when he hears that your worship is returning to his castle, where he still remains with my lady duchess!"

"I know you not, friend," answered Don Quixote; "nor can I conceive who you are, unless you tell me." "Signor Don Quixote," answered the courier, "I am Tosilos, the duke's lacquey; the same who would not fight with your worship about Donna Rodrigeuz' daughter." "Heaven defend me!" exclaimed Don Quixote, "are you he whom the enchanters, my enemies, transformed into the lacquey, to defraud me of the glory of that combat?" "Softly, good sir," replied the messenger; "there was neither enchantment nor change in the case. Tosilos the lacquey I entered the lists, and the same I came out. I refused fighting, because I had a mind to marry the girl; but it turned out quite otherwise; for your worship had no sooner left the castle than, instead of a wife, I got a sound banging, by my lord duke's order, for not doing as he would have had me in that affair; and the end of it all is, that the girl is turned nun, and Donna Rodriguez packed off to Castile; and I am now going to Barcelona with a packet of letters from my lord to the viceroy; and if your worship will please to take a little of the dear creature, I have here a calabash full at your service, with a slice of good cheese that will awaken thirst, if it be sleeping." "I take you at your word," quoth Sancho; "and, without more ado, let us be at it, good Tosilos, in spite of all the enchanters in the Indies."

"In truth, Sancho," quoth Don Quixote, "thou art a very glutton, and, moreover, the greatest simpleton on earth, to doubt that this courier is enchanted, and a counterfeit Tosilos. But, if thou art bent upon it, stay, in Heaven's name, and eat thy fill, while I go on slowly, and await thy coming." The lacquey laughed, unsheathed his calabash and unwalleted his cheese; and taking out a little loaf, he and Sancho sat down upon the grass, and in peace and good-fellowship quickly dispatched the contents, and got to the bottom of the provision-bag, with so good an appetite that they licked the very packet of letters because it smelt of cheese.

While they were thus employed, "Hang me, friend Sancho," said Tosilos, "if I know what to make of that master of yours—he must needs be a madman." "Need!" quoth Sancho; "faith, he has no need; for if madness pass current, he has plenty to pay every man his own. That I can see full well, and full often I tell him of it; but what boots it? — especially now that it is all over with him; for he has been worsted by the Knight of the White Moon."

Tosilos begged him to relate what had happened to him; but Sancho excused himself, saying it would be unmannerly to keep his master waiting; but that, another time, if they should meet again, he would tell him the whole affair. He then rose up, shook the crumbs from his beard and apparel, and took leave of Tosilos; then driving Dapple before him, he set off to overtake his master, whom he found waiting for him under the shade of a tree.

CHAPTER LXVII.

)f the resolution which Don Quixote took to turn shepherd, and lead a pastoral life, till the promised term should be expired; with other incidents truly diverting and good.

I<small>F</small> the mind of Don Quixote had been afflicted and disturbed before his defeat, how greatly were his sufferings increased after that misfortune! While waiting for Sancho, as before mentioned, a thousand thoughts rushed into his head, buzzing about like flies in a honey-pot; some dwelling on the disenchantment of Dulcinea, and others on the life he should lead during his forced retirement. On Sancho's coming up, and commending Tosilos as the civilest lacquey in the world, " Is it possible, Sancho," said he, " that thou shouldst still persist in his being really a lacquey? It seems to have quite escaped thy memory that thou hast seen Dulcinea transformed into a country wench, and the Knight of the Mirrors into the bachelor Sampson Carrasco:—all the work of the enchanters who persecute me. But tell me, didst thou inquire of that man touching the fate of Altisidora? Doth she still bewail my absence, or hath she already consigned to oblivion the amorous thoughts that tormented her whilst I was present?"

" Troth, sir," quoth Sancho, " I was too well employed to think of such fooleries. Body of me! is your worship now in a condition to be inquiring after other folks' thoughts — especially on love matters?" " Observe, Sancho," quoth Don Quixote, " there is a great deal of difference between love and gratitude. It is very possible for a gentleman not to be in love; but, strictly speaking, it is impossible he should be ungrateful. Altisidora, to all appearance, loved me; she gave me three nightcaps, as thou knowest; she also wept at my departure; she cursed me, vilified me, and, in spite of shame, complained publicly of me: certain proofs that she adored me; for in such maledictions the anger of lovers usually vents itself. I had neither hopes to give her, nor treasures to offer her, for mine are all engaged to Dulcinea; and the treasures of knights-errant, like those of fairies, are delusory, not real; and therefore, to retain her in remembrance is all I can do for her, without prejudice to the fidelity I owe to the mistress of my soul, who every moment suffers under thy cruelty in neglecting to discipline that flesh of thine—would to Heaven the wolves had it!—since thou wouldst rather keep it for the worms, than apply it to the relief of that poor lady."

"Sir," answered Sancho, "to deal plainly with you, I cannot see what the lashing of my body has to do with disenchanting the enchanted. It is just as if you should say, 'When your head aches, anoint your knee-pans;' at least, I dare be sworn that, of all the histories your worship has ever read of knight-errantry, none ever told you of anybody being unbewitched by flogging. However, be that as it will, when the humour takes me, and time fits, I'll set about it, and lay it on to some tune."

"Heaven grant," said Don Quixote, "and give thee grace to understand how much it is thy duty to relieve my lady, who is also thine, since thou belongest to me."

Thus conversing, they travelled on till they arrived at the very spot where they had been trampled upon by the bulls. Don Quixote, recollecting it, "There, Sancho," said he, "is the meadow where we met the gay shepherdesses and gallant shepherds, who proposed to revive, in this place, another pastoral Arcadia. The project was equally new and ingenious, and if thou thinkest well of it, Sancho, we will follow their example, and turn shepherds; at least for the term of my retirement. I will buy sheep, and whatever is necessary for a pastoral life; and I, assuming the name of the shepherd Quixotiz, and thou that of the shepherd Panzino, we will range the woods, the hills, and the valleys, singing here, and sighing there; drinking from the clear springs or limpid brooks, or the mighty rivers; while the oaks, with liberal hand, shall give us their sweetest fruit—the hollow cork trees lodging—willows their shade—and the roses their delightful perfume. The spacious meads shall be our carpets of a thousand colours; and, ever breathing the clear, pure air, the moon and stars shall be our tapers of the night, and light our evening walk; and thus, while singing will be our pleasure and complaining our delight, the god of song will provide harmonious verse, and love a never-failing theme—so shall our fame be eternal as our song!"

"'Fore gad!" quoth Sancho, "that kind of life squares and corners with me exactly; and I warrant, if once the bachelor Sampson Carrasco and Master Nicholas the barber catch a glimpse of it, they will follow us, and turn shepherds too: and Heaven grant that the priest have not an inclination to make one in the fold—he is so gay and merrily inclined." "Thou sayest well," quoth Don Quixote; "and if the bachelor Sampson Carrasco will make one amongst us, as I doubt not he will, he may call himself the shepherd Samsonino or Carrascon. Master Nicholas the barber may be called Niculoso, as old Boscan called himself Nomoroso. As for the curate, I know not what name to bestow upon him, unless it can be one derived from his profession, calling him the shepherd Curiambro. As to the shepherdesses who are to be the objects of our love, we may pick and choose their names as we do pears; and since that of my lady accords alike with a shepherdess and a princess, I need not be at the pains of selecting one to suit her better. Thou, Sancho, mayest give to thine whatever name pleaseth thee best." "I do not intend," answered Sancho, "to give mine any other than Teresona, which will fit her fat sides well, and is so near her own, too, that when I come to put it in my verses, everybody will know her to be my own wife, and commend me for not coveting other men's goods, and seeking for better bread than wheaten. As for the priest, he must be content without a mistress, for good example's sake; and, if the bachelor Sampson wants one, his soul is his own."

"Heaven defend me!" quoth Don Quixote, "what a life shall we lead, friend Sancho! what a melody we shall have of bagpipes and rebecks, and pipes of Zamora! And if to all this we add the albogues, our pastoral band will be nearly complete." "Albogues!" quoth Sancho, "what may that be? I never heard of such a thing." "Albogues," answered Don Quixote, "are concave plates of brass, like candlesticks, which, being struck against each other, produce a sound, not very agreeable, it is true, yet not offensive; and it accords well enough with the rusticity of the pipe and tabor. Albogues, Sancho, is a Moorish word, as are all those which in Spanish begin with *al;* as Almoaza, Almorzar, Alhambra, Alguacil, Aluzema, Almacen, Alcancia, with some others: our language has only three Moorish words ending in *i,* which are, Borzegui, Zaquizami, and Maravedi; Alheli and Alfaqui, both by their beginning and ending, are known to be Arabic. This I just observe by the way, as the mention of albogues brought it to my mind. One circumstance will contribute much to make us perfect in our new profession, which is my being, as thou well knowest, somewhat of a poet, and the bachelor Sampson Carrasco an excellent one. Of the priest I will say nothing; yet will I venture a wager that he too has the points of a poet; and Master Nicholas the barber, also, I make no doubt, for most or all of that faculty are players on the guitar and song makers. I will complain of absence; thou shalt extol thyself for constancy; the shepherd Carrascon shall complain of disdain; and the priest Curiambro may say or sing whatever he pleaseth: and so we shall go on to our hearts' content."

"Alas! sir," quoth Sancho, "I am so unlucky that I shall never see those blessed days! Oh, what neat wooden spoons shall I make when I am a shepherd! What curds and cream! what garlands! what pretty nick-nacks! An old dog I am at these trinkums, which, though they may not set me up for one of the seven wise men, will get me the name of a clever fellow. My daughter Sanchica shall bring our dinner to us in the field—but hold there: she's a sightly wench, and shepherds are sometimes roguishly given; and I would not have my girl go out for wool and come back shorn. Your love doings and wanton tricks are as common in the open fields as in crowded cities, in the shepherd's cot as in the palaces of lords and princes. Take away the opportunity, and you take away the sin; what the eye views not the heart rues not; a leap from behind a bush may do more than the prayer of a good man."

" Enough, Sancho, no more proverbs," quoth Don Quixote, "for any one of those thou hast cited would have been sufficient to express thy meaning. I have often advised thee not to be so prodigal of these sentences, and to keep a strict hand over them; but it is preaching in the desert; 'the more my mother whips me, the more I rend and tear.' "

" Faith and troth, sir," cried Sancho, "is not that the pot calling the kettle smut? You chide me for speaking proverbs, and you string them yourself by scores."

"Observe, Sancho," answered Don Quixote, "this important difference between thy proverbs and mine : when I make use of them they fit like a ring to the finger; whereas by thee they are dragged in by the head and shoulders. I have already told thee, if I mistake not, that proverbs are short maxims of human wisdom, the result of experience and observation, and are the gifts of ancient sages; yet the proverb which is not aptly applied, instead of being wisdom, is stark nonsense. But enough of this at present : as night approaches, let us retire a little way out of the high road to pass the night, and God knows what to-morrow may bring us."

They accordingly retired, and made a late and scanty supper, much against Sancho's inclination, for it brought the hardships of knight-errantry fresh upon his thoughts, and he grieved to think how seldom he encountered the plenty that reigned in the house of Don Diego de Miranda, at the wedding of the rich Camacho, and at Don Antonio Moreno's; but again reflecting that it could not be always day nor always night, he betook himself to sleep, leaving his master thoughtful and awake.

CHAPTER LXVIII.

Of the bristly adventure which befell Don Quixote.

THE night was rather dark, for though the moon was in the heavens, it was not visible : Madam Diana is wont sometimes to take a trip to the antipodes, and leave the mountains and valleys in the dark.

Don Quixote followed nature, and, being satisfied with his first sleep, did not solicit more. As for Sancho, he never wanted a second, for the first lasted him from night to morning; indicating a sound body and a mind free from care ; but his master, being unable to sleep himself, awakened him, saying, "I am amazed, Sancho, at the torpor of thy soul; it seems as if thou wert made of marble or brass, insensible of emotion or sentiment ! I wake whilst thou sleepest, I mourn whilst thou art singing, I faint with long fasting, whilst thou canst hardly move or breathe from pure gluttony ! It is the part of a good servant to share his master's pains, and, were it but for decency, to be touched with what affects him. Behold the serenity of the night and the solitude of the place, inviting us to intermingle some watching with our sleep : get up, good Sancho, I conjure thee, and retire a short distance from hence, and, with a willing heart and grateful courage, inflict on thyself three or four hundred lashes, upon the score of Dulcinea's disenchantment; and this I ask as a favour : I will not come to wrestling with thee again, for I know thou hast a heavy hand; and that being done, we will pass the remainder of the night in singing—I of absence, thou of constancy; commencing from this moment the pastoral occupation which we are henceforth to follow."

" Sir," answered Sancho, " I am neither monk nor friar, to start up in the middle of the night and discipline myself at that rate; neither do I think it would be an easy matter to be under the rod one moment, and the next to begin singing. Talk not of whipping, I beseech you, sir, and let me sleep, or you will make me swear never to touch a hair of my coat, much less of my flesh." " Oh, thou soul of flint!" cried Don Quixote; " Oh, remorseless squire! Oh, bread ill-bestowed! A poor requital for favours already conferred and those intended! Through me thou hast been a governor; through me art thou in a fair way to have the title of an earl, or some other equally honourable, and which will be delayed no longer than this year of obscurity; for *Post tenebras spero lucem.*"

" I know not what that means," replied Sancho; " I only know that while I am asleep I have neither fear nor hope, nor trouble nor glory. Blessings light on him who first invented sleep!—it covers a man all over, body and mind, like a cloak; it is meat to the hungry, drink to the thirsty, heat to the cold, and cold to the hot; it is the coin that can purchase all things; the balance that makes the shepherd equal with the king, the fool with the wise man. It has only one fault, as I have heard say, which is, that it looks like death; for between the sleeper and the corpse there is but little to choose."

" I never heard thee talk so eloquently, Sancho," quoth Don Quixote, " which proves to me the truth of that proverb thou often hast cited : ' Not with whom thou art bred, but with whom thou art fed.' " " Odds my life, sir!" replied Sancho, " it is not I alone that am a stringer of proverbs—they come pouring from your worship's mouth faster than from mine. Your worship's, I own, may be more pat than mine, which tumble out at random; yet no matter—they are all proverbs."

Thus were they engaged, when they heard a strange, dull kind of noise, with harsh sounds, issuing from every part of the valley. Don Quixote started up, and laid his hand to his sword; and Sancho squatted down under Dapple, and fortified himself with the bundle of armour on one side of him, and the ass's pannel on the other, trembling no less with fear than Don Quixote with surprise. Every moment the noise increased as the cause of it approached, to the great terror of one at least —for the courage of the other is too well known to be suspected. Now, the cause of this fearful din was this :—some hog-dealers, eager to reach the market, happened at that early hour to be driving above six hundred

The wide-spreading host of grunters came crowding on, and threw down both master and man,
demolishing Sancho's entrenchment, and laying even Rozinante in the dust!

of these creatures along the road to a fair, where they were to be sold;
which filthy herd, with their grunting and squeaking made such a horrible noise that both the knight and squire were stunned and confounded,
and utterly at a loss how to account for it.

The wide-spreading host of grunters came crowding on, and, without
showing the smallest degree of respect for the lofty character of Don
Quixote, or of Sancho his squire, threw down both master and man,
demolishing Sancho's entrenchment, and laying even Rozinante in the
dust! On they went, and bore all before them, overthrowing pack-
saddle, armour, knight, squire, horse, and all; treading and trampling
over everything without remorse. Sancho with some difficulty recovered
his legs, and desired his master to lend him his sword, that he might slay
half a dozen at least of those unmannerly swine—for he had now discovered what they were; but Don Quixote admonished him not to hurt
them. "Heaven," said he, "has inflicted this disgrace upon my guilty
head: it is no more than a just punishment that dogs should devour,
hornets sting, and hogs trample on a vanquished knight-errant."

"And Heaven, I suppose," quoth Sancho, "has sent fleas to sting
and bite and hunger to famish us poor squires, for keeping such knights
company. If we squires were the sons of the knights we serve, or their

kinsmen, it would be no wonder that we should share in their punishments, even to the third and fourth generation; but what have the Panzas to do with the Quixotes? Well, let us to our litter again, and try to sleep out the little that is left of the night, and God will send daylight, and mayhap better luck." "Sleep thou, Sancho," said Don Quixote, "who wert born to sleep, whilst I, who was born to watch, allow my thoughts to range till daybreak, and give a tuneful vent to my sorrow in a little madrigal which I have just composed." "Methinks," quoth Sancho, "that a man cannot be suffering much when he can turn his brain to verse-making. However, madrigal it as much as your worship pleases, and I will sleep as much as I can." Then measuring off what ground he wanted, he rolled himself up and fell into a sound sleep; neither debts, bails, nor troubles of any kind disturbed him. Don Quixote, leaning against a beech or cork tree (for Cid Hamet Benengeli does not specify the tree), to the music of his own sighs, sang as follows:

> "O love, when, sick of heart-felt grief,
>   I sigh, and drag thy cruel chain,
> To death I fly, the sure relief
>   Of those who groan in lingering pain.

> "But, coming to the fatal gates,
>   The port in this my sea of woe,
> The joy I feel new life creates,
>   And bids my spirits brisker flow.

> "Thus, dying every hour I live,
>   And living I resign my breath:
> Strange power of love, that thus can give
>   A dying life and living death!"

The many sighs and tears that accompanied this tuneful lamentation proved how deeply the knight was affected by his late disaster and the absence of his lady. Daylight now appeared, and the sun, darting his beams full on Sancho's face, at last awoke him; whereupon, rubbing his eyes, yawning, and stretching his limbs, he perceived the swinish havoc made in his cupboard, and heartily wished the drove at the devil, and even went further than that in his wishes.

The knight and squire now started again, and journeyed on through the whole of that day, when towards evening they saw about half a score of men on horseback, and four or five on foot, making directly towards them. Don Quixote was much agitated by the sight of these men, and Sancho trembled with fear, for they were armed with lances and shields, and other warlike implements. "Ah, Sancho," said Don Quixote, "had I my hands at liberty, I would make no more of that hostile squadron than if it were composed of gingerbread. However, matters may not turn out so bad as they promise." The horsemen soon came up, and instantly surrounded the knight and the squire, and in a threatening manner presented the points of their lances at their prisoners. One of those on foot putting his finger to his lips, as if commanding Don Quixote to be mute, seized on Rozinante's bridle, and drew him out of the road ; while the others, in like manner, took possession of Dapple and his rider, and the whole then moved on in silence. Don Quixote several times would have inquired whither they meant to take him, but scarcely had he moved his lips to speak when they were ready to close them with the points of their spears. And so it was with Sancho : no sooner did he show an inclination to speak, than one of those on foot pricked him with a goad, driving Dapple in the same manner, as if he also wished to speak.

Night advancing, they quickened their pace, and the fear of the prisoners likewise increased ; especially when they heard the fellows ever and anon say to them, " On, on, ye Troglodytes ! Peace, ye barbarian slaves ! Pay, ye Anthropophagi ! Complain not, ye Scythians ! Open not your eyes, ye murderous Polyphemuses — ye butcherly lions ! " With these and other such names they tormented the ears of the unhappy master and man. Sancho went along muttering to himself— " What ! call us ortolans ! barbers ! slaves ! Andrew popinjays ! and Polly famouses !—I don't like the sound of such names—a bad wind this to winnow our corn ; mischief has been lowering upon us of late, and now it falls thick, like kicks to a cur. It looks ill, God send it may not end worse ! " Don Quixote proceeded onwards, quite confounded at the reproachful names that were given to him, and he could only conclude that no good was to be expected, and much harm to be feared. In this perplexing situation, about an hour after nightfall they arrived at a castle, which Don Quixote presently recollected to be that belonging to the duke, where he had lately been. " Heaven defend me ! " said he, as soon as he knew the place, " what can this mean ? In this house all is courtesy and kindness !—but, to the vanquished, good is converted into bad, and bad into worse." On entering the principal court they saw it decorated and set out in a manner that added still more to their fears, as well as to their astonishment, as will be seen in the following chapter.

CHAPTER LXIX.

Of the newest and strangest adventure of all that befell Don Quixote in the whole course of this great history.

No sooner had the horsemen alighted than, assisted by those on foot, they seized Don Quixote and Sancho in their arms, and placed them in the midst of the court, where a hundred torches, and above five hundred other lights, dispersed in the galleries around, set the whole in a blaze ; insomuch that, in spite of the darkness of the night, it appeared like day. In the middle of the court was erected a tomb, six feet from the ground, and over it was spread a large canopy of black velvet ; round which, upon its steps, were burning above a hundred wax tapers in silver candlesticks. On the tomb was visible the corpse of a damsel, so beautiful as to make death itself appear lovely. Her head was laid upon a cushion of gold brocade, crowned with a garland of fragrant flowers, and in her hands, which were laid crosswise upon her breast, was placed a green branch of victorious palm. On one side of the court was erected a theatre, where two personages were seated, whose crowns on their heads and sceptres in their hands denoted them to be kings, either real or feigned. On the side of the theatre, which was ascended by steps, were two other seats, upon which Don Quixote and Sancho were placed. This was performed in profound silence, and by signs they were both given to understand they were to hold their peace : though the caution was needless, for astonishment had tied up their tongues.

Two great persons now ascended the theatre with a numerous retinue, and seated themselves in two chairs of state, close to those who seemed to be monarchs. These Don Quixote immediately knew to be the duke and duchess who had so nobly entertained him. Everything he saw filled him with wonder, and nothing more than his discovery that the corse lying extended on the tomb was that of the fair Altisidora ! When the duke and duchess had taken their places, Don Quixote and Sancho rose up, and made them a profound reverence, which their highnesses returned by a slight inclination of the head. Immediately after, an officer crossed the area, and, going up to Sancho, threw over him a robe of black buckram, painted over with flames, and, taking off his cap, he put on his head a pasteboard mitre, three feet high, like those used by the penitents of the Inquisition; bidding him, in a whisper, not to open his lips, otherwise he would be either gagged or slain. Sancho viewed himself from top to toe, and saw his body covered with flames ; but finding they did not burn him, he cared not two straws. He took off his mitre, and saw it painted all over with devils ; but he replaced it again on his head, saying within himself, " All is well enough yet ; these flames do not burn, nor do these imps fly away with me." Don Quixote also surveyed him, and in spite of his perturbation he could not forbear smiling at his strange appearance.

And now in the midst of that profound silence (for not a breath was heard), a soft and pleasing·sound of flutes stole upon the ear, seeming to proceed from the tomb. Then, on a sudden, near the couch of the dead body appeared a beautiful youth, in a Roman habit, who in a sweet and clear voice, to the sound of the harp, which he touched himself, sang the two following stanzas :

> " Till Heaven, in pity to the weeping world,
> Shall give Altisidora back to day,
> By Quixote's scorn to realms of Pluto hurled,
> Her every charm to cruel death a prey ;
> While matrons throw their gorgeous robes away,
> To mourn a nymph by cold disdain betrayed ;
> To the complaining lyre's enchanting lay,
> I'll sing the praises of this hapless maid,
> In sweeter notes than Thracian Orpheus ever played.

" Nor shall my numbers with my life expire,
Or this world's light confine the boundless song :
To thee, bright maid, in death I 'll touch the lyre,
And to my soul the theme shall still belong.
When, freed from clay, the flitting ghosts among,
My spirit glides the Stygian shores around,
Though the cold hand of death has sealed my tongue,
Thy praise the infernal caverns shall rebound,
And Lethe's sluggish waves move slower to the sound."

" Enough," said one of the kings, " enough, divine musician ! it were an endless task to describe the graces of the peerless Altisidora—dead, as the ignorant world believes, but still living in the breath of fame, and through the penance which Sancho Panza, here present, must undergo, in order to restore her to light : and therefore O Rhadamanthus ! who,

Immediately six duennas were seen advancing in procession along the court.

with me, judgest in the dark caverns of Pluto, since thou knowest all that destiny has decreed touching the restoration of this damsel, speak— declare it immediately ; nor delay the promised felicity of her return to the world."

Scarcely had Minos ceased, when Rhadamanthus, starting up, cried, " Ho, there ! ye ministers and officers of the household, high and low, great and small ! Proceed ye, one after another, and mark me Sancho's face with four and twenty twitches, and let his arms and sides have twelve, and thrust therein six times the pin's sharp point ; for in the due performance of this ceremony depends the restoration of that lifeless corse."

Sancho, hearing this, could hold out no longer. " I vow to Heaven," cried he, " I will sooner turn Turk than let my flesh be so handled ! Body of me ! how is the mauling of my visage to give life to the dead ? ' The old woman has had a taste, and now her mouth waters.' Dulcinea is enchanted, and to unbewitch her I must be whipped ! And now here

Altisidora dies of some disease that God has sent her; and, to bring her to life again, my flesh must be tweaked and pinched, and corking-pins thrust into my body! No, put these tricks upon a brother-in-law: I am an old dog, and am not to be coaxed with a crust."

" Relent!" said Rhadamanthus, in a loud voice, " relent, tiger, or thou diest! Submit, proud Nimrod! Suffer and be silent, monster! Impossibilities are not required of thee: then talk not of difficulties. Twitched thou shalt be; pricked thou shalt feel thyself, and pinched even to groaning. Ho, there! officers, do your duty—or, on the word of an honest man, thy destiny shall be fulfilled!"

Immediately six duennas were seen advancing in procession along the court, four of them with spectacles, and all of them with their right hands raised, and four fingers' breadth of their wrists bared, to make their hands seem the longer, according to the fashion. No sooner had Sancho got a glimpse of his executioners than, bellowing aloud, he cried, " Do with me whatever you please; pour over me a sackful of mad cats to bite and claw me, as my master was served in this castle; pierce and drill me through with sharp daggers; tear off my flesh with red-hot pincers, and I will bear it all with patience to oblige your worships; but the devil may fly away with me at once before a duenna shall put a finger upon my flesh!"

Don Quixote could no longer keep silence. " Have patience, my son," said he; " yield to the command of these noble persons, and give thanks to Heaven for having imparted to thy body a virtue so wonderful that, by a little torture, thou shouldst be able to break the spells of enchanters and restore the dead to life."

By this time, Sancho was surrounded by the duennas; and, being softened and persuaded by his master's entreaties, he fixed himself firmly in his chair, and held out his face and beard to the executioners. The first gave him a dexterous twitch, and then made him a low courtesy. " Spare me your complaisance, good madam, and give less of your slabber-sauce; for, Heaven take me! your fingers stink of vinegar." In short, all the duennas successively performed their office, and after them divers other persons repeated the same ceremony of tweaking and pinching, to all of which he submitted; but when they came to pierce his flesh with pins, he could contain himself no longer; and, starting up in a fury, he caught hold of a lighted torch, and began to lay about him with such agility that all his tormentors were put to flight. " Away!" he cried; " scamper, ye imps of the devil! Do you take me to be made of brass, and suppose I cannot feel your cursed torments?"

At this moment Altisidora (who must have been tired with lying so long upon her back) turned herself on one side; upon which the whole assembly cried out with one voice, " She lives! she lives! Altisidora lives!" Rhadamanthus then told Sancho to calm his rage, for the work was accomplished. The moment Don Quixote perceived Altisidora move, he went to Sancho, and, kneeling before him, said, " Now is the time, dear son of my bowels, rather than my squire, to inflict on thyself some of those lashes for which thou art pledged in order to effect the disenchantment of Dulcinea. This, I say, is the time, now that thy virtue is seasoned, and of efficacy to operate the good expected from thee." "Why, this," replied Sancho, "is tangle upon tangle, and not honey upon fritters! A good jest, indeed, that pinches and prickings must be followed by lashes! Do, sir, take at once a great stone and tie it about my neck, and tumble me into a well: better kill me outright than break my back with other men's burdens. Look ye, if you meddle any more with me, as I have a living soul, all shall out!"

Altisidora had now raised herself, and sat upright on her tomb, whereupon the music immediately struck up, and the court resounded with the cries of "Live, live, Altisidora! Altisidora, live!" The duke and duchess arose, and with Minos, Rhadamanthus, Don Quixote, and Sancho, went to receive the restored damsel, and assist her to descend from the tomb. Apparently near fainting, she bowed to the duke and duchess and the two kings; then casting a side-glance at Don Quixote, she said, "Heaven forgive thee, unrelenting knight! by whose cruelty I have been imprisoned in the other world above a thousand years, as it seems to me, and where I must have for ever remained had it not been for thee, O Sancho! Thanks, thou kindest and best of squires, for the life I now enjoy; and, in recompense for thy goodness, six of my smocks are at thy service, to be made into as many shirts for thyself; and, if they are not all whole, at least they are all clean." Sancho, with his mitre in his hand, and his knee on the ground, kissed her hand. The duke ordered him to be disrobed and his own garments returned to him; but Sancho begged his grace to allow him to keep the frock and the mitre, that he might carry them to his own village, in token and memory of this unheard-of adventure. Whereupon the duchess assured him of her regard, and promised him that the frock and the mitre should certainly be his. The court was now cleared by the duke's command; all the company retired, and Don Quixote and Sancho were conducted to the apartments which they had before occupied.

CHAPTER LXX.

Which treats of matters indispensable to the perspicuity of this history.

Sancho slept that night on a truckle-bed, in the same chamber with Don Quixote — an honour he would gladly have avoided; well knowing that he should be disturbed by his master's ill-timed questions, which he was then in no mood to answer. Still smarting from the penance he had undergone, he was sullen and silent, and at that time would rather have lain in a hovel alone than in that rich apartment, so accompanied. His fears were well founded, for no sooner was his master in bed than he opened upon the squire. "What thinkest thou, Sancho," said he, "of this night's adventure? Great and terrible are the effects of love rejected, as thine own eyes can testify, which beheld Altisidora dead, not by sword or dagger, or other mortal weapon—no, nor poisonous draught—but simply my disregard of her passion!"

" She might have died how and when she pleased," answered Sancho, " so that she had left me alone; for I neither loved nor slighted her. In truth, I cannot see what the recovery of Altisidora, a damsel more light-headed than discreet, should have to do with the tweaking and pinching of Sancho Panza's flesh! Now, indeed, I plainly see that there are enchanters and enchantments in the world, from which, good Lord, deliver me, since I know not how to deliver myself. But all I wish for now is, that your worship would let me sleep, and not talk to me, unless you would have me jump out of the window." " Sleep, friend Sancho," answered Don Quixote, " if the prickings and pinchings thou hast endured will give thee leave." " No smart, sir," replied Sancho, " is equal to the disgrace of being fingered by duennas—confound them! But I would fain sleep it off, if your worship would let me ; for sleep is the best cure for waking troubles." " Then do so," quoth Don Quixote, " and Heaven be with thee!"

Both master and man were soon asleep; and Cid Hamet, the author of this grand history, took the opportunity to inform the world what had moved the duke and duchess to think of contriving the solemn farce which had just been enacted. Accordingly, he says that the bachelor Sampson Carrasco, not forgetting his overthrow when Knight of the Mirrors, by which all his designs had been baffled, was inclined to try his hand again, in the hope of better fortune ; and gaining intelligence of Don Quixote's route from the page who was charged with the letter and presents to Teresa Panza, he procured a better steed and fresh armour, with a shield displaying a White Moon. Then placing his arms upon a mule, which was led by a peasant (not choosing to trust his former squire, lest he should be discovered by Sancho Panza), he set off, and arrived at the duke's castle, where he was informed by his grace of the knight's departure, the road he had taken, and his intention to be present at the tournaments of Saragossa. He related to him also the jests which had been put upon him, with the project for disenchanting Dulcinea at the expense of Sancho's back. The bachelor was also told of the imposition which Sancho practised upon his master, in making him believe that the Lady Dulcinea was transformed into a country wench ; and also that the duchess afterwards made Sancho believe his own lie. The bachelor was much diverted at what he heard, and wondered afresh at the extraordinary madness of the knight and the shrewdness and simplicity of his squire. The duke requested him, whether he was victorious or not, to call at the castle on his return, to acquaint him with the event. This the bachelor promised ; and, departing, he proceeded straight to Saragossa, where not finding the knight, he continued the pursuit, and at length overtook him ; the result of which meeting has been already told.

On the bachelor's return, he stopped at the castle, agreeable to his promise, and informed the duke of what had passed, and also that Don Quixote, intending honourably to fulfil the conditions of the combat, was now actually on his return home, where he was bound to remain twelve months, in which time he hoped the poor gentleman would recover his senses; declaring, moreover, that nothing but the concern he felt on seeing the distracted state of so excellent an understanding could have induced him to make the attempt. He then took leave of the duke, expecting to be shortly followed by the vanquished knight.

The duke, who was never tired with the humours of Don Quixote and his squire, had been tempted to amuse himself in the manner which has been described; and to make sure of meeting them on their return, he dispatched servants on horseback in different directions, with orders to convey them, whether willing or not, to the castle; and the party whose chance it was to fall in with them, having given the duke timely notice of their success before they appeared, everything was prepared so as to give the best effect possible to the fiction. And here Cid Hamet observes that, in his opinion, the deceivers and the deceived in these jests were all mad alike, and that even the duke and duchess themselves were within two fingers' breadth of appearing so, for taking such pains to make sport with these two wandering lunatics; one of whom was then happily sleeping at full swing, and the other, as usual, indulging his waking fancies; in which state they were found when day first peeped into their chamber, giving Don Quixote an inclination to rise; for whether vanquished or victorious, he took no pleasure in the bed of sloth.

About this time Altisidora—so lately, in Don Quixote's opinion, risen from the dead — entered his chamber, her head still crowned with the funereal garland, her hair dishevelled, clad in a robe of white taffeta flowered with gold, and supporting herself by a staff of polished ebony, she stood before him. The knight was so amazed and confounded at this unexpected sight that he was struck dumb; but, being determined to show her no courtesy, he covered himself well over with the sheets. Altisidora then sat down in a chair at his bed-side, and, heaving a profound sigh, in a soft and feeble voice she said, "When women of virtue and of a superior order, in contempt of all the rules of honour and virgin decency, can allow their tongues openly to declare the secret wishes of their heart, they must indeed be reduced to great extremities. I, Signor Don Quixote de la Mancha, am one of those unhappy persons, distressed, vanquished, and enamoured, but withal patient, long-suffering, and modest, to such a degree that my heart burst in silence, and silently I quitted this life. It is now two days since, O flinty knight, harder than marble to my complaints! that the sense of your unfeeling cruelty brought death upon me, or something so like it that all who saw me concluded my soul was fled to another world; and had not Love, in pity, placed my recovery in the sufferings of this good squire, there it must for ever have remained!"

"Truly," quoth Sancho, "if Love had given that business to my Dapple, I should have taken it as kindly. But pray tell me, signora — so may Heaven provide you with a more tender-hearted lover than my master — what saw you in the other world? What did you find in purgatory? for whoever dies in despair must needs go thither, whether they like it or not." "To tell you the truth," quoth Altisidora, "I did not quite die, and therefore I did not go so far; for, had I once set foot therein, nothing could have got me out again, however much I might have wished it. The fact is, I got to the gate, where I observed about a dozen devils playing at tennis, in their waistcoats and drawers, their shirt-collars ornamented with Flanders lace, and ruffles of the same, with four inches of their wrists bare, to make their hands seem the larger, in which they held rackets of fire; and what still more surprised me was, that instead of the common balls, they made use of books that seemed to be stuffed with wind and wool — a marvellous thing, you will allow. But what added to my wonder was to see that, instead of the winners rejoicing and the losers complaining, as it is usual with game-sters, they all grumbled alike, cursing and hating one another with all their hearts!"

"There is nothing strange in that," quoth Sancho; "for devils, play or not play, win or not win, can never be contented." "That is true," quoth Altisidora; "but there is another thing I wonder at—I mean I wondered at it then—which was, that a single toss seemed always to demolish the ball; so that, not being able to use it a second time, the volumes were whipped up in an astonishing manner. To one in parti-cular that I noticed, which was spick-and-span new, and neatly bound, they gave such a smart stroke that out flew the contents, in leaves fairly printed, which were scattered about in all directions. 'Look,' said one devil to the other, 'how it flies! see what book it is.' ''T is the Second Part of Don Quixote de la Mancha,' cried the other: 'not that by Cid Hamet, its first author, but by an Arragonese, who calls himself a native of Tordesillas.' 'Away with it,' quoth the other devil, 'and down with it to the bottomless pit, that it may never be seen more.' 'Is it so bad, then?' said the other. 'So bad,' replied the first, 'that had I endeavoured to make it worse I should have found it beyond my skill.' So they went on tossing about their books; but having heard the name of Don Quixote, whom I love and adore, I retained this vision in my memory."

"A vision, doubtless, it must have been," quoth Don Quixote, "for I am the only person of that name existing, either dead or alive, and just so the book you speak of is here tossed about from hand to hand, re-maining in none:—every one has a kick at it. Nor am I concerned to hear that any phantom, assuming my name, should be wandering in darkness or in light, since I am not the person mentioned in the book you saw shattered to pieces. The history that is good, faithful, and true, will survive for ages; but should it have none of these qualities, its passage will be short between the cradle and the grave."

Altisidora was then about to renew her complaint against the obdu-rate knight, when he interrupted her. "Madam," said he, "I have often cautioned you against fixing your affections on a man who is utterly incapable of making you a suitable return. I was born for Dul-cinea del Toboso: to her the fates, if any there be, have devoted me; and, being the sole mistress and tenant of my soul, it is impossible for any other beauty to dispossess her. This, I hope, may suffice to show the fallacy of your hopes, and recall you to virtue and maidenly decorum; for it is wild to expect from man what is impossible." "God's my life!" exclaimed Altisidora, in a furious tone, "thou stock-fish! soul of marble! stone of date! more stubborn and insensible than a courted clown! Monster! I'd tear your eyes out if I could come at you! Have you the impudence, Don Cudgelled! Don Beaten-and-battered! to suppose that I died for love of your lantern jaws? No! no such matter, believe me; all that you have seen to-night has been sheer counterfeit: I am not the woman to let the black of my nail ache, much less to die, for such a dromedary as thou art!" "By my faith, I believe thee," quoth Sancho, "for as to dying for love, it is all a jest: folks may talk of it, but as for doing it, believe it, Judas."

At this time the musical poet joined them, who had sung the stanzas composed for the solemnities of the night; and, approaching Don Quixote, with a profound reverence, he said, "I come, Sir Knight, to request you will vouchsafe to number me among your most humble servants: an honour which I have been long ambitious to receive, both on account of your fame and your wonderful achievements." "Pray, sir," replied Don Quixote, "inform me who you are, that I may duly acknowledge your merits." The young man said that he was the musician and panegyrist of the preceding night. "Truly, sir," quoth Don Quixote, "your voice is excellent; but what you sang did not seem to me applicable to the occasion: for what have the stanzas of Garcilasso to do with the death of this lady?" "Wonder not at that, sir," answered the musician; "for, among the green poets of our times, it is common to write as the whim guides, whether to the purpose or not: picking and stealing wherever it suits; and every senseless thing sung or said is sure to find its apology in poetical license."

Don Quixote would have replied, but was prevented by the entrance of the duke and duchess, who had come to visit him. Much relishing conversation then passed between them, in the course of which Sancho extorted fresh admiration from their graces, by his wonted shrewdness and pleasantry. In conclusion, Don Quixote besought them to grant him leave to depart that same day; for a vanquished knight like himself should rather dwell in a sty with hogs than in a royal palace. His request was granted, and the duchess desired to know whether Altisidora had attained any share in his favour. "Madam," said he, "your ladyship should know that the chief cause of this good damsel's suffering is idleness, the remedy whereof is honest and constant employment. Lace, she tells me, is much worn in purgatory; and since she cannot but know how to make it, let her stick to that; for while her fingers are assiduously employed with her bobbins the images that now haunt her imagination will keep aloof, and leave her mind tranquil and happy. This, madam, is my opinion and advice." "And mine, too," added Sancho, "for I never in my life heard of a lacemaker that died for love; for your damsels that bestir themselves at some honest labour think more of their work than of their sweethearts. I know it by myself: when I am digging I never think of my Teresa, though, God bless her! I love her more than my very eyelids."

"You say right, Sancho," quoth the duchess, "and it shall henceforth be my care to see that Altisidora is well employed; she knows how to make use of her needle, and it shall not lie idle." "There is no need, madam," answered Altisidora, "of any such remedy; the cruel treatment I have received from that monster is quite sufficient to blot him out of my memory, without any other help; and, with your grace's leave, I will withdraw, that I may no longer have before my eyes, I will not say that rueful, but that abominable, hideous, and horrible figure." "I wish," quoth the duke, "this may not confirm the saying, 'A lover railing is not far from forgiving.'"

Altisidora, then, pretending to wipe the tears from her eyes, and making a low courtesy to her lord and lady, went out of the room. "Poor damsel!" quoth Sancho, "I forbode thee ill-luck, since thou hast to do with a soul of rushes, and a heart as tough as oak—i' faith, had it been me thou hadst looked on with kindness, thy pigs would have been brought to a better market." Here the conversation ceased: Don Quixote arose and dressed himself, dined with the duke and duchess, and departed the same afternoon.

CHAPTER LXXI.

Of what befell Don Quixote and his squire Sancho on the way to their village.

THE vanquished knight pursued his journey homeward, sometimes overcome with grief, and sometimes joyful; for if his spirits were depressed by the recollection of his overthrow, they were again raised by the singular virtue that seemed to be lodged in the body of his squire, still giving him fresh hopes of his lady's restoration: at the same time, he was not without some qualms respecting Altisidora's resurrection. Even Sancho's thoughts were unpleasant and gloomy, for he was not at all pleased that Altisidora should have paid no regard to her solemn promise concerning the smocks. Full of his disappointment, he said to his master, "Faith and troth, sir, there never was a more unlucky physician than I am. Other doctors kill their patients and are well paid for it, though their trouble be nothing but scrawling a piece of paper with directions to the apothecary, who does all the work; whilst I give life to the dead at the expense of my blood, and the scarification of my flesh to boot: yet the never a fee do I touch. But I vow to Heaven, the next time they catch me curing people in this way, it shall not be for nothing. 'The abbot must eat that sings for his meat;' besides, Heaven, I am sure, never gave this wonderful trick of curing, without meaning that I should get something by it."

" Thou art in the right, friend Sancho," answered Don Quixote, " and Altisidora behaved very ill in not giving thee the smocks which she promised, although the faculty whereby thou performest these miracles was given thee *gratis*, and costs thee nothing in the practice but a little bodily pain. For myself, I can say, if thou wouldst be paid for disenchanting Dulcinea, I should readily satisfy thee. Yet I know not whether payment be allowed in the conditions of the cure, and I should be grieved to cause any obstruction to the effects of the medicine. However, I think there can be no risk in making a trial; therefore, Sancho, consider of it, and fix thy demand, so that no time may be lost. Set about the work immediately, and pay thyself in ready money, since thou hast cash of mine in thy hands."

At these offers Sancho opened his eyes and ears a span wider, resolving to strike the bargain without delay. " Sir," said he, " I am ready and willing to give you satisfaction, since your worship speaks so much to the purpose. You know, sir, I have a wife and children to maintain, and the love I bear them makes me look to the main chance: how much, then, will your worship pay for each lash?" " Were I to pay thee, Sancho," answered Don Quixote, " in proportion to the magnitude of the service, the treasure of Venice and the mines of Potosi would be too small a recompense; but examine and feel the strength of my purse, and then set thine own price upon each lash." " The lashes to be given," quoth Sancho, " are three thousand three hundred and odd; five of that number I have already given myself—the rest remains. Setting the five against the odd ones, let us take the three thousand three hundred, and reckon them at a quartil* each—and, for the world, I would not take less—the whole amount would be three thousand three hundred quartils. Now the three thousand quartils make one thousand five hundred halfreals, which comes to seven hundred and fifty reals, and the three hundred quartils make a hundred and fifty half-reals, or seventy-five reals; which, added to the seven hundred and fifty, make, in all, eight hundred and twenty-five reals. That sum, then, I will take from your worship's money in my hands, and with it I shall return home rich and contented, though soundly whipped: but trouts are not to be caught† with dry breeches." " O blessed Sancho! O amiable Sancho!" replied Don Quixote, " how much shall Dulcinea and I be bound to serve thee as long as Heaven shall be pleased to give us life! Should she be restored to her former state, as she certainly will, her misfortune will prove a blessing—my defeat a most happy triumph! And when, good Sancho, dost thou propose to begin the discipline? I will add another hundred reals for greater dispatch." " When?" replied Sancho; "even this very night, without fail: do you take care to give me room enough, and open field, and I will take care to lay my flesh open."

So impatient was Don Quixote for night, and so slowly it seemed to approach, that he concluded the wheels of Apollo's chariot had been

---

* A small coin about the fourth of a real.
† The entire proverb is, " They do not catch trouts with dry breeches."

broken, and the day thereby extended beyond its usual length ; as it is with expecting lovers, who always fancy time to be stationary. At length, however, it grew dark; when, quitting the road, they seated themselves on the grass under some trees, and took their evening's repast on such provisions as the squire's wallet afforded. Supper being ended, Sancho made himself a powerful whip out of Dapple's halter, with which he retired about twenty paces from his master. Don Quixote, seeing him proceed to business with such resolution and spirit, said to him, " Be careful, friend, not to lash thyself to pieces ; take time, and pause between each stroke : hurry not thyself so as to be overcome in the midst of thy task. I mean, I would not have thee lay it on so unmercifully as to deprive thyself of life before the required number be completed. And that thou mayest not lose by a card too much or too little, I will stand aloof, and keep reckoning upon my beads the lashes thou shalt give thyself: so Heaven prosper thy pious undertaking ! " " The good paymaster needs no pledge," quoth Sancho ; " I mean to lay it on so that it may smart, without killing me ; for therein, as I take it, lies the secret of the cure."

He then stripped himself naked from the waist upwards, and, snatching up the whip, began to lash it away with great fury, and Don Quixote to keep account of the strokes. But Sancho had not given himself above six or eight, when, feeling the jest a little too heavy, he began to think his terms too low, and stopping his hand, he told his master that he had been deceived, and must appeal, for every lash was well worth half a real, instead of a quartil. " Proceed, friend Sancho," quoth Don Quixote, "and be not faint-hearted : thy pay shall be doubled." " If so," quoth Sancho, " away with it, in God's name, and let it rain lashes." But the sly knave, instead of laying them on his back, laid them on the trees, fetching, ever and anon, such groans, that he seemed to be tearing up his very soul by the roots. Don Quixote, besides being naturally humane, was now fearful that Sancho would destroy himself, and thus, by his indiscreet zeal, the object would be lost ; and therefore he cried out, " Hold, friend Sancho—let the business rest there, I conjure thee ; for this medicine seems to me too violent when so administered ; take it, friend, more at leisure : Zamora* was not gained in one hour. Thou hast already given thyself, if I reckon right, above a thousand lashes : let that suffice at present—for the ass (to speak in homely phrase) will carry the load, but not a double load." " No, no," answered Sancho, "it shall never be said of me, ' the money paid, the work delayed.' Pray, sir, get a little farther off, and let me give myself another thousand lashes at least ; for a couple of such bouts will finish the job, and stuff to spare." " Since thou art in so good a disposition," quoth Don Quixote, " go on, and Heaven assist thee : I will retire a little."

Sancho returned to his task with the same fury as before, and with so much effect did he apply the lash, that the trees within his reach were

---

* This was a town in the kingdom of Leon, a long while disputed for by the Arabs and Christians.

already disbarked. At length, exalting his voice, in accompaniment to a prodigious stroke on the body of a beech, he cried, " Down, down with thee, Samson, and all that are with thee!" The frightful exclamation and blow were too much for the knight's tenderness, and he ran immediately, and, seizing hold of the twisted halter, said, " Heaven forbid, friend Sancho, that thy death, and the ruin of thy helpless family, should be laid at my door!—let Dulcinea wait for another opportunity, and I will myself restrain my eagerness for her deliverance within reasonable bounds, and stay till thou hast recovered fresh strength, so as to be able to finish thy task with safety." " Since it is your worship's pleasure that I should leave off, be it so, in Heaven's name : and pray fling your cloak over my shoulders, for I am all in a sweat, and am loath to catch cold, as new disciplinants are apt to do." Don Quixote took off his cloak, and did as Sancho desired, leaving himself in his doublet; and the crafty squire, being covered up warm, fell fast asleep, and never stirred until the sun waked him.

The knight and squire now pursued their journey, and having travelled about three leagues, they alighted at the door of an inn, which, it is to be remarked, Don Quixote did not take for a turreted castle, with its moat and drawbridge: indeed, since his defeat, he was observed at times to discourse with a more steady judgment than usual. He was introduced into a room on the ground-floor, which, instead of tapestry, was hung with painted serge, as is common in country places. In one part of these hangings was represented, by some wretched dauber, the story of Helen's elopement with Paris; and in another was painted the unfortunate Dido, upon a high tower, making signals, with her bed-sheet, to her fugitive lover, who was out at sea, crowding all the sail he could to get away from her. Of the first the knight remarked that Helen seemed not much averse to be taken off, for she had a roguish smile on her countenance ; but the beauteous Dido seemed to let fall from her eyes tears as big as walnuts. " These two ladies," said he, " were most unfortunate in not being born in this age, and I above all men unhappy that I was not born in theirs ; for, had I encountered those gallants, neither had Troy been burnt nor Carthage destroyed :—all these calamities had been prevented simply by my killing Paris."

" I will lay a wager," quoth Sancho, " that, before long, there will not be either victualling-house, tavern, inn, or barber's shop, in which the history of our exploits will not be painted ; but I hope they may be done by a better hand than the painter of these." " Thou art in the right, Sancho," quoth Don Quixote ; " for this painter is like Orbaneja of Ubeda, who, when he was asked what he was painting, answered, ' As it may happen ;' and if it chanced to be a cock, he prudently wrote under it, ' This is a cock,' lest it should be mistaken for a fox. Just such a one, methinks, Sancho, the painter or writer (for it is all one) must be, who wrote the history of this new Don Quixote, lately published: whatever he painted or wrote was just as it happened. Or he is like a poet some years about the court, called the Mauleon, who answered all questions extempore ; and, a person asking him the meaning of *Deum de Deo*, he answered '*Dé donde diere.*' * But setting all this aside, tell me, Sancho, hast thou any thoughts of giving thyself the other brush to-night? and wouldst thou rather it should be under a roof, or in the open air?"

"Faith, sir," quoth Sancho, " for the whipping I intend to give myself, it matters little to me whether it be in a house or in a field; though methinks I had rather it were among trees, for they seem to have a fellow feeling for me, as it were, and help me to bear my suffering marvellously." " However, now I think of it, friend Sancho," said Don Quixote, " to give you time to recover your strength, we will defer the remainder till we reach home, which will be the day after to-morrow at farthest."

" That shall be as your worship pleases," quoth Sancho : " for my own part, I am for making an end of the job, out of hand, now I am hot upon it, and while the mill is going, for delay breeds danger. Pray to God devoutly, and hammer away stoutly; one ' take' is worth two ' I'll give thee's;' and a sparrow in hand is better than a vulture on the wing." " No more proverbs, for God's sake," quoth Don Quixote ; " for methinks, Sancho, thou art losing ground, and returning to *Sicut erat.* Speak plainly, as I have often told thee, and thou wilt find it worth a loaf per cent. to thee." " I know not how I came by this unlucky trick," replied Sancho ; " I cannot bring you in three words to the purpose without a proverb, nor give you a proverb which, to my thinking, is not to the purpose :—but I will try to mend." And here the conversation ended for this time.

CHAPTER LXXII.

How Don Quixote and Sancho arrived at their village.

THAT day Don Quixote and Sancho remained at the inn, waiting for night ; the one to finish his penance in the open air, and the other to witness an event which promised the full accomplishment of all his wishes. While they were thus waiting, a traveller on horseback, attended by three or four servants, stopped at the inn. " Here, Signor Don Alvaro Tarfe," said one of the attendants to his master, " you may pass the heat of the day ; the lodging seems to be cool and cleanly." " If I remember right, Sancho," said Don Quixote, on hearing the gentleman's name, " when I was turning over the book called the second part of my history, I noticed the name of Don Alvaro Tarfe." " It may be so," answered Sancho : " let him alight, and then we will put the question to him."

The gentleman alighted, and the landlady showed him into a room on the ground-floor adjoining to that of Don Quixote, and, like his, also

---

* "Wherever it hits." Cervantes, in his "Dialogue between two Dogs," quotes these words from the same Mauleon, calling him " Foolish Poet," although belonging to the Academy of Imitators.

hung with painted serge. This newly-arrived cavalier undressed and equipped himself for coolness, and stepping out to the porch, which was airy and spacious, where Don Quixote was walking backwards and forwards, he said to him, " Pray, sir, whither are you bound?" " To my native village, sir," replied Don Quixote, " which is not far distant. Allow me, sir, to ask you the same question." "I am going, sir," answered the gentleman, " to Grenada, the country where I was born." " And a fine country it is," replied Don Quixote. " But pray, sir, will you favour me with your name? for I believe it particularly imports me to know it." " My name is Don Alvaro Tarfe," answered the new guest. " Then, I presume," said Don Quixote, " you are that Don Alvaro Tarfe mentioned in the Second Part of the history of Don Quixote de la Mancha, lately printed and published?" " The very same," answered the gentleman, " and that Don Quixote, the hero of the said history, was an intimate acquaintance of mine; and it was I indeed who drew him from his home —I mean, I prevailed upon him to accompany me to Saragossa, to be present at the jousts and tournaments held in that place: and in truth, while we were there, I did him much service, in saving his back from being well stroked by the hangman for being too daring." " But pray, sir," said Don Quixote, " am I anything like that Don Quixote you speak of?" " No, truly," answered the other, " the farthest from it in the world." " And had he," said the knight, " a squire named Sancho Panza?" " Yes, truly," answered Don Alvaro, " one who had the reputation of being a witty comical fellow, but for my part I thought him a very dull blockhead." " Gad! I thought so," quoth Sancho, abruptly, " for it is not everybody that can say good things, and the Sancho you speak of must be some pitiful ragamuffin, some idiot and knave, I'll warrant you; for the true Sancho Panza am I :—'t is I am the merry-conceited squire, that have always a budget full of wit and waggery. Do but try me, sir—keep me company but for a twelvemonth, and you will bless yourself at the notable things that drop from me at every step;— they are so many, and so good too, that I make every beard wag without meaning it, or knowing why or wherefore. And there, sir, you have the true Don Quixote de la Mancha—the staunch, the famous, the valiant, the wise, the loving Don Quixote de la Mancha; the righter of wrongs, the defender of the weak, the father of the fatherless, the safeguard of widows, the murderer of damsels; he whose sole sweetheart and mistress is the peerless Dulcinea del Toboso : here he is, and here am I, his squire; all other Don Quixotes and all other Sancho Panzas are downright phantoms and cheats."

" Now, by St. Jago! honest friend, I believe it," said Don Alvaro, " for the little thou hast now said has more of the spice of humour than all I ever heard from the other, though it was much. The fellow seemed to carry his brains in his stomach, for his belly supplied all his wit, which was too dull and stupid to be diverting; indeed, I am convinced that the enchanters, who persecuted the good Don Quixote, have out of spite sent the bad one to persecute me. Yet I know not what to make of this matter, for I can take my oath that I left one Don Quixote under the surgeon's hands, at the house of the nuncio in Toledo, and now here starts up another that has no resemblance to him!"

"I know not," said Don Quixote, "whether I ought to avow myself the good one, but I dare venture to assert that I am not the bad one; and, as a proof of what I say, you must know, dear Signor Alvaro Tarfe, that I never in my life saw the city of Saragossa; so far from it, that having been informed this usurper of my name was at the tournaments of that city, I resolved not to go thither, that all the world might see and be convinced he was an impostor. Instead, therefore, of going to Saragossa, I directed my course to Barcelona — that seat of urbanity, that asylum of strangers, the refuge of the distressed, birthplace of the brave, avenger of the injured, the abode of true friendship, and moreover the queen of cities for beauty and situation. And though certain events occurred to me there that are far from grateful to my thoughts—indeed, such as excite painful recollections — yet I bear them the better for having had the satisfaction of seeing that city. In plain truth, Signor Don Alvaro Tarfe, I am Don Quixote de la Mancha; it is I whom fame has celebrated, and not the miserable wretch who has taken my name, and would arrogate to himself the honour of my exploits. I therefore hope, sir, that you, as a gentleman, will not refuse to make a deposition before the magistrate of this town, that you never saw me before in your life till this day; and that I am not the Don Quixote mentioned in the Second Part which has been published, nor this Sancho Panza my squire the same you formerly knew."

"That I will with all my heart," answered Don Alvaro; "though I own it perplexes me to see two Don Quixotes and two Sancho Panzas, as different in their nature as alike in name, insomuch that I am inclined to believe that I have not seen what I have seen, nor has that happened to me which I thought had happened." "Past all doubt," quoth Sancho, "your worship is enchanted, like my lady Dulcinea del Toboso; and would to Heaven your disenchantment depended upon my giving myself another such three thousand and odd lashes, as I do for her!—I would do your business, and lay them on, without fee or reward." "I do not understand what you mean by lashes," quoth Don Alvaro. Sancho said it was a tale too long to tell at that time, but he should hear it if they happened to travel the same road.

Don Quixote and Don Alvaro dined together; and as it chanced that a magistrate of the town called at the inn, accompanied by a notary, Don Quixote requested they would take the deposition of a gentleman there present, Don Alvaro Tarfe, who proposed to make oath that he did not know another gentleman then before them, namely, Don Quixote de la Mancha, and that he was not the man spoken of in a certain book called "The Second Part of Don Quixote de la Mancha, written by such a one De Avellaneda, a native of Tordesillas." In short, the magistrate complied, and a deposition was produced according to the regular form, and expressed in the strongest terms, to the great satisfaction of Don Quixote and Sancho — as if the difference between them and their spurious imitators had not been sufficiently manifest without any such attestation. Many compliments and offers of service passed between Don Alvaro and Don Quixote, in which the great Manchegan showed so much good sense, that Don Alvaro Tarfe was convinced he had been deceived, and also that there was certainly some enchantment in the case, since he had touched with his own hand two such opposite Don Quixotes.

In the evening they all quitted the inn, and after proceeding together about half a league, the road branched into two—the one led to Don Quixote's village, and the other was taken by Don Alvaro. During the short distance they had travelled together, Don Quixote informed him of his unfortunate defeat, the enchantment of Dulcinea, and the remedy prescribed by Merlin, to the great amusement of Don Alvaro, who, after embracing Don Quixote and Sancho, took his leave, each pursuing his own way.

Don Quixote passed that night among trees, to give Sancho an opportunity to resume his penance, in the performance of which the cunning rogue took special care, as on the preceding night, that the beech trees should be the sufferers; for the lashes he gave his back would not have brushed off a fly from it. The cheated knight counted the strokes with great exactness, and reckoning those which had been given him before, he found the whole amount to three thousand and twenty-nine. The sun seemed to rise earlier than usual to witness the important sacrifice, and to enable them to continue their journey. They travelled onward, discoursing together on the mistake of Don Alvaro, and their prudence in having obtained his deposition before a magistrate, and in so full and authentic a form. All that day and the following night they proceeded without meeting with any occurrence worth recording, unless it be that when it was dark Sancho finished his task, to the great joy of Don Quixote, who, when all was over, anxiously waited the return of day, in the hope of meeting his disenchanted lady; and for that purpose, as he pursued his journey, he looked narrowly at every woman he came near, to recognize Dulcinea del Toboso; fully relying on the promises of the sage Merlin.

Thus hoping and expecting, the knight and squire ascended a little eminence, whence they discovered their village; which Sancho no sooner beheld than, kneeling down, he said, " Open thine eyes, O my beloved country ! and behold thy son, Sancho Panza, returning to thee again, if not rich, yet well whipped ! Open thine arms, and receive thy son Don Quixote, too ! who, though worsted by another, has conquered himself, which, as I have heard say, is the best kind of victory ! Money I have gotten, and though I have been soundly banged, I have come off like a gentleman." " Leave these fooleries, Sancho," quoth Don Quixote, " and let us go directly to our homes, where we will give full scope to our imagination, and settle our intended scheme of a pastoral life." They now descended the hill, and went straight to the village.

CHAPTER LXXIII.

Of the omens which Don Quixote met with at the entrance into his village; with other matters which adorn and illustrate this great history.

AT the entrance of the village, as Cid Hamet reports, Don Quixote observed two boys standing on a threshing-floor, disputing with each other. "You need not trouble yourself, Perquillo," said one of them, "for you shall never see it again." Don Quixote hearing these words, said, "Dost thou mark that, Sancho? Hearest thou what he says? 'You shall never see it again!'" "Well, and what then?" said Sancho. "What!" replied Don Quixote, "dost thou not perceive that, applying these words to myself, I am to understand that I shall never more behold my Dulcinea?"

Sancho would have answered, but was prevented by seeing a hare come running across the field, which, pursued by a number of dogs and sportsmen, took refuge between Dapple's feet. Sancho took up the fugitive animal and presented it to Don Quixote, who immediately cried out, "*Malum signum! Malum signum!*—a hare flies, dogs pursue her, and Dulcinea appears not!" "Your worship," quoth Sancho, "is a strange man; let us suppose, now, that this hare is the Lady Dulcinea, and the dogs that pursue her those wicked enchanters who transformed her into a scurvy wench: she flies, I catch her, and put her into your worship's hands, who have her in your arms, and pray make much of her. Now, where is the harm of all this?"

The two boys who had been quarrelling now came up to look at the hare, when Sancho asked one of them the cause of their dispute, and was told by him who said, "you shall never see it again," that he had taken a cage full of crickets from the other boy, which he intended to keep. Sancho drew four maravedis out of his pocket, and gave them to the boy for his cage, which he also delivered to Don Quixote, and said, "Look here, sir, all your omens and signs of ill luck are come to nothing; to my thinking, dunce as I am, they have no more to do with our affairs than last year's clouds; and, if I remember right, I have heard our priest say that good Christians and wise people ought not to regard these trumperies; and it was but a few days since that your worship told me yourself that people who minded such signs and tokens were little better than fools. So let us leave these matters as we found them, and get home as fast as we can."

The hunters then came up and demanded their hare, which Don Quixote gave them and passed on; and in a field adjoining the village, they met the curate and the bachelor Sampson Carrasco repeating their breviary. It must be mentioned that Sancho Panza, by way of sumpter cloth, had thrown the buckram robe painted with flames, which he had worn on the night of Altisidora's revival, upon his ass. He likewise clapped the mitre on Dapple's head,—in short, never was an ass so honoured and bedizened. The priest and bachelor, immediately recognizing their friends, ran towards them with open arms. Don Quixote alighted, and embraced them cordially. In the meantime the boys, whose keen eyes nothing can escape, came flocking from all parts. "Ho!" cries one, "here come Sancho Panza's ass as gay as a parrot, and Don Quixote's old horse, leaner than ever!"

Thus surrounded by the children, and accompanied by the priest and the bachelor, they proceeded through the village till they arrived at Don Quixote's house, where at the door they found the housekeeper and the niece, who had already heard of his arrival. It had likewise reached the ears of Sancho's wife Teresa, who, half naked, with her hair about her ears, and dragging Sanchica after her, ran to meet her husband; and seeing him not so well equipped as she thought a governor ought to be, she said, "What makes you come thus, dear husband? methinks you come afoot, and foundered! This, I trow, is not as a governor should look." "Peace, wife," quoth Sancho, "for the bacon is not so easily found as the pin to hang it on. Let us go home, and there you shall hear wonders. I have got money, and honestly too, without wronging anybody." "Hast thou got money, good husband?—nay, then, 't is well, however it be gotten, for, well or ill, it will have brought up no new custom in the world."

Sanchica clung to her father, and asked him what he had brought her home, for she had been wishing for him as they do for showers in May. Teresa then taking him by the hand on one side, and Sanchica laying hold of his belt on the other, and at the same time pulling Dapple by the halter, they went home, leaving Don Quixote to the care of his niece and housekeeper, and in the company of the priest and the bachelor.

Don Quixote, without waiting for a more fit occasion, immediately took the priest and bachelor aside, and briefly told them of his having been vanquished, and the obligation he had consequently been laid under to abstain from the exercise of arms for the space of twelve months, and which he said it was his intention strictly to observe, as became a true knight-errant. He also told them of his determination to turn shepherd, and during the period of his recess to pass his time in the rural occupations appertaining to that mode of life; that while thus innocently and virtuously employed, he might give free scope to his thoughts of love. He then besought them, if they were free from engagements of greater moment, to follow his example, and bear him company; adding that it should be his care to provide them with sheep, and whatever was necessary to equip them as shepherds; and moreover, that his project had been so far matured, that he had already chosen names that would suit them exactly. The priest having inquired what they were, he informed him that the name he proposed to take himself was the shepherd Quixotiz; the bachelor should be the shepherd Carrascon; and he, the curate, the shepherd Curiambro; and Sancho Panza, the shepherd Panzino.

This new madness of Don Quixote astonished his friends; but to prevent his rambling as before, and hoping also that a cure might in the meantime be found for his malady, they entered into his new project, and expressed their entire approbation of it; consenting also to be companions of his rural life. "This is excellent!" said the bachelor; "it will suit me to a hair, for, as everybody knows, I am a choice poet, and shall be continually composing love ditties and pastorals to divert us as we range the flowery fields. But there is one important thing to be done, which is, that each of us should choose the name of the shepherdess he intends to celebrate in his verses, and inscribe it on the bark of every tree he comes near, according to the custom of enamoured swains." "Certainly," said the knight, "that should be done: not that I have occasion to look out for a name, having the peerless Dulcinea del Toboso, the glory of these banks, the ornament of these meads, the flower of beauty, the cream of gentleness, and, lastly, the worthy subject of all praise, however excessive!"

"That is true," said the priest; "but as for us, we must look out shepherdesses of an inferior stamp, and be content; if they square not with our wishes, they may corner with them; and, when our invention fails us in the choice of names, we have only to apply to books, and there we may be accommodated with Phillises, Amarillises, Dianas, Floridas, Galateas, and Belisardas in abundance, which, as they are goods for any man's penny, we may pick and choose. If my mistress, or rather, my shepherdess, should be called Anna, I will celebrate her under the name of Anarda; and if Frances, I will call her Francesina; and if Lucy, Lucinda; and so on: and if Sancho Panza make one of our fraternity, he may celebrate his wife Teresa Panza by the name of Teresona." Don Quixote smiled at the turn given to the names; the priest again commended his laudable resolution, and repeated his offer to join the party whenever the duties of his function would permit. They then took their leave, entreating him to take care of his health by every means in his power.

No sooner had his friends left him than the housekeeper and niece, who had been listening to their conversation, came to him. "Bless me, uncle!" cried the niece, "what has now got into your head? When we thought you were coming to stay at home, and live a quiet and decent life, you are about to entangle yourself in new mazes, and turn shepherd forsooth!—in truth, uncle, 'the straw is too hard to make pipes of.'" Here the housekeeper put in her word. "Lord, sir! how is your worship to bear the summer's heat and winter's piercing cold, in the open fields? And the howling of the wolves—Heaven bless us! No, good sir, don't think of it; this is the business of stout men, who are born and bred to it:—why, as I live, your worship would find it worse even than being a knight-errant. Look you, sir, take my advice—which is not given by one full of bread and wine, but fasting, and with fifty years over my head—stay at home, look after your estate, go often to confession, and relieve the poor; and, if any ill come of it, let it lie at my door."

"Peace, daughters," answered Don Quixote, "for I know my duty;

only help me to bed, for methinks I am not very well; and assure yourselves that whether a knight-errant or a shepherd-errant, I will not fail
to provide for you, as you shall find by experience." The two good
creatures—for they really were so—then carried him to bed, where
they brought him food, and attended upon him with all imaginable care.

CHAPTER LXXIV.

How Don Quixote fell sick, made his will, and died.

As ALL human things, especially the lives of men, are transitory, ever
advancing from their beginning to their decline and final termination,
and as Don Quixote was favoured by no privilege of exemption from the
common fate, the period of his dissolution came—and when he least
thought of it. Whether that event was hastened by the melancholy
occasioned by the recollection of his defeat, or that his destined hour
was come, true it is that he was seized with a fever, which, after six days'
confinement to his bed, terminated his mortal course. During that time
he was often visited by his friends the priest, the bachelor, and the
barber; and his trusty squire Sancho Panza never quitted his bed-side.
Supposing that the mortification of being vanquished, and the disappointment of his hopes as to the restoration of Dulcinea, were the
causes of his present malady, they endeavoured by all possible means to
revive his spirits. The bachelor bid him be of good courage and to
think soon of beginning their pastoral life; telling him that he had
already composed an eclogue on the occasion, which would eclipse all
that Sannazarius had written, and that he had also bought of a shepherd
of Quintanar two excellent dogs to guard the flock, the one called Bar-
cino and the other Butron. Nevertheless, Don Quixote's dejection still
continued: it was therefore thought necessary to send for a physician,
who, perceiving some unfavourable symptoms in his pulse, advised his
patient to look to his soul's health, for that of his body was in danger.
Don Quixote heard this admonition with more tranquillity than those
about him; for his housekeeper, his niece, and his squire began to weep
as bitterly as if he were already dead and laid out before their eyes.
Grief and other troublesome cares, the doctor told them, had brought
him to this pass.
Don Quixote now feeling an inclination to sleep, desired that he might
be left alone. They complied, and he slept full six hours at a stretch
(as it is termed), so that the niece and housekeeper thought he would
never awake more. At the end of that time, however, he awaked, and
immediately exclaimed in an audible voice, "Praised be Almighty God,
who has vouchsafed me so great a blessing!—Boundless are His mercies;
nor can the sins of men either lessen or obstruct them!"

The niece listened attentively to her uncle's words; for she thought she had perceived in him, especially since his illness, more consistency than usual, and she said to him, " What is it you say, sir ? Has anything extraordinary happened ? What mercies and what sins do you speak of? " " My good niece," replied Don Quixote, " the mercies I mean are those which God hath, in this instance, been pleased to show me, though my sins are so many. My judgment is now clear, and freed from the dark clouds of ignorance with which the continual reading of those detestable books of chivalry had obscured it. I now see their extravagance and folly, and am only grieved that this discovery happens so late as to leave me no time to profit by such books as might improve and enlighten my soul. I feel myself, niece, at the point of death, and I would fain wash away the stain of madness from my character; for though in my life I have been deservedly accounted a lunatic, I earnestly desire that the truth thereof shall not be confirmed at my death. Go, therefore, dear child, and call hither my good friends the priest, the bachelor Sampson Carrasco, and Master Nicholas the barber; for I would fain make my confession and my will."

Fortunately, at that moment his three friends entered. As soon as Don Quixote saw them, he exclaimed, " Give me joy, good gentlemen, that I am no longer Don Quixote de la Mancha, but Alonzo Quixano, the same whom the world, for his fair and honest life, was pleased to surname the Good. I am now an utter enemy to Amadis de Gaul and all his generation. Now the senseless and profane histories of knight-errantry are to me disgusting and odious ; I now acknowledge my folly, and perceive the danger into which I was led by reading them; and now, through the mercy of God, and my own dear-bought experience, I abhor them."

When his three friends heard him speak thus, they imagined that some new frenzy had seized him. " What! Signor Don Quixote," said the bachelor, " now that we have news of the Lady Dulcinea being disenchanted, do you talk at this rate ? And now that we are just upon the point of becoming shepherds, to sing and live like princes, would you turn hermit ? Think not of it—be yourself again, and leave these idle stories." " Such, indeed," replied Don Quixote, " were the stories that to me have proved so baneful; but my death, with Heaven's assistance, shall convert them to my good. I feel, good sirs, that death advances fast upon me ; let us, then, be serious, and bring me a confessor, and a notary to draw up my will; for a man in my state must not trifle with his soul. Let the notary be sent for, I beseech you. while my friend here, the priest, is taking my confession."

They looked at each other in surprise at his expressions, and, though still dubious, they were inclined to believe him, and could not but regard as a fatal symptom this sudden change from madness to sanity. He then conversed again in so rational and Christian a manner, that no doubt remained of the perfect restoration of his intellects. The priest desired all the rest to leave the room, and when alone, he received his confession. The bachelor went for the notary, and presently after returned with him,

*Torrents of tears issued from the swollen eyes of the housekeeper, his niece,
and Sancho Panza his trusty squire.*

followed by Sancho Panza, who having learned from the bachelor the
hopeless situation of his master, and seeing the niece and housekeeper in
tears, he also began to weep like the rest. The priest, having taken his
dying friend's confession, came out of the room, and told them that the
good Alonzo Quixano was near his end, and certainly in his right senses:
he therefore advised them to go in, as it was full time that his will should
be made. This sad intelligence opened still wider the sluices of grief, and
torrents of tears issued from the swollen eyes of the housekeeper, his
niece, and Sancho Panza his trusty squire, and from the bottom of their
aggrieved hearts a thousand sighs and groans; for, in truth, as it hath
been said before, both while he was plain Alonzo Quixano and while he
was Don Quixote de la Mancha, he was ever of an amiable disposition,

and kind and affable in his behaviour; so that he was beloved, not only by those of his own family, but by all who knew him.

The notary now entered the room with the others, and after the preamble of the will had been written, and Don Quixote had disposed of his soul in the usual Christian forms, coming to the distribution of his worldly goods, he directed the notary to write as follows: namely—— "*Item*, it is my will that, in regard to certain monies which Sancho Panza, whom in the wildness of my folly I called my squire, has in his custody, there being between him and me some reckonings, receipts, and disbursements, he shall not be charged with them, nor called to any account for them; but if, after he has paid himself, there should be any overplus, which will be but little, it shall be his own, and much good may it do him: and if, as in my distracted state I procured him the government of an island, I could, now that I am in my senses, procure him that of a kingdom, I would readily do it; for the simplicity of his heart, and the fidelity of his dealings, well deserve it." Then turning to Sancho, he said, " Forgive me, friend, for perverting thy understanding, and persuading thee to believe that there were, and still are, knights-errant in the world."

"Alas! good sir," replied Sancho, "do not die, I pray you; but take my advice, and live many years; for the greatest folly a man can commit in this world is to give himself up to death without any good cause for it, but only from melancholy. Good your worship, be not idle, but rise and let us be going to the field, dressed like shepherds, as we agreed to do: and who knows but behind some bush or other we may find the Lady Dulcinea disenchanted as fine as heart can wish? If you pine at being vanquished, lay the blame upon me, and say you were unhorsed because I had not duly girthed Rozinante's saddle; and your worship must have seen in your books of chivalry that nothing is more common than for one knight to unhorse another, and that he who is vanquished to-day may be the conqueror to-morrow."

" It is so, indeed," quoth the bachelor; " honest Sancho is very much in the right." " Gentlemen," quoth Don Quixote, " let us proceed fair and softly; look not for this year's birds in last year's nests. I was mad; I am now sane: I was Don Quixote de la Mancha; I am now, as formerly, styled Alonzo Quixano the Good, and may my repentance and sincerity restore me to the esteem you once had for me!—now let the notary proceed."

"*Item*, I bequeath to Antonia Quixano, my niece, here present, all my estate, real and personal, after the payment of all my debts and legacies; and the first to be discharged shall be the wages due to my housekeeper for the time she has been in my service, and twenty ducats besides for a suit of mourning.

" I appoint for my executors Signor the Priest and Signor Bachelor Sampson Carrasco, here present. *Item*, it is also my will that, if Antonia Quixano my niece should be inclined to marry, it shall be only with a man who, upon the strictest inquiry, shall be found to know nothing of books of chivalry; and, in case it shall appear that he is acquainted with such books, and that my niece, notwithstanding, will and doth marry him, then shall she forfeit all I have bequeathed her, which my executors may dispose of in pious uses as they think proper. And finally, I beseech the said gentlemen, my executors, that if haply they should come to the knowledge of the author of a certain history, dispersed abroad, entitled, 'The Second Part of the Exploits of Don Quixote de la Mancha,' they will, in my name, most earnestly entreat him to pardon the occasion I have unwittingly given him of writing so many and such gross absurdities as are contained in that book; for I depart this life with a burden upon my conscience, for having caused the publication of so much folly."

The will was then closed; and being seized with a fainting-fit, he stretched himself out at length in the bed, at which all were alarmed, and hastened to his assistance; yet he survived three days: often fainting during that time in the same manner, which never failed to cause much confusion in the house: nevertheless, the niece ate, the housekeeper drank, and Sancho Panza consoled himself—for legacies tend much to moderate grief that nature claims for the deceased. At last, after receiving the sacrament, and making all such pious preparations, as well as expressing his abhorrence, in strong and pathetic terms, of the wicked books by which he had been led astray, Don Quixote's last moment arrived. The notary was present, and protested he had never read in any book of chivalry of a knight-errant dying in his bed in so composed and Christian a manner as Don Quixote, who, amidst the plaints and tears of all present, resigned his breath—I mean to say, he died. When the priest saw that he was no more, he desired the notary to draw up a certificate, stating that Alonzo Quixano, commonly called Don Quixote de la Mancha, had departed this life and died a natural death; which testimonial he required, lest any other authors beside Cid Hamet Benengeli should raise him from the dead, and impose upon the world with their fabulous stories of his exploits.

This was the end of that extraordinary gentleman of La Mancha, whose birthplace Cid Hamet was careful to conceal, that all the towns and villages of that province might contend for the honour of having produced him, as did the seven cities of Greece for the glory of giving birth to Homer. The lamentations of Sancho, the niece, and the housekeeper, are not here given, nor the new epitaphs on the tomb of the deceased knight, except the following one, composed by Sampson Carrasco:

> Here lies the valiant cavalier
> Who never had a sense of fear:
> So high his matchless courage rose,
> He reckoned death among his vanquished foes.
>
> Wrongs to redress, his sword he drew,
> And many a caitiff giant slew;
> His days of life, though madness stained,
> In death his sober senses he regained.

The sagacious Cid Hamet, now addressing himself to his pen, said, " Here, O my slender quill ! whether well or ill cut—here, by this brass wire suspended, shalt thou hang upon this spit-rack, and live for many long ages yet to come, unless presumptuous or wicked scribblers take thee down to profane thee.   But, before they lay their vile hands upon thee, tell them, as well as thou art able, to beware of what they do ; say to them, ' Off—off, ye caitiffs !   Approach me not ! for this enterprise, good king, was reserved for me alone.'   For me alone was Don Quixote born, and I for him : he knew how to act, and I to record : we were destined for each other, in despite of that bungling impostor of Tordesillas, who has dared with his clumsy and ill-shaped ostrich-quill to describe the exploits of my valorous knight—a burden much too weighty for his shoulders—an undertaking too bold for his impotent and frozen genius.   Warn him, if perchance occasion offers, not to disturb the wearied and mouldering bones of Don Quixote ; nor vainly endeavour, in opposition to all the ancient laws and customs of death, to show him again in Old Castile, impiously raking him out of the grave, wherein he lies really and truly interred, utterly unable ever to make another sally or attempt another expedition ; for enough has been done to expose the follies of knight-errantry by those he has already happily accomplished, and which in this and other countries have gained him so much applause. Thus shalt thou have fulfilled thy Christian duty, in giving salutary admonition to those who wish thee ill ; and I shall rest satisfied, and proud also, to have been the first author who enjoyed the felicity of witnessing the full effects of his honest labours ; for the sole object of mine was to expose to the contempt they deserved the extravagant and silly tricks of chivalry, which this of my true and genuine Don Quixote has nearly accomplished ; their credit in the world being now actually tottering, and will doubtless soon sink altogether, never to rise again. Farewell.